# A MIGHTY FORTRESS

## TOR BOOKS BY DAVID WEBER

*Off Armageddon Reef*
*By Schism Rent Asunder*
*By Heresies Distressed*
*A Mighty Fortress*

# A
# MIGHTY
# FORTRESS

# DAVID
# WEBER

**TOR**®

A TOM DOHERTY ASSOCIATES BOOK
NEW YORK

A MIGHTY FORTRESS

Copyright © 2010 by David Weber

Maps by Ellisa Mitchell

A Tor Book
Published by Tom Doherty Associates, LLC
175 Fifth Avenue
New York, NY 10010

www.tor-forge.com

Tor® is a registered trademark of Tom Doherty Associates, LLC.

ISBN 978-0-7653-1505-2

First Edition: April 2010

Printed in the United States of America

0  9  8  7  6  5  4  3  2  1

For Bobbie Rice.
Wait for us, Grandmommy-in-law. We miss you,
but Sharon and the kids and I will be along.

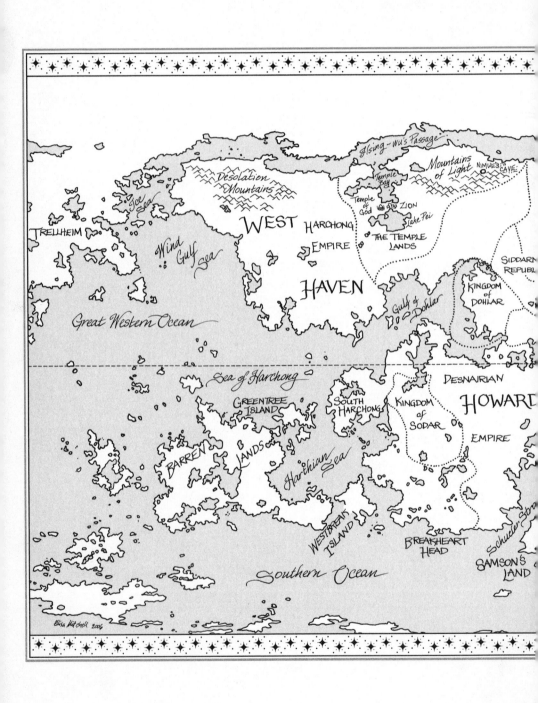

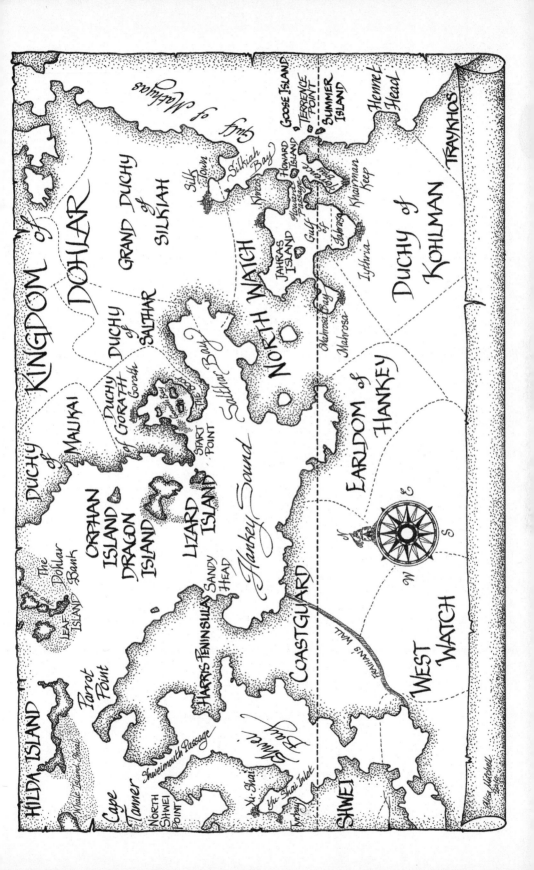

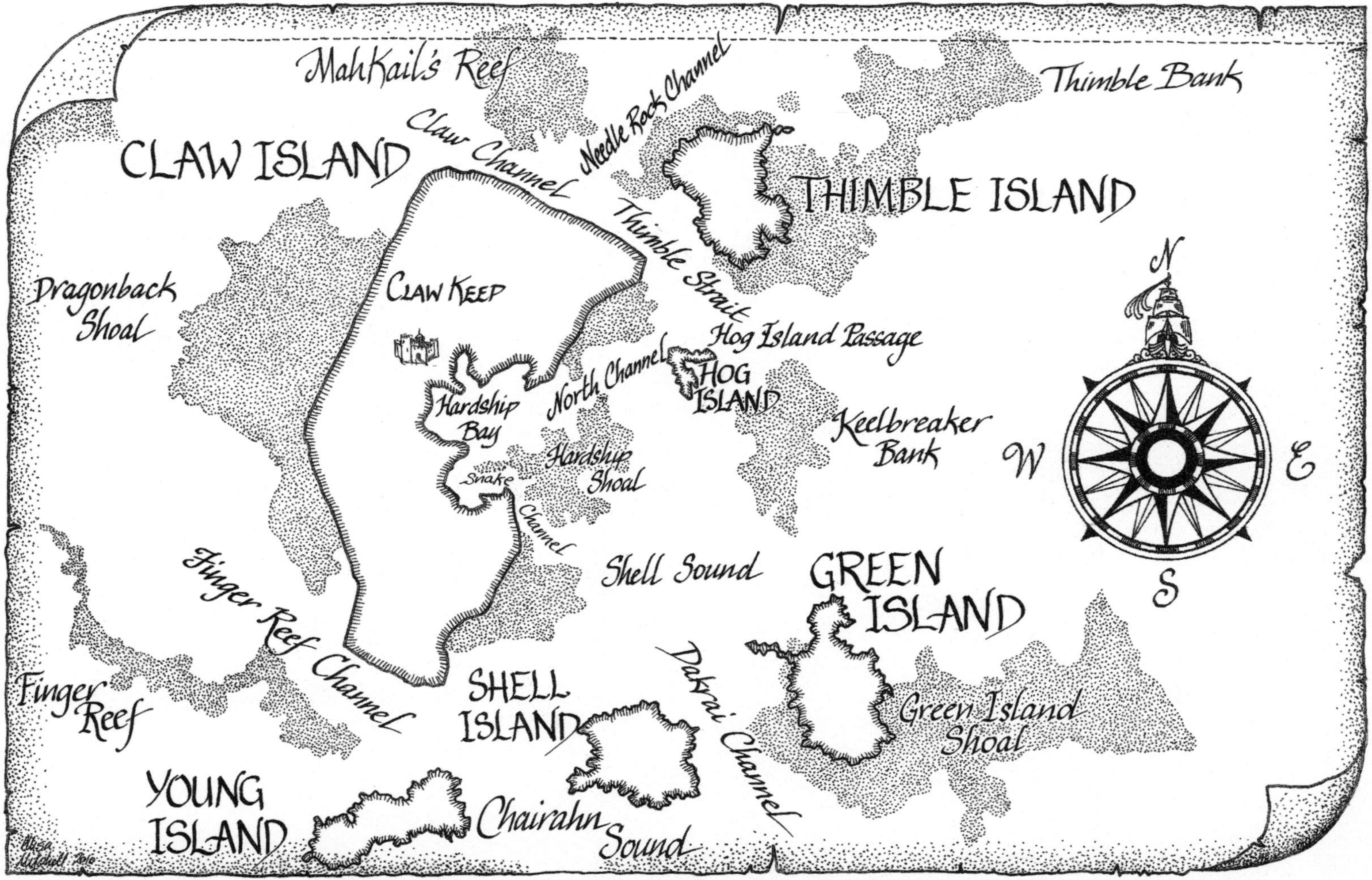

Mahkail's Reef
Needle Rock Channel
Thimble Bank
Claw Channel
CLAW ISLAND
THIMBLE ISLAND
Thimble Strait
Claw Keep
Dragonback Shoal
Hog Island Passage
North Channel
HOG ISLAND
Hardship Bay
Keelbreaker Bank
Hardship Shoal
Snake Channel
N
W
E
S
Shell Sound
GREEN ISLAND
Finger Reef Channel
SHELL ISLAND
Dakrai Channel
Green Island Shoal
Finger Reef
YOUNG ISLAND
Chairahn Sound

# SEPTEMBER,
# YEAR OF GOD 893

S o I don't know about *you* people, but *I've* had more than enough of this dragon shit!" Paitryk Hainree shouted from his improvised speaker's perch on the municipal fire brigade cistern.

*"Bastards!"* a voice came back out of the small crowd gathered outside the tavern. It was early in the morning, on a Wednesday, and like every other tavern on the face of Safehold, all the taverns of the city of Manchyr were closed and would stay that way until after morning mass. The sun was barely up, the narrow streets were still caverns of shadow, but the clouds overhead already promised rain by afternoon, and the humidity was high.

As, Hainree noted, were tempers. It wasn't a huge crowd, in fact it was considerably smaller than the one he'd hoped for, and probably at least half the men in it were there more out of curiosity than commitment. But the ones who *were* committed—

"Fucking murderers!" someone else snarled back.

Hainree nodded vigorously, hard enough to make sure everyone in his angry audience could recognize the gesture. He was a silversmith, by trade, not an actor or an orator, and certainly not a priest! But over the last few five-days he'd had the opportunity to profit by the experience and advice of quite a few men who *were* trained priests. He'd learned how voice projection and "spontaneous" body language could support and emphasize a message—especially when that message was backed by genuine, burning outrage.

"Yes!" he shouted back to the last speaker. "Damned right they're murderers, unless you want to believe that lying bastard Cayleb!" He flung up his hands in eloquent contempt. "Of course *he* didn't do it! Why, what possible motive could *he* have had to order Prince Hektor's murder?"

A fresh chorus of outrage, this time formed of pure anger rather than anything as artificial as words, answered him, and he smiled savagely.

"Goddamned butchers!" yet another voice shouted. "Priest-killers! *Heretics!* Remember Ferayd!"

"Yes!" He nodded his head again, just as vigorously as before. "They can *say* what they want—this new 'archbishop' of ours and *his* bishops—but *I'm* not so sure you aren't right about Cayleb's precious 'Church of Charis'! Maybe there *are* some priests who've abused their offices. No one wants to believe that—*I* don't want to, do you? But remember what Archbishop Wyllym said in his report about the Ferayd Massacre! There's no doubt Cayleb lied about how terrible the original attack was, and it's for *damned* sure he and all his other bootlickers have been lying about how 'restrained' their response to it was. But even so, Mother Church herself acknowledged that the priests who were hanged—hanged impiously, with no proper Church trial, by 'Archbishop Maikel's' own *brother*, mind you!—were guilty of wrongdoing. *Mother Church* said that, and the Grand Vicar imposed a personal penance on the Grand Inquisitor *himself* for letting it happen! Does that sound to *you* like Mother Church can't be trusted? Like we can't rely on *her* to deal with abuses and corruption? Like the only answer is to defy God's own Church? Cast down the vicarate Langhorne himself ordained?"

There was another snarl of fury, yet this one, Hainree noted, was less fiery than the one before. He was a bit disappointed by that, but not really surprised. Corisandians, by and large, had never felt directly threatened by the policies of the Church of God Awaiting and the Knights of the Temple Lands. Certainly not the way Charisians had felt when they discovered their entire kingdom had been condemned to fire and the sword by that same Church. Or, at least, by the men who controlled it.

Still, it would have been inaccurate—and foolish—to pretend there weren't plenty of Corisandians who had their own reservations about the Church's current rulership. Manchyr was a long way from the Temple or the city of Zion, after all, and Corisandians as a whole were undoubtedly more independent-minded in matters of religion than the Inquisition or the vicarate at large would truly have approved. For that matter, plenty of Corisandians had had sons or brothers or fathers killed in the Battle of Darcos Sound, and it was common knowledge that Darcos Sound had been the disastrous consequence of a war which had seen Corisande and its allies conscripted to act as the Church's proxies. Among those for whom religious fervor and orthodoxy were major motivators, they burned with a blinding, white-hot passion that surpassed all others. The majority of Corisandians, however, were far less passionate about those particular concerns. *Their* opposition to the Church of Charis stemmed far more from the fact that it was the Church of *Charis*, linked in their own minds with the House of Ahrmahk's conquest of their princedom, than from any outraged sense of orthodoxy. For that matter, Corisande undoubtedly harbored its own share of the reform-minded, and *they* might well find themselves actively attracted to the breakaway church.

*Best not to dwell too heavily on the heresy, Paitryk,* Hainree told himself. *Leave the ones already on fire over that to burn for themselves. Father Aidryn's right about that; they'll be hot enough without you. Spend your sparks on other tinder.*

"I've no doubt God and Langhorne—and the Archangel *Schueler*—will deal with that, in time," he said out loud. "That's God's business, and Mother Church's, and I'll leave it to them! But what happens *outside* the Church—what happens in Corisande, or here on the streets of Manchyr—that's *man's* business. *Our* business! A *man's* got to know what it is he stands for, and when he knows, he has to truly *stand,* not just wave his hands about and wish things were *different.*"

The last word came out in a semi-falsetto sneer, and he felt the fresh anger frothing up.

"Hektor!" a wiry man with a badly scarred left cheek shouted. Hainree couldn't see him, but he recognized the voice easily enough. He should have, after all. Rahn Aimayl had been one of his senior apprentices before the Charisian invasion ruined Hainree's once thriving business, along with so many other of the besieged capital's enterprises, and Hainree had been there when a cracked mold and a splash of molten silver produced the scar on Aimayl's cheek.

"Hektor!" Aimayl repeated now. *"Hektor!"*

"Hektor, Hektor!" other voices took up the shout, and this time Hainree's smile could have been a slash lizard's.

"Well," he shouted then, "there's a hell of a lot more of *us* than there are of *them,* when all's said! And I don't know about you, but I'm not ready— yet—to assume that *all* of our lords and great men and members of Parliament are ready to suck up to Cayleb like this so-called *Regency Council!* Maybe all they *really* need is a little indication that some of the *rest* of us aren't ready to do that, either!"

▼    ▼    ▼

"Hek-*tor!* Hek-*tor!*"

Sergeant Edvard Waistyn grimaced as the crowd streamed closer and its chant rose in both volume and anger. It was easy enough to make out the words, despite the majestic, measured tolling of the cathedral's bells coming from so close at hand. Of course, one reason it might have been so easy for him to recognize that chant was that, unfortunately, he'd already heard quite a few other chants, very much like it, over the last few five-days.

*And it's not anything I'm not going to be hearing a lot* more *of over the next few five-days, neither,* he thought grimly.

The sergeant, one of the scout-snipers assigned to the First Battalion, Third Brigade, Imperial Charisian Marines, lay prone on the roof, gazing up along the narrow street below his perch. The crowd flowing down that street, through the shadows between the buildings, still seemed touched by just a bit of hesitancy. The anger was genuine enough, and he didn't doubt they'd started out in the full fire of their outrage, but now they could see the cathedral's dome and steeples rising before them. The notion of . . . registering their unhappiness was no longer focused on some future event. It was almost *here* now, and that could have unpleasant consequences for some of them.

*Still and all, I'm not thinking this is one as'll just blow over with only a little wind. There's rain in this one—and some* thunder, *too, like as not.*

His intent eyes swept slowly, steadily across the men and boys shaking their fists and hurling imprecations in the direction of the rifle-armed men formed up in front of Manchyr Cathedral in the traditional dark blue tunics and light blue trousers of the Charisian Marines. Those Marines formed a watchful line, a barrier between the shouters and another crowd—this one much quieter, moving quickly—as it flowed up the steps behind them.

So far, none of the sporadic "spontaneous demonstrations" had intruded upon the cathedral or its grounds. Waistyn was actually surprised it hadn't happened already, given the ready-made rallying point the "heretical" Church of Charis offered the people out to organize resistance to the Charisian occupation. Maybe there'd been even more religious discontent in Corisande than the sergeant would have thought before the invasion? And maybe it was just that even the most belligerent rioter hesitated to trespass on the sanctity of Mother Church.

*And maybe* this *crowd's feeling a little more adventurous than the last few have,* he thought grimly.

"Traitors!" The shout managed to cut through the rhythmic chant of the assassinated Corisandian prince's name. "Murderers! *Assassins!*"

"Get out! Get the hell out—and take your murdering bastard of an *'emperor'* with you!"

"Hek-*tor!* Hek-*tor!*"

The volume increased still further, difficult as that was to achieve, and the crowd began to flow forward once again, with more assurance, as if its own bellowed imprecations were burning away any last-minute hesitation.

*I could wish General Gahrvai had his own men down here,* Waistyn reflected. *If this goes as bad as I think it could . . .*

A group of armsmen in the white and orange colors of the Archbishop's Guard marched steadily down the street towards the cathedral, and the volume of the shouts ratcheted still higher as those same protesters caught sight of the white cassock and the white-cockaded priest's cap with its broad orange ribbon at the heart of the guardsmen's formation.

"Heretic! *Traitor!*" someone screamed. "Langhorne knows his own—*and so does Shan-wei!*"

*Perfect,* Waistyn thought disgustedly. *Couldn't've come in the* back *way, could he now? Don't be daft, Edvard—of* course *he couldn't! Not today, of all days!* He shook his head. *Oh, isn't* this *going to be fun?*

▼　　▼　　▼

Down at street level, Lieutenant Brahd Tahlas, the youthful commanding officer of Second Platoon, Alpha Company, found himself thinking very much the

same thoughts as the veteran sergeant perched above him. In fact, he was thinking them with even more emphasis, given his closer proximity to the steadily
swelling mob.

And his greater responsibility for dealing with it.

"I can't say I'm liking this all that much, Sir," Platoon Sergeant Zhak
Maigee muttered. The platoon sergeant was half again Tahlas' age, and he'd first
enlisted in the Royal Charisian Marines when he was all of fifteen years old.
He'd been a lot of places and seen a lot of things since then—or, as he was occasionally wont to put it, "met a lot of interesting people . . . and killed 'em!"—and
he'd learned his trade thoroughly along the way. That normally made him a reassuring presence, but at the moment his face wore that focused, intent-on-the-
business-in-hand expression of an experienced noncom looking at a situation
which offered all sorts of possibilities . . . none of them good. He'd been careful to keep his voice low enough only Tahlas could possibly have heard him, and
the lieutenant shrugged.

"I don't much care for it myself," he admitted in the same quiet voice,
more than a little surprised by how steady he'd managed to keep it. "If you
have any suggestions about how to magically convince all these idiots to just
disappear, I'm certainly open to them, Sergeant."

Despite the situation, Maigee snorted. He rather liked his young lieutenant, and whatever else, the boy had steady nerves. Which probably had
something to do with why he'd been selected by Major Portyr for his current
assignment.

And Maigee's of course.

"Now, somehow, Sir, I can't seem to come up with a way to do that just
this very minute. Let me ponder on it, and I'll get back to you."

"Good. In the meantime, though, keep your eye on that group over there,
by the lamppost." Tahlas flicked one hand in an unobtrusive gesture, indicating
the small knot of men he had in mind. "I've been watching them. Most of
these idiots look like the sort of idlers and riffraff who could have just sort of
turned up, but not those fellows."

Maigee considered the cluster of Corisandians Tahlas had singled out and
decided the lieutenant had a point. Those men weren't in the crowd's front ranks,
but they weren't at the rear, either, and they seemed oddly . . . cohesive. As if they
were their own little group, not really part of the main crowd. Yet they were
watching the men about them intensely, with a sort of focus that was different
from anyone else's, and some of those other men were watching them right back.
Almost as if they were . . . waiting for something. Or *anticipating* it, maybe.

▼  ▼  ▼

The cluster of Church armsmen was closer, now, Waistyn observed, and the
quantity of abuse coming from the crowd swelled steadily. It couldn't get a

whole lot louder, but it was getting more . . . inclusive as shouts and curses with a clear, definitely religious content added themselves to the ongoing chant of Prince Hektor's name.

"All right, lads," the sergeant said calmly to the rest of the squad of scout-snipers on the roof with him. "Check your priming, but no one so much as moves an eyelash without *I* give the order!"

A quiet chorus of acknowledgment came back to him, and he grunted in approval, but he never took his eyes from the street below him. Despite his injunction, he wasn't concerned by any itchy trigger fingers, really. All of his Marines were veterans, and all of them had been there when Major Portyr made his instructions perfectly—one might almost have said *painfully*—clear. The last thing anyone wanted was for Charisian Marines to open fire on an "unarmed crowd" of civilians in the streets of Corisande's capital. Well, maybe that was the *next* to last thing, actually. Waistyn was pretty sure that letting anything unfortunate happen to Archbishop Klairmant would be even less desirable. That, after all, was what Waistyn's squad had been put up here to prevent.

*Of course, unless we're ready to start shooting anyone as soon as they get in range of him, it's possible we might just be a* tad *late when it comes to the "preventing" part,* he thought with profound disgust.

▼　▼　▼

*"Blasphemers!"* Charlz Dobyns shouted, waving his fist at the oncoming Archbishop's Guard. His voice cracked—it still had an irritating tendency to do that at stressful moments—and his eyes glittered with excitement.

Truth to tell, Charlz didn't really feel all that strongly one way or the other about this "Church of Charis" nonsense. In fact, he hadn't chosen his own war cry—that had been suggested by his older brother's friend, Rahn Aimayl. And he wasn't the only person using it, either. At least a dozen others in the crowd, most of them no older than Charlz himself, had begun shouting the same word, just as they'd rehearsed, the moment someone caught sight of Archbishop Klairmant's approach.

From the way some of the people around them were reacting, Rahn had been right on the mark when he explained how effective the charge of blasphemy would be.

Personally, Charlz wasn't even entirely certain exactly what "blasphemy" was—except for the way his mother had always clouted him over the ear for it whenever he took Langhorne's name in vain. And he had no idea how the Church of Charis' doctrine might be at odds with that of the rest of the Church. He was no priest, that was for sure, and he knew it! But even he found it difficult to believe the more spectacular stories about orgies on altars and child sacrifice. Stood to reason that nobody could get away with that right here in the

Cathedral without *everyone* knowing it was happening, and he'd yet to meet anyone who'd actually seen it. Or anyone he would have trusted to tell him whether or not it was raining, at any rate!

As far as the rest of it went, though, for all he knew this new "church" of theirs could have a point. If even a quarter of what some folks were saying about the so-called "Group of Four" was true, he supposed he could understand why some people could be upset with them. But that didn't matter, either. They were the *Vicars,* and so far as Charlz could see, what the Vicars said, went. *He* certainly wasn't going to argue with them! If someone else wanted to, that was their affair, and he knew quite a few Corisandians seemed to agree with the Charisians. In fact, at this particular moment, there were a Shan-wei of a lot more people *inside* the Cathedral than there were standing outside it shouting at them.

For that matter, Charlz's own mother was the housekeeper for the rectory at Saint Kathryn's. He knew where *she* was this morning, and from what she'd said in the last few five-days, Father Tymahn seemed to be leaning heavily towards this new Church of Charis, as well.

But that was really beside the point, as far as Charlz was concerned. In most ways, he shared his mother's immense respect for Father Tymahn, yet in this case, she was missing the true point. No. The *true* point—or at least the one which had brought Charlz here this morning—wasn't doctrine, or who wore the archbishop's priest's cap here in Manchyr. Or it *wouldn't* have been about who wore the cap . . . except for the fact that the man who did had sworn fealty to the *Empire* of Charis, as well as the *Church* of Charis, in order to get it.

It wasn't so much that Charlz was a fanatic Corisandian patriot. There really weren't all that many Corisandian "patriots," in the sense that someone from the millennium-dead Terran Federation might have understood the term. Loyalties in most Safeholdian realms—there were exceptions, like Charis and the Republic of Siddarmark—tended to be purely local. Loyalties to a specific baron, or earl, or duke, perhaps. Or to a prince, or an individual monarch. But not to the concept of a "nation" in the sense of a genuine, self-aware nation-state. Young Charlz, for example, thought of himself first as a Manchyrian, a resident of the city of that name, and then as (in descending order of importance) a subject of the Duke of Manchyr and as a subject of Prince Hektor, who had happened to be Duke of Manchyr, as well as Prince of Corisande.

Beyond that, Charlz had never really thought all that deeply, before the Charisian invasion, about where his loyalties lay or about relations between Corisande and the Kingdom of Charis. In fact, he still wasn't entirely clear on exactly what had provoked open warfare between Corisande and Charis. On the other hand, he was only sixteen Safeholdian years old (fourteen and a half, in the years of long-dead Terra), and he was accustomed to being less than fully clear on quite a few issues. What he did know was that Corisande had been invaded; that the city in which he lived had been placed under siege; that the Corisandian Army had been soundly defeated; and that Prince Hektor—the one clearly visible (from his perspective, at any rate) symbol of Corisandian unity and identity—had been assassinated.

That was enough to upset anyone, wasn't it?

Still, he'd have been inclined to leave well enough alone, keep his own head down, and hope for the best if it had been solely up to him. But it wasn't. There were plenty of other people here in Manchyr who definitely *weren't* inclined to leave well enough alone, and some of them were getting steadily louder and more vociferous. It seemed pretty obvious to Charlz that sooner or later, if they had their way, people were going to have to choose up sides, and if he had to do that, he knew which side *he* was going to choose. Whatever had started the quarrel between Corisande and Charis, he didn't need any dirty foreigners poking any sticks into hornets' nests here in *his* hometown.

(And they had to be *dirty* foreigners, didn't they? After all, *all* foreigners were, weren't they?)

"*Blasphemers!*" he shouted again.

"*Blasphemers!*" he heard someone else shouting. It wasn't one of his friends this time, either. Others were starting to take up the cry, and Charlz grinned as he reached under his tunic and loosened the short, heavy cudgel in his belt.

▼     ▼     ▼

"*That's enough!*"

Rather to Paitryk Hainree's surprise, the voice of the young Charisian officer in front of the cathedral was actually audible through the crowd noise. It probably helped that he was using a leather speaking trumpet, but more likely, Hainree reflected, it had to do with the fact that he'd been trained to be heard through the thunder of a field of battle.

What surprised him even more was that the front ranks of his crowd—*No, mob, not "crowd,"* he thought. *Let's use the honest word, Paitryk*—actually seemed to hesitate. His eyes widened slightly as he saw it, then narrowed again as he recognized at least part of the reason. The Charisian had raised his voice to be heard, true, but it wasn't a bellow of answering anger. No, it was a voice of . . . exasperation. And the young man's body language wasn't especially belligerent, either. In fact, he had one hand on his hip, and it looked as if he were actually tapping his toe on the cathedral's steps.

*He looks more like an irritated* tutor *somewhere than an army officer confronting a hostile mob,* Hainree realized.

"It's Wednesday morning!" the Charisian went on. "You should all be *ashamed* of yourselves! If you're not in church yourselves, the least you can do is let other people go to mass in peace!"

"What d'*you* know about mass, heretic?!" somebody—he thought it might have been Aimayl—shouted back.

"I know *I'm* not going to throw rocks through a cathedral's windows," the Charisian shouted back. "I know that much!" He gave a visible shudder. "Langhorne only knows what my mother would do to me if she found out about *that!*"

More than one person in the crowd surprised Hainree—and probably themselves—by laughing. Others only snarled, and there was at least a spatter of additional shouts and curses as Archbishop Klairmant passed through the cathedral doors behind the Marines.

"Go home!" The Charisian's raised voice sounded almost friendly, tinged more with resignation than anger. "If you have a point to make, make it someplace else, on a day that doesn't belong to God. I don't want to see anybody hurt on a Wednesday! In fact, my orders are to avoid that if I possibly can. But my orders are *also* to protect the cathedral and anyone in it, and if I have to hurt someone *outside* it to do that, I will."

His voice was considerably harder now, still that of someone trying to be reasonable, but with an undertone that warned them all there was a limit to his patience.

Hainree glanced around the faces of the four or five men closest to him and saw them looking back at him. One of them raised an eyebrow and twitched his head back the way they'd come, and Hainree nodded very slightly. He wasn't afraid of going toe-to-toe with the Marines himself, but Father Aidryn had made it clear that it was Hainree's job to nurture and direct the anti-Charis resistance. That resistance might well require martyrs in days to come, yet it would need *leaders* just as badly. Possibly even more badly.

The man who'd raised the eyebrow nodded back and turned away, forging a path towards the front of the now-stalled crowd. Hainree watched him go for a moment, then he and several of the others began filtering towards the back.

▼　　▼　　▼

*Damn me if I don't think the lad's going to do it!* Platoon Sergeant Maigee thought wonderingly.

The sergeant wouldn't have bet a single Harchong mark on Lieutenant Tahlas' being able to talk the mob into turning around and going home, but Tahlas had obviously hit a nerve by reminding them all it was Wednesday. Maigee had expected that to backfire, given the shouts of "blasphemer" and "heretic" coming out of the crowd, yet it would appear the lieutenant had read its mood better than he had.

"Go on, now," Tahlas said, his tone gentler as the mob's volume began to decrease and he could lower his own voice level a bit. "Disperse, before anyone gets hurt. I don't want that. For that matter, whether you believe it or not, Emperor Cayleb doesn't want that; Archbishop Klairmant doesn't want that; and it's for *damned* sure—if you'll pardon my language—that *God* doesn't want that. So what say you and I make all those people happy?"

▼      ▼      ▼

Charlz Dobyns grimaced as he felt the mood of the crowd around him shift. Somehow, this wasn't what he'd anticipated. This Charisian officer—Charlz had no idea how to read the man's rank insignia—was supposed to be furious, screaming at them to disperse. *Threatening* them, making his contempt for them clear. He certainly wasn't supposed to be just *talking* to them! And *reasoning* with them—or pretending he was, at any rate—was just too underhanded and devious to be believed.

And yet, Charlz wasn't completely immune to the Charisian's manner. And the other man had a point about its being Wednesday. Not only that, but the Charisian's mention of his mother had reminded Charlz forcibly of his *own* mother . . . and how she was likely to react when she found out what her darling boy had been up to when he was supposed to be at mass himself.

He didn't know what thoughts were going through the minds of the rest of the crowd, but he could sense the way the entire mob was settling back on its heels, losing the forward momentum which had carried it down the street. Some of the people in it—including some of Charlz's friends—were still shouting, yet their voices had lost much of their fervor. They sounded shriller, more isolated, as if those voices' owners felt their own certainty oozing away.

Charlz took his hand away from the truncheon under his tunic and was a bit surprised to discover he was actually more relieved than regretful at the way things had so unexpectedly shifted.

He started to turn away, then paused, his eyes widening in shock, as the man who'd just walked up behind him brought something out from under his own tunic.

Charlz had never seen one of the new "flintlocks" which had been introduced into the Corisandian Army, but he recognized what he had to be seeing now. It was a short, squat weapon—a musket whose stock had been cut down and whose barrel had been sawn down to no more than a couple of feet. It was still far bigger and clumsier than the pistols which equipped the Charisian Imperial Guard, and it must have been extraordinarily difficult to keep it hidden, but the flintlock which had been fitted in place of its original matchlock didn't need a clumsy, smoldering, impossible-to-hide, lit slow match. That had probably helped a lot where concealing it was concerned, a corner of Charlz's mind thought almost calmly.

He watched, frozen, as the weapon rose. It poked over the shoulder of another young man, no more than a year or so older than Charlz himself, standing beside him. The other young man twitched in astonishment, turning his head, looking across and down at the muzzle as it intruded into the corner of his field of vision . . . just as the man holding it squeezed the trigger.

▼　　▼　　▼

The sudden gunshot took everyone by surprise, even experienced noncoms like Waistyn and Maigee. Perhaps it shouldn't have taken the sergeants unaware, but Tahlas' obvious success in calming the crowd had lulled even them just a bit, as well.

The man behind that musket had marked the Marine lieutenant as his target. Fortunately for Brahd Tahlas, however, no one would ever have described the would-be murderer's weapon as a precision instrument. It was a smooth-bore, with a very *short* barrel, and loaded with meal powder, not corned powder. Less than a quarter of the slow-burning, anemic propellant had actually been consumed before the rest was flung out of the barrel in a huge, blinding cloud, and the bullet's flight could only be characterized as . . . erratic.

The unfortunate young man who'd been looking at the muzzle at the moment it was fired screamed in agony as his face was savagely burned. He staggered back, clutching at his permanently blinded eyes, and four or five more people who'd been unlucky enough to be standing directly in front of him cried out in pain of their own as blazing flakes of gunpowder seared "coalminer's tattoos" into the backs of their necks. One especially luckless soul actually had his hair set on fire and went to his knees, howling in panic and pain as he beat at the flames with both hands.

Charlz Dobyns was far enough away to escape with only minor singeing, and his head snapped around, looking for the musket's target.

▼　　▼　　▼

"Shit."

Lieutenant Tahlas wondered if Platoon Sergeant Maigee even realized he'd spoken out loud. The single word was pitched almost conversationally, after all. Not that it was going to make a lot of difference.

The musket ball had almost certainly been meant for him, the lieutenant realized, but it hadn't found him. Instead, it had slammed into the chest of one of his privates, a good four feet to his right. The Marine went down, clutching at the front of his suddenly bloody tunic, and Tahlas realized something else. Major Portyr's orders had been perfectly explicit on the matter of what Tahlas was supposed to do if firearms or edged weapons were used against any of his troops.

"Fix bayonets!" he heard his own voice command, and the men of his platoon obeyed.

He saw many of those in the crowd suddenly trying to back away as steel clicked and the long, shining blades sprouted from the ends of his Marines' rifles. Some of them managed it; others found their escape blocked by the mass of bodies behind them, and still others reacted quite differently. Expressions snarled, truncheons and clubs came out from under tunics, and the front of the mob seemed to solidify somehow, drawing together. It seemed clear the people in those front ranks were ready for a fight.

*For now,* Brahd Tahlas thought grimly. *For now, perhaps.*

He looked at his bleeding private, and his jaw tightened as his expression hardened into something far less youthful than his years. He'd seen dead men enough at Talbor Pass. He looked away again, meeting Maigee's eye, and his youthful voice was a thing of hammered iron.

"Sergeant Maigee, clear the street!" he said.

### .II.
### Maikelberg,
### Duchy of Eastshare,
### Kingdom of Chisholm

So," General Sir Kynt Clareyk, Imperial Charisian Army, late Brigadier Clareyk of the Imperial Charisian Marines and recently knighted and ennobled as the Baron of Green Valley, said as he poured wine into his guest's cup, "what do you think, *Seijin* Merlin?"

"Of what, My Lord?" the tall, blue-eyed Imperial Guardsman in the black and gold of the House of Ahrmahk asked mildly.

He picked up his cup and sipped appreciatively. Clareyk's taste in wine had always been good, and his promotion hadn't changed the ex-Marine in that respect. Or in any other respect that Merlin Athrawes could see. He was still the same competent officer he'd always been, with the same willingness to roll up his sleeves and dig into a new assignment. The tent in which they currently sat while icy autumn rain pounded down against its (nominally) waterproofed canvas canopy was evidence of that. The day after tomorrow would be Cayleb and Sharleyan Ahrmahk's first anniversary, which also made it the anniversary of the creation of the Empire of Charis, and Merlin couldn't help comparing the chill, wet misery outside Green Valley's tent to the brilliant sunshine, tropical heat, and flowers of that wedding day.

The difference was . . . pronounced, and while Green Valley might be a mere baron, and one of the Empire's most recently created peers to boot (he'd held his new title for less than four five-days, after all), it was no secret Emperor Cayleb and Empress Sharleyan both thought very highly of him. In fact, it was no secret that he'd been hauled back to Chisholm from the newly conquered (more or less) Princedom of Corisande precisely *because* of how highly they regarded him. Given all of that, one might reasonably have assumed that a man with his connections could have found comfortable quarters in the nearby city of Maikelberg rather than ending up stuck under canvas with winter coming on quickly.

*And a* northern *winter, at that,* Merlin thought dryly, glancing at the large, dripping spot in one corner of the tent where its roof's theoretical waterproofing had proved unequal to the heavy rain. *He's a southern boy, when all's said and done, and he's not going to enjoy winter in Chisholm one bit. The rain's bad enough, but there's worse coming. Snow? What's that?!*

Which, as Merlin understood perfectly well, was the real reason Green Valley had taken up residence in this tent instead of a luxurious townhouse, or at least a comfortable room in one of the city's more respectable inns. An awful lot of other Charisian ex-Marines were about to spend a Chisholmian winter under less than ideal conditions, and Green Valley wouldn't be moving out of his tent until the last man under his command had been provided with dry, *warm* space of his own in the barracks being hastily thrown up.

"'Of what,' is it?" the general repeated now, sitting back in his folding camp chair beside the cast-iron stove which was doing its best—successfully, at the moment—to maintain a fairly comfortable temperature inside the tent. "Now, let me see . . . what could I *possibly* have been asking about? Hmmm. . . ."

He frowned in obvious, difficult thought, scratching his chin with his eyes screwed half-shut, and Merlin chuckled. There weren't all that many people on the planet of Safehold who felt comfortable enough with the fearsome *Seijin* Merlin to give him grief, and he treasured the ones who did.

"All right, My Lord!" He acknowledged defeat with a grin, then let the grin fade slowly. "Actually," he went on in a considerably more serious tone, "I've been impressed. You and Duke Eastshare seem to be managing the integration process even more smoothly and quickly than Their Majesties had anticipated. It's my impression that you're basically comfortable with the emerging command relationships, as well."

His tone made the final sentence a question, and Green Valley snorted.

"I'd expected a somewhat more . . . visionary comment out of you, Merlin," he said. "In fact, I'm a little surprised His Majesty felt it was necessary to send you all the way up here to look things over with your own eyes, as it were."

Merlin managed not to wince, although that was coming to the point with a vengeance. On the other hand, it was a reasonable enough observation, given that Green Valley was one of the relatively small number of people who knew *Seijin* Merlin was far more than merely Emperor Cayleb Ahrmahk's personal armsman and bodyguard.

Over the last few years, virtually everyone in what had become the Empire of Charis had learned that all of the old fables and fairy tales about the legendary *seijin* warrior-monks were not only true, but actually understated their lethality. There was absolutely no question in anyone's mind that *Seijin* Merlin was the most deadly bodyguard any Charisian monarch had ever possessed. Given the number of assassination attempts he'd thwarted, and not just on the emperor, it was no wonder he was kept constantly at Cayleb's back, watching over him, protecting him both in the council chamber and on the field of battle.

But what Green Valley knew—and very few of his fellow Charisians even suspected—was that Cayleb and Sharleyan had another and very special reason for keeping Merlin so close.

The *seijin* had visions. He could see and hear far distant events, know what was happening thousands of miles away even as it happened. His ability to literally sit in on the war councils and political deliberations of Charis' enemies was a priceless advantage for the beleaguered empire, and his role as Cayleb's bodyguard was a perfect cover. He truly was the deadly and efficient guardian everyone thought he was, but that very deadliness provided ample reason for his permanent proximity to Cayleb and Sharleyan. After all, not even a *seijin* could protect someone from an assassin if he wasn't there to do the protecting, now could he? And so any potentially suspicious souls understood exactly why Captain Athrawes, with his eyes of "unearthly *seijin* blue," was constantly at the emperor's elbow, and it obviously had nothing at all to do with visions. Merlin was a bodyguard, not an adviser and an oracle. Any village idiot could figure *that* much out!

Green Valley knew better than that. Indeed, he'd come to suspect that Merlin was as much mentor as adviser. That most of the radical innovations which had provided the margin—so far—for Charis' survival in the face of its enemies' overwhelming numerical advantages had come from the *seijin*'s "suggestions" to the Charisians who had actually developed them into workable propositions. The baron suspected that for the excellent reason that he'd *been* one of those Charisians. It had been Green Valley, as a major in the Royal Charisian Marines, who'd played the lead role in developing revolutionary new infantry tactics built around the field artillery and rifled flintlock muskets which had "just happened" to appear in Charis shortly after one Merlin Athrawes' arrival. He'd worked closely with Merlin in the process of accomplishing that task, and they'd worked even more closely together, in many ways, during the Corisande campaign. In fact, the victory which had won Green Valley his title (and his knighthood) and sealed Prince Hektor of Corisande's defeat had been possible only because Merlin had revealed his ability to see visions to him.

And, so, yes—Baron Green Valley knew far more than the vast majority of his fellow subjects about Merlin Athrawes. But what he *didn't* know—what Merlin devoutly hoped he didn't even *suspect*—was how much more Merlin truly was.

*I'd really like to get him added to the inner circle,* the *seijin* reflected, *and I know*

*Cayleb and Sharleyan both agree with me, too. In fact, I think we have to get him added. It simply doesn't make sense not to bring him all the way inside, and I don't think we have to worry about any crises of religious conscience on his part.*

That last thought really did almost make him wince, given its direct bearing on the reason he was here.

"Their Majesties actually sent me for several reasons, My Lord," he said. "One of them, in many ways probably the most important, was to let me evaluate your progress—yours and Duke Eastshare's, I mean—firsthand. When I can actually ask questions, maybe even make a few suggestions in His Majesty's name. It's hard to do that if all you're doing is watching a vision."

"I can see where that would be true," Green Valley agreed. He didn't seem at all upset by the notion of Merlin's "evaluating" his progress in his new assignment, the *seijin* noted.

"And the second reason, almost equally important," Merlin admitted, "is to get me close enough to Eastshare to . . . interact with him."

This time, Green Valley only nodded. Merlin wasn't especially surprised— the baron had always been an astute and diplomatic fellow. He understood that, even with him, Merlin could scarcely come right out and say "They want me to see whether or not Eastshare is a traitor . . . too."

The good news was that Merlin was almost certain Eastshare wasn't. The bad news was that, despite all the *seijin*'s "unfair" advantages, Merlin was *only* almost certain he wasn't. And, unfortunately, the fact that the duke was effectively Empress Sharleyan's uncle by marriage, that he was the brother-in-law of the recently deceased Duke of Halbrook Hollow, and that he'd been Halbrook Hollow's senior general, second in command of the Royal Chisholmian Army, for the better part of fifteen years, meant that "almost certain" wasn't nearly good enough.

Not in the wake of Halbrook Hollow's treason.

"May I ask what your impressions have been so far?" Green Valley asked politely. "In a general sense, of course. I wouldn't want to ask you to get too specific about any particularly deserving ex-Marines—assuming there are any of those around, of course—and embarrass me with your effusive praise," he added, and Merlin snorted.

"You know, My Lord," the *seijin* said in an almost meditative tone, "I've always heard that a certain . . . brashness, one might say, is an integral part of any Marine's personality. You wouldn't happen to know how that rumor might have gotten started, would you?"

"Me?" Green Valley widened his eyes innocently. "I'm not a *Marine, Seijin* Merlin! I'm an officer in the Imperial Army. In fact, I've got a written commission around here somewhere to prove it. So what would a bluff, honest, naturally modest Army officer know about Marines and their overinflated self-images?"

"Oh, an excellent point," Merlin agreed. "I can't imagine what could have come over me to ask such a question."

"I should certainly hope not," Green Valley said a bit severely as he picked up the wine bottle and topped off Merlin's cup once more.

"Well, at any rate, in answer to your question, my impressions so far have been just about universally good." Merlin's tone and expression had both turned serious once again. "To be honest, I hadn't really realized quite how good the Chisholmian Army was. I should have, I suppose, given the role it played under King Sailys. Not to mention keeping Queen Sharleyan on the throne—and alive—after Sailys' death, of course. I mean, two-thirds of its senior officers are veterans of Sailys' campaigns, after all, and it's obvious Eastshare—and Halbrook Hollow, for that matter—did an excellent job of training and equipping them in the first place."

Green Valley nodded slowly, his gaze thoughtful, and Merlin shrugged.

"Obviously," he continued, "their equipment hasn't been as good as what we took to Corisande with us—but, then, no one's has, when you come down to it. And just as you've undoubtedly been discovering, their formations and drill are all oriented around tactics which have just become obsolete. But, again, they're scarcely alone in that. Given the weapons available to everybody a few years ago, my impression is that Eastshare's troops could at least hold their own against any of the mainland armies, man-for-man, and probably kick their arses for them, for that matter. Except for Siddarmark, of course."

It was Green Valley's turn to snort. The Republic of Siddarmark's army was widely acknowledged—with good reason—as the most effective armed force in Safehold's history. On land, at least. Siddarmark's navy was virtually nonexistent, and the Royal Charisian Navy had reigned supreme upon Safehold's seas even before Merlin Athrawes' arrival in Tellesberg. Anyplace a Siddarmarkian pike phalanx could find a place to stand, though, *it* reigned supreme. Which explained the Republic's successful, sustained expansion southward towards the Desnairian Empire over the past hundred and fifty Safeholdian years or so. That expansion had been halted only when the Knights of the Temple Lands guaranteed the frontiers of the Grand Duchy of Silkiah, in the Treaty of Silk Town, in 869.

Silkiah was at least nominally independent, although its grand duke paid a substantial yearly tribute to Desnair. He also paid one to the Knights of the Temple Lands every year, although *that* one was called a "tithe" and, until very recently, had been paid by every Safeholdian ruler. Not officially to the "Knights of the Temple Lands," of course, but that was only because the Knights of the Temple Lands all just happened to be members of the Church of God Awaiting's Council of Vicars, as well. Their dual role as both secular and temporal rulers gave them a significant unfair advantage, yet it imposed certain disadvantages, as well. Especially now. The Knights of the Temple Lands had been nervous for a long, long time about that magnificent Siddarmarkian Army just on the other side of their shared frontier, and over the years, they'd used their power as princes of the Church to help discourage any adventurism on the part of a succession of the Republic's lords protector. The Treaty of Silk Town might be the most flagrant example of their intervention, but it was scarcely the only one. That hadn't exactly helped the Church's relations with the Republic, although it had scarcely seemed likely to provoke an open breach, whatever some of the vicars might have thought, given the Church's unassailable supremacy.

But now . . . now that the Church's supremacy *had* been assailed, all of the anxieties which had been entertained by decades of Church chancellors had just acquired an entirely new point. There was no real evidence of any general movement of Siddarmarkians to embrace the Church of Charis, yet that didn't keep the Group of Four—the quartet of powerful vicars who truly ruled the Church—from worrying about what might yet happen.

*I wish it* would *happen,* Merlin thought more than a bit wistfully, *but however much Stohnar resents the Church—or the Group of Four, at least—he's not about to climb out on a limb with Charis. I don't think it's because he disagrees with Charis' accusations of Church corruption or because he has any illusions about the "sanctity" of the Group of Four and their motivations. But he's pragmatic as hell, and as well aware of the balance of power as anyone. In fact, he's* better *aware of it than almost anyone else. Besides, from what I've seen, he doesn't think any move to break with the Church would find general support in Siddarmark. And, for the moment at least, it looks like he's right about that.*

"The thing that impresses me most about the Chisholmians, to be honest," the *seijin* continued out loud, "is how readily and smoothly they seem to be adapting to the *new* tactics."

He raised one eyebrow at Green Valley, inviting comment, and the baron nodded.

"You're right about that," he agreed. "It seems to me that their officers are grasping the reasons behind the new tactics even faster than *our* troops did. And they're not just going through the motions in order to keep Their Majesties happy. For that matter, they're not even just duplicating what we've got to teach them, either. Instead, they're thinking about *why* we made the changes we've made and looking for ways to make what we've already accomplished even more effective."

"That's been my impression, too," Merlin acknowledged.

"As a matter of fact, I haven't seen a sign of what I was most worried about," Green Valley said. Merlin's eyebrow rose again, and the baron shrugged. "Charis has never had anything anyone in his right mind would call an 'army,' Merlin. We had a *navy* second to none, and nobody wanted to face our Marines at sea, but in terms of anything a land power would describe as an army, Charis wasn't even on the map.

"Here in Chisholm, though," he continued, sitting back in his chair, his expression intent, "the Army's clearly the senior service. It was the Army that broke the power of the great nobles and provided the stability here at home that let the Empress' father—and her, in her turn, of course—build the King-dom's prosperity. King Sailys may have started building a navy as soon as he could, since Chisholm needed it to protect its commerce against Corisandian privateers, but it was only the prosperity created by the Army which let him do that. So while we Charisians have tended to lavish our admiration and pride—not to mention the dragon's share of our wealth—on the Navy, it's been the other way around in Chisholm."

He shrugged again.

"Under those circumstances, what I was most afraid of was that the Chisholmians would automatically reject our advice about the new tactics. Af-ter all, what could a bunch of *Marines* know about the *real* conditions and re-quirements of fighting a war on *land?* In a lot of ways, that would only have been a reasonable question, too. For that matter, I imagine more than a few Charisian naval officers felt exactly that way where the Chisholmian *Navy* was concerned, when you come down to it. And the fact that it was our Marines who did all the actual fighting in Corisande—that their Army was completely left out, sitting here at home—could very well have fanned their resentment. Oh, they *said* they accepted the logistics arguments. That they understood we could only supply so many men across so many miles of ocean, which meant we couldn't afford to take along anyone who wasn't already equipped and trained with the new weapons. But I was afraid that, whatever they might have said, they would have resented being treated like some kind of farm team and left sitting in the dugout while the big-league players went off to war.

"As a matter of fact, that was what I *expected* to happen, and not just be-cause of any petty concern about the Army's 'honor,' either. You know as well as I do that prestige—and the ability to point to past accomplishments—plays a big role in how big a budget an army or a navy can expect to see coming its way. This is a professional army, with a professional officers corps, Merlin. They have to have been worried that being left home while someone else did all the fighting was going to . . . adversely effect their career prospects, one might say. I've seen a distinct undertone of resentment out of quite a few *civil-ian* Chisholmian bureaucrats who seem to think Charis has gotten an unfair share of the power and advantages under the Empire, so I don't think it would have been unreasonable for the Army to've felt that way."

"I know." Merlin nodded. "I've seen the same thing—from the bureaucrats, I mean—although, for some strange reason, they seem a bit more leery about showing their resentment around the Emperor or the Empress."

"No, really? I wonder why that might be?" Green Valley mused with an innocent smile, and Merlin snorted.

"As I say, I really was concerned about the Army's possible resentment over being 'left out' of the Corisande campaign," Green Valley went on. "And I have seen a little bit of it, but not very much, thank Langhorne."

"So they don't seem to be upset about the sudden infusion of all the Marines, either?" Merlin asked.

He was watching Green Valley attentively. The baron had been chosen for his present assignment, despite his relative youth—he was still well short of forty—and painfully new elevation to the aristocracy, not simply because he was so good at his job, but because of the acuity of his insights. Now Green Valley gave the *seijin* a wry headshake, as if admonishing him for having asked a question to which they both so obviously already knew the answer.

"No, it hasn't," he said out loud. "Partly, I think that's because of their professionalism. They're more interested in learning how to do their jobs even better than in defending their reputation for how well they already do them. In that respect, they remind me a lot of our naval officers like Earl Lock Island and Baron Rock Point. They're professionals first and prima donnas second, or even third.

"But, as I say, that's only *part* of the reason." Green Valley's eyes were narrow now, his expression intent. "I think probably an even bigger reason is that, aside from its very uppermost ranks, such a huge percentage of the Army's officers are commoners. One of the things I think most frustrates the great nobles who are so unhappy with the Emperor and the Empress is the way they've been shut out of any real positions of power in the Army. It would be stupid of them to be *surprised* by that, I suppose, since the whole reason King Sailys and Baron Green Mountain—and Halbrook Hollow, to give the man his due—created the Royal Army in the first place was to restore the Crown's prerogatives at the expense of the nobility. After the amount of fighting that took, I don't think it should astonish anyone that they decided against handing out generalships to any noblemen whose loyalty to the Crown they weren't totally sure of. And the fact that lowborn soldiers could—and *have*—risen to high rank in the Army helps explain how enthusiastically the commons support it. Here in Chisholm, the Army holds exactly the same position—as far as the commons are concerned, at any rate—as the Navy does in Charis, and it's young enough and professional enough to be genuinely flexible." He shook his head. "I honestly never expected just how flexible it really is."

Merlin nodded in agreement. He'd been a bit more optimistic about the Royal Chisholmian Army's willingness to adopt the new weapons and tactics than some Charisians had been, but even he had been pleasantly surprised by the Chisholmians' *enthusiasm* for the changes.

And, the *seijin* thought, Green Valley had an even better point than the baron himself might realize about the Army's importance in the eyes of the Empire's Chisholmian subjects.

By and large, the majority of Chisholmians appeared firmly united behind the decision to fuse the kingdoms of Chisholm and Charis (now almost universally referred to as "Old Charis," just to keep things straight) into the new Charisian Empire. Not all of them were, however. Some—and especially those who were most prone to think in terms of their own power and influence—doubted that the promised equality between Chisholm and Old Charis could (or would) truly be maintained. Old Charis boasted half again the population of Chisholm, and its economic wealth was at *least* four times that of Chisholm. Its manufactories and merchants had held a dominant position in *Chisholm's* economy even before the two kingdoms had united, the Charisian merchant marine dominated all the seas and oceans of Safehold, and the Royal Chisholmian Navy had disappeared—almost without a trace—into the much larger Royal Charisian Navy, even if the resulting union was officially called the *Imperial* Navy.

Under the circumstances, it probably wasn't unreasonable for at least some Chisholmians to nourish a few doubts about how long it would be before Chisholm openly became the junior partner—one might almost say the *second-class* partner—in the imperial relationship.

Cayleb and Sharleyan were determined to prevent that from happening. The fact that Sharleyan was Cayleb's *co*-ruler, that she had governed the entire Empire in her own name from Tellesberg while Cayleb was off at war in Corisande, and that it was *she*—not Cayleb—who had overseen the creation of the new Imperial Parliament had gone quite some way towards accomplishing that goal. The fact that the imperial capital would be located in Cherayth, the capital of the Kingdom of Chisholm, for half the year, and in Tellesberg, the capital of the Kingdom of Charis, for the other half of the year, went even further. It assured the citizens of Chisholm that Charisian viewpoints would not be allowed to dominate the imperial government simply because the people arguing for those viewpoints enjoyed a far better, far closer, and uninterrupted access to the emperor and empress.

The formation of the Imperial Army was intended to be yet another reassurance. The Chisholmian Crown's two great supports under King Sailys and Queen Sharleyan had been the fierce loyalty of the Chisholmian Commons and the Royal Army. As Green Valley had just pointed out, it had been the Army, backed by the political and financial support of the commons and with its ranks filled primarily by commoners, with which King Sailys had broken the arrogant power of the Charisian aristocracy's great magnates. It was that same Army and the even fiercer loyalty—the love—of those same commoners for the dauntless courage of the child-queen who had succeeded Sailys after his untimely death which had allowed Sharleyan to survive. And those same deep reservoirs of support were what had carried them with her in her decision to wed Cayleb and create the Empire.

She and Cayleb were both fully aware of that, which was why, just as Cayleb had insisted Chisholmian merchants and manufacturers must have equal access to the Empire's markets, both foreign and domestic, the two of them had decreed that it was Chisholm which would take the lead in the formation of the Imperial Army. There were those among the Royal Charisian Marines who had objected (although they'd been wise enough to do it quietly, in most cases) to that decision. Whose sense of pride in their own organization, in the way it had grown so explosively, the fashion in which it had smashed its opposition in Corisande, was deeply offended by the notion that the Marines should not only go back to being purely a shipboard and amphibious force but also transfer the majority of the Corisande campaign's veterans to the Army.

Those who'd been sufficiently foolish to make an issue of their objections had been . . . found other duties, however.

"I think probably still another part of it," the *seijin* said out loud now, "is the fact that Cayleb and Sharleyan have made it so abundantly clear that whereas Charis is reasonably going to take the lead where naval affairs are concerned, it only makes sense to give that same role to Chisholm where the *Army* is concerned. Which is why *you're* an Army officer now, of course. The decision to fold the bulk of the Imperial Marines over into the Army—and respect the seniority of the Army's existing officers in the process—wasn't an easy one, but Cayleb and Sharleyan were right to insist on it, I think."

"Absolutely!" Green Valley's nod was more vigorous and emphatic than Merlin's had been. "The officers I'm working with obviously see that decision as proof Their Majesties meant what they said about the organization of the Empire's armed forces. Especially after—well . . ."

The baron's voice trailed off on a most unusual note of something that was almost—not quite, but *almost*—embarrassment, and Merlin smiled without any trace of humor.

"Especially after the Army's top commander conspired with the Temple Loyalists to murder—or at least kidnap—Sharleyan, you mean?"

"Well, yes, actually," Green Valley admitted. He shook his head slightly. "Hard to blame them for worrying about it, really. In their place, *I'd* certainly have been afraid the Crown would entertain serious doubts about the Army's basic reliability. Especially given how popular Halbrook Hollow was—with the common troopers, not just the officer corps. He's the one who *built* this entire Army, Merlin. He shaped it, he commanded it in most of its critical battles, and he led its soldiers to victory in every campaign. How could they not have worried about whether or not the Crown would feel it couldn't afford to trust their loyalty after something like that? For that matter, a lot of them felt *shamed* by his actions. *They* hadn't done anything wrong, but he was their *commander*, and at least some of them feel his treason has stained them, as well."

"I know exactly what you mean," Merlin said soberly.

*And the truth is,* he told himself silently, *that at least some of the Army's officers* do *entertain the same doubts Halbrook Hollow did. Like the noble Earl of Swayle, for example.*

Barkah Rahskail, the Earl of Swayle, was young, only thirty-seven Safeholdian years old. He was also very tall for a Safeholdian, within an inch or so of Merlin's own height, and rakishly good-looking with his fair hair, dark eyes, and sun-bronzed complexion. Back when Merlin Athrawes had been Nimue Alban, she would definitely have given Swayle a close look.

But in addition to his good looks and noble birth, Swayle was a dyed-in-the-wool Temple Loyalist. He'd done a better job of hiding it than quite a few of his fellows, including Halbrook Hollow, but Merlin had no doubts about his fundamental beliefs. What he didn't know yet was where Swayle's ultimate loyalties lay. Would his repulsion against the Church of Charis' "apostasy" and "heresy"—and, quite possibly, the death in disgrace of an army commander he'd deeply admired and respected—drive him into treason of his own? Or would his and his family's long-standing loyalty to the House of Tayt—unusual, actually, among the high Chisholmian nobility—and his oath as an officer of the Royal Army hold firm against those forces?

Merlin was afraid he could guess which way Swayle would jump in the end. But he hadn't jumped yet, and neither Cayleb nor Sharleyan was in the habit of punishing people for what they *might* do.

Which suited Merlin Athrawes just fine, when it came down to it.

*I'm keeping an eye on all of the ones we know shared at least some of Halbrook Hollow's doubts,* he reminded himself. *And if Cayleb and Sharleyan aren't going to hammer anyone until and unless someone decides to emulate Halbrook Hollow, they won't hesitate if the time ever comes to bring that hammer down, either. I know they hope they won't have to, but they'll do it if they* do *have to. And at least it looks like the ones with Temple Loyalist leanings are definitely in the minority . . . for now.*

"And Duke Eastshare?" he asked out loud. "What's your read of how *he* feels about all this, My Lord?"

"You're asking me to comment about my commanding officer, *Seijin* Merlin," Green Valley said with a sudden—and unaccustomed—edge of severity, and he frowned. "I understand why you'd be concerned, but, to be honest, I don't think it's really appropriate for me to be passing judgment on His Grace's loyalty to the Crown."

Merlin allowed one of his eyebrows to arch in mild surprise. He started to respond, then stopped.

Actually, he thought, Green Valley's . . . stiffness *was* a judgment on Eastshare's loyalty. Particularly since it clearly didn't stem from any reluctance to risk antagonizing a powerful noble in the extraordinarily unlikely event that word of any criticism on his part would ever make it back to Eastshare.

*What it is, is an indication of just how much he's discovered he respects Eastshare,*

Merlin told himself. *If he had any doubts about Eastshare's loyalty, he wouldn't respect him, either, no matter how flexible the Duke might be in a professional sense. So the fact that he doesn't want to answer is an answer.*

"I understand, My Lord," he said out loud, rather more formally than had become the norm for his conversations with Green Valley. The baron looked at him for a moment, then gave an almost imperceptible nod, and his frown vanished.

"So, overall, you're satisfied?" Merlin continued in a more normal tone, and Green Valley nodded again, more firmly.

"Overall, I'm very satisfied. I wish—and so does Duke Eastshare—that we could have provided even more Marines as cadre, but we both understand why Their Majesties had to leave General Chermyn a big enough garrison force in Corisande. I also wish we could get the new rifle shops and cannon foundries set up here in Chisholm more quickly, but Chisholm simply doesn't have the pool of experienced mechanics and craftsmen Old Charis does. At least the first couple of shipments of rifles have already come in, so not *everyone* is drilling with broom handles.

"On the plus side, in addition to everything else we've just been talking about, I have to admit that the Duke and his officers seem to have a better grasp of the realities of fighting on land than we do—than *I* do, and I'm the fellow who developed all our new infantry tactics." He snorted. "They pay me a flattering amount of attention, and they listen damned carefully to everything I say, particularly given the fact that, unlike them, I actually have field experience with the new weapons. But the truth is, they've already pointed out a lot of places where my ideas—and not just about tactics, either; they've got a lot more experience with army *logistics* than we have—could stand some improving. In some cases, a *lot* of improving."

*And it says very good things about you, My Lord, that you not only recognize the truth when you see it but that you're willing to admit it—to others, and not just yourself, too,* Merlin thought.

"So you think I'll be able to go back to Cherayth and tell Their Majesties the great army integration project is going well?" he said out loud.

"Yes," Green Valley said, looking steadily into the *seijin's* blue eyes, making it plain just how many levels he was actually speaking on. "Yes, I think you can tell them it's going *very* well."

W hat do you think they really want, Phylyp?"
Irys Daykyn's tone was calm as she gazed across the dinner table's
empty plates at her legal guardian, but the hazel eyes she'd inherited from her
dead mother were darker than could have been explained solely by the lamps'
dimness.

"Mostly, I think, what they've said, Your Highness." Phylyp Ahzgood, Earl
of Coris, shrugged. "Oh, I don't doubt they've got more in mind than they've
actually said so far. But as far as what that 'more' might be, your guess is almost
certainly as good as mine," he said. And he meant it, too. Irys Daykyn might be
only seventeen years old—not quite *sixteen,* in the years of the planet upon
which humanity had actually evolved—but she was scarcely a typical seventeen-
year-old. Not even a typical seventeen-year-old princess.

"I don't expect they've issued their . . . invitation, let's call it, because of
their vast concern for Daivyn, though." Coris' tone was biting. He wouldn't
have let anyone else hear him using it about the Group of Four, but neither he
nor Irys had any illusions about that particular quartet, and no one else was present. "At the same time," the man who had been Prince Hektor of Corisande's
spymaster for so many years continued, "I think it could probably be worse than
it actually is. At least they're not insisting the two of you accompany me!"

"Why should they bother to invite *me,* whatever their motives?"

Irys' face had tightened, and Coris found himself nodding in acknowledgment. He'd meant his final sentence at least partly as an attempt at humor, but he
wasn't really surprised, after the fact, that it had fallen flat. And he no more
doubted than Irys did that, as far as the Group of Four was concerned, she herself had very little value. Her little brother Daivyn was the legitimate Prince of
Corisande—even Cayleb and Sharleyan of Charis acknowledged that much—
even if he was currently in exile. But Irys? She was simply a sort of unimportant second thought. She had no intrinsic value as a political pawn in the Group
of Four's eyes, and they certainly weren't going to waste any time worrying
about what a fugitive princess in exile, subsisting solely (so far as they knew, at
any rate) upon the niggardly generosity of distant relatives, might think.

Which was incredibly foolish of them, in Phylyp Ahzgood's opinion, no
matter how reasonable *they* obviously thought it was.

So far, anyway. It was entirely possible they would eventually learn the error of their ways. Probably quite painfully, he thought with a certain undeniable satisfaction.

"I'm afraid you have a point about that, from their perspective, at least," he said in answer to her question. "On the other hand, my own point stands, I think. If they had any immediate plans where Daivyn is concerned, they'd probably insist I drag him along, as well."

Despite the very real affection in which she held her "guardian," and despite her own worries, Irys couldn't quite keep from grinning at Coris' sour tone. It wasn't really funny, of course—a journey of the next best thing to nine thousand miles would scarcely have been a mere jaunt in the country, even in the middle of summer. With winter coming on fast, it was going to be a highly unpleasant experience no matter what happened. And its final stage had the potential to be actively dangerous, for that matter.

"You don't think it's just because of how hard the trip's going to be?" she asked, indirectly voicing her own worry where Coris was concerned.

"No, I don't." The earl's lips tightened, and he shook his head. "Duchairn would probably worry about that, especially given Daivyn's age. Even Trynair *might* consider it, for that matter, if only because of his awareness of Daivyn's potential value. I doubt it would even cross Maigwair's mind to worry about dragging a nine-year-old through hip-deep snow, though. And Clyntahn—"

Coris broke off and shrugged, and it was Irys' turn to nod. Vicar Zahmsyn Trynair was probably as cold-blooded and calculating a chancellor as the Church of God Awaiting had ever produced in all the nine dusty centuries since the Day of Creation. He was far more likely to regard Daivyn Daykyn purely as a potential political asset than as a little boy whose father had been brutally murdered. And, by all reports, Allayn Maigwair, the Church's Captain General, had about as much imagination as a worn-out boot. Expecting it to occur to *him* to worry about Daivyn would have been as foolish as it would futile.

And then there was Zhaspahr Clyntahn. Irys no more doubted than Coris did that the Grand Inquisitor would simply have looked blankly at anyone who might have had the temerity to suggest he should bother his own head one way or the other about Daivyn's well-being.

"If they were contemplating any significant change in their calculations where he's concerned, they might want him in Zion, where he'd be handy," the earl continued. "For that matter, I think Clyntahn, at least, would want the opportunity to . . . impress Daivyn with just how serious an interest the Inquisitor and his associates take in him." He shook his head. "No, I'm inclined to think it's pretty much exactly what Trynair's message suggests it is. They want to be sure *I* fully understand their plans for him. And to get my own impressions of the situation in Corisande, of course."

For a moment, Irys looked as if she wanted to spit, and Coris didn't blame her a bit.

"I'm sure they've got better sources than I do—than *we* do," he said. "Or, at least, that their sources can get their reports to Zion faster than our agents can get reports to us. But anything they know about Corisande is secondhand, at best, even if it is more recent than anything we've heard. I'm not surprised they'd want to pick the brain of one of your father's councilors."

"Especially his spymaster's brain, you mean." Irys' lips twitched a brief smile. It was *very* brief, though. "And especially now that Father's dead. No doubt they want your impression of how our people are likely to have reacted when Cayleb assassinated him."

This time, Coris only nodded. He'd watched Irys Daykyn grow up. In fact, as he'd once admitted to her, he'd been present on more than one occasion when her diaper had been changed. He knew exactly how close she'd been to her father, exactly how she'd taken his murder. And although he'd tried his very best to keep her mind open to other possibilities, he knew exactly who she blamed for that murder.

Personally, Coris' suspicions lay in a somewhat different direction. But there were dangers, especially for her, in laying those suspicions too plainly before her.

"I'm sure that's one of the things they'll want to discuss," he agreed. "At any rate, though, I think this probably means they're planning on leaving you and Daivyn here in Talkyra with King Zhames, at least for the foreseeable future. It's going to take me better than two months just to get to Zion, and I don't have any idea how long they plan on my staying once I get there. Since I don't think they're contemplating separating me permanently from Daivyn, or that they're likely to be planning on sending him anywhere without me along as his guardian, that probably means they expect to leave him right here for at least five or six months. Probably longer, actually."

"I can't say I'd be entirely sorry if they did." Irys sighed and shook her head. "Neither of us really likes it here, but he needs some stability, Phylyp. Needs some time in one place to heal."

"I know." Coris reached across the table and patted the back of her left hand gently. "I know. And I'll do my best to convince *them* of that, as well."

"I know you will."

Irys smiled at him, hoping he didn't see the edge of fear behind her expression. She knew Phylyp Ahzgood. Despite the reputation some assigned him, she knew how loyal he'd always been to her father, and she herself trusted him implicitly. Probably more than she really ought to, she thought sometimes. Not because she thought there was truly any likelihood of his betraying her trust, but simply because—as her father had always said—no one who sat on a throne, or who was responsible for supporting someone who did, could ever afford to *completely* trust anyone.

But there was a reason her father had selected Coris as her own and Daivyn's guardian. And part of that reason was that in Phylyp Ahzgood's case, at least, he'd set aside his own injunction against trusting too deeply.

*Which is* exactly *why they'll try to separate us from you, if they realize the truth, Phylyp,* she thought. *For right now, they may well believe all those stories you and Father always encouraged about your own ambitions and sinister motivations. But if they ever figure out where your true loyalties lie, that you* aren't *prepared to cheerfully sacrifice Daivyn for your own advantage, or to curry favor with them, you'll become a potential liability, not an asset. And if that happens, Trynair and Clyntahn won't hesitate for an instant about declaring us—or Daivyn, at least—official wards of the Council of Vicars.*

She looked across the table at him in the lamplight, studying his expression and, for a moment, at least, feeling every bit as young as the rest of the world thought she was. Wishing she were still young enough to climb up into his lap, put her head down on his shoulder, and let him hug away her fears while he promised her everything would be all right.

But everything *wasn't* going to be "all right," ever again, and she knew it.

*Don't let them take you away from me, Phylyp,* she thought. *Whatever else happens, don't let them take you away.*

.IV.
### City of Manchyr,
### Duchy of Manchyr,
### Princedom of Corisande

*CORISANDIANS!*

*CITIZENS OF MANCHYR!*

The Blood of your slain Prince cries out from the very stones of your City! The boots of the slaves and lackeys of the Monster who shed that Blood march through your streets! The voices of Apostate Priests speak in your Churches! The Defenders of the True Faith are driven into silence and hiding!

How much longer will you endure these Insults? These Affronts to both God and Man? How much longer . . .

Paitryk Hainree frowned in concentration as he considered the composing stick and the current line of type. As a silversmith, he was a skilled engraver, but he'd discovered (not to his surprise) that there were very few similarities between engraving and typesetting. For one thing, he still had trouble reading the mirror-imaged letters. There was no problem identifying each letter as he took it from the proper pigeonhole of the job case (although he still had to look to be sure it *was* the proper pigeonhole), and it was easy enough—ahead of time—to chart out which letters had to go where on the composing stick before they were transferred to the forme and bound together. But his brain still persisted in reading each word as he set up the type, and he'd discovered that it tried to trick him into reading the letters in the "correct" order instead of in the reversed order they had to go into for the press.

Still, it wasn't an impossible skill to acquire, and if it wasn't the same as silversmithing, there were similarities. He'd always liked the detail work, the concentration on the little things, working with metals, the fine coordination of hand and eye. The printer's was a different art, but it was still an art, and he'd found that the part of him which had never expected to become a street agitator treasured the retreat back into an artisan's role, even if it was only temporary.

He reached for the next letter, and behind his focus on the task in hand his mind was busy. This broadsheet would be transported from the carefully hidden basement press through a network of dedicated supporters. Copies of it would be tacked up all over the city by tomorrow night. Of course, parties of the City Guard would be busy tearing them down by the following dawn. Not all of those City Guardsmen would agree with their orders in that regard— Hainree was sure of that—but they'd obey them. The "Regency Council" and that traitorous bastard Gahrvai would see to that!

Hainree discovered his jaw was clenching once more and ordered it to relax. It obeyed . . . after a fashion, and he drew a deep breath. Just thinking about Sir Koryn Gahrvai was enough to send rage pulsing through every vein. Gahrvai's effortless defeat at the hands of Cayleb Ahrmahk and his army could have been put down to mere feckless incompetence. In his more charitable moments, Hainree would even have been prepared to put at least some of it down to simple bad luck, or to the fact that Shan-wei looked after her own. But Gahrvai's decision to actually accept command of the traitorous forces prepared to do Ahrmahk's will here in Corisande had to make a man wonder. Had he truly been simply unlucky, or incompetent, or had there been something more sinister at work? Some quiet little understanding between him and the invaders?

Had his treason against Corisande and the House of Daykyn begun only after his defeat . . . or before it?

Most of the time, Hainree was willing to accept that Gahrvai's present position was a case of opportunism after the fact, not an indication of treason *before* the fact. And he'd realized, even without Father Aidryn's gentle hints, that accusing Gahrvai and his father of having plotted with Cayleb ahead of time would be . . . premature, at this point. In the fullness of time, that might change, especially as the debate over exactly whose hand had hired the assassins to strike down Prince Hektor and his eldest son matured. Personally, it seemed obvious to Hainree that those who'd profited the most by the prince's murder were those most likely to have *planned* that murder. And, taken all together, he couldn't think of anyone who'd profited more heavily than the members of the "Regency Council" set up to govern the Princedom according to Ahrmahk's demands. They could call themselves Prince Daivyn's council all they wanted to, but that didn't change who they truly answered to . . . or the fact that they'd somehow managed not simply to survive but to come out with even more power than they'd had before.

Nor did it change the supine surrender of the Princedom's Parliament, Hainree thought, scowling down at the composing stick. He supposed it was unreasonable to expect Parliament to defy Ahrmahk's will, as dutifully expressed through the "Regency Council," with the Charisian Viceroy General Chermyn and the better part of sixty thousand Charisian Marines occupying Corisande. Chermyn had twenty thousand of those Marines right here in Manchyr, and while he'd made some effort to avoid parading them too blatantly through the streets of the city, everyone knew they were there. As did the members of the House of Lords and the House of Commons. So, no, it wasn't surprising Parliament had voted to give Ahrmahk everything he asked for.

On the other hand, there might well be a difference between what they'd *voted* for and what they really intended to do. By all reports, Parliament would be breaking up shortly, with all of its members returning to their homes, out from under the eye—and the bayonets—of the occupation. It would be interesting to see what happened *then*. He knew the hard skeleton of organized resistance had already come together here in Manchyr, and his own contact from that skeleton assured him the same thing was happening outside the city. It remained to be fleshed out with sinew and muscle, but those other things would come in time. And not all of them from sources Hainree might have expected. In fact, from a few stray words his contact had let drop, Hainree strongly suspected that the resistance's leadership had already made discreet contact with several members of Parliament, as well. No doubt they'd planted quite a few equally discreet seeds that would bear fruit in due time.

In the meanwhile, Paitryk Hainree would concentrate on cultivating and fertilizing his own little plot right here in the capital.

▼ ▼ ▼

Hainree was far too intent on his work to have noticed the tiny device perched in one corner of the basement's ceiling. Even if he hadn't been distracted by the printing press, it was extremely unlikely he would have seen the thing. It was the next best thing to microscopically small, although even at that, it was larger than some of its still smaller brethren, and if anyone had told him what it was capable of doing, he would have dismissed the claims as something out of a fairy tale.

Unfortunately for him, he would have been wrong, and later that evening, in the far distant city of Cherayth, an Imperial Guardsman with a fierce mustache and a neatly trimmed dagger beard leaned back, eyes closed, and rubbed the scar on his cheek with a thoughtful finger as he contemplated the imagery that tiny surveillance platform had transmitted to him.

*I'd really like to pay a visit to Master Hainree,* Merlin Athrawes reflected without ever opening his eyes. *He and his friends are getting just a little bit better organized than I could wish. On the other hand, we're building up a pretty detailed organizational chart on them. Of course, it would help if we could tell someone in Corisande that we are, but I suppose you can't have* everything.

He grimaced sourly at the thought, yet he also knew he was correct. He didn't like how much of his own—and Owl's, and Cayleb's, and Sharleyan's—time was being consumed by the project, but he'd spread his SNARCs' remote platforms thickly throughout the Corisandian capital. As each member of the emerging resistance cadre was identified, one of the parasite platforms was assigned to him full-time, and these people's internal organization wasn't nearly as sophisticated as it could have been. Aidryn Waimyn—and there was someone Merlin *really* wanted to have a word with—had done his best to instill a cellular organization, at least at the very top. Unfortunately for him, he had to make do with what was available, and at least some of his . . . associates were too direct for that sort of sophistication. They had far more enthusiasm than professional detachment. And, as far as Merlin could tell, very few members of the Earl of Coris' intelligence services had so far been co-opted by Waimyn.

*Of course, we don't know how long that's going to* last, *now do we?* he reminded himself.

There were times when Merlin was deeply tempted to hop into his recon skimmer, buzz down to Manchyr, and personally eliminate Waimyn. It wouldn't be particularly difficult. In fact, it would be childishly simple and, under the circumstances, one of the more pleasant chores he could have assigned himself. Unfortunately, unless he was prepared to remain in Corisande full-time and spend his nights doing nothing but eliminating resistance leaders, he'd be rather in the position of King Canute. Worse, he would deprive the resistance of its *organized* leadership, and he didn't want that. Far better to leave Waimyn in position for now, however irritatingly competent and industrious he was proving, rather than shatter the resistance's cohesion. That might change, yet for now it was far more useful to know exactly who its leaders were, exactly where they might be found when the time came, and exactly what sort of plans it was making and what information it was passing to its various satellites. Breaking up the current organization would almost certainly deprive it of its increasing effective-ness, but only at the cost of replacing it with a formless, *unorganized* movement which would be almost impossible to monitor the way they could monitor the present situation. Not to mention one which would be far more difficult to up-root when the moment to take action against it finally arrived.

*I only wish,* he thought, returning his attention to the SNARC's imagery, *that I didn't expect them to do so much damage in the interim.*

▼　　▼　　▼

"I know it's a pain in the arse," Hauwyl Chermyn growled, standing with his hands clasped behind him while he gazed out his office window at a vista of cloudy rain. "And, truth to tell, what I'd really like to be doing is shooting the bastards the instant they turn up!"

Brigadier Zhoel Zhanstyn, commanding officer of the Imperial Charisian Marines Third Brigade, looked at his superior's back with a faint smile. It was mostly a smile of affection, although it might have held just a trace of amuse-ment, and possibly just a *little* exasperation. If it did, though, that last emotion was directed at the situation, not at Viceroy General Chermyn.

*And if the Old Man needs to vent his spleen at someone, I suppose I'm the logical candidate,* Zhanstyn reflected. *It's not like there's anyone else he can let down his guard with.*

That would probably have been true with just about any senior officer in Chermyn's unenviable position, the brigadier thought. Combining the roles of occupation force commander and official viceroy for Emperor Cayleb and Em-press Sharleyan would have been a stiff enough challenge for almost anyone. Given Chermyn's distaste for politics, coupled with his previous lifelong suc-cess at avoiding anything that even smacked of duty at court, it would have been difficult to find someone who felt less suited to the task.

Fortunately for the Empire of Charis, it had never occurred to Hauwyl Chermyn to decline his present post. And the reason that was fortunate was that no matter how ill-suited he might have considered himself, he was almost certainly the very best man available for the job. The viceroy general might not *like* politics, and he might be unpolished (to say the very least) by courtly stan-dards, but that didn't mean he didn't *understand* politics, and his iron sense of duty and integrity was coupled with a bulldog pugnacity any fool could sense from clear across a room.

There was no doubt that the noblemen and commoners who'd assembled in Parliament here in Manchyr had sensed it, at any rate, and none of them had been stupid enough to challenge him. Not openly, at any rate. Zhanstyn had no doubt that quite a few conversations in various cloakrooms and private apart-ments had centered on clandestine ways to evade Chermyn's determination to enforce the policies Emperor Cayleb had laid out before his own departure for

Chisholm. For the moment, though, the viceroy general had his hand firmly around the throat of Corisande's great lords.

That had been made easier by the fact that, like the wealthier members of the House of Commons, the great aristocrats had too much to lose. That made them cautious, unwilling to attempt open resistance, especially after Chermyn— in his blunt, unpolished, uncourtly, yet crystal-clear style—had made it abundantly plain what he intended to do to any noble who violated his new oath of fealty to the Charisian Crown. The fact that diplomatic circumlocution was so utterly foreign to him had gone a great way towards making certain no one in his audience doubted for a moment that he'd meant every word he said. And that any excuses about oaths to the excommunicated not being binding would leave him remarkably unmoved when he and his siege artillery turned up outside any oathbreaker's castle walls.

"But pain in the arse or not," Chermyn continued now, swinging away from the window to face the brigadier, hands still clasped behind him, "it's the way it's got to be. For now, at least." He grimaced. "Mind you, I'd like nothing better than to get my hands on the damned ringleaders! There's not much doubt in *my* mind that most of these poor bastards're being more or less led around by the nose." He made a disgusted sound midway between a snort and a snarl. "And I've read the damned broadsides, same as you. Somebody's stirring this pot, and I've no doubt His Majesty was right about what it is they're after. Which is why I'm not going to give it to them."

"Yes, Sir," Zhanstyn acknowledged. Although, truth to tell, it wasn't exactly as if he'd objected to the viceroy general's instructions or policy. On the other hand, he was pretty sure Chermyn knew he understood his superior's "explanation" was more in the nature of a way for Chermyn to let off pressure of his own before it did him a mischief.

"The last thing we need to offer up to the bastards behind all this are martyrs," Chermyn growled now, turning his head to look back at the water-streaming panes of glass. "I think most of these people are at least willing to keep their heads down, if the troublemakers'll just leave them alone. I'm not saying we could keep the lid on the pot forever, but all we really have to do is keep it screwed down until Anvil Rock, Tartarian, and the rest of the Regency Council get their feet on the ground. Build up at least a little legitimacy. That business at the Cathedral the other day"—he turned his head back, his eyes meeting Zhanstyn's suddenly—"that could've turned nasty. Bad enough to lose one of our own, but if that young lad of yours—Lieutenant Tahlas, wasn't it?" He paused until Zhanstyn nodded, then snorted again. "If the boy had lost control, let his men stack the bodies the way I've no doubt they *wanted* to instead of settling for cracked skulls and a few broken bones, it would've given the bastards on the other side exactly what they wanted."

"I've already commended Lieutenant Tahlas, Sir," Zhanstyn said, making no effort to hide how pleased he'd been by the viceroy general's remembering the young man's name. "And I agree with what you've just said. All the same, Sir, if they keep pushing, and especially if we lose more men, we're going to have to push back. It's one thing to show restraint; it's another thing if the other side decides restraint is really weakness."

"Agreed." Chermyn nodded grimly. "That's one reason I want Gahrvai's formations stood up as quickly as possible. I'd rather put a Corisandian face on this whole confrontation, drop us back into a support role." He showed his teeth in a thin smile. "D'you suppose any of these people are going to realize just how much we don't want to kill any more of them than we can help?"

"In a perfect world, Sir, I'm sure they would. In the world we've got—?"

The brigadier shrugged, and Chermyn chuckled harshly. Then he squared his shoulders and marched back across to his desk. He settled into the chair behind it and picked up the first of the folders piled on his blotter.

"Well, as you've just suggested, it's an *imperfect* world, Brigadier," he observed. "And that being the case, I suppose it's time we dealt with some of those imperfect little details. Starting with this request from Brigadier Myls." He tapped the top sheet of paper and the folder with an index finger. "I think he's got a point about being spread too thin."

"I agree, Sir." Zhanstyn grimaced. "That's not to say I like it, but I agree he's got a problem. And, unfortunately, I can already see where you're thinking about finding the manpower to solve it for him."

"Sharp as a tack, that's you," Chermyn said with another, much more cheerful-sounding chuckle. "Now, where do you think I should start robbing you?"

"Well, Sir, I was thinking that if we took Alpha Company out of Second Battalion of the Third, then took Charlie Company out of First Battalion of Fourth, we'd have a pretty good mix of experience and enthusiasm. Then, if we added—"

# OCTOBER,
# YEAR OF GOD 893

Empress Sharleyan of Charis had been prepared for marvels—or she'd thought she was, anyway. But the reality was so far beyond what she'd expected that she'd discovered all her preparations had been in vain.

She sat in the "recon skimmer's" passenger compartment, with her nose perhaps two inches from the inside of the clear "armorplast" which covered it like some perfectly transparent bubble, staring out at the night-struck sky. The moon rode high and clear, shining like a new, incredibly bright silver coin against the blackest heaven she had ever imagined, spangled with stars that were even more impossibly bright than the moon. They were odd, those stars, burning with pinprick clarity, without even the faintest trace of a twinkle. She'd never seen stars that sharp, that clear, even on the coldest winter night, and she shivered as she remembered Merlin's explanation.

*We're so high there's not even any air out there. Not enough to matter, anyway.* She shook her head. *It never even occurred to me that the only reason they "twinkle" is because we're seeing them through so many miles of air that it distorts our view. I always thought "clear as air" meant really clear, but it doesn't, really, after all. And now I'm up above all of that. I'm on the very threshold of what Merlin calls "space."*

No other Safehold-born human being, she knew, had ever been as high before. Not even Cayleb on his journey between Corisande and Charis. She stared down, down, to where the planet itself had become a vast, curved globe. To where the cloud tops so very far below the skimmer were silver and deepest black, drifting across The Anvil, that stormy sweep of water between Chisholm and Hammer Island. She couldn't make out the surface from this height, not in the dark, not using her own merely mortal eyes. She knew it was there, though, and all she had to do was turn her head and look at the "visual display" to see that vast, wind-ruffled stretch of saltwater in perfect detail. Merlin had shown her how to manipulate the display's controls, and the skimmer's computer-driven sensors happily generated daylight-bright, true-color imagery of anything she cared to gaze upon. She could focus closer—"zoom in," Merlin called it—until even the most distant objects below seemed little more than arm's-length away, too.

And yet, as Cayleb had warned her would be the case, that marvel, that

God's eye view, paled beside what her own eye saw when she gazed out through the armorplast.

*It's because the "imagery" is magic,* she thought. *Merlin can call it whatever he wants, but it is magic, and my emotions know it, whatever my mind may be trying to tell them. It's like something out of a child's tale, something that's not quite . . . real. But this—the moon, these stars, those clouds—I'm seeing them with my own eyes, and that means they* are *real. And I'm seeing them from thousands upon thousands upon* thousands *of feet in the air. I'm actually* up *here, flying among them, and they're really, really* out *there, all above and about and beneath me.*

She drew a deep breath, smiling more than a bit crookedly, as that thought reminded her of the previous evening. . . .

▼    ▼    ▼

Sharleyan finished throwing up (she hoped) and wiped her face with the hot, damp towel. Her mouth, she reflected, tasted as bad as she could remember anything's ever tasting. Her stomach heaved again at the thought, but she suppressed the sensation sternly. Muscles hovered on the brink of revolt for a few precarious seconds, then subsided . . . for the moment, at least.

"Better?" a voice asked, and she looked up from the basin in her lap with a wan smile.

Despite both the fire crackling behind her husband and the embedded tile pipes circulating heated water under the bedroom's tile floor, the air was chilly, to say the least, and the fresh towel he'd just taken from the kettle on the bedroom hearth steamed in his hand. Under the circumstances, it was understandable that the emperor had wrapped a blanket around himself as he stood beside their bed, however unregal he might look at the moment. In fact, Sharleyan was of the opinion that it went beyond unregal to something approaching silly.

*On the other hand,* she thought, *he did* climb *out of bed and hand me a towel the instant he heard me throwing up. That's got to count for something . . . even if the whole thing* is *his fault.*

"Better . . . I think," she said, adding the conditional when her stomach gave another tentative heave.

"Good."

He whisked the towel with which she'd wiped her face—and which had already cooled markedly—out of her hand and replaced it with the one he'd just wrung out. The used towel went back into the kettle, and he carried the basin into the adjacent bathroom. A moment later, she heard the toilet flush. Then he returned, setting the basin carefully on the bedside table beside her before he climbed back into the bed himself and wrapped his arms around her.

"Ow!" she objected as cold feet wiggled their way under her.

"Well," Cayleb Zhan Haarahld Bryahn Ahrmahk, Duke of Ahrmahk, Prince of Tellesberg, Prince Protector of the Realm, King of Charis, and by

God's Grace Emperor of Charis, said reasonably to Sharleyan Alahnah Zheny-fyr Ahlyssa Tayt Ahrmahk, Duchess of Cherayth, Lady Protector of Chisholm, Queen of Chisholm, and by God's Grace *Empress* of Charis, "they got frozen in *your* service. The least you can do is help me thaw them out again!"

"And if the shock of being poked with two lumps of ice makes me throw up again?" she inquired darkly.

"At the rate you're throwing up, whether I poke you with ice or not isn't going to make any difference," he told her philosophically. "Besides, you're facing the other way."

Some things could not be allowed to pass by any self-respecting empress, and Cayleb squawked as she whipped around and slender, vengeful fingers found his armpits. In one of the universe's less fair dispensations, he was far more ticklish than she was, and she pressed her despicable advantage ruthlessly.

"All right! *All right!*" he gasped finally. "I surrender! I'll thaw my own feet out, you ungrateful and unreasonable wench!"

"Ooooh! *'Wench'* is it?" she retorted, and he shouted with laughter as she redoubled her attack. Then he rolled back over, caught her wrists, and pinned them down. She started to wiggle, only to stop as he bent over her and kissed her forehead.

"But you're my very most *favorite* wench in all the world," he told her softly, and she shook her head with a smile.

"You really need to work on your technique, Your Majesty," she told him. "On the other hand, considering the source—and the fact that that's probably the very best your poor, primitive male brain can do—I accept your apology."

"'Apology'?" He quirked one eyebrow. "I don't remember making any apol—"

She smacked her hip into him sideways, and he paused in midword, his expression thoughtful.

"What I meant to say," he corrected himself in a dignified tone, "was that I'm gratified—*deeply* gratified—by your forgiveness."

"Which is why you'll live to see another dawn," she told him sweetly.

"A consideration which did cross my own mind," he conceded, and gave her forehead another kiss before he settled back.

Given the way her own mouth tasted, she couldn't fault his kisses' placement, she admitted as his right arm went back under and around her and he drew her head down on his right shoulder. She nestled close, treasuring the warmth of their blankets, inhaling the smell of him, and he raised his arm behind her in a hug which happened to let his right hand caress her hair.

"Seriously," he said, "how long do you expect this to go on?"

"*Too* long, however long it is," she said darkly, then shrugged. "I'm not sure. Mother says she was never morning sick at all, and neither was Grandmama, as far as Mother recalls, so that's no help. Or particularly *fair*, now that I think about it. And according to Sairaih, *her* mother was morning sick for at least *ten* months. Or was it an entire year? *Two* years?" The empress shrugged again. "Something like that anyway."

She grimaced fondly, and Cayleb chuckled in sympathy. Sairaih Hahlmyn had been Sharleyan's personal maid since she'd been a little girl, and she seemed to be enjoying the present moment rather more than the empress was. She was certainly hovering for all she was worth, and no matter what Father Derahk, the palace healer, might say, Sairaih could be relied upon to think of one of her innumerable female ancestors who had experienced the same problem, only incomparably worse. No doubt she fondly imagined she was reassuing her charge by telling her how lucky she was that things were so much less bad than they could have been.

Or something.

"Well, maybe Merlin can give us an estimate," Cayleb said.

"Maybe." Sharleyan knew her tone sounded a bit tentative, but she also figured she was entitled to at least a little anxiety, given the nature of her projected itinerary.

"Nervous?" Cayleb asked gently, as if he'd just read her mind . . . not that it would have required any esoteric talent to be able to figure out exactly what she'd been thinking.

"A little," she admitted, nestling more comfortably against him. "It's not something *I've* ever done before, after all."

"Well, I've only done it twice myself—once, really, if you're talking about round trips," Cayleb said. "On the other hand, Merlin's done it a lot. Of course, he didn't take *me* 'out of atmosphere' "—the emperor pouted for a moment—"but he didn't have as far to go then as he does this time. And if he's confident his 'stealth systems' are up to the trip, *I'm* not going to argue with him."

"Very big of you, since *you're* not the one making this particular trip," she pointed out dryly.

"No, I'm not," he agreed. "In fact, I wish I were." He hugged her more tightly against himself for just a moment. "Still, given that he can only fit in one passenger, I think you may actually be a better choice for this first trip than I'd be, in some ways. And I know Father Derahk says everything is just fine, that all this morning sickness is perfectly natural, but I'll still feel better having Owl say the same thing."

"Me, too," she acknowledged, then giggled just a little nervously against his shoulder. "Still, it does feel a bit strange to be talking about getting a . . . machine's opinion."

"Just 'strange'?" Cayleb asked softly.

"All right," she said after a moment, her own voice more serious, "I'll admit it worries me a little, too. I can't help that. I know, up here," she raised one hand to tap her temple," that everything the Church ever taught us is a lie. I *know* that, and I truly believe it. But I was still raised a daughter of Mother Church, Cayleb. Somewhere down inside, there's that little girl reciting her catechism who can't help being a little scared when she thinks about walking into the very lair of Shan-wei herself. I know it's silly, but . . ."

She let her voice trail off, and his arm tightened around her.

"I don't think it's 'silly' at all," he told her. "It's been less than five months since you found out about Merlin and all the rest of it. As a matter of fact, I think that's one reason you make a better choice than I do just now. After all, I've had a lot longer than you have to adjust—as much as anyone *can,* at least—although I'd be lying if I said I don't still have my own worried moments. And I understand exactly what you mean. It's not a matter of having doubts, just a matter of realizing how completely and totally you've broken with everything you were brought up knowing you were *supposed* to believe. On the other hand, I've found it helps to ask myself if someone like 'the Archangel Langhorne' is supposed to've been would ever have let someone like the Group of Four take over his church if he actually existed!"

"There's that," Sharleyan agreed grimly.

Cayleb was right, she thought. And as he'd said, it wasn't that she had any doubts about the truthfulness of everything Merlin Athrawes had told them, either. On the other hand, the occasional spasms of deeply programmed anxiety *she* felt left her less than totally confident about how the rest of the planet Safehold's population was going to react when the time finally came to reveal the full truth about the Church of God Awaiting. It was going to be ugly, at the very least, and deep inside, she felt sinkingly certain it would turn out to be much worse than that, in the end.

It couldn't be any other way, really. Not when every human being on the entire planet had been taught the same things she'd been taught. Believed the same things she'd always believed. Believed in the *Holy Writ*'s version of God's plan for Safehold, and in *The Testimonies'* description of the Day of Creation. And how could they not believe those things? The "Adams" and "Eves" who'd written those testimonies had told the absolute truth, as far as they knew it. Of course, they hadn't known their memories had been altered during their long cryonic journey (she still had trouble understanding how *that* bit had worked) from a doomed planet called Earth to their new home. They hadn't known the "Archangels" who'd appeared to them in human form as God's messengers and deputies had actually been members of the colonizing expedition's command crew.

And they hadn't known the "Archangel Langhorne" and the "Archangel Bédard" had deliberately and cold-bloodedly murdered Dr. Pei Shan-wei and everyone else who'd disagreed with Langhorne's plan to lock Safehold into a pre-technical civilization forever.

So it wasn't a bit surprising that their totally accurate accounts of what they had seen and experienced, thought and felt, after awakening here on Safe-hold should be so damnably consistent and convincing. Worse, there were lit-erally millions of them . . . and not one of them disputed the Church's official version.

*Well, maybe* one *of them did,* she reminded herself, thinking of the journal of Saint Zherneau. It wasn't part of the official *Testimonies,* and there was no question in her mind what the Inquisition would do, if it should ever discover that journal's existence. But Saint Zherneau—Jeremiah Knowles—had *also* been an Adam, and his version of events didn't agree with the *Writ, The Testi-monies,* or Mother Church herself. Of course, that was because he'd been part of Pei Shan-wei's Alexandria Enclave. He'd known the truth about Safehold, about the genocidal Gbaba who had destroyed something called the Terran Federation and driven this last remnant of the human race into hiding. He'd known what was supposed to happen here on Safehold—known the mission planners had never intended for all memory of the Gbaba to be lost. That they'd recognized that sooner or later mankind and the Gbaba would meet again, and that while it was essential for humanity to temporarily abandon technology while it hid among the trackless stars, it was just as essential for that technology to reemerge once more in the fullness of time.

And it was for knowing that truth—for refusing to *abandon* that truth—that Pei Shan-wei and every other living soul in the Alexandria Enclave had been slaughtered by Langhorne's *rakurai*—the cataclysmic kinetic bombardment which had transformed Alexandria into the officially damned and accursed Armageddon Reef.

But Knowles, his wife, and his brother-in-law and sister-in-law had sur-vived, hidden away in a tiny colony settlement called Tellesberg which would one day become the capital of the Kingdom of Charis. They'd written their own testimony, their history of what had really happened, and hidden it, hop-ing that when it was rediscovered, centuries later, someone would be willing to recognize the truth when he finally saw it.

Someone had been, and the Brethren of Saint Zherneau had guarded that knowledge for over four hundred years, passing it on, nurturing it in secret, working by gradual degrees to undermine the crushing political and spiritual tyranny of the "Church" Langhorne and Bédard had created. There'd never been many of them, and they'd always had to be insanely cautious, yet they'd never given up.

The fact that they'd believed Knowles' journal when they read it still awed Sharleyan, in many ways. The intellectual and spiritual integrity it had taken to accept that lone voice of dissent was staggering, whenever she thought about it. She hoped she would have been able to do the same thing, yet deep inside, she doubted it. Put her faith in a single voice of protest, however passionate, rather than the massed testimony of eight *million* other Adams and Eves? Accept the word of someone who'd died almost seven hundred years before Sharleyan's own birth, rather than the word of the living, breathing Church of God Awaiting? *Reject* every single belief about the will of God she herself had been taught from girlhood?

No. Despite her own deep disappointment over the Church's failings, despite her recognition of the degeneracy and venality of the men who controlled that Church, despite her deep-seated conviction that the Church had to be somehow, impossibly purged of its corruption, she'd never once questioned the fundamental, underlying "truth" she'd been taught about Langhorne and Bédard. And, if she was going to be honest, she never would have . . . if she hadn't met someone who'd been dead even longer than Jeremiah Knowles.

Merlin Athrawes. *Seijin* Merlin. The most deadly warrior in the world, seer of visions, Cayleb's protector, mentor, friend, and guide. All of those things . . . and also a PICA—the "personality integrated cybernetic avatar" which housed the memories, hopes, and dreams of a young woman who had once been named Nimue Alban.

Merlin, the one being on the planet of Safehold who knew the truth about the Terran Federation and its destruction because he had seen it with Nimue's own eyes. Because Nimue herself had died over nine hundred years ago, deliberately sacrificing her life so that this planet, Safehold, might someday become not simply mankind's refuge, but the cradle of humanity's rebirth.

*No, I would never have believed it without Merlin,* she admitted. *I would've wanted to, I think, but I wouldn't have. Despite how much I love Cayleb, I don't think even he could have convinced me of it. But I've got Merlin. We've got him. And given that, how could I not believe?*

▼　　▼　　▼

"I wish you were here, Cayleb," she said now, wistfully, and heard a soft chuckle in her ear.

"I wish I were, too," her husband said from their bedroom in Cherayth . . . well over six thousand miles away. "And not just because Edwyrd and I are going to find it a bit difficult to explain where you are if someone happens to notice you're away."

The water-clear earpiece tucked into her right ear relayed his voice from the "security com" she wore on a golden chain around her neck.

"Fortunately," a second, deeper voice observed, "you're one of the most talented . . . fabricators I've ever encountered, Cayleb."

"Any diplomat learns to lie with the best of them, Merlin," the emperor replied.

"Why do I suspect that *you* learned to 'lie with the best of them' trying to explain away little things like broken windows, stolen apples, and all those other childhood infractions of which you were undoubtedly guilty?" Merlin Athrawes inquired from the skimmer's forward cockpit.

"Because you know him?" Sharleyan suggested innocently.

"Probably," Merlin said dryly, and Sharleyan chuckled.

*Well, maybe the "commmunicator" is magic,* she thought. *But if it is, at least it's magic I've started getting used to. I wonder if I'll ever get to the point of taking it for granted the way Merlin does, though?*

Sometimes, she suspected she would; other times, she was positive it would never happen. It was simply too marvelous, too impossible, for that. Yet there were also those moments when her own lack of familiarity with Merlin's miraculous toys actually became an advantage.

The com she wore around her neck was a case in point. It was considerably smaller than the one Merlin had originally given her, and her lips twitched in another, less crooked smile as she considered why that was. It hadn't occurred to her, at first, that coms *could* be smaller than the one he'd initially shown her, but as she'd encountered more examples of the often incredibly tiny bits and pieces of "technology" Merlin had shared with her and Cayleb, a possibility had crossed her mind.

From the beginning, she'd decided that figuring out ways to conceal things like the communicators had to be one of their highest priorities. Small as the original, handheld units Merlin had given them might be, they were still obviously—and dangerously—alien-looking. They didn't belong to Safehold's homegrown (and allowable) technology, and anyone who saw one of them would realize that. It might not be very likely anyone ever *would* see one of them, but unlikely wasn't the same thing as impossible, and as Merlin himself had pointed out, if the Group of Four ever discovered their enemies truly were dabbling in the proscribed knowledge of Shan-wei, the consequences could be disastrous.

Especially if they could prove it.

So she'd asked Merlin if there were smaller, even easier to hide "coms" tucked away in "Nimue's Cave." There hadn't been, but as Merlin considered her question, he'd realized there was no inherent reason he couldn't make one smaller. Most of the existing units' size was more a consequence of having to provide something large enough for a human hand to manipulate comfortably than of any unavoidable technological constraints. The same basic capabilities could be provided by something far smaller, if those manipulation requirements were removed. In fact, they had been, prior to the Federation's destruction, in the form of the surgically implanted communicators the Terran military had issued to its personnel. Of course, he didn't have any of those, and surgically installing something which would cause the eyebrows of any healer who discovered it to become permanently affixed to his hairline would probably have been a bad idea, anyway. But if he had Owl redesign a com to respond only to spoken commands—for "voice activation," as he described it—even an external com could be made little larger than the end joint of Sharleyan's slender thumb.

Which was precisely what he'd done, using the "fabrication unit" in the cave where Pei Shan-wei and Commodore Pei had hidden Nimue's PICA (and all the other tools they'd provided for Merlin's use) to manufacture the new devices. Just as he'd used the same fabrication unit to hide Sharleyan's com in the golden pectoral scepter she wore about her neck. Cayleb wore a matching scepter—they were exact duplicates, down to the maker's stamp and the tiniest scratch, of the pectorals she'd commissioned as a welcome-home gift for his return from Corisande—and they'd have to be literally smashed apart to reveal the forbidden technology concealed at their hearts.

While he was at it, he'd produced yet another marvel in the form of the "contact lenses" Sharleyan wore at this very moment. At first, the thought of actually sticking something into her own eye—even something as clear and tiny as a "contact lens"—had been more than she was prepared to undertake. Cayleb had been more adventurous, however, and his delight had been so great Sharleyan had gathered her courage and taken the same plunge.

She was glad she had, since the tiny lenses not only corrected the slight but irritating farsightedness which had been growing worse over the last couple of years, but also permitted her new, tiny com to project its imagery directly onto the lenses. She could view remote imagery, transmitted to her over the com, without the betraying "hologram" the original, larger com had produced. In fact, she and Cayleb could now view images garnered by Merlin's SNARCs— those "Self-Navigating Autonomous Reconnaissance and Communication" platforms she still understood only poorly—which was actually letting them assist Merlin and the artificial intelligence called Owl in the endless struggle to cope with all the intelligence material Merlin's network of SNARCs made available.

Merlin had followed up the same idea and provided the same ability to everyone else who'd been added to what Cayleb had dubbed "the inner circle"— the list of people who knew the entire truth and had been cleared to use the coms. There weren't many of them, unfortunately, but the list was growing slowly. In some ways, that only made it more frustrating, of course. The ability to stay in close, instant communication with people literally thousands of miles away—not to mention communicating with Owl, or the ability to view Merlin's "visions" for themselves—was an advantage whose importance would have been literally impossible to overstate. At the same time, it was something which had to be used with extraordinary care. They couldn't afford to have too many of the wrong people start wondering just exactly how it was that they managed to coordinate so perfectly over such vast distances, for example. And, in some ways, the ability to talk to *some* of their closest allies only made their inability to do the same thing with *all* of them even more incredibly frustrating.

Still—

*Stop that, Sharley!* she told herself severely. *You're letting your mind wander on purpose, and you know it.*

Which, she admitted, probably wasn't too surprising, under the circumstances.

She looked ahead and saw the vast curve of Safehold stretching out before them. It was beginning to grow lighter, she realized, and felt a fresh stir of awed delight as she realized they really were catching up to the day which had already left Chisholm so far behind.

"How much longer to your cave, Merlin?" she asked, and heard his quiet, amused chuckle over the com. Apparently she hadn't managed to pitch her voice quite as casually as she'd intended.

"About twenty-five minutes, Your Majesty," he replied. "Just over another seventy-five hundred miles or so."

.II.

### Nimue's Cave,
### The Mountains of Light,
### The Temple Lands

Sharleyan knew she was gaping like a child witnessing a stage conjuror's illusions for the first time, but she couldn't help it. For that matter, she hadn't particularly *cared,* either, as she'd watched in breathless, unalloyed delight while Merlin brought the recon skimmer down into the thicker air and bright daylight of the Mountains of Light.

*"Thicker air,"* indeed! She snorted at her own thought. *You're still high enough you'd pass out almost instantly—not to mention* freezing *to death almost as quickly—if you weren't locked up inside Merlin's skimmer, you silly twit!*

The mountain peaks reaching up toward them were crowned with thick, eternal blankets of snow. It was already high winter in these latitudes, but those mountains would have been snow-covered whatever the time of year, she thought, and adjusted the visual display, shivering inside as she gazed at their bleak, icy summits and the glaciers oozing ever so slowly down their flanks, and watched ice crystals blow on the thin winds, glittering in the bright sunlight.

It was the first time she'd ever been to the continent of East Haven. In fact, it was the first time she'd ever been to the mainland at all. She'd always intended to make the pilgrimage to Zion and the Temple, just as the *Writ* enjoined all of God's children to make it, but there'd always been too many charges on her time, too many decisions to make. Too many political crises for the first true reigning queen in Chisholm's history to deal with.

*And the* last *thing I need is to be making any "pilgrimages" to the Temple* now, *isn't it?* she thought bitterly. *Somehow, I don't think I'd enjoy the Inquisition's greetings. On the other hand, Vicar Zhaspahr, the day is coming when a lot of Charisians are going to be heading for Zion, whether the Inquisition wants to see us there or not.*

"You're sure no one's going to see us, Merlin?" she asked, glancing at the secondary display that showed Merlin's face.

"I'm sure, Your Majesty," Merlin replied, smiling reassuringly back at her out of the same display. "Nobody really lives here, even in the summer, and the SNARCs have the entire area under observation. Trust me, there's no one down there. And even if there were, I've got the skimmer in full stealth mode. We'd be invisible, as far as they were concerned."

"I don't mean to dither," she said half-apologetically.

"Your Majesty—Sharleyan—you're doing one hell of a lot better than I imagine *I'd* be doing if our positions were reversed," he assured her.

"I doubt that, somehow," she said dryly. "It's probably just that I've learned to *pretend* better than you realize. I think it comes with being a queen. Mahrak always told me it was vital to convince people you were calm and in charge, no matter how scared you really were."

"Father always told me the same thing," Cayleb agreed in her ear, and she heard a sharper edge of envy in his voice. She knew he was watching the imagery relayed from the skimmer, but she also knew that wasn't the same thing as actually being there.

*And I'm probably the only person who wishes he were here more than* he *does!*

She suppressed a nervous chuckle at the thought.

"Either way, it won't be much longer," Merlin assured her. "Watch."

"Watch wh—?" Sharleyan began, then froze, her eyes wide, as Merlin flew straight into a sheer vertical face of stone.

They weren't actually moving all that quickly, a corner of her brain realized. Certainly not compared to the velocity of their flight here, at any rate! But they were going quite fast enough for her heart to leap up into her throat. She felt herself tensing uselessly for impact, then exhaled explosively as a portal literally *snapped* open in front of them.

"*Merlin!*"

"Sorry."

There was genuine apology in the deep voice . . . but there was also an undeniable edge of amusement, and Sharleyan made a mental note to find out whether or not it was possible to throttle a PICA. And, for that matter, to throttle her insufferable lout of a husband, she thought as she listened to him laughing over the com.

"I suppose you think that was astonishingly funny, don't you, Cayleb?" she inquired in a dangerously affable tone as the skimmer swept down the center of a huge, perfectly circular, brightly lit tunnel.

"Ah, no. No, not actually," the emperor said instantly, once again demonstrating his acumen as a tactician.

"Good," she told him. "As for *you*, Merlin Athrawes—!"

"I know you're going to make me pay for it," he told her. "But . . . it was worth it."

Cayleb laughed again, and this time, Sharleyan discovered she had no choice but to join him. Her pulse was decelerating towards normal once more, and she shook her head as the tunnel stretched on and on ahead of them. They were moving slowly enough now for her to see that the stone walls around them were smooth and polished, almost like mirrors, reflecting the impossibly bright glow of the endless line of overhead lights running down the center of its curved roof. There was room enough for at least half a dozen craft the skimmer's size to have passed through it abreast, and she found herself feeling very small—almost tiny—as they drifted onward through it.

"How far down does this go?" she asked.

"Well, the cave is underneath Mount Olympus," Merlin told her. "At the moment, we're still about two miles from the mountain itself, coming in from the north. And when we get there, we'll be just over twelve thousand meters—that's about seven and a half miles—down."

"Seven and a half *miles?*" Sharleyan repeated very carefully, and Merlin chuckled. There wasn't a good deal of genuine humor in the sound, she noticed, and wondered why.

"Well, that's seven and a half miles below the *summit,* not below sea level," he pointed out before a reason for the pain shadowing his chuckle had occurred to her. "Still, I suppose it's deep enough to be going on with." She sensed his shrug. "Commodore Pei and Shan-wei wanted to make certain no one would stumble across me before I woke up."

Sharleyan started to respond, then stopped herself as she suddenly grasped the reason for the pain in his voice. It was hard for her to remember, sometimes, that people who had been dead for the better part of a millennium, as far as she was concerned, had died only a handful of years ago, as far as the man who had once been Nimue Alban was concerned.

"Anyway," Merlin went on after a moment, his tone deliberately brighter, "after they tucked me away, they filled the entire complex with an inert atmosphere. Which means there wasn't really anything down here that a flesh-and-blood human being could have breathed. But Owl's got the environmental plant up and running, so there's going to be plenty of air when we get there."

"Well, *that's* a relief," Sharleyan said dryly, wondering exactly what an "inert atmosphere" was.

"We strive to please, Your Majesty," Merlin assured her. "And speaking of getting there . . ."

Even as he spoke, the recon skimmer slid out of the tunnel into a far vaster chamber, and Sharleyan inhaled sharply as still more overhead lights came on, illuminating a stupendous cavern shaped like a flattened hemisphere. Its walls curved up and inward, smooth as the tunnel had been, to join an equally smooth, flat roof a good two hundred feet overhead. Yet tall as it was, it was much, much wider, and as the skimmer drifted out into it, she realized its vast, pavement-flat floor was crowded with dozens of devices and machines which looked at least as marvelous as the recon skimmer itself. The skimmer slid gracefully onward for another few moments, then floated smoothly into a landing beside a duplicate skimmer, nestled in the lee of another, far larger aircraft of some sort. They touched down under the sweep of an enormous wing that dwarfed their own vehicle, and as Sharleyan stared up at the chamber's roof, she realized the cavern was at least a thousand yards across.

"My God," she heard herself murmur.

"What *is* that thing, Merlin?" Cayleb asked over the com, and she heard the wonder in his voice, as well.

"Which 'thing'?" Merlin asked.

"The one you just landed next to!"

"Oh." Merlin shrugged. "That's what we call an 'assault shuttle,'" he said. "Think of it as one of the landing craft we took to Corisande, but designed to move troops from orbit down to a planetary surface."

"How *many* troops?" Cayleb's voice was suddenly more intent, more calculating, and Merlin's and Sharleyan's images looked at one another with matching smiles as the emperor's military instincts engaged.

"Only a couple of hundred," Merlin replied in a deliberately casual tone.

"*Only* a couple of hundred, is it?" Cayleb repeated dryly.

"More or less," Merlin agreed, and Sharleyan straightened as the skimmer's twin canopies opened.

Cool air, fresh-smelling but with just a whisper of a stone-edged tang, flowed about her, and Merlin climbed out onto the self-extending boarding ladder and held out a hand to her.

She took the hand and let him guide her down the ladder, though she was scarcely so old and feeble—or pregnant—that she needed the assistance. On the other hand, she realized, maybe she *did* need a little help. She was so busy gawking at all of the wonders around her that she didn't realize she'd reached the bottom of the ladder until her questing toes jarred against solid ground instead of finding the next rung, and she stumbled, on the brink of falling, until that hand lifted her effortlessly back upright.

She gave herself a shake, then smiled at Merlin.

"I'm impressed," she said.

"Oh, you haven't seen anything yet," he assured her.

▼    ▼    ▼

"—and this is the medical unit," Merlin told Sharleyan the better part of an hour later.

They didn't have an unlimited amount of time, but he'd deliberately taken long enough to let her settle down a bit. Her ability to cope with the wonders coming at her had both impressed and surprised him, although it probably shouldn't have. He'd already known she was one of the smartest, toughest-minded people he'd ever met. Still, all of this had to be more than a minor shock to the system, however well prepared she'd thought she was, and they had long enough to let her regain her mental balance before she faced the examination for which she'd come the next best thing to halfway around the planet.

"I see," she said now, tilting her head to one side to regard the gleaming curves of the diagnostic instruments above the comfortably padded, recliner-like couch. There might have been the very slightest edge of a tremor in the two words, but even with his PICA's hearing, Merlin wouldn't have sworn to it. She gazed at the unit for a few moments, arms crossed in front of her, palms rubbing her forearms gently, as if against a slight chill, then smiled crookedly at him.

"Somehow this doesn't look like any healer's office I've ever visited," she observed.

"I know." Merlin smiled sympathetically. "I promise the doctor is 'in,' though." He raised his voice slightly. "Owl?"

"Yes, Lieutenant Commander Alban?"

Sharleyan recognized the voice of the AI—the "artificial intelligence"—Merlin had named "Owl." She'd heard that voice quite often, now, over the earpiece of her com. She'd even discussed things with its owner . . . and discovered along the way that Merlin had a point about how literal-minded and unimaginative Owl was. He still seemed miraculous enough to Sharleyan, but he *could* be a little slow. Yet this was the first time she'd heard that voice speaking to her from the open air, and she looked around quickly. Almost, she thought a moment later, as if she expected to see some wizened little scholar pop out of a cupboard somewhere.

The thought made her smile, and she shook her head at Merlin.

"Hello, Owl," she said out loud.

"Good morning, Your Majesty," the computer replied. "Welcome."

Sharleyan saw one of Merlin's eyebrows rise at the last word and wondered why, but she had other things on her mind at the moment.

"I trust you won't feel offended if I seem a little . . . anxious, Owl," she said. "I mean, I don't doubt your competence for a moment, but this is all new to me."

"And to me, Your Majesty," the computer returned, and Sharleyan snorted. Now *that* was a reassuring thing for her "healer" to be telling her at a moment like this!

"Owl may never have personally done this before," Merlin put in, shooting a nasty look at a tiny glowing light Sharleyan suddenly realized probably indicated the location of Owl's visual pickup. "But that's because he's basically a tactical computer. Until he ended up as my librarian, he was in charge of dealing with weapons, not health issues. The *medical* computer which will actually be handling the examination did this hundreds of times before the Commodore and Dr. Pei stripped it out of its transport and parked it down here, though. All Owl is going to be doing is telling it to get started."

"I see." Sharleyan regarded Merlin gravely, fighting a desire to smile at his obvious exasperation with the AI. "But how much practice has it had *since?*" she asked, putting a deliberate edge of anxiety into her own voice.

"Well, as far as pregnancies are concerned, not all that much," Merlin admitted. Rather against his will, she thought, and gave him a look that was just as worried as she could possibly manage. "It's fully up to the job, though," the PICA went on reassuringly. "And it's already got your medical records on file."

"Really?" Sharleyan blinked. "How did that happen?" she asked, her eyes narrowing as her lively curiosity was piqued and distracted her from teasing Merlin to get even for that trick with the cliffside.

"Oh." For a moment, Merlin looked nonplussed. Then he shook himself. "Uh, well, actually," he said, "I had to give it your full profile. I used one of the remote diagnostic units one night. When you were asleep," he added.

"When I was asleep?" She gave him the sort of look nannies gave young children who insist *they* certainly don't know anything about any missing cookies. No, Ma'am! Not *them!* "And just why did you do that, *Seijin* Merlin?" she inquired rather tartly. "Without mentioning it to me, I mean."

"Well, at the time, the Brethren still hadn't agreed you could be told about the Journal," Merlin said. "That meant I couldn't explain it to you."

"That meant you couldn't explain it to me *then*," she pointed out implacably. "It doesn't say a word about why you couldn't have explained it to me *since*. Nor does it answer the really important question. That would be the one about why you did it at all."

Merlin looked at her for a long moment, then shook his head. He'd known this moment was going to come, he reminded himself. And he didn't really expect her to be *too* upset with him. . . .

Sure *you don't*, he thought dryly. *That's why you've been in such a tearing rush to come clean, isn't it, Seijin Merlin? And why the hell does Owl have to suddenly *start displaying spontaneous autonomous responses right this minute? If he'd just kept his damned mouth shut, like usual. . . .*

"All right," he sighed. "The reason I gave the medicomp your records—and yours, too, Cayleb," he added to the emperor he knew was listening in from Cherayth, "was so that it could manufacture standard nanotech for both of you."

" 'Nanotech'?" Cayleb repeated over the com, pronouncing the word very carefully, and Merlin nodded.

"Yes. Nanotechnology consists of very, very tiny machines—so tiny you couldn't see them with the most powerful magnifying glass any Safehold optician could possibly grind. In this case, they're *medical* machines, designed to work inside the human body to keep it healthy."

"There are machines *inside* us?" Sharleyan knew she sounded a bit shaken by the idea, but that was fair enough. She *was* shaken. And not just a little bit, if she was going to be honest about it, either.

"Yes. But they're so tiny no one would ever realize they were there," Merlin assured her hastily. "And they won't hurt you—or anyone else—in any way!"

"Should I assume from what you've just said that you put these . . . machines inside both of us?" Cayleb asked, and there was a faint but undeniable sternness in the question.

"Yes," Merlin said again, and squared his shoulders. "You and your father were both going off to war, Cayleb, and I *needed* you both." His face hardened and his voice grew harsher, harder. "I lost your father, anyway," he grated, unable, even now, to fully forgive himself for that, "and I don't plan on losing *you,* too. Certainly not to anything I can prevent! So I injected you with the standard Federation nanotech when you were asleep. And I did the same thing to Sharleyan after she arrived in Tellesberg. And"—he shrugged again—"if this is the time for coming clean, I suppose I should admit I did it for Maikel and Domynyk and . . . a few others, too."

"But . . . why?" Sharleyan asked.

"Because it will keep you from getting sick."

"Sick from what?" Cayleb asked.

"From anything," Merlin said simply.

"What?" Sharleyan blinked at him again. Surely he didn't mean—

"From anything," Merlin repeated. "You'll never have cancer, or pneumonia, or even a cold again. And if you're injured, it will help you heal more quickly. A *lot* more quickly, in fact. Actually, that was one reason I hesitated to inject it. If a healer happens to notice how fast one of you recovers from a cut or a broken bone, it could lead to . . . questions."

"Wait a minute," Cayleb said. "Just wait a minute. You mean neither of us will ever be sick again? Not *ever?*"

"Exactly." Merlin sighed yet again. "I don't have the anti-aging drugs to go with it, even if we dared to use them in the first place, but that much, at least, I could do. And you were both too important to what we're trying to accomplish for me *not* to do it, too." He shook his head, and his expression was still hard, like something hammered from old iron. "I can't keep you or Sharley from being killed in an accident, Cayleb, and we've already had proof enough I can't guarantee you won't get killed in some stupid battle. But I will be *damned* if I lose either of you one minute before I have to to something as stupid as a frigging *germ!*"

Sharleyan felt her own expression soften as she recognized the raw, genuine emotion behind that response. She still wasn't entirely certain what a "germ" was, although she thought she had a pretty good idea. But that wasn't really the point, and she knew it. No, the point was that Merlin Athrawes was still Nimue Alban, as well, and that Nimue had lost her entire universe nine hundred years before. Just as Merlin Athrawes knew he was going to lose *his* entire universe— or all the people in it who mattered to him, at least—as well. She'd tried before (without, she knew, succeeding) to imagine what that must be like, how it had to *feel,* for someone who so obviously and deeply loved the friends he knew must all ultimately die and leave him behind. Now, as she looked into those sapphire eyes—and they were *eyes,* damn it, not bits of glass and metal and "technology!"—she knew that however important she and Cayleb might have been to Merlin's great task here on Safehold, that was only a part—and not the greatest one—of his true motivation.

Silence hovered in the buried stillness of "Nimue's Cave," and then Sharleyan Ahrmahk reached out. She touched the PICA in which her friend lived gently on the forearm. And she smiled.

"I hope you won't be offended if I point out that it's just a little cool in here—even for a Chisholmian girl—to be taking off my clothes, Doctor."

"Oh, that won't be necessary," Merlin assured her with an answering smile, his blue eyes softening as he recognized the deliberate change of subject. Or of emphasis, at least. He put his hand lightly over the slender one on his arm for a moment, then waved the same hand at the waiting examination chair. "Just stretch out on the couch, here. Owl will handle everything from there."

Sharleyan looked at the elevated chair again and shrugged, and he extended that same hand once more. She took it, stepped up onto the stool beside the chair, and seated herself. The examination couch's surface moved under her, conforming to the shape of her body, but that much she took in stride. She'd already experienced the same sensation with the recon skimmer's flight couch, after all.

"So I just lie here? That's all?"

"That's all," Merlin confirmed.

She gazed at him for perhaps another two seconds, then drew a deep breath and leaned back into the couch's embrace.

"Just go ahead and relax," Merlin encouraged her, and her eyebrows rose as the *seijin*'s voice shifted. Its deep, masculine timbre flowed higher, shifting into a throaty contralto Sharleyan had never heard before. It remained recognizably Merlin's voice, somehow, yet the empress realized suddenly that who she was actually hearing, for the very first time, was *Nimue Alban,* not Merlin Athrawes.

She turned her head, looking at him, and he smiled. It was a gentle, oddly sad smile, and she cocked her head, looking a question at him.

"I haven't gotten to be Nimue in a long time, Sharleyan," that contralto voice said, "and it occurred to me you might be a bit more comfortable with her than with Merlin, under the circumstances. Besides, you're here for something Nimue always wanted to experience. Children—babies . . . They weren't something responsible people were bringing into the world when she was alive. Not when everyone knew the Gbaba were going to kill us all, anyway."

Sharleyan reached out, laying her hand gently on Merlin/Nimue's forearm once more as she recognized the sorrow behind that smile.

"I always knew I'd never have a child," Nimue said quietly from behind Merlin's face and mustachios. It was the most bizarre thing Sharleyan had ever witnessed, yet there was a strange, perfect "rightness" to it, as well.

"I knew it was something that could never happen to me. But I never realized, never imagined, I'd be standing here today, watching someone who *is* going to become a mother." Nimue laughed sadly. "It's ironic, isn't it? I always expected to die young. Now I'm nine hundred years old, and—who knows?—I could be around for another nine hundred. And I'll still never have a child of my own."

"Oh, yes you will," Sharleyan said softly. "*This* child is yours, Merlin . . . Nimue. This child will live, will grow up, only because of you. Cayleb and I would never have met without you. I would have died at Saint Agtha's without you. Charis would be a burned and slaughtered ruin without you. The Group of Four would win—*Langhorne* would win . . . without you. *The Writ* says a child is more than just flesh of its parents' flesh, and the fact that it lies about so many other things doesn't mean it lies about *everything*. Whatever else happens, Cayleb and I will always remember, always know, this is a child we share with you, as well as with each other. And I swear to you, Nimue," brown eyes looked deep into eyes of sapphire blue, seeking the centuries-dead young woman behind them, "that one day, whether Cayleb and I live to see it or not, all the world will know that, too."

They looked at one another for several long, silent moments, and then Merlin smiled again. There was still sorrow in that smile, but there was more than that, as well, and gentleness, and the swordsman's sinewy fingers patted the slender, female hand on his mailed forearm.

"Well, in that case, why don't we go ahead and get this done?"

D*amn, it's cold enough to freeze the balls off a mountain slash lizard,* Sahlahmn Traigair, the Earl of Storm Keep, thought as he climbed down from the saddle at last.

October was summer, not winter in Corisande, but no one could have proved it by the cold, icy rain pounding the streets and roofs of Serabor. The same icy mountain rain which had pounded him and his companions for the entire day just past. It wasn't as if Storm Keep was unfamiliar with the local weather. His own earldom lay just to the northeast of Larchros, and he'd been a fairly frequent visitor here over the years. More than that, the jagged Marthak Mountains formed the border between Larchros and the Earldom of Craggy Hill. Despite the fact that the equator passed directly across the northern Marthaks, there was snow on their highest peaks almost year-round, and the Barcor Mountains, in whose foothills Serabor nestled, were even taller.

*It's not* really *cold enough to freeze anyone, I guess,* he admitted grudgingly, reaching back to massage his posterior as the rest of their sizable party of servants, retainers, and guards dismounted around him. *It sure as hell* feels *that way, though!*

"Welcome to Castle Mairwyn, My Lord," a voice said, and Storm Keep turned to the speaker. Rahzhyr Mairwyn, Baron Larchros, was just as wet—and looked almost as miserable—as Storm Keep felt, but he still managed a smile. "If you're not too thoroughly frozen, I expect there's a fire and hot chocolate—or maybe even something a bit stronger—waiting for us."

"Now *that*, Rahzhyr, sounds like the best idea *I've* heard all day!" Storm Keep said with a smile of his own.

"Then let's go find both of them," Larchros invited, and waved for Storm Keep to accompany him as efficient grooms led their mounts away.

The earl nodded, and the two of them headed out of the brick-paved stable yard, across the castle's main courtyard, and up the steps to the massive, old-fashioned central keep. Castle Mairwyn was well over three centuries old, and despite the enlarged, many-paned windows which had replaced most of the keep's upper firing slits, the old fortress looked its age. Personally, Storm Keep preferred his own much newer residence in the city of Telitha, looking out over the sparkling blue waters of Telith Bay. He certainly preferred the scenery, at any rate. However picturesque they might be, Serabor's narrow, twisting streets were a far cry from Telitha's broad, straight avenues. But that was because Serabor was perched atop a "hill" which would probably have been called a mountain anywhere except in the Barcors. The last mile or so to the city's gate had been a steady uphill slog which had been pure, undistilled misery for their horses, and the castle itself crowned the solid plug of granite Serabor had been built around so long ago.

*Still,* Storm Keep thought, *whoever picked this as the place to build a castle knew what he was doing. Just getting at it would be an unmitigated pain in the arse. And actually* storming *the place would be a hell of a lot* worse *than that!*

That wasn't a consideration he would have spent a great deal of time on as little as three months ago; at the moment, though, it loomed large in his thinking.

They reached the top of the steps and entered the keep's main hall. Lady Larchros was waiting for them, smiling in welcome, and Storm Keep was delighted to see that she was, indeed, holding a steaming cup of hot chocolate in each hand.

"Welcome home!" Raichenda Mairwyn said, smiling at her husband, then switched her attention to Storm Keep. "And twice welcome for the visitor, My Lord! The watch warned me you were coming, and given the weather, I was sure both of you would appreciate this."

She extended the steaming cups, and Storm Keep smiled broadly as he cupped both chilled hands around the welcome warmth.

"You are a hostess among hostesses, Lady Raichenda," he said, then raised the cup and sipped appreciatively. The warmth seemed to flow through him, and he sighed in bliss. "Langhorne will reward you in Heaven," he assured her.

"Perhaps so, My Lord." Her voice and expression had both turned sober. "It's to be hoped it will be for more than a simple cup of chocolate, though."

"May it be so, indeed," he murmured, meeting her eyes levelly. Apparently she was even deeper into her husband's confidence than Storm Keep had anticipated.

*Well, you've known for years that he dotes on her,* he reminded himself. *And woman or not, she's one of the smarter people you know, for that matter. Even if he hadn't told her a word, she'd've guessed what's toward soon enough.*

"In the meantime, though," she continued, "I've had hot baths drawn for both of you. Mairah"—she nodded to one of the serving women hovering in the background—"will show you to your room, My Lord. I imagine there's a fair chance your baggage is at least a little damp, given the weather. But you and Rahzhyr are much the same size, I believe, and I've had a selection of his garments laid out for you. I'll have your valet sent up to join you as soon as he comes in from the stables. For now, please—go soak the chill out of your bones!"

▼    ▼    ▼

An hour or so later, and feeling almost sinfully warmed and comfortable, Storm Keep found himself seated in a richly upholstered chair in the chamber Larchros used as an office. The baron's clerk was nowhere in sight, but Father Airwain Yair, Larchros' chaplain and confessor, sat in a marginally plainer chair on the far side of the fireplace. Rain pattered against the windows and gurgled musically through gutters and downspouts, a coal fire seethed quietly in a shallow grate, decorative cut crystal glittered on the marble mantel above the fire, and all three of them had snifters of brandy at their elbows. It was as peaceful and welcoming a scene as Storm Keep could have imagined, yet Yair's expression was anxious as he looked at Larchros.

"So the traitors have truly decided to capitulate to Cayleb, My Lord?" The priest sounded as if even now he found it difficult to believe.

"In fairness, Father," Storm Keep said before the baron could speak, "it's not as if the Regency Council had a great deal of choice. With Prince Hektor and his son both dead, Daivyn out of the Princedom, and Cayleb besieging the capital, their only real options were surrender or standing a siege which could end only one way."

"True enough, Sahlahmn," Larchros' voice was considerably harsher than the earl's had been, "but there's a difference between a tactical decision to surrender a city and what Father Airwain has so aptly called 'capitulating.'"

"There, I can't argue with you," Storm Keep conceded, his own voice bleaker. "Mind you, I do think there's some point to Anvil Rock's argument. With no army left in the field, with our navy sealed up in port, and with Cayleb in position to bring in still more troops whenever the urge struck him, what were we supposed to use to stop him from doing whatever he wanted? He already had thousands of men in the Princedom, and he hadn't even begun deploying any Chisholmian troops here, so he still had every single soldier in Sharleyan's army—a considerably larger and even more professional army than the one he'd already brought with him, I might add—in reserve. I, on the other hand, have less than eighty armsmen in my entire guard. How many do you have?"

Larchros growled, but he couldn't dispute the earl's point. It had taken Prince Fronz, Prince Hektor's father, the better part of twenty years to complete the process of stripping his nobles of their feudal levies, but he'd managed it in the end. And, truth to tell, Storm Keep and most of his fellow aristocrats had seen the wisdom of his policy—after the fact, at least. After all, the Royal Army, with its core of professional, long-term troops, would have made mincemeat out of any levies one of them (or even an alliance of several of them) could have put into the field against it, anyway. None of them could afford to maintain a force which could have changed that, even assuming Fronz had been willing to let them try. Which he hadn't been. He'd made that point rather firmly, and the plain truth was that most of his magnates had been just as happy to avoid the sort of occasional fratricide which had wracked parts of Corisande with dreary predictability under Fronz's father and grandfather. At least this way each of them was spared the expense of maintaining his own private troops while the Army saw to it that none of his fellows were in a position to threaten him.

Unfortunately, that policy of Prince Fronz's had just come home to roost with a vengeance.

"The largest force any of us—even someone like one of the dukes—can command is barely enough to keep the peace in his own lands, and not one of us has any of the new weapons," the earl pointed out remorselessly. "Would you like to try to stand up to a battalion or two of Charisian Marines, with their damned rifles and artillery, with *that?*"

There was silence for a moment, profound enough for all of them to hear the patter of the persistent rain against the chamber's windows. Then Larchros shook his head.

"No," he said. "Or . . . not *yet,* at least."

"Exactly," Storm Keep said very, very quietly, and he and the baron looked at one another.

It wasn't as if they hadn't discussed the situation at length during the endless ride from Cherayth to Serabor. They'd had to be at least a little circumspect, since there was no telling which set of ears, even among their own retainers, might be eager to curry favor with the Charisian occupiers by carrying tales. But they'd known one another for a long time. Neither of them had been left in any doubt about where the other stood. On the other hand . . .

"It's going to have to be handled carefully," Storm Keep pointed out softly.

"Oh, I agree entirely." Larchros grimaced. "Unless I'm mistaken, at least some of those southerners are actually willing to stand in line to lick Cayleb's hand . . . or his arse, for that matter!" He shook his head in disgust. "And I never thought I'd say this, but I'm pretty sure Anvil Rock is, too."

"Truly, My Lord?" Yair shook his head. "I confess, I always thought the Earl was completely loyal to Prince Hektor. Not to mention Mother Church!"

"So did I, Airwain." Larchros shrugged. "From the way he reacted to any suggestion we play for time, though, I'm beginning to think we were both wrong about that. Either that or the guts have gone out of him. Not to mention his damned *son!*"

Storm Keep considered pointing out that Sir Koryn Gahrvai, the Earl of Anvil Rock's son, had probably done as well as anyone could have in the face of the Charisians' crushing tactical superiority. Blaming Gahrvai for his army's defeat, however satisfying it might be, was scarcely an exercise in fair-mindedness.

*On the other hand, fair-mindedness isn't exactly what we need just now, either,* the earl reminded himself. *And if being pissed at Anvil Rock and Gahrvai helps . . . motivate Rahzhyr or some of the others, then so be it.*

"At any rate, Father," he said out loud, looking at the priest, "Anvil Rock, Tartarian, and North Coast have made it clear enough they aren't prepared to countenance any sort of armed resistance. And before he left for Chisholm, Cayleb—damn his soul!—made it even clearer than that that anyone who wasn't prepared to swear fealty to him would be deprived of his titles and his lands." He shrugged. "I can't say it came as any great surprise. That was the reason he summoned us all to Manchyr in the first place, after all. And however bitter the pill may taste, he's also the one who won the damned war, so I don't suppose anyone should be astonished when he acts the part."

"And this . . . abomination, My Lord? This 'Church of Charis' of his?"

"And he delivered the same ultimatum to the clergy, Father," Storm Keep admitted heavily. "I'm sure you'll be hearing from your bishop—your new bishop, I suppose I should say—to that effect soon enough."

"Bishop Executor Thomys has *accepted* the schism?" Yair stared at the earl in disbelief.

"No. In fact, the Bishop Executor and Father Aidryn apparently managed to get out of Manchyr, despite the siege lines," Baron Larchros answered for Storm Keep. "No one seems to know exactly how they did it, but the fact that they seem to've done it suggests 'Emperor Cayleb' isn't quite as infallible as he'd like us to believe!"

"Then who—?"

"Bishop Klairmant. Or, I suppose, I should say '*Archbishop* Klairmant,' " Larchros said bitterly, and Yair blanched visibly.

Klairmant Gairlyng, the Bishop of Tartarian, one of the Princedom of Corisande's most respected prelates, came from the Temple Lands themselves. To be sure, the Gairlyngs scarcely constituted one of the truly great Church dynasties. If they had, Klairmant would undoubtedly have ended up with a more prestigious bishopric. But he was still at least a distant cousin of several current vicars, which had always given him a great deal of moral authority within the ranks of Corisande's clergy. Worse, he'd served his see for sixteen years now, without taking a single vacation trip back to Zion, and earned a reputation for unusual piety in the process. Having *him* acknowledge the primacy of the heretic Staynair constituted a serious blow to the Church's authority, and one of Yair's hands rose. It signed the Scepter of Langhorne, and Baron Larchros barked a laugh which contained very little humor.

"I'm afraid the good bishop isn't the only servant of Mother Church who's turned his coat—or should I say his cassock?—Father," he said flatly. "In fact, I think that may've been the most disturbing thing about this 'Special Parliament' of Cayleb's, when you come down to it. Over a third—almost half, really—of the Princedom's bishops were prepared to proclaim their loyalty to the 'Church of Charis.'" His lips worked in disgust. "And where bishops led the way, is it any surprise the rest of the priesthood followed suit?"

"I can't . . ." Yair shook his head. "I can't believe—"

He broke off, and Storm Keep reached out to pat his knee with a comforting hand.

"It's early days yet, Father," he said quietly. "Yes, I'm afraid Gairlyng truly intends to . . . reach an accommodation, shall we say, with Cayleb and Staynair. I don't pretend to know what all of his motives are. On the one hand, he's known Tartarian for years, and as far as I know, they've always been on excellent terms. That might be part of it. And, to give Shan-wei her due, I suppose it's possible he's at least partly trying to head off any sort of pogrom here in Corisande. The Charisian version of the Inquisition is hardly likely to treat any open resistance by 'Temple Loyalists' gently, after all."

*Although,* he admitted to himself a bit grudgingly, *this "Viceroy General" Chermyn's Marines have been a lot "gentler" than I would have expected . . . so far, at least. Musket butts and bayonets are bad enough, but bullets are worse, and he's been mighty sparing with* those, *under the circumstances.*

"And maybe Gairlyng, Anvil Rock, and Tartarian all see an opportunity to feather their own nests, and Shan-wei while heading off any 'pogroms,'" Larchros said bitingly in response to the earl's last observation.

"And maybe that, as well," Storm Keep conceded.

"You said over a third of the bishops have accepted Staynair's authority, My Lord," Yair said to Larchros. "What's happened to those who refused?"

"Most of them have gone into hiding like Bishop Amilain, I imagine," the baron replied, and this time there was at least a hint of genuine humor in his thin smile.

Amilain Gahrnaht, the Bishop of Larchros, had "mysteriously disappeared" before Larchros set out for Cherayth. The baron didn't officially know exactly where Gahrnaht had taken himself off to, but he knew Father Airwain did. So did Storm Keep. That, in fact, was the main reason the earl was prepared to speak so frankly in front of a mere chaplain he scarcely knew personally.

"With the semaphore stations in the hands of Gairlyng's sycophants," the baron continued more somberly, "it's hard to know what's really going on, of course. A lot of bishops and upper-priests refused—like Bishop Amilain—to obey Cayleb's summons at all. In the case of bishops who refused, he and Gairlyng appointed replacements before he left, and 'Viceroy General' Chermyn's announced his intention to send troops along with each of those replacements. He *says* there will be no mass arrests or persecutions of 'Temple Loyalists' as long as they refrain from acts of 'rebellion.'" Larchros snorted viciously. "I can just imagine how *long* that's going to last!"

"But . . . but Cayleb and Staynair have been excommunicated!" Yair protested. "No oath to either of them can be binding in the eyes of God or man!"

"A point I bore in mind myself," Larchros agreed with a grim smile.

"And I," Storm Keep said. "In fact, I imagine quite a few of Prince Daivyn's nobles were thinking about that. For that matter, I'm quite certain Bishop Mailvyn was, as well."

"Indeed?" Yair perked up noticeably. Mailvyn Nohrcross was the Bishop of Barcor. Unlike Gairlyng, he was a native-born Corisandian. In fact, he was a cousin of the Baron of Barcor, and his family wielded considerable influence both within the Church and in secular terms, as well.

"I wouldn't say we've actually discussed it, you understand, Father," Storm Keep said, "but from a couple of 'chance remarks' he managed to let fall in my presence, it's my belief Bishop Mailvyn believes it will be wiser, for now, to pay lip service to this Church of Charis. At any rate, I feel reasonably confident he'll do his best to . . . buffer the blows to those who remain privately loyal to Mother Church."

"In fact," Larchros looked at his chaplain rather pointedly, "if anyone were to have the opportunity to discuss it with Bishop Amilain, I suspect Bishop Mailvyn would be prepared to quietly extend his protection to a fellow prelate unjustly deprived of his office."

Yair looked back at him for a moment, then nodded, and Storm Keep shrugged.

"The truth is, Father Airwain, that no one really knows what's going to happen. My understanding is that Cayleb intends to leave affairs here in Corisande in the hands of the Regency Council . . . 'advised' by his Viceroy General Chermyn, of course. Apparently he cherishes the belief—or the *hope,* perhaps—that now that he's taken himself off to Chisholm, people may forget he had Prince Hektor murdered. That's the real reason we all spent so many five-days parked in Manchyr even after he sailed for Cherayth. Anvil Rock, Tartarian, and the others were busy hammering all of us over the head with how deeply committed they are to doing their best to preserve the Princedom intact and defend its ancient prerogatives. They *say* Cayleb has promised them he'll leave Corisande as much self-rule 'as possible.' I leave it to you to judge just how much 'self' there's going to be in *that* 'rule'!"

The priest's nostrils flared with contempt, and the earl nodded.

"Precisely," he said. "For now, at least, though, he's left Anvil Rock and Tartarian to deal with maintaining order while he dumps the . . . thorny problem, shall we say, of settling the Church's affairs into Gairlyng's hands. There were rumors swirling around Manchyr that Staynair himself may be visiting us in a few months' time. For now, two or three upper-priests from Charis are playing the part of Gairlyng's intendants, and no doubt keeping an eye on him for Staynair's version of the Inquisition. Unless I'm seriously mistaken, Cayleb figures his best chance is to at least pretend he plans to ride Corisande with a light rein, if only we'll let him."

"You think that's why he's agreed to accept Daivyn as Prince Hektor's heir, My Lord?"

"I think that's part of it, certainly." Storm Keep waved one hand slowly, like a man trying to fan a way through fog. "To be honest, though, I don't see what other option he had. He's made it clear enough that whether we want it to or not, Corisande's just become part of this 'Charisian Empire' of his. That would have been a hard enough pill to force down the Princedom's throat under any circumstances; after Prince Hektor's murder, it's going to be even harder. If he'd set straight out to put one of his favorites in the Prince's place, or claimed the crown directly in his own name, he knows the entire Princedom would have gone up in flames. This way, he and the 'Regency Council' can hide behind Daivyn's legitimacy. He can even pretend he's looking out for the boy's best interests, since, after all, *he* never had anything to do with Prince Hektor's assassination, now did he? Oh, no, of *course* he didn't!"

The earl's irony was withering.

"And then there's the consideration that with Daivyn safely out of the Princedom, he's neatly deprived any potential resistance of a rallying point here in Corisande," Larchros pointed out. "Worse, Anvil Rock and Tartarian can claim they're actually looking after Daivyn's claim to the crown when they move to crush any resistance that *does* arise! Look at the cover it gives them! And if Daivyn is ever foolish enough to come back into Cayleb's reach, he can always go the same way his father and older brother did, once Cayleb decides he doesn't need him anymore. At which point we *will* get one of his damned favorites on the throne!"

"In a lot of ways, I don't envy Cayleb the mouthful he's bitten off here in Corisande," Storm Keep said frankly. "Murdering the Prince and young Hektor was probably the stupidest thing he could have done, but Langhorne knows enough hate can make a man do stupid things. I can't think of any two men who hated one another more than he and Prince Hektor hated each other, either, especially after Haarahld was killed at Darcos Sound. And let's not even get started on how *Sharleyan* felt about the Prince! So maybe he simply figured the personal satisfaction of vengeance was going to be worth any political headaches it created. And if he didn't know Daivyn was already out of the Princedom, he probably figured controlling a little boy would be easier than controlling someone young Hektor's age, so killing the Crown Prince may have seemed sensible to him, too . . . at the time. For that matter, as you just pointed out, Rahzhyr, he could always have had Daivyn suffer one of those 'childhood accidents' that seem to happen to unwanted heirs from time to time." The earl's expression was grim, and he shrugged. "But now he doesn't have Daivyn in his hands, after all, and that leaves the entire situation in a state of flux."

"What do you think is going to happen, My Lord?" Yair asked quietly. "In the end, I mean."

"At this point, I truly don't know, Father," the earl said. "If the Regency Council can keep a lid on things for the next several months, and if Gairlyng and the other Church traitors can cobble together some sort of smooth-seeming transition into this Church of Charis, he may actually make the conquest stand up. I think the odds are against that, and to be honest," he showed his teeth in a smile which contained absolutely no humor, "I intend to do everything I can to make them worse, but he *might* manage to pull it off. For a while, at least. But in the long run?"

He shrugged.

"In the long run, as long as Daivyn stays free, there's going to be a secular rallying point for resistance. It may be located somewhere else, and any sort of direct contact between us and him may be all but impossible to maintain, but the *symbol* will still be there. It doesn't matter if the 'Regency Council' claims to be acting in his name or not, either. As long as he's outside the Princedom and 'his' council is obviously taking its orders from Cayleb, its legitimacy is going to be suspect, to say the very least. And the same thing is true for Bishop Executor Thomys, as well. As long as the true Church's hierarchy remains, even if it's driven underground, then any effort to replace it with the 'Church of Charis' is going to be built on sand. Eventually, Cayleb and his cat's paws are going to find themselves face-to-face with a genuine popular uprising, Father. When that happens, I think they'll find their authority runs a lot less deeply than they thought it did. And it's the nature of that sort of thing that one uprising plants the seeds for the next one, whether *it* succeeds or not. So when the day comes that Cayleb is forced to pull his troops off of Corisandian soil, and recall his ships from Corisandian waters, to deal with threats closer to home, I think those of us who have been planning and working and waiting for that day will be in a position to give him a *most* unwelcome surprise."

.IV.
King Ahrnahld's Tower,
Royal Palace,
City of Gorath,
Kingdom of Dohlar

Lywys Gardynyr, the Earl of Thirsk, was in a less than cheerful mood as the guardsmen saluted and their commanding officer bowed him through the open door.

*Langhorne, how I hate politics—especially court politics,* he thought harshly. *And especially court politics at a time like this!*

Of course, he admitted a bit grudgingly as one of the Duke of Fern's innumerable secretaries met him with a deep bow, just inside King Ahrnahld's Tower, it could have been worse. In fact, for the last two years or so, it *had* been worse—a lot worse. Things were in the process of looking up enormously, at least for him personally, and he was grateful that was true. On the other hand, he could have wished they'd started looking up a bit sooner . . . and at not quite so cataclysmic a cost for everyone else.

The secretary led him down a short, broad hall, turned a corner, ascended a shallow flight of stairs, and knocked gently on an ornately carved wooden door.

"Enter!" a deep voice called, and the secretary pushed the lavishly decorated panel wide.

"Earl Thirsk is here, Your Grace," he announced.

"Excellent. Excellent! Come in, My Lord!"

Thirsk obeyed the deep voice's invitation and stepped past the secretary into a luxurious, sunlit office. The walls of King Ahrnahld's Tower were over three feet thick, but some remodeler had laboriously cut windows, reaching almost from floor to ceiling, through the thick masonry. They filled the chamber with light and at least the illusion of warmth. It was a welcome illusion, given the icy weather outside. The reality of the fire crackling on a wide hearth did considerably more to hold off the chill, however, and he was grateful for it, even if the chimney did seem to be smoking just a bit.

"Thank you for coming so promptly, My Lord," the owner of the deep voice said, rising to stand behind his desk.

Samyl Cahkrayn, the Duke of Fern, was a man of medium height, thick-chested, with still-powerful arms and hands, despite the years he'd spent in offices very like this one. His hair had silvered with age, yet it was still thick and curly, despite the fact that he was several years older than the grizzled, gray Thirsk. Those sinewy hands were soft and well manicured these days, though, without the sword calluses they'd boasted when he was younger, and he'd discovered that a quill pen was a far more deadly weapon than any blade he'd ever wielded.

"My time is His Majesty's, Your Grace," Thirsk said, bowing to the Kingdom of Dohlar's first councilor, "and sea officers learn early that nothing is more precious than time." He straightened once more with a smile which was decidedly on the thin side. "Changing tides have little compassion, and winds have been known to shift whenever the mood takes them, so a seaman learns not to dawdle when they're favorable."

"I see." Fern returned the earl's smile with one which was even thinner, then gestured gracefully to the other man who'd been waiting in the office. "As a matter of fact," he continued, "Duke Thorast and I were just discussing that. Weren't we, Aibram?"

"Yes, we were," Aibram Zaivyair, the Duke of Thorast, replied. There was no smile at all on his face, however, and the "bow" *he* bestowed upon Thirsk was far closer to a curt nod.

"You were, Your Grace?" Thirsk asked, raising one eyebrow slightly in Thorast's direction. It probably wasn't wise of him, yet under the circumstances, he couldn't quite refrain from putting a certain innocent curiosity into his tone.

"Yes, we were," Fern said before his fellow duke could respond. The words were identical to Thorast's, but there was a small yet pronounced edge to them. Thirsk heard it, and met the first councilor's eyes. The message in them was plain enough, and the earl nodded in acknowledgment and acceptance.

*He's probably right, too,* Thirsk reflected. *Much as I'd like to watch the bastard squirm, I'm still going to have to work with him, so rubbing too much salt into the wounds probably isn't the very smartest thing I could do. But,* damn, *it felt good!*

"As you say, Your Grace," he said out loud. "And, to be honest, I can't say I'm completely surprised to hear it. It's not as if any of us have an unlimited supply of time, is it?"

"No, we don't," Fern agreed, and waved his hand at a large armchair set facing his desk. "Please, be seated, My Lord. We have a great deal to discuss."

"Of course, Your Grace."

Thirsk seated himself in the indicated chair and leaned back, his expression attentive. Although Fern's formal note hadn't stated the official reason for his summons to the first councilor's private office, he'd been fairly certain what it was about. Finding Thorast waiting with the first councilor—and looking like a cat-lizard passing fish bones, into the bargain—confirmed the earl's original surmise. What remained to be seen was exactly how far Thirsk was about to be formally "rehabilitated."

"As I'm sure you're aware, My Lord," Fern began after a moment, "Mother Church's Captain General, Vicar Allayn, determined some months ago that our initial shipbuilding programs required a certain degree of . . . modification."

*Well, that's one way to put it,* Thirsk thought sourly. *After all, it would hardly do to say,* "The fucking idiot finally got his thumb out of his arse and realized he'd wasted Langhorne only knows how many marks building exactly *the wrong damned ships,*" *even if it* would *be considerably more accurate.*

"Although I'm sure many of the galleys we originally laid down will still prove useful," Fern continued, "it's apparent that, as Vicar Allayn has pointed out, we're going to require a galleon fleet of our own when the time comes to take Mother Church's war back to the apostate."

*Which is exactly the point I* made to the moron in my reports—my *detailed reports—eighteen months ago, if memory serves,* Thirsk reflected.

Of course, it had been made tactfully but firmly—very firmly—clear to him that he was to keep his mouth shut about how long Vicar Allayn Maigwair had totally ignored his own warnings about what Cayleb Ahrmahk's heavy, gun-armed galleons had done to the Royal Dohlaran Navy's galleys in the battles of Rock Point and Crag Reach.

"As I'm sure you're aware, the Captain General ordered a major shift in our building plans six months ago," the first councilor said. "It took some five-days for that change in direction to be integrated into our own efforts here in Gorath"—in fact, it had taken over two months, as Thirsk knew perfectly well— "but we've undertaken a large-scale conversion program on existing merchant galleons. Work is well under way on the new ships now, as well, and several of our original vessels are being altered on the ways. Duke Thorast"—Fern nodded in Thorast's direction—"tells me the first of our converted galleons will be ready for service within the month and that the first of our new galleons will be launching quite soon after that, although it will obviously take rather longer than that to get them rigged and ready for sea. When they *are* ready for sea, however, My Lord, I intend to call upon you to command them."

"I'm honored, Your Grace," Thirsk said quietly. "May I ask, however, if I am to command them in King Rahnyld's service, or in that of the Temple?"

"Does it matter?" Thorast asked, his tone sharp, and Thirsk looked at him calmly.

"In many ways, not at all, Your Grace," he replied. "If my impression of the number of ships to be manned is correct, however, we'll have no choice but to impress seamen. Just finding experienced officers is going to be extremely difficult, assuming it's possible at all, and our supply of experienced *sailors* may well be even more limited, relative to the numbers I'll require."

Thorast's lips tightened. He seemed about to say something, then glanced at Fern and clearly changed his mind.

*Probably just as well I didn't point out that his idiot brother-in-law, Malikai, is one of the main reasons we're so short of sailors,* the earl reflected dryly. *Especially since he's done everything he could for the last two years to hang responsibility for that fiasco around my neck! And what Cayleb's privateers have done to our merchant fleet—on his own watch—hasn't done one thing to help the shortage, either. Not to mention considerably reducing the potential supply of those converted galleons Fern was just talking about.*

"And your point is, My Lord?" Fern inquired as if he were totally unaware of Thirsk's thoughts . . . which he most definitely was not.

"My point, Your Grace, is that it will make quite a bit of difference whether those seamen are being impressed by the Kingdom of Dohlar or by Mother Church. While I realize no one likes to admit it, many of His Majesty's subjects have little or no compunction about avoiding the Navy's press gangs, and I regret to say that not a few of their fellow subjects have no compunction about helping them do it. Frankly, it would be unreasonable to expect anything else, I'm afraid, given the common seaman's lot aboard a ship of war.

"If, however, they're being impressed for service in *Mother Church*'s name, I think it likely many who might otherwise attempt to avoid service will be more willing to come forward. Moreover, I believe it's even more likely that those who might otherwise assist the . . . less enthusiastic in avoiding the press gangs are far less likely to do so if that would run counter to Mother Church's commands."

Fern frowned thoughtfully. Although the first councilor had never himself served at sea, he had risen to high rank in the Royal Army before turning to a political career. He understood the question Thirsk was really asking.

"I see your point, and it's well taken, My Lord," the duke conceded after several seconds. "Unfortunately, I can't answer it at this moment."

"May I speak frankly, Your Grace?"

"Of course, My Lord." Fern sat back in his chair slightly, his eyes narrowing, and Thirsk gave a small shrug.

"Your Grace, I realize Grand Vicar Erek has not yet chosen to decree Holy War against Charis." Thorast stiffened noticeably, but Fern only sat there, and Thirsk continued in the same calm voice. "Among ourselves, however, as the men who will be responsible for answering Mother Church's summons when it comes, a certain degree of bluntness is in order, I think. No one in the entire Kingdom can possibly doubt why Mother Church is building such an enormous fleet. Given the Charisians' actions over the last couple of years, it's inevitable that Mother Church is going to move openly against Cayleb and Sharleyan as soon as it's practicable to do so. I'm positive *Cayleb and Sharleyan* realize that, as well, unless all of their spies have been miraculously rendered deaf and blind. That being the case, I believe it would be better to acknowledge from the beginning exactly whom the ships—and their crews—will serve, and why. Pretending otherwise will fool no one, yet may make it more difficult to get the ships manned. Under the circumstances, I would vastly prefer to be able to tell my officers and men what they will be called upon to do from the start."

There was silence in the office for the better part of a minute. Even Thorast looked more thoughtful than belligerent—for the moment, at least. Finally, Fern nodded slowly.

"Again, I see your point, My Lord," he said. "And I confess I'm inclined to agree with you. At the moment, however, I have no instructions from the Captain General or the Chancellor in this regard. Without such instructions, it would undoubtedly be . . . premature, shall we say, to begin unilaterally declaring our belief that Holy War is coming. That being the case, I don't believe we can authorize you to begin impressing men in Mother Church's name. Not yet, at least. But what I can do is ask Bishop Executor Ahrain to consult with the Captain General by semaphore. I'll inform Vicar Allayn that I'm in agreement with you on this matter. I'm inclined to think that while the Grand Vicar may not wish to declare Holy War quite this soon, Vicar Allayn"—*or the rest of the Group of Four, at least,* the first councilor carefully did not say aloud—"will agree that it's self-evident the fleet is being raised in Mother Church's service."

"Thank you, Your Grace," Thirsk murmured.

"You're welcome." Fern gave him a smile which looked mostly genuine, then turned to other matters.

"Something you may *not* be aware of, My Lord," he said briskly, "is that the Grand Inquisitor has personally ruled that the new artillery mountings do not constitute any infringement of the Proscriptions. While I'm sure all of us could wish this point had been clarified sooner, all of our new artillery will be modified as it's cast to incorporate these 'trunnions.' In addition, I've been informed that a technique has been devised for adding 'trunnions' to existing guns. I'm scarcely an artisan myself, so the details of the process don't mean much to me, but I feel confident that an experienced sea officer like yourself will understand them.

"In addition, we'll be adopting the new sail plans, and I've been informed that our gunsmiths will soon be beginning construction of a new and improved musket, as well. Taken all together, I believe this means—"

.V.
## Archbishop's Palace,
## City of Tellesberg,
## Kingdom of Charis

Another glass, Bynzhamyn?" Archbishop Maikel Staynair invited, reaching out a long arm to lift the brandy decanter and arching one salt-and-pepper eyebrow suggestively.

"I suppose, under the circumstances, it couldn't hurt, Your Eminence," Bynzhamyn Raice, Baron Wave Thunder, agreed.

The baron was a large man, with a completely bald head and a powerful nose, who had risen from humble beginnings to his present position on the Royal Council of Old Charis. Although Prince Nahrmahn of Emerald had become the official *Imperial* Councilor for Intelligence, Wave Thunder had been King Haarahld's spymaster before Cayleb ascended to the Charisian throne, and he continued to hold what was almost certainly the most sensitive of the new Empire of Charis' intelligence positions. He held that position because he was so very good at what he did, although he'd recently acquired certain advantages he had never previously dreamed might exist.

He and Staynair sat in the cleric's third-floor study in the Archbishop's Palace beside Tellesberg Cathedral, listening to the background sounds of the benighted city through the study's open windows. The night was relatively cool—for Tellesberg in October, at any rate—which was a relief after the day's heat, and the city noises were muted this late in the evening. They would never quite cease, of course. Not in Tellesberg, the city that never quite slept. But they were definitely diminishing as the night deepened, and the palace was far enough from the eternally busy docks for the noises which continued to be hushed by distance.

The archbishop's official residence sat in a stately park of just under three wooded, beautifully landscaped acres, which were worth a not-so-small fortune in their own right, given the price of real estate in Tellesberg. The palace itself was a magnificent building, having been built of golden-hued Ahrmahk marble and designed to house one of Mother Church's archbishops in the splendor appropriate to his high office, but Staynair's tastes were rather simpler than those of most of Old Charis' previous prelates. The magnificent furnishings with which his immediate predecessor had filled this study, for example, had been removed early in Staynair's tenure. He'd replaced them with furniture he and Ahrdyn Staynair, his years-dead wife, had assembled during their lives together. All of that was tasteful enough, but it was also old, comfortable, and (obviously) well loved.

At the moment, Staynair lay tipped back, half lying in a recliner his wife, Ahrdyn, had commissioned for him when he was first ordained a bishop. He'd had it recovered at least twice since then, and from the condition of the fabric, he was going to have to have it reupholstered yet again sometime soon. The reason he was going to have to do that (this time) lay contentedly curled in his lap, purring in happy possessiveness. The snow-white cat-lizard whose claws had shredded the upholstery of the recliner-shaped scratching post with which he had been so obligingly provided—and whose name was also Ahrdyn, despite the fact that he happened to be male—was clearly in no doubt as to who owned who, whatever any silly humans might think.

Now Ahrdyn-the-lizard interrupted himself in mid-purr and raised his head to look disapprovingly up at Staynair as the archbishop leaned far enough to the side to pour fresh brandy into Wave Thunder's proffered glass. Fortunately for the cat-lizard's view of the proper organization of the universe, the refilling process didn't take long, and his mattress' anatomy settled back into the appropriate position relatively quickly. Better yet, the hands which had been distracted from their proper function resumed their dutiful stroking.

"It's such a relief to realize that the Empire's spiritual shepherd is made of such stern stuff," Wave Thunder observed dryly, gesturing with his glass at the large, powerful hands rhythmically stroking the cat-lizard's silky pelt. "I'd hate to think you could be readily manipulated—or, God forbid, allow yourself to be dominated!"

"I have no idea what you're talking about," Staynair replied with a serene smile.

"Oh, of course not!" Wave Thunder snorted, then allowed a fresh sip of brandy to roll across his tongue and send its honeyed fire sliding down his throat. He savored the sensation, but then his expression sobered as he returned his attention to the true reason for this evening's visit.

"I understand the logic behind your travel plans, Maikel," he said soberly, "but I'd be lying if I didn't say I have some significant reservations about them, as well."

"I don't see how the man charged with your responsibilities could feel any other way." Staynair shrugged very slightly. "In fact, in many ways, I'd really prefer to stay right here at home, myself. And not just because of the possibility of lurking assassins, or any of the more mundane hazards involved in the trip, or even of the fact that I anticipate spending quite a bit of it being ineffably bored." He grimaced. "On the other hand, and even giving all of those reasons I should stay home their just weight, I still can't possibly justify *not* going. First, because it's my spiritual responsibility as Archbishop of the Church of Charis. We've had more than enough of absentee archbishops who visit their archbishoprics for a single month or two each year! God's children deserve better than that, and I intend to see that—to the best of my own ability—they get it."

Staynair's lips tightened, and his eyes darkened. Wave Thunder knew better than most that Maikel Staynair was one of the most naturally gentle men the human race had ever produced. At that moment, though, looking into those eyes, seeing that expression, he realized yet again what a vast gulf lay between the words "gentle" and "weak."

"And even if that weren't true—which it is, and you know it as well as I do," Staynair resumed after a moment, "it's absolutely essential that people outside Old Charis have a face to put with my name. Or, rather, with my *office*. It's not going to be very much longer before the Group of Four does manage a counterattack. When it does, the Church of Charis will face the first true test of its strength and stability. And, frankly, at this particular moment, the extent of that strength and stability is still very much an unknown quantity. I'm confident about the state of the Church here in Old Charis, and I'm *optimistic* about Emerald and Chisholm, given my correspondence and the . . . other intelligence avenues available to us. But it would be terribly unfair to people like Archbishop Fairmyn in Emerald or Archbishop Pawal in Chisholm to expect them to stand firm in the face of a tempest like that one is going to be—and hold their own clergy with them—without at least having had the opportunity to meet *their* Archbishop face-to-face."

"I said I understood the logic," Wave Thunder pointed out. "But I may be just a bit more focused on those assassination possibilities than you are. I know you're going to have your own guardsmen along, and frankly, the fact that you'll be a moving target is actually going to make any sort of coordinated attack, like the one on Sharleyan, more difficult to put together. It could still happen, though, Maikel, and I'm not going to be very happy about that possibility until you're either safely under Merlin's eye in Chisholm or back here, where *I* can keep an eye on you. There are too many people, completely exclusive of the Group of Four, who'd really, really like to see you dead about now. If I have my way, though, they're going to go on being disappointed in that regard, if you don't object too strongly."

He gave the archbishop a stern look, which turned into something a bit more like a glower when Staynair answered it with one of complete tranquility. They looked at one another for a second or two, and it was Wave Thunder who abandoned the struggle first.

"In addition to that little area of concern, however," he continued, "having you out of the Kingdom for so long is going to cause its own share of problems that don't relate directly to the Church—or any potential assassins—in any way, and you know it. For one thing—"

He tapped the lobe of his right ear with an index finger, and Staynair nodded, his own expression rather more sober than it had been. Like Wave Thunder's, his own ear held the almost invisible earplug for one of Merlin Athrawes' security coms. The baron had been one of his own very first nominees to be added to Cayleb's "inner circle" when Merlin made the devices available after the attempt to assassinate Sharleyan had come so terrifyingly close to success.

In the almost five months since the assassination attempt, both Staynair and Wave Thunder had become accustomed to the many advantages the coms provided. Indeed, the archbishop often thought Wave Thunder found those advantages even greater than he himself did, which was hardly surprising, given the nature of the baron's duties. As a priest, Staynair couldn't be entirely happy about the degree of intrusiveness into others' lives which Merlin's SNARCs made possible, but he also knew that Merlin, with Cayleb's and Sharleyan's strong approval, had set up "filters" (whatever *they* might be, which was a subject still well beyond Staynair's current understanding) to limit that as much as possible. For that matter, and despite the fact that any man might have been tempted by expediency after spending as long as Wave Thunder had spent managing all of the Charisian spy networks, Staynair trusted the baron's integrity enough to not spend too many nights lying awake worrying over what privacies *he* might be violating. He knew the baron habitually spent at least an hour every night now conferring with Owl and reviewing the day's intelligence information, but he also knew he was more than content to leave the actual monitoring of the various reconnaisance platforms up to the computer. If Wave Thunder looked at something, it was only because it fell into the parameters he'd defined for Owl—parameters designed to insure it was really important—and not out of any sort of voyeurism.

Unfortunately, the number of other people in Old Charis who had been cleared for the level of information available to the two of them literally could have been counted on the fingers of one hand. (Assuming Ahrdyn had been prepared to relinquish one of Staynair's hands long enough for the computation to be accomplished.) In fact, the only people so far equipped with the communication devices were Staynair himself; Wave Thunder; Dr. Rahzhyr Mahklyn at the Royal College; Admiral Sir Domynyk Staynair, the Baron of Rock Point (and Maikel Staynair's brother); Sir Ehdwyrd Howsmyn, who was undoubtedly the Empire of Charis' wealthiest single subject; and Father Zhon Byrkyt, the Prior of the Monastery of Saint Zherneau. There were others Staynair would desperately have preferred to see added to that list, but that decision was neither his, nor Cayleb's and Sharleyan's, alone. And, despite his own impatience, he had to agree with Cayleb's original decision to set things up that way. Maddening though it might so often be, he was prepared to admit the overwhelming force of the arguments in favor of proceeding with almost insane caution where the expansion of the inner circle was concerned.

*Which is about the only thing that lets me maintain a semblance of patience with Zhon and the rest of the Brethren,* he reminded himself. *The fact is, though, that someone has to be that voice of caution. And let's be honest with ourselves, Maikel. At this point, it's a lot more important we not tell someone it turns out we couldn't trust after all than that we add everybody we'd like to the list.*

"Domynyk is already out of the Kingdom," Wave Thunder continued, "Howsmyn is pretty much anchored to his foundry right now—which, I might point out, is the next best thing to eleven hundred miles from where we happen to be sitting at the moment, in case it's slipped your mind—and Father Zhon is about as close to a hermit as someone living in the middle of Tellesberg gets. So when *you* leave the Kingdom, that will leave the Emperor or Empress with direct access to only me and Rahzhyr, here in the capital. Rahzhyr isn't a member of the Council at all—yet, at least—and, to be brutally frank, I don't have the amount of influence with Rayjhis that you do. He and I are friends and colleagues, and he trusts my judgment in a lot of specific areas. But I don't begin to have the status *you* have with him. Or with the rest of the Council, for that matter. If they head off in some wrong direction, I'm not going to be able to rein them in the way you could."

"Agreed."

Staynair nodded, and his eyes darkened for a moment. Wave Thunder was entirely correct about his own influence with Sir Rayjhis Yowance, the Earl of Gray Harbor and First Councilor of the Kingdom of Old Charis. The two of them had known one another almost literally since boyhood, and they trusted one another implicitly. Yet that wasn't the only reason why Gray Harbor trusted *Archbishop* Maikel Staynair's judgment so deeply.

*Just as it isn't the only reason I haven't even considered suggesting Rayjhis be added to the "inner circle,"* he thought with more than a trace of sorrow, then grimaced at his own perversity. *It's really pretty stupid for an archbishop to regret the depth of a kingdom's first councilor's personal faith,* he told himself severely.

Perhaps it was, yet he *did* regret it, in some ways, and he was too self-honest to deny it, especially in the privacy of his own thoughts. Like every other living Safeholdian, Gray Harbor had been brought up in the Church of God Awaiting, and despite his burning hatred for the Group of Four and the other men who had corrupted that Church, his faith ran deep. It was an absolutely essential part of who he was, of what made him such a strong and honorable man.

And it was the reason Sir Rayjhis Yowance could never be told the truth about "the Archangel Langhorne" and the entire perverted lie upon which Langhorne's Church rested. It would destroy him. Or perhaps it wouldn't. He was a strong man, and his faith was powerful. He might weather the storm . . . but Staynair was certain the struggle would be a terrible one. One which would, at the very least, thrust him into an agonizing crisis of conscience that would paralyze the strong, confident decisiveness which was so much a part of him—the very things which had made him so very outstanding in his present position.

Personally, Staynair would have breathed a deep, heartfelt prayer of gratitude if all it cost them was the most effective first councilor to have served the Kingdom of Charis in at least two generations. Perhaps that was shortsighted of him as an archbishop, but he'd been a priest long before he was a bishop, and he prayed nightly that he would never become more concerned with "matters of state" than with individual souls. Yet the priest in him was dreadfully afraid that a first councilor would *not* be all it cost them . . . and in that fact lay a microcosm of Maikel Staynair's true quandary as a man of God.

There was no question in Staynair's mind that God had to recognize the strength and passion of the faith of a man like Rayjhis Yowance, however that faith had been distorted by the very people who'd been charged with nurturing his soul. As Staynair himself had once told Merlin Athrawes, God might demand much from some of His servants, but whatever else He might be, He wasn't stupid. He would never condemn a man like Rayjhis for believing as he had been taught to believe.

Yet when—and how—did Staynair and the others like him, who knew the truth, *proclaim* that truth? That day must eventually come. Ultimately, faith could not be based upon a deliberate lie, and those who knew the lie had been told *must* expose it. But how? When? And at what cost to those who had been reared to believe the lie? Despite his own faith, Maikel Staynair never doubted for a moment that when the truth was told, there would be many who decided God Himself must be a lie, as well. He dreaded that moment, dreaded the possible cost to all of those souls, yet he knew it must be done, anyway. Just as he knew that the religious conflict which *that* schism would bring to life would, in many ways, dwarf the present one.

Which was why they first had to destroy the Group of Four and break the Church of God Awaiting's stranglehold on all of Safehold.

Which, in turn, brought him back to the problem of his own impending departure and the hole that would leave in the Council.

"To tell the absolute truth, Bynzhamyn, I'm not really that worried about Rayjhis," he said. "It's not as if you and I have had to spend all of our time 'steering him' into doing the things we know Cayleb and Sharleyan want done, after all. I mean, he's already *doing* them, and God knows he's demonstrated often enough how competent he actually is. Besides, there are practical limits to the amount of 'steering' we could do. Unless *you* want to stand up in the middle of the next Council meeting and announce that you 'hear voices'?"

"Not likely!" Wave Thunder snorted.

"Well, there it is, then, when you come down to it." Staynair shrugged again. "Rayjhis isn't the sort to go charging off in some idiosyncratic direction without at least discussing it with the rest of the Council first. When that happens, if you think, based on something you know that he doesn't, that he's about to make a mistake, you're just going to have to do the best you can. I wouldn't push it too hard, if I were you, until you've had a chance to discuss it directly with Cayleb and Sharleyan, in any case. It may well be that if we all put our heads together, we can come up with some way to . . . restrain his enthusiasm, let's say. And, knowing Rayjhis, even if we can't find a way to do that, he's hardly likely to do anything stupid or risky enough to create a genuine danger."

"You're probably right about that," Wave Thunder conceded. "No, you *are* right about that. All the same, I really don't like having the Court in Cherayth this way." He grimaced. "I'm sure Green Mountain and Queen Mother Alahnah felt pretty much the same way when the Court was here in Tellesberg, and I know it's something we're all going to have to get used to, but that doesn't mean I enjoy it."

"No, it doesn't," Staynair agreed. "In fact, sheer distance—and how long it takes for messages to cross between its various parts, openly, at least—is the Empire's biggest weakness, and we all know it. I'm pretty sure the Group of Four does, too, and I imagine anyone as smart as Trynair and Clyntahn is going to do his best to take advantage of it. Of course," Staynair showed his teeth in a most un-archbishop-like smile, "they don't know quite everything, do they? We may be sitting here fretting about how to 'steer' Rayjhis, but *they* don't have a clue of the fact that you or I can discuss a situation 'face-to-face' with Cayleb and Sharleyan anytime we have to!"

"Which only makes it even more frustrating when we can't talk to someone *else* anytime we have to," Wave Thunder growled, and the archbishop chuckled.

"The *Writ* says patience is one of the godly virtues," he pointed out.

"Interestingly enough, so do all of the other religions Owl and I have been reading about. So you're not going to get a lot of sympathy from me just because it's a virtue which *you* notably lack, Bynzhamyn!"

"I hope you still find it humorous when you're sitting on a becalmed galleon in the middle of the Chisholm Sea," Wave Thunder replied, dark eyes gleaming. "*Patience,* I mean."

"Somehow I suspect being becalmed in the Chisholm Sea is going to be one of the least of my problems in the middle of the winter," Staynair said wryly. "I've been advised to pack a lot of golden-berry tea, for some reason."

The gleam in Wave Thunder's eyes turned into a snort of amusement. Golden-berry tea, brewed from the leaves of the golden-berry tree, which grew to a height of about ten feet and thrived in almost any climate, was the standard Safeholdian treatment for motion sickness.

"*You* may find the thought amusing," Staynair said severely, "but I rather doubt I'm going to feel the same way when we're looking at waves as high as a cathedral spire!"

"Probably not," Wave Thunder acknowledged with a grin. He leaned back in his own chair and sipped more brandy for several moments, then looked back across at Staynair.

"And Nahrmahn?" he asked. "Have you pressed Father Zhon about *that* recently?"

"Not really," Staynair confessed. "I'm still in two minds, myself, if the truth be told. I understand how valuable Nahrmahn could be, but I don't really have a good enough feel for him yet—as a man, and not just a prince—to feel comfortable predicting how he'd react to the complete truth."

"He's handled the 'Merlin has visions' version of the truth well enough," Wave Thunder pointed out.

"So has Rayjhis," Staynair countered. "Oh, don't get me wrong, Bynzhamyn. If there's anyone who's . . . mentally flexible enough, let's say, to accept the truth, it's got to be Nahrmahn. And I'm very much inclined to believe Merlin—and Cayleb, for that matter—are correct about where he's placed his fundamental loyalties now. Maybe the problem's just that Emerald was the enemy for so long. I mean, it's possible I'm carrying around some kind of automatic prejudice towards all things Emeraldian, including the *Prince* of Emerald, myself. I don't *think* I am, but that doesn't mean I'm not. I'm just . . . uncomfortable in my own mind about how . . . stable his loyalties are. That's not the right word." The archbishop waved one hand, his expression that of a man unaccustomed to being unable to express himself with precision. "I guess what it comes down to is that I haven't really been able to spend enough time with him to feel I truly *know* him."

"Well, that's fair enough," Wave Thunder conceded. Prince Nahrmahn had spent no more than a month and a half in Tellesberg before departing for the Corisande campaign with Emperor Cayleb. He'd returned to Old Charis two months ago, but he'd stayed in Tellesberg for less than two five-days before departing for Emerald. No reasonable person could have complained about his priorities, given the fact that he'd seen neither his wife nor his children in the better part of a year, but it did mean that Staynair—and Wave Thunder, for that matter—had enjoyed precious little opportunity to truly get to know him.

"Maybe you'll have the opportunity to get better acquainted during your pastoral visit," the baron pointed out, and Staynair nodded.

"I plan to make a point of it," he said. "For that matter, I think it's entirely possible he may end up sailing back to Chisholm with me, as well. And as you so tactfully pointed out a few moments ago," the archbishop grimaced, "that ought to give me *plenty* of time to get 'acquainted.'"

"I understand ocean cruises are supposed to be an excellent opportunity to make lifelong friendships," Wave Thunder observed, and Staynair snorted. Then the archbishop's expression turned a bit more thoughtful.

"Actually," he said in the tone a man used to admit something he found at least mildly surprising, "I think a genuine friendship with Nahrmahn is definitely a possibility." He shook his head with a bemused air. "Who would've thought that a year or two ago?"

"Not me, that's for sure!" Wave Thunder shook his own head rather more forcefully, then glanced at the clock. "Well," he set his brandy snifter back down, "I suppose I ought to be getting back home. I'd like to say Leahyn is going to be wondering where I am. Unfortunately, the truth is that she already *knows* where I am, and she's probably got a pretty fair idea of what the two of us have been up to." He grimaced. "I don't doubt that she's going to give my breath the 'sniff test' as soon as I come in the door."

Staynair chuckled. Leahyn Raice, Lady Wave Thunder, was sometimes described as "a redoubtable female," which was accurate enough as far as it went. She was almost as tall as her husband, and no one had ever accused her of being frail. She also had strong opinions on quite a few subjects, a sharp tongue she wasn't at all afraid to use, and a keen intelligence which had quite often helped her husband solve a particularly perplexing problem. She was also warmhearted and deeply caring, as the priest who'd been her bishop for so long knew better than most. She went to considerable lengths to disguise the fact, however. She wasn't really all that good at it, though. She and Bynzhamyn had been married for the better part of twenty-five years, and while Staynair knew it amused Wave Thunder to play the "wyvern-pecked husband" to his friends, everyone who knew them recognized that the truth was distinctly different. Still, there was no denying that Leahyn Raice had a distinctly proprietary attitude where the care and feeding of her husband were concerned.

"The real reason she picks on you is that heart attack, you know," the archbishop said now, mildly.

"Of course I know that!" Wave Thunder smiled wryly. "On the other hand, that was six *years* ago, Maikel! The healers have all said a little wine now and then—or even whiskey, in moderation—won't hurt me a bit. In fact, they say it's probably good for me!"

"If I didn't know they'd given you permission, I wouldn't have invited you to deplete my stock," Staynair pointed out.

"Well, I just wish one of them would have another talk with *her!*"

"Nonsense!" Staynair shook a finger at him. "Don't try to mislead *me*. This is part of the game you two have been playing for years, and I'm really not sure which of you enjoys it more." He eyed Wave Thunder shrewdly. "Most of the time, I think it's *you,* actually."

"That's ridiculous." The spymaster's voice was less than fully convincing as he pushed himself up out of his chair, Staynair noticed. "But, in any case, I do need to be getting home."

"I know," Staynair replied, but something in his manner stopped Wave Thunder halfway to his feet. The baron's eyebrows rose, and then he settled back again, his head cocked.

"And what did you just decide you were going to mention to me after all, Maikel?" he asked.

"We *have* known each other for quite a while, haven't we?" Staynair observed a bit obliquely.

"Yes, we have. And I know that expression. So why don't you go ahead and tell me instead of sitting there while I pull something you already know you're going to tell me about out of you by inches?"

"Actually," Staynair's voice was unwontedly serious, almost hesitant, "this is a bit difficult for me, Bynzhamyn."

"Why?" Wave Thunder asked in a markedly different tone, his eyes narrowing with concern as the archbishop's genuine—and highly unusual—discomfort registered.

"Tomorrow morning," Staynair said, "Father Bryahn will be at your office bright and early to deliver a half-dozen crates to you. They aren't very large, but they're fairly heavy, because they're packed almost solid with paper."

"Paper," Wave Thunder repeated. He leaned back in his chair again, crossing his legs. "What *sort* of paper, Maikel?"

"Documents," Staynair replied. "Files, really. Collections of memoranda, depositions, personal letters. You can think of them as . . . evidence."

"Evidence of what?" Wave Thunder asked intently.

"Something like twenty years' worth of documented corruption within the vicarate and the Inquisition." Staynair's voice was suddenly very flat, his eyes cold. "Evidence of specific acts of extortion, blackmail, theft—even rape and murder. And evidence that Zhaspahr Clyntahn, at least, knew about quite a few of those acts and conspired to conceal them."

Despite his many years of experience, Wave Thunder felt his jaw drop. He stared at his old friend for several seconds, literally speechless, then shook himself violently.

"You're not joking, are you? You really mean it!"

"I do." Staynair sighed. "And I really wasn't going to tell you I had it, either. Unfortunately, accidents do happen, and I am going to be making some rather lengthy voyages in the next few months. So I decided I had to hand it to someone before I sail, just in case."

"And how long have you had it?" Wave Thunder asked in a careful tone.

"I've been examining it for about a month now," Staynair admitted. "It took a while to get here from— Well, never mind about that."

"And you weren't going to tell anyone about it?" Wave Thunder shook his head slowly. "Maikel, if your description of what you have is accurate, then you have to realize even better than I do just how critical that sort of evidence could be. Especially if we can *document* it."

"To be honest, that's part of the problem." Staynair leaned back in his own chair. "What I have are *duplicates* of the original evidence. I'm personally completely convinced of its authenticity, but there's no way I could prove all of it isn't simply a clever forgery, and that definitely makes it a double-edged sword. Frankly, I think we could do ourselves enormous damage in the propaganda war between us and Zion by publishing allegations we can't *prove*."

"Maybe," Wave Thunder conceded. "On the other hand, no matter what kind of 'proof' we had, the Group of Four and its mouthpieces would swear up and down that it was all a forgery, anyway. I mean, it doesn't matter how much *genuine* proof we have; people on both sides are going to make their minds up based on what they already believe. Or what they're *willing* to believe, at any rate."

"I know. And I thought about that. But there's another issue involved, as well."

"What sort of 'issue'?" Wave Thunder asked warily.

"This information was delivered to me under the seal of the confessional," Staynair said. "The person who delivered it to me agreed to trust my discretion about the use I might choose to make of it, but I was told the source of the documentation in my role as a priest. And the person who gave it to me doesn't wish the identity of the source to become known."

"Not even to Cayleb or Sharleyan?"

"Not to *anyone*." Staynair's expression was somber. "I think the person who delivered this to me is probably being overly cautious, Bynzhamyn, but that isn't my decision to make. And I have to agree, given what I've been told—and what I've already seen of the documentation itself—that if the Group of Four should suspect, even for a moment, that we have this information and—especially!— how it came into our possession, the consequences for a very courageous person would be devastating. For that matter, the consequences would be fatal, and quite probably for a large number of other people, as well."

The archbishop's eyes, Wave Thunder realized, were as troubled as the baron had ever seen them.

"In many ways, I really ought to hand this over to Hainryk for safekeeping, I suppose," Staynair said slowly. "I thought about that . . . hard. But in the end, I decided this was an occasion where finding the best way to balance my responsibilities to the Empire and my responsibilities to God required very careful consideration. I'm not fully satisfied with the answer I've come to, but it's the best I've been able to do after praying and meditating about as hard as I've ever prayed or meditated in my life."

Wave Thunder nodded slowly. Hainryk Waignair, the Bishop of Tellesberg, was the second-ranking member of the Church of Charis' episcopate here in Old Charis. In fact, Waignair would be the acting Archbishop of Charis until Staynair returned. He was also a Brother of Saint Zherneau, which meant that—like Wave Thunder and Staynair—he knew the truth behind the lie of "the Archangel Langhorne" and the Church of God Awaiting. He and Staynair were very old friends, as well as colleagues and brothers of the same order, and Wave Thunder knew that Staynair trusted Waignair implicitly, both as a man and as a priest. The baron had no doubt that it must have taken a great deal of prayer and meditation, indeed, to bring the archbishop to the point of leaving this with him, and not with Waignair.

"Speaking as a member of the Imperial Council, and as the Archbishop of Charis, and as Cayleb's and Sharleyan's adviser, there's absolutely no question in my mind that I should already have handed all of this information over and told you and them exactly where it came from, Bynzhamyn," Staynair continued. "But speaking as Father Maikel—as a *priest*—I cannot violate the sanctity of the confession. I *won't*. The Church of God Awaiting may be a lie, but God isn't, and neither is the faith of the person who trusted me in this matter."

Wave Thunder had started to open his mouth to argue. Now he closed it again as he recognized the unyielding armor of Maikel Staynair's faith and integrity. Speaking purely for himself, Bynzhamyn Raice had found he was considerably less confident of the existence of God following his discovery of the truth about the Church of God Awaiting. He wasn't comfortable admitting that, even to himself, yet there was that nagging suspicion—possibly a product of his spymaster's necessary cynicism—that if one religion could have been deliberately fabricated, then all of them might have been. He was too intellectually self-honest to deny that doubt to himself, but it didn't keep him up at night, unable to sleep, either. Whether God existed or not, the Empire of Charis was still locked in a death struggle with the Group of Four, and laying itself open to charges of atheism (a word Wave Thunder had never even heard of until he gained access to

Owl's computer records) would only hand someone like Clyntahn a deadly weapon.

But whatever doubts he might find himself entertaining, he knew there was no doubt at all in Maikel Staynair. The archbishop was as far removed from a fanatic as a human being could possibly be. Wave Thunder was pretty sure Staynair was aware of his own doubts, but he was even more confident that if the archbishop *was* aware of them, he would never condemn the baron for them. That simply wasn't the way Staynair worked, and Wave Thunder had found himself hoping that the God Maikel Staynair believed in—the God who could *produce* a man like Maikel Staynair—*did* exist. But if Staynair had given his word as a priest, then he would die before he broke it.

*Which, when you come down to it, is the real difference between him and someone like Clyntahn, isn't it?* Wave Thunder thought. *Clyntahn believes in the* Church. *In the* power *of the Church, not of God, despite the fact that no one has ever shown him a scrap of evidence to cast doubt on God's existence. Maikel* knows *the Church is a lie . . . but his faith in God has never wavered for a moment.*

"All right, Maikel," he said quietly. "I understand your thinking. And I respect it. But if you deliver this evidence to me, then it's going to be my duty to make use of it. Or, at least, to examine it all very carefully. You know how much insight we got into the Church and the Inquisition from the files Domynyk captured in Ferayd. From what you're saying, *these* documents could tell us a hell of a lot more—if you'll excuse the language—than they did."

"I realize that. It's one of the reasons I hesitated so long about giving them to you. I even considered leaving them here to be delivered to you only in the event that something *did* happen to me, along with a cover letter explaining what they were. In the end, though, I decided I needed to explain to you in person, and I decided that for many of the same reasons I decided to leave it with you and not Hainryk. Hainryk is my brother in God and one of my dearest friends, and he has the courage of a great dragon, yet his deepest and truest joy lies in his priesthood, in ministering to the needs of his flock. That's a great deal of what made him such a perfect choice as the Bishop of Tellesberg—well, to be honest, that and the fact that I knew I could place complete trust in his loyalty. But if I left this with him, it would put him in a most uncomfortable position. I *think* he would recognize the same issues I recognize, yet I can't be certain of that, and I refuse to put him in the position of carrying out binding instructions from me which might violate his conscience as a priest.

"From a more practical perspective, he truly detests politics—even Church politics, though he knows he has to be aware of them. Secular politics, diplomacy, and strategy are things he would far rather leave in other hands, however. Which means he's far less well informed and aware of the . . . imperial realities, shall we say, than you or I. He would definitely not be the best person to be evaluating the information in these files for its possible significance and value to the Empire.

"You, on the other hand, have a very keenly developed sense for all of those things. If there's a single person in all of Old Charis who could more accurately judge the value of this material, I have no idea who he might be. Which is why I decided to leave it with you . . . and to make you aware of the reasons I can't tell you exactly where they came from, or who delivered them to us. I trust your discretion, and I know you'll handle them with extraordinary care. And"—Staynair looked levelly into Wave Thunder's eyes—"I know you won't tell a soul where *you* got them until and unless I give you permission to do so."

The baron wanted to argue, but he recognized an exercise in futility when he saw it. And the fact that Staynair trusted him enough to hand him something like this meant it was unthinkable that he should violate that trust.

"All right," he said again. "You have my word, in that regard. But on one condition, Maikel!"

"And that condition is?"

"If something *does* happen to you—God forbid—then I'll do what seems best in my own judgment with this evidence." Wave Thunder held Staynair's eyes as levelly as the archbishop had just held his. "I'll do my best to protect your source, whoever it is, and I'll be as cautious as I can. But I won't accept something like this without the understanding that my own duties and responsibilities will require me to decide what to do with it if *you're* no longer around to make the call. Is that understood?"

"Of course," Staynair said simply.

"Good."

There were a few moments of silence, and then Wave Thunder snorted quietly.

"What?" the archbishop asked.

"Well, it just occurred to me to wonder if you're planning on telling Cayleb and Sharleyan about this?"

"I'm not in any tearing rush to do so," Staynair said wryly. "I'm sure they'd respect the responsibilities of my office. That's not the same thing as saying they'd be *happy* about it, though. So, if it's all right with you, I'm just going to let that sleeping dragon lie."

"As a matter of fact," Wave Thunder smiled crookedly, "I think that may be the best idea I've heard all night!"

There were rather more people than Father Tymahn Hahskans was accustomed to seeing in his church every Wednesday.

Saint Kathryn's was always well attended, especially for late mass. And, he knew (although he did his best to avoid feelings of undue satisfaction), especially when *he* officiated at that service, rather than the dawn mass he truly preferred. The *Writ* enjoined humility in all men. Father Tymahn strove diligently to remember that, yet he wasn't always successful in that effort. He was as mortal and fallible as any man, and the number of guest members who attended when the schedule board outside Saint Kathryn's announced that he would be preaching that Wednesday sometimes touched him with the sin of pride. He did his very best to put that unseemly emotion aside, yet it would have been dishonest to pretend he always managed it. Especially when one of his parishioners told him they'd heard one of his sermons being cited by a member of some other church.

Yet this morning, as he stood in front of the altar, just inside the sanctuary rail, listening to the choir at his back and looking out at the crowded pews and the standing-room-only crowd piled against Saint Kathryn's outer wall, he felt more anxious than he'd felt in decades. Not because he had any doubts about what he was going to say—although he didn't expect this sermon to be wildly popular in all quarters of the city, to say the very least—but because he was finally going to *get* to say it. He'd been silenced often enough over the years, warned far more often than he cared to remember to keep his mouth shut on certain subjects and called on the carpet whenever he strayed too close to those limitations.

*And now, when you're finally in a position to speak from the heart at last, Tymahn, at least half of your audience is going to figure you're a Shan-wei-damned traitor currying favor with the occupation!*

He felt his face trying to grimace, but he smoothed the expression back out with the ease of long practice. At fifty-six, he'd held Saint Kathryn's pulpit for over ten years. He was hardly some newly ordained under-priest, and he knew better than to demonstrate anything which could be misconstrued by even the most inventive as uncertainty or hesitation. Not in the pulpit. There, he spoke with God's own voice, at least in theory. By and large, Hahskans had always felt confident God would give him the words he needed, yet he also had to admit there'd been times he'd found it difficult to hear God's voice behind the Church's message.

This time, at least, he didn't have that particular problem. Of course, as the *Writ* itself warned in more than one passage, delivering God's message wasn't always the best way to make oneself popular with God's *children*. Men had a tendency to decide God ought to be clever enough to agree with them . . . and to ignore anything He might have to say on a subject if it *didn't* agree with them. In fact, sometimes the messenger was lucky if *all* they did was to ignore him.

At least Archbishop Klairmant and Bishop Kaisi had promised him their support if—when—things got ugly. That was quite a change from Bishop Executor Thomys' attitude where this particular subject was concerned, although Hahskans wasn't entirely clear yet on who was going to support *them*. The new archbishop and the new Bishop of Manchyr were making waves enough of their own, already, and he suspected there was going to be more than enough ugliness to go around before they all safely reached port once more.

Assuming they did.

Which was another thing the *Writ* had never promised would always happen, now that he thought about it.

The choir drew towards the end of the offeratory hymn and Hahskans raised his right hand and signed the Scepter of Langhorne.

"Lift up your hearts, my children."

The liturgy's familiar, beloved words rolled from his tongue as the organ's final note followed the choir's voices into silence. The simple injunction was quiet in that stillness, yet he felt its comfort strengthening his voice as it always did.

"We lift them up unto the Lord, and to the Archangels who are His servants."

The massed answer rumbled back in unison, filling the ancient church, bouncing back down from the age-blackened beams overhead.

"Let us now give thanks unto the God Who made us, and unto Langhorne, who was, is, and always shall be His servant," he said.

"It is meet and right so to do."

All those extra voices gave the reply additional power, yet there was more to that strength than simple numbers. The formal response carried a fervency, spoke to a need, that went far beyond the ordinary comfort and fellowship of the mass. These were no longer simply the words of a well-worn, perhaps overly familiar liturgy. This time, today, in this church, the people behind that response knew themselves as God's children in a world afloat upon the proverbial sea of troubles. They were frightened, and they turned—as always—to Mother Church and her clergy for comfort and guidance.

"It is very meet, right, and our bounden duty, that we should at all times and in all places give thanks unto You, O Lord, Creator and Builder of the Universe, Everlasting God. Therefore, with the Archangel Langhorne and the Archangel Bédard, and all the blessed company of Archangels, we laud and magnify Your glorious Name; evermore praising You and saying—"

"Holy, holy, holy," the congregation gave back, their voices joining and enveloping his own in their merged majesty, "Lord God of hosts, heaven and earth are full of Your glory: Glory be to You, O Lord Most High. Amen."

"Amen," Hahskans finished quietly into the silence after those massed voices, and smiled as the tranquility of his vocation flowed through him yet again.

*It's all right,* he thought. *Whatever happens, wherever it leads, it's all right, as long as You go with me.*

"Be seated, my children," he invited, and feet shuffled and clothing rustled throughout the church as those in the pews obeyed him. Those standing against the wall could not, although he sensed many of them leaning back against the solid stonework and ancient wooden paneling. And yet, in many ways, the congregation's relaxation was purely physical. Only an easing of muscles and sinews so that minds and souls might concentrate even more fully on what was to come.

He smiled and crossed to the pulpit, where he opened the enormous copy of the *Holy Writ* waiting there. The massive volume was considerably older than Hahskans. In fact, it had been donated to Saint Kathryn's in the memory of a deeply beloved mother and father by one of the parish's few truly wealthy families three years before his own father had been born, and it had probably cost close to twice Hahskans' annual stipend even then. It was one of Saint Kathryn's treasures—no mass-printed copy, but a beautiful, hand-lettered edition, with illuminated capitals and gorgeous illustrations filling the margins and flowing down the gutters between columns of words. The scent of candle wax and incense was deeply ingrained into the jewel-set cover and the heavy, creamy, rich-textured pages. As he opened the book, that scent rose to Hahskans like the very perfume of God, and he drew it deep into his lungs before he looked back up at the waiting congregation.

"Today's scripture is taken from the fifth chapter of *The Book of Bédard*, beginning at the nineteenth verse," he told that sea of faces, and took some extra comfort from it. Perhaps it was a good omen that this Wednesday's text was drawn from the book of his own order's patron.

"Behold," he read. "I will tell you a great truth, worthy of all men and sacred unto the Lord. Hear it, and heed, for on the Final Day, an accounting shall be demanded of you. The Church is created of God and of the Law of Langhorne to be the keeper and the teacher of men's souls. She was not ordained to serve the will of Man, nor to be governed by Man's vain ambitions. She was not created to glorify Man, or to be used by Man. She was not given life so that

that life might be misused. She is a great beacon, God's own lamp, set upon a mighty hill in Zion to be the reflector of His majesty and power, that she might give her Light to all the world and drive back the shadows of the Dark. Be sure that you keep the chimney of that lamp pure and holy, clean and unblemished, free of spot or stain. Recall the Law you have been given, the will of God that will bring you safe to Him at the last, utmost end of time. Guard her always, keep true to the *Writ,* and all will be well with you, and with your children, and with your children's children, until the final generation, when you shall see Him and We who are His servants face-to-face in the true Light which shall have no ending."

He looked up into a silence which had suddenly become far more intense than it had been, and he smiled.

"This is the Word of God, for the Children of God," he told them.

"Thanks be to God, and to the Archangels who are His Servants," the congregation replied, and he closed the *Writ,* folded his hands on the reassuring authority of that mighty book, and faced them.

His earlier fear, his earlier anxiety, had disappeared. He knew both of them would return, for he was merely mortal, not one of the Archangels come back to Safehold. Yet for now, for this day, he was finally free to deliver the message which had burned in his heart of hearts for so long. A message he knew burned in the hearts of far more of God's priests than those who wore the orange of the vicarate might ever have suspected.

"My children," he began in a deep, resonant voice, "it has not been given to us to live in tranquil times. Unless, of course, you have a somewhat different definition of 'tranquil' than I've been able to locate in any of *my* dictionaries!"

His smile broadened, and a deep mutter of amusement—almost but not quite laughter—went through the church. He treasured it, but then he allowed his smile to fade into a more somber expression and shook his head.

"No," he said then. "Not tranquil. Not peaceful. And so, frightening. And let us be honest with one another, my children. These *are* frightening times, and not just for ourselves. What father doesn't strive with all his might to keep his children fed and safe? What mother fails to give all she has within her to guard her children from harm? To banish the shadows of the nightmare and the bad dream? To bind up all the hurts of the spirit, as well as the scraped knees and stubbed toes of childhood? All that is within us cries out to keep them from danger. To protect them. To guard them and keep every threat far, far away from those we love."

The silence in the church was profound, and he turned his head slowly, letting his eyes sweep the congregation, making direct contact with as many other eyes as possible.

"It is Mother Church's task to keep all of *her* children from harm, as well," he told them. "Mother Church is the fortress of the children of God, raised and ordained by the Archangels to be God's servant in the world, established as the great teacher to His people. And so, in times of danger—in times of pestilence, of tumult, of storm and fire and earthquake . . . and war—the children of God turn to God's Holy Church as a child seeks his father's arms in the windstorm, his mother's embrace when nightmare rules his night. She is our home, our refuge, our touchstone in a world too often twisted by violence and cruelty and the ambition of men. As the Holy Bédard herself tells us, she is a great lamp set high on a hill, illuminating all of us as she illuminates every inch of God's creation with the reflection of His holy Light."

He paused once more, feeling them, feeling the weight behind their eyes as his words washed over them, and he inhaled deeply.

"This is one of those times of tumult and war," he said quietly. "Our Princedom has been invaded. Our Prince lies slain, and his son and heir with him. We have been occupied by a foreign army, and the clergy of a strange church—a *schismatic* church, separated and apart from Mother Church, at *war* with Mother Church—have come to us with frightening, heretical words. Thousands of our fathers and sons and brothers were slain at the Battle of Darcos Sound, or fell in battle here, defending their own soil, their own homes. And as we look upon this tide of catastrophes, this drumroll of disasters, we cry out to God, to the Archangels—to Mother Church—seeking that promised guidance and protection, begging for the inner illumination which will lead all of us to the Light in the midst of such Darkness. Allow us to make some sort of sense of the chaos and somehow find God's voice amid the thunder.

"I know there are many in this Princedom, in this very city, who call upon us to rise in just resistance, in defiance of the foreign swords and bayonets about us. To cast off the chains and dishonor of oppression. And I know that many of you, my children, are torn and frightened and confused by the sight of Mother Church's own priesthood splitting, tearing apart into opposing factions. Into factions being denounced—and denouncing one another—as traitors, heretics, apostates. 'Blasphemer!' some shout, and 'Corrupter of innocence!' others return, and when the shepherds assail one another, where shall the sheep find truth?"

He unfolded his hands and very, very gently, reverently, caressed the huge book lying closed in front of him.

"*Here,* my children."

He spoke so softly those farthest from the pulpit had to strain to hear him, yet still his superbly trained voice carried clearly.

"Here," he repeated. "In this Book. In the word of God Himself, and of the Archangels He sent into His world to do His work and to carry His Law to us. *Here* is where we will find truth.

"And yet," his voice gained a little strength, a little power, "as Langhorne himself warned us would be the case, the truth is not always pleasant hearing. The truth does not always come to us in the guise we would prefer. It does not always tell us we have been correct, that it must be someone *else* who has been in error, and it is not always safe. It demands much, and it brooks no self-deception. If we fall from a tree, the truth may be a bruise, or a sprain, or a broken limb . . . or neck. If we do not heed the word of God in time of peace, if we ignore His truth in times of tranquility, then we must learn it in the tempest. He will send His truth in whatever form He must in order to make us—His stubborn, willful, self-absorbed children—hear it, and that form can include foreign warships, foreign swords and bayonets, and even 'heretical' priests forced upon us at sword's point by foreign rulers."

The silence was as deep, as attentive, as ever, yet it had changed, as well. It was . . . harder, tenser. It was wary and watchful, holding its breath, as if the people behind that stillness were aware he was about to say something he had never before been permitted to say.

"The Holy Bédard tells us in today's scripture that Mother Church is not the servant of Man. That she is not to be perverted and used for the vain, corrupt ambition of this world. That she is to be kept without spot or blemish. We do not wish to believe she could ever be anything else. That God would ever permit *His* Church to fall into evil. Permit *His* great lamp to become a source not of illumination, but of Darkness. We cry out in anger if anyone dares to tell us our wishes are in vain. We brand those who tell us such things can happen to Mother Church with every vile label we can conceive—blasphemer, heretic, apostate, excommunicate, accursed of God, servant of Darkness, spawn of Shan-wei, child of evil . . . the list goes on forever. And yet, much though it grieves me, bitterly though my heart weeps within me, it is not the 'heretics' who have lied to us. It is not the Church of Charis which has become the handmaiden of Shan-wei.

"It is Mother Church."

A deep, hoarse almost-sound of protest swept through the congregation. It was bone-deep, filled with pain, and yet no one listening to him found the words to give that protest shape and form. No one cried out in rejection. And that failure, the fact that the protest was inchoate, unformed—a cry of grief, not one of *denial*—told Tymahn Hahskans a great deal about the sheep of his flock.

Tears burned behind his eyes as he felt the conflicting tides sweeping through his congregation's hearts. As he recognized their sorrow, the fear not simply of what he had already laid out before them, but of what they sensed was yet to come, and the soul-deep dread which was the precursor of acceptance.

"I am not the only one of Mother Church's priests who has longed to cry out against her oppression," he told them. "Not the only one of her loving children whose eyes have seen the corruption growing and festering at her very heart. There are more of us than you may ever have guessed, and yet we have been ordered to keep silence. To tell no one we've seen the blemishes growing, the chimney of her lamp begrimed. To pretend we haven't seen worldly power, wealth, and the pomp and secular glory of princes become more important to those charged to keep her safe and clean of spot than their own duty to God and to the Archangels."

His voice rose, gaining steadily in power, touched with the denuncitory power of the visionary, and his dark eyes flashed.

"We have been ordered—*I* have been ordered—to keep silent about all these things, yet I will keep silent no more. I will open my mouth, and I will tell you, yes. *Yes!* My children, I *have* seen all of those things, and my eyes, made sharp by sorrow and disappointment, have grown disillusioned. I have seen the evil hiding beneath the fairness of Mother Church's surface. I have seen the men called to the orange who have turned their backs upon God's true message, given their hearts not to God but to their own power and ambition. I have seen her captivity, and heard her cries for succor, and grieved for her bondage in the dark hours of the night, as have others, and our hearts are heavy as stones, for if *she* can give harbor to corruption, then surely anything can. If *she* is not proof against evil, then surely nothing is, and there is no hope in us. No help *for* us, for we have failed the Holy Bédard's great charge, and God's own Church has been defiled. Mother Church herself has become the doorway of evil, the portal for Shan-wei's dark poison of the soul, and we—*we,* my children!—are the ones who have let that terrible, terrible transformation come to pass. By our silence, by our acceptance, by our *cowardice,* we have become the accomplices of her defilers, and do not doubt for one moment that at the end of all things, we shall be called to account for our most grievous faults!

"And yet . . ."

His voice trailed off into stillness, and he let that stillness linger. Let it build and hang heavily, filling Saint Kathryn's like some throbbing thunderhead, pregnant with the very *rakurai* of God. And then, at last, after a tiny eternity, he spoke again.

"Oh, yes, my children . . . and yet. The great 'and yet.' The *glorious* 'and yet'! Because God *has* sent us hope once more, after all. Sent it in the most unlikely guise of all. In the words of the 'apostate,' in the division of the 'schismatic,' and in the teachings of the 'heretic.' I know how shocked many of you must be to hear that, how dismayed. How frightened. And yet, as I examine the doctrine of this 'Church of Charis,' I find no evil in it. I find anger. I find rebellion. I find denunciation and defiance. But none of that, my children—*none of it!*—do I find directed against God. Or against the *Writ.* Or against what Mother Church was ordained to be and, with God's help, will one day be again!

"I do not say the Empire of Charis came to our shores solely out of the love all children of God are called to share with one another. I will not tell you worldly ambition, the contest of princes squabbling over baubles and the illusion of power, has played no part in what has happened here . . . or in what happened in Darcos Sound when the corrupt men in Zion sent our sons and brothers to destroy those who had dared to reject their own corruption. Men are men. They are mortal, fallible, imperfect, prey to ambition and to the hatreds of this world. They are all of that. Yet even so, they live in God's world, and God can—and will—use even their weaknesses for His great purpose. And as I look upon His world, as I meditate upon His word," again, the hands gently caressed the great book before him, "I see Him doing precisely that. I tell you now, and no 'foreign heretic' has put the words into my mouth, what the Church of Charis tells you about the corruption, the decadence, the *evil,* of the 'Group of Four' and those who serve their will is God's own truth, carried to us in the tempest of war because God's Church would not hear Him in the time of tranquility. The men in Zion, the *men* who think of themselves as the masters of *God's* Church, are not shepherds, but wolves. They serve not the Light, but the deepest, blackest Dark. And they are not the keepers of men's souls, but the enemies of God Himself, set free to wreak Shan-wei's ruin upon us all . . . unless those who *do* serve the Light stop them and cast them down utterly.

"God's sword has been loosed in the world, my children. We are fated to live in the shadow of that sword, and it is up to each of us to decide where *we* will stand when His truth demands an accounting of us. That choice lies before each and every one of us. We ignore it at our peril, for those who do not choose to stand *for* the Light will find themselves, in the fullness of time, given *to* the Dark. I beseech you, as you face this time of tumult, choose. *Choose!* Take your stand for God as God gives you the power to see it, and gird yourself for the greater and still sterner test to come."

▼    ▼    ▼

Merlin Athrawes shook himself and opened his eyes, letting the imagery recorded by the tiny sensors deployed inside Saint Kathryn's Church slip away from him. He sat up in his chair in Cherayth, thousands of miles from Manchyr, feeling the sleeping quiet of the palace all around him, and something deep within his moly-circ heart seemed to be beating against the confining cage of his chest's synthetic composites.

The power and the passion of Tymahn Hahskans' sermon echoed inside him, driven by the man's personal, burning faith. A part of Merlin, even now, wanted to mock and deride that faith, because, unlike Hahskans, he knew the lie upon which it rested. He knew what Adorée Bédard had truly been like. Knew that, in many ways, Zhaspahr Clyntahn and Zahmsyn Trynair were far, far closer to Eric Langhorne than someone like Maikel Staynair could ever be.

He longed—longed with a depth and a strength which shocked him more than a little, even now—to hate Tymahn Hahskans for worshipping mass murderers like Bédard and Langhorne.

Yet he couldn't. He literally *could* not do it, and he smiled crookedly as he contemplated the sublime irony of it all. Adorée Bédard had been personally responsible for brainwashing every single colonist planted on the planet of Safehold into believing that he or she had been created, given the breath of life itself, in the very instant their eyes opened on this world for the first time. She'd built the entire lie, brick by brick. Every word of *"The Book of Bédard,"* whether she'd actually written it herself or it had simply been attributed to her after her own death, had been dedicated to supporting that lie, shoring up the coercive edifice of the Church's tyranny.

And yet, despite all of that, it was the Order of Bédard—men like Tymahn Hahskans, like Maikel Staynair—who were the spearheads of the Reformist movement. Who insisted on taking the words of Adorée Bédard and actually *applying* them. Insisted upon holding those who corrupted the Church's power accountable.

Merlin Athrawes wasn't going to make the mistake of assuming that anyone who supported the Church of Charis automatically supported the *Empire* of Charis, as well. The world—and the workings of the human heart—were too complicated, too complex, for that simple a parallelism to govern. Yet Merlin had also known, thanks to the unique perspective his SNARCs conferred upon him, that the anger against the Group of Four's corruption had never been limited solely to the Kingdom of Charis. Even he had failed to fully appreciate the power of that anger as it bubbled away beneath the surface, for the coercive power of the Church—and especially of the Inquisition—had *kept* it beneath the surface. Unseen and unheard, where it was not permitted to challenge the authority and power of those who had made themselves masters of the Church.

There were others like Hahskans. Merlin had known that from the beginning of this struggle. He never doubted that they would demand the right to speak their minds and their hearts where the Church of Charis was concerned, as well, but he'd known they recognized the evils which afflicted the Temple. He'd hoped they would find their voices when the Inquisition's stifling hand was lifted from their mouths, and he'd been deeply pleased when Tymahn Hahskans' name had headed the list of reconfirmed parish priests in Klairmant Gairlyng's first proclamation as Archbishop of Corisande. Whether Hahskans himself realized it or not, Merlin's SNARCs had revealed to him long ago that the rector of Saint Kathryn's was one of the most respected priests in all of Manchyr. And there was a reason that was so, a reason Hahskans deserved every bit of respect the laity of the Corisandian capital gave him, and not simply because he was a gifted preacher. He was that, of course, but the true reason he was so respected—even beloved—was that only the blindest or most cynical of people could possibly have denied the intellect, the integrity, and the limitless love which filled that man of God.

*He is a man of God, too,* Merlin thought now. *Filtered through the prism of the Church of God Awaiting or not, Hahskans truly has found his own way to God. As he himself says, he's not the only priest in Corisande who's seen the corruption in Zion, but there's damned well not another man in Manchyr who could possibly have seen it more clearly . . . or denounced it more fearlessly. And if I'd ever doubted there truly is a God, finding a man like this in a church in the middle of* Manchyr, *of all places, would prove there is.*

The man who had once been Nimue Alban shook his head again and then, although he would never again need oxygen, drew a deep and cleansing breath.

"All right, Owl," he murmured. "Now let's see the take from Manchyr Cathedral. I doubt Archbishop Klairmant's going to be able to beat that one, but let's give him the chance to try."

"Of course, Lieutenant Commander," the distant AI replied obediently, and Merlin closed his eyes once more.

.VII.
IHNS *Ice Lizard,*
City of Yu-Shai,
Shwei Province,
Harchong Empire

"W elcome aboard, My Lord."

"Thank you, Captain—?" Phylyp Ahzgood replied, arching one eyebrow as he returned the bow of the stocky, bearded man in the uniform of the Imperial Harchong Navy who'd been waiting for him at the inboard end of the boarding plank.

"Yuthain, My Lord. Captain Gorjha Yuthain, of His Imperial Majesty's Navy, at your service." The officer bowed again, more deeply, with that certain special flourish of which only the Harchongese seemed truly capable.

"Thank you, Captain Yuthain," Earl Coris repeated, acknowledging the introduction, and smiled with genuine if weary gratitude.

This wasn't his first visit to Yu-Shai, and he hadn't really cared much for the city the first time round. It wasn't the townsfolk that bothered him, but both the city and the provincial administration possessed every bit of the arrogance and insufferable sense of superiority stereotype assigned to all Harchongese bureaucrats. The permanent bureaucracy which administered the Empire was highly skilled. When properly motivated, it could accomplish amazing feats with astonishing skill and efficiency. Unfortunately, it was equally corrupt, and that skill and efficiency tended to vanish like snow in summer when the proper "spontaneous gifts" weren't offered. The fact that he and his royal charges had been little more than political fugitives—and fugitives who were very, very far from home, at that—had meant the local officialdom had expected considerably more generous "gifts" than usual, and Phylyp Ahzgood had a constitutional objection to being gouged.

This Captain Yuthain, however, was something else again. Coris recognized a type he'd seen often enough back home in Corisande—a professional seaman, with quite a few years of tough naval service behind him and a marked lack of patience with the sort of bureaucrats who'd extorted every mark they could out of the earl the first time through. Coris doubted Yuthain would turn up his nose at the possibility of garnering a few extra marks here and there. He might even not be completely above a little judicious smuggling—or above looking the other way while someone else did the smuggling, at any rate. But any venality on his part would be little more than surface deep, unless Coris missed his guess, and his competence—and his own confidence *in* that competence—were obvious.

That was good, and the gleam of humor the earl seemed to detect in Yuthain's eye was another good sign. Unless Coris was mistaken, Captain Yuthain was going to need a good sense of humor—and all that competence— in the next few five-days. The icy wind was brisk enough down here by the docks, in the shelter of the breakwaters and the waterfront buildings. It was going to be a lot *brisker* once they cleared the port, too. There was a reason a trip by galley across the Gulf of Dohlar in the teeth of a West Haven winter was nothing to look forward to. Not only that, but what waited after his arrival in the port of Fairstock, in the Empire's Malansath Province, promised to be substantially less pleasant even than that.

Coris was perfectly well aware of that, yet after more than a full month's travel by coach and horseback, the thought of spending three or four five-days aboard a ship was positively alluring. The deck might move under his feet, probably fairly violently, at least once during the voyage. But Phylyp Ahzgood had been born and raised in an island princedom. He'd discovered early on that he was actually a very good sailor . . . and he'd just once again amply proved that he was *not* a good equestrian. In fact, it took all the self-restraint he possessed to keep himself from kneading his aching posterior.

"I can tell you've had a less than restful journey so far, My Lord, if you'll pardon my saying so," Yuthain observed, brown eyes twinkling ever so slightly as he took in Coris' mud-streaked boots and slightly bowlegged stance. "*Ice Lizard*'s no fine cruiseship, and I'm afraid that this time of year she's likely to live up to her name, too, once we're clear of the land. But we'll not be sailing until tomorrow morning's tide, so if you'd care to get your gear stowed aboard, you can get at least one good night's sleep tied up wharf-side. For that matter," he twitched his head towards the lamp-lit windows of a tavern at the end of the wharf, "the Copper Kettle sets a good table, and it's got a decent bath-house attached out back. A man who's spent the last few five-days aboard a saddle might be thinking a good, hot, steaming bath would be the best way to start his evening."

"He might indeed, Captain," Coris agreed with a smile which was even more grateful, and glanced over his shoulder at the equally travel-worn servant at his heels.

Rhobair Seablanket was a tall, thin man, probably close to fifty years old, with stooped shoulders, brown hair, dark eyes, and a full but neatly trimmed beard. He also boasted a long nose and a habitually lugubrious expression. He looked, to be brutally honest, like the compulsive-worrier sort of man no one had ever heard tell a joke, but he was a competent, if occasionally overly fussy, valet, and he was also Corisandian. That hadn't been a minor consideration when Coris hired him after Captain Zhoel Harys had safely delivered the earl and his two royal charges to Yu-Shai for their first visit to the city, on their way to Delferahk. There'd been no question of taking servants with them aboard the cramped merchant galley *Wing,* given their humble cover identities, and Coris had been delighted, for several reasons, to engage Seablanket when the Harchongese hiring agency turned him up. The man's accent was a comforting reminder of home, and his competence—in more than one area—had been more than welcome in the long, weary five-days since Coris had engaged him.

"Yes, My Lord?" Seablanket asked now, correctly interpreting his employer's glance.

"I think Captain Yuthain's advice is excellent," Coris said. "I fully intend to take advantage of that hot bath he just mentioned. Why don't you go ahead and get our gear stowed aboard? If I've got a dry change of clothes, unpack it and bring it over to the—the Copper Kettle, was it, Captain?" Yuthain nodded, and Coris turned back to Seablanket. "Bring it over so I'll have something to put on, and if the kitchen looks as good as Captain Yuthain is suggesting, bespeak dinner for me, as well."

"Of course, My Lord."

"And don't forget to bring a change for yourself, too," Coris admonished, raising one forefinger and wagging it in the valet's direction. "I imagine you're just as frozen as I am, and I'm sure they've got more than one tub."

"Yes, My Lord. Thank you!"

Seablanket's normal expression lightened noticeably, but Coris merely shrugged his gratitude aside.

"And now, Captain," the earl said, returning his attention to Yuthain, "please don't think me rude, but the sooner I get into that hot tub of yours, the better. And while I'm sure *Ice Lizard* is an admirably well-found vessel, I'm also going to be spending quite a bit of time as your guest. I'm sure we'll have entirely too much time to get to know one another between here and Fairstock."

▼    ▼    ▼

The Copper Kettle's bathhouse was plainly furnished, but well built and fully equipped. Coris spent the better part of an hour immersed up to the neck, eyes half-closed in drowsy content as steaming water soaked the ache out of his muscles. He'd endured more time on horseback—or in one of the bouncing, jouncing stagecoaches that bounded between posting houses on the more heavily traveled stretches—over the past few months than in his entire previous existence, and he felt every weary mile of it deep in his bones. To be fair, the high roads here in Howard were far better designed, built, *and* maintained than their ostensible counterparts in Corisande had ever been. Broad, stone-paved, with well-designed drainage and solid bridges, they'd made it possible for him to maintain an average of just over a hundred miles a day. He could never have done that on Corisandian roads, and to be honest, he wished he hadn't had to do it on Howard's roads, either. The fact that it was *possible* didn't make it anything remotely like *pleasant,* and the earl's lifetime preference for sea travel had been amply reconfirmed over the month since his departure from Talkyra.

Of course, that had been the *easy* part of his projected journey, he reminded himself glumly as he hoisted himself out of the water at last and reached for the towel which had been warming in front of the huge tiled stove that heated the bathhouse. The Gulf of Dohlar in October was about as miserable a stretch of seawater as anyone could ever hope to find. And while Coris had formed a high initial impression of Captain Yuthain's competence, *Ice Lizard* was a galley, not a galleon. She was shallow draft, low-slung, and sleek . . . and it was obvious to the earl's experienced eye that she was going to be Shan-wei's own bitch in a seaway.

Assuming they survived the passage of the Gulf (which seemed at least an even bet, if Captain Yuthain proved as skilled as Coris thought he was), there was the delightful prospect of another thirteen hundred miles of overland travel—this time through the belly-deep snows of November—just to reach the southern shores of Lake Pei. And then there was the even more delightful prospect of the four-hundred-mile trip *across* the lake. Which would undoubtedly be frozen over by the time he got there, which—in turn—meant he would have to make the entire trip—oh, joy!—by iceboat.

*That* experience, he had no doubt, would make *Ice Lizard* look *exactly* like the fine cruiseship Yuthain had assured him she wasn't.

*It's a good thing you're not fifty yet, Phylyp,* he told himself glumly as he finished toweling off and reached for the linen drawers Seablanket had thoughtfully placed to warm in front of the stove. *You'll probably survive. It's a good thing you made sure your will was in order ahead of time, but you'll probably survive. Until you actually get to Zion, at least.*

And that was the crux of the matter, really, wasn't it? What *was* going to happen once he reached Zion and the Temple? The fact that the writ summoning him had been signed by the Grand Inquisitor, as well, not just the Chancellor, hadn't exactly put his mind at ease. Not surprisingly, he supposed, since he rather doubted it had been intended to do anything of the sort. Trynair and Clyntahn couldn't possibly see Daivyn as anything more than a potentially useful pawn. Someday, if he could finally, somehow reach the chessboard's final file, he might be elevated—converted into something more valuable than that. But Daivyn Daykyn was only a very *little* boy, when all was said, and Clyntahn, at least, would never forget for a moment that pawns were meant to be sacrificed.

Coris had done his best to reassure Irys, and he knew the princess far too well to serve up comforting lies in the effort. In the earl's opinion, the girl was even smarter than her father had been, and she wasn't afraid to use the wit God and the Archangels had given her. She had all her father's ability to carry a grudge until it died of old age, then have it stuffed and mounted someplace where she could admire it at regular intervals, but—so far, at least—she'd usually shown a fair amount of discretion in choosing which grudges to hold. That might well change—indeed, might *already* have changed—given how her world had been shattered into topsy-turvy ruin in the last year or so, but despite her youth, she was just as capable as Coris himself when it came to reading the political wind, recognizing the storm clouds gathering about her younger brother. That was why he'd told her the absolute truth when he'd said he doubted the Group of Four had any *immediate* plans for how they might most profitably utilize Daivyn. Yet sooner or later, they *would* have plans, and that was the reason they'd decided to drag him all these thousands of miles through a mainland winter.

When the time came, they would want to be certain Phylyp Ahzgood understood his place. Recognized his true masters, with a clear vision, unblinkered by any lingering, misplaced loyalty to the House of Daykyn. They intended to underscore that to him . . . and to see him for themselves, form their own judgment of him. And if that judgment proved unfavorable, they would remove him from his position as Daivyn's and Irys' guardian. If he was quite unreasonably lucky, he might even survive the removal rather than be quietly and efficiently disappeared. At the moment, he'd give odds of, oh, at least one-in-fifty that he would.

*Well, Phylyp, my boy,* he thought, slipping into an embroidered steel thistle silk shirt, *you'll just have to see that they form a favorable opinion, won't you? Shouldn't be all that hard. Not for an experienced, conniving liar such as yourself. All you have to do is keep any of them from getting close enough to figure out what you really think. How hard can it be?*

▼   ▼   ▼

"I've got to be getting back to the Copper Kettle," Rhobair Seablanket said. "He's bound to be finished with his bath by now. He'll want his dinner, and as soon as I get it served, he'll wonder why I'm not in the bathhouse myself." He grimaced. "For that matter, *I'll* wonder why I'm not neck-deep!"

"I understand," the man on the other side of the rickety desk in the small dockside warehouse office replied.

The office wasn't exceptionally clean, nor was it particularly warm, and its tiny window was so thoroughly covered with grime no one could possibly have seen through it. All of which only served to make it even better suited to their purposes.

"I understand," the other man repeated, "and so far, at least, I think my superiors are going to be satisfied. At any rate, I don't think anyone's going to want to give you any . . . more proactive instructions."

"I hope not," Seablanket said with obvious feeling. The other man arched an eyebrow, and the valet snorted. "This man is no fool, Father. I'm confident of everything I've reported so far, and I think your 'superiors'' original estimate of his character probably wasn't far wrong. But I'd *really* rather not be asked to do anything that might make him start wondering about me. If he ever realizes I'm reporting everything he does to someone else, he's likely to do something drastic about it. Please don't forget he was Hektor's spymaster. You know—the one all of Hektor's *assassins* reported to?" Seablanket grimaced. "Corisandian intelligence was never too shy about dropping suitably weighted bodies into handy lakes or bays—or swamps, for that matter—and the two of us are about to sail across the Gulf of Dohlar in winter. I'd sort of like to arrive on the other side."

"Do you think it's really likely he'd react that way?" The other man actually seemed a bit amused, Seablanket noted sourly.

"I don't know, and if it's just the same to you, Father, I'd rather not find out. It's always possible he'd exercise a little restraint if he figured out who planted me on him the last time he was in Yu-Shai, but he might not, too. For that matter, he might not *care* who it was."

"Well, we can't have that!" The other man stood, straightening his purple, flame-badged cassock, and raised his right hand to sign Langhorne's Scepter in blessing. "My prayers will go with you, my son," he said solemnly.

"Oh, *thank* you, Father."

It was, perhaps, a sign of just how preoccupied Seablanket truly was with the more immediate threat of the Earl of Coris' possible reactions that he allowed his own irritation to color his tone. Or it might simply have been how long he'd known the other man. Perhaps he realized it wasn't actually quite as risky as someone else might have thought.

After all, even one of the Grand Inquisitor's personal troubleshooters could have a sense of humor, when all was said.

# NOVEMBER,
# YEAR OF GOD 893

.I.

Imperial Palace,
City of Cherayth,
Kingdom of Chisholm,
and
HMS *Dawn Wind*, 54,
Dolphin Reach

W hat do you think about Merlin's and Owl's latest reports on Corisande, Maikel?" Sharleyan asked.

She and Cayleb sat in Prince Tymahn's Suite, the rooms just down the hall from their own suite which had been converted into a combined library and office. It lacked the remodeled, heated floors of their bedroom, but a brand-new cast-iron stove from the Howsmyn Ironworks had been installed, and the coal fire in its iron belly gave off a welcome warmth.

"You've both seen the same imagery I have from Merlin's SNARCs," Maikel Staynair pointed out over the plug in her right ear. His voice sounded remarkably clear for someone better than four thousand miles, as the wyvern flew, from Cherayth. "What do you think?"

"No you don't," Cayleb shot back with a grin. "We asked *you* first!"

"Harumpf!" Staynair cleared his throat severely, and Sharleyan grinned at her husband. Their contact lenses brought them the archbishop's image as he sat in his shipboard cabin, looking out over a sunset sea, with Ahrdyn draped across his lap. His own lenses showed him her grin, as well, and he made a face at her. But then he shrugged, and his tone was more serious as he continued.

"As far as the Church goes, I think we've been *extremely* blessed with Gairlyng and—especially—men like Father Tymahn," he said very soberly. "We're not going to find any Charisian 'patriots' in Corisande, even among the clergy, anytime soon, but the reform element in the Corisandian hierarchy's proved rather stronger than I'd dared hope before the invasion. And the really good news, in many ways, is how many of those Reformists are native-born Corisandians, like Father Tymahn. That puts a Corisandian face on voices of reason, and that's going to be incredibly valuable down the road.

"From a more purely political perspective," the archbishop continued, "I think General Chermyn and Anvil Rock and Tartarian are about as on top of things as we could reasonably ask, Your Majesty. That's Bynzhamyn's opinion, too, for that matter. Neither of us sees how anybody could be doing a *better* job, anyway, given the circumstances of Hektor's murder and the fact that there probably aren't more than a half-dozen people in all of Corisande—even among the most reform-minded members of the priesthood—who think Cayleb wasn't behind it."

"Agreed," Cayleb said, his own expression sober. "All the same, I have to admit I'd feel a lot better if the Brethren would let us go ahead and bring Hauwyl fully inside. If we'd been able to give *somebody* in Corisande one of Merlin's coms, I'd sleep a lot more soundly at night."

Sharleyan nodded, although, truth to tell, she wasn't entirely certain she would have been in favor of giving Hauwyl Chermyn a communicator. It wasn't that she doubted the Marine general's loyalty, intelligence, or mental toughness in the least. No, the problem was that despite Chermyn's genuine hatred for the Group of Four, he still believed—deeply and completely—in the Church's doctrine. As with Rayjhis Yowance and Mahrak Sahndyrs, there was simply no way to know how he might react if they tried to tell him the truth.

*And it's not as if they're the only ones that's true of,* she acknowledged unhappily to herself. *Or as if they were the only ones who could be so much* more *capable if we only dared to tell them everything we know.*

Unfortunately, they couldn't, despite the difficulties that created. It was bad enough that they couldn't tell Gray Harbor, given his position as the effective First Councilor of the Charisian Empire, but Sahndyrs, the Baron of Green Mountain, was at least equally important in light of his duties as First Councilor of the Kingdom of Chisholm.

*Not to mention the tiny fact that he's Mother's lover (whether I'm supposed to know that or not)* and *the man who taught me everything I know about being a queen,* she thought unhappily. *Why, oh why, couldn't the two political advisers Cayleb and I both lean most heavily upon have just a* little *bit less integrity . . . where the Church is concerned, at least?*

"I've done my best to ginger up Zhon and the others, Your Grace," Staynair told Cayleb, his tone a bit wry. "And I have to say, in the interests of fairness, that they've actually become much more flexible about approving additions to your inner circle. After being so miserly with their approval for so long—for so many entire *generations* of the Brethren, when you come down to it—that's really quite remarkable, when you think about it."

"Agreed," Cayleb said once more, acknowledging his archbishop's slightly pointed but unmistakably admonishing tone. "Agreed! And however irritating it may sometimes be, I have to admit that having someone put the brakes on my own occasional bursts of . . . excessive enthusiasm isn't exactly a bad thing." The emperor made a face. "I think all monarchs have a tendency to fall prey to expediency, if they aren't careful. And sometimes I think the rest of the Brethren might've had a point when they worried about that 'youthful impatience' of mine while they debated telling *me* about it."

"I don't think I'd go quite that far," Staynair replied. "At the same time, though, I won't pretend I'm not relieved to hear you say that, either."

"Oh, I'm maturing, I am," Cayleb assured him dryly. "Having Merlin and

Sharley right here at hand to whack me over the head at the drop of a hat tends to have that effect, you know."

"Maybe it would, if your skull wasn't quite so thick," his wife told him, smiling as she ran her fingers through his hair. He smiled back at her, and she snorted in amusement. But then she leaned back in her own chair and shook her head.

"At least, where Corisande is concerned, you and I are closer than Telles-berg, at the moment," she pointed out aloud. "And even with the over-water links, the sempahore between here and there—or from here to Eraystor, for that matter—works for *us* now, not the Group of Four. We can get dispatches to Manchyr a lot quicker from Cherayth."

"That helps," Cayleb agreed. "In fact, as far as the semaphore's concerned, we're actually better placed here than we would be in Tellesberg, since Cher-ayth's much closer to our geographic center. It's not the same as being there to keep an eye on things in Corisande myself, though. And, for that matter, I'm none too delighted at having to send them overland through Zebediah, even if we did personally vet the semaphore managers," he added a bit sourly.

"No, it's not the same as being there," she acknowledged. On the other hand, they both knew why he wasn't still in Manchyr, personally overseeing the restive princedom's incorporation into the Empire. And completely leaving aside all of the personal reasons she was glad he wasn't—including the one which was just beginning to affect her figure—the cold-blooded political calculation which had brought him "home" to Cherayth seemed to be proving out in practice. Sharleyan wasn't foolish enough to think Earl Anvil Rock and Earl Tartarian were going to keep the lid nailed down on the conquered prince-dom's many and manifold boiling resentments forever. The "spontaneous" street demonstrations in Manchyr—and quite a few of them truly were spontaneous, she admitted, completely independent of the activities of people like Paitryk Hainree—were an ominous indication of heavy weather just over the horizon. But it was obvious from Merlin's SNARCs that it would have been even worse if Cayleb had remained in Corisande. At least, unlike Cayleb, Anvil Rock and Tartarian were also Corisandians themselves. And at least they were governing Corisande (officially, at any rate) as the regents of Prince Daivyn, not in the name of a foreign conqueror. Everyone might still see that foreign conqueror lurking just behind Daivyn's (empty) throne, yet it still gave them a degree of le-gitimacy in Corisandian eyes which Viceroy General Chermyn simply could not have enjoyed.

Of course, that was its own jar of worms. And a particularly *squirmy* jar it was, too.

*I wish I didn't sympathize with Irys as much as I do,* she thought grimly. *And I know I can't afford to let that sympathy influence me. But I also know what it's like to have your father murdered. I know exactly what that can do to someone, and however much I may have loathed and hated Hektor Daykyn, he was her father. She loved him, loved him as much as I loved mine, and she's never going to forgive Cayleb for having him assassinated any more than I ever forgave Hektor for buying my father's murder.*

Sharleyan Ahrmahk was only too well aware of the bitterly ironic parallels between herself and Irys Daykyn, and despite her own burning hatred for Hektor of Corisande, she truly did feel a deep, pain-laced sympathy for Hektor's surviving, orphaned children. And if there was one person on the face of Safehold who would never underestimate just how dangerous a "mere girl's" blazing determination to avenge that murder could truly be, it was Sharleyan of Chisholm.

*Which only makes me worry even more about Larchros, Storm Keep, and all of their damned friends and neighbors. If only we could just go ahead and arrest them all for what we know they're doing.*

That, however, was the one thing they absolutely couldn't do. Cayleb had been right when he'd decided he couldn't simply replace conquered princes and nobles with people who would inevitably be seen as his favorites. No, he had to leave legitimate nobles who had sworn fealty to him in place . . . unless and until he had incontrovertible proof the princes and nobles in question had been guilty of treason. Which, since they couldn't possibly present evidence from the SNARCs in any open court, meant all they could do was to keep a wary eye on what Merlin had christened the "Northern Conspiracy."

And, if she were honest, she wished even more passionately that they could move openly even against the street agitators. She supposed there really wasn't any reason they couldn't arrest commoners "on suspicion," assuming there'd been some way to identify them to General Chermyn. Or to Koryn Gahrvai. But just how did one go about identifying them to anyone outside the inner circle without raising all sorts of potentially disastrous questions? And even leaving aside that not-so-minor consideration, did they really want to start down that road? She didn't doubt there might come a time when they'd have no choice, but as Cayleb had just pointed out, it was always tempting (and seldom wise) to succumb to expediency. As far as she was concerned, she'd prefer to delay that time when they had no choice for as long as possible.

Of course, there were some other weighty, purely pragmatic arguments in favor of their current "hands-off" approach, as well. The "database" of agitators Merlin had Owl building continued to grow steadily, and there were many advantages in letting that proceed undisturbed . . . up to a point, at least. Not only would they know where to find their organized enemies when the moment finally came, but letting the other side do its recruiting undisturbed also served to draw the most dangerous opposition together in one group, to give them a single target they could decapitate with a single strike.

*And,* she reflected, *sifting through Owl's reconnaissance "take," as Merlin calls it, helps us evaluate* why *someone joined the resistance. I never realized how valuable that could be, until he pointed it out. Knowing what motivates people to actively oppose you is incredibly useful when it comes to evaluating the effectiveness of your policies. Or how other people* perceive *those policies, at any rate. And it doesn't hurt to be able to judge the character of your opponents, either. Not everyone who joins up with people like Hainree and Waimyn belongs in the same basket with them. There are good and decent people on the other side—people who genuinely think what they're doing is the right thing, what God wants them to do. It's hard enough remembering that even with the proof right in front of us. Without it, I don't think I'd be able to remember at all when sentencing time rolls around.*

At least the effort wasn't burning up as much of their time as it might have. Now that Merlin had gotten the process up and running, Owl routinely assigned parasite sensors to each additional anti-Charis activist as he was identified. At this point, neither Merlin nor Cayleb or Sharleyan were trying to keep track of everyone being added to the files. If the "filters" Merlin had put in place were doing their jobs, Owl would identify any important Corisandian churchman, noble, or member of Parliament who crossed the path of anyone in the database. At that point, those involved would be brought to Merlin's attention and flagged for closer future observation. Several of the more important (or more *active,* at least) of the street agitators had also been added to the "special watch" list, and Owl routinely notified Merlin of anyone new who crossed those people's paths, regardless of the newcomer's rank. For the most part, though, all they were really doing was developing their list of active opponents and continuing to chart the slowly growing, steadily more sophisticated organization those opponents were putting in place. And hard as it was watching it grow when they couldn't nip it in the bud, none of them were foolish enough to think they could have prevented it from happening, in one form or another, whatever they did.

*And sooner or later, we* will *be in a position to break their organization, too,* Sharleyan thought. *In fact, sooner or later we'll* have *to, and not just in Manchyr, either. The "Northern Conspiracy" is going to be on our little list, too. Eventually, they* will *give us evidence we can use, once we "discover it" through more acceptable avenues. And when we do,* they'll *discover just how efficient our headsmen are.*

She was rather looking forward to that day, actually.

"Well," she said, "at least it doesn't look like Corisande's going up in flames tomorrow morning. It doesn't hurt that you're on your way for your first pastoral visit both here and in Corisande, either, Maikel. And I imagine"—her voice turned just a bit smug, undeniably it turned smug—"that once word gets out that we're *finally* about to produce an heir it's going to upset certain people I could mention almost as much as it's going to reassure all of *our* people."

"Oh, I'm sure it is," Cayleb agreed in a tone of profound satisfaction. "I'm sure it is."

"And neither is Emerald," Staynair told them both. "Going up in flames, I mean."

None of them were speaking loudly, but the archbishop's voice was lower pitched than either Cayleb's or Sharleyan's. They had the advantage of thick stone walls, and of a heavy door of solid nearoak, warded by two Imperial Guardsmen personally selected for their duty by Merlin Athrawes and Edwyrd Seahamper. No one was going to get close enough to eavesdrop on them.

Staynair, on the other hand, was ensconced in the admiral's cabin aboard HMS *Dawn Wind,* one of the Charisian Navy's newer galleons. As quarters went aboard cramped, overcrowded warships, it was a spacious abode, well suited to the archbishop's dignity and the privacy the duties of his office—not to mention his own need for meditation and prayer—frequently required. Of course, it *was* aboard one of the aforementioned cramped, overcrowded warships. Which was to say that the bulkheads were thin, the doors were anything *but* solid nearoak, and people were likely to inadvertently intrude upon his privacy at any moment. Fortunately, he'd already firmly established a tradition of retiring to his cabin every evening to enjoy the sunset through the stern windows and meditate. By now, his staff was accustomed to protecting his privacy during those moments. As long as he kept his voice down—and the cabin skylight closed—it was extremely unlikely anyone would hear his voice over the inevitable sounds of a sailing ship underway. And even less likely that anyone who heard him speaking would be able to make out words. The logical assumption would simply be that he was praying, and anyone who thought that was what was happening would get themselves out of eavesdropping range as quickly as they could.

"In fact," the archbishop continued now, "I think Emerald is going to be almost as happy to hear about your pregnancy as anybody in Old Charis or Chisholm, Sharleyan. They're committed now—they know that—and they're as eager to see the succession secured as anyone else."

"Really?" Sharleyan said. "I think that's been my own impression," she admitted, "but I also have to admit I've been a little afraid it was my impression because that was the impression I *wanted* to have, if you follow me." She grimaced slightly. "In some ways, I think, having all this access courtesy of Merlin's SNARCs only makes it harder to figure out what people are really thinking. I've spent years training myself to estimate things like that accurately on the basis of second- and third-hand reports. Interpretively, I suppose you might say. Now I'm actually trying to look at people directly and decide for myself, and I've discovered that it's *hard* to get some sort of objective feel for what that many people are really thinking from direct observation. No wonder Merlin's tended to get himself buried under the 'data overload.'"

Her voice softened with the final sentence, and Cayleb nodded in agreement. He still didn't fully understand how the "high-speed data interface"

Merlin's PICA body had once possessed had functioned, but he didn't have to understand how it had *worked* to understand what it had *done*. Or to understand how bitterly Merlin regretted its loss. Having had personal experience now of the sheer quantity of imagery and audio recordings flooding in through Merlin's planet-circling network of reconnaissance platforms, he only wished *he* had a "high-speed interface."

Fortunately, they were making at least a little progress. And while Cayleb wasn't positive, he suspected Owl was getting progressively better at sorting and prioritizing information. Whatever *Owl* was doing, though, the ability to assign specific portions of what Merlin called the "intel take" to someone besides just Merlin had helped enormously. There were limitations, of course. No one else had Merlin's built-in com equipment; they had to speak out loud, instead of subvocalizing, if they wanted to communicate with Owl (or anyone else), which severely limited where and when they could interact with the AI. And all of them were also creatures of flesh and blood, prey to all the weaknesses of the flesh—including the need for food and at least a reasonable amount of sleep.

For that matter, even Merlin had discovered the hard way that he did need at least the equivalent of rest if he was going to maintain his *mental* focus. More to the point, *Cayleb* had figured that out, as well, and ordered him to take the "downtime" he needed to stay fresh and alert.

Which, in fact, was precisely what he was doing at this very moment. Or he'd damned well better be, at any rate, because if Cayleb or Sharleyan caught him listening in when he was supposed to be "sleeping"—and Owl had been ordered to report him, if it happened—there'd be hell to pay.

"Well, in this case, Your Majesty, I think your impression is accurate," Staynair told her. "As a matter of fact, I suppose I might as well go ahead and admit I was hugely relieved by my own observations here."

"Here" wasn't actually quite the correct word anymore, Sharleyan reflected. *Dawn Wind* had sailed from Eraystor Bay on the afternoon tide. At the moment, she was making her way—slowly, especially for someone who had experienced Merlin's recon skimmer—out into the western half of Dolphin Reach, and she was no wyvern, able to ignore reefs, shoals, islands, currents, and unfavorable winds. If they were lucky, and if *Dawn Wind* managed—oh, unlikely event!— to avoid any major storms and made a relatively quick passage for this time of year, she would cover the seventy-three-hundred sea miles to Cherayth in "only" about ten five-days.

Sharleyan hated—absolutely *hated*—having Staynair stuck aboard a ship for that long, yet she'd been forced to agree with him that it wasn't really as if they had a lot of choice. It was essential for the ordained head of the Church of Charis to visit all of the new empire's lands, and unlike the Church of God Awaiting, the Church of *Charis* had decreed from the outset that its bishops and archbishops would be permanent residents of their sees. Instead of making brief annual visits to the souls committed to their care, they would make one—and *only* one—visit to the Church of Charis' annual convocation each year. The rest of their time would be spent at home, seeing to their own and their flocks' spiritual needs, maintaining their focus on what truly mattered. And the Church's annual convocation would be held in a different city every year, not allowed to settle permanently into a single location which would, inevitably, become an imperial city—the Charisian equivalent of the city of Zion—in its own right.

That meant the Archbishop of Charis would be traveling most years just as surely as any of his subordinate prelates. It would have been unthinkable for any Grand Vicar to make the same sort of journey and subject himself to all the wearying effort involved in it—or, for that matter, the inescapable perils of wind and weather inherent in such lengthy voyages—but that was fine with Maikel Staynair. The greater and more numerous the differences between the Church of Charis and the Church of God Awaiting, the better, for a lot of reasons, as far as he was concerned, and he was determined to establish the pattern firmly. Firmly enough that no empire-building successor of his would find the tradition easy to subvert.

His current tour was part of building that tradition. Yet it was more than that, too, for he was determined to personally visit every capital of every political unit of the Charisian Empire—and as many more of the major cities as he could manage, as well. As Wind Thunder had so grumpily pointed out before his departure for Emerald, it was a security nightmare, in many respects. God only knew how many Temple Loyalists would simply have loved to stick something sharp and pointy between the ribs of "Arch Heretic Staynair," as the Loyalist broadsides had dubbed him, but the number had to be enormous. The attempt had already been made once, right in his own cathedral. Who knew what kind of opportunities might arise—or might be manufactured—in someone *else's* cathedral? On the other hand, he was right. He had to establish that kind of personal contact with as much as possible of the new Church's clergy if he expected that clergy to accept that he truly cared about its worries, its concerns, its agonizing crises of conscience, as it coped with the spiritual demands of schism.

*And he does care,* Sharleyan thought. *He truly does. He understands what he's asking of them. I don't believe anyone not completely blinded by intolerance and hatred could fail to recognize that after five minutes in his presence, and that's the exact reason he has to be doing this, however much what I really want to do is lock him up safe and sound inside Tellesberg Cathedral and the Archbishop's Palace.*

"So you're satisfied about Emerald, at least. Where the Church is concerned, I mean," Cayleb said, and Staynair nodded.

"I don't think Prince Nahrmahn's Emeraldians have quite as much . . . fire in their bellies, let's say, as we have back home in Tellesberg," he said. "On the other hand, they weren't the people the Group of Four intended to have raped and murdered, either. At the same time, though, I was deeply gratified by how clearly people in Emerald already recognized the fundamental corruption that let the Group of Four come to power in the first place. It's become increasingly evident to me that many—indeed, I'm tempted to say most, if that's not a case of letting my own optimism run away with me—of Emerald's churchmen saw the Temple's corruption long before Nahrmahn ever decided to swear fealty to the two of you, at any rate. And, believe me, those who did recognize it know they could have been Clyntahn's *next* target, even if they weren't the first time around. In fact, I'm coming to the conclusion that we may discover a larger Reformist movement and commitment than we'd initially anticipated in most places."

"A *Reformist* commitment," Cayleb repeated, and Staynair nodded again, far more serenely than Sharleyan suspected she would have been able to in response to the same question.

"One step at a time, Cayleb," the archbishop said calmly. "One step at a time. Merlin was right when he said God can creep in through the cracks whenever He decides to, but we're going to have to let Him do this in His own good time, I think. First, let us correct the gross, obvious abuses. Once we have people in the habit of actually *thinking* about matters of doctrine and church policy it will be time to begin suggesting . . . more substantive changes."

"He's right, Cayleb," Sharleyan said quietly. Cayleb looked at her, and she reached across to touch the side of his face. It was a conversation they'd had often enough, and she knew how bitterly it grated upon his sense of responsibility that he literally dared not rip away the mask, expose the full, noisome extent of the lies and perverted faith which were the entire foundation of the Church of God Awaiting. *Not* doing that was going to be the true supreme challenge of his life.

"I know he is, love," Cayleb replied. "I don't have to like it—and I won't pretend I do—but I know he's right."

"In the meantime, I'm starting to think young Saithwyk might actually make a good candidate for the inner circle, in a year or two," Staynair said.

"You're joking!" Sharleyan realized she was sitting bolt upright in her chair, her eyes wide.

"I don't know why you should think anything of the sort, Your Majesty."

Staynair's tone was imperturbability itself, although there was a slight twinkle in his eyes, and Sharleyan felt her own eyes narrowing. Fairmyn Saithwyk was the newly consecrated Archbishop of Emerald. Barely forty years old—less than thirty-seven in Terran Standard Years, in point of fact—he came from a conservative family, and his nomination had been firmly supported by Emerald's House of Lords. That was scarcely the pedigree of a rebellious radical, she thought. Yet as she studied Staynair's expression—

"You're *not* joking," she said slowly.

"No, I'm not." He smiled gently at her. "You might want to remember that I'm the one with primary responsibility for evaluating Owl's reports about the senior clergy," he pointed out. "Given that, I don't suppose it should be too surprising for me to have a somewhat different perspective. On the other hand, you should also remember who it was who nominated him in the *first* place."

"Nahrmahn," Cayleb said thoughtfully.

"Precisely, Your Grace." Staynair bobbed his head in Cayleb's direction in a half bow. "You, of course, were never faced with the necessity of making a nomination, given my own fortuitous—and vastly qualified—presence right there in Tellesberg."

Cayleb made an indelicate sound, and Staynair chuckled. But then his expression sobered.

"You didn't have that luxury in Corisande, though, Cayleb. And Sharleyan didn't have it in Chisholm. Or Nahrmahn in Emerald. Mind you, I've been quite satisfied with everything I've seen of Braynair. Both by the way he supported me and the Crown when Sharleyan organized the Imperial Parliament here in Tellesberg, and by the way he's supported both of you—and me—there in Cherayth, since. And I think *you've* been quite satisfied with him, too."

He held Cayleb's eye until the emperor nodded, then shrugged.

"We take what God gives us, and we do the best with it that we can, Cayleb," he said simply. "And in this case, I think He's given us some sound timber to work with. Pawal Braynair is a good, solid, reliable man. He's loyal to God and to Sharleyan, in that order, and however much he might have wished it weren't so, he recognizes how corrupt the vicarate's become. I'm sorry to say I don't think he'll ever be ready for the complete truth, any more than Rayjhis or Baron Green Mountain, but he's just as good a man as they are.

"Yet I'm actually inclined to think Nahrmahn may have found an even greater treasure in Saithwyk." The archbishop's lips seemed to twitch for a moment, and he shook his head. "I'm not at all certain, mind you, but I rather had the impression he was probing to see just how . . . revolutionary, in a doctrinal sense, *I* was prepared to be. I don't have any idea yet where it is *he* wants to go, although I'm sure I'll get around to figuring it out soon enough. I'll want a little longer to watch him in action, mind you, but I'm serious. I think that ultimately he may make a very good candidate for the inner circle. And let's face it, the more senior churchmen we can recruit, the better."

"Well, I doubt anyone could argue with *that*," Sharleyan conceded. Then she shook herself and stood.

"And on that note, Archbishop Maikel, I'm going to call this conference to an end and drag my husband off to bed before he decides to break out the whiskey and stay up all night carousing with you long distance."

"*Carousing?*" Cayleb repeated in injured tones. "I'll have you know that one doesn't '*carouse*' with an archbishop!"

"I didn't say *he'd* be the one doing the carousing, either," she pointed out with a stern twinkle. "And while it's barely the twentieth hour where he is, it's well past twenty-*fourth* here. An empress in my delicate condition needs her sleep, and if I'm going to get any sleep, I need my hot-water bottle. I mean, my beloved husband." She grinned at him. "I can't imagine how I came to . . . misspeak myself that way."

"Oh, no?" Cayleb climbed out of his own chair, eyes laughing while both of them heard Staynair chuckling over the com. Sharleyan regarded him with bright-eyed innocence and shook her head.

"Absolutely," she assured him. "I would *never* think of you in such purely utilitarian and selfish terms! I can't *imagine* how a phrase like that could have somehow slipped out that way!"

"Well, *I* can," he told her ominously. "And I assure you, young lady—there's going to be a penalty."

"Really?" She cocked her head, then batted her eyes at him. "Oh, goody! Should I ask one of the guardsmen to find us the peach preserves? After all, it's not going to be all that much longer before I start losing the athleticism to really enjoy them, you know."

Cayleb made a strangled sound, his face turning a rather alarming shade of red as he fought his laughter, and she giggled delightedly, then looked at the archbishop and smiled sweetly.

"And on that note, Maikel, goodnight."

## .II.
## Archbishop's Palace,
## City of Manchyr,
## Princedom of Corisande

S o, My Lord," Archbishop Klairmant Gairlyng kept his tone rather lighter than he actually felt at this particular moment, "now that you've been here for a five-day, what do you think?"

"In what regard, Your Eminence?" Bishop Zherald Ahdymsyn responded blandly as the archbishop and his two guests stepped into Gairlyng's study.

"Zherald . . ." Bishop Kaisi Mahkhynroh said, raising one chiding index finger, and Ahdymsyn chuckled. Then he looked back at Gairlyng.

"Forgive me, Your Eminence." There was an edge of contrition in his voice. "I'm afraid my sense of humor sometimes betrays me into unbecoming levity.

I think that's at least partly a response to the fact that I used to take myself much too seriously. And, as the *Writ* says, God made Man to smile, as well as to weep."

"That's true enough, My Lord," Gairlyng agreed. "And sometimes, laughter is the only way to *avoid* weeping, I think." He walked around the desk to the comfortable swivel chair behind it, and a courteous sweep of his right hand indicated the even more comfortable armchairs facing it. "Please, My Lords. Make yourselves easy. May I offer you any refreshment?"

"Not for me, thank you, Your Eminence." Ahdymsyn seated himself in one of the indicated chairs. "After we've finished our discussions here, I'm dining with Earl Anvil Rock and his son. I understand Earl Tartarian and at least one or two other members of the Regency Council will be joining us, as well." He grimaced humorously. "As a bishop *executor* of Mother Church, I developed a remarkably hard head. Now, as a lowly bishop once more, and given to somewhat more abstemious habits, I don't seem to have quite the capacity where alcohol is concerned before my jokes become a bit too loud and my judgment becomes somewhat less reliable than I think it is." He frowned thoughtfully, rubbing one eyebrow. "Or that's *one* possibility, at any rate. Another is that I never was quite as immune to its effects as I thought I was, but no one had the nerve to point it out to me."

He smiled broadly, but then his expression sobered and he looked very levelly into Gairlyng's eyes across the archbishop's desk.

"Odd, isn't it, how no one seems to want to challenge the judgment of Mother Church's senior clergy?"

Silence hovered for a moment or two, and then Gairlyng looked up at the aide who had escorted him and his guests from Manchyr Cathedral to the Archbishop's Palace.

"I think that will be all, Symyn," he said. "If I need you, I'll call."

"Of course, Your Eminence."

The dark-haired, dark-complexioned young under-priest's brown cassock bore the Scepter of the Order of Langhorne, as did Gairlyng's orange-trimmed white cassock, and there was a sort of familial resemblance about them, although the under-priest was obviously a native-born Corisandian. Had he been several years younger, or had Gairlyng been several years older, he might have been the archbishop's son. As it was, Ahdymsyn was relatively certain it was simply a case of a young man modeling his own behavior and demeanor upon that of a superior whom he deeply respected.

*And it would appear there's quite a bit* to *respect about the Archbishop*, Ahdymsyn thought. *Rather more than there was to respect about* me *in the good old days, at any rate!*

His lips twitched again, remembering certain conversations which had once passed between him and then-Bishop Maikel Staynair. It was, he reflected (for far from the first time), a very fortunate thing that Staynair's sense of humor was as lively as his compassion was deep.

The door closed behind the departing aide, and Gairlyng returned his attention to his guests. He'd gotten to know Mahkhynroh surprisingly well over the past month or two. Or perhaps not *surprisingly* well, given how closely he'd been compelled to work with the other man since his own elevation to the primacy of Corisande and Mahkhynroh's installation as the Bishop of Manchyr. He wouldn't have gone quite so far as to describe the two of them as friends yet. "Colleagues" was undoubtedly a better term, at least this far. They shared a powerful sense of mutual respect, however, and he'd come to appreciate that Mahkhynroh had been chosen for his present position at least in part because he combined a truly formidable intellect with a deep faith and a remarkably deep well of empathy. Despite his installation by a "foreign, heretical, schismatic church," he'd already demonstrated a powerful ability to *listen* to the priests—and laity—of his bishopric. Not simply to listen, but to convince them he was actually hearing what they said . . . and that he would not hold frank speaking against them. No one would ever accuse him of weakness or vacillation, but neither could any honest person accuse him of tyranny or intolerance.

Ahdymsyn, on the other hand, was so far a complete unknown. Gairlyng knew at least the bare bones of his official history, yet it was already obvious there were quite a lot of things that "official history" had left out. He knew Ahdymsyn had been Archbishop Erayk Dynnys' bishop executor in Charis before Dynnys' fall from grace and eventual execution for heresy and treason. He knew Ahdymsyn came from a merely respectable Temple Lands family, with considerably fewer—and lower placed—connections than Gairlyng's own family could boast. He knew Ahdymsyn, as bishop executor, had more than once reprimanded and disciplined Archbishop Maikel Staynair when Staynair had been simply the Bishop of Tellesberg, and that he had been imprisoned—or, at least, placed under "house arrest"—following the Kingdom of Charis' decision to openly defy the Church of God Awaiting. And he knew that since that time, Ahdymsyn had become one of Staynair's most trusted and valued "troubleshooters," which explained his current presence in Corisande.

What Gairlyng did *not* know, and what it was becoming rapidly evident to him he'd been mistaken about, was how—and why—Zherald Ahdymsyn had made that transition. He thought about that for a few seconds, then decided forthrightness was probably the best policy.

"Forgive me, My Lord," he said now, returning Ahdymsyn's level regard, "but I've begun to suspect that my original assumptions about how you . . . come to hold your present position, shall we say, may have been somewhat in error."

"Or, to put it another way," Ahdymsyn said dryly, "your 'original assumptions' were that, having seen the way the wind was blowing in Charis, and realizing that, whatever defense I might present, the Grand Inquisitor and the Chancellor were unlikely to be overjoyed to see me again in the Temple or Zion, I decided to turn my coat—or would that be my cassock?—while the turning was good. Would that be about the size of it, Your Eminence?"

That, Gairlyng decided, was rather more forthrightness than he'd had in mind. Unfortunately . . .

"Well, yes, actually," he confessed, reminding himself that however he'd become one, he was an *arch*bishop while Ahdymsyn was merely a bishop. "As I say, I've begun to think I was wrong to believe that, but while I don't believe I'd have phrased it quite that way, that was more or less my original assumption."

"And, no doubt, exactly the way it was presented to you here in Corisande before the invasion," Ahdymsyn suggested.

"Yes," Gairlyng said slowly, his tone rather more thoughtful, and Ahdymsyn shrugged.

"I don't doubt for a minute that the Group of Four's presented things that way, whatever they truly think. But neither, in this case, do I doubt for a moment that that's exactly what they think happened." He grimaced once more. "Partly, I'm confident, because that's precisely the way *they* would have been thinking under the same circumstances. But also, I'm very much afraid, because they've spoken with people who actually knew me. I hate to admit it, Your Eminence, but my own attitudes—the state of my own faith—at the time this all began *ought* to make that a very reasonable hypothesis for those who were well acquainted with me."

"That's a remarkably forthright admission, My Lord," Gairlyng said quietly, his chair squeaking ever so softly as he leaned back in it. "One I doubt comes easily to someone who once sat as close to an archbishop's chair as you did."

"It comes more easily than you might think, Your Eminence," Ahdymsyn replied. "I don't say it was a pleasant truth to face when I first had to, you understand, but I've discovered the truth is the truth. We can hide from it, and we can deny it, but we can't *change* it, and I've spent at least two-thirds of my allotted span here on Safehold ignoring it. That doesn't give me a great deal of time to work on balancing the ledger before I'm called to render my accounts before God. Under the circumstances, I don't think I should waste any of it in pointless evasions."

"I see," Gairlyng said. *And I'm beginning to think I see why Staynair trusted you enough to send you here in his name,* the archbishop added silently. "But since you've been so frank, My Lord, may I ask what actually led you to 'face the truth,' as you put it, in the first place?"

"Quite a few things," Ahdymsyn replied, sitting back in his own chair and crossing his legs. "One of them, to be honest, *was* the fact that I realized what sort of punishment I would face if I ever did return to the Temple Lands. Trust me, that was enough to give anyone pause . . . even before that butcher

Clyntahn had Archbishop Erayk tortured to death." The ex-bishop executor's face tightened for a moment. "I doubt any of us senior members of the priesthood ever actually gave much thought to having the Penalty of Schueler levied against *us*. That was a threat—a club—to hold over the heads of the laity in order to frighten *them* into doing God's will. Which, of course, had been revealed to *us* with perfect clarity."

Ahdymsyn's biting tone could have chewed chunks out of the marble façade of Gairlyng's palace, and his eyes were hard.

"So I hadn't actually anticipated that *I* might be tortured to death on the very steps of the Temple," he continued. "I'd accepted that my fate was going to be unpleasant, you understand, but it never crossed my mind to fear *that*. So I'd expected, at least initially, that I'd be incarcerated somewhere in Charis, probably until the legitimate forces of Mother Church managed to liberate me, at which point I would be disciplined and sent to rusticate in disgrace, milking goats and making cheese in some obscure monastic community up in the Mountains of Light. Trust me, at the time I expected that to be more than sufficient punishment for someone of my own exquisite epicurean tastes."

He paused and looked down, and his eyes softened briefly, as if at some memory, as he stroked one sleeve of his remarkably plain cassock. Then he looked back up at Gairlyng, and the softness had vanished.

"But then we learned in Tellesberg what had happened to the Archbishop," he said flatly. "More than that, I received a letter from him—one he managed to have smuggled out before his execution." Gairlyng's eyes widened, and Ahdymsyn nodded. "It was written on a blank page he'd taken from a copy of the *Holy Writ*, Your Eminence," he said softly. "I found that remarkably symbolic, under the circumstances. And in it, he told me his arrest—his trial and his conviction—had brought *him* face-to-face with the truth . . . and that he hadn't liked what he'd seen. It was a brief letter. He had only the single sheet of paper, and I think he was writing in haste, lest one of his guards surprise him at the task. But he told me—*ordered* me, as my ecclesiastic superior—*not* to return to Zion. He told me what his own sentence had been, and what mine would undoubtedly be if I fell into Clyntahn's hands. And he told me Clyntahn's Inquisitors had promised him an easy death if he would condemn Staynair and the rest of the 'Church of Charis'' hierarchy for apostasy and heresy. If he would confirm the Group of Four's version of the reason they'd chosen to lay waste to an innocent kingdom. But he refused to do that. I'm sure you've heard what he actually said, and I'm sure you've wondered if what you heard was the truth or some lie created by Charisian propagandists." He smiled without any humor at all. "It would certainly have occurred to *me* to wonder about that, after all. But I assure you, it was no lie. From the very scaffold on which he was to die, he rejected the lies the Group of Four had demanded of him. He rejected the easy death they'd promised him because that truth he'd finally faced was more important to him, there at the very end of his life, than anything else."

It was very quiet in Gairlyng's study. The slow, measured ticking of the clock on one of the archbishop's bookcases was almost thunderous in the stillness. Ahdymsyn let that silence linger for several moments, then shrugged.

"Your Eminence, I knew the reality of the highest levels of Mother Church's hierarchy . . . just as I'm sure you've known them. I *knew* why Clyntahn had the Archbishop sentenced, why for the first time *ever* the Penalty of Schueler was applied to a senior member of the episcopate. And I knew that, whatever his faults—and Langhorne knows they were almost as legion as my own!—Erayk Dynnys did not deserve to die that sort of death simply as a way for a hopelessly corrupt vicarate to prop up its own authority. I looked around me in Charis, and I saw men and women who believed in *God,* not in the corrupt power and ambition of men like Zhaspahr Clyntahn, and when I saw that, I saw something *I* wanted to be. I saw something that convinced me that, even at that late a date, I—even *I*—might have a true vocation. Langhorne knows, it took God a while to find a hammer big enough to pound that possibility through a skull as thick as mine, but He'd managed it in the end. And, in my own possibly long-winded way, that's the answer to your question. It's not the answer to all of *my* questions— not yet—I'm afraid, but it's something just as important. It's the *start* of all my questions, and I've discovered that, unlike the days when I was Mother Church's consecrated vice regent for Charis, with all the pomp and power of that office, I'm *eager* to find answers to those questions."

Ahdymsyn drew a deep breath, then he shrugged.

"I'm no longer a bishop executor, Your Eminence. The Church of Charis doesn't have those, but even if it did, I wouldn't be one again. Assuming anyone would trust me to be one after the outstanding job I did *last* time around!"

It was no smile, this time. It was a broad, flashing grin, well suited to any youngster explaining that fairies had just emptied the cookie jar. Then it faded again, but now the eyes were no longer hard, the voice no longer burdened with memories of anger and guilt. He looked at Gairlyng from a face of hard-won serenity, and his voice was equally serene.

"I'm something far more important than a 'bishop executor,' now, Your Eminence. I'm a priest. Perhaps for the first time in my entire life, really, I'm a *priest.*" He shook his head. "Frankly, that would be far too hard an act for any high episcopal office to follow."

Gairlyng gazed back at him for a long, thoughtful moment, then looked at Mahkhynroh. None of that had been the answer he'd expected out of Zherald Ahdymsyn, yet somehow it never occurred to him for a moment to doubt the other man's sincerity.

*Which is the biggest surprise of all, really,* he thought. *And where does that leave you, Klairmant?*

He thought about that carefully. He was the consecrated Archbishop of Corisande, as far as the Church of Charis was concerned. Which, of course, made him an utterly damned apostate heretic where the Church of God Awaiting was concerned. After what had happened to Erayk Dynnys, as Ahdymsyn had just reminded him, there was no doubt in his mind what would happen if he or Ahdymsyn or Mahkhynroh ever fell into the hands of the Inquisition. That was a thought fit to wake a man wrapped in the cold sweat of nightmares, and it had, on more than one occasion. In fact, it had awakened him often, making him wonder what in the world—what in God's name—he'd thought he was doing when he accepted his present office.

And now this.

As archbishop, he was Ahdymsyn's ecclesiastic superior. Of course, Ahdymsyn wasn't assigned to his archbishopric, so he'd properly come under Gairlyng's orders only when those orders did not in any way conflict with instructions he'd already received from Maikel Staynair. Still, in this princedom, in this archbishopric, and this office, Ahdymsyn could neither give Gairlyng orders nor pass judgment upon him. All he could do was report back to Staynair, who was thousands of miles away in Chisholm, assuming he'd met his planned travel schedule, or even farther away than that, in Emerald or in transit between Eraystor and Cherayth, if his schedule had slipped. Yet Ahdymsyn was Staynair's personal representative. He was here specifically to smooth the way, prepare the ground, for Staynair's first pastoral visit to Corisande. Despite everything, Gairlyng had expected a far more overtly political representative, especially given Ahdymsyn's hierarchical pedigree. But what he'd gotten . . . what he'd gotten raised almost as many questions in his own mind—questions about *himself*—as they'd answered about Zherald Ahdymsyn.

"My Lord," he said finally, "I'm honored by the honesty with which you've described your own feelings and beliefs. And I'll be honest and say it had never occurred to me that you might have . . . sustained that degree of genuine spiritual regeneration." He raised one hand, waving it gently above his desk. "I don't mean to imply that I believed you'd accepted your present office solely out of some sort of cynical ambition, trying to make the best deal that you could out of the situation which had come completely apart for you in Charis. But I must confess I'd done you a grave disservice and assumed that that *was* much of what had happened. Now, after what you've just said, I find myself in a bit of a quandary."

"A quandary, Your Eminence?" Ahdymsyn arched one eyebrow, and Gairlyng snorted.

"Honesty deserves honesty, My Lord, especially between men who both claim to be servants of God," he said.

"Your Eminence, I doubt very much that you could—in honesty—tell me anything that would come as a tremendous surprise," Ahdymsyn said dryly.

"For example, I *would* be surprised—enormously surprised—to discover that you had accepted your present archbishopric solely out of a sense of deep loyalty and commitment to the Empire of Charis."

"Well," Gairlyng's voice was even drier than Ahdymsyn's had been, "I believe I can safely set your mind to rest upon that point. However," he leaned forward slightly and his expression became far more serious, even somber, "I must admit that despite my very best efforts, I felt more than one mental reservation when I took the vows of my new office."

Ahdymsyn cocked his head to one side, and Gairlyng glanced quickly at Mahkhynroh. This wasn't something he'd admitted to the Bishop of Manchyr, yet he saw only calm interest in the other man's eyes before he looked back at Ahdymsyn.

"First, I would never have accepted this office, under any circumstances, if I hadn't agreed Mother Church—or the vicarate, at least—has become hopelessly corrupt. And when I say 'hopelessly,' that's exactly the word I meant to use. If I'd believed for one moment that someone like Zahmsyn Trynair might demand reform, or that someone like Zhaspahr Clyntahn would have permitted it if he had, I would have refused the archbishopric outright and immediately. But saying I believe Mother Church has been mortally wounded by her own vicars isn't the same thing as saying I believe the Church of *Charis* must automatically be correct. Nor does it mean I'm somehow magically free of any suspicion that the Church of Charis has been co-opted by the *Empire* of Charis. Mother Church may have fallen into evil, but she was never intended to be the servant of secular political ambitions, and I won't willingly serve any 'Church' which is no more than a political tool." He grimaced. "The spiritual rot in Zion is itself the result of the perversion of religion in pursuit of power, and I'm not prepared simply to substitute perversion in the name of the power of *princes* for perversion in the name of the power of *prelates*."

"Granted." Ahdymsyn nodded. "Yet the problem, of course, is that the Church of Charis can survive only so long as the Empire of Charis is able to protect it. The two are inextricably bound up with one another, in that respect, at least, and there are inevitably going to be times when religious policy is shaped by and reflects political policy. And the reverse, I assure you."

"I don't doubt that for a moment." Gairlyng reached up and squeezed the bridge of his nose gently between thumb and forefinger. "The situation is so incredibly complicated, with so many factions, so many dangers, that it could hardly be any other way." He lowered his hand and looked directly at Ahdymsyn. "Still, if the Church is seen as a creature of the Empire, she will never gain general acceptance in Corisande. Not unless something changes more dramatically than I can presently imagine. In that regard, it would have been far better if she had been renamed the 'Reform Church,' perhaps, instead of the Church of *Charis*."

"That was considered," Ahdymsyn told him. "It was rejected because, ultimately, the Group of Four was inevitably going to label it the 'Church of Charis,' whatever *we* called it. That being so, it seemed better to go ahead and embrace the title ourselves—I speak here using the ecclesiastic 'we,' of course," he explained with a charming smile, "since I was not myself party to that particular decision. And another part of it, obviously, was that mutual dependence upon one another for survival which I've already mentioned. In the end, I think, the decision was that honesty and forthrightness were more important than the political or propaganda nuances of the name."

"Perhaps so, but that doesn't magically expunge the unfortunate associations in the minds of a great many Corisandians. Or, for that matter, in my own mind, and I was scarcely born here in Corisande, myself." Gairlyng shook his head. "I don't claim to understand all of my own motivations myself, My Lord. I think any man who pretends he does is guilty of self-deception, at the very least. However, my *primary* reasons for accepting this office were four.

"First, my belief, as I've already said, that Mother Church has gone too far down the path of corruption under her current hierarchy to be internally reformed. If reform is even possible for her at this late date, it will happen only because an external threat has forced it upon the vicarate, and as I see it, the Church of Charis represents that external threat, that external demand for change.

"Second, because I desire, above almost all other things, to prevent or at least mitigate the religious persecutions and counterpersecutions I dread when I look at a conflict such as this one. Men's passions are seldom so inflamed as when they grapple with issues of the soul, My Lord. Be you personally ever so priestly—be Archbishop Maikel ever so gentle—violence, vengeance, and countervengeance will play their part soon enough. That isn't an indictment of you, nor even an indictment of the Church of Charis. The Group of Four began it, not you, when they launched five other princedoms at the Kingdom of Charis' throat. But, in its way, that only proves my point, and what happened at Ferayd only underscores it. I do not wish to see that cycle launched here in Corisande, and when this office was offered to me, I saw it as my best opportunity to do something to at least moderate it in the Princedom which has become my home."

He paused, regarding Ahdymsyn steadily until the other man nodded slowly.

"Third," Gairlyng resumed, "I know there are far more members of the Corisandian priesthood who share my view of the state of Mother Church's soul than anyone in the Temple or in Zion has ever dreamed. I'm sure I need hardly tell you this, after what you've seen in Charis, and in Emerald, and in Chisholm, yet I think it deserves to be stated anyway. The Group of Four, and the vicarate as a whole, have made the serious, serious error of assuming that if they can suppress internal voices of criticism—if they can use the power of the

Inquisition to *repress* demands for reform—then those voices and those demands have no strength. Pose no threat. Unfortunately for them, they're wrong, and there are pastors in this very city who prove my point. Bishop Kaisi is already aware of several of them, but I hope, My Lord, you'll take the opportunity to attend mass at Saint Kathryn's soon. I think you'll hear a voice you recognize in Father Tymahn's. I hope, however, that you'll also recognize that what you're hearing is a *Corisandian* voice, not that of a man who considers himself a Charisian."

He paused once more, raising one eyebrow, and Ahdymsyn nodded again, more firmly.

"A valid distinction, and one I'll strive to bear in mind," the bishop acknowledged. "On the other hand, I scarcely thought of myself as 'a Charisian' when all of this began. I imagine that, in the fullness of time, your Father Tymahn may actually make something of the same transition on his own terms."

"He may, My Lord." Gairlyng's tone conveyed something less than confidence in that particular transition, and he grimaced.

"I'll be honest," the archbishop went on, "and admit that the sticking point for quite a few Corisandians is the assassination of Prince Hektor and the Crown Prince. Whatever his faults from the perspective of other princedoms, and I'm probably more aware of them than the vast majority of Corisandians, Prince Hektor was both respected and popular here in Corisande. Many of his subjects, especially here in the capital, bitterly resent his murder, and the fact that the Church of Charis hasn't condemned Cayleb for it makes the Church, in turn, suspect in their eyes. And, to be brutally honest, it's a point upon which those trying to organize opposition to both the Church and the Empire are playing with considerable success."

"The Church," Ahdymsyn said, and for the first time there was a hard, cold edge in his voice, "hasn't condemned Emperor Cayleb for the murder of Prince Hektor because the Church doesn't believe he was responsible for it. Obviously, condemning the rulers of the Church's sole secular protector for an act of cold-blooded murder would be politically very difficult and dangerous. Nonetheless, I give you my personal assurance that Archbishop Maikel—and I—genuinely and sincerely believe the Emperor had nothing at all to do with Prince Hektor's assassination. If for no other reason than because it would have been so incredibly stupid for him to have done anything of the sort! In fact—"

He closed his mouth with an almost audible snap and made an angry, brushing-away gesture before he sat back—firmly—in his armchair. The office was very still and quiet for several seconds, until, finally, Gairlyng stirred behind his desk.

"If you'll recall, My Lord," he said, and his tone was oddly calm, almost mild, considering what had just passed between him and Ahdymsyn, "I said I had four primary reasons for accepting this office. I fully realize that what you were about to say, what you *stopped* yourself from saying because you realized how self-serving it would sound, is that you believe it was *Mother Church* who had Prince Hektor killed."

Ahdymsyn seemed to stiffen in his chair, but Gairlyng met his gaze levelly, holding him in place.

"I do not believe Mother Church ordered Prince Hektor's murder," the Archbishop of Corisande said very, very quietly, his eyes never wavering from Ahdymsyn's. "But neither do I believe it was Emperor Cayleb. And that, My Lord, is the *fourth* reason I accepted this office."

"Because you believe that, from it, you'll be in a position to help discover who did order it?" Ahdymsyn asked.

"Oh, no, My Lord." Gairlyng shook his head, his expression grim, and made the confession he'd never intended to make when these two men walked into his office. "I said I don't believe Mother Church had Prince Hektor killed. That, however, is because I'm morally certain in my own mind who did." Ahdymsyn's eyes widened, and Gairlyng smiled without humor. "I don't believe it was Mother Church . . . but I do believe it was Mother Church's *Grand Inquisitor,*" he said softly.

"You do?" Despite all of his formidable self-control, and all of his years of experience, Ahdymsyn couldn't quite keep the surprise out of his voice, and Gairlyng's thin smile grew ever so slightly wider without becoming a single degree warmer.

"Like you, My Lord, I can imagine nothing stupider Cayleb could possibly have done, and the young man I met here in Manchyr is anything but stupid. And when I consider all the other possible candidates, one name suggests itself inescapably to me. Unlike the vast majority of the people here in Corisande, I've actually met Vicar Zhaspahr. May I assume you've done the same?"

Ahdymsyn nodded, and Gairlyng shrugged.

"In that case, I'm sure you'll understand when I say that if there is one man in Zion who is simultaneously more prepared than Zhaspahr Clyntahn to embrace expediency, more certain his own prejudices accurately reflect God's will, and more confident his intellect far surpasses that of any other mortal man, I have no idea who he might be. Prince Hektor's murder, his instant transformation from one more warring prince to a martyr of Mother Church, would strike Clyntahn as a maneuver with absolutely no disadvantages, and I'm as certain as I'm sitting here that he personally ordered the assassinations. I can't prove it. Not yet. In fact, I think it's probable no one will ever be able to *prove* it, and even if someday I could, it wouldn't suddenly make the notion of being subordinated to Charisian control magically palatable to Corisandians. But knowing what I know of the man, believing what I believe about what he's already done—and what that implies about what he's prepared to do in the future—I had no choice but to oppose him. In that respect, at least, I'm as loyal a son of the Church of Charis as any man on the face of the world."

Zherald Ahdymsyn sat back once more, regarding him for several silent moments, then shrugged.

"Your Eminence, that's precisely the point at which I began my own spiritual journey, so I'm scarcely in a position to criticize you for doing the same thing. And as far as the Church of Charis is concerned, I think you'll find Archbishop Maikel is perfectly prepared to accept that starting point in anyone, even if it should transpire that you never reach the same destination I have. The difference between him and Zhaspahr Clyntahn doesn't have anything to do with their confidence they'll someday reach God's goals. Neither one of them is ever going to waver in that belief, that determination. The difference is that Clyntahn is prepared to do whatever he must to reach the goal he's dictated to God, while Archbishop Maikel trusts God to reach whatever goal *He* desires. And"—the bishop's eyes warmed—"if you can actually meet Archbishop Maikel, spend a five-day or two in his presence, and not discover that any Church he's responsible for building is worthy of your wholehearted support, then you'll be the first person *I've* met who can do that!"

.III.
### Royal Palace,
### City of Manchyr,
### Princedom of Corisande

Sir Koryn Gahrvai sighed with relief as he entered the palace's heat-shedding bulk and got out of the direct path of the sun's ferocity. November was always warm in Manchyr, but this November seemed determined to set a new standard.

*Which we don't exactly need, on top of everything else,* he thought as he strode briskly down the hall. *Langhorne knows we've got enough other things generating "warmth" all over the damned princedom!*

Indeed they did, and Gahrvai was—unfortunately—in a far better position to appreciate that minor fact than he might have preferred.

The guards standing outside the council chamber door came to attention at his approach, and he nodded back, acknowledging the military courtesy. He recognized both of them. They'd been part of his headquarters detachment before that . . . unpleasantness at Talbor Pass, which was the main reason they'd been chosen for their present duty. Just at the moment, the number of people he could trust behind him with a weapon was limited, to say the least, he thought as he passed through the garden door.

"Sorry I'm late," he said as his father looked up from a conversation with Earl Tartarian. "Alyk's latest report arrived just as I was getting ready to leave my office."

"Don't worry about it," his father said just a bit sourly. "You haven't really missed much, since it's not like we've managed to accomplish a whole hell of a lot so far today."

Gahrvai wished the sourness in that response could have come as a surprise, but Sir Rysel Gahrvai, the Earl of Anvil Rock, had a lot to feel sour about. As the senior of the two designated co-regents for Prince Daivyn, he'd wound up head of the prince's Regency Council, which had to be the most thankless task in the entire princedom. Well, probably aside from Sir *Koryn* Gahrvai's new assignment, that was.

If there were six nobles in the entire Princedom who genuinely believed Anvil Rock hadn't cut some sort of personal deal with Cayleb Ahrmahk, Gahrvai didn't have a clue who they might be. Aside from Tartarian (who was probably as thoroughly detested these days as Anvil Rock himself), Gahrvai could think of exactly three of the deceased Prince Hektor's councilors who genuinely believed Anvil Rock and Tartarian weren't solely out for themselves.

Fortunately, Sir Raimynd Lyndahr, who continued to serve as the Keeper of the Purse, was one of those three. The other two—Edwair Garthin, the Earl of North Coast, and Trumyn Sowthmyn, the Earl of Airyth—had both agreed to serve on the Regency Council, as well (although with a marked lack of enthusiasm on North Coast's part), because they'd realized someone had to do it. Archbishop Klairmant Gairlyng, whose position automatically made him a member of the Council, as well, appeared to agree with North Coast and Airyth where Anvil Rock and Tartarian were concerned, but he'd never been one of Hektor's councilors. The Council's final two members, the Duke of Margo and the Earl of Craggy Hill—neither of whom were present at the moment—*had* held positions on Hektor's council . . . and shared the rest of the nobility's general suspicion about Anvil Rock's and Tartarian's motives to the full.

*Not having them here today isn't going to make them any happier when they find out about this meeting, either,* Gahrvai thought as he walked across to his own place at the circular council table. *On the other hand, I can't think of anything that would* make them happy.

Sir Bairmon Chahlmair, the Duke of Margo, was the Regency Council's highest-ranking nobleman. He'd also been a distant—*very* distant—cousin of Prince Hektor, and it probably wasn't too surprising that he resented having a mere earl as Daivyn's regent instead of himself. Wahlys Hillkeeper, the Earl of Craggy Hill, on the other hand, was quite a different breed of kraken. It was entirely possible Margo nursed a few ambitions of his own, under the circumstances. Gahrvai didn't think he did, but he well might, and not without at least some justification, given the current, irregular circumstances. Yet if there was an edge of doubt about him in Gahrvai's mind, there was none at all about Craggy Hill. The earl's ambition was far more poorly hidden than he obviously thought it was, despite the fact that, unlike Margo, he possessed not even a shred of a claim on the Crown.

The good news was that the two of them were outnumbered six-to-two whenever it came down to a vote. The bad news was that their very inability to influence the Council's decisions had only driven them closer together. Worse, one of them—*at least* one of them—was leaking his own version of the Council's deliberations to outside ears.

*Which probably explains why Father didn't make any particular effort to get the two of them here today,* Gahrvai reflected.

"Actually, Rysel, saying we haven't accomplished *anything* today isn't entirely fair," Tartarian said in a rather milder tone.

"Oh, forgive me!" Anvil Rock rolled his eyes. "So far we've managed to agree on how big a stipend to set aside for Daivyn from his own income. Of course, we haven't figured out how we're going to *get* it to him, but I'm sure we'll come up with something . . . eventually."

"I realize you're probably even more worn out with all of this than I am," Tartarian said. "And I don't blame you, either. But the truth is that we've at least managed to handle the correspondence from General Chermyn."

"Handle?" Anvil Rock repeated. "Just exactly how did we 'handle' that, Taryl? If I recall correctly, it was more a matter of getting our marching orders than 'handling' anything."

Obviously, Gahrvai thought, his father was in one of his moods. Not surprisingly.

"I'd scarcely call them 'marching orders,'" Tartarian replied calmly. "And neither would you, if you weren't so busy pitching a snit."

Anvil Rock's eyes opened wide. He started to shoot something back, then visibly made himself pause.

"All right," he conceded grudgingly. "Fair enough. I'll try to stop venting my spleen."

"A *little* venting is perfectly all right with us, Rysel," Lyndahr told him with a slight smile. "It's not as if the rest of us don't feel exactly the same way from time to time. Still, Taryl has a point. From my read, the Viceroy General"—it was clear to Gharvai that Lyndahr had used Chermyn's official title deliberately—"is still doing his best to avoid stepping on us any harder than he has to."

Anvil Rock looked as if he would have liked to dispute that analysis. Instead, he nodded.

"I have to admit he's at least taking pains to be courteous," he said. "And, truth to tell, I appreciate it. But the unfortunate fact, Raimynd, is that he's not telling us anything we don't know. And the even more unfortunate fact is that, at the moment, I don't see a damned thing we can *do* about it!"

He looked around the table, as if inviting suggestions from his fellows. None, however, seemed to be forthcoming, and he snorted sourly.

"May I assume the Viceroy General was expressing his concern over the latest incidents?" Gahrvai asked after a moment, and his father nodded.

"That's exactly what he was doing. And I don't blame him, really. In fact, if *I* were in his position, I'd probably be doing more than just expressing concern by this point."

Gahrvai nodded soberly. Given the white-hot tide of fury which had swept Corisande following Prince Hektor's assassination, it wasn't surprising the princedom seethed with resentment and hatred. Nor was it especially surprising that the resentment and hatred in question should spill over into public "demonstrations" which had a pronounced tendency to slide over into riots. Riots which seemed to be invariably punctuated by looting and arson, as well, if the City Guard or (more often than Gharvai liked) Chermyn's Marines didn't get them quenched almost immediately.

By an odd turn of fate, the people suffering most frequently from that arson tended to be merchants and shopkeepers, many of whom had been blamed for profiteering and price gouging once the Charisian blockade of Corisande had truly begun to bite. Gahrvai was certain quite a few long-standing, private scores (which had damn all to do with loyalty to the House of Daykin) were being settled under cover of those riots—and, for that matter, that some of that arson was intended to destroy records of just who owed what to whom—although he was in no position to prove anything of the sort. Yet, at least. But even if some of the motivation was somewhat less selfless than outraged patriotism and fury over Hektor's assassination, there was no denying the genuine anger at Charis' "foreign occupation" of Corisande which was boiling away at the bottom of it.

And, inevitable or not, understandable or not, the unrest that anger engendered had equally inevitable consequences of its own. The terms Emperor Cayleb had imposed were far less punitive than they could have been, especially in light of the decades of hostility between Charis and Corisande. All the same, Gahrvai was certain they were more punitive than Cayleb would really have preferred. Unfortunately, the emperor had been able to read the writing on the wall as clearly as anyone else.

"I agree, Father," he said out loud. "I suppose it's a good thing, under the circumstances, that the Viceroy General recognizes the inevitability of this sort of thing. At least he isn't likely to overreact."

"Yet, at least," North Coast said.

The earl was a thickset man, getting a bit thicker through the belly as he settled into middle age. His thinning hair still held a few embers of the fiery red of his youth, and his gray eyes were worried.

"I don't think he's likely to *over*react no matter what happens, My Lord," Gahrvai said frankly. "Unfortunately, if we can't get a handle on this unrest, I think he's going to feel forced to take considerably more forceful steps of his own. Frankly, I don't see that he'll have any choice."

"I have to agree with you, Koryn," Earl Airyth said somberly. "But when he does, I'm afraid it's only going to make things worse."

"Which is undoubtedly why he's showing restraint, so far," Lyndahr pointed out. He shifted in his chair slightly, facing Gahrvai more squarely. "Which, in turn, brings us to you, Sir Koryn."

"I know," Gahrvai sighed.

"You said you had a report from Alyk?" Anvil Rock asked.

"Yes. In fact, that report is probably the closest thing to good news I've gotten lately. He says his mounted constables are just about ready."

"That *is* good news," Anvil Rock said, although his feelings were obviously at least somewhat mixed, for which Gahrvai didn't blame him a bit.

Sir Alyk Ahrthyr, the Earl of Windshare, had a reputation as something of a blunt object. A well-deserved reputation, if Gahrvai was going to be honest about it. He'd been accused, on more than one occasion, of thinking with his spurs, and no dictionary was ever going to use "Windshare" to illustrate the words "calmly reasoned response."

On the other hand, he was aware he wasn't the most brilliant man ever born, and Gahrvai knew better than most that the impetuous earl had actually learned to stop and think—for, oh, *at least* thirty or forty seconds—before charging headlong into the fray. In many ways, he was far from the ideal commander for the mounted patrols about to assume responsibility for maintaining order in the countryside, yet he had two shining qualifications which outweighed any limitations.

First, whatever anyone else might think, the survivors of Gahrvai's army trusted Windshare as implicitly as they trusted Gahrvai himself. *They* knew, whether the rest of the Princedom was prepared to believe it or not, that no one could have done a better job, under the circumstances, than Gahrvai, Windshare, and Sir Charlz Doyal had done. That the combination of the Charisian Marines' rifles, the long range of the Charisian artillery, and the deadly amphibious mobility of the Charisian Navy had been too much for any merely mortal general to overcome. And they knew another commander, other generals, might very well have gotten far more of them killed proving that. As a consequence, they were willing to continue to trust their old commanders, and that trust—that loyalty—was more precious than rubies.

And, second, just as important as the troops' trust in Windshare, *Gahrvai* had complete faith in the earl. Perhaps not without a few reservations about Windshare's *judgment,* he conceded, although he did have rather more confidence in that judgment than some of the Regency Council's members. But whatever reservations he might quietly nurse about the earl's . . . sagacity, he had complete and total faith in Alyk Ahrthyr's loyalty, integrity, and courage.

*So maybe he doesn't have the sharpest brain in the Princedom to go with them. These days, I'll take three out of the four and thank Langhorne I've got them!*

"What about the rest of the army, Koryn?" Tartarian asked.

"It could be better, it could be worse." Gahrvai shrugged. "General Chermyn's reissued enough muskets for our total permitted force, and we've converted all of them to take the new bayonets. At the moment, we still don't have any artillery, and, to be honest, I can't really blame him for that. And, all the muskets are still smoothbores. On the other hand, they're a hell of a lot better than anyone else is going to have. That's the 'could be worse' side of things— none of the troublemakers we're likely to face are going to have anything like the firepower we do. Unfortunately, I don't have anywhere near as many men as I wish I had. As many as I'm pretty damn sure we're going to *need* before this is all over, the way things seem to be headed, in fact. And the ones I do have were all trained initially as *soldiers,* not city guardsmen. Until we actually see them in action, I'm not as confident as I'd like to be that they aren't going to react like combat troops instead of guardsmen, which could get . . . messy. That's the 'could be better' side."

"How many do you have? Do *we* have?" North Coast asked. Gahrvai looked at him, and he shrugged. "I know you sent us all a memo about it. And I read it— really I did. But, to be honest, I was paying more attention to the naval side of things when I did."

Well, that made sense, Gahrvai supposed. North Coast's earldom lay on Wind Daughter Island, separated from the main island of Corisande by East Margo Sound and White Horse Reach. Wind Daughter was very nearly half Corisande Island's size, but it boasted less than a quarter as many people. Much of it was still covered in old-growth forest, and ninety percent of the population lived almost in sight of the water. Wind Daughter's people tended to regard inhabitants of "the big island" as foreigners, and (so far, at least) they seemed far less incensed than the citizens of Manchyr over Prince Hektor's assassination. Under the circumstances, it didn't really surprise Gahrvai that North Coast had been more concerned over how the Charisian naval patrols were likely to affect his fishermen than over the size of garrison the island might be going to receive.

"Our total force—*field* force, that is—is going to be a little under thirty thousand," he said. "I know thirty thousand sounds like a lot of men and, frankly, I'm more than a little amazed that Cayleb agreed to let us put that many Corisandians back under arms at all. But the truth is that it isn't really that big a number. My Lord—not when we're talking about something the size of the entire Princedom. As long as I can keep them concentrated, they can deal with anything they're likely to face. If I have to start dividing them into smaller forces, though—and I *will,* just as sure as Shan-wei—the odds start shifting. Frankly, I don't see any way I'm going to be able to put detachments everywhere we're really going to need them. Not if I'm going to keep them big enough, new muskets or not, to make any of us happy."

North Coast nodded somberly.

"The real problem," Anvil Rock observed, "is that we're going to have enough combat power to stomp on any fires that spring up, but we're not going to have enough *numbers* to give us the sort of coverage that might keep the sparks from flaring up in the first place." He looked unhappy. "And the real problem with stomping on fires is that everything else in the vicinity tends to get stomped on as well."

"Exactly, Father. Which is why I was so glad to see Alyk's report. I'm going to start deploying his men to the other major towns, especially down here in the southeast, as quickly as possible. He's not going to be able to make any of his detachments as big as we'd all like, but they'll be more mobile than any of our infantry. They'll be able to cover a lot more ground, and, frankly, I think cavalry is going to be more . . . reassuring to the local city guardsmen."

" 'Reassuring'?" His father smiled thinly. "Don't you mean more *intimidating*?"

"To some extent, I suppose I do," Gahrvai admitted. "On the other hand, a little intimidation for the people who'd be most likely to give those guardsmen problems is a good thing. And I'm not going to complain if the constables suggest to the local guard officers that remembering they're supposed to be maintaining public order instead of leading patriotic insurrections would be another good thing."

"I'm not, either," Anvil Rock said. "Even though there's a part of me that would rather be doing exactly that—leading a patriotic insurrection, I mean—instead of what I *am* doing."

No one responded to that particular remark, and after a moment, the earl shrugged.

"All right, Raimynd," he said. "Now that Koryn has his troops ready to deploy, I suppose it's time we figure out how we're going to pay them, isn't it?" His smile was wintry. "I'm sure *that's* going to be lots of fun, too."

.IV.
HMS *Rakurai*, 46,
Gorath Bay,
Kingdom of Dohlar,
and
HMS *Devastation*, 54,
King's Harbor,
Helen Island,
Kingdom of Old Charis

T he brisk afternoon wind had a whetted edge as it swept across the dark blue waters, ruffling the surface with two-foot waves. Here and there a crest of white foam broke almost playfully, and the sharp-toothed breeze hummed in the rigging. Gorath Bay was a well-sheltered anchorage, and it was always ice-free year round. But the present air temperature was barely above freezing, and it took very little wind to make a man shiver when it came slicing across the vast, treeless plain of the bay.

The Dohlaran seamen assembled on the deck of HMS *Rakurai* were certainly doing their share of shivering as they stood waiting for orders.

"Down topgallant masts!"

Captain Raisahndo's voice rang out from the converted merchantman's quarterdeck in the official preparatory order, and petty officers gave their working parties warning glances. Earl Thirsk had decided to grace *Rakurai* with his presence this afternoon, and it had been made thoroughly clear to everyone aboard that today would be a very bad day to be less than perfect.

"Topgallant yardmen in the tops!"

Feet thudded across the deck as the designated topmen flooded up the ratlines. They swept up them like monkey-lizards, fountaining upward into the rigging, yet the dulcet tones of petty officers gently encouraged them to be still speedier.

"Aloft topgallant yardmen!"

The fresh command came almost before they'd finished collecting in the tops and sent them scurrying still higher, swarming up to the level of the topmast cap.

"Man topgallant and mast ropes!"

More seamen moved to their stations at deck level, manning the ropes run through leading blocks on deck, then through blocks hooked to one side of each topmast cap and down through bronze sheaves set into the squared-off heels of the topgallant masts. Each mast rope then ran up its mast once more, to the other side of the topmast cap and a securing eyebolt. The result was a line rigged through the topgallant mast heel, designed to support the mast's weight as it slid down from above and controlled by the deck party assigned to each mast. Other hands eased the topmast stays and shrouds, loosening them slightly, and the next command rang out.

"Haul taut!"

Tension came on the mast ropes, and the officer in charge of each mast examined his own responsibility critically, then raised his hand to signal readiness.

"Sway and unfid!"

Seamen threw still more weight onto the mast ropes, and high above the deck, each topmast rose slightly as the rope rove through its heel lifted it from below. Its heel rose just far enough through the square hole ( just barely large enough to allow the heel to move in it) in the topmast trestletrees for a waiting hand to extract the fid—the tapered hardwood pin which normally passed through the heel and rested on the trestletrees to support the topgallant's weight and lock it in place.

"Lower away together!"

The topgallant masts slid smoothly, gracefully down in almost perfect unison as the men on the mast ropes obeyed the command. Breeching lines and heel ropes both guided and restrained the masts, although the anchorage was sheltered enough, even with the brisk breeze, that there was no real danger of the yard going astray.

The purpose of the exercise wasn't to bring the masts clear down on deck and stow them, and their downward progress ended when their heels came to a point just above the hounds on their respective lower masts. At the same time the spars came down, the topmen tended to the topgallant rigging. They eased the stays and backstays carefully as the masts descended, then secured them on the topmast caps. If the topgallants had been going to remain struck for any period of time, a capstan bar would have been pushed through the secured stays and lashed into place to help keep things under control. No one bothered with that particular refinement this afternoon, however. There wasn't much point, since all hands knew they were to enjoy the pleasure of completing the evolution at least three more times before the day was over.

"Lay down from aloft!"

The order brought the topmen back down, even as a heavy lashing was passed through the fid hole and secured around the topmast to hold it in place. The ship looked truncated with her topgallant masts and topmasts doubled that way, but the topgallant was securely stowed in a manner which reduced the height of her rigging by almost a third. The result was to reduce wind resistance aloft and to reduce her rigging's center of gravity, which might well prove the margin between survival and destruction in the teeth of a winter storm.

The last line was passed, the last lashing secured, and all hands watched tensely as the captain and the admiral surveyed their handiwork. It was a moment of intense stillness, a sort of hushed watchfulness burnished by the sounds of wind and wave, the whistles of wyverns and the cries of gulls. Then Earl Thirsk looked at Raisahndo and nodded gravely.

No one was foolish enough to cheer at the evidence of the admiral's satisfaction. Even the pressed men of the ship's company had been aboard long enough to learn better than that. But there were broad grins here and there, born of combined relief (none of them had wanted to consider how the captain would react if they'd embarrassed him in front of the admiral) and pride, the knowledge that they'd done well. Completing an evolution like this in harbor was child's play compared to accomplishing it at sea, in the dark, in a pitching, rolling vessel. Most of them knew that—some, the relatively small number of seasoned seamen scattered amongst them, from intensely unpleasant personal experience—but they also knew it was something they were going to have to do eventually. None of them were any more enamored of the notion of sweating for the sake of sweating than the next man, but the majority of them preferred to master the necessary skills here rather than trying to pick them up at the last minute in the face of a potentially life-or-death emergency at sea.

That was an unusual attitude, in many ways, especially for crews which contained such large percentages of inexperienced landsmen. Sailors who'd been snapped up by the press gangs tended to resent being dragged away from their snug homes ashore—and from wives and children who depended upon them for support. Given the risks of battle, not to mention the vagaries of disease or accident, the odds were little better than even that they would ever see those wives and children again. That was enough to break any husband or father's heart, but it didn't even consider the fact that their impressment generally rendered their families destitute overnight. There was no guarantee the ones they loved would manage to survive in their men's absence, and even if they did, hardship and hunger were all but guaranteed for most of them. Under the circumstances, it was scarcely surprising that, more often than not, pressed men had to be driven to their tasks, frequently with calculated brutality, until they fused into a cohesive ship's company. Sometimes they never achieved that fusion at all, and even many of those who eventually would find their places simply lacked the experience—so far, at least—to understand why relentless training was important to *them,* and not simply to their demanding, hectoring officers and hard-fisted petty officers. That wasn't the sort of attitude which normally evoked cheerful eagerness for swarming up and down masts on an icy cold afternoon when they could have been below decks, out of the cutting wind.

The attitude of *Rakurai*'s company was quite different from that, however. In fact, it was different from that which would previously have been seen aboard almost any Dohlaran warship with so many pressed men. Partly that was because this time there'd been relatively little brutality, and that which had been employed had been carefully calculated, fitted to the circumstances which demanded it and administered with ruthless equity. There'd still been at least a few incidents where it had been unnecessary, where a bosun's mate of the "old school" had resorted to the use of fists or the overenthusiastic employment of his "starter" (a knotted length of rope used to whip "laggards" along), but they'd been remarkably few compared to what would have happened in most other Dohlaran fleets.

Partly that was because so many of the Navy's "old school" bosun's mates (and captains, for that matter) had been lost in the disastrous campaign which had ended at Rock Point and Crag Hook. Mostly, though, it was because the fleet's new commander had explained his position on that particular point, among others, with crystalline clarity. And because it had turned out he'd actually *meant* it, as well. So far, eleven captains who'd made the mistake of assuming he wasn't serious about his orders concerning unnecessary punishment or brutality had been relieved in disgrace. Given the fact that two of those captains had been even better born than the earl, and that one of them had enjoyed the patronage of the Duke of Thorast himself, none of his remaining captains were inclined to doubt he'd meant what he said the first time.

There was another reason, as well, though—one that grew out of acceptance from below even more than out of restraint from above, and one which had won Earl Thirsk a degree of devotion almost unheard of among impressed seamen. No one knew exactly how word of it had gotten out, but it was common knowledge in the fleet that the earl had personally argued that since the fleet was being manned for Mother Church's service, Mother Church ought to assume responsibility for the well-being of the pressed men's families. The wage of a common sailor in the Royal Dohlaran Navy wasn't much, but Mother Church would see to it that the money was paid directly to a man's family during his absence, if that was his request. More than that, and totally unprecedented, the Church had promised to pay a pension to the widow of any impressed seaman who died on active service and to provide for the support of his minor children, as well.

All of which helped to explain why there were remarkably few groans of resignation as the captain and the admiral returned to *Rakurai*'s poop deck and the captain reached for his speaking trumpet yet again.

"*Up* topgallant masts!"

▼   ▼   ▼

"They're getting better at that than I'd really like," Sir Domynyk Staynair, the Baron of Rock Point, observed quietly.

The one-legged admiral leaned comfortably back in an overstuffed armchair, the wooden peg which had replaced the calf of his right leg resting on a footstool in front of him. Kraken-oil lamps burned brightly, hanging from the deckhead, and the sleeping bulk of his new flagship was quiet about him as she lay at anchor while he watched the recorded imagery play out before his eyes. The lowered topgallant masts were moving back up into position as smoothly as they'd descended, as if controlled by a single hand, and he shook his head.

"Agreed," Merlin Athrawes' voice replied in his right ear, speaking from his palace bedchamber in Cherayth, the better part of seven thousand miles away. It was just past midnight in King's Harbor, but the first, very faint traces of an icy winter dawn could be seen out of Merlin's window. "Of course, it's all still drill, under pretty much ideal circumstances. And they still aren't as good at it as our people are."

"Maybe not," Rock Point conceded. "Then again, *nobody's* as good at it as our people are, and I'd just as soon keep it that way." He shook his head again. "Proficiency builds confidence, Merlin, and the last thing we need is for these people to start feeling confident about facing us at sea." He paused for a moment, head cocked as if in thought, then snorted. "Allow me to correct myself. The *next* to last thing we need is for them to start feeling confident about their competence. The *last* thing we need is for them to actually develop that competence. And that, unfortunately, is exactly what Thirsk seems to be doing."

"Agreed," Merlin repeated, this time in something much more like a sigh. "I've discovered that, despite myself, I rather admire Thirsk," he continued. "Still, I've also discovered that I can't quite help wishing he'd encountered a round shot at Crag Hook. For that matter, I can't help wishing King Rahnyld had gone ahead and had him executed as a scapegoat for Armageddon Reef. It would've been grossly unfair, but the man's entirely too good at his job for my peace of mind."

"I suppose it's inevitable they could turn up at least one competent sailor if they looked long enough and hard enough," Rock Point agreed sourly.

"I don't think all the time he spent on the beach hurt any, either," Merlin pointed out. Rock Point raised an interrogative eyebrow, and Merlin grimaced. "The man's got a brain that's probably at least as good as Ahlfryd's," he pointed out, "and he's got more actual sea experience than almost anyone else the Church can call on. I think it's pretty obvious he spent the time they left him ashore to rot using that brain and that experience to analyze all the mistakes Maigwair and idiots like Thorast have been making. They were stupid to park him there, and I'm just as glad they did, but the downside is that they gave him plenty of time to think. Now he's putting the fruits of all that thinking to work."

Rock Point made an irate sound of acknowledgment—something midway between a grunt and a growl. Like Merlin and Cayleb, the baron had come to the conclusion that Thirsk was almost certainly Charis' most dangerous current adversary. As Merlin had just pointed out, the man had a brain, and a dangerously competent one. Worse, he wasn't a bit afraid of what Merlin called "thinking outside the box." His insistence that the Church provide for the families of impressed seamen was unheard of, for example. There'd been bitter resistance to the entire notion, and not just from the Church. Quite a few of the Dohlaran Navy's senior officers had mounted a ferocious attempt to defeat the suggestion. Some of that resistance had been pure reflex in defense of "the way things have always been." Some of it had stemmed from a fear that the practice would become customary—that the *Navy* would be expected to assume the same financial responsibilities in the future. But more of it had arisen from simple resentment of the authority and support which both the Duke of Fern and Captain General Maigwair had thrown behind Thirsk. And from Thirsk's willingness to use that support to smash his way through their sullen resistance. Reformers were seldom beloved, and the degree to which they were resented and loathed was usually in direct proportion to how desperately reform was needed.

*There's a lesson there,* Merlin reflected. *Or a damned sharp bit of irony, at any rate, given how unpopular "reformers" like Cayleb Ahrmahk and Maikel Staynair are proving in the Temple just now!*

"You realize," the baron said after a second or two, "if he actually manages to get their navy reorganized for them, Thorast and the others will toss him to the krakens just as soon as they figure they can possibly get along without him."

"Of course they will," Merlin agreed a trifle sadly. "I think he knows it, too. Which only makes him even more dangerous, from our perspective."

"So we'll just have to do something about him ourselves," Rock Point said more briskly. "Gwylym's about ready to sail."

"I know." Merlin frowned. "In a lot of ways, though, I wish you were going, instead."

"Gwylym's just as capable as I am," Rock Point pointed out. There might have been a touch of stiffness in his tone, and Merlin shook his head quickly.

"It's not a matter of capabilities, Domynyk," he said. "Believe me, no one has more respect for Gwylym than I do! It's just that I'd rather the fellow in charge of singeing King Rahnyld's beard had access to the SNARCs. Especially given how competent we've just agreed Thirsk is turning out to be."

Rock Point nodded in acknowledgment, although the acknowledgment in question was obviously a bit grudging. Still, he really couldn't argue the point. Admiral Sir Gwylym Manthyr had been Cayleb's flag captain at the battles of Rock Point, Crag Hook, and Darcos Sound. He was an experienced seaman, possessed of a singular attention to detail and an iron nerve. He was *not,* however, one of the "inner circle" who had been cleared for the truth about Merlin, which meant he wasn't going to be examining any "satellite imagery." Nor, for that matter, would anyone assigned to his staff.

Unfortunately, Rock Point himself was the only one of Cayleb and

Sharleyan's senior naval officers who *was* part of the inner circle. Getting some of the others on board was a high priority, but, again, not something which could be rushed. Rock Point himself had argued strongly in favor of adding High Admiral Bryahn Lock Island to the list, and both he and Merlin were confident that the Brethren of Saint Zherneau would approve Lock Island's admission quite soon. Of course, the question then arose of just who would inform Lock Island. With Cayleb, Sharleyan, and Archbishop Maikel all out of Old Charis, it would be virtually impossible to find the right messenger—somebody with the authority to make Lock Island *listen* if he didn't take it well, and somebody he'd trust enough to believe when he did listen. Baron Wave Thunder *might* serve in a case of dire emergency, but still. . . .

"I could probably talk Bryahn into sending me, instead of Gwylym," the baron said after a moment, but his expression was unhappy and his tone was tentative.

"No." Merlin shook his head again. "Cayleb and Sharleyan are right about that. We need you right where you are, too. Or, rather, where you're about to be. And let's face it, Dohlar's a worry, but Tarot's right next door. And White Ford is no slouch, either."

It was Rock Point's turn to grimace, but he couldn't disagree.

The Imperial Charisian Navy was the largest, most powerful fleet any single Safeholdian realm had ever boasted. It was rising rapidly to a strength of over ninety galleons, and it continued to expand. Unfortunately, it wasn't going to find itself matched against any other single Safeholdian realm; it was going to face the combined fleets of virtually *every* mainland realm. Worse, the Church of God Awaiting had poured out staggering sums to subsidize those fleets, although not all of the various kingdoms' and empires' building programs were equally advanced. The Temple Lands and the more northern ports of the Harchong Empire were considerably behind the shipyards of Dohlar and the Desnairian Empire, and that situation wasn't going to improve for the Church anytime soon. But the plain, ugly truth was that even with an unlimited budget (which it didn't have) the Charisian Empire couldn't possibly have matched the mainland realms' combined building capacity. Nor was the Charisian supply of manpower unlimited, either. Ninety galleons, each with a crew of roughly five hundred, required forty-five thousand men. So far, the Navy had managed to meet its manpower requirements without resorting to impressment of its own, largely because it had always followed policies similar to the ones Thirsk had forced upon Dohlar and the Church. That was about to change, however, because there were only so many volunteers who could be attracted no matter what the inducement, and the manning situation was only going to get worse as the size of the fleet continued to climb.

And it was going to have to climb. Assuming the Church completed its current construction programs, it would command a fleet of over three hundred and ninety galleons—better than four times the current Charisian strength. A hundred and fifty of them would be converted merchant ships, but so were a quarter of the Charisian Navy's galleons. And that didn't even consider the two hundred–plus galleys the Church had built before it realized just how outclassed galleys had become. They might not be well suited to decisive broadside duels, but they more than doubled the total number of hulls the Church could throw at its opponents, and if they were free to operate while the Church's galleons neutralized *Charis'* galleons. . . .

The good news was that the ships in question were scattered between five widely separated navies. No single kingdom or empire could match the Charisians' numbers, although Harchong would come close once its winter-delayed construction could be completed. Concentrating those widely dispersed squadrons would be at least as difficult as it had been to concentrate the forces detailed for the Group of Four's original plans for Old Charis' destruction. And even after they were concentrated, their companies would be sadly inexperienced compared to the Imperial Navy's crews.

Earl Thirsk, at least, obviously recognized that fact. So did Gahvyn Mahrtyn, the Baron of White Ford, King Gorjah of Tarot's senior admiral. Unfortunately, from the Church's perspective, they were the only two fleet commanders still available to it who had ever faced the Charisian Navy in battle. The Duke of Black Water, the Corisandian commander at Darcos Sound, had died there, and Gharth Rahlstahn, the Earl of Mahndyr, and Sir Lewk Cohlmyn, the Earl of Sharpfield, who had commanded the Emeraldian and the Chisholmian components of Black Water's fleet, were now in Charisian service. Even more unfortunately (for the Church), the fact that Thirsk and White Ford had been devastatingly defeated by then-Crown Prince Cayleb had caused their advice to be discounted by almost all of their fellow flag officers.

That was clearly changing in Thirsk's case, but neither Harchong, nor the Desnairian Empire, nor the Temple Lands seemed overly inclined to profit by Dohlar's example. Tarot did, but King Gorjah continued to languish under a cloud of disapproval. It seemed clear that the Group of Four continued to blame Tarot for the disastrous intelligence leak which had permitted King Haarahld of Charis and his son to deduce the Church's strategy and come up with a counterstrategy to defeat it in detail. That was grossly unfair, although with no knowledge of Merlin's SNARCs, it was understandable enough. Particularly given Charis' efforts to encourage exactly that reaction.

As a consequence, none of the Church's galley fleet had been laid down in Tarotisian shipyards. Following the Group of Four's belated switch to a galleon-based fleet, Tarot had been admitted to the building program, yet even then the Tarotisian component remained the smallest of all. And White Ford—

who was quite possibly an even better combat commander than Thirsk—had been almost totally ignored.

Under the circumstances, the Church's numerical advantage was considerably less overwhelming than it might appear. To set against that, however, the Empire of Charis was a very large, very vulnerable target. Charis and Chisholm, in particular, were six thousand miles apart, as the wyvern flew, and it was over two thousand miles from Port Royal, in Chisholm, to Corisande's Cape Targan. A ship deployed to defend Charis was a minimum of a month from Chisholm under even the most favorable conditions of wind and weather, and it would take almost that long for a ship stationed in Chisholm to reach Manchyr, in Corisande.

Distances and transit times like that prevented High Admiral Lock Island from concentrating his own forces in a central position. In fact, he'd been forced to station twenty galleons in Chisholm, under Admiral Sharpfield and supported by the Chisholmian Navy's surviving galleys. Another ten galleons and twenty-five galleys had been stationed in Corisandian waters under Earl Mahndyr, and Lock Island had retained twenty galleons under his own command, covering Rock Shoal Bay and the approaches to Howell Bay and the Sea of Charis.

That left barely forty galleons for other service, and freeing up even that many had been possible only because the Church's war fleet was so widely scattered . . . and still so far short of completion. As more of the Church's galleons became available for service, the various Charisian defensive fleets would have to be strengthened, which would reduce the strength available for other tasks still further.

Unless something could be done in the meantime to reduce the numbers opposed to them.

That was supposed to be Manthyr's and Rock Point's assignment. Manthyr, with eighteen galleons and six thousand Marines, was bound for the Sea of Harchong. More specifically, he was bound for Hardship Bay, on the largely uninhabited Claw Island. There were reasons very few people lived on Claw Island. It wasn't very big—barely a hundred and twelve miles in its longest dimension. It was also little more than two hundred miles south of the equator, and its barren, mostly treeless expanses of rock and sand were about as welcoming as an oven the same size. On the other hand, Hardship Bay offered a good deep-water anchorage, and the small city of Claw Keep would offer his squadron a home port . . . of sorts, at any rate. Even more importantly, it was better than twenty-one-thousand sea miles from Tellesberg, which put it "barely" five thousand sea miles from Gorath Bay. It also lay off the western coast of South Harchong, however, where a quarter of the Harchong Empire's galleons were under construction, and it was less than fifteen hundred miles from the mouth of the Gulf of Dohlar.

The voyage to Claw Island would actually have been slightly shorter if he sailed east, by way of Chisholm, instead of west, past Armageddon Reef and around the southern tip of the continent of Howard, but he'd have both favorable winds and currents going west, especially this time of year. He'd probably average at least fifty or sixty miles more a day on his projected course . . . and it would *still* take him better than three months to complete the voyage.

Once he got there, his Marines ought to be more than sufficient to capture Claw Keep and garrison the island, especially since the only reliable source of water on the entire sun-blasted spit were the artesian wells that served Claw Keep itself. That would provide him with a secure base from which to operate against both Dohlar and Harchong. He'd be a long way from home, although he'd be within nine thousand miles of Chisholm, but he'd be well placed to blockade the Gulf of Dohlar and intercept any effort to combine Thirsk's galleons with the Harchongese contingent building farther south around Shipwreck Bay, in the provinces of Queiroz, Kyznetsov, and Selkar. Even if he did nothing but sit there (and Merlin was confident that an officer of Manthyr's abilities and personality should find all manner of ways to make himself an infuriating pest), it was unlikely the Church—or King Rahnyld or Emperor Waisu, for that matter—would be prepared to tolerate a Charisian presence that close to them.

His galleons would be substantially outnumbered—by almost four-to-one by Dohlar, alone, assuming the Dohlarans got all of their own warships completed and manned—but the greater experience of his crews and captains would offset much of that disadvantage. And the simple fact that Charis was once again taking the initiative, despite its numerical disadvantage, would have profound implications for the confidence and morale of his opponents.

And if worse came to worst, he could always load his Marines back aboard his transports and withdraw.

*That's the idea, at least,* Merlin thought. *And as a way to throw a spanner into the Church's plans, it's got a lot to recommend it. But I'd still feel better with Domynyk in command. Or if we could give Gwylym a com, at least! I hate having that big a chunk of the Navy out at the end of a limb that long when we can't even talk to its CO.*

Unfortunately, as he himself had just pointed out, they were going to need Rock Point closer to home. He and the remaining twenty galleons currently available to Charis would be moving their base of operations to Hanth Town on Margaret Bay, which would put him across the Tranjyr Passage from the Kingdom of Tarot. His new base would be well placed to assist Lock Island in meeting any threat against Old Charis from East Haven or Desnair. More importantly, however, he'd be in a position to operate directly against Tarot.

*And Sharleyan was right about that, too,* Merlin reflected. *It's more important than ever to . . . induce Gorjah to consider joining the Empire voluntarily. Or, failing that, to present him with a somewhat more forceful argument. Neutralizing Tarot would be worthwhile in its own right. Gaining Tarot as a forward base right off the East Haven coast would be even more worthwhile. And getting our hands on the galleons Gorjah's building for the Church wouldn't hurt a damned thing, either!*

"I'd like to be able to do a lot of things we can't do right now," he said out loud. "Desnair's starting to worry me, for one thing, and I *really* wish we could get at Harchong and the Temple Lands yards! But we can't afford to uncover Old Charis and Chisholm, and that's just the way it is. If Gwylym can keep Dohlar busy long enough for you and Gray Harbor to convince Gorjah to see the light, it'll help a lot, though."

"Then we'll just have to see what we can do about that, won't we, *Seijin* Merlin?" Rock Point said with a smile. "We'll just have to see what we can do."

## .V.
## City of Fairstock,
## Province of Malansath,
## West Harchong Empire

The falling snow was so thick no one could see more than a ship's length or two in any direction.

The Earl of Coris found that less than reassuring as *Snow Lizard* crept cautiously into the Fairstock roadstead. Captain Yuthain had furled his sail and gone to oars as soon as the leadsman in the bow found bottom at ten fathoms. Sixty feet represented considerably more depth of water than *Snow Lizard* required, but only a fool (which Yuthain had conclusively demonstrated he was not) took liberties with the Fairstock Channel. It measured the next best thing to two hundred and fifty miles from north to south, and if most of it was easily navigable, there were other bits which were anything but. And there wasn't a lot of room to spare. At its narrowest point, which also happened to offer some of the nastiest, shifting sandbanks, it was barely fourteen miles wide . . . at high water. Fairstock Bay itself was a superbly sheltered anchorage, well over two hundred miles wide, but getting into it could sometimes prove tricky.

Especially in the middle of a snowstorm.

Frankly, Coris would have preferred to lay-to off the entrance of the channel until the weather cleared. Unfortunately, there was no guarantee the weather *would* clear anytime soon, and Captain Yuthain was under orders to deliver his passenger to Fairstock as quickly as possible. So he'd crept very cautiously and slowly inshore until he'd been able to run a line of soundings which let him locate himself by matching them with the depths recorded on his chart. Even after he was confident he knew where he was, however, he'd continued to proceed with a caution of which Coris had wholeheartedly approved. Not only was it distinctly possible, in these visibility conditions, that *Snow Lizard* wasn't really where he thought she was, but there was always the equally unpleasant possibility that they might meet another vessel head-on. The narrowness of the channel and the atrocious visibility only made that even more likely, and Phylyp Ahzgood hadn't come this far at the summons of the Council of Vicars just to get himself drowned or frozen to death.

"By the mark, seven fathom!"

The cry floated back from the bow, oddly muffled and deadened by the falling snow, and despite his thick coat and warm gloves, Coris shivered.

"I imagine you'll be happy to get ashore, My Lord," Captain Yuthain remarked, and Coris turned to face him quickly. He'd been careful not to intrude on the captain's concentration while Yuthain conned *Snow Lizard* cautiously up-channel. It wasn't the sort of moment at which one joggled someone's elbow, he reflected.

Something of his thoughts must have shown in his expression, because Yuthain grinned through his beard.

"This next little bit's not all that bad, My Lord," he said. "I wouldn't want to sound overconfident, but I'd say the really tricky parts are all safely past us. Not but what I imagine there was a time or two when you were less than confident we'd get this far."

"Nonsense, Captain." Coris shook his head with an answering smile. "I never doubted your seamanship or the quality of your ship and crew for a moment."

"Ah, now!" Yuthain shook his head. "It's kind of you to be saying so, but I'm not so sure telling a fearful lie like that is good for the health of your soul, My Lord."

"If it *were* a lie, perhaps it wouldn't be good for my spiritual health. Since it happens to have been a completely truthful statement, however, I'm not especially concerned, Captain."

Yuthain chuckled, then cocked his head, listening to the leadsman's fresh announcement of the depth. He frowned thoughtfully down at the chart, obviously fixing his position afresh in his brain, and Coris watched him with the respect a professional deserved.

As it happened, what he'd just said to Yuthain really had been the truth. On the other hand, despite his recognition of the captain's skill and the capability of his crew, there'd been more than one moment when Coris had strongly doubted they would ever reach Fairstock. The Gulf of Dohlar in winter had proved even uglier than he'd feared, and once they'd cleared the passage between Cliff Island and Whale Island, they'd encountered a howling gale which he'd been privately certain was going to pound the low-slung, frail, shoal-draft galley bodily under. The steep, battering seas had been almost as high as the galley's mast, and at one point they'd been forced to lie to a sea anchor for two full days with the pumps continuously manned. There'd been no hot food for those two days—not even Yuthain's cook had been able to keep his galley fire lit—and icy water had swirled ankle deep through the earl's cabin more than once as the ship fought for her very life. They'd survived that particular crisis after all, yet that had scarcely been the end of the foul weather—or the crises—they'd faced. Snow, bad visibility, and icy rigging had only made things still worse, and Coris' respect for Yuthain and his men had grown with each passing day.

Despite which, he could hardly wait to get off the ship. It would have been tiresome enough to spend an entire month in such confined quarters under any circumstances. Under the conditions associated with a winter passage of the Gulf, "tiresome" had quickly given way to something much closer to "intolerable."

*Of course, there is the little fact that every foot closer to Fairstock brings me that much closer to Zion and the Temple, as well,* he reminded himself. *On the other hand, as the Archangel Bédard said, "Sufficient unto the day is the evil thereof." If I get off this damned ship alive, I'll be perfectly prepared to let future problems take care of themselves!*

"I make it about another three hours to our anchorage, My Lord," Yuthain said, reemerging from his contemplation of the chart. "If the visibility were better, we'd probably already have a pilot boat coming alongside. As it is, I won't be so very surprised if we have to feel our way all the way in on our own. Either way, though, I think we'll have you ashore in time for supper."

"I appreciate that, Captain. I doubt anyone could have taken better care of me on the passage than you have, but I trust I won't offend you if I admit I'd really like to sleep in a bed that isn't moving tonight." He grimaced. "I doubt I'll get more than one night—maybe two, if I'm really lucky—but I intend to enjoy it to the fullest!"

"Well, I can't say as I blame you," Yuthain said. "Mind you, I've never really understood why anyone prefers sleeping ashore when he's the option. Although, to be honest, back before I had my own cabin, and my own cot, I felt rather differently about it, I believe. Fortunately for my sea-dog image," he grinned at his passenger again, "that's been long enough ago now that my memory's none too clear!"

"I'm sure that for a seasoned sailor like yourself the ship's motion is just like a mother rocking a cradle," Coris responded. "Still, though, I think it's an

acquired taste. And if it's all the same to you, it's one I'd just as soon not acquire."

"To each his own, My Lord," Yuthain agreed equably.

▼      ▼      ▼

As it happened, Yuthain's prediction was accurate. They had to make their
own way until they saw the blurred, indistinct shapes of other vessels, riding
at anchor, and dropped their own anchor. In fact, they'd passed close enough
aboard one of the other ships to draw an irate shout of warning from its anchor watch.

"Oh, hold your noise!" Yuthain had bellowed back through his speaking
trumpet. "This is an Emperor's ship on Church business! Besides, if I'd wanted to
sink your sorry arse, you silly bastard, I'd've hit you square amidships, not passed
across your misbegotten bow!"

The noise from the other vessel had ended abruptly, and Yuthain had
winked at Coris.

"Truth to tell, My Lord," he'd admitted in a much lower voice, "I never
even saw 'em until the last moment. I think I'm as surprised as they are that
I didn't cut their cable! Not that I'd ever admit it to them, even under torture!"

"Your secret's safe with me, Captain," Coris had assured him, then gone
below to be certain Seablanket had everything packed up to go ashore.

"I've checked and double-checked, My Lord," the habitually gloomy-
faced valet had said then. "Still and all, I don't doubt I've forgotten something.
Or misplaced it. Or that one of Captain Yuthain's sticky-fingered sailors has
relieved us of it when I wasn't looking."

"I promise I won't hold you responsible for someone else's pilferage,
Rhobair," Coris had assured him. If the promise had done anything to lighten
Seablanket's gloom, Coris hadn't noticed it. On the other hand, his valet knew
their itinerary as well as he did, and he rather doubted Seablanket was any more
eager than he was for the final stage of the journey.

Now, as the earl sat on the midships thwart of the ten-oared launch which
had (eventually) turned up to ferry him ashore, he found his own thoughts
dwelling on the prospect of the journey in question. He was, by nature, a less
gloomy fellow than Seablanket, but at the moment he'd discovered his mood
was very much in tune with the valet's. The one good thing about the weather
was that there was very little wind, yet that didn't keep an open boat from feeling like Shan-wei's own icehouse, and he felt confident the bitter cold he was
feeling at the moment was only a mild foreshadowing of what it was going to
be like when they reached Lake Pei.

*Or, for that matter, how cold it's going to be* between *here and Lake Pei,* he told
himself sourly. *Langhorne, I hope I really* do *get at least two nights in a row under a
roof in a warm bed that isn't simultaneously pitching and rolling under me!*

"Easy all!" the launch's coxswain called. "In oars . . . and bear off forward there, Ahndee!"

Coris looked up to see a long stone quay looming up close at hand. The tide had turned long enough ago to leave the high-water garland of weed and shellfish a good foot and a half clear of the harbor, and the launch slid alongside a set of stone steps, leading down into the sea. The two or three lowest of the exposed steps looked decidedly treacherous, covered with a slushy mix of residual seawater and falling snow (where they weren't still regularly sloshed over by the weary-looking swell), but the upper steps didn't look a lot better. There'd been enough traffic to pack the snow into ice, and it didn't look as if anyone had spread fresh sand across them in the last several hours.

"Mind the footing, My Lord," the coxswain warned, and Coris nodded in acknowledgment. He also reached into his purse to add an extra quarter-mark to the boat crew's tip. That was probably exactly what the coxswain had hoped would happen, and the earl knew it, but that didn't change his gratitude for the reminder.

"And you mind *your* footing, too, Rhobair," he tossed over his shoulder as he stood and stepped cautiously onto solid stone for the first time in a month.

The solid stone in question seemed to be curtsying and dipping underfoot, and he grimaced at the sensation. *That* wasn't going to help him get up these damned stairs undrenched, undrowned, and unfractured, he reflected glumly.

"I don't want to be fishing you—or the baggage—out of the damned harbor," he added as one of the launch's oarsmen helped the valet move Coris' carefully balanced trunk.

"If it's all the same to you, My Lord, I'd just as soon you didn't have to, either," Seablanket replied, and Coris snorted, took a firm (and grateful) grip on the hand rope rigged through eyebolts set into the side of the quay to serve as a railing, and made his way carefully up the slippery steps.

He inhaled in relief as he finally reached the quay's broad, flat surface intact. Everything still seemed to be moving under his feet, and he wondered how long it was going to take him to regain his land legs this time. Given how extended (and lively) the passage across the Gulf had been, he wouldn't be surprised if it took considerably longer than usual.

He stepped away from the head of the stair, trying not to move too gingerly across the apparently swaying quay, then turned to watch Seablanket and one of the launch's oarsmen carrying the baggage cautiously up. The valet's expression was even more lugubrious than usual, and his long nose—red with cold—seemed to quiver, as if he could actually smell some sort of accident or dropped trunk stealing surreptitiously closer under cover of the veiling snow.

Despite any trepidation Seablanket might have felt, however, Coris' trunks and valises made the hazardous journey up onto the quay unambushed by disaster.

Seablanket had just clambered back down the slippery steps after his own more modest traveling bag when someone cleared his throat behind the earl.

He found himself facing a man wearing the blue-trimmed brown cassock of an under-priest of the Order of Chihiro under a thick, obviously warm coat. The priest seemed on the young side for his clerical rank, and although he was actually only very slightly above average in height, he also seemed somehow just a bit larger than life. The badge of Chihiro's quill on the left shoulder of his coat was crossed with a sheathed sword, further identifying him as a member of the Order of the Sword. Chihiro's order was unique in being divided into two sub-orders: the Order of the Sword, which produced a high percentage of the Temple Guard's officers, and the Order of the Quill, which produced an almost equally high percentage of the Church's clerks and bureaucrats. Coris rather doubted, given this fellow's obviously muscular physique and the calluses on the fingers of his sword hand, that anyone really needed the shoulder badge to know which aspect of Chihiro's order *he* served.

"Earl Coris?" the under-priest inquired in a courteous voice.

"Yes, Father?" Coris replied.

He bowed in polite acknowledgment, hoping his face didn't show his dismay. Having someone pop up clear down here at quayside, in the middle of a snowfall, on a freezing-cold day, when no one could possibly have known *Snow Lizard* would choose today for her arrival, did not strike him as a good sign. Or not, at least, where his hope of spending a day or two in a snug, warm room was concerned.

"I'm Father Hahlys Tannyr, My Lord," the under-priest told him. "I've been waiting for you for several days now."

"I'm afraid the weather was less than cooperative," Coris began, "and—"

"Please, My Lord!" Tannyr smiled quickly. "That wasn't a complaint, I assure you! In fact, I know Captain Yuthain quite well, and I'm confident he got you here as swiftly as humanly possible. In fact, given what I expect the weather was like, he made rather better time than I expected, even from him. No, no." He shook his head. "I wasn't complaining about any tardiness on your part, My Lord. Simply introducing myself as the fellow responsible for seeing you through the next, undoubtedly unpleasant leg of your journey."

"I see."

Coris considered the under-priest for a moment. Tannyr couldn't be more than thirty-five, he decided, and probably not quite that old. He was dark-haired and brown-eyed, with a swarthy complexion and the lean, lively features of a man who would never find it difficult to attract female companionship. There was what looked suspiciously like humor dancing in the depths of those eyes, and even simply standing motionless in the snow, he seemed to radiate an abundance of energy. And competence, the earl decided.

"Well, Father Hahlys," he said after a handful of seconds, "since you've been so forthright, I won't pretend I'm looking forward to the . . . rigors of our trip, shall we say?"

"Nor should you be," Tannyr told him cheerfully. "The bad news is that it's the better part of thirteen hundred miles as the wyvern flies from here to Lakeview, and we're not wyverns. It's a bit better than seventeen hundred by road, and what with snow, ice, and the Wishbone Mountains squarely in the way, it's going to take us very nearly a month just to get there. At least the high road follows the Rayworth Valley, so we won't have to spend all our time climbing up and down. And I've arranged for relays of snow lizards to be waiting at the Church post houses all along our route, so we'll make fair time, I imagine, as long as we're not actively weatherbound. But even the Valley's a good seven or eight hundred feet higher than Fairstock, so I think we can safely assume the weather's going to be miserable enough to keep us off the roads for at least the equivalent of a five-day or so, anyway."

"You make it sound delightful, Father," Coris said dryly, and Tannyr laughed.

"The *Writ* says truth is always better than lies, My Lord, and trying to convince ourselves it'll be better than we know it will isn't going to make us any happier when we're stuck in some miserable little village inn in the Wishbones waiting for a blizzard to pass, now is it?"

"No, I don't imagine it is," Coris agreed. And, after all, it wasn't as if Tannyr were telling him anything he hadn't already realized.

"The *good* news, such as it is," Tannyr said, "is that I think you'll be in for a bit of a treat once we finally do get to Lakeside."

"Indeed?" Coris cocked his head, and Tannyr nodded.

"It's been a hard winter, My Lord, and according to the semaphore, the Lake's already frozen pretty hard. By the time *we* get there, we won't have to worry about hitting any open water on our way across. Well," he corrected himself with a judicious air which was only slightly undermined by the twinkle in his eyes, "we *probably* won't have to worry about it. You can never be entirely certain when a lead's going to open up unexpectedly."

"So we definitely will be taking an iceboat from Lakeview to Zion?" Coris shook his head just a bit doubtfully. "I've been to sea often enough, but I've never gone ice-sailing."

"That we will, and I think you'll find the experience . . . interesting," Tannyr assured him. The under-priest had obviously noticed Coris' mixed feelings, and he smiled again. "Most people do, especially the first time they make the trip. *Hornet's* quite a bit smaller than *Snow Lizard,* of course, but she's much faster, if I do say so myself."

"Ah?" Coris cocked an eyebrow. "That sounded rather possessive, Father. Should I take it you're going to be my captain across the Lake, as well as shepherding me safely from here to Lakeview?"

"Indeed, My Lord." Tannyr gave him a sort of sketchy half bow. "And I can assure you that I have never—yet—lost a passenger during a winter passage."

"And I assure *you* that I am suitably comforted by your reassurance, Father. Even if it did seem to contain at least a hint of qualification."

Tannyr's smile became a grin, and Coris felt himself relaxing a bit more. He still wasn't looking forward to the journey, but Hahlys Tannyr was about as far as anyone could have gotten from the grimly focused Schuelerite keeper he'd expected to encounter for the final stage of his journey.

"Seriously, My Lord," Tannyr continued, "*Hornet* is much faster than you may have been assuming. She doesn't have a galley's hull drag, so the same wind will push her a lot faster, and the prevailing winds will be in our favor, this time of year. Not to mention the fact that we're far enough into the winter now that the ice's been pretty well charted and marked, so I can afford to give her more of her head than I could earlier in the year. I won't be surprised if we average as much as thirty miles an hour during the lake crossing itself."

"Really?"

Despite himself, Coris couldn't hide how impressed he was by the speed estimate. Or by the fact that it radically revised downward his original estimate of how long it would take to cross Lake Pei. Of course, that was a two-edged sword. It meant he'd spend less time shivering and miserable on the ice, but it also meant he'd be meeting with Chancellor Trynair and the Grand Inquisitor that much more quickly, as well.

And it wasn't going to make the month-long journey from Fairstock to Lakeview any less arduous than the under-priest had already promised.

*I suppose I should spend some time thanking Langhorne I'm still young enough to have a realistic prospect of surviving the experience,* he thought sourly.

"Really, My Lord," Tannyr assured him, answering his last question. "In fact, running with the wind in a good lake blizzard, I've had her up to better than fifty miles per hour—that's average speed, over a twenty-mile course, too, so I'm sure we were higher than that, at least in bursts—on more than one occasion. I'll try not to inflict any weather quite that spectacular on you this time around. It's not exactly something for the faint of heart—or, as my mother would put it, for the reasonably sane." He winked. "Still, I think I can promise you'll find the crossing memorable."

The under-priest smiled with obvious pride in his vessel, then turned his head, watching Seablanket emerge onto the quay once more with the final piece of baggage. He gazed at the valet with a thoughtful expression for several seconds, then looked back at Coris, and there was an almost conspiratorial gleam in his eye.

"I realize, My Lord, that you undoubtedly wish to complete your journey as quickly as possible. I have no doubt your impatience to set forth again is greater than ever in light of the current inclement weather and the obviously strenuous nature of the voyage you've just completed. I'm afraid, however, that I'm not entirely satisfied with the lizard team reserved for the first leg of our journey. Not only that, but I've been having a few second thoughts about our planned stopping points along the way. I've come to the conclusion that the entire trip could have been a bit better planned and coordinated, and I think we'll probably complete it more quickly, in the long run, if I spend a little time . . . tweaking my present arrangements. I apologize profusely for the delay, but as the person charged with delivering you safe and sound, I really wouldn't feel comfortable setting out on a journey as long as this one without first making certain all of our arrangements are going to be as problem-free as possible."

"Well, we certainly couldn't have you feeling pressured into anything precipitous, Father," Coris replied, making no effort to hide his sudden gratitude. "And I'm certainly prepared to defer to your professional judgment. We can't have you skimping on your preparations if you feel any of them could stand improvement, now can we? By all means, see to it before we set out!"

"I appreciate your willingness to be so understanding, My Lord. Assuming the weather gives us a window for the semaphore, I expect tidying things up should take no more than, oh"—Tannyr looked at the earl consideringly, like an assayer, almost as if he could physically measure Coris' fatigue—"a day or two. Possibly three. In fact, we'd better *count* on three. So I'm afraid you're probably going to have to spend at least four nights here in Fairstock. I hope that won't disappoint you too deeply."

"Believe me, Father," Coris said, looking him in the eye, "I believe I'll manage to bear up under my disappointment."

.VI.<br>
Off Hennet Head,<br>
Gulf of Mathyas

Someone from the planet humanity had once called Earth might have described it as "Force Six" from the old Beaufort scale. Ensign Hektor Aplyn-Ahrmahk, the Duke of Darcos, had never heard of the Beaufort scale, but he had been at sea for almost five of his fourteen years. Well, thirteen years and nine months, since his birthday was next month. And to his experienced eye, the eleven-foot waves, with their white foamy crests, and the high humming sound whining through the stays were the products of what a seaman would have called either a strong breeze or a stiff topsail breeze, which still had another four or five miles per hour to go before it officially became a near gale.

Hektor suspected that most landsmen would have found the ship's motion, the way she leaned to her canvas and the flying spray bursting up around her cutwater as she drove hard, rising in showers of diamonds when the early morning sun caught it, alarming. In fact, there'd been a time—though he couldn't really remember it now—when *he* would have found it distinctly so. Now, though, he found it exhilarating (especially with his stomach so freshly wrapped around a breakfast of toasted biscuit and well-sweetened, raisin-laced oatmeal), despite the sharp, icy teeth of the wind, and he clapped his gloved hands together and beamed hugely as he looked up at the reefed topsails and topgallants, then turned to the senior of the two men on the wheel.

"How does she feel, Chief?" he asked.

"Well enough, Sir."

Chief Petty Officer Frahnklyn Waigan was closing in on three times the youthful ensign's age, and Hektor was about as junior as an officer got. Once upon a time, all of three or four months ago, he would have been referred to not as an "ensign," but as a "passed midshipman"—a midshipman who had successfully sat his lieutenant's examination but not yet received his commission—since he legally *couldn't* be granted a full lieutenant's commission until he was at least sixteen years old. The new "ensign" rank had been introduced as part of the Navy's enormous expansion, and the fleet was still in the process of getting used to it. But if Waigan felt any exasperation at being interrogated by an officer of Ensign Aplyn-Ahrmahk's tender years and lack of seniority he showed no sign of it.

"She's takin' a bit more weather helm nor I'd like," Waigan added, "but not s' much as all that."

Hektor nodded. Any sailing vessel carried at least a little weather helm when she came close to the wind, and at the moment *Destiny* was close-reaching to the east-northeast on the starboard tack under single reefed topgallants and topsails with the wind out of the south-southeast, just over three points abaft the beam. That was very close to close-hauled for HMS *Destiny*; Hektor doubted they could have edged more than another point or so closer to the wind, and damned few other square-riggers could have come *this* close.

Of course, it made for a lively ride, but that was part of the exhilaration, and even with her reduced sail, the ship had to be making good close to seven knots—well, over six and a half, at least. That was an excellent turn of speed, although she could probably have carried more sail and shown a little more speed if Captain Yairley had decided to shake out the topgallant reefs and press her.

*Not that he's likely to do anything of the sort without a damned good reason,* Hektor thought with a small, inner smile. *It would never suit his fussy worrier's image!*

The truth was that Hektor recognized just how fortunate he'd been to be assigned to Yairley's command in the first place. And not just because of the captain's abilities as a mentor in tactics and seamanship, either. Hektor doubted there could have been a better teacher in the entire fleet for either of those skills, yet as appreciative as he was of that training, he was even more grateful for the time Yairley had taken to teach one Hektor Aplyn-Ahrmahk certain other, equally essential skills.

Despite his present exalted patent of nobility, Hektor Aplyn had most definitely not been born to the aristocracy. His was a family of sturdy, hard-working merchant seamen, and young Hektor's appointment as a midshipman in the Royal Charisian Navy had represented a significant step upward for the Aplyns. He'd hoped to make a decent career for himself—the Charisian Navy was really the only one on Safehold where a commoner had an excellent chance of rising to even the highest ranks, and more than one man as commonly born as he had ended up with a knighthood and an admiral's streamer, when all was said. He could think of at least a half dozen who'd earned baronetcies, and at least one who'd died an earl, for that matter. But he'd never dreamed for a moment that *he* might end up a duke!

Then again—his amusement dimmed—he'd never expected to have his king die in his arms, or to live with the knowledge that his monarch had received his fatal wound fighting to protect *him*. Never anticipated that he would be one of only thirty-six survivors of the entire crew of King Haarahld VII's flagship. In fact, three of those survivors had eventually died of their wounds in the end, after all, despite all the healers could do, and of the thirty-three who hadn't, eleven had been so badly wounded they would never go to sea again. The odds that he might simply have survived that level of carnage, far less remained on active duty after it, would have struck him as tiny enough on their own. The possibility of his being adopted into the House of Ahrmahk, of becoming legally the son of Emperor Cayleb himself, would never have occurred to him in the wildest delirium. And if anyone had ever suggested the possibility to him, he would have run screaming in terror from the prospect. What could *he,* the son of a merchant galleon's first officer, possibly have in common with the *royal family*? The very idea was absurd!

Unfortunately, it had happened. Probably, in the fullness of time, Hektor was going to come to consider that a good thing. He was perfectly prepared to admit the possibility—he wasn't *stupid,* after all—but his immediate reaction had been one of abject panic. Which was why he was so grateful he'd wound up in *Destiny*. Sir Dunkyn Yairley was scarcely from the rarefied heights of the nobility himself, but he was at least related, albeit it distantly, to three barons and an earl. More to the point, he'd taken pains from the outset to personally instruct young Midshipman Aplyn-Ahrmahk in the etiquette which went with his towering new aristocratic rank.

*Starting with which fork to use,* Hektor reflected, grinning again as he remembered how the captain had rapped him sharply across the knuckles with his own fork when he reached for the wrong one. *I thought sure he'd broken them! But I suppose—*

"Sail ho!" the hail came down from the lookout perched in the mainmast crosstrees, a hundred and ten feet above the deck. From there, the horizon was almost eleven and a half miles farther away than it was from deck level, and on a clear day like today, he could undoubtedly see that far.

"*Two* sail, five points to larboard!" the lookout amplified a moment later.

"Master Aplyn-Ahrmahk!" a closer, deeper voice said, and Hektor turned to find himself facing Lieutenant Rhobair Lathyk, *Destiny's* first lieutenant, who had the watch.

"Aye, Sir?" Hektor touched his chest with his right fist in salute. Lathyk was a tall man—tall enough he had to mind his head constantly under the ship's deck beams—and he had a short way with slackers. He insisted on proper military courtesy at all times, especially out of extremely junior officers. But he was also a fine seaman, and he didn't (usually) go out of his way to find fault.

"Get aloft, Master Aplyn-Ahrmahk," Lathyk said now, handing him the watch spyglass. "See what you can tell us about these fellows."

"Aye, aye, Sir!"

Hektor seized the telescope, slung its carrying strap over his shoulder, and leapt nimbly for the ratlines. Lathyk could easily have sent one of the galleon's midshipmen, but Hektor was glad he hadn't. One of the things he missed, thanks to his recent promotion and appointment as *Destiny's* acting fifth lieutenant, was that no lieutenant—not even one who was really a lowly ensign—was allowed to race his fellows up and down the rigging the way mere midshipmen could. Unlike many of his fellows, Hektor had been born with an excellent head for heights. He'd loved spending time in the tops, and laying out along the yard, even in the roughest weather, had never truly bothered him. *Scared* him sometimes, yes, but always with that edge of exhilaration to keep the terror company, and now he went scampering up the humming weather shrouds like a monkey-lizard.

He ignored the lubber's hole when he reached the maintop, hanging from his fingers and toes as he climbed the futtock shrouds *around* the top instead, then swarmed on up the topmast shrouds. Wind whistled chill around his ears and burned cold in his lungs, and his eyes were bright with pleasure as the shrill whistle of one of the sea wyverns following the ship, perpetually hopeful of snapping up some tasty tidbit of garbage, floated to him.

"Where away, Zhaksyn?" he asked the lookout as he reached the sailor's dizzying roost. The lookout was perched on the crosstrees, one leg dangling nonchalantly between the weather hounds, one arm wrapped around the foot of the topgallant mast, and he grinned as his eyes met Hektor's.

It was colder up here, and the wind always grew fresher as one climbed higher above the deck. (That much was a known fact, although Hektor had no idea why it should be so.) Despite the exertion of his climb, he was grateful for his thick watch coat, heavy gloves, and the soft, knitted muffler Princess Zhanayt had given him last Midwinter Day. The main topmast head was almost a foot and a half in diameter where its upper end passed through the cap above the crosstrees, which helped support the topgallant mast, and it shivered against his spine as he leaned back against it, vibrating like a living thing with the force of wind and wave. When he looked straight down, he saw not *Destiny*'s deck but the gray-green and white water creaming away from her leeward side as she leaned to the press of her canvas. If he fell from his present position, he'd hit water, not planking. Not that it would make much difference. As cold as that water was, his chances of surviving long enough for anyone aboard ship to do anything to save him would be effectively nonexistent.

Fortunately, he had no intention of doing anything of the sort.

"There, Sir," the lookout said, and pointed.

Hektor followed the pointing finger, nodded, and hooked one knee securely around the topmast head as he used both gloved hands to raise the heavy telescope and peered through it.

Steadying something the size of a powerful telescope, especially while one swept through a dizzying arc with the ship's motion, was not a task to be lightly undertaken. The fact that Hektor would never be a large, powerfully built man like Lathyk didn't make it any easier, either. On the other hand, his slender boy's frame was filling out steadily into a well-muscled wiriness, and he'd had lots of practice. He supported the tube on his left forearm, swinging it through a compensating arc, and captured the pale flaw of the distant ships' topsails with a steadiness a landsman would have found difficult to credit.

Even from here, the ships to whom those sails belonged remained hull-down. He could see only their topsails fully, although the tops of their main courses came into sight when both they and *Destiny* happened to rise simultaneously. Assuming their masts were the same length as Destiny's, which would put their main yards about fifty feet above the water, that made them about fourteen and a half miles distant.

He studied them carefully, patiently, evaluating their course and trying to get some feel for their speed. His eye ached as he stared through the spyglass, but he neither blinked nor lowered the glass until he was satisfied. Then he sighed in relief, let the glass come back to hang from its shoulder strap once more, and rubbed his eye.

"What d'you make of 'em, Sir?" the seaman asked.

Hektor turned his head to arch one eyebrow at him, and the sailor grinned. It was unlikely, to say the least, that he would have been forward enough to pose the same question to Lieutenant Lathyk, and Hektor knew some of his fellow officers—Lieutenant Garaith Symkee, *Destiny*'s second lieutenant, came rather forcibly to mind—would have been quick to depress the man's "pretension." For that matter, he supposed a mere ensign had even more reason than most to be sure he guarded his authority against overfamiliarity from the men he commanded. Captain Yairley, on the other hand, who never seemed to have any particular difficulty maintaining *his* authority, would simply have answered the question, and if it was good enough for the captain . . .

"Well," Hektor said, "it's still a bit far away to be making out details, even with the glass, but unless I'm mistaken, at least the nearer of them is flying a Church pennant."

"You don't say, Sir!" Zhaksyn's grin grew considerably broader. He actually rubbed his hands together in anticipation, since the presence of the Church pennant automatically made the ship flying it a legitimate prize, waiting to be taken, and Hektor grinned back at him. Then the ensign allowed his smile to fade into a more serious expression.

"You did well to spot them, Zhaksyn," he said, patting the older man (although, to be fair, Zhaksyn was only in his late twenties; topmen were generally chosen from the youngest and fittest members of a ship's company) on the shoulder.

"Thank'ee, Sir!" Zhaksyn was positively beaming now, and Hektor nodded to him, then reached for the shrouds once more. He was strongly tempted to slide down the backstay, but the youthful exuberance of his midshipman's days was behind him now—Lieutenant Lathyk had made that point rather firmly just last five-day—and so he descended in a more leisurely fashion.

"Well, Master Aplyn-Ahrmahk?" the first lieutenant inquired as he reached the ship's rail, hopped down onto the deck, and made his way aft once more.

"There are definitely two of them, Sir—that we can see so far, at any rate. Galleons, ship-rigged, but not as lofty as we are, I think. They aren't carrying royal masts, anyway. I make the range about fourteen or fifteen miles, and they're sailing on the wind, almost exactly northwest by north. They're showing their courses and topsails, but not their topgallants, and I think the closer of the two is flying a Church pennant."

"Is she, now?" Lathyk mused.

"Yes, Sir. And as she lifted, I could just catch a glimpse of her mizzen. I couldn't see her headsails, so I can't say for sure that she's got the new jibs, but she's definitely got a gaff spanker. She's wearing new canvas, too—it's hardly weathered at all—and I think she's big, Sir. I'd be surprised if she were a lot smaller than we are."

Lathyk's eyes narrowed, and Hektor could almost *feel* him following the same logic chain Hektor had already explored. Then the first lieutenant nodded, ever so slightly, and turned to one of the midshipmen hovering nearby.

"My respects to the Captain, Master Zhones, and inform him that we have sighted two galleons, bearing almost due north, distance about fourteen miles, running northwest by north, and Master Aplyn-Ahrmahk"—the first lieutenant smiled slightly at Hektor—"is *firmly* of the opinion that at least one of them is a large, *newly rigged* galleon in the service of the Church."

"Aye, aye, Sir!" young Zhones squeaked. He couldn't have been more than twelve years old, which struck Hektor as absurdly young . . . despite the fact that he himself had been at sea for three years by the time he'd been that age.

The midshipman started for the hatch at a semi-run, then froze as Lathyk cleared his throat loudly enough to be heard even over the sounds of wind and wave. The boy peered at him for a second, huge-eyed, then hastily straightened and came to attention.

"Beg pardon, Sir!" he said, and then repeated Lathyk's message word for word.

"Very good, Master Zhones," Lathyk confirmed with a nod when he'd finished, and the midshipman darted away again. Hektor watched him go and remembered a time when *he'd* garbled a message, and not to any mere master-after-God captain, either. He'd been positive he was going to die of humiliation right on the spot. And, assuming he'd survived that, he'd *known* Captain Tryvythyn would give him The Look, which would be considerably worse, when *he* heard about the transgression.

*I suppose it was just as well,* the ensign reminded himself, managing not to smile as Zhones disappeared down the main hatch, *that His Majesty forgave me after all.*

▼ ▼ ▼

"So, Ruhsail, what do you make of her?" Commodore Wailahr inquired as he stepped out from under the break of the poop deck, and Captain Ruhsail Ahbaht, commanding officer of the Imperial Desnairian Navy galleon *Archangel Chihiro,* turned quickly to face him.

"Beg your pardon, Sir Hairahm." The captain saluted. "I didn't realize you'd come on deck."

"Well, I hadn't, until this very minute," Wailahr said just a bit testily. The commodore was a solidly built man, his dark hair starting to silver at the temples. There were a few strands of white in his neatly trimmed beard, as well, but his dark eyes were sharp and alert.

He was accompanied by Father Awbrai Lairays, his chaplain, in the purple, flame-badged cassock of the Order of Schueler.

"Yes, Sir. Of course you hadn't," Ahbaht replied quickly, but his voice still held that same edge of half-apprehensive apology, and he looked so much as if he were planning to salute yet again that Wailahr found it difficult not to grimace. He knew he was lucky to have a flag captain of Ahbaht's experience, but he did wish that, after more than three thousand miles and three and a half five-days at sea, the captain would forget he was related—distantly, and only by marriage—to the Earl of Hankey.

"No reason you should have realized I was here, until I spoke." The commodore tried (mostly successfully) to keep any exaggerated patience out of his tone and glanced rather pointedly up at the lookout whose report had summoned him to the deck.

"It sounds like it's probably a Charisian galleon, Sir," Ahbaht said in response to the hint. "The lookout ought to have sighted her sooner, but she's still a good eleven or twelve miles clear. Still, she's close enough for us to get a good look at her canvas, and she's obviously got the new rig. She's also carrying a lot of sail for these weather conditions, and she's making straight for us." He shrugged very slightly. "Given that almost all the armed ships cruising these waters have been Charisian for the better part of a year, I doubt anyone but a Charisian would be making sail to overhaul anyone she hadn't definitely identified as a friend."

Wailahr nodded slowly as he considered Ahbaht's analysis of the other galleon captain's thinking. It made sense, he decided, and after twenty-six years in the Crown's service, he had more than enough experience as an officer himself to appreciate what his flag captain had offered about the probable Charisian's thought processes. Unfortunately, he was far less well qualified to evaluate some of the other factors involved in the developing situation, since almost all of his own experience had been ashore, most of it as a cavalry commander in the Imperial Army. As in the majority of Safeholdian realms, traditional Desnairian practice had always been to assign army commanders to its warships (of which it had possessed precious few), each with an experienced seaman to translate his decisions and commands into action. It was a warship commander's job to *fight*, after all, and a professional military man had more important things to worry about than the technical details of making the boat go where it was supposed to go.

*Or that's the theory, at any rate,* Wailahr told himself sourly. *And I suppose if I'm going to be fair, it's always worked well enough against other people who do the same thing. Unfortunately*—there was that word again—*Charis doesn't. And it hasn't, not for a long time.*

As a loyal subject of Mahrys IV and an obedient son of Mother Church, Sir Hairahm Wailahr was determined to make a success of his present assignment, but he had few illusions about his own knowledge of things naval. He was out of his depth (he grimaced mentally at his own choice of phrase) as the commander of one of the Navy's new galleons, much less an entire squadron, which was the reason he was so grateful for Ahbaht's experience.

Even if he did want to kick the captain in the arse from time to time.

"You say he's making for us, Captain," Wailahr said after a moment. "Do you mean he's *pursuing* us?"

"Most likely, Sir." Ahbaht swept one arm in a half circle in the general direction of the other ship, still invisible from *Archangel Chihiro*'s deck. "There's a lot of ocean out there, Sir Hairahm, and not much shipping on it since the damned Charisians started privateering. It wouldn't be unreasonable for a merchant galleon to be making for Terrence Bay, just as we are. But, as I say, without positively knowing we were friendly, I'd expect any merchant skipper to keep his distance. He'd certainly have reduced sail to maintain our current separation, I'd think, even if he's headed for Silk Town or for Khairman Keep, like we are. And even though the lookout isn't positive, he thinks this fellow has made *more* sail."

"He isn't *positive* about something like that?" Wailahr raised one eyebrow.

"He says he isn't, Sir. I can get him down here to speak to you personally, of course." The flag captain gave another of those small shrugs. "I had Lieutenant Chaimbyrs speak with him already, though. It's the Lieutenant's opinion that what really caught the lookout's eye in the first place was this other ship's setting additional canvas."

"I see."

Ahbaht's response had just neatly encapsulated both his greatest strength and, in Wailahr's opinion, his greatest weakness as a flag captain. Or as any sort of military commander, for that matter. From his tone and his body language he was completely prepared to summon the lookout to the deck so that Wailahr could personally browbeat the man, yet he'd also had Lieutenant Zhustyn Chaimbyrs, *Archangel Chihiro*'s second lieutenant, interrogate the sailor first. Chaimbyrs was himself an excellent young officer—one Wailahr already had an eye on for promotion—and he would have gotten the lookout's very best estimate out of him without intimidating him. It was just like Ahbaht to have made exactly the right choice about how to get the most accurate information possible, on the one hand, and yet to be willing to allow a possibly irritated superior to vent his spleen on the seaman who'd provided it, on the other. Especially if that superior had the sort of court influence which might benefit his own career.

*Be fair, Hairahm,* the commodore reminded himself for perhaps the thousandth time. *Unlike you, Ahbaht has no connections at all, and the man's already— what? Forty-three? Whatever. Old enough at any rate to expect he's not going to climb much higher without someone to give him a boost. Although I'd think the fact that they picked him to command one of the very first galleons ought to go at least a little way towards reassuring him.*

On the other hand, the Navy had never been exactly glamorous in Desnairian eyes. Quite a few of the career naval officers Wailahr had met over the last several months seemed to find it a bit difficult to grasp just how much that was about to change.

"All right, Ruhsail," he said out loud after several seconds' thought. "What do you recommend?"

"Recommend, Sir?" Ahbaht's eyes flitted sideways for a moment, towards Lairays.

"Do we let him catch us, or do we make more sail of our own?" Wailahr expanded in a slightly dangerous tone.

Ahbaht's eyes came back to the commodore's face, and Wailahr managed not to sigh in exasperation. As far as he could tell, there was nothing at all wrong with Ahbaht's physical courage, but it was obvious he had no more intention of putting his foot wrong in front of Lairays than he did of offending Wailahr himself.

Which, Wailahr was forced to concede upon more mature consideration, was probably wise of him, in many ways, after all. Lairays hadn't been the commodore's own choice as chaplain. He'd been *assigned* to Wailahr by Bishop Executor Mhartyn Raislair, and his presence was a clear statement of exactly who *Archangel Chihiro* actually belonged to. She might fly Desnair's black horse on a yellow field, but there was a reason Mother Church's pennant flew above the national colors. For the moment, no one was talking a great deal about that reason—not openly, at any rate. But only a complete moron (which, despite his obsequiousness, Ahbaht clearly wasn't) could have failed to realize that all the rumors about the imminence of Holy War had a very sound basis, indeed.

It was fortunate, in Wailahr's opinion, that there seemed to be little of the fanatic about Father Awbrai. Zealotry, yes, which was only to be expected in the priest the bishop executor had chosen as his personal eyes and ears on Wailahr's staff, but not fanaticism. He was unlikely to hold Ahbaht's honest opinion against the flag captain, whatever it was, but Wailahr supposed he shouldn't really blame Ahbaht for being cautious in front of him.

"I suppose, Sir, that that depends on what it is we want to accomplish," the flag captain said finally. "If our sole concern is to collect the bullion from Khairman Keep, then I would advise against accepting action." His eyes tried to flick to Lairays again, but he kept his voice commendably firm as he continued. "While there are two of us and only one of him, it's entirely possible—even probable—that we'd suffer at least some damage even against one of their privateers. If this is one of their war galleons, the chance of that goes up considerably. And any damage we might suffer would have to be put right again before we could sail with the bullion, which would undoubtedly delay its delivery."

*A reasonable answer,* Wailahr reflected. *And a well-taken point, for that matter.*

He didn't know the precise value of the gold shipment awaiting his two ships, but he knew it was large. In fact, it was a substantial portion of Desnair's annual tithe to Mother Church, actually. Which, considering the incredible outlays the Temple had been making to pay for the new warships building all over Hauwerd and Haven, lent a certain urgency to getting that gold safely delivered to the Temple's coffers in Zion. Vicar Rhobair's Treasury needed all the cash it could get, and given typical winter road conditions, it made sense to send it by sea for as much of its journey as possible. Or it would have, at least, if not for the omnipresent Charisian privateers, and if the ships building in the Gulf of Jahras, conveniently close to Khairman Keep, had been near enough to ready for sea to take it. As it happened, however, those Charisian privateers did, indeed, seem to be just about everywhere, and none of the new construction at Iythria or Mahrosa had been far enough advanced for the task. Which explained why he and the first two fully operational ships of his squadron had been dispatched all the way from the imperial capital at Desnair the City (so called to distinguish it from the rest of the empire) to fetch it.

*We're already behind schedule, too, and Bishop Executor Mhartyn won't thank me if I'm even later,* he thought. *There are two of us, though, and sooner or later we have to cross swords with them. Langhorne knows the sheer terror of the Charisians' reputation is one of their most effective weapons! Deservedly so, I suppose. But they're only mortals, when all's said, and we need to start chipping away at that reputation. . . .*

He glanced at "his" chaplain.

"Father, I'm inclined to let this fine gentleman overhaul us, if that's his intention. Or to let him get at least a bit closer, at any rate. Close enough for us to see who he really is. If he's only a privateer, I imagine he'll sheer off once he realizes he's been chasing a pair of *war* galleons, and, to be honest, I'd like to get him close enough we'd have a chance to catch him if he runs."

"And if he's a war galleon himself, Commodore?" Lairays' deep voice sounded even deeper coming from someone as youthful looking as the underpriest, and the brown cockade of his priest's cap fluttered in the stiff breeze whipping across *Archangel Chihiro*'s quarterdeck.

"If he's a war galleon, then I suppose it's possible he'll keep right on coming," Wailahr replied. "If he does, as the Captain's just pointed out, there are two of us, which should give us a considerable advantage if we can entice him into engagement range. Do you think His Eminence would be willing to put up with a little delay while we repair any battle damage in return for taking or sinking one of Cayleb's warships?"

▼　　▼　　▼

"Deck, there! The nearer chase is shortening sail!"

Captain Sir Dunkyn Yairley looked up at the mizzen crosstrees and frowned slightly as the announcement came down from above.

"She's takin' in her topgallants, Sir!" the lookout continued. "Both of 'em are!" he added a minute or so later, and Yairley's frown deepened.

It was merely a *thoughtful* frown, however, Hektor Aplyn-Ahrmahk observed, and set his own mind to following the captain's thoughts.

It *could* be that the other ship had simply decided she was carrying too much sail for safety. The other two galleons had come to a more northerly heading, about north-northwest, and set their topgallants once they realized *Destiny* was pursuing them, but that didn't mean their commander had been happy about his own decision. His ships' rigs might be considerably more powerful than they would have been two or three years ago, but very few vessels in the world had sail plans as powerful—and well balanced—as those of the present Charisian Navy.

*Destiny*'s masts were taller, proportionately, and included the lofty royal masts her quarry lacked, yet it wasn't simply a matter of more mast height, either. If she'd set every scrap of canvas she had, including all her fore-and-aft staysails and all three jibs, she would have shown twenty-five sails. Not only that, the new water-powered Charisian looms meant her sails had a much tighter weave, which let them capture more of the wind's power, *and* they were cut to the new, flat pattern Sir Dustyn Olyvyr had introduced. The ships she was pursuing didn't carry royals or staysails; they would have shown only ten under the same circumstances. Those sails were still cut to the old "bag sail" pattern, acting like rounded sacks to catch the wind, rather than the flatter, more perpendicular—and hence more efficient—surface of *Destiny*'s. Hektor had to admit that the bag sails *looked* as if they should have been more powerful, but the superiority of Olyvyr's new patterns had been conclusively demonstrated in competitve sailing tests in Howell Bay.

The proportions of the other ships' sails were significantly different, as well, for *Destiny*'s topsails had both a greater hoist and a broader head, which gave each of them significantly more area and made them more powerful. In fact, her topsails were actually her principal sails, whereas the courses set below them remained the primary sails for the ships she was pursuing.

Of course, there was a vast difference between the total canvas a ship could set under *optimum* conditions and the amount it was safe to carry in any given sea state. In some respects, in fact, *Destiny* and her sisters were actually oversparred. It would have been easy to set too much sail, drive her too hard—even dangerously too hard—under the wrong circumstances. Besides, there was a point at which crowding on more sail actually *slowed* a ship, by driving her head too deeply into the sea or heeling her so sharply it distorted the water flow around her hull, even if it didn't actually endanger her. So, in most respects, how many sails a ship had mattered less than the total sail area she could show under the current strength of wind and wave.

But it did matter how that area was *distributed,* because of how it affected the ship's motion. At the moment, for example, one reason Captain Yairley had set the fore course was that, unlike the ship's other square sails, the fore course actually tended to *lift* the bow slightly, easing the vessel's motion, rather than driving the bow down deeper and harder. A captain had to think about the blanketing effect of his sails, as well, and, generally speaking, the higher a sail, the greater its heeling effect. So in heavy weather, the standard order of reducing sail would be to take in first the royals (assuming the ship carried them in the first place), then the topgallants, the courses, and finally the topsails. (The courses came off before the higher topsails because of their greater size and the difficulty in handling them, despite the greater heeling effect of the topsails.)

Hektor's own initial estimate that the other galleons were as large as *Destiny* appeared to have been in error, too. The other ships were at least a little smaller than he'd thought, although not greatly so, which meant *Destiny* could safely carry more canvas than they could under these conditions. Captain Yairley had been doing just that, having shaken out his reefs and set the fore course (the main course was brailed up to keep it from blanketing the foremast, with the wind dead aft on her new course), and even without her own royals, *Destiny*'s speed had risen to almost eight knots. She'd been steadily overhauling the other vessels for the past five hours now, despite the fact that they'd both put on extra sail of their own once they finally noticed they were being pursued, so it was certainly possible—likely, in fact—the chases had decided they couldn't outrun *Destiny* after all. And if that was the case, there was no point in their risking damage to sails or rigging by carrying too much canvas. Particularly not since it was always possible something would carry away aloft in *Destiny,* in which case they might be able to outsail her yet.

On the other hand, the topgallants would have been the first sails to be furled if a captain decided to shorten for *any* reason, not simply because of weather concerns. So it was also possible the other ships had simply decided to allow *Destiny* to overtake them. Which would require either a very stupid merchant skipper, given the depredations of Charisian privateers and naval cruisers, or else a—

"I believe we'll clear the ship for action in about another . . . three hours, I think, Master Lathyk," Yairley said calmly. "We'll be coming up on lunch shortly, I believe, so there's no point rushing things. But see to it all hands get something hot to eat, and plenty of it, if you please."

"Aye, Sir," the first lieutenant acknowledged. He beckoned to one of the midshipmen and started giving the lad crisp instructions, and Yairley glanced at Hektor.

"You don't think they're merchantmen after all, do you, Sir?" Hektor asked quietly. Some captains would have bitten the head off of any officer, be he ever so well connected to the aristocracy, for having the impertinence to ask him such a question uninvited. Hektor wasn't concerned about that, though, and not because of his own noble title.

"No, Master Aplyn-Ahrmahk, I don't," Yairley replied. He nodded ahead to where the other ships' sails were visible now from the deck as *Destiny* rose with the waves. "Both those fellows are *inviting* us to catch up with them, and no merchant skipper would do that, even if they haven't seen our colors by now. Which they well may not have."

He glanced up to where the Empire's banner streamed out, stiff and hard-looking, from the mizzen yard. On *Destiny*'s new course, running almost directly before the wind as she charged after the other ships, it was entirely possible that her colors were hidden from her quarry by the canvas on her foremast and mainmast.

"They may not realize we're a king's ship—I mean, an emperor's ship"—Yairley grimaced as he made the self-correction—"but they have to assume we're at least a privateer. Under the circumstances, merchant vessels would go right on running for all they were worth in hopes of staying away from us until dark. Mind you, I don't think they'd succeed, but they might, and no one ever knows what the wind's going to do."

He paused, one eyebrow raised, and Hektor recognized the cue.

"So if they aren't running as hard as they can—if they've decided they want us to catch up with them while we'll both have daylight still in hand—you think *they're* war galleons, too, Sir," he said.

"I think that's very likely, Master Aplyn-Ahrmahk." Yairley nodded slightly, with the satisfaction of a teacher whose student had drawn the proper conclusion. "I'd thought for a moment, before they *both* shortened, that it might be a merchant with an escort dropping astern of the ship under his protection. But no escort would be foolish enough to keep his charge in close company if he'd decided to drop back to engage us, so it seems to me we have to assume they're both warships. According to Baron Wave Thunder's latest estimates, Desnair should have at least a dozen of their converted galleons about ready for sea. There's no way to be positive yet, but I'll be quite surprised if these aren't two of them. The only question in my mind," the captain continued, his voice becoming a bit dreamy as his eyes unfocused in thought, "is what two of them would be doing out here by themselves."

"They might simply be working up, Sir," Hektor suggested diffidently, and Yairley nodded.

"Indeed they might, but not this far out to sea, I'm thinking." He indicated the brisk wind, the motion of the hard-driven ship, with a twitch of his head. "These conditions are a bit lively for a lubberly lot like the Desnairian Navy, wouldn't you say, Master Aplyn-Ahrmahk? I'd expect them to stay closer to home if all they're after is sail drill, especially if there are only two of them. We're a good six hundred and fifty leagues from their shipyards at Geyra—and over a hundred leagues off Hennet Head, for that matter. It's possible they're from the ships building in the Gulf of Jahras instead of the Geyra yards. God knows they're building a lot more of their total navy in the Gulf than they are at Geyra. But even that would be an awful long way to come just to drill their crews, and I'd think Baron Jahras would be a tad nervous about having just two of his meet a squadron or two of our galleons when they decided to venture out into deeper water. He's certainly been . . . cautious enough about things like that so far, at least. So I wonder . . ."

The captain stood thinking for several more moments, then nodded again,

this time obviously to himself, before he glanced once more at the youthful ensign standing beside him.

"I can think of one good reason for them to be here, Master Aplyn-
Ahrmahk," he said with a slight smile. "And if I'm right, the men are going to
be just a bit unhappy that we sighted them when we did, instead of a few days
later."

"Sir?" Hektor suppressed an urge to scratch his head in puzzlement, and
Yairley's smile broadened.

"Now then, Master Aplyn-Ahrmahk! A captain has to maintain at least a
few little secrets, don't you think?"

▼    ▼    ▼

"Excuse me, Sir."

Captain Ahbaht turned, raising one eyebrow, to face Lieutenant Laizair
Mahrtynsyn, *Archangel Chihiro*'s first lieutenant.

"Yes, Laizair? What is it?" Ahbaht's tone was a bit brusque. He and Mahrtynsyn normally got along quite well, but at the moment, as the pursuing vessel's
lower masts began to loom above the horizon, even from deck level, the captain
had a few things on his mind. The distance to the other ship was down to little
more than seven miles, and given their present speeds, she would be up to
*Archangel Chihiro* in no more than two or two and a half hours. For that matter, she'd be into extreme gunshot in little more than ninety minutes.

"Master Chaimbyrs"—Mahrtynsyn twitched his head slightly in the direction of the mizzen top, where Lieutenant Chaimbyrs was ensconced watching
the other ship—"reports that he's just seen her colors, Sir. She's flying the
Charisian banner . . . and a commission streamer."

Ahbaht's expression tightened ever so slightly. Only someone who knew
the captain well would have noticed, but Mahrtynsyn *did* know him well. And
he also knew exactly what Ahbaht was thinking. The fact that Chaimbyrs had
finally seen the colors which had been masked by her canvas only confirmed
the captain's previous near certainty that she had to be Charisian. But the commission streamer . . . *that* was something else entirely. No privateer would have
been flying that. Only ships of the Royal Charisian Navy—or, rather, the Imperial Charisian Navy, these days—flew those.

"I see," Ahbaht said, after a moment. "And has he had an opportunity to
estimate her force?"

"We've not seen her ports yet, Sir, but she's carrying at least ten or twelve of
their short guns on her weather deck. Probably more. And," Mahrtynsyn added
almost apologetically, "Master Chaimbyrs says she doesn't look merchant-built
to him."

The tightening around the captain's eyes was more noticeable this time. If
Chaimbyrs' estimates were correct—and the second lieutenant was quite a

competent officer—then their pursuer wasn't simply an imperial warship, but one of the Charisian Navy's new, purpose-built galleons, whereas both of Wailahr's ships were converted merchant vessels.

"I see," Ahbaht repeated, nodding to his first officer. "Thank you, Master Mahrtynsyn."

Mahrtynsyn touched his chest in salute, then withdrew to the larboard side of the quarterdeck while Ahbaht clasped his hands behind his back and turned to the rail, gazing out across the crested waves in obvious thought.

The lieutenant didn't envy his captain at the moment. On the other hand, he didn't feel an enormous amount of sympathy, either. For the most part, he respected Ahbaht as a seaman, although for all his years of naval service, the captain had precious little experience with galleons. Virtually all of his previous time had been served aboard the Desnairian Navy's limited number of *galleys,* and his ship-handling skills, while adequate, weren't as good as Mahrtynsyn's own. In fact, that was one reason Mahrtynsyn had been assigned as his first lieutenant.

In terms of *military* experience, though, Ahbaht was far more qualified to command than Mahrtynsyn was, and the lieutenant knew it. Of course, no one in Desnairian service had any experience at all in broadside gunnery tactics, but at least Ahbaht had smelled powder smoke in actual combat, which was more than Mahrtynsyn had. Given that experience, Ahbaht had to be (or damned well *ought* to be, at any rate) even better aware of the looming confrontation's balance of combat power than Mahrtynsyn was.

Not to mention the minor fact that an officer with his experience should, perhaps, have been just a bit more careful about, spent a little more time thinking over, what he had recommended to Commodore Wailahr.

At first glance, Wailahr's two ships ought to have had the advantage. There *were* two of them, after all. But that wasn't all that was involved here—not by a long shot.

One of the Charisian Navy's new galleons would mount at least fifty guns (and probably more) to *Archangel Chihiro*'s forty. Worse, they'd be *heavier* guns. *Archangel Chihiro,* like her consort, *Blessed Warrior,* carried twenty-six lizards on her gundeck and fourteen falcons on her upper deck. That might seem to give her eighty percent of the Charisian's broadside, and all of their guns not only had the new trunnions and carriages but used the new bagged powder charges the Charisians had introduced, so they ought to be able to match the other ship's rate of fire, as well. So far, all well and good, Mahrtynsyn thought dryly. But the lizards' round shot weighed only a bit over twenty pounds each, and the falcons' weighed less than nine, while if the reports about the Charisians were correct, the other ship would mount long *thirty*-pounders on her gundeck and short thirty-pounders—what the Charisians called "carronades"—on her upper deck.

Which would give her over twice *Archangel Chihiro*'s weight of metal. In fact, she'd carry a heavier weight of broadside than both the Desnairian ships *combined* . . . in a much more heavily framed and planked hull. And that changed Ahbaht's earlier calculations significantly. Not only would each hit be far more destructive than he almost certainly had been expecting, but her heavier hull would take substantially less damage from each hit she received in return.

Of course, two lighter ships, if well handled, ought to be able to outmaneuver a single opponent, and it was extremely unlikely the Charisian carried a big enough crew to fully man both broadsides—especially if she had to reserve hands to manage her own sails. If they could get to grips with her from both sides simultaneously, they ought to be able to overpower her in fairly short order. But while the sail-handling skills of *Archangel Chihiro*'s crew had improved hugely since they'd left Desnair the City, Mahrtynsyn very strongly doubted they could even come close to an experienced *Charisian* crew's level of competence.

He felt fairly confident that, since the other ship had been cruising alone, with no one else in company with her, Ahbaht had assumed she was most likely a privateer, not a regular man-of-war. It would have been a reasonable enough assumption, in many ways, and had it proved accurate, she would have been far more lightly gunned, while the quality of her ship's company would have been much more problematical, as well. Besides, privateers weren't in the business of taking hard knocks if they could avoid it. If a privateer's skipper had realized he was pursuing two Desnairian *warships,* rather than a pair of fat merchant prizes, he would almost certainly have decided his time could be more profitably spent elsewhere. A Charisian Navy captain was likely to feel a bit differently about that.

*But just how does the Captain break the news to the Commodore?* Mahrtynsyn wondered a bit sardonically. *"Excuse me, Commodore, but it turns out that's a war galleon back there, instead. And I'm just a* bit *less confident about beating her than I was about beating a privateer."* The lieutenant snorted mentally. *Sure, I can just* hear *him saying* that!

No. Ahbaht wasn't going to risk pissing Wailahr off by turning cautious at this point. And since Wailahr lacked the seagoing experience to realize exactly how weight of metal and—especially—relative ship-handling skills really factored into a sea battle, it was unlikely he was going to recognize just how dicey this entire situation could turn. He certainly wasn't going to decide to try avoiding action at this point. Not without Ahbaht suggesting it, at any rate.

Which meant things were going to get just a bit *lively* in the next two hours or so.

▼     ▼     ▼

Sir Dunkyn Yairley gazed ahead at the towering canvas of the Desnairian ships and scratched his chin thoughtfully. As always, the prospect of battle created a hollow, unsettled feeling in his belly. None of his officers and men appeared to share his apprehension, and it was, of course, unthinkable for him to reveal it to them. He often wondered if he was truly fundamentally different from them in that regard, or if they were simply better at hiding their emotions than he was.

Not that it mattered at the moment.

"Well," he remarked out loud, permitting neither his voice nor his expression to hint at any internal trepidation, "at least they seem to have figured out we're not just some deaf, dumb, and blind merchant ship!"

The men manning the quarterdeck carronades heard him, as he'd intended, and grinned. Some of them nudged each other in amusement, and a couple actually chuckled. No sign *they* felt anything but confident anticipation!

Cheerful *idiots, aren't they?* Yairley thought, but there was as much affectionate amusement of his own as exasperation in the reflection.

He pushed the thought aside as he reconsidered his position.

He was confident he had an accurate appraisal of the other ships' armament, now, and he rather wished he'd been up against a few less guns. His own were heavier, and he had no doubt his gun crews were far more experienced, and almost certainly better drilled, into the bargain. But eighty guns were still eighty guns, and he had only fifty-four.

*I wonder if that's a galley commander over there?* he mused.

It could well make a difference, given the habits of thought involved. Galley captains thought in terms of head-on approaches—since their chase armament, which always mounted the heaviest guns, fired only directly ahead—and boarding tactics. And a galley captain would almost certainly be less skilled when it came to maneuvering a fundamentally clumsy thing like a square-rigged galleon. Besides, galleys had oars. Captains accustomed to being able to row directly into the wind tended to have a less lively appreciation for the value of the weather gauge.

Yairley stopped scratching his chin and clasped his hands behind him, his expression distant as he contemplated the narrowing stretch of water between *Destiny* and her adversaries. The Desnairians weren't quite in line. The wind had backed about five points—from south-southeast to east-southeast—during the long hours since the chase had begun, and the rearmost of the two ships was a good two hundred yards to leeward and astern of her consort as they sailed along on the starboard tack. Yairley wondered if that was intentional or simply sloppy stationkeeping. Or, for that matter, if it simply represented lack of experience on his opponents' part. The Desnairian Empire did still follow the tradition of putting army officers in charge of warships, after all.

*Let's not get too overconfident in that respect, Dunkyn,* he reminded himself. *Still, we can hope, can't we?*

Two hundred yards might not sound like an enormous distance to a lands-man, but Yairley was no landsman. To an artillerist accustomed to thinking in terms of land battles fought on nice, motionless pieces of dirt, two hundred yards would equate to easy canister range, where it would be difficult for any semi-competent gun crew to miss a target fifty-plus yards long, six or seven yards high, and the next best thing to ten yards wide. For a seaman, accustomed to the fact that his gun platform was likely to be moving in at least three differ-ent directions simultaneously, completely irrespective of his *target's* motion, a two-hundred-yard range was something else entirely.

*Like a perfectly good range to completely waste powder and shot at,* the captain thought dryly. *Which means those two fellows over there are out of effective support range of one another. Unless I'm obliging enough to sail directly* between *them, at any rate!*

He glanced up at his own sails, and decided.

"Master Lathyk."

"Yes, Sir?"

"Let's get the t'gallants off her, if you please."

"Aye, aye, Sir!" The first lieutenant touched his chest in salute, then raised his leather speaking trumpet. "Hands to reduce sail!" he bellowed through it, and feet thundered across the deck planking in response.

▼    ▼    ▼

Laizair Mahrtynsyn watched the Charisian through narrow eyes from his sta-tion on *Archangel Chihiro*'s quarterdeck. She was sweeping steadily closer, with her starboard battery run out while she angled towards *Archangel Chihiro*'s lar-board quarter, which didn't surprise Mahrtynsyn a great deal. It didn't *please* him, but it didn't surprise him, either. The one thing of which he was com-pletely confident was that Cayleb Ahrmahk wasn't in the habit of assigning his most powerful warships to people who didn't know what to do with them, and that Charisian captain over there obviously recognized the huge maneuver ad-vantage his possession of the weather gauge bestowed upon him. Because of his position to windward, the choice of when and how to initiate action lay completely in his hands, and he clearly understood exactly what to do with that advantage.

Mahrtynsyn only wished he was more confident that Captain Ahbaht un-derstood the same thing.

Whether Ahbaht understood that or not, it was already painfully evident to Mahrtynsyn that the Charisian galleon was being far more ably handled than his own ship. *Archangel Chihiro*'s sail drill had improved immeasurably during her lengthy voyage from Desnair. Despite that, however, the precision of the other ship's drill as she reduced canvas only underscored how far *Archangel Chi-hiro*'s own company still had to go. The Charisian's fore course was brailed up and her topgallants disappeared with mechanical precision, as if whisked away by the wave of a single wizard's magic wand. Two of her jibs disappeared, as well, as she reduced to fighting sail, yet even with her sail area drastically reduced, she continued to forge steadily closer.

Her speed had dropped with the reduction of sail, but that didn't make Mahrtynsyn a lot happier. *Archangel Chihiro* and *Blessed Warrior* had taken in their own courses in preparation for battle, and that had cost them even more speed than the Charisian had given up. She still had an advantage of close to two knots, and she was only eight hundred yards astern. In fifteen minutes, give or take, she'd be right alongside, and it was evident what her captain had in mind. He intended to keep to leeward of *Archangel Chihiro,* engaging her larboard broadside with his own starboard guns. With the shift in the wind, both ships were heeling harder now, so his shots might tend to go high, but it would allow him to engage the flagship in isolation, where *Blessed Warrior* would be unable to engage him closely. In a straight broadside duel, the heavier Charisian galleon would almost certainly overpower *Archangel Chihiro* in relatively short order.

*Still, if the Captain and the Commodore's plans work out, it won't be a straight broadside duel, now will it?*

No, it wouldn't. Unfortunately, Lieutenant Mahrtynsyn suspected that that Charisian captain over there might just have a few plans of his own.

▼    ▼    ▼

"All right, Master Lathyk," Sir Dunkyn Yairley said, "I think it's about time."

"Aye, Sir," the first lieutenant responded gravely, and beckoned to Hektor.

"Stand ready, Master Aplyn-Ahrmahk," he said, and Hektor nodded—under the rather special circumstances obtaining at the moment, he'd been specifically instructed *not* to salute in acknowledgment where anyone on the enemy ship might see it—and moved idly a bit closer to the hatch gratings at the center of *Destiny*'s spar deck. He glanced down through the latticework at the gundeck below. The long thirty-pounders were run out and waiting to starboard, and he smiled as he noted the gun crews' distribution.

It was not a particularly pleasant expression.

"Man tacks and braces!" he heard Lathyk shout behind him.

▼    ▼    ▼

Commodore Wailahr stood on *Archangel Chihiro*'s poop deck, gazing at the steadily approaching Charisian ship.

It was evident to him that Captain Ahbaht had been less than delighted to discover just how powerful their adversary actually was. Well, Wailahr hadn't been tempted to turn any celebratory cartwheels himself. And although all of the commodore's previous combat experience might have been solely on land, his ships had conducted enough gunnery drills for him to suspect their accuracy was going to prove dismal. To some extent, though, that should be true for both sides, and the fact that he had almost twice as many total guns ought to mean he'd score more total hits, as well.

Assuming he could bring all of them into action.

*So far, he's doing what Ahbaht predicted, Hairahm,* he reminded himself. *Now if he just goes on doing it. . . .*

At least before they'd separated to their present distance from one another, *Archangel Chihiro* and *Blessed Warrior* had been able to come close enough together for Wailahr and Ahbaht to confer with Captain Tohmys Mahntain, *Blessed Warrior*'s commanding officer, through their speaking trumpets. Mahntain was a good man—junior to Ahbaht, and a little younger, but also the more aggressive of the two. And he'd understood exactly what Ahbaht and Wailahr had in mind. The commodore was confident of that, and also that he could rely on Mahntain to carry through on his instructions.

More than that, it was evident Ahbaht's prediction that the enemy would attempt to engage just one of Wailahr's ships if the opportunity were offered had been accurate. By deliberately opening a gap between the two Desnairian galleons, he and Wailahr had offered up *Archangel Chihiro* as what had to be a tempting target. If the Charisian kept to larboard, closing in on *Archangel Chihiro*'s downwind side, she could range up alongside Wailahr's flagship and pound her with her superior number and weight of guns when none of *Blessed Warrior*'s guns could be brought to bear in the flagship's support.

But when the enemy ship took the offered advantage, Mahntain would execute the instructions he'd been given earlier. *Blessed Warrior* would immediately alter course, swinging from her heading of north-northwest to one of west by north or even west-southwest, taking the wind almost dead abeam. That course would carry her directly across the Charisian ship's bow, giving her the opportunity to rake the larger, heavier galleon from a position in which none of the Charisian's guns could bear upon her in reply.

As soon as he'd crossed the Charisian's course, Mahntain would come back onto his original heading . . . by which time (if all had gone according to plan) the Charisian and *Archangel Chihiro* would have overtaken *Blessed Warrior*. The bigger galleon would be trapped between Wailahr's two lighter vessels, where their superior number of guns ought to prove decisive.

*Of course, it's unlikely things* will *go exactly "according to plan,"* Wailahr reminded himself. *On the other hand, even if we don't pull it off exactly, we should still end up with the tactical advantage.*

The Charisian wouldn't be able to turn away to prevent *Blessed Warrior* from raking her from ahead without exposing her equally vulnerable—and even more fragile—stern to *Archangel Chihiro*'s broadside. She wouldn't have much choice but to remain broadside-to-broadside with the flagship. So unless

*Archangel Chihiro* took crippling damage to her rigging in the opening broadsides, or unless someone collided with someone else, the advantage should still go to the Desnairians.

*And a* collision *will work to our advantage, too,* Wailahr thought grimly. Good as the Imperial Charisian Marines were, Wailahr's crews would outnumber the Charisians by two-to-one. A collision that let him board the larger ship and settle things with cold steel wouldn't exactly be the worst outcome he could imagine.

▼      ▼      ▼

Captain Yairley watched the tip of *Destiny*'s jibboom edging steadily closer to the Desnairian galleon. He could read the other ship's name off her counter now—*Archangel Chihiro,* which didn't leave much doubt about who she'd actually been built to serve—and even without his spyglass, he could make out individual officers and men quite clearly.

*Archangel Chihiro,* despite her shorter, stubbier length, stood higher out of of the water than *Destiny*, which undoubtedly made her crankier and more leewardly. She also had less tumblehome (undoubtedly a legacy of her merchant origins), and her forecastle and aftercastle had both been cut down at least somewhat during her conversion. She'd retained enough height aft, however, for a complete poop deck, and in some ways, Yairley wished *Destiny* had possessed the same feature. *Destiny*'s helmsmen's quarterdeck position left them completely exposed—to musketry, as well as cannon fire—whereas *Archangel Chihiro*'s wheel was located under the poop deck, where it was both concealed and protected.

As if to punctuate Yairley's reflections, muskets began to fire from the other vessel. They were matchlocks, not flintlocks, which gave them an abysmally low rate of fire. They were also smoothbores, which wasn't going to do any great wonders for their accuracy, although pinpoint precision wasn't much of a factor firing from one moving ship at personnel on the deck of another moving ship. Whether or not any particular target was actually hit under those circumstances was largely a matter of chance, although it was just a bit difficult to remember that when a musket ball went humming past one's ear.

As one had just done, a corner of his mind observed.

Marine marksmen in the fore and maintops began returning fire, and if their rifled weapons weren't a lot more accurate under the conditions which obtained, the fact that they were armed with flintlocks, not matchlocks, at least gave them a substantially higher rate of fire. Someone screamed at one of the midship starboard carronades as one of those matchlocks did find a target, and Yairley saw a body pitch over the side of *Archangel Chihiro*'s mizzentop and smash down on the poop deck with bone-pulverizing force as one of his Marines returned the compliment.

*I think we're just about close enough, now,* he mused, and glanced at Lathyk.

"Now, Master Lathyk!" he said crisply, and the first lieutenant blew his whistle.

▼   ▼   ▼

Sir Hairahm Wailahr didn't even turn his head as the seaman's body crashed onto the poop deck behind him. The man had probably been dead even before he fell; he was almost certainly dead now, and it wouldn't have been the first corpse Wailahr had ever seen. He paid no more attention to it than he did to the splinters suddenly feathering the planking around his feet as three or four Charisian musket balls thudded into the deck. The other ship's marksmen had obviously recognized him as an officer, he noted, even if they didn't realize exactly how rich a prize he would make. Yet it was a distant observation, one which was not allowed to penetrate below the surface of his mind. The commodore was scarcely unaware of his own mortality, but he had other things to worry about as the tip of the Charisian's long, lance-like jibboom started to creep level with *Archangel Chihiro*'s taffrail.

*Langhorne, this is going to hurt!* he told himself. The Charisian was coming even closer than he'd anticipated. It looked as if the other galleon's captain intended to engage from a range of no more than thirty yards. At that range, not even Wailahr's relatively inexperienced gunners were likely to miss, and he grimaced as he considered the carnage which was about to be inflicted.

*But on both of us, my heretical friend,* he thought grimly. *On* both *of us.*

Another few minutes, and—

▼   ▼   ▼

"Larboard your helm!" Sir Dunkyn Yairley snapped. "Roundly, now!"

"Helm a-lee, aye, Sir!" Chief Waigan acknowledged, and he and his assistant spun the big double-wheel's spokes blurringly to larboard.

The motion of the wheel moved the ship's tiller to larboard, which kicked her rudder in the opposite direction. Which, in turn, caused the ship to turn abruptly to *starboard*.

▼   ▼   ▼

Wailahr's eyes widened as the Charisian suddenly altered course. It was the last thing he'd expected, especially since it sent her turning *away* from *Archangel Chihiro*—turning up to windward across his flagship's wake, and not ranging alongside to *leeward* as he'd expected. Her yards tracked around with metronome precision as her heading altered, continuing to drive her, yet she slowed drastically as her new course brought her up closer to the wind, and Wailahr's initial surprise began to turn into a frown of confusion as he found himself looking at the Charisian galleon's larboard gunports.

Her *closed* larboard gunports, since it was her *starboard* broadside she'd run out when she cleared for action.

▼    ▼    ▼

"Roundly, lads! *Roundly!*" Hektor shouted down through the hatch gratings.

The admonition probably wasn't necessary. The officers and men in charge of *Destiny*'s main armament had undoubtedly heard Lieutenant Lathyk's whistle almost as well as the carronade gunners on the spar deck weapons. Captain Yairley wasn't the sort to take chances on something like that, however. It was one of his fundamental principles that a competent officer did everything he could *before* the battle to minimize the chance of errors or misunderstandings. They were going to happen, anyway, once battle was fairly joined, but a *good* officer did his best to see to it there were as few as possible . . . and that they didn't happen any earlier than they had to.

And this particular evolution presented plenty of opportunity for things to go wrong.

As the ship rounded up to windward, the seamen who'd been ostentatiously manning the weather carronades (as any wall-eyed idiot on the other ship could plainly see) turned as one and charged, obedient to Lathyk's whistle, to the opposite side of the deck. The short, stubby carronades of the larboard battery, already loaded and primed, were run out quickly, in plenty of time, but the heavier gundeck weapons were both much more massive and far less handy.

The good news was that no one aboard *Archangel Chihiro* had been able to see *Destiny*'s gundeck. Captain Yairley had been able to send full gun crews to his larboard battery without giving away his intentions. Now the larboard gunports snapped open, gun captains shouted orders, and men grunted with explosive effort as they flung their weight onto side tackles. Gun trucks squealed like angry pigs as they rumbled across planking which had been sanded for better traction, and the long, wicked snouts of the new-model krakens thrust out of the suddenly open ports.

There wasn't much time to aim.

Fortunately, HMS *Destiny*'s gun captains had enjoyed plenty of practice.

▼    ▼    ▼

The world came apart in a deafening bellow of lightning-shot thunder.

Sir Hairahm Wailahr had never imagined anything like it. To be fair, no one who had never experienced it *could* have accurately imagined it. He stood on the tall, narrow poop deck of his flagship—a deck little more than forty feet long and barely twenty feet across at its widest point—and twenty-seven heavy cannon exploded in a long, unending drumroll, spitting fire and blinding, choking smoke as *Destiny* crossed *Archangel Chihiro*'s stern and her broadside came to bear from a range of perhaps fifty feet. The two ships were so close together that

*Destiny*'s jibboom had actually swung *across* her enemy's poop, barely clearing *Archangel Chihiro*'s mizzen shrouds, as she altered course almost all the way to northeast-by-east, and the concussive force of that many cannon, firing at that short a range, each gun loaded with a charge of grape on top of its round shot, was indescribable. He actually felt the heat of the exploding powder, felt vast, invisible fists of muzzle blast punching his entire body with huge bubbles of overpressure. Felt the fabric of his flagship bucking and jerking—slamming upward against his feet as if some maniac were pounding the soles of his shoes with a baseball bat—as the Charisian fire crashed into her. Planking splintered, the glass of *Archangel Chihiro*'s big stern windows simply disappeared, and the screams and high-pitched shrieks of men who'd been taken just as completely by surprise as Wailahr himself ripped at his ears even through the incredible thunder of *Destiny*'s guns.

Cleared for action, *Archangel Chihiro*'s gundeck was one vast cave, stretching from bow to stern. A cavern edged with guns, nosing out through the open ports, waiting for a target to appear before them. But the target wasn't there. It was *astern* of them, where the gunners crewing those guns couldn't even *see* it, far less fire back at it, and six-inch iron spheres came howling down that cavern's length like Shan-wei's own demons.

Half a dozen of the galleon's lizards took direct hits, their carriages disintegrating into clouds of additional splinters, the heavy bronze gun tubes leaping upward, then crashing back down to crush and mangle the survivors of their crews. Human beings caught in the path of one of those round shot were torn in half with casual, appalling ease. Splinters of the ship's fabric—some of them as much as six feet long and three or four inches in diameter—slammed into fragile flesh and blood like spears hurled by some enraged titan. Men shrieked as they clutched at torn and riven bodies, and other men simply flew backwards, heads or chests or shoulders destroyed in explosions of gore as grapeshot—each almost three inches in diameter—smashed into them.

That single broadside killed or wounded almost half of *Archangel Chihiro*'s crew.

▼    ▼    ▼

"Bring her back off the wind, Waigan!"

The captain had to raise his voice to be heard, yet it seemed preposterously calm, almost thoughtful, to Chief Waigan.

"Aye, aye, Sir!" the petty officer replied sharply, and the wheel went over in the opposite direction as *Destiny*'s rudder was reversed.

The galleon didn't like it, but she answered like the lady she was. Her hull heaved awkwardly as she swung back to the west, across the waves, but Yairley had timed the maneuver almost perfectly, and the wind helped push her back around.

*Destiny* came back before the wind, then swept even farther to larboard, taking the wind on her larboard quarter instead of her starboard beam, and her topsail yards swung with machine-like precision as they were trimmed back around.

She'd lost a great deal of her speed through the water, and *Archangel Chihiro*'s motion had continued to carry her away from Yairley's ship, along her earlier course. But there was far too much confusion aboard the Desnairian ship for Captain Ahbaht—or, rather, Lieutenant Mahrtynsyn, since Ruhsail Ahbaht had encountered one of *Destiny*'s round shot—to even consider altering heading. Her officers were still fighting to reestablish control after the incredible carnage of that first broadside when *Destiny* swept across *Archangel Chihiro*'s stern yet again, this time from northeast to southwest, rather than southwest to northeast.

There hadn't been time for her gun crews to reload, but they didn't have to. The starboard guns had been loaded before they were run out, and even with so many hands detailed to man the braces, the starboard battery's officers had been left more than enough crewmen to fire the already loaded weapons. The range was much greater—well over a hundred yards this time. Closer to a hundred and fifty, actually. But not *enough* closer to a hundred and fifty.

▼    ▼    ▼

"Clear away that wreckage! Get it over the side—*now!*" Sir Hairahm Wailahr shouted.

A commodore had no business allowing himself to be distracted from his responsibilities as a flag officer. Wailahr might not be a sailor, but he knew that much. Unfortunately, there was damn-all else he could do at the moment, and he actually grabbed one end of the broken length of gangway which had fallen across the upper-deck guns himself. He heaved, grunting with effort, fighting to clear away the wreckage blocking the guns, then wheeled back around, his head coming up, his eyes darting to the wind-shredded smoke astern of his flagship, as HMS *Destiny* fired her second broadside.

The next best thing to thirty more heavy round shot came screaming at him. The range was much greater this time, and, unlike the last broadside, many of these shot missed *Archangel Chihiro* entirely. But some of them didn't, and one of those which didn't crashed into the mizzenmast, cutting it cleanly in two eight feet above the deck. It toppled forward, smashing into the mainmast with all its own weight added to the driving pressure of the wind, and the mainmast went with it. *Archangel Chihiro* shuddered like a mortally wounded prong lizard, then heaved as a torrent of shattered spars and shredded canvas came crashing down across her decks or plunged into the sea alongside. She surged wildly, rounding to the sudden sea anchor of her own rigging, and fresh screams echoed as still more of her crew were crushed under the falling spars or torn apart by the Charisian fire.

Wailahr staggered clear of the broken mizzen, right hand clutching his left arm. That arm was almost as badly broken as his flagship, a corner of his brain reflected—not that it mattered a great deal at the moment.

He watched, his eyes bitter with understanding, as the Charisian galleon altered course yet again. She swung back, coming fully back before the wind, her spars once more tracking around as if controlled by a single hand. She leaned to the wind, driving hard as she accelerated once more, and he saw the topgallants blossoming above her topsails. They fell like curtains, then hardened as sheets and tacks were tended, and *Destiny* came storming past *Archangel Chihiro*.

Wailahr turned, looking for *Blessed Warrior*.

He knew Captain Mahntain must have been taken at least as much aback by the Charisians' unexpected maneuvers as Ahbaht and he himself had been. *Blessed Warrior* had altered course almost automatically when *Destiny* opened fire, swinging around onto a westerly heading as originally arranged. Unfortunately, that was the only part of Wailahr's original arrangements which had worked as planned. Worse, neither *Destiny* nor *Archangel Chihiro* were where he'd expected them to be when he planned his original tactics. Now *Blessed Warrior* was well to the southwest of her original track . . . and *Destiny*, edging around to north by northwest, was already heading to pass *astern* of her—and with the advantage of the weather guage, as well—rather than finding herself broadside-to-broadside with both of her opponents at once.

The Charisian galleon's starboard broadside flamed and thundered yet again as she swept past *Archangel Chihiro,* heading for her second victim. The foremast, already weakened by the loss of the stays which had once led aft to the vanished mainmast, pitched over the side, leaving *Archangel Chihiro* completely dismasted. The ship rolled madly, drunkenly, corkscrewing indescribably as the sudden loss of all her tophamper destroyed any vestige of stability, only to snub savagely as she brought up short against the wreckage still anchored to her side by the broken shrouds. Lieutenant Mahrtynsyn was still on his feet, somehow, shouting commands, driving parties of his surviving seamen to clear away the wreckage. Axes flashed and thudded, chopping through tangled cordage, fighting to free the ship even while other sailors and Marines dragged sobbing, screaming, or silently writhing wounded out of the debris.

*Destiny*'s passing broadside added still more torn and broken bodies to her cruel toll, but it was obvious *Archangel Chihiro* had become little more than an afterthought to the Charisian vessel. Wailahr's flagship was a broken ruin, so badly mangled, with so many of her people dead or wounded, that she could be gathered in anytime *Destiny* got around to it. The enemy had more important concerns at the moment, and Hairahm Wailahr's jaw clenched with something far worse than the pain of his broken arm.

He knew Tohmys Mahntain. If there was a single ounce of quitter in Mahntain's entire body, Wailahr had never seen even a hint of it, and *Blessed*

*Warrior* was already altering course. Her sail drill lacked *Destiny*'s polished precision, and the ship wallowed around to her new heading unhappily, sails flapping and thundering in protest. Her maneuver managed to turn her stern away from her enemy before *Destiny* could rake her as she had *Archangel Chihiro,* and her starboard guns ran out defiantly. Yet gallant and determined as Mahntain undoubtedly was, the awkwardness with which his ship came onto her new heading only emphasized how little comparison there was between the skill level of his crew and that of the Charisian galleon slicing towards him. He wasn't simply outgunned and outweighed; he was out*classed,* and a part of Sir Hairahm Wailahr wished he still had an intact mast and signal halyards. Wished he could order Mahntain to break off the action and run for it.

*Or surrender,* he admitted to himself with bleak, terrible honesty as he watched Sir Dunkyn Yairley's ship stoop upon her fresh prey like a hunting wyvern. *He* can't *break off—can't outrun her or avoid her. And since he can't—*

Fresh thunder rolled across the icy afternoon sea as the Charisian galleon, as merciless as the kraken emblem of the Ahrmahks flying from its mizzen yard, opened fire yet again.

.VII.

## Archbishop's Palace,
## City of Tairys,
## Province of Glacierheart,
## Republic of Siddarmark

It was the coldest winter Zhasyn Cahnyr could remember . . . in more than one way.

Cahnyr was a lean man, and God had wasted very little fat when He designed him. As a result, he usually felt the cold more badly than many others did, and he'd always thought his assignment to the Archbishopric of Glacierheart, in the mountains of Siddarmark, was evidence that God and the Archangels had a sense of humor.

Of late, that humor had seemed somewhat harder to find.

He stood gazing out of his office window on the second floor of his palace in the city of Tairys. It wasn't much of a palace as the great lords of Mother Church usually reckoned such things. For that matter, Tairys, despite its unquestioned status as Glacierheart Province's largest city, was actually little more than a largish town by the standards of wealthier, more populous provinces.

The people of Cahnyr's archbishopric tended to be poor, hardworking, and devout. Most of the limited wealth Glacierheart could boast came from the province's mines—which, unfortunately, produced not gold, silver, sapphires, or rubies, but simply coal. Cahnyr had nothing against coal. In fact, in his opinion, it had far greater intrinsic value than any of those more pricey baubles, and Glacierheart's coal was good, clean-burning anthracite. It was an . . . honest sort of product. The sort which could be set to purposes of which he was fairly confident God approved. One that provided homes with desperately needed warmth in the midst of winter ice and snow. One that at least a few foundry owners here in Siddarmark were beginning to experiment with, turning it into coke in emulation of the current Charisian practice.

Yet there were times when the archbishop could have wished for something a bit gaudier, a bit more in keeping with the vain desires of the world. One that would have provided his hardworking, industrious parishioners with a greater return. And one which did not, despite all the Order of Pasquale could do, send all too many of those parishioners to early graves with black lung.

Cahnyr's mouth twitched at the familiar thought, and he shook his head.

*Of course you wish that, Zhasyn,* he scolded himself, although the scold was on the mild side, its hard edges worn down by frequent repetition. *Any priest worth his cap and scepter wants his people to live longer, healthier, richer lives! But be grateful God at least gave them coal to mine and a way to get it to market.*

That thought drew his eyes to the Tairys Canal, frozen hard now, which connected the city to the Graywater River. The Graywater was navigable—for barge traffic, at least—for most of its four-hundred-mile length, although there were several spots where locks had been required. It linked Ice Lake, northwest of Tairys, with Glacierborn Lake, two hundred miles to the southwest. From there, the mighty Siddar River ran sixteen hundred miles, snaking through the final mountains of Glacierheart, then through the foothills of Shiloh Province, and into Old Province to the capital city of Siddar itself. Which meant barges of Glacierheart coal could be floated down the rivers all the way to Siddar, where it could be loaded aboard coasters and blue-water galleons for destinations all over the world.

Most of it was used right here in the Republic, either dropped off at one of the river ports as it passed, or carried clear to Siddar City before it was sold. Of the portion that wasn't disposed of in any of those places, the majority was shipped up the East Haven coast as far as Hsing-wu's Passage, then west, through the passage, to serve the insatiable winter appetite of the city of Zion. The fact that it could be sent by water the entire way made its delivery price competitive with overland sources, even when those sources were much closer to hand and even in far off Zion, and its quality made it highly prized by discerning customers. Most of its purchase price got soaked up by the merchants, shippers, and factors through whose hands it passed, of course. Very little of the final selling price found its way into the hands—the gnarled, callused, broken-nailed, coal-dust-ingrained hands—which had actually wrested it from the bowels of Glacierheart's mountains. But it was enough, if only barely, and the people of Cahnyr's archbishopric were grateful to get it. They were a provincial people, with only the most imperfect knowledge of the world beyond the craggy, snow-topped palisades of their mountain horizons, yet they knew they were better off than many other people on Safehold.

That was one of the things Cahnyr loved about them. Oh, he loved their piety, as well. Loved the pure joy in God which he heard in their choirs, saw in their faces. But as much as he loved those things, as much as he *treasured* them, it was their sturdy independence, their stubborn self-reliance, that truly resonated somewhere deep inside him. They had a sense of self-sufficient *integrity*. Always quick to help a neighbor, always generous even when their own purses were sadly pinched, there was something in them that demanded they stand upon their own two feet. They knew what it meant to earn their own livelihoods by the sweat of their brows, by backbreaking labor in the deep and dangerous mines. They entered the labor force early, and they left it late, and along the way, they learned to value themselves. To recognize that they had given good value and more for those livelihoods. That they had managed to put food on their families' tables. That they had met their obligations, and that they were beholden to no one but themselves.

*Clyntahn and Trynair and Rayno have never understood why I love these people so,* the archbishop thought now, his eyes sweeping the mist-shrouded, snow-covered mountains. *Their ideal is what Rayno gets in Harchong—serfs, beaten-down people who "know their place."* Cahnyr's face hardened. *They like knowing their "flocks" aren't going to get uppity. Aren't going to argue with their secular and temporal masters. Aren't going to start thinking for themselves, wondering why it is that Mother Church is so incredibly wealthy and powerful while her children starve. Aren't going to start demanding the princes of Mother Church remember that they serve God . . . and not the other way around.*

Cahnyr knew the vast majority of his fellow prelates had never understood why he insisted on making two lengthy pastoral visits to his archbishopric every year, instead of the one grudging flying visit per year most of them made. The fact that he voluntarily spent the winter in Glacierheart, away from the amenities of the Temple, the diversions of Zion, the political maneuvering and alliance building which were so central to the vicarate's existence, had always amused them. Oh, one or two of them realized how he'd come to love the spectacular beauty, the cragginess of towering mountains, snowcaps, and dense evergreen forests. Waterfalls that tumbled for hundreds of feet through lacy banners of spray. The deep, icy cold lakes fed by the high mountain glaciers from which the province took its name. A few others—mostly men he'd known in seminary, when he'd been far younger—knew of his long-standing interest in geology, the way he'd always loved studying God's handiwork in the bones of the world, his pleasure in spelunking, and the hushed cathedral stillness he'd found in deep caverns and caves.

Yet even the ones who knew about those sides of his nature, who could dimly grasp what a man like him might see in an archbishopric like his, still found his preference for Glacierheart and his lengthy visits to its uncouth, country-bumpkin inhabitants difficult to understand. It was so eccentric. So . . . quaint. They'd never understood the way he drew strength and sustenance from the faith which burned so brightly here in Glacierheart.

Nor had they ever understood that the people of Glacierheart—nobles (such as they were and what there were of them) and commoners alike—knew he genuinely cared about them. Those other archbishops, and those vicars, didn't worry about such minor matters. Even the best of them, far too often, considered that they'd done their jobs and more by keeping tithes within survivable bounds, seeing to it that enough other priests were sent to their archbishoprics to keep their churches and their priories filled, making certain their bishop executors weren't skimming too much off their parishioners. They were no longer village priests; God had called them to greater and more important duties in the administration of His Church, and there were plenty of other priests who could supply the pastoral care they no longer had time to give.

*Which is precisely how this entire business in Charis managed to take all of them so completely by surprise,* Cahnyr thought grimly. He shook his head, eyes hard on the horizon—harder than the ice and snow upon which they gazed. *The idiots. The fools! They sneer at efforts to reform Mother Church because she's working just fine . . . for them. For their families. For their power, and for their purses. And if she's working for them, then, obviously, she must be working for everyone else. Or for everyone else who matters, at least. Because they're right. They aren't priests anymore . . . and they don't even realize what an abomination in God's eyes a bishop or a vicar becomes when he forgets that first, last, and always, he's a pastor, a shepherd, a protector and teacher. When he gives up his priesthood in the name of power.*

He made himself step back from the anger. Made himself draw a deep breath, then gave himself a shake and turned away from the window. He crossed to the fireplace, opened the screen, and used the tongs to position a couple of fresh lumps of coal on the grate. He listened to the sudden, fierce crackling sound as the flame explored the surfaces of the new fuel and stood warming his hands for a few moments. Then he replaced the screen, walked back to his desk, and seated himself behind it.

He knew the real reason his anger against the corrupters of Mother Church turned so easily into a white-hot fury these days, crackling and roaring up like the flames on his grate. And he knew his anger was no longer the simple product of outrage. No, it was rather more pointed and much more . . . personal now.

He closed his eyes, traced the sign of the scepter across his chest, and murmured yet another brief, heartfelt prayer for his friends in Zion. For the other members of the Circle who he'd been forced to leave behind.

He wondered if Samyl Wylsynn had discovered the traitor's identity. Had he uncovered the deadly weakness in the walls of the Circle's fortress? Or was he still guessing? Still forced to keep his knowledge to himself lest Clyntahn realize he knew what was coming and strike even more quickly and more ruthlessly?

*I shouldn't say it, Lord,* the archbishop thought, *but thank You for sparing me Samyl's burden. I ask You to be with him and protect him, and all of my brothers. If they can be saved, then I ask You to save them, because I love them, and because they are such good men and love You so dearly. Yet You are the Master Builder of all this world. You alone know the true plan of Your work. And so, in the end, what I ask most is that You will strengthen me in the days to come and help me to be obedient to whatever plan You have.*

He opened his eyes again, and leaned back in his chair. That chair was the one true luxury Cahnyr had permitted himself—the one extravagance. Although, to be fair, it would have been more accurate to say it was the one true extravagance he had allowed himself to *accept.* Eight years earlier, when Gharth Gorjah, his longtime personal secretary, had told him the people of the archbishopric wanted to buy him a special Midwinter gift and asked him for suggestions, Cahnyr had commented that he needed a new chair for his office because the old one (which was probably at least a year or two older than Father Gharth) was finally wearing out. Father Gharth had nodded and gone away, and the archbishop hadn't thought very much about it. Not until he arrived for his regular winter pastoral visit—the long one, when he always spent at least two months here in Glacierheart—and found the chair waiting for him.

His parishioners had ordered it from Siddar City itself. It had cost—easily—the equivalent of a year's income for a family of six, and it had been worth every mark of its exorbitant price. Cahnyr had discovered only later that Fraidmyn Tohmys, his valet, had provided his exact measurements so that the craftsman who had built that chair could fit it exactly to him. It was in many ways an austere design, without the bullion-embroidered upholstery and gem-set carvings others might have demanded, but that suited Cahnyr's personality and tastes perfectly. And if no money had been wasted on ostentatious decoration, it was the most sinfully comfortable chair in which Zhasyn Cahnyr had ever sat.

At the moment, however, its comfort offered precious little comfort.

His lips twitched sourly as he realized what he'd just thought, but that didn't make his current situation any more amusing, and the brief flash of humor faded quickly.

He'd been deeply touched when Wylsynn told him about his suspicions, about his growing certainty that the Circle had been compromised, betrayed to Clyntahn and the Inquisition. The fact that Samyl had trusted him enough to tell him, had known *he* wasn't the traitor, had filled him with an odd sort of joy even as the terror of that treachery's consequences flooded through him. And Samyl had been as blunt and forthright as ever.

"One reason I'm telling you, Zhasyn," he'd said, "is that unlike any of the rest of us, you have the perfect reason to leave Zion in the middle of winter. Everyone knows about your 'eccentricities,' so no one—not even Clyntahn—will think it's out of character for you to return to Glacierheart as usual. I'm going to do what I can to get as many as possible of our other archbishops and bishops out of harm's way, but if we've been as thoroughly betrayed as I think we have, all of us are going to be marked for the Inquisition. That includes you."

Wylsynn had looked into his eyes, then reached out and rested one hand on each of Cahnyr's shoulders.

"You got Erayk Dynnys' final letters out of his cell, Zhasyn. And we got them to his wife—his widow—in Charis. This isn't going to be that simple. This time they know about us. But I don't think they're likely to make an open move against us for at least another month or two. So you'll have some time once you get to Glacierheart. *Use* it, Zhasyn." The hands on his shoulders had shaken him with powerful, gentle emphasis. "Use it. Make your plans, however you can, and then disappear."

Cahnyr had opened his mouth to protest, only to find Wylsynn shaking him again.

"You couldn't accomplish anything here even if you stayed," the vicar had told him. "All you could do would be to die right along with the rest of us. I know you're prepared to do that, Zhasyn, but I think God has more in mind for you yet than martyrdom. Much though I hate to admit it, I've come to the conclusion that the 'Church of Charis' has become our only true hope. Well, not *ours,* so much, since I don't see much Staynair or Cayleb could do to save the Circle even if they knew about our predicament. But our only hope for what we set out to accomplish in the first place. The rot's gone too deep here in the Temple. Clyntahn and Trynair—but especially Clyntahn—are too corrupt. They're actively committed to maintaining the very evils that are turning Mother Church into an abomination, and if *we* ever truly had any hope of stopping them, we've lost it now. We've run out of time. So the only hope I see is that the Charisians will succeed in challenging them. That the example of Charis from without will force reform from within. What that ultimately means for the universality of Mother Church is more than I can say, yet I've come to the conclusion that it's more important she be *God's* Church, be she broken into however many pieces, than that she remain one unbroken entity enslaved to the power of the Dark."

Cahnyr had seen the pain in Wylsynn's eyes, recognized the bitterness of that admission. And in that recognition, he'd realized Wylsynn had come to speak for him, as well. His very soul quailed from the thought of schism, the nightmare of the religious strife—the enormous scope for doctrinal error—that must sweep over the world if Mother Church dissolved into competing sects. And yet even that was preferable to watching God's Church slide deeper and deeper into corruption, for that was the worst and darkest "doctrinal error" of which Zhasyn Cahnyr could possibly conceive.

Yet even though he'd found himself in unwilling agreement with Wylsynn's analysis, and even though he'd shared every bit of Wylsynn's urgency, he'd had no idea how he might contrive to escape the Inquisition in the end. True, he'd probably have at least a slightly better chance from Glacierheart than he would in the Temple itself, but that wasn't saying a great deal.

He was positive Father Bryahn Teagmahn, the Glacierheart intendant, was at least generally aware of Clyntahn's suspicions. The intendant, like all intendants, had been assigned to Glacierheart by the Office of the Inquisition, and, also like all intendants, he was a member of the Order of Schueler. He was also a cold, harsh-minded disciplinarian. Cahnyr had tried to get him replaced several times, and each time his request had been denied. That was unusual, to say the least, and bespoke an interest at a very high level within the Inquisition in keeping Teagmahn here, all of which meant there was no question in Cahnyr's mind where "his" intendant's loyalties lay. Yet, sad to say, Teagmahn wasn't exactly the most deft agent Clyntahn could possibly have selected. Perhaps the Grand Inquisitor had felt sufficient dedication would substitute for a certain lack of subtleness? Or had he decided that only a moderate degree of competence would be required to keep an eye on an obviously addled "eccentric" like Cahnyr? Whatever the logic, Teagmahn had been doing a very poor job of late of disguising the suspicion with which he regarded his nominal superior. He was ever so much more attentive than he'd normally been, constantly calling upon the archbishop, checking with him, making certain he had no unexpected needs or tasks for his loyal intendant. As ways of keeping an eye on someone went, it was about as subtle as throwing a cobblestone through a window. Which, unfortunately, made it no less effective.

Worse, that very brute-force technique told Cahnyr a great deal. It told him Clyntahn was confident he had the archbishop under his thumb, ready to be snapped up whenever the moment came. Which meant Teagmahn would be alert for any arrangements Cahnyr might make, and Tairys was a small enough city that it wouldn't be difficult for the intendant and the Inquisition to monitor his actions. He'd had absolutely no idea what he was going to do after he reached his archbishopric, not even the first faint glimmering of a plan.

Which was one reason he'd been astonished when he arrived here and discovered that, apparently, he wasn't the only one who'd been thinking about that.

Now he reached into the inner pocket of his cassock and withdrew the letter once more.

He didn't know who'd sent it, and he didn't recognize the handwriting. He supposed it was entirely possible it had been sent to him on Clyntahn's orders as a means of provoking him into a false move to help justify his own arrest when the time came, but it seemed unlikely. The degree of subtleness such a strategy implied went far beyond anything Clyntahn or the Inquisition had ever before wasted on him.

Besides, there was no need for the Grand Inquisitor to manufacture or provoke some sort of self-incriminating action on Cahnyr's part. He had the authority to order Cahnyr's arrest whenever he chose to, and he could always count upon the skill and energy of his Inquisitors to produce whatever "evidence" he might feel he required. Given that, and given the contempt with which he so obviously regarded Cahnyr, setting some sort of complex, subtle trap would have been totally out of character.

Which left the perplexing question of exactly who *else* might have sent the letter.

He was positive it wasn't from Wylsynn. First, because the letter had beaten him here. If Wylsynn had wanted to communicate its contents to him, he could simply have spoken to him face-to-face, directly, without the letter's protective obliqueness, before he ever left Zion. Second, if Wylsynn had actually sent it after Cahnyr left Zion for some reason, he would have sent it in cipher, and he wouldn't have spent so much time speaking in what amounted to riddles.

Now Cahnyr unfolded it, and his eyes narrowed as he reread the single page yet again.

"I realize you have reason for anxiety at this time, Your Eminence, and I understand from a mutual friend why that is. I realize also that you have no idea who I am, and I wouldn't blame you for simply burning this letter immediately. In fact, burning it might well be your best choice, although I would like to think you'll read it in full first. But our mutual friend has shared his concerns with me. I believe he's been willing to do so because I have never been a member of his inner circle, one might say. Nonetheless, I am aware of your hopes and aspirations . . . and of your current difficulties. It is possible I may be able to be of some assistance with those difficulties.

"I have taken the liberty of suggesting a few alternatives. The degree to which any one of these may be applicable will, of course, depend on many factors which I cannot possibly properly evaluate at this time from so far away. And the fact that I'm unable to give you a return address will make it impossible for you to inform me as to which, if any, of my suggested alternatives strike you as most workable.

"Because of that, I have also taken the liberty of making a few definite arrangements. The critical point, Your Eminence, is that any successful travel plans on your part will require you to be in one of three locations within a specific window of time. If you can contrive to reach one of those locations at the appropriate time, I believe you'll find a friendly face waiting for you. Precisely how things might proceed beyond that point is more than I dare commit to writing at this time. We can only trust in God for that. Some might say that seems a futile trust, given the darkness you—and we all—face, I suppose. Yet despite that present Darkness, there is always a far greater Light waiting to receive us. With that in our hearts, how can we not risk a little loss in this world if that should be the price of setting our hands to the work we know God has prepared for us?"

There was no second or third page to the letter. Or, rather, there was *no longer* any second or third page. Cahnyr had taken his mysterious correspondent's advice to heart in that much, at least. But he'd kept the first page. It was his talisman. More than that, it was the physical avatar of hope. Of *hope,* that most fragile and most wonderful of commodities. If the author of that letter had written truly—and despite a conscientious effort to remain skeptical, Cahnyr believed he had—then there were people in God's world still willing to act as they believed He wanted them to. Still willing to set their hands to that task, even knowing all Clyntahn and the twisted power of the Inquisition might do to them.

That was why he'd kept that single sheet of paper written in an unknown hand, and why he carried it in the pocket of his cassock, close against his heart. Because it reminded him, restored his hope, that Light was mightier than the Dark. And the reason Light was mightier was that it resided in the human heart, and the human soul, and the human willingness to risk *everything* to do what was right.

*And as long as even a flicker of that willingness burns in a single heart, illuminates a single soul, the Dark cannot win,* Zhasyn Cahnyr thought as he refolded that single priceless sheet and placed it almost reverently back in the pocket next to his heart once more.

# FEBRUARY,
# YEAR OF GOD 894

D amnation!"
Daivyn Bairaht, the Duke of Kholman and Emperor Mahrys IV's
senior councilor for the Imperial Desnairian Navy, balled the sheet of paper
into a crushed wad and hurled it at the trashcan. The improvised projectile's
aerodynamic qualities left a great deal to be desired, and it landed on his office
carpet, bounced twice, and sailed under a bookcase.

"Shit," the duke muttered in disgust, then slumped back in the chair behind his desk and glowered at the man sitting in the chair facing it.

His guest—Sir Urwyn Hahltar, Baron Jahras—was a short, compactly built
man, brown hair going salt-and-pepper gray at the temples. A study in physical
contrast with the taller, silver-haired Kholman, he had a full beard, rather than
the duke's neatly groomed mustache. He was also more than ten years younger,
with a much more weathered-looking complexion.

And, not to his particular comfort at the moment, he was Admiral General
of the Imperial Desnairian Navy. It was a magnificent-sounding title. Unfortunately, it was also an office with which no Desnairian had any previous experience, since there'd never before been any need for it. The Desnairian Navy had
never been particularly "Imperial" before the recent unpleasantness between
the Kingdom of Charis and the Knights of the Temple Lands. In fact, it had
never boasted more than forty ships at its largest. Worse, that somewhat less
than towering level of power had been attained almost seventy years before; the
Navy's strength as of the Battle of Darcos Sound had been only *twelve* ships,
and all of them had been purchased somewhere else, rather than built in any
Desnairian shipyard. Despite the magnificent harbors of the Gulf of Jahras,
Desnair had never been a maritime power—especially over the past century
and a half or so of its competition with the equally land-oriented Republic of
Siddarmark.

Baron Jahras, however, was something of an oddity for a Desnairian noble.
He'd served—adequately, if not outstandingly—in the Imperial Army, as any
senior aristocrat was expected to do, but his family had been far more active in
trade than most well-born Desnairians. In fact, they'd been even more active
than they'd been prepared to admit to most of their noble relatives and peers.
Jahras, in fact, had controlled the largest merchant house in the entire Desnairian

Empire, and (however disreputable it might have been for a proper nobleman) that merchant house had owned a fleet of no less than thirty-one trading galleons.

Which was how he had come to find himself tapped to command Emperor Mahrys' newborn navy.

*Of course,* he thought now from behind a carefully expressionless face, *it would help if I'd ever commanded a naval warship before I found myself commanding the entire damned Navy! Or, for that matter, if there were a single Desnairian who had a clue how to organize a navy.*

"His Majesty isn't going to be happy about this, Urwyn," Kholman said finally, in a calmer tone. And, Jahras reflected, with monumental understatement.

"I know," the baron said out loud. Despite the vast gulf between their titles, Jahras, even though a mere baron, was very nearly as wealthy as Kholman. He was also married to Kholman's first cousin, a combination which, thankfully, made it possible for him to speak frankly, which he now proceeded to do.

"On the other hand," he continued, "I can hardly say I'm surprised." He shrugged. "Wailahr was a good man, but he didn't have any more experience commanding a galleon than any of the rest of our senior officers."

Kholman snorted. He couldn't disagree with that particular statement, although he could have added that none of their senior officers had any particular experience commanding *galleys,* either. Which, given the apparent differences between galleys and galleons, might not necessarily be a bad thing. He only wished that he, as the imperial councilor directly charged with building and running the emperor's new navy, had some idea of exactly what those differences were.

"That may be true," the duke said now. "But when His Majesty gets his copy of *that*"—he jabbed an index finger in the direction of the vanished ball of paper—"he's going to hit the roof, and you know it. Worse, Bishop Executor Mhartyn's going to do the same thing."

"I do know it," Jahras agreed, "but, frankly, they should have seen this—or something like it—coming when they decided to send the tithe by sea." He shrugged unhappily. "I've had enough experience with what happened to my own merchant galleons to know what Charisian privateers and naval cruisers can do."

"But according to that," Kholman's finger stabbed the air again, "*one* of their galleons just beat the shit out of *two* of ours. And ours were under the command of what you yourself just described as 'a good man.' In fact, one of our *better* men."

"It's what I've been trying to explain from the beginning, Daivyn," Jahras said. "Sea battles aren't like land battles, and we just aren't trained for them. By the time a Desnairian nobleman's eighteen, he has at least some notion about how to lead a cavalry charge, and the Army has a well-developed organization with at least some experience in how to supply cavalry and infantry in the field. We know how long it's going to take to get from Point A to Point B, how many miles we can expect an army to advance over what sort of roads and in what kind of weather, how many horseshoes and nails we're going to need, what kind of wagons, how many farriers and blacksmiths. We can make plans based on all of that. But how many casks of powder does a galleon need? How much spare cordage and canvas and spars? For that matter, how long will it take a galleon to sail from Geyra to Iythria? Well, that depends. It depends on how fast it is, how skilled its captain is, what the weather's like—all sorts of things none of His Majesty's officers really have any experience at all with."

The baron shrugged again—not nonchalantly, but with a certain helplessness.

"When we think about taking Charis on at sea, we're talking about fighting someone else's kind of war," he said. "I'd love the chance to face them on land, no matter what kind of ridiculous stories we're hearing out of Corisande. But at sea, there's no way we can match their experience and training any more than they could match *ours* in a cavalry melee. Until we've had a chance to *build up* some experience, it's going to stay that way, too."

Kholman managed not to swear again, although it wasn't easy. On the other hand, one of the good things about Jahras (aside from the fact that he was family) was that he was willing to speak his mind plainly, at least to Kholman. And he had a point. To be honest, the duke had never been overly impressed with his cousin-in-law's military prowess, but Jahras had one of the Desnairian Empire's better brains when it came to managing anything which had to do with trade, shipping, or manufactories. Well, one of the better *aristocratic* brains when it came to dealing with such matters, but that was pretty much the same thing. It was, after all, unthinkable that anyone who *wasn't* an aristocrat should be given the sort of authority the Admiral General of the Navy required.

It was a testimonial to Kholman's inherent mental flexibility that he was even vaguely aware that there might have been a non-aristocrat somewhere in Desnair with more expertise in those matters than he or Jahras possessed. The very notion would never have occurred to the vast majority of his fellow nobles, and it never occurred even to Kholman that anyone except a nobleman should hold his or Jahras' current offices. The sheer absurdity of such an idea would have been sufficient to keep it from crossing his brain in the first place. And if someone else had suggested it, he would have rejected it immediately, since it would have been impossible for that theoretical common-born officer to exercise any effective authority over "subordinates" so much better born than he was.

But the fact that Jahras had what was probably the best brain available when it came to the problems involved in building a navy from scratch didn't necessarily mean he was really up to the task. For that matter, in Kholman's estimation, the Archangel Langhorne might not have been up to *this* task!

"I don't disagree with anything you've just said, Urwyn," the duke said after a moment. "Langhorne knows we've discussed it often enough, at any rate. And it's not anything we haven't warned His Majesty and the Bishop Executor about, either. But that's still not going to solve our problem when the Emperor and Bishop Executor Mhartyn hear about this."

Jahras nodded. The good news was that Emperor Mahrys and the bishop executor were in Geyra, thirteen hundred miles from Kholman's Iythria office. There were times when that physical distance between Kholman's headquarters and the imperial court worked against them, especially given the nasty infighting which so often marked Desnairian politics. Rivals had much easier and quicker access to the imperial ear, after all. On the other hand, most of those rivals had quickly realized that despite the enormous opportunities for graft inherent in building a navy from scratch, it was likely to prove a thankless task. However optimistically belligerent Emperor Mahrys and—especially—Bishop Executor Mhartyn might be, Jahras doubted that any Desnairian aristocrat ever born could possibly look forward to the notion of fighting the *Charisian* Navy at sea. No one who'd ever done that had enjoyed the experience . . . a point which had been rather emphatically underscored by what the Charisians had recently done to the combined fighting strength of five other navies.

Under the circumstances, while Kholman's enemies would undoubtedly seize upon any opportunity to damage his credibility with the Crown with unholy glee, they'd be careful not to do it in a way which might end up with *them* being chosen to take his place. For that matter, Jahras' position, despite his far less lofty birth, was even more secure. In fact, if he'd been able to think of any way to avoid it himself in the first place, he would have done so in a heartbeat. But at least the sheer distance between them and Geyra gave them a pronounced degree of autonomy, without rivals or court flunkies constantly peering over their shoulders. So the two of them were far enough away from the imperial capital, and well enough insulated against removal, to be reasonably confident of not simply surviving their monarch's anger but retaining their current positions.

*Oh, joy,* he thought ironically.

"Let's be honest, Daivyn," he said out loud. "*Nothing* is going to make the Emperor or the Bishop Executor any less angry about what's happened to Wailahr. That's a given. In fact, I think we should use this to underscore the fact that we've always warned everyone we're bound to get hurt, at least initially, going after Charisians in their own element. We're not the only ones who know Wailahr, or who understand his reputation as a good commander's well deserved. All right. Let's make that point to His Majesty—that one of our *better* commanders, with two of our best vessels under his command, was defeated by a single Charisian galleon in less than forty-five minutes of close action. Don't blame him for it, either. In fact, let's emphasize the fact that he fought with great gallantry and determination. For that matter, as far as I can tell from this Captain Yairley's message, that's exactly what Wailahr did! Tell the Emperor we're making great progress in *building* the Navy, but that it's going to take a lot longer to *train* it."

Kholman frowned thoughtfully. There was a great deal to what Jahras had just said. In fact, the economies of the Gulf of Jahras and Mahrosa Bay had attained an almost Charisian bustle since the Church of God Awaiting had begun pouring money into the creation of shipyards there. Skilled carpenters, smiths, ropemakers and sailmakers, lumberjacks, seamstresses, gunpowder makers, foundry workers, and farmers and fishermen to provide the food to feed all of them, had swarmed into the area. The locals might not think much of the Harchong "advisers" who'd been sent in to (theoretically) help them, but they'd buckled down with a will to the task itself, propelled by an enthusiasm built almost equally out of religious zeal and the opportunity for profit.

For that matter, Kholman and Jahras had increased their own families' fortunes enormously in the process. Of course, that was one of the standard, accepted perquisites of their birth and position, and their own share of the graft had been factored into the Navy's original cost estimates. With that in mind, they were actually ahead of schedule and marginally under budget where the actual building programs were involved, and the local metalworking industry was booming. It wasn't precisely mere happenstance that almost all of the expanded foundries—and every single one of the *new* foundries—supplying artillery to the ships building in Iythria, Mahrosa, and Khairman Keep were located in the Duchy of Kholman, but there were actually some valid logistical arguments to support the far more important moneymaking arguments in favor of that. And production was rising rapidly. The guns coming out of those foundries might cost more than twice as much as the same guns would have cost from Charisian foundries, and they might have been two or three times as likely to burst on firing, but they were still being cast and bored far more quickly than *Desnairian* artillery had ever before been produced, and they were arriving in numbers almost adequate to arm the new construction as it came out of the yards.

"We can tell them that," the duke said. "And, for that matter, whether His Majesty wants to admit it or not, he'll almost certainly realize that it *is* going to take time to crew and train this many ships. But he's still going to want some kind of an estimate as to how *long* it's going to take, and I don't think he's going to settle for generalities much longer. Even if he'd like to, Bishop Executor Mhartyn isn't going to stand for it."

"Probably not," Jahras agreed.

The baron sat gazing at one of the paintings on Kholman's office wall for several seconds, stroking his beard while he thought. Then he shrugged and returned his attention to the other man.

"I think we need to tell the Bishop Executor that whether it's going to be convenient or not, we're going to have to send the tithe overland to Zion this year. I'll give you an official report and recommendation to that effect. And then, I think, we need to point out that we're actually managing to build and arm the ships faster than the people responsible for providing crews can get the men to us. When I write up my recommendation to send the tithe overland, I'll also point out how what's happened to Wailahr underscores the obvious need for longer and more intensive training even after we get the crews assembled. And as the men come in, let's assign them proportionately to *all* of the ships ready to commission, rather than fully crewing a smaller number of them."

Kholman's eyes narrowed, and he felt himself beginning to nod slowly. If they announced that they had even a limited number of new galleons fully manned, they would almost inevitably come under pressure to repeat the same disastrous sort of experiment which had just recoiled so emphatically on Wailahr. As long as they could report—honestly—that the ships' crews remained seriously understrength, there'd be no pressure (or none that couldn't be resisted, at any rate) to send them to sea in ones and twos where the Charisians could snip them off like frost-killed buds.

*And if we spread the men between as many ships as possible, we can do that while still sending in manpower returns that show we're making use of every man they send us. That it's not* our *fault the supply won't stretch to cover all our requirements, however hard we try. . . .*

"All right," he agreed. "That makes sense. And if they press us for a definite schedule, anyway?"

"Our first response should be to say we'll have to see how successful they are in sending us the men we require," Jahras replied promptly. "That's only the truth, by the way. Tell them we're going to need some time—probably at least a month or two—to form some kind of realistic estimate of how long it will take to fully man the ships we need at the rate they can provide the crews.

"After that, we'll need time to train them. I imagine that will take at least several more months, and it's already February." The baron shrugged again. "Under the circumstances, I'd say August or September would be the soonest we could possibly expect to really be prepared, and even then—and I'll mention this, tactfully, of course, in my report to you, as well—we're going to be inexperienced enough that it would be unrealistic to expect us to win without a significant numerical advantage. Obviously," his lips twitched in a faint smile, "it would be wisest to avoid operations which would permit the Charisians to whittle away at our own strength until we can be reinforced with enough of the ships building elsewhere to provide us with that necessary numerical advantage."

"Of course," Kholman agreed.

*August or September, eh?* he thought, restraining a smile of his own. *Heading into October, really, with the inevitable—and explainable—schedule slippage, aren't you, Urwyn? Slippage we can blame, with complete justification, on the people who aren't getting us the manpower we need. More probably even next November . . . which will just happen to be about the time Hsing-wu's Passage freezes solid. At which point none of those ships "building elsewhere" will be able to reinforce us until spring.*

It hadn't escaped the duke's thoughts, as he considered what Jahras had just said, that stretching out the schedule would also present the opportunity to funnel still more of the Church's bounty into his own and the baron's purses. In truth, however, that calculation was little more than a spinal reflex, inevitable in any Desnairian noble. What was more important, at least in so far as Kholman's conscious analysis was concerned, was that acting too precipitously—being the *first* swimmer to plunge into a sea full of Charisian-manned krakens— would be an unmitigated disaster for the navy he and Jahras were supposed to be building. Far better to be sure there were at least other targets for those krakens to spread their efforts between.

"Go ahead and write your report," the Duke of Kholman told his admiral general. "In fact, I think it would be a good idea to backdate at least some of it. We really have been thinking about this for a while, so let's make that clear to His Majesty." The duke smiled thinly. "It wouldn't do to have him decide we're just trying to cover our arses after what happened to Wailahr, after all."

.II.
Ice Ship *Hornet*,
Lake Pei,
The Temple Lands

The Earl of Coris had never been colder in his entire life. Which, after the last few months of winter travel, was saying quite a lot. At the moment, however, he didn't really care. In fact, at the moment, he wasn't even worrying about the imminence of his arrival in the city of Zion or what was going to happen after he finally got there. He was too busy trying not to whoop in sheer exuberance as the iceboat *Hornet* went slicing across Lake Pei's endless plain of ice like Langhorne's own razor in a scatter of rainbow-struck ice chips.

He'd never imagined anything like it. Even the descriptions Hahlys Tannyr had shared with him over meals or an occasional tankard of beer on the wearisome overland trip from Fairstock to Lakeview had been inadequate. Not for lack of trying, or because Father Hahlys had lacked either the enthusiasm or the descriptive gift for the task, but simply because Coris' imagination had never been given anything to use for comparison. If anyone had asked him, he would have simply discounted out of hand the possibility that anyone could ever travel faster than, say, fifteen miles an hour. To be honest, even that would have seemed the next best thing to starkly impossible, except possibly in a sprint by specially bred horses. Slash lizards were faster than that when they charged—he'd heard estimates that put their speed in a dash as high as forty miles an hour—but no human being had ever *ridden* a slash lizard . . . except very briefly in certain fables whose entire purpose was to demonstrate the unwisdom of making the attempt.

Now, as showers of ice flew like diamond dust from the iceboat's screaming runners and the incredible vibration hammered into him through his feet and legs, Coris was finally experiencing what Tannyr had tried to explain to him, and a corner of the earl's mind went back over the past, wearisome five-days of travel which had brought him to this moment.

▼      ▼      ▼

The sheer, slow, slogging misery of their journey along the Rayworth Valley where it formed the open north-south "V" at the heart of the Wishbone Mountains had only served to make Tannyr's descriptions of his iceboat's speed even less believable. The only redeeming aspect of the trip, perversely enough, had been the snowy conditions with which they'd been forced to cope. The outsized sleighs Tannyr had procured had made surprisingly good time—indeed, better time than carriages or even mounted men might have made over those winter-struck roads—behind the successive teams of six-limbed snow lizards the under-priest had arranged via the Church's semaphore system.

The snow lizards, unlike the sleighs' passengers, hadn't minded the icy temperatures and snow at all. Their multi-ply pelts provided near perfect insulation (not to mention, Coris had discovered at one of the posting houses in which they had overnighted, the most sinfully sensual rugs any man had ever walked barefoot across), and their huge feet, with the webs between their pads, carried them across even the deepest snow. They were considerably smaller than the mountain lizards used for draft purposes in more temperate climes, but they were close to twice the size of a good saddle horse. And while they would have found it difficult to match a horse in a sprint, they had all of lizard-kind's endurance, which meant they could maintain almost indefinitely a pace which would have quickly exhausted, or even killed, any horse.

The snow lizards would have been perfectly happy padding along into the very teeth of a Wishbone Mountains blizzard. Assuming the wind had gotten too bad even for them, they would simply have curled up into enormous balls—two or three of them huddling together, whenever possible—and allowed the howling wind to cover them in a comfortable blanket of snow. Human beings, unfortunately, were somewhat more poorly insulated, and so, even with the snow lizards' help, Coris and Tannyr had found themselves weatherbound on three separate occasions—once for almost three days. Mostly, they'd used Church posting houses, since most of the inns (which seemed to be considerably larger than those to which Coris was accustomed) appeared to have closed their doors for the winter. Not surprisingly, he'd supposed, given how the weather had undoubtedly inspired all but the hardiest—or most lunatic—of travelers to stay home until spring. Even the posting houses had been both larger and rather more luxurious than he would have anticipated, but given the number of high-ranking churchmen who frequently traveled this route, he'd realized he shouldn't have been particularly surprised by that discovery.

The weather delays had been frustrating enough, despite the comfort of the posting houses, but the shortness of the winter days hadn't helped, either, even though the snow lizards had been perfectly happy to keep going even in near total darkness. They'd stretched their travel time each day as far as they could, yet there'd been stretches—even in the sheltered and (relatively) low-lying valley—where the roads had been far too sinuous, steep, and icy for anyone but an idiot to traverse them in darkness. Considering all that, the earl hadn't been particularly surprised to find Tannyr's original estimate of how long the trip would take had actually been a bit optimistic.

Despite that, they'd finally reached Lakeview, once again (inevitably) in the middle of a dense snowfall. Night had already fallen by the time they arrived, and the ancient city's buildings had seemed to huddle together, hunching shoulders and roofs against the weather. Many of the city's windows had been shuttered against the cold, but the glow of lamplight streaming from others had turned the falling snowflakes into a dancing, swirling tapestry woven by invisible sprites. Their traveling sleighs had slowed dramatically once they reached Lakeview's streets, yet the darkness and the weather had already urged most of the city's inhabitants inside, and they'd quickly reached The Archangels' Rest, the harborside inn where rooms had been reserved for them.

It was a huge establishment, a full six stories tall, with palatial sleeping chambers and a full-fledged ground-floor restaurant. In fact, The Archangels' Rest dwarfed anything Coris had ever seen in Corisande or even the largest of the outsized inns they'd passed en route from Fairstock. For that matter, he was pretty sure it was larger than anything he'd ever seen *anywhere,* short of a cathedral in some capital city. It hardly seemed proper to describe it as a mere "inn," and he supposed that was why someone had coined the word "hotel" to describe it, instead.

At the moment, however, it was clearly operating with a much-reduced staff. He'd mentioned that to Tannyr, and the under-priest had chuckled.

"During the summer, the place is usually packed," he'd explained. "In fact, they usually wish they had even more rooms to let. Didn't you notice how much bigger the inns were along the high road?" Coris had nodded, and Tannyr had shrugged. "Well, that's because when everything's not covered with ice and snow, there are usually thousands of pilgrims using the high road to make their way to or from the Temple at any given time. All of them need someplace to spend the night, after all, and *all* the roads to Lake Pei from the south come together here, which makes Lakeview the lakeside terminus for anyone traveling to Zion or the Temple by road, just like Port Harbor is the major landfall for anyone traveling there by way of Hsing-wu's Passage. Trust me, if you were here at midsummer, you'd swear every adult on Safehold was trying to get to the Temple . . . and that every one of them was trying to stay at the Rest. This time of year, the top three floors are completely closed down, though. For that matter, I'd be surprised if more than a third—or even a quarter—of the rooms which haven't been closed for the winter are occupied at the moment."

"How in the world do they justify keeping it open at all, if they lose so much of their business during the winter?" Coris had asked.

"Well, the quality of their restaurant helps a lot!" Tannyr had laughed. "Trust me, you'll see that for yourself at supper. So they manage to keep their kitchen staff fully occupied, no matter what time of year it is. As for the rest"—he'd shrugged—"Mother Church has a partial ownership in the Rest, and the Temple Treasury helps subsidize expenses over the winter months. In fact, Mother Church has the same arrangement with quite a few of the larger inns and hotels here in Lakeview. And in Port Harbor, for that matter."

Coris had nodded in understanding. For that matter, he'd realized he should have thought of that possibility for himself. Obviously, the Church would have a powerful interest in providing housing for those performing the pilgrimage to the Temple enjoined upon all of the truly faithful by the *Holy Writ*.

*And,* he'd thought just a bit more cynically, *I'll bet the profit the Treasury turns during the peak pilgrimage months is more than handsome enough to cover the costs of keeping the places open year-round.*

However that might have been, he'd been forced to admit The Archangels' Rest had provided the most comfortable and luxurious travel accommodations he'd ever encountered, and the contrast between it and the conditions they'd endured all too frequently elsewhere during their rigorous journey had been profound. He was certain that few of the hotel's other suites were quite as luxurious as the ones to which he and Tannyr had been escorted, and the restaurant had been just as excellent as Tannyr had promised. In fact, Coris had found himself wishing rather wistfully that they could have spent more than a single night as its guests.

Unfortunately, he'd known they couldn't, and he'd tried to project an air of cheerful acceptance as he followed Tannyr down to the docks the next morning. From the under-priest's obvious amusement, it had been clear he'd failed to fool the other man, but despite Tannyr's lively sense of humor (and the ridiculous), he'd managed somehow to refrain from teasing his charge.

Coris had appreciated the under-priest's forbearance, and he suspected that his reaction when he finally set eyes on *Hornet* for the first time had constituted a sort of reward for Tannyr's patience.

He'd actually stopped dead, gazing at the iceboat in astonishment. Despite all the descriptions he'd heard, he hadn't been prepared for the reality when he saw the rakish vessel sitting there on the gleaming steel feet of its huge, skate-like runners. The mere thought of how much each of those runners must have cost was enough to give a man pause, especially if the man in question had firsthand experience in things like foundry costs because he'd recently been involved in an effort to build a galleon-based, cannon-armed navy from scratch. Again, though, he'd realized, he was looking at an example of the Church's enormous financial resources.

Iceboats like *Hornet* weren't just exorbitantly expensive. They were also highly specialized propositions, and their sole function was to cross Lake Pei after the enormous sheet of water had frozen solid. It was almost four hundred and fifty miles from Lakeview to Zion, and every year, when winter truly set in, the lake became only marginally navigable. Indeed, once it had fully iced over, it was completely closed to normal shipping, and iceboats became the only way in or out of Zion. They couldn't begin to carry the amount of cargo conventional ships could, so a vast fleet would have been required to ship in any significant supply of foodstuffs or fuel, which meant neither Zion nor the Temple could count on importing large amounts of either from their usual southern sources after the lake had begun freezing in earnest. But at least some freight—mostly luxury goods—and quite a few passengers still needed to cross, regardless of the season. And Mother Church had a monopoly where iceboat ownership was concerned.

*Hornet* herself looked a great deal like a Church courier galley on enormous skates. There were some differences, yet her courier-ship ancestry had been clearly recognizable. And made some sense, Coris had supposed, given that there were occasions—especially early in the ice season—when, as Tannyr had suggested, it wasn't unheard of for one of the iceboats to encounter a still-open lead of unfrozen lake water. Or, for that matter, to rather abruptly discover that a sheet of ice was thinner than it had appeared. The ability to float in an instance like that was undoubtedly a good thing to have.

Coris had never heard of something a native of Old Terra would have called a "hydrofoil," but in many respects, that would have been a reasonable analogue for what he was looking at. *Hornet*'s outriggers extended much farther beyond the footprint of her hull, because unlike a hydrofoil, they had to plane across the surface of the ice rather than relying on hydrodynamics for stability. Aside from that, however, the principle was very much the same, and as he'd looked at the iceboat's lean, rakish grace, he'd realized Hahlys Tannyr was exactly the right sort of man to captain such a vessel. In his case, at least, the Church had slipped a round peg neatly into an equally round hole, and Coris had found himself wondering just how typical of the Lake Pei iceboat captains Tannyr truly was.

The under-priest's pride in his command had been readily apparent, and the earl's obvious admiration—or awe, at least—had clearly gratified him. His crew's cheerfulness at seeing him had also been apparent, and they'd gotten Coris, Seablanket, and their baggage moved aboard and settled quickly.

"The wind looks good for a fast passage, My Lord," Tannyr had told him as the two of them stood on *Hornet*'s deck, looking out across the frozen harbor. Despite the snow which had fallen overnight, wind had kept the ice scoured clear, and Coris had been able to see the scars of other iceboats' passages leading across the wide, dark sheet of ice and out through the opening in the Lakeview breakwater. At the moment, there had seemed to be very little breeze stirring at dockside, however, and he'd quirked an eyebrow at the under-priest.

"Oh, I know there's not much wind right here," Tannyr had replied with a grin. "Out beyond the breakwater, though, once we get out of Lakeview's lee . . . Trust me, My Lord—there's plenty of wind out there!"

"I'm quite prepared to believe it," Coris had replied. "But just how do we get from here to there?"

"Courtesy of *those,* My Lord." Tannyr had waved a hand, and when Coris turned in the indicated direction, he'd seen a team of at least thirty snow lizards headed for them. "They'll tow us out far enough to catch the breeze," Tannyr had said confidently. "It'll seem like that takes forever, but once we do, I promise, you'll think we're *flying.*"

▼    ▼    ▼

Now, remembering the under-priest's promise, Coris decided Tannyr had been right.

The earl had declined Tannyr's offer to go below to the shelter of *Hornet*'s day cabin. He'd thought he'd seen approval for his decision in the under-priest's eyes, and Tannyr had entrusted him to the charge of a grizzled old seaman—or was that properly "iceman"? Coris had wondered—with instructions to find the earl a safe spot from which to experience the journey.

The "tow" away from the docks hadn't been nearly as laborious-seeming an affair as Tannyr's description might have suggested. That could have been because Coris had never before experienced it and so had no backlog of wonder-dulling familiarity to overcome. Unlike Tannyr and his crew, he'd been seeing it for the very first time, and he'd watched in fascination as the snow lizards were jockeyed into position. It had been obvious the lizards had done this many times before. They and their drovers had moved with a combination of smooth experience and patience, and heavy chains and locking pins had clanked musically behind the frothing surface of commands and encourage-ment as the heavy traces were attached to specialized towing brackets on *Hor-net*'s prow. Given the complexity of the task, they'd accomplished it in a remarkably short time, and then—encouraged by much louder shouts—the snow lizards had leaned into their collars with the peculiar, hoarse, almost bark-ing whistles of effort with which Coris had become familiar over the last month or so. For a moment, the iceboat had refused to move. Then the runners had broken free of the ice and she'd begun to slide gracefully after the strain-ing snow lizards.

Once they'd had her in motion, she'd moved easily enough, and as they'd eased steadily away from the docks, Coris had felt the first, icy fingers of the freshening breeze which Tannyr had promised waited for them out on the lake. It had taken them the better part of three-quarters of an hour to get far enough out to satisfy Tannyr, but then the snow lizards had been unhooked, the senior drover had waved cheerfully, and the tow team had headed back to Lakeview.

Coris had watched them go, but only until crisp-voiced commands from the cramped quarterdeck had sent *Hornet*'s crew to their stations for making sail. The closer-to-hand fascination of those preparations had drawn his atten-tion away from the departing snow lizards, and he'd watched as the iceboat's la-teen sail was loosed. In some ways, his familiarity with conventional ships had only made the process even more bizarre. Despite the fact that his brain had known there were probably hundreds of feet of water underneath them, he hadn't been able to shake the sense of standing on dry land, and there'd been an oddly dreamlike quality to watching sailors scurrying about a ship's deck when the gleaming ice had stretched out as far as the eye could see with rock-steady solidity.

But if he'd felt that way, he'd obviously been the only one on *Hornet*'s deck who did. Or perhaps the others had simply been too busy to worry about such fanciful impressions. And they'd certainly known their business. That much had been clear as the sail had been loosed. The canvas had complained, flapping heavily in the stiff breeze whistling across the decks, and *Hornet* had stirred un-derfoot, as if the iceboat were shivering with eagerness. Then the sail had been sheeted home, the yard had been trimmed, and she'd begun to move.

Slowly, at first, with a peculiar grating and yet sibilant sound from her run-ners. The motion underfoot had been strange, vibrating through the deck plank-ing with a strength and a . . . hardness Coris had never experienced aboard any *water*borne vessel. That wasn't exactly the right way to describe it, but Coris hadn't been able to think of a better one, and he'd reached out, touching the rail, feeling that same vibration shivering throughout the vessel's entire fabric and dancing gently in his own bones.

The iceboat had gathered way slowly, in the beginning, but as she'd slid steadily farther out of Lakeview's wind shadow, she'd begun to accelerate steadily. More quickly, in fact, than any galley or galleon, and Coris had felt his lips pursing in sudden understanding. He should have thought of it before, he'd realized, when Tannyr first described *Hornet*'s speed to him. On her runners, the iceboat avoided the enormous drag water resistance imposed on a normal ship's submerged hull. Of course she accelerated more rapidly . . . and without that selfsame drag, she had to be much faster in any given set of wind conditions.

Which was exactly what she'd proven to be.

▼　　▼　　▼

"Enjoying yourself, My Lord?"

Hahlys Tannyr had to practically bellow in Coris' ear for the question to be heard over the slithering roar of the runners. Coris hadn't noticed him approaching—he'd been too busy staring ahead, clinging to the rail while his eyes sparkled with delight—and he turned quickly to meet *Hornet*'s captain's gaze.

"Oh, I certainly am, Father!" the earl shouted back. "I'm afraid I didn't really believe you when you told me how fast she was! She must be doing—what? Forty miles an hour?"

"Not in this wind, My Lord." Tannyr shook his head. "She's fast, but it would take at least a full gale to move her *that* quickly! We might be making thirty, though."

Coris had no choice but to take the under-priest's word for it. And, he admitted, he himself had no experience at judging speeds this great.

"I'm surprised it doesn't feel even colder than it does!" he commented, and Tannyr smiled.

"We're sailing *with* the wind, My Lord. That reduces the apparent wind speed across the deck a lot. Trust me, if we were beating up to windward, you'd feel it then!"

"No doubt I would." The earl shook his head. "And I'll take your word for our speed. But I never imagined that *anything* could move this quickly—especially across a solid surface like this!"

"It helps that the ice is as smooth as it is out here," Tannyr replied.

He waved one arm, indicating the ice around them, then pointed at yet another of the flagstaffs, all set upright in the lake's frozen surface and supporting flags of one color or another, which *Hornet* had been passing at regular intervals since leaving Lakeside.

"See that?" he asked, and the earl nodded. This particular staff boasted a green flag, and Tannyr grinned. "Green indicates smooth ice ahead, My Lord," he said. "Only a fool trusts the flags completely—that's why we keep a good lookout." He twitched his head at a distinctly frozen-looking man perched in

*Hornet's* crow's nest. "Still, the survey crews do a good job of keeping the flags updated. We should see yellow warning flags well before we come up on ridge-ice, and the ridges themselves will be red-flagged. And the flags also provide our piloting marks—like harbor buoys—for the crossing."

"How in Langhorne's name do they get the flags planted in the first place?" Coris half shouted the question through the exuberant roar of their passage, and Tannyr's grin grew even broader.

"Not too hard, really, once the ice sets up nice and hard, My Lord! They just chop a hole, stand the staff in it, then let it refreeze!"

"But how do they keep the staff from just keeping going right down into the water?"

"It sits in a hollow bracket with crossbars," Tannyr replied, waving his hands as if to illustrate what he was saying. "The brackets are iron, about three feet tall, with two pairs of crossbars, set at right angles about halfway along their length. The bars are a lot longer than the width of the hole, and they sit on top of the ice, holding the bracket in position while the hole freezes back over. Then they just step the flagstaff in the bracket. When we get closer to spring, they'll buoy each bracket to keep it from sinking when the ice melts, so they can recover them and use them again next winter."

Coris nodded in understanding, and the two of them stood side by side for several minutes, watching the ice blur past as *Hornet* slashed onward. Then Tannyr stirred.

"Assuming my speed estimate's accurate—and I modestly admit that I'm actually very good at estimating that sort of thing, My Lord—we're still a good eleven or twelve hours out from Zion," he said. "Normally, I'd be guessing even longer than that, but the weather's clear, and we'll have a full moon tonight, so we're not going to have to reduce speed as much when we lose the daylight. But while I'm glad you're enjoying yourself up here, you might want to think about going below and getting something hot to drink. To be honest, I'd really like to get you delivered unfrozen, and we'll be coming up on lunch in another couple of hours, as well, for that matter."

"I'd prefer arriving unfrozen myself, I think," Coris replied. "But I'd really hate to miss any of this!"

He waved both arms, indicating the sunlight, the deck around them, the mast with its straining sail braced sharply, and the glittering ice chips showering away from the steadily grating runners as they tore through the bright (although undeniably icy) morning.

"I know. And I'm not trying to *order* you below, My Lord!" Tannyr laughed out loud. "To be honest, I'd be a bit hypocritical if I did, given how much *I* enjoy it up here on deck! But you might want to be thinking ahead. And don't forget, you've got a full day of this to look forward to. Believe me, if you think it's exhilarating right now, wait till you see it by moonlight!"

Silent snowflakes battered against the floor-to-ceiling windows like lost ghosts. The brilliant, mystic lighting which always illuminated the outside of the Temple turned the swirling flakes into glittering gems until the wind caught them and swept them to their rendezvous with the window. Hauwerd Wylsynn watched them changing from gorgeous jewels into feathery ghosts and felt a coldness, far deeper than that of the night beyond the windows, whispering, whispering in the marrow of his bones.

He looked away from the transmuting snowflakes at the luxurious suite assigned to his brother. Every vicar had personal apartments in the enormous, majestic sweep of the Temple, and as apartments went, Samyl Wylsynn's were not particularly huge. They weren't *tiny*, either, yet they were substantially more modest than a vicar of Samyl's seniority might have demanded.

They were more plainly and simply furnished, too, without the sumptuous luxury other vicars required. Zhaspahr Clyntahn, the current Grand Inquisitor, was a case in point. It was rumored (almost certainly correctly) that the art treasures in his chambers, alone, were probably worth the total annual income of most baronies. And that didn't even consider the fact that Clyntahn had demanded and received one of the coveted corner apartments, with windows looking both east and north, allowing him to survey the roofs, towers, and buildings of the city of Zion through one set and the magnificent dome and colonnade of the main Temple through the other.

Hauwerd supposed that one could make the argument—as Clyntahn obviously did—that such quarters were merely in keeping with the office of the man responsible for overseeing the state of Mother Church's soul. More than once, he'd heard Clyntahn piously declaiming about the need to properly support the authority and prestige of the Grand Inquisitor. Of the need to emphasize the necessary—always necessary—extent of that official's authority over all of Mother Church's children in ways which even the most worldly soul might recognize. To reach out to those too easily impressed by the trappings and power of this world in ways which even they could not ignore. It was *never* about his own gluttonous, greedy, debauched, power-mongering personal lifestyle or desires. Oh, Langhorne, no!

Hauwerd felt his lips tightening, and acid churned in his stomach as he compared his brother's chosen simplicity—the absence of statuary, the dearth of priceless carpets, the lack of stupendous oil paintings by the greatest masters Safehold had ever produced—with Clyntahn's. There were paintings on Samyl's walls, but they were portraits of both his first and his current wife, his three sons, his two daughters, his son-in-law, and his first grandchild. The furniture was comfortable, and certainly not cheap, yet it was only furniture, selected *because* it was comfortable and not to emphasize the importance of its owner. And the artworks which adorned *his* bookshelves and prayer desk were modest and understated, almost all exquisitely wrought, but most of them by lessser known artists he had chosen to support with his patronage because something about the pieces had touched his own heart, his own soul and faith.

*If Samyl had only won the election,* Hauwerd thought bitterly. *He came so close. In fact, I'm still not convinced Clyntahn really won. That lickspittle Rayno was in charge of the vote count, after all, and look where* he *wound up!*

Of course, if Samyl had won, if *he'd* become the new Grand Inquisitor instead of Clyntahn, the vast gulf between the fashion in which he would have furnished his apartments in the Temple and the fashion in which Clyntahn had done the same thing would have been the least of Mother Church's differences.

*For one thing, this damned schism would never have happened. Samyl would never have signed off on Clyntahn's casual proposal to completely destroy an entire kingdom just because it had pissed him off. For that matter, Clyntahn wouldn't have been in any position to be tossing off suggestions like that, in the first place! Of course,* Hauwerd admitted grimly, *it's probably at least as likely that if he'd won he would have been assassinated by now. It's happened to more than one of our ancestors, after all. So at least we were spared that much.*

*Not that it's going to make any difference in the end.*

He drew a deep breath, and his hard eyes softened as he glanced at his brother. He and Samyl had always been close, despite the almost ten years between their ages. He'd always admired Samyl, always known Samyl was fated to do great things for God and Mother Church.

He knew his mother had been dismayed when Samyl chose the Schuelerites. She might not have been a Wylsynn by birth, but she'd scarcely been blind to the way in which the heritage of the family into which she had married had pitted so many of its members against Church corruption over the last three or four centuries. She'd understood what had drawn Samyl into the Order of Schueler, recognized his burning desire to do something to fight the evils he saw gathering about the Temple . . . and she'd remembered what had happened to his great-grandfather, just over a hundred years ago, now. Saint Evyrahard's grand vicarate had been the shortest in history, and whatever the official histories might say, no one ever doubted that his "accidental fall" had been the direct result of *his* efforts to reform the vicarate. And the grand vicarate of Grand Vicar Tairhel, Samyl and Hauwerd's granduncle, had been almost as short. There were no rumors to suggest Tairhel's death had been arranged, but he'd been old and in ill health when he'd been raised to Lang-horne's Throne, without the vigor and energy which had characterized Evyra-hard. His fellow vicars may have felt they could simply wait for natural causes to put an end to *his* reform efforts. Of course, it was also always possible the "natural causes" which had finally killed him had been nudged along just a bit, despite what anyone might have thought.

*Well, Mother,* Hauwerd thought now. *You were right to worry. I'm just glad you and Father won't be here to see what happens. I'm sure you'll know anyway, but the* Writ *says that from God's side, all things make sense. I hope that's true, because from where I sit right this minute, there's neither sense nor sanity in what's about to happen. And there sure as Shan-wei isn't a trace of justice in it!*

"What did you think of the wine?" Samyl asked calmly, and Hauwerd snorted.

"I thought it was excellent. Saint Hyndryk's, wasn't it? The '64?" Samyl nodded serenely, and Hauwerd snorted again, louder. "Well, at least that's *one* thing Clyntahn won't get his pig-hands on!"

"Not exactly the reason I chose to serve it tonight, but a thought worth re-membering, I suppose." Samyl agreed so serenely a corner of Hauwerd's inner-most soul wanted to scream at him in frustration. That serenity, that total, always grounded faith, was one of the things Hauwerd had always most admired in his brother. At the moment, however, it rasped on his nerves almost as much as it comforted him. And the real reason it did, however little he might want to ex-amine the truth, was that Samyl's serenity—his acceptance of God's will—actually made Hauwerd question his own faith.

He'd fought that doubt with all his strength, yet he'd never been able to completely vanquish it. Surely, a truly just God, Archangels who truly served the Light, would never have abandoned a man as good as his brother, one who longed only to serve God and love his fellow man. Not simply *abandon* him, but deliver him into the hands of a vile, corrupt, *evil* man like Zhaspahr Clyn-tahn. Into the hands of a man prepared to slaughter an entire kingdom. The hands of a man who was armed with every terrible punishment of *The Book of Schueler* . . . and perfectly willing, *eager,* to inflict every single one of them upon blameless children of God whose only crime had been to resist his own corruption.

Hauwerd Wylsynn knew his own weaknesses, his own shortcomings. He couldn't really honestly say he thought any of them were so terrible as to jus-tify the fate Clyntahn had in mind for *him,* either, yet he was prepared to admit that he, too, had been prey to the sin of ambition. That, on occasion, he had al-lowed the seductive power of his birth and his office to lead him into taking the easy course, accepting the shortcut, *using* God instead of using *himself* in God's service. But he also knew Samyl hadn't done that. That Samyl truly had been the spiritual heir of Saint Evyrahard, and not just his descendant. What could God possibly be *thinking* to let the man who should have been His champion, the man who would willingly have embraced his own death to redeem His Church, come to an end like this one?

That wasn't the sort of question *anyone,* far less someone consecrated to the orange, was supposed to ask of God. And a vicar of the Church of God Awaiting wasn't supposed to rail at God, indict Him for abandoning even the most blameless of His servants. That was what faith was supposed to be for. To help a man accept what he could not understand.

He started to say just that. To take his doubt, his anger, to Samyl as he'd done so often before, knowing his brother would listen without condemnation, then offer the quiet words of comfort (or the gently stern words of admonition) he needed to hear. But this time, no words could comfort the questions burning deep inside Hauwerd Wylsynn, just as no words of admonition could banish them. And this time, he would not—*could* not—add the burden of his own doubt to the weight already crushing down upon his brother.

*At least we got as many of the junior members of the Circle as we could out of Zion before the snows really set in,* he reminded himself. *And along the way, I think, some of the other vicars must have realized what Samyl was doing. I hope some of them did, anyway. That they were able to come up with plans which might give them at least a tiny hope of escaping when the Inquisitors come for us all. That's the only reason I can think of for so many of their families to have "disappeared," at least.*

His eyes went back to the portraits of his brother's family. *They* had vanished, as well, although he didn't think Samyl had arranged it. In fact, he'd been there when his brother received the letter from his wife, Lysbet, informing him that she would be coming to the Temple this winter after all . . . in spite of his specific instructions that she stay away. He'd seen the way Samyl's facial muscles had sagged, despite his best effort to hide his reaction, and he'd understood exactly why his brother had just aged five years in front of him. But then, still three days' journey short of Zion, Lysbet and the children had disappeared one night.

There'd been evidence of a struggle, but no sign of who the struggle might have been with, and Lysbet, her two boys, and her daughter had simply vanished. At first, Samyl had looked even older and more . . . defeated than before, but then gradually, he'd realized that whatever else had happened, his family had *not* been quietly taken into custody by the Inquisition, after all. No one seemed to have the least idea what had happened to them, and there'd been at least some expressions of sympathy, but it was Zhaspahr Clyntahn's barely hidden fury which had convinced Hauwerd the Inquisition truly hadn't had a thing to do with Samyl's family's "abduction."

Obviously, the kidnapping of a *vicar's* family had sparked one of the most intense manhunts in the history of Mother Church, yet not one single sign of the culprits had been discovered. Over the five-days which had followed,

Samyl had born up nobly under the strain as day after day passed with no ransom demand, no threat, no word at all. Hauwerd was quite certain the Inquisition was still watching his brother like king wyverns waiting to pounce, hoping for some break, some communication, which would lead it to Lysbet. After so long, though, even Clyntahn's agents seemed to be giving up hope of that.

And it was probably Lysbet's disappearance which had inspired some of the Circle's other members to make arrangements for their own families. Hauwerd hoped those arrangements had been in time and that they were going to prove effective.

*And I hope—pray—the others understand why we couldn't warn them directly.*

In his own mind, Hauwerd had narrowed the suspects to no more than half a dozen. The problem was that he didn't know which of those half dozen might have turned informant, betrayed them all to Clyntahn, revealed the existence—and membership—of the organization of Reformists. For that matter, he might have been wrong. The traitor might *not* be one of the people he was convinced it had to be. And they could warn none of the Circle's members without warning all of them . . . including the traitor.

Had they done that, Clyntahn would have struck with instant, vicious power rather than waiting until what he judged to be the perfect moment. Waiting, Hauwerd was certain, so that he could savor the sweet bouquet of his coming triumph over the men who had dared to challenge his authority.

And so they'd said nothing, using the time while Clyntahn waited to do what little they could to mitigate the blow when he finally pounced. Getting all of the junior bishops and archbishops they could out of Zion where they might be safe. Alerting their network of correspondents and agents *outside* the innermost circle to quietly prepare the deepest boltholes they could contrive.

*Thank God I never married,* Hauwerd thought. *Maybe that was another way I had less faith than Samyl, because I was never willing to trust God enough to give up those hostages to someone like Clyntahn.*

"I understand Coris arrived this evening," he said out loud, and Samyl smiled faintly at his younger brother's obvious effort to find something "safe" to talk about.

"Yes, so I heard," he replied, and shook his head. "That must have been a nightmare of a journey this time of year."

"I'm sure it was, but I doubt the thought particularly bothered Clyntahn or Trynair," Hauwerd said sourly. "I suppose we should be grateful they didn't insist he drag the boy along with him!"

"I'm sure they saw no need to." Samyl shrugged. "He's only a little boy, Hauwerd. For at least the next several years, Daivyn's going to do what he's told by his elders simply because that's what he's accustomed to doing. I imagine Clyntahn figures there's plenty of time to . . . impress him with the realities of his position, let's say, before he gets old enough to turn into a headstrong young prince."

"Assuming he and Trynair are willing to let the boy grow up at all." Hauwerd's tone was harsh, bitter, yet it was less bitter than his eyes.

"Assuming that, yes," Samyl was forced to concede. "I've prayed about it. Of course, I'd feel more optimistic if it didn't seem so evident God has decided to let things work their own way out."

Hauwerd's jaw muscles tightened again as he fought down yet another stab of anger. Still, as Samyl had pointed out more than once, God wouldn't have given man free will if He hadn't expected him to use it. And that meant those who chose to do evil *could* do evil. Which automatically implied that other men—and even little boys—could and would suffer the consequences of those evil actions. No doubt it truly was all part of God's great plan, but there were times—like now—when it seemed unnecessarily hard on the victims.

"Well, I hope Coris is as smart as I've always heard he is," Hauwerd said after a moment. "That boy—and his sister—are going to need every edge they can find if they're going to survive."

This time, Samyl only nodded, his eyes softening briefly with affection. So like his brother, he thought, to be worrying about a little boy and a teenaged girl he'd never even met. That was the Temple Guardsman in him, the pugnacious, protective streak which had driven him to serve God first with a sword, and only later with his heart and mind. He was glad Hauwerd already knew how deeply he loved him, that neither of them had to say it at this time, in this place.

"And on that note," Hauwerd said, glancing at the clock on the wall—the clock which, like every other clock in the Temple, always kept perfect, precisely synchronized time—and then climbing out of his chair, "I'm afraid I have to be going. I've got a couple of errands I need to take care of tonight."

"Anything I can help with?" Samyl asked, and Hauwerd snorted yet again, this time much more gently.

"You may not believe this, Samyl, but I've been buttoning my own shirt and tying my own shoes for, oh, *years* now."

"Point taken." Samyl chuckled softly. "And I know you have. So go see to your errands. Supper tomorrow night at your place?"

"It's a date," Hauwerd said, then nodded to his brother and left.

▼　▼　▼

"Haaaaahhhhhh—chhheeewwwwww!"

The sneeze seemed to have taken the top right off of Vicar Rhobair Duchairn's head. Not even the Temple's sacred, always comfortable precincts seemed capable of defeating the common cold. This was the third cold Duchairn had already entertained this winter, and this one looked like being worse than either of its predecessors.

He paused long enough to get out his handkerchief and blow his nose—taking the opportunity to recover from the sneeze at the same time—then resumed his progress along the corridor. He was already late for the scheduled meeting, although timing wasn't actually all that critical. He *was* the Church of God Awaiting's Treasurer, after all.

The people waiting for him all reported to him, and it wasn't as if they could start things without him. And it wasn't as if he were really looking forward to the conference, for that matter. The Treasury had been hemorrhaging money ever since the Kingdom of Charis smashed the initial attack upon it, and he didn't see that situation getting better anytime soon. Especially not with the blow the Church's cash flow had taken. Not only had the Kingdoms of Charis and Chisholm and the Princedoms of Emerald and Corisande—not to mention the Grand Duchy of Zebediah—abruptly stopped paying their tithes (which, in Charis' case, had been very *large* tithes), but Charis' relentless destruction of its enemies' commerce had dealt severe damage to the economies of those enemies. And as their economies slowed, so did their ability to generate tithes. According to Duchairn's latest estimates, the cash flow from the mainland kingdoms' annual tithes had dropped by somewhere around ten percent . . . and total tithes, including those which should have been coming in from the lands now in rebellion against Mother Church, had fallen by over a third. It was fortunate the Church had so many other lucrative sources of income, but there was a limit to how much slack could be squeezed out of those other sources. For the first time in mortal memory, the Church of God Awaiting was spending money faster than it was taking money in, and that sort of thing couldn't be sustained forever.

Which, unfortunately, certain of his colleagues seemed to find difficult to grasp.

His expression darkened as he thought about those other colleagues. Neither Trynair nor Clyntahn had mentioned to him that they intended to "interview" the Earl of Coris this morning. He was fairly confident he had sources neither of those two suspected he possessed, but he wasn't going to risk revealing those sources' existence by challenging his "colleagues" on something he wasn't supposed to know anything about. He doubted either of them would have been prepared to make an issue out of it if he'd suddenly turned up for their "interview," yet he was quite positive they'd deliberately timed things so it just *happened* to fall opposite his already-scheduled Treasury meeting. Both of them, each for his own reasons, would have found Duchairn's presence for the discussion they had in mind decidedly unwelcome.

And that, unfortunately, neatly underscored the differences between him and them . . . and the dangers yawning about him *because* of those differences.

He paused, looking out the windows which formed one entire side of the hallway. The snow had stopped shortly after dawn, and brilliant sunlight sparkled

and bounced from the new, deeper layers of trackless white which had blan-
keted the Temple's grounds. The mystic, unbreakable, perfectly insulated crystal of the windows muted the snow glare, however, and the icy vista's pristine
purity made him acutely aware of the warm air moving gently about him.

And made him think about all the people outside the Temple, especially
the city of Zion's many poor, who were anything but warm and comfortable
this freezing cold morning, as well. That was yet another thought he was unprepared to share with his erstwhile colleagues in the Group of Four. Not because they didn't already realize it would have occurred to him, but because it
would have done no good and might do quite a lot of harm.

Zahmsyn Trynair would simply have looked at him with a certain impatient incomprehension. If the Church of God Awaiting's Chancellor ever
thought of Zion's poor at all, it was undoubtedly to remember the passage from
*The Book of Langhorne* in which the Archangel had warned that they would have
the poor with them always. If that had been good enough for Langhorne, it was
good enough for Trynair.

Allayn Maigwair, on the other hand, probably wouldn't even notice that
Duchairn had mentioned them. These days, especially, all of the Church's Captain General's thoughts and efforts were fully concentrated on building up the
fleet needed to crush the upstart Empire of Charis once and for all. The fact
that he'd started out building the *wrong* fleet, and that Duchairn's Treasury had
disbursed a staggering sum to pay for hundreds of galleys which were effectively useless, lent a certain emphasis to his concentration, no doubt. Of course,
Maigwair had never been overburdened with intellect in the first place. Concentrating the entire, scant store of it he possessed shouldn't require all *that*
great an effort. He should have been able to spare at least a little thought for the
men and women and children—especially the children—for whom every vicar
was supposed to be responsible.

And then there was Clyntahn. The Grand Inquisitor. The one member of
the Group of Four who would have regarded Duchairn's concern over the poor
with neither incomprehension nor indifference. Duchairn sometimes wished
he himself had felt called to the Order of Bédard instead of the Order of Chihiro. He was pretty sure any Bédardist who wasn't terrified of the Grand Inquisitor would have unhesitatingly diagnosed him as a paranoiac, and one whose
paranoia was growing steadily deeper, as well. Of course, finding any Bédardist
who was insane enough *not* to be terrified of Clyntahn would probably have
been an impossible task. Still, Duchairn would have liked to have something
besides his own layman's opinion—where matters of the mind were concerned, at least—to go on.

Not that it mattered a great deal. He didn't need a formal diagnosis to know
Clyntahn would have taken any comment about the *Writ*'s injunction to care
for the poor and the least fortunate of God's children as a criticism of the

Church's record in that regard. As a matter of fact, he would have been perfectly correct if he'd done so, too, Duchairn admitted. But at this particular moment, when Zhaspahr Clyntahn had divided the entire world into just three categories—those who were his allies, those who had an at least fleeting value as tools, and those who must be exterminated without mercy—suggesting that any aspect of the Church's stewardship might be found wanting was dangerous.

Duchairn had discovered there were times when he really didn't care about that. When his anger, his outrage, the pain stemming from his refound faith's recognition of his own blood guilt, actually drove him to *seek* confrontation with Clyntahn. When he found himself almost yearning for destruction, even martyrdom, with all that would entail, as some sort of expiation for his own life. For his own acceptance of the vicarate's corruption. His own lifelong eagerness to profit by that corruption. For the fact that he'd stood there and not simply accepted Clyntahn's proposal to destroy the Kingdom of Charis utterly but actually *acquiesced* in it. Helped to arrange it.

Duchairn made himself resume his progress towards his waiting underlings, but his eyes were as bleak as the snow beyond the hallway's windows as he once more admitted his guilt to himself. He wouldn't pretend he wasn't terrified of what Clyntahn would have done to him if it had come to an open confrontation. That he didn't know precisely how savage an example Clyntahn would make of any member of the Group of Four who seemed to have turned against him. Yet it wasn't *that* fear which drove him to bite his tongue, keep his furious denunciation of Clyntahn's vileness lodged behind his clenched teeth. No, it was quite a different fear that kept him silent: the fear that if he allowed himself to be too easily destroyed he would commit the still more grievous sin of dying without at least trying to undo the terrible, terrible damage he had helped to unleash upon God's own world.

*Not that I've figured out how to go about undoing any of it yet,* he admitted desolately. *Maybe that's part of my penance? Is it part of my punishment to be forced to watch things getting worse and worse without seeing any way to make them* better *again? But the* Writ *says God will always find a way, whether man can or not. So maybe what He really* wants *me to do is to stop trying so hard, stop being so arrogant as to think I can somehow fix a disaster on a worldwide scale. Maybe He wants me to finally accept that I need to let* Him *show* me *what to do, and then—*

Rhobair Duchairn's thoughts were abruptly interrupted as he walked full tilt into a wall someone had inconsiderately left in the exact center of the hallway.

That was what it *felt* like, at any rate, although the wall's sudden "Oof!" suggested it might not actually have been the solid granite obstruction it appeared to be.

He staggered backwards, almost falling. In fact, he *would* have fallen if someone's hands hadn't caught him by the upper arms and held him upright.

He shook his head, cold-clogged ears ringing, and his eyes widened as they refocused on the face of the man he'd run into.

Duchairn was not a short man, but neither was he a giant. In fact, he'd always been on the slender side, and his had been a decidedly sedentary life for the last twenty or thirty years. The man with whom he'd just collided was half a head taller than he, broad-shouldered and powerfully built, and he'd obviously spent the last several years of his own life exercising to maintain the physical toughness he'd enjoyed as a senior officer of the Temple Guard. He must outweigh Duchairn by a good forty or fifty pounds, and very little of that weight advantage was fat.

And he also happened to be named Hauwerd Wylsynn.

Duchairn found himself temporarily paralyzed, staring into eyes of Wylsynn gray. They were hard, those eyes, with polished, quartz-like purpose. The eyes of a man who, unlike Rhobair Duchairn, had never compromised with the Temple's corruption. Of a man who had every reason to fear Zhaspahr Clyntahn . . . and no reason at all to fear God.

"You want to be a bit more careful, Rhobair," Wylsynn said, setting him fully back on his feet before he released his grip on Duchairn's arms. He patted the smaller man almost gently, as if to be certain there was no breakage, and his smile was thin. "You might do yourself a mischief running into people like that. Life's too short to take that sort of chance, don't you think?"

Wylsynn cocked his head slightly with the question, and Duchairn felt an icicle run through his veins. There was something about Wylsynn's tone, something about the glitter of those hard eyes.

*He knows,* Duchairn thought. *He* knows *I warned his brother. And, God help me, he knows Clyntahn is going to kill both of them. And that I don't have the courage to try to stop him.*

The Church's Treasurer felt his mouth open without having the least notion of what was going to come out of it, but then Wylsynn shook his head. It was a quick gesture, one that stopped whatever Duchairn might have been about to say cold.

"Of course it is," the doomed man said. "Too short, I mean. There are too many things we all need to do to just throw away the time to do them in. Doesn't the *Writ* say God sets the course for every man to run?"

"Yes," Duchairn heard himself say. "Yes, it does."

"Well, then I don't imagine He's through with any of us until we've finished running it. So be more careful." He actually smiled faintly, wagging an index finger under Duchairn's nose. "Watch where you're walking, or else you won't have time to do all the running God has in mind for you."

It took every ounce of Duchairn's self-control to clamp his mouth on what he wanted to say. He looked into those gray eyes, and he didn't really trust himself to speak at all when he realized what was truly looking back at him out of them. Wylsynn only smiled at him again, gently this time, and gave him another pat, then turned and walked away.

▼    ▼    ▼

"The Earl of Coris, Your Holiness," the upper-priest said as he bowed Phylyp Ahzgood into the small, private meeting chamber.

It wasn't very much of a bow, Coris reflected. Then again, the upper-priest was assigned to the Chancellor's office. He probably saw dukes by the dozen and earls by the score, and God only knew how many bevies of mere barons he might encounter every year. Not to mention the fact that most of the dukes and earls who crossed his path weren't dispossessed exiles living on someone else's charity.

"So I see," a voice replied. "Come in, My Lord."

Coris obeyed the summons and found himself facing a tallish, lean man with an angular face, a closely trimmed beard, and deep, intelligent eyes. He wore the orange cassock of a vicar, and he matched the description of Vicar Zahmsyn Trynair quite well.

Trynair extended his hand, and Coris bent to kiss the sapphire ring, then straightened.

"Your Holiness," he acknowledged.

"We appreciate the promptness with which you've responded to our summons, My Lord, especially at this time of the year," Trynair said. His smile never touched his eyes. "Would that all of Mother Church's sons were so mindful of their duty to her."

"I won't pretend it wasn't an arduous journey, Your Holiness." Coris allowed himself a slight, wry smile of his own. "But as a boy, I was always taught that when Mother Church calls, her sons answer. And it was also interesting, especially the voyage across Lake Pei, while the opportunity to finally visit the Temple is an added blessing."

"Good."

The single, perfunctory word came not from Trynair, but from the shorter, portly, silver-haired, heavy-jowled vicar who hadn't bothered to rise when Coris entered. There was no doubt about his identity, either, the earl thought, although he was just a bit surprised to realize Zhaspahr Clyntahn matched so completely the descriptions he'd received. Right down to the spots spilled food had left on his cassock.

*There ought to be a rule that real villains aren't allowed to look like stereotypical villains,* Coris thought, and felt a tiny shiver run through him as he realized how he'd just allowed himself to describe Clyntahn. It wasn't really a *surprise*; he'd been headed in that direction for years, after all. Yet there was an odd sense of commitment to the moment, as if he'd crossed some irrevocable bridge, even if he was the only one who realized he had.

*And you'd damned well better make sure you stay the only one who realizes you have, Phylyp!* he told himself.

From Clyntahn's expression, he didn't much care what might be going through Coris' mind at the moment. Nor did he appear to feel tempted to expend any courtesy on their visitor. Where Trynair's eyes held the cool dispassion of a chess master, Clyntahn's glowed with the fervor of a zealot. A fervor which confirmed Coris' long-standing opinion that Clyntahn was, by far, the more dangerous of the two.

"Please be seated, My Lord," Trynair invited, indicating the single chair on Coris' side of the meeting-room table.

It was the simplest chair Coris had yet seen inside the Temple—a straight-backed, apparently unpadded, utilitarian piece of furniture. It was certainly a far cry from the throne-like chairs in which Trynair and Clyntahn were ensconced, yet when he settled onto it, he almost jumped back to his feet in astonishment as what had appeared to be a simple wooden surface seemed to *shift* under him. It moved—*flowed*—and he couldn't keep his eyes from widening as the chair shaped itself perfectly to the configuration of his body.

He looked up to see Trynair regarding him speculatively, and made himself smile at the Chancellor. It was an expression which blended an admission of surprise with a sizable dollop of boyish enjoyment, and Trynair allowed himself the small chuckle of a host who has successfully surprised a guest.

Clyntahn—predictably, probably—seemed completely oblivious to the small moment, Coris noted.

*Best not to assume anything of the sort, Phylyp,* he told himself. *I wouldn't be a bit surprised if Clyntahn's long since figured out just how useful it can be to have potential opponents underestimate one's powers of observation. The only thing in the world more dangerous than a fool, especially when it comes to the "great game," is a smart man you've assumed is stupid. Nahrmahn should certainly have taught you that much!*

"Well," Trynair began briskly after a moment, "now that you're here, My Lord, I suppose we ought to get right down to business. As you know, I have, as Mother Church's Chancellor, and acting on Grand Vicar Erek's specific instructions, formally recognized young Prince Daivyn as the rightful ruler of Corisande. Given his tender years, it struck us as unnecessary to bring him all the way to the Temple to discuss his future with him. You, on the other hand, are his legal guardian. Since we do not—and never will—recognize that travesty of a 'Regency Council' Cayleb and Sharleyan have foisted upon God, we also regard you as the closest thing Daivyn has at this time to a true regent."

He paused, as if inviting comment, but Coris wasn't about to rush into that particular snare. He contented himself with a slow nod of understanding and an attentive expression, instead.

"In light of the circumstances," the Chancellor resumed a few seconds later, "we think it's essential to . . . regularize Daivyn's position. While he would appear to be safe enough for the moment under the protection of King Zhames, especially given the fact Delferahk is already at war with the apostates, there are certain aspects of his situation which we feel require formal clarification."

He paused once more, and this time it was obvious he intended to stay paused until Coris responded.

"'Formal clarification,' Your Holiness?" the earl obediently repeated. "May I ask what sort of clarification?"

"Oh, come now, My Lord!" Clyntahn entered the discussion, waving one hand in a dismissive gesture. "You were Prince Hektor's spymaster. You know how the game is played, if anyone does!"

"Your Holiness," Coris replied, choosing his words more carefully than he'd ever chosen words in his life before, "you're right. I was Prince Hektor's spymaster. But, if you'll forgive me for saying so, my perspective from a single princedom that far from the Temple couldn't possibly be the same as your perspective from right here, at the heart of all of Mother Church's concerns *and* at the focus of all of the avenues of information Mother Church possesses. I'll admit I've spent a lot of time trying to analyze the information I do have in an effort to anticipate what it is you and the Chancellor have called me here to explain. I'm not foolish enough, however, to assume for a moment that I have *enough* information to make any sort of truly informed deductions. I can think of several aspects of Prince Daivyn's current situation which might require 'clarification,' but without a better understanding of precisely how Prince Daivyn—and I, of course—can best serve Mother Church, I truly don't know how you and Vicar Zahmsyn may wish to proceed."

Trynair's eyes had flickered with what might have been irritation when Clyntahn spoke up. Now the Chancellor sat back in his own chair, folding his hands together on the table before him, his expression thoughtful. Clyntahn, on the other hand, gave Coris an oddly triumphant little smile, as if the earl's response had passed some sort of test.

"We're naturally relieved to learn you've been thinking about how best Daivyn—and you yourself—can serve Mother Church," the Grand Inquisitor said, and the emphasis on the word "you" was as unmistakable as the glow in his eyes. "I feel confident we'll be able to rely as fully upon your intelligence and diligence as Prince Hektor ever did."

*"And we'd damned well* better *be able to,"* eh, Your Holiness? Is that it? Coris thought trenchantly. However intelligent Clyntahn might actually be, he was dangerously transparent in at least some ways. Of course, when a man controlled all the levers of power that came together in the office of the Grand Inquisitor, he could probably afford a certain degree of transparency, at least when it suited his own purposes to come straight to the point.

"I'll certainly do my very best to justify your confidence, Your Holiness," he said out loud.

"Then I hope you'll understand that what I'm about to say reflects no lack of confidence in you personally, My Lord," Trynair said. Coris looked back at him, and the Chancellor shrugged very slightly. "Under the circumstances, the Grand Vicar deems it best to formally vest authority as Prince Daivyn's regent in the vicarate, rather than in any secular noble. His father was martyred by the champions of apostasy and impious heresy. The Grand Vicar believes it is incumbent upon Mother Church to openly—and expressly—extend her protection to Prince Hektor's heir."

"Of course, Your Holiness," Coris replied.

He was confident Trynair would assume—accurately—that he recognized that business about Grand Vicar Erek as pure fiction. Trynair had hand-selected the current Grand Vicar from a short list of suitable puppets years ago, and if Erek had ever cherished a single independent thought since assuming the Grand Vicar's throne, that thought had undoubtedly perished of loneliness long since.

"In many ways," Trynair continued, "that change will represent little more than a technicality. As I suggested earlier, there's no need to further destabilize young Daivyn's life at this time. Better to leave him where he is, under the care of someone he trusts and knows is looking out for his best interests."

*Especially if the someone he trusts is looking out for the interests of the Church—or of the Group of Four, at least—instead,* Coris thought.

"And, to be frank, My Lord," Clyntahn said, "we're of the opinion that it won't hurt a bit to have a man with your particular set of skills and experiences watching over him." Coris looked at him, and the Grand Inquisitor shrugged his beefy shoulders. "After all, Cayleb's already murdered the boy's father. There's no telling when someone like him—or that bitch Sharleyan—might decide the time's come to make a clean sweep of the entire House of Daykyn. I understand they're confronting considerable popular unrest in Corisande. They might just come to the conclusion that it would be a good idea to remove young Daivyn as a potential focus for the more restive elements of the Princedom's population."

"I see, Your Holiness." Coris prayed that the icicle which had just danced down his spine wasn't apparent to either of the vicars. "Obviously, I discussed Prince Daivyn's security with King Zhames before I left Talkyra. As you say, I don't think we could be too careful where his safety is concerned. And I assure you that once I return to Delferahk, I'll exercise personal oversight of his security arrangements."

"Good!" Clyntahn smiled broadly. "I feel confident our decision to rely upon you and your judgment will prove well placed, My Lord."

"As do I," Trynair seconded. "In the meantime, however, we have several other points to discuss," the Chancellor went on. "I'm sure it will take us several sessions to cover all of them, and you will, of course, remain the Temple's honored guest until we've completed them. For the moment, what we'd really like to do, though, is to pick your brain a little bit. Obviously, we've had many reports about the situation in Corisande and the attitude of the Corisandian people, but you're a Corisandian yourself. And one who was extremely well placed to see the consequences of Cayleb's invasion from Corisande's view-point. No doubt there have been many changes since your own departure from the Princedom, but you still represent a priceless resource from our perspective. There are many points on which we would greatly appreciate hearing anything you can tell us. For example, which of Prince Hektor's—I mean Prince *Daivyn's,* now—nobles do you think would be most likely to organize effective resistance against the Charisian occupation?"

*Well, I can see* this *is going to take some time,* Coris thought dryly. *Still, best to be careful about how we proceed, especially when we don't know how much information they've already got.*

"That's a complicated question, Your Holiness," he began. "I can think of at least a dozen of Prince Hektor's closer allies among the Corisandian Lords who are almost certainly thinking in those directions. Without a better feel than I have at this time—please do recall that I've been traveling for the better part of four months, which has prevented me from setting up any sort of proper network—I would suspect those farther from Manchyr would be in a better po-sition to *act* upon such thoughts, however.

"Bearing that in mind, I'd be inclined to think the Earl of Storm Keep and the Earl of Craggy Hill have probably already begun to take steps along exactly those lines. Neither of them are going to feel particularly well disposed towards Cayleb and Sharleyan, and both are located well up to the north, out of easy reach from the capital.

"Moving back to the south, and west," he continued, "I wouldn't be dreadfully surprised to find Duke Black Water—that would be Sir Adulfo, the new Earl—is headed in the same direction. For that matter, the Duke of Bar-cair is probably similarly inclined, and—"

▼ ▼ ▼

"So, Master Seablanket. I see you've succeeded admirably in your assignment once again."

"I've certainly attempted to, Your Eminence."

Rhobair Seablanket bowed over Archbishop Wyllym Rayno's hand, kissing the proffered ring, then straightened. His expression was politely attentive, waiting for Rayno's questions to begin, and the archbishop smiled very slightly.

Rayno was short, dark, and slender. As always, he wore the habit of a simple monk in the Order of Schueler's dark purple. But that habit bore the flame-crowned sword of the Schuelerite Adjutant General, which made him Vicar Zhaspahr Clyntahn's second-in-command and a very dangerous man, indeed. He was always a bit amused by the way the Inquisition's various agents reacted to him. More to the point, he'd learned over the years that those reactions offered a valuable yardstick for evaluating an agent's capabilities. Take Seablanket, for example. No one who'd risen as high in the Inquisition's service as he had was going to be foolish enough to take the adjutant general lightly, nor could he be unaware of the potential consequences of disappointing him, yet the Corisandian's eyes met Rayno's levelly, and his composure appeared genuine.

*Maybe he really is as calm as he looks,* the archbishop thought. *And maybe he isn't. I wonder which it is? If he's really that comfortable meeting me for a face-to-face interview for the very first time, he could be more foolish than I'd expected.* No one's *conscience is so clear that they shouldn't feel at least a little anxiety under these circumstances. On the other hand, if he's able to* appear *this comfortable under those same circumstances, then his ability to dissemble is even greater than his file indicates. And in that case, I'm sure I can find profitable employment for an agent of his caliber elsewhere once he's no longer needed to keep an eye on Coris.*

"I've read your reports," Rayno continued out loud. "I must say that, compared to some of the accounts which cross my desk, yours have been clear, concise, and comprehensive. And the grammar's actually been correct!"

His whimsical smile didn't touch his eyes, and Seablanket managed to restrain any unseemly temptation to laughter.

"From those reports," Rayno continued, "it would appear Earl Coris is both aware of the political realities of Prince Daivyn's position and also . . . pragmatic enough, shall we say, to be aware of how those realities might impinge upon his own future. At the same time, he seems to be even more competent than I'd anticipated. I suppose I really shouldn't be too terribly surprised by that, given how long he held his position under Prince Hektor. However, I have several specific questions I'd like to address, and I've discovered over the years that even the best written reports are sometimes . . . incomplete."

Seablanket stirred slightly, and Rayno raised his right hand in a gentle, fluttering gesture.

"I'm not suggesting anything was intentionally omitted, Master Seablanket. I have seen that happen on occasion, of course," he smiled again, thinly, "but what I really meant was that written reports are no substitute for oral reports in which questions can be asked, individual points can be more fully explained, and I can be certain I've actually understood what you meant to say the first time."

He paused, head cocked slightly, expression expectant, and Seablanket nodded.

"I take your meaning, Your Eminence. And, obviously, if you have any questions or any points you'd like more thoroughly gone into, I'm at your service. I would, though, point out that the Earl will be expecting to find me in his chambers when he returns from his interview with Vicar Zahmsyn and Vicar Zhaspahr."

"An excellent point to bear in mind," Rayno agreed. "On the other hand, the Chancellor and the Grand Inquisitor are going to be picking his brain about Corisande's internal politics for quite some time. I estimate that the process will take at least two or three hours, and to be frank, Master Seablanket, as important as this is in many ways, I'm afraid I don't have two or three hours to devote to it this morning."

"Of course, Your Eminence," Seablanket murmured with a small bow.

Rayno nodded, satisfied the Corisandian had taken the point. It never hurt to encourage brevity and concision in an agent's report.

"In that case, Master Seablanket, let us begin." Rayno settled into the comfortable chair behind his desk without offering Seablanket a seat. He tipped back, resting his elbows on the chair arms, and steepled his fingers across his chest. "First," he said, "your reports indicate Prince Daivyn seems to trust Coris implicitly. Would you care to expand briefly on why you think that?"

"Your Eminence, the Prince is a very little boy at the moment," Seablanket responded without hesitation. "He knows his father is dead and that his own life would be in danger if Charisian assassins could reach him."

The agent's eyes met Rayno's again, and the archbishop's respect for the other man inched up another notch. Obviously, Seablanket had his own suspicions about who'd actually been behind Hektor's assassination. Equally obviously, he had no intention of ever voicing those suspicions aloud. Yet he was also smart enough to know what Rayno was truly interested in discovering.

"Under those circumstances, and given the fact that he's known the Earl for his entire life—not to mention the fact that he knows his father specifically named the Earl as his legal guardian—it's hardly surprising Daivyn should trust the man. And, frankly, the Earl's done everything he could to encourage that trust." Seablanket smiled ever so slightly. "He was Prince Hektor's spymaster for years, Your Eminence. Convincing a little boy to view him as his best friend, as well as his protector, is child's play after something like that."

"So it's your opinion Coris is deliberately encouraging the boy's dependency on him?"

"I wouldn't actually put it precisely that way, Your Eminence." Seablanket pursed his lips slightly, eyes narrowed in thought as he searched for exactly the words he wanted.

"He doesn't have to encourage the Prince's *dependency* on him," the agent went on after a moment. "It's already clear to everyone, including Daivyn and Princess Irys, that both of them are completely dependent on him. King Zhames may be their official protector, but to be perfectly honest, I doubt His Majesty is even half as smart as Earl Coris." Seablanket shrugged. "It's only a matter of time before the Earl has the entire court at Talkyra dancing to his tune, whoever may officially be in charge. So it's not so much a case of his encouraging Daivyn's dependency as much as it is encouraging Daivyn's *trust*. Of getting the boy to regard him as not simply his primary adviser but as his *only* adviser. I'm sure at least some of it is for the Prince's own good," Seablanket smiled piously, "but the upshot is that when the time comes for the Earl to 'recommend' a course of action to Prince Daivyn, the boy isn't going to hesitate for a moment. And he's going to take the Earl's advice regardless of what anyone else, even his sister, might have to say about it."

"So you believe Coris is going to be in a position to control the boy?"

"I believe he'll be in a position to control the boy's *decisions,* Your Eminence. At the moment, King Zhames controls the boy's physical security." Seablanket met the archbishop's eye again. "If His Majesty should decide for some reason that it might be . . . advantageous for Prince Daivyn to fall into someone else's hands, I doubt the Earl would be in a position to prevent it."

"And do you believe there is some danger of King Zhames making such a decision?" Rayno's eyes had narrowed, and Seablanket shrugged.

"Your Eminence, I'm not in King Zhames' service, and my insight where he's concerned is far more limited than anything I might be able to tell you about the Earl. I'm not attempting to suggest His Majesty has any plans at all for Prince Daivyn—other than any he may have already discussed with you and the Grand Inquisitor, of course—but it's no secret in Talkyra that he's under a great deal of pressure at the moment. The Charisian Navy has completely wiped out his merchant marine, and Charisian raiding parties are operating freely all along his coasts. His army isn't being any more successful at stopping them ashore than his navy's been at stopping them at sea, either. Under those circumstances, who can say how he might eventually be tempted to play a card like Prince Daivyn?"

Rayno nodded slowly. That was an excellent point, and the fact that Seablanket had made it was another indication of the man's intelligence and general capability. And his suggestion that Zhames might not be the most reliable of guardians . . . that might be distressingly well taken, given what had already happened with certain other rulers (Prince Nahrmahn of Emerald came rather forcibly to mind) who'd found themselves in Cayleb of Charis' path. Still . . .

"I don't think we need concern ourselves too deeply with King Zhames at the moment," he observed, half to Seablanket and half simply thinking out loud. "I doubt very much that he's likely to disregard any directives from the Temple where Daivyn is concerned."

"I'm certain he wouldn't, Your Eminence," Seablanket agreed, yet there was something about his tone, a slight edge of . . . something. Rayno cocked his head, frowning, and then his own eyes widened. Could the Corisandian be suggesting—?

"Naturally," the archbishop said, "we have to be at least a bit concerned about Daivyn's current security. After all, his father's security in Manchyr seemed quite adequate. And I suppose we really ought to be thinking in terms of multiple layers of protection for the boy. It's sadly true that human nature is easily corrupted, and the possibility always exists that someone responsible for protecting him might be suborned by those more interested in *harming* him. Or in . . . transferring him to someone else's custody, shall we say."

"Exactly so, Your Eminence." Seablanket bowed once more. "And, if I may be so bold, it couldn't hurt to be doubly certain the man in charge of the Prince's security sees his own first and primary loyalty as belonging to Mother Church."

Rayno's eyes narrowed again, this time with more than a little surprise. Seablanket hadn't been chosen for his present assignment solely because he was a Corisandian who could be placed in Yu-Shai in time to be hired as Coris' valet. He'd handled more than one politically sensitive mission for the Inquisition over the years, but the archbishop hadn't expected him to be quite so willing to bring up that particular point.

"And do you believe Coris' 'first and primary loyalty' is to Mother Church?" the adjutant general asked softly.

"I believe the Earl's first and primary loyalty *was* to Prince Hektor," Seablanket replied with the air of a man choosing his words very carefully. "I'm not prepared to speculate on how much of that loyalty might have been owed to his own ambition and the power he enjoyed as one of Prince Hektor's closest advisers, but I believe it was genuine. Prince Hektor is dead now, however, Your Eminence, and the Earl's lands in Corisande have been seized by Cayleb and Sharleyan. He's a man accustomed to wielding power, and that's been taken away from him with the fall of Corisande and his own exile. He's not foolish enough to believe Cayleb or Sharleyan would ever trust anyone who was as close to Hektor as he was, so even if he were tempted to try to reach some sort of an arrangement with them—and I don't believe for a moment that he is— he'd know the effort was probably pointless, at best. At worst, Cayleb might happily agree to give him whatever he asked for . . . until, at the least, he could get the Earl within reach.

"More than that, Your Eminence, it seems apparent to me that the Earl recognizes that, ultimately, Charis can't possibly win. I don't think he's likely to be very tempted to sell his allegiance to the side which is bound to lose in the end. That being the case, I can't escape the feeling that worldly ambition—in addition to spiritual loyalty—would incline him towards casting his lot with Mother Church. And he's a very pragmatic man." Seablanket shrugged very slightly. "I'm sure that as Hektor's spymaster he came to realize long ago that sometimes certain . . . practical accommodations have to be made."

"I see."

Rayno considered Seablanket's words for several seconds. He'd been a bit concerned himself, from time to time, about the possibility of Coris' seeking some arrangement with Cayleb. After all, the earl was in a position to deliver Prince Daivyn to Charis, and Cayleb—and Sharleyan, damn her soul—had to be aware of how valuable a counter Daivyn had become. On the other hand, any attempt to hand the youthful prince over to Charis would be fraught with difficulty and danger, and Coris couldn't possibly be unaware of what Mother Church would do to him if he made such an attempt and failed.

Yet Rayno hadn't fully considered the other two points Seablanket had just raised. It truly was unlikely Cayleb, and especially Sharleyan, would ever repose an ounce of trust in the Earl of Coris. For one thing, Sharleyan was never going to forget that Coris had been Hektor's spymaster when her father was killed—that it was Coris who'd actually arranged to hire the mercenary "pirates" responsible for King Sailys' death. And even leaving that consideration aside, there was Seablanket's assessment of Coris' estimate of who was ultimately going to win this war. Unless something happened to catastrophically shift the balance of power between the two sides, Charis couldn't possibly win against Mother Church. It was conceivable, little though Rayno liked to admit it, that an independent Charis might *survive* Mother Church's ire, but nothing short of divine intervention could create circumstances under which Charis could actually *defeat* the Church and its effectively limitless resources. From everything he'd ever seen or heard about the Earl of Coris, the man was certainly smart enough to have reached the conclusions Seablanket had just ascribed to him. And a man who'd lost everything he'd spent his life building had to be thinking in terms of restoring at least a little of what had been taken from him.

*It's certainly worth bearing in mind,* the archbishop told himself. *All my reports on Coris suggest Seablanket's right when he says the Earl is far smarter than Zhames. Which means he's a lot less likely to be tempted to do something outstandingly stupid. Leaving him right where he is as Daivyn's guardian could be the smartest thing we could do. Always assuming Seablanket's reading of his character is reliable.*

He thought about it for a few more moments, then gave a mental shrug. Trynair and Clyntahn would undoubtedly be forming their own opinions about Coris and his reliability over the next few five-days. They'd probably rely more on their own judgment than on any outside advice, but it would be a good idea for Rayno to have his own recommendation ready if it should be asked for.

He put that consideration aside, tucking it into a mental pigeonhole for future contemplation, and returned his attention to Seablanket.

"Those are some very interesting observations, Master Seablanket," he conceded. "However, there are several other points I need to discuss with you, and I'm afraid time is pressing onward. So, bearing that in mind, what can you tell me about Prince Daivyn's own attitude towards Charis?"

"As I've already said, Your Eminence, he's a very young boy whose father has been murdered, and whatever denials Cayleb and Sharleyan may have issued, I don't believe there's any doubt in Daivyn's mind who was responsible. Under those circumstances, I don't think it's very surprising that he hates and distrusts—and fears—Cayleb with every fiber of his being. It hasn't been difficult for Earl Coris and King Zhames to encourage those emotions, either." Seablanket gave another of those tiny shrugs. "Under the circumstances," he said, his tone ever so slightly edged with irony, "encouraging him to feel that way can only contribute to his own chances of survival, of course."

He met Rayno's gaze yet again, and this time the archbishop found himself unable to totally restrain an unwilling smile. He was definitely going to have to find future employment for Seablanket, he thought. The man was even more perceptive and (even more valuable in an agent) willing to share those perceptions than Rayno had expected.

"Having said that," the Corisandian continued, "Daivyn's also angry enough to be looking for any possible way to hurt Cayleb or Charis. Admittedly, he's only a boy, but that won't be true forever. By the time he comes to young manhood—assuming he can avoid Charisian assassins long enough for that—he's going to be fully committed to the destruction of this 'Charisian Empire' and all its works. In fact, I think—"

Wyllym Rayno sat back in his chair, listening attentively. He might well have to cancel his next appointment after all, he thought. Given the acuity of Seablanket's insight into the inner workings of the Corisandian court in exile in Talkyra, it might be very much worthwhile to get the man's impressions of the cities and provinces through which he and Coris had passed on their way to the Temple. Rayno had plenty of reports from Inquisitors and intendants throughout all of the mainland realms, but Seablanket clearly had a sharp and discerning eye, and Coris' rank had been high enough to get Seablanket inside the highest circles of the lands through which they had traveled. True, he was only the earl's valet, but any spymaster knew servants made the very best spies. They saw and heard everything, yet their betters tended to think of them as part of the landscape, little more than animate furniture. All of which meant Seablanket's perspective on the reports from Rayno's agents in place could be extremely valuable.

*I really have to keep an eye on this one,* the archbishop told himself, listening to Seablanket's report. *Spies who can actually* think *are too rare—and valuable—to waste on routine duties.*

▼　　▼　　▼

Rhobair Duchairn sat back, rubbing his forehead wearily. Another half hour, he thought, and they could finally break for lunch. He was looking forward to it, and not just because he'd skimped on breakfast that morning. His head throbbed, the congestion in his ears was worse than ever (the clerk who was currently speaking sounded as if he were in a barrel underwater), and he dearly wanted a little time in privacy to consider his unexpected encounter with Hauwerd Wylsynn.

Not that he expected to feel a great deal of comfort after he'd done the considering, he thought.

He felt his nose start to drip and muttered a short, pungent phrase which went rather poorly with the dignity of his august office. He *hated* blowing his nose in public, but the alternative seemed worse. So he reached into his pocket for his handkerchief—

—and froze.

For just an instant, not a single muscle moved, and then he forced himself to relax, one nerve at a time. He hoped no one had noticed his reaction. And when he thought about it, there was no reason anyone should have, really. But that didn't prevent him from feeling as if he had somehow, in that instant, pasted an enormous archer's target onto his own back.

Or, perhaps, had someone else paste it there.

His fingertips explored the small but thick envelope which had somehow come to be nestled under his handkerchief. It hadn't been there when he left his suite this morning, and he knew *he* hadn't put it there since. In fact, he could think of only one person who'd been close enough to find the opportunity to slide anything unobtrusively into his pocket.

And just at this moment, he couldn't think of a single gift that person could have given him that wouldn't be at least potentially more deadly than its own weight in cyanide.

*Odd,* a corner of his brain thought. *For someone who was so hungry a few seconds ago, I seem to have lost my appetite remarkably quickly.*

.IV.
Royal College,
Tellesberg Palace,
City of Tellesberg,
Kingdom of Old Charis

Baron Seamount is here, Doctor."

Rahzhyr Mahklyn looked up from the notes in front of him as Dairak Bowave poked his head through the office door. Bowave was a cheerful young man, not that many years older than Emperor Cayleb, and when he wasn't working directly with Mahklyn, he tended to spend his time with Mahklyn's son-in-law, Aizak Kahnklyn, in the Royal College's library. There was certainly plenty to do there, Mahklyn reflected grimly. They'd accomplished a lot since the College's original home had been burned to the ground eleven months earlier, yet their current collection remained little more than a shadow of what it had been, and organizing the new material as it came in was a huge task.

Of course, even though Aizak and Bowave didn't know it, what Mahklyn now had access to dwarfed everything they'd lost.

Not that he could tell either of them.

"Ask the Baron to come in, please, Dairak," he said out loud.

"Of course." Bowave smiled, nodded, and disappeared, and Mahklyn started jogging the handwritten pages neatly together.

The notes in question were from Sahndrah Lywys. He'd been scanning them in preparation for this very meeting, and he was amused by how easily he'd been able to follow them . . . now. Dr. Lywys' writing style had always been clear and concise, even elegant, but her handwriting was also what might charitably be called "spidery," and Mahklyn's nearsightedness—"myopia," as Merlin Athrawes called it—had been getting steadily worse for years. Despite the best lenses which could be ground, he'd found it harder and harder to read even the printed word. Until very recently, that was. Now the "contact lenses" Merlin had provided to go with Mahklyn's "com" had also corrected his vision to miraculous clarity. In fact, Mahklyn suspected it was better than it had been even in the days of his now-distant youth. Of course that youth had been long enough ago the golden glow of memory could well be playing tricks on him, but he *knew* his ability to see things in poor light had improved enormously. He still didn't have the low-light acuity Merlin Athrawes did, yet he saw far better than anyone else could.

"Baron Seamount, Doctor," young Bowave said, ushering a rather short, pudgy officer in the sky-blue tunic and loose black trousers of the Imperial Charisian Navy into the large, sunlit room.

"Ahlfryd!" Mahklyn stood behind his desk, holding out his right hand, and the two men clasped forearms.

They'd known one another only slightly before Merlin Athrawes arrived in Charis, but over the last three years they'd become critical members of the small, slowly growing cadre of advisers and innovators Emperor Cayleb had gathered together. Unlike Mahklyn, Seamount still didn't know the full truth about Merlin. Or, for that matter, the *full* truth about the ultimate nature of Charis' life-and-death fight against the Group of Four. None of which had kept him from making enormous contributions to Charis' survival.

*And if Byrkyt can finally bring the rest of the Brethren around, we'll get him admitted to the inner circle. And past damned time we did, too,* Mahklyn thought grumpily.

"Rahzhyr," Sir Ahlfryd Hyndryk returned the greeting with a smile of his own. "I'm glad you could fit me in."

"I imagine His Majesty would've had a little something to say if I *hadn't* found it possible to 'fit you in,' despite my massively crowded schedule," Mahklyn said dryly, waving for the baron to seat himself in the armchair facing his desk. "And even if His Majesty hadn't, I know damned well *Her* Majesty would have."

Mahklyn added the final sentence just a bit feelingly, and Seamount chuckled. Empress Sharleyan had shown a deep interest in the baron's many projects. Not only did she have a keen appreciation for the advantages and tactical implications of his efforts, but her agile, ever-active brain had produced quite a few eminently worthwhile suggestions of her own. And, in the process, a genuine friendship had sprung up between her and the baron.

"On the other hand," Mahklyn continued, "it really didn't take the threat of potential imperial displeasure to get you in to see me." He shrugged. "I never have time to keep completely abreast of your memos, Ahlfryd, but I keep up well enough to know you and those Helen Island minions of yours are making all kinds of waves again. Thank God."

"We try," Seamount acknowledged. "Although I have to admit the tempo seems to slow down just a bit with Captain Athrawes out of the Kingdom." The look he gave Mahklyn was more than a little speculative, but the civilian had become accustomed to the pudgy commodore's occasional probes where Merlin was concerned.

"He does seem to have that . . . *fertilizing* effect, doesn't he?" he said in reply.

"I hadn't realized you had such a command of understatement," Seamount observed with a thin smile.

"We academics inevitably become masters of the language," Mahklyn said with a matching smile, then tipped back in his swivel chair. "So, what's managed to pry you loose from King's Harbor?"

"Actually, the main thing I want to do, as I believe I mentioned in my note, is to spend a little time with Dr. Lywys. I've got a couple of questions I need her to answer for me, if she can. But I also wanted to get *you* broadly informed about where we are at the moment."

Mahklyn nodded. Given the fact that the Royal College's pursuit of knowledge had always skirted a little too close to the edge of the Proscriptions of Jwo-jeng for some of the clergy's comfort, it had seemed like a good idea to keep it well separated from the Crown when old King Cayleb I originally endowed it. By the time Mahklyn became the College's head, that separation had become a firm tradition, and despite his own involvement in the original innovations Merlin Athrawes had midwifed, he'd seen no reason to change it.

Until, that was, arsonists had destroyed the original College and very nearly murdered Mahklyn himself in the process. At which point Emperor Cayleb— only he'd still been *King* Cayleb at the time—had decided the time for such nonsense was past. He'd moved the College onto the grounds of Tellesberg Palace, assigned responsibility for its security to the Royal Guard, and brought one Rahzhyr Mahklyn fully inside his own inner circle. One of the outward signs of that change was the fact that Mahklyn had also been formally named to head the "Imperial Council of Inquiry" when Empress Sharleyan created it.

"So inform me," he invited now, clasping his hands behind his head and leaning still farther back in his chair.

"Well," Seamount began, "first, I finally got my Experimental Board—you know, the one I've been kicking around as a concept for so long?—set up. Took me a while, I admit, but a lot of that was because of how long it took to find the right man to head it. I finally have, though, I think. I can't remember— have you ever actually met Commander Mahndrayn?"

" 'Mahndrayn'?" Mahklyn repeated slowly, frowning thoughtfully. Then his eyes narrowed. "Tall, skinny, young fellow, with black hair? Always looks like his trousers are about to catch on fire?"

"I don't know that I'd describe him exactly like that." Seamount's lips quivered, although he managed not to laugh out loud. "Still, he *is* a bit fidgety, so I'd say you've got the right man."

Mahklyn nodded, although "a bit fidgety" fell well short of the young man *he* remembered. His own impression of Mahndrayn had been of a man possessed of an abundance—one might almost have called it a *super*abundance—of nervous energy. Physically, the commander could have been deliberately designed as Seamount's antithesis, but Mahklyn could see far greater and more important similarities under the skin.

"At any rate," the commodore continued, "I've assigned Urvyn—that's his first name—to ride herd on my other clever young officers. In fact, I told him I wanted him to start out by examining everything we think we already know."

"What we think we already know?" Mahklyn raised one eyebrow, and it was Seamount's turn to nod.

"Exactly. The thing is, Rahzhyr, we've changed so much so quickly over the last few years that I'm not comfortable in my mind about how systematically we've approached the situation. Oh," he waved his left hand, the one missing its first two fingers, courtesy of a long-ago gunpowder accident, "I'm satisfied that we're enormously far out in front of anyone else. But we've moved so fast, covered so much ground, that I'm almost certain at least some of the things we've done are . . . less than optimal. So I asked Urvyn to start with a clean set of assumptions. To look at what we've done and see if he can spot any profitable avenues we passed up on our way by. Or, for that matter, choices we made which, with the benefit of hindsight, may not have been the best ones. Places where we might have chosen differently if we'd had more time to think about it."

"I see." Mahklyn swung his chair gently from side to side while he considered what Seamount had just said. And as he considered, he realized just how much sense the commodore was making.

*In fact, I should have suggested something like this months ago,* he admitted. *I wonder why it never even occurred to me?* He snorted mentally. *No, you don't,* he told himself. *You know* exactly *why it didn't. It's because you know the truth about Merlin. You know about all the "computer records" Owl has tucked away, so you know Merlin has all the answers at his fingertips. Which is why you've been assuming he must have given you the "right answers" to our various problems.*

*But what Merlin's been after from the beginning almost certainly means he* hasn't *always gone out of his way to just hand us the "best answer" to a problem, now doesn't it? He wants us to have to* work *for it . . . and to recognize the potentials to find better solutions on our own, without his leading us to them by the hand.* Mahklyn gave a mental headshake. *He's right—we do have to develop and cultivate that kind of thinking of our own, but I wonder how hard it must be to not just* tell *us how to do something? Especially something which could turn out to be critical in the end, whatever it seems like at the moment?*

His already vast respect for the man who had been Nimue Alban clicked up another notch at the thought, and he returned his mental focus to Seamount.

"That sounds to me like an excellent idea," he said firmly. "Has anything startling come to light yet?"

"Actually, I think there are going to be several things. Some of them I'm going to have to discuss with Admiral Lock Island and Dustyn Olyvyr, but I wouldn't be surprised if we wind up making some design changes in the next class of galleons." He shook his head, his expression ruefully bemused. "I suppose we shouldn't be surprised, given how radically we've stood traditional naval architecture on its head, but it turns out—if Urvyn and the rest of the Experimental Board are right—that we've been guilty of trying for too much of a good thing, in at least a couple of ways.

"They're also carrying out those detailed artillery experiments I've been trying to find time to supervise for the last year and a half." He shook his head again, and this time there was more than a trace of exhaustion in his eyes. "That's one reason—the main one, really—I wanted the Board, Rahzhyr. There just aren't enough hours in a day for me to personally see to everything that needs seeing to. I realized several months ago that I've actually turned myself into a bottleneck by trying to do that. I think Urvyn's going to help a lot in that respect."

"Personally, I'm in favor of reducing your workload any way we can," Mahklyn said a bit gently. "In fact, if I'd thought about it—and if I'd thought I could talk you into it—I probably would have suggested something like this to you myself. I'm ashamed to admit that I *didn't* think about it, though."

"Well, it's not as if we haven't all had a few other things on our minds," Seamount observed dryly.

"No, it's not," Mahklyn agreed. And, he reflected, it must be extraordinarily difficult to voluntarily step back in a situation like this. Especially for someone who was so damned good at what he did. It *had* to be hard for a competent man, doing something he loved as much as Seamount obviously loved his own work, to let anyone else come between him and any of the "hands-on" aspects of it.

"At any rate, I think we're going to have the Board's first formal report for you and the Inquiry Council in the next five-day or so. That's the first thing I wanted to mention to you. The second thing I wanted to talk to you about, though, and the real reason I want to sit down with Dr. Lywys this afternoon, is that while Urvyn's been getting started on that, I've found myself with some extra time to think about the new artillery."

"And?" Mahklyn let his chair come most of the way back upright, propping his elbows on the arms and interlacing his fingers across his stomach.

"Well, the first thing is that Dr. Lywys' new compound seems to perform as promised."

Seamount beamed, and Mahklyn felt himself smiling back. Sahndrah Lywys was the College's senior chemist, although now that Mahklyn had access to Owl's computer library, he supposed the proper term would probably be "alchemist" at this point. The College had been groping its way towards what Merlin called the "scientific method of inquiry" even before his own arrival, but the conditions Eric Langhorne and Adorée Bédard had established in the *Holy Writ* had made the process . . . difficult, to say the least. And dangerous.

When they'd created the Church of God Awaiting, Langhorne and Bédard had realized that simply telling people what God *forbade* them to do would never be sufficient to stifle human curiosity forever, which was why they'd provided "miraculous" explanations for an incredible breadth of phenomena which might otherwise have provoked eternally inquisitive human beings into wondering *why* things happened. By offering up those explanations under the infallible imprimatur of the Archangels—and, for that matter, God Himself—they'd done a remarkably good job of short-circuiting those "why" questions. Not too surprisingly, perhaps, when doubting or challenging those explanations equated to doubting God, which was unthinkable for anyone raised under the aegis of Holy Mother Church and her Inquisition.

At the same time, though, the potential seeds for those very sorts of questions had been buried in the *Writ* itself, in the directions which had been required for the successful colonization of a planet humanity hadn't originally been designed to live upon. Merlin called the process "terraforming," and it was a stupendous task for any world without advanced technology.

It was also one which had left the "Archangels" with something of a dilemma. The original colonists (and their descendants) had absolutely required at least some technological tools if they were to spread out from their initial enclaves, claim the entire surface of the planet, and—above all—survive. Which, after all, had been the point of establishing the colony in the first place. Even lunatics like Langhorne and Bédard had been forced to admit that much! And if those tools weren't provided from the beginning, the need for them would very soon force their indigenous development . . . thus sparking the very innovation the two of them were determined to prevent. So the "Archangels" had found themselves with no choice but to give "divine instructions" for things like animal husbandry, fertilizing techniques, hygiene, basic preventive medicine, certain "cottage-level" manufacturing processes, and a whole host of other necessary skills and techniques.

The fact that those instructions always worked, if they were followed properly, had served to buttress and powerfully reinforce the "miraculous," fundamentally unscientific worldview which had gripped Safehold for so many centuries. Yet people were still people. There were always those who wanted to delve a little deeper, understand things even more thoroughly, and despite the eagle eye the Inquisition kept on those inquisitive souls, sometimes the questions got asked anyway.

Despite that, progress in evolving anything like the scientific method had remained glacially slow, even in the Royal College. Under King Haarahld, however, the process had gained both speed and increased acceptance . . . in Charis, at least. Which, Mahklyn suspected, might well have had quite a bit to do with Zhaspahr Clyntahn's personal and corrosive hatred for the distant kingdom.

Since Merlin's arrival—and the eruption of open conflict between Charis and the Group of Four—the process had accelerated enormously, and Dr. Lywys was one of its most enthusiastic devotees, although her actual knowledge of chemistry remained basically empirical. She knew what would happen in any number of chemical reactions, and she knew how to produce a very large number of useful chemical compounds, but she did not—yet, at least—understand why those reactions occurred or those particular compounds formed. Unless Mahklyn was mistaken, that was going to change over the next several years. In fact, it was already changing, but for now, any answers she might come up with for Seamount's questions would still be based on that purely empirical knowledge.

"The compound's not any harder to manufacture than gunpowder, really," the commodore continued. "A bit touchier, in some ways—less so, in others. The good news is how many of the ingredients were already available in bulk from places like the fertilizer makers. The bad news is that, like gunpowder itself, *mixing* those ingredients can get just a bit hazardous." He snorted. "Could hardly be otherwise, I guess, given that the whole notion was to come up with something that would reliably ignite from friction. And it *does* do that!"

He shook his head, his expression one of wry amusement.

"Is it *too* touchy?" Mahklyn asked. "Too sensitive?"

"No. No, not really." Seamount shook his head. "In fact, it seems just about ideal—as the basis for an artillery fuse, at least. Urvyn's running a test program on that for me right now. We don't have nearly enough actual shells to play around with—not when Ehdwyrd's people have to make each of them individually for us—but he's come up with some ingenious ways to test our current fuse design, and reliability is really, really impressive so far, Rahzhyr."

Mahklyn nodded. The basic design Seamount was talking about was actually at least partly Empress Sharleyan's work. Seamount was the one who'd come up with the notion of using a friction-detonated compound inside a sealed tube. He'd realized the most reliable method for fusing a rifled shell would be to coat the inside of the tube with a properly combustible compound, then let an iron ball inside the tube fly forward when the shell hit its target, striking the inside of the tube, igniting the compound, and detonating the shell.

It was Sharleyan, however, who had suggested anchoring the ball in the middle of the tube with a length of wire designed to shear off as the shell accelerated down the bore of the gun. The wire kept the ball firmly in place, helping to prevent accidental detonations, until the shell was fired. At that point, acceleration forces sheared the wire, and the ball flew to the rear (and uncoated) end of the tube and stayed there until the shell reached its target. At that point, the ball—freed of the wire's restraint—tried to keep going forward, slammed into the *front* of the tube, ignited the compound which coated it, and—*Boom!*

It was an elegantly simple solution . . . assuming someone managed to come up with a suitable incendiary compound, that was. There were any number of possibilities which could be ignited by friction or shock; the difficulty was finding one which could be made to do so *reliably* and counted upon *not* to do that at . . . inconvenient moments. That search had been assigned to Sahndrah Lywys, and her response had been to go back to the *Writ*, looking for cautionary admonitions about various compounds and processes the "Archangels" had made available as part of those terraforming requirements. For example, phosphorus had been produced for use as a fertilizer from the Day of Creation itself, and although no citizen of the long-dead Terran Federation would ever have considered the production methods used anything but hopelessly primitive, they'd worked well enough for Safehold's purposes. Nor were they the only production techniques the *Holy Writ* had laid out for Mother Church's children. Saltpeter had been used in both fertilizers and in food preservation, for example, and "Schueler's tears" (which someone from the Federation would have called "nitric acid") had been used in metallurgy, as a cleaning compound, and even as a way to remove clogs from plumbing.

No one had ever had any idea of the actual chemical processes involved in producing any of those things, however. That meant there was no way for Safeholdians to recognize potential hazards on their own, which could very easily have gotten a lot of people killed, over the centuries. Even worse—from Langhorne's perspective, at least—if people suffered disasters from following the "Archangels'" directions, it was likely to make someone *question* those directions . . . or, at the very least, start looking for alternate methods. Which would have kicked off the entire innovation process Langhorne had been determined to stifle.

To head that off, the "Archangels" had incorporated precautions against things like accidental explosions—or other potential dangers—into their directions. For example, *white* phosphorus was actually simpler to manufacture than *red* phosphorus, yet the *Writ* strictly prohibited white phosphorus' use for most purposes under pain of the Curse of Burning Jaw. What Mahklyn hadn't known, until Owl's library became available to him, was that the horrible symptoms of "Burning Jaw" had nothing to do with the Archangel Pasquale's curse for the misuse of the banned white phosphorus. In fact, it was a condition which had been known, on a planet which had once been called Terra, as "phosphorus necrosis of the jaw" or "phossy jaw," and it was a completely natural consequence of overexposure to white phosphorus' vapors. There was no vengeful Archangel of healing, lashing out to punish sinners, behind the process which caused jawbones to abscess and actually begin to glow in the dark . . . and led eventually to death if the afflicted bones weren't surgically removed.

Of course, "Burning Jaw" was only one example of the many "curses" which waited for those who sinned by violating the Archangels' solemn rituals and admonitions. The various Curses of Pestilence—the periodic outbreaks of disease which always followed, sooner or later, upon the violation of Pasquale's directives for public hygiene—were another, as were diseases like scurvy and rickets which followed upon violation of the *Writ*'s dietary laws. There were literally hundreds of curses, and the rules and "religious laws" to which they were attached impinged upon almost every aspect of Safeholdian life.

What Lywys had done was to hunt down all the prohibitions punishable by things like spontaneous combustion and explosions of "the Archangels' Wrath" and use them to point her towards things which could be *made* to explode. At the moment, she and Seamount were using a combination of what a chemist would have called potassium chlorate, antimony sulfide, gum, and starch.

"So far, the fuse failure rate is only about one in a thousand," Seamount continued. "And Dr. Lywys' suggestions about our powder mills—those 'quality control issues' Merlin was talking about—have been extraordinarily useful, too."

He shook his head again, and this time his smile was decidedly tart.

"I was pretty proud of the quality and consistency of our powder," he admitted. "And rightfully so, I think, compared to the kind of crap everybody else was turning out. But every lot is still at least a little bit different from every other lot. Dr. Lywys says it's because nobody can guarantee uniform quality for the saltpeter or the charcoal—or, for that matter, even the sulfur—we're using. But she's managed to make some significant improvements in that area—mostly by insisting on inspection and processing standards fanatical enough to satisfy Jwo-jeng herself! And she's also come up with some really good suggestions about ways we can proof each lot of powder. We're firing representative charges from each lot now, using a testing high-angle gun at a fixed elevation, and measuring the ranges we obtain. That lets us label each lot with the range achieved using a standard proof charge, so the poor damned gunner who has to use it in action is going to be able to judge ranges and accuracy a lot more effectively."

"That sounds like Sahndrah," Mahklyn acknowledged with a smile of his own.

"She made another suggestion that's turned out to have some . . . interesting implications, too," Seamount told him.

"What kind of implications?" Mahklyn asked a bit warily.

"Well, way back when Merlin first suggested the possibility of corned powder to us, he told me that one reason corned powder was more powerful than meal powder was because there's more space between each grain, since the space meant the fire—and all gunpowder really does is to burn very quickly—can burn even *more* quickly and completely. According to Dr. Lywys, that's not entirely accurate, though."

"It's not?" Mahklyn asked, and tried not to frown.

"No, it's not," Seamount said. "Mind you, it describes the *consequences* of what happens accurately enough, and I've come to the conclusion that he was explaining it in a way that would make sense to me. But according to Dr. Lywys—and my own experiments, working on trying to stabilize burning rates for combustion fuses—*smaller*-grained powder actually burns faster than larger-grained powder, yet the larger grains produce far more power. Before we started producing corned powder, we were using a *thirty*-pound charge in the long thirty-pounders; now we're using a nine-and-a-half-pound charge. That's how much more powerful the new powder is, despite the fact that the grains are burning *slower,* not faster, as they get bigger. So I've come to the conclusion that what Merlin told me was actually completely accurate, even if it wasn't."

"Excuse me?" Mahklyn blinked at him, and Seamount chuckled.

"Corning the powder helps a lot with consistency and those 'quality control' issues of Merlin's. The biggest thing is the way it keeps the ingredients from separating, and corning it makes it less susceptible to damp, too—especially since we've started glazing the grains the way Dr. Lywys suggested. But the other thing it does is to expose more of the surface area of the powder to ignition simultaneously. And that allows more of the powder to ignite before it starts throwing *unburned* powder down the barrel in front of the explosion. In other words, even though the actual combustion rate is lower, we're burning more of it *simultaneously,* and that means we're burning more of the powder, in a shorter length of barrel, than we ever managed before. Which, by the way, also means the powder is leaving a lot less fouling—less ash—behind because it *is* burning more completely. Does that make sense?"

"As a matter of fact, it does," Mahklyn said slowly.

"And I think it's exactly the sort of thing Merlin wants us to figure out on our own . . . for some reason."

"You're probably right," Mahklyn agreed, carefully not noticing the sharp look the commodore gave him.

"Well," Seamount continued when Mahklyn failed to rise to the bait, "what I hadn't really considered until Urvyn and I started talking this over with Dr. Lywys was that, logically, making the grains even bigger should give us even greater power for a given weight of charge."

"Which is going to push bore pressures even higher," Mahklyn said thoughtfully.

"Oh, believe me, we've been thinking about *that* aspect of it, too." Seamount rolled his eyes. "The good news there is that I've just had another letter from Howsmyn, and he says Merlin's suggestion about using wire to reinforce the gun tubes should be perfectly workable, according to his mechanics. They say producing that much wire's going to be a royal pain in the arse, but he's got them working on new wire-drawing machinery—and the machinery to wind the wire uniformly around the gun tube under a high enough tension, too—and he's confident they'll manage it . . . eventually. Once they do, he says, he'll be producing guns which are going to be both lighter, stronger, *and* a hell of a lot cheaper. Unfortunately, his best estimate is that it's going to take at least a year, and in the meantime, the gun foundries are still the major bottleneck where the Navy's concerned. We can build ships faster than we can cast as many guns as we're going to need, and he's not certain what shifting over to rifled pieces will do to our production schedules. And then there're all the little problems involved in making—and filling—hollow shells with enough quality control to keep them from being as dangerous to *us* as to their targets."

"Wonderful."

"Actually, it could be worse." Seamount shrugged. "At least by the time he's ready to start making guns and shells using the new techniques, we should've had time to finish tweaking our powder's performance still further."

"I can see that." This time, Mahklyn nodded with firm, unqualified approval. "And that was what Sahndrah suggested to you?"

"Oh, no." Seamount's headshake surprised him. "I suppose if I'm really going to be accurate, it wasn't so much something she suggested we *do* so much as something she suggested we *not* do."

"If your object is to confuse me, Ahlfryd, you're succeeding quite nicely," Mahklyn said a bit tartly, and the baron chuckled.

"Sorry! What I meant is that Dr. Lywys is a very . . . thorough woman. She sent us a list of just about everything that could conceivably have been used to fuse our shells. We're satisfied—so far, at least—with the one we've tentatively settled on, but there were quite a few others. Including some which she warned us would almost certainly be far too sensitive or unsuitable for some other reason."

"That sounds like her," Mahklyn said with a slight smile.

"Well, something she included was what she called 'fulminated quicksilver.'"

He raised an eyebrow at Mahklyn, who very carefully showed no reaction at all, aside from a polite nod inviting his visitor to continue.

"She warned us that fulminated quicksilver was much too sensitive for something as . . . lively as an artillery shell. We tested it, of course—cautiously!—and I agree with her entirely. But a couple of days ago, one of my other clever young officers suggested to Urvyn that even though it's too sensitive for inclusion in a shell, there ought to be some way to use it as a priming composition. Something that could actually replace flintlocks."

Mahklyn let his chair come fully upright, making no attempt now to disguise his sudden, intent interest. "Fulminated quicksilver"—what an Old Terran would have called "fulminate of mercury"—was scarcely anything *he* would have wanted to work with, if only because of the potential health risks. But it had some very interesting properties, and those properties had led it to be used in Old Terra's firearms for a long, long time. He'd discovered them for himself, using his com and Owl's research assistance on one of the unfortunately frequent nights when his aging bones found sleep elusive. There were other, safer ways to achieve the same effect, but this one was already *here,* ready to hand, if only someone would recognize the implications. As he'd skimmed over Lywys' most recent reports, he'd wondered how he might casually bring some of those properties to her attention. Was it possible . . . ?

"Go on," he urged.

"This stuff is sensitive enough you can set it off just by dropping it, which is going to pose some problems," Seamount said, leaning forward himself and waving his mutilated hand in what Mahklyn considered rather pointed emphasis. "I'll be surprised if there's not a way to figure out solutions for most of them, though. And if we can . . . ! Rahzhyr, you can actually set it off *under-water*! If we can figure out a way to make it work, our Marines' rifles would fire just as reliably in the middle of a Tellesberg thunderstorm as on a sunny day! Not only that, but I think it would decrease the lock time—the interval between when the hammer falls and the main charge explodes. And if it does, it should also increase individual accuracy."

"I see." Mahklyn nodded his head energetically. "I think your 'clever young officer' is onto something very important here, Ahlfryd. This is something we need to follow up on immediately!"

"I agree entirely," the baron said, then snorted. "He really *is* a clever fellow, too. In fact, he's also come up with another interesting application of Dr. Lywys' fuse compound."

"He has?"

"Oh, yes. As a matter of fact, I think he may be going to put tinderbox makers out of business," Seamount said, and chuckled at Mahklyn's baffled expression. "He tried putting some of the new compound on the end of a splinter and discovered he could ignite it by scratching it across a rough surface. It's almost like magic, in a lot of ways. The damned thing will strike almost anywhere, and if he coats the splinter in a little paraffin to give it some reliable fuel, it not only waterproofs the compound, but the splinter itself burns a lot hotter—and a lot longer—than anything I've ever seen out of a tinderbox or a regular fire striker, too."

"Really? That sounds like it could have a lot of uses outside the Navy!"

"I imagine it will, but it's going to take some getting used to. It ignites a bit . . . energetically, and it throws sparks like crazy. In fact, you have to be a bit cautious about using one of the things. And talk about *stinking*—!" He grimaced, then grinned suddenly. "Somehow, I don't think the Group of Four is really likely to approve of the nickname the Board's hung on the thing, either."

"What sort of nickname?" Mahklyn asked.

"Well, given the sparks and the stink—it smells just like brimstone, actually—they're calling the things 'Shan-wei's candles,'" Seamount said with another grimace. "I'm not so sure we want to be encouraging anyone to use that particular nickname when the Group of Four is busy accusing us all of heresy and Shan-wei worship!"

"Probably not," Mahklyn agreed. "Probably not."

Yet even as he agreed, another thought was passing through a very private corner of his brain.

*You may be right about not using it* now, *Ahlfryd. In fact, I'm sure you are! But whether they know it or not, your "bright young officers" have hung* exactly *the right name on it. Because that "candle" is part of what's going to blow the Church of God Awaiting's tyranny apart, and wherever she is, Pei Shan-wei is going to be cheering us on the entire way.*

O h, it's *good* to actually see you, Maikel!"

Empress Sharleyan held out her arms to Maikel Staynair, who was considerably taller than she was. She seemed to disappear momentarily as he embraced her, and Cayleb was pretty certain, as he waited for his own turn to embrace Staynair, that neither his wife's nor his archbishop's eyes were completely dry.

"It's good to see you, too, Your Majesty," Staynair replied after a moment, standing back far enough to rest his hands on Sharleyan's shoulders and looking deep into her eyes. "The last time, it hadn't been all that long since those maniacs tried to kill you."

"I know." Sharleyan's eyes darkened briefly, and she reached up to pat the hand on her right shoulder. Then her expression turned more lively once more, and she shook her head severely at him. "I know," she repeated, "but don't think the pleasure of seeing you again is going to cause me to overlook the impropriety of your chosen form of address!"

For a second, Staynair actually seemed a bit taken aback, but then his own eyes began to twinkle and he stepped back to bow to her in mock contrition.

"Forgive me . . . Sharleyan," he said.

"Better," she told him, and he chuckled as he turned to greet Cayleb, in turn.

With most men, Cayleb would have settled for clasped forearms, but this was Maikel Staynair, whom he hadn't seen face-to-face in over a year, and his own eyes weren't totally dry as he hugged the archbishop fiercely.

"Easy, Cayleb! *Easy!*" Staynair gasped. "Mind the ribs! They're no younger than the rest of me, you know!"

"They—and you—are tougher than an old boot, Maikel!" Cayleb returned a bit huskily.

"Now there's a respectful way to describe an archbishop," Staynair observed, and Cayleb laughed and waved at the armchair waiting in front of the coal fire quietly seething on the grate.

"Well, we'll just have to see if we can't make amends. Knowing you as well as I do, I expect *this* to make a pretty good start." He indicated the whiskey decanter on the end table between the armchair and the small couch beside it. "West Isle blended, as a matter of fact. It was hard to get Sharley to agree to part with it—this is the twenty-four-year grand reserve—but she agreed it would probably be the best way to get your undivided attention."

"The two of you obviously have a deplorably low—and frighteningly accurate—view of my character," Staynair said.

The archbishop followed his hosts across to the waiting chair and allowed himself to be seated before either of them. Most—not all, by any means, but definitely most—of the Church of God Awaiting's archbishops would have demanded precedence over any mere monarch. Would have *expected* his hosts to remain standing until he'd taken his seat. Staynair didn't . . . which was one reason they insisted on doing it anyway.

Once they had him ensconced in the comfortable chair, Sharleyan curled up on one end of the couch, kicking off her shoes and tucking her feet under her, while Cayleb busied himself pouring three substantial glasses of the pungent, amber whiskey. He added water to all three, and a little ice (something Chisholm produced in bulk, during the winter months) to his and Staynair's glasses. Sharleyan, having been taught the *proper* way to appreciate fine drink by Baron Green Mount, regarded the contamination of perfectly good whiskey with ice as a Charisian perversion. When she was in a better mood than usual she was prepared to concede that, given the warmth of Old Charis' year-round climate, the barbarous custom might have *some* justification under truly extreme conditions, but that didn't make it the sort of thing in which decent people wanted to indulge. A little spring water to tone down the alcohol just enough to bring out the full array of scents and flavors was quite another thing, of course.

"Oh, my," Staynair sighed, eyes half-closed in bliss, as he lowered his glass a few moments later. "You know, it's not often something actually exceeds its reputation."

"I have to admit, Chisholm's distilleries really are better than ours in Charis," Cayleb agreed. "I'm still in the process of sampling and developing my palate properly. And the good news is that it's going to take me *years* to try all of them."

"It's incredibly smooth," Staynair said, taking another sip and rolling it gently over his tongue before swallowing.

"They triple-distill it," Cayleb told him. "And most of the distilleries char the insides of the casks, too. The West Isle distillery's just outside Traynside, and they add just a little peat to the drying kiln—that's where that little touch of a smoky taste comes from. Merlin says that, aside from the peat, it reminds him a lot of something they used to call 'Bushmills' back on Old Terra."

"Somehow, when he told us that, it did more than almost anything else—for me, at least—to drive home the connection between us, right here today on Safehold, and where we all truly came from in the beginning," Sharleyan said quietly. "We're not only still distilling whiskey, but someone who was there—on Old Terra—*recognizes* it when we do."

"Recognizes the *taste,* anyway." Cayleb's smile was as crooked as it was sad. "Apparently, a PICA can't really appreciate alcohol, anymore. And for me, that drives home what Merlin's given up just to be here."

"Amen," Staynair said quietly, and the single word was as much prayer as simple agreement. The archbishop sat for a handful of seconds, looking down into his glass, then deliberately sipped again and sat back in his chair.

"Speaking of Merlin—?" he said, one eyebrow arched.

"He'll be here for supper," Cayleb assured him. "He's taking care of an errand with Ahlber Zhustyn and Earl White Crag."

"Ah?" Staynair's other eyebrow rose.

Sir Ahlber Zhustyn was the Chisholmian equivalent of Bynzhamyn Raice, and Hauwerstat Thompkyn, the Earl of White Crag, was Chisholm's Lord Justice. Zhustyn and White Crag worked closely together, because the espionage function was distributed rather differently under the Chisholmian tradition. Zhustyn was responsible for spying on *other* people, while one of White Crag's responsibilities was to keep other people from spying on *Chisholm.*

"May I ask the nature of the errand?" the archbishop inquired.

"Actually, he's mostly preparing the ground for Nahrmahn's conference with them tomorrow," Sharleyan replied, and made a small face. "I'm afraid that, even now, Hauwerstat finds it difficult to contemplate welcoming Nahrmahn with open arms. Something about how many years he spent trying to fend off Emeraldian spies."

"Now why could that possibly be?" Staynair wondered dryly.

"I don't have the least idea," Cayleb said even more dryly, then snorted a chuckle. "You should've seen the two of them when we stopped off here in Cherayth on our way to Chisholm last year, Maikel!" He shook his head. "No one could possibly have been politer, but somehow, every time Nahrmahn started getting a little close to discussing any of the things White Crag's spent so long keeping his nose out of, the Lord Justice suddenly discovered something else he absolutely, positively had to do right then."

"I've scolded him about that since I got home." Sharleyan looked a little embarrassed. "He's promised he'll behave better this time. But, to be perfectly honest, I'd rather have him being overly suspicious rather than too complacent."

"Oh, no argument there." Cayleb nodded vigorously. "And Nahrmahn obviously understood. Besides, White Crag was perfectly willing to share any intelligence he had with *me,* so Nahrmahn got it all secondhand, anyway. Still, we really do need for our imperial councilor for intelligence to have *direct* access to all of the intelligence coming our way. Which is what Merlin—and Ahlber, who's a bit more . . . flexible about these things—are emphasizing to White Crag right this minute." The emperor shrugged. "By now, everyone here in Chisholm regards Merlin as my own personal messenger. And Sharley's, for that matter. They're all prepared to accept that he's speaking directly for us, but he can be a bit franker than either of us can without things turning officially sticky. And, for that matter, people can be 'franker' in responding to him while everybody pretends it's not going to get back to us."

"I see." Staynair shook his head and chuckled. "Somehow, it's a bit hard to think of Merlin playing go-between."

"Really?" Cayleb cocked his head at the archbishop with a peculiar expression, half smile and half grimace. "Trust me, 'go-between' is a pretty good description of a couple of things he's got in mind."

"What sort of things?" Staynair asked more than a bit warily, but Cayleb only shook his head.

"Oh, no, Maikel! We're not going to trot that particular little discussion out until Merlin's here to take part in it himself. For that matter, he's been being a bit mysterious even with Sharley and me, so we're looking forward to hearing what he's *really* up to at the same time you do!"

Staynair looked at his monarchs thoughtfully. There were times when he had to remind himself that Merlin Athrawes had his own agenda. Or perhaps it would have been more accurate to say Nimue Alban had *her* own agenda. Better yet, her own *mission*. The archbishop never doubted Merlin's loyalty to Charis and the people who had become his friends, his family. Yet under all of that—sometimes obscured by that loyalty though it might be—lay the granite purpose which had sent Nimue Alban knowingly to her death so that, nine centuries later, her PICA might walk the soil of a planet she herself would never see. There had to be times, Staynair thought, when Merlin found the imperatives of Nimue's mission clashing with his own loyalties here on Safehold. It could scarcely be any other way, and the archbishop hoped whatever he had in mind this time didn't fall into that category. Yet if it did, he knew, Merlin would meet that challenge as unflinchingly as he'd met every other challenge, and Staynair found himself murmuring a silent, heartfelt prayer for the soul which had accepted such a burden.

"Well," he said then, holding out the whiskey glass which had somehow mysteriously become empty, "I suppose I should probably fortify my nerve a little more before I find myself subjected to such a stressful revelation."

"Oh, what a marvelous rationale, Maikel!" Sharleyan laughed. "Wait a minute while I finish my glass and I'll join you!"

"Don't get too fortified, either of you," Cayleb said sternly. "Or not before we're finished with our immediate business, at least."

" 'Immediate business'?" Staynair repeated.

"Oh, I know what he's talking about," Sharleyan said. The archbishop looked at her, and she shrugged. "Nahrmahn."

"Nahr—?" Staynair began, then nodded in sudden understanding. "You mean whether or not he should be admitted to the inner circle?" Cayleb nodded, and the archbishop looked at him curiously. "I'm just a bit surprised you want to discuss it when Merlin isn't here to put in his quarter-mark's worth."

"Merlin," Cayleb said, "has already voted. And, I might add, treated Sharley and me to some fairly . . . pithy comments on the Brethren. Something about decision processes, glaciers, cranky old men, and watched pots."

"Oh, my," Staynair said again, in a rather different tone, and shook his head with a chuckle. "I wondered why he hadn't been pestering Zhon about it lately. It hadn't occurred to me that it might be because of something as un-Merlin-like as *tact,* though!"

"I wouldn't go quite that far, myself," Cayleb said dryly. "I think it may have been more a matter of not trusting himself to remain civil. He's pretty damned adamant about it, actually. And, to be honest, I think part of that's because he's pretty sure Nahrmahn has already figured out even more than we've told him." Staynair's eyes widened with what might have been an edge of alarm, but the emperor waved his hand in a brushing-away gesture. "Oh, I don't think even Nahrmahn could've gotten too close to guessing what's *really* going on. For that matter, I'm pretty sure that if he had, you'd have been in a better position than anyone else to notice it, given where the two of you have been for the last few months. But I do think Merlin has a point about his having put together enough to at least be asking himself questions we haven't gotten around to answering for him yet. And as we all know, Nahrmahn has a distinct tendency to eventually get answers when he goes looking for them."

*Now that,* Staynair thought, *is an* outstanding *example of understatement.*

There might have been one or two men on Safehold who were smarter than Nahrmahn Baytz, the archbishop reflected. He was quite certain, though, that there weren't *three* of them. If he'd ever entertained any doubts on that head, they'd been firmly laid to rest during the long days of the lengthy voyage from Emerald to Chisholm. With Nahrmahn's cousin, the Earl of Pine Hollow, to keep an eye on matters of state in Emerald, the rotund little prince had been perfectly willing to return to Chisholm. Mostly, Staynair suspected, because that was where the Court was and Nahrmahn simply couldn't stand being away from the "great game," even if he had found himself drafted onto someone else's team after his own was eliminated early in the playoffs. The only thing he'd insisted upon was that his wife, Princess Ohlyvya, join him this time, and watching the two of them together during the voyage, Staynair had understood that perfectly, as well.

As a matter of fact, Staynair had been very much in favor of Ohlyvya's coming along. He strongly suspected that Nahrmahn's wife—who was one of the shrewdest women the archbishop had never met—helped to keep the sometimes potentially too-bright-for-his-own-good Nahrmahn centered, and that was a very good thing. Of course, it could present a few additional difficulties of its own, under the circumstances.

"As a matter of fact, Cayleb, I agree with your assessment of Nahrmahn," he said out loud. "And with Merlin's, for that matter. And, unlike Merlin, I have been pressing Zhon for a decision. Which, I might add, he hasn't given me yet."

"No?"

Cayleb sat back, gazing at the archbishop. The short silence seemed considerably longer than it actually was, and then the emperor grimaced.

"He may not have given you an answer *yet,* Maikel. This time, though, I think he's going to have to."

At that particular moment, Staynair thought, Cayleb looked a great deal like his father. There was very little humor in his brown eyes, and—at least as importantly—Sharleyan's expression was as serious as her husband's.

"I don't want to get up on my Emperor's high dragon with the Brethren any more often than I have to," Cayleb continued, "but in this instance, I think I do have to. They've been debating this particular decision for months. They started on it well before you ever left for Emerald, for God's sake, and I can't afford to let it go on any longer. I'm going to have to insist they give me a decision—now."

Staynair looked at both of his monarchs for a long, silent moment, then dipped his head in an unusual formal gesture of respect. But then he looked up again, meeting their eyes steadily.

"If you wish a decision, Your Grace, then you'll have one," he said gravely. "But you have considered the consequences if the Brethren agree and it goes . . . poorly?"

"We have," Sharleyan said, grimly, before Cayleb could reply. Staynair turned toward her, and she returned his regard with equal steadiness. "If we tell Nahrmahn the truth, and it turns out we've misjudged his reaction, we both know what we'll have to do, Maikel. I pray it won't come to that. And if it does, I'm sure I'll spend the rest of my life regretting it, and asking God's forgiveness. But if the decision has to be made, we *will* make it." She smiled bleakly. "After all, we've faced the same possibility with everyone we've 'brought inside.' So far, we've 'come up golden' every time, as Cayleb likes to put it. And, to be honest, part of that is probably exactly *because* the Brethren's first instinct is always to go slow and think things through as thoroughly as possible. But we've always known that, sooner or later, we're almost certain to be mistaken. And we've always known what the price of that mistake will be . . . just as we've accepted that there are some people we'll *never* be able to tell the complete truth."

"Very well, Your Majesty. You'll have your answer, one way or the other, this very day."

▼  ▼  ▼

"That, Harvai—as always—was delicious," Sharleyan said with simple sincerity, several hours later, as the servants finished clearing the dessert plates. "You spoil us shamelessly, you know. You and all the staff. Which is probably why we appreciate you all so much. Thank you . . . and please pass that on to Mistress Bahr and the rest of the kitchen staff, as well."

"Of course, Your Majesty," Sir Harvai Phalgrain agreed with a smile and a deep bow. Phalgrain, the palace's majordomo, saw to it that its organization ran with the sort of smooth efficiency any military command might have envied . . . and few could have attained. Given the identities of the emperor and empress' dinner guests, he'd taken personal charge of tonight's supper to make certain *nothing* went wrong, and he was obviously pleased by Sharleyan's compliments.

"And now," Cayleb said, "I think we can take care of ourselves for a while, Harvai. Just leave the bottles on the side table, and we'll ring if we need anything else."

He smiled as he spoke, and Phalgrain smiled back. Then the majordomo bowed once again—this time a more general courtesy, directed at all of the diners—and withdrew.

Cayleb watched him go until the door closed behind him, then returned his attention to his and Sharleyan's guests.

In some ways—many ways, if he were going to be honest—he wished there were only two of those guests, not three. He supposed they could have insisted this would be a "working supper" to which Princess Ohlyvya was not invited. In fact, they'd started to do exactly that. But then they'd thought about it a bit more and realized just how unwise that might have proved.

First, it would have been uncharacteristically rude. He and Sharleyan would have regretted that, but they could have lived with it. Unfortunately, Ohlyvya Baytz was a very, very smart woman. If she'd been excluded from the invitation and . . . something happened to Nahrmahn, she was more than capable of asking exactly the sorts of questions Nahrmahn himself would have asked. It was entirely possible she'd get answers to them, too, and even if she didn't, turning *her* against Charis would be only marginally less disastrous than turning *Nahrmahn* into an enemy would have been.

Second, though, Nahrmahn and Ohlyvya, in their own ways, were at least as close as Cayleb and Sharleyan themselves. The steadying influence she exercised upon him grew out of that closeness, the strength of that commitment and love. Not telling her after they'd told Nahrmahn would put the portly little prince in a position just as invidious as Cayleb's had been before Sharleyan finally learned the truth. And, on top of all that, it was distinctly possible that telling both him and Ohlyvya at the same time would make it easier for both of them to accept the truth.

Neither Cayleb nor Sharleyan were entirely happy with the decision they'd finally reached, but, in the end, it had been the only one they could reach.

*Well, if Merlin's right about both of them, it's not going to be a problem,* Cayleb told himself yet again. *Of course, Merlin would be the first to admit that he* has *made a mistake or two along the way.*

Speaking of which . . .

"Why don't you come over here and join us, Merlin?" he invited, looking over his shoulder at the tall, blue-eyed guardsman standing just inside the dining-room door.

▼     ▼     ▼

Merlin Athrawes smiled slightly as Ohlyvya Baytz looked up just that little bit too quickly from her quiet conversation with Sharleyan. Princess Ohlyvya had spent decades married to a reigning head of state. Along the way, she'd learned to conceal little things like surprise far better than most mere mortals ever did.

Normally, at least.

Nahrmahn, on the other hand, had had ample opportunity to watch Cayleb and Merlin interact during the Corisande campaign. In fact, he'd already been informed that the *seijin* saw "visions." That his function as seer and adviser was even more important than his function as Cayleb's personal bodyguard. Along the way, he'd also come to understand that Captain Athrawes' relationship with both Emperor Cayleb and Empress Sharleyan was even closer than most other people would ever have surmised.

That was something he'd learned to factor into his analyses of Merlin's "visions." It was not, however, knowledge he had ever shared with his wife, and the fact that the emperor and empress had apparently decided it was time for Ohlyvya to discover at least part of what he himself already knew had to have come as a significant surprise for him, as well. If so, it wasn't evident. He simply cocked his head with a mildly speculative expression which would probably have fooled just about anyone. Merlin had come to know the plump little prince at least as well as Nahrmahn had come to know him, however, and he could almost literally see the thoughts flickering through that agile brain.

"Of course, Your Grace," he murmured out loud, and crossed to the table. Cayleb's wave indicated a chair between himself and Maikel Staynair, and Merlin bowed in acknowledgment. He unbuckled his weapons harness, standing his sheathed katana and wakazashi against the wall, then pulled back the indicated chair and seated himself in it.

"Wine, Merlin?" Staynair inquired with a whimsical smile.

"If you please, Your Eminence," Merlin replied, and watched Princess Ohlyvya's bemused expression from the corner of one eye as the primate of the

Church of Charis poured wine for a mere bodyguard. The archbishop passed the glass across, and Merlin nodded in gratitude and took a sip.

"Nahrmahn, Ohlyvya," Cayleb said then, gathering back up the prince's and princess' attention, "as I'm sure both of you have already deduced, Sharleyan and I invited Merlin to join us at table to make a point. And that point, as I'm sure both of you have also already realized, is that Merlin is quite a bit more than simply my bodyguard. In fact, Ohlyvya, Nahrmahn was already acquainted with that minor fact, although I'm aware he hasn't shared that knowledge with you."

"Indeed he hasn't, Your Grace," Ohlyvya said when he paused for a moment, and despite herself, there was an edge of anxiety in her voice.

"We know that," Sharleyan said quickly, reaching out to touch the older woman's arm reassuringly. Ohlyvya looked at her, and the empress smiled. "Trust me—when I say we *know* Nahrmahn has never betrayed a single one of our confidences, even to you, we truly do. You'll understand what I mean after Merlin completes his explanation."

"Explanation, Your Majesty?" Ohlyvya's confusion showed much more clearly this time, and Sharleyan nodded. Then she glanced at Merlin.

"Why don't you go ahead and begin?" she invited.

"Of course, Your Majesty." Merlin bent his head in acknowledgment, then looked across the table at Ohlyvya. "Prince Nahrmahn has already heard a part of this, Your Highness," he said, "but most of it will be equally new to him. Or, perhaps I should say he's about to discover that the information he's already been given was . . . incomplete. I apologize for that, Your Highness," he said, shifting his attention to Nahrmahn for a moment, "but it was one of those 'need to know' items, as I feel confident you'll understand when I finish explaining."

"Should I assume something has changed and given me the 'need to know' after all, *Seijin* Merlin? And, for some reason, Ohlyvya, as well?" Nahrmahn asked the question calmly, but he also reached out to take his wife's hand reassuringly. There was something profoundly touching about the protectiveness in that small gesture, Merlin thought, and felt his heart warming to the pudgy Emeraldian.

"It's not so much something that's changed as a decision process which has worked its way through, Your Highness," Merlin told him. "There were more people involved in making that decision than even you can have suspected, I think. And most of those other people lacked the . . . unfair advantages, you might say, which you were already aware I myself possess. That tended to make them more hesitant—well, *cautious* would actually be a better word—than they might have been otherwise."

"But not *you?*" Nahrmahn murmured with a smile, and Merlin shrugged.

"We wouldn't be having this conversation if Cayleb, Sharleyan, and Archbishop Maikel weren't already quite confident about how it will work out, Your Highness. None of us is infallible, so it's possible we're all wrong about that. I don't think that's very likely, though."

"Well, I suppose *that's* a relief," Nahrmahn said. "On the other hand, perhaps you should go ahead and begin that explanation. Now."

"Certainly, Your Highness."

Despite the potential gravity of the moment, Merlin found it difficult not to chuckle at the mingled exasperation, impatience, and humor in Nahrmahn's tone. Then the temptation faded, and he leaned forward in his chair, folding his hands around the base of his wineglass as he looked soberly at Nahrmahn and Ohlyvya.

"I realize, better than either of you probably even begin to suspect, just how disillusioned both of you are with the Group of Four," he said very levelly. "I know—I don't suspect, I don't think, I don't estimate, I *know*—that Princess Ohlyvya is just as disgusted and heartsick and angry as Cayleb or Sharleyan themselves over the way Clyntahn and Trynair are using and abusing the Church's authority and the faith of every Safeholdian. By the same token, I know your own disgust over the Group of Four's blatant corruption and taste for tyranny is far deeper than you'd really like anyone else to guess, given that cynical, pragmatic, ruthless politician's image you've spent so long cultivating, Your Highness." He smiled faintly at Narhmahn's slightly affronted expression, yet no trace of his amusement touched his somber tone as he continued. "But what neither of you know is that the Group of Four are scarcely the first to abuse the faith of all Safeholdians for their own purposes. In fact, they're following in a tradition that was established even before the Day of Creation."

The husband and wife sitting across the table from him stiffened in unison, their eyes widening in confusion, and this time his smile was far, far grimmer.

"You see, just over a thousand years ago—"

▼    ▼    ▼

The silence in the dining room was profound when Merlin finished his explanation two hours later. The faint, icy sigh of the winter wind, plucking at cornices, battlements, and gables, tapping invisible fingers on the closed windowpanes, was clearly audible, despite the solidity of the palace's ancient stony bulk.

Nahrmahn and Ohlyvya Baytz sat side by side, holding hands as they had from the moment Merlin began, and Ohlyvya's eyes were huge, dark pools in the lamplight, as they clung to the communicator, the compact holographic projector, and the bare wakazashi lying on the table before her. Merlin wondered, looking at her, which of his bits of story-proving technological evidence she'd found most convincing. In some ways, he suspected, it had probably been the wakazashi. The communicator and the projector both *looked* alien, strange, even magical. The wakazashi didn't, yet she'd watched him use the impossibly sharp battle steel blade to whittle long slivers of iron off the poker he'd selected from the dining-room fireplace tools. The fact that the wakazashi *didn't* look alien yet obviously was had probably made it even more . . . impressive.

*And I'd better make damned sure that poker disappears for good*, he reminded himself. *Better for the servants to wonder where it went than find it chopped up like a Christmas goose.*

He felt a brief pang at his own choice of similes and wondered if it was his recitation of humanity's true history which had recalled it to his thoughts.

Nahrmahn's expression gave away much less than his wife's did. Her wonder, and the ghost-haunted eyes that went with it, were plain. Nahrmahn's eyes were merely hooded, thoughtful, his lips pursed as if he were pondering an everyday conundrum rather than a complete and fundamental shift in the universe he'd always thought existed.

"Well?" Cayleb said quietly, at last, into the silence.

Ohlyvya's head snapped up, her eyes flitting to the emperor like startled rabbits. Nahrmahn simply looked at Cayleb, but his free hand reached across to join the one already holding his wife's. He patted the back of her hand gently, reassuringly, then looked across the table at Merlin.

"It wasn't Her Majesty's bodyguards who saved her life, after all, was it, *Seijin* Merlin?" he asked calmly. "Not entirely."

"Not entirely, no, Your Highness." Merlin's voice was low, his sapphire PICA eyes dark. "Without them, I would've been too late, though . . . and it's my fault so many of them died. I dropped the ball badly that day."

Sharleyan stirred in her chair, as if she wanted to dispute his verdict, but she didn't, and Nahrmahn smiled faintly.

"I've just been replaying that entire morning in my mind." His tone was almost whimsical. "Here I thought you'd explained so much, when it turns out there was so much *more* you didn't even touch on!" He shook his head. "I have to admit that a few things make a lot more sense now than they did then, though. For one thing, I've been persistently perplexed by the extent to which Their Majesties seem to think so much alike. Mind you, I've had enough experience of how well a man and a wife can learn to read one another's minds. And"—the skin around his eyes crinkled as he smiled briefly but warmly at Ohlyvya—"of the way they can still surprise one another, even after years. But you two"—he transferred his gaze back to Cayleb and Sharleyan—"haven't been together that long, which is why you've amazed me, more than once, by how smoothly your actions and decisions have coordinated despite the fact that you were months of travel time apart. The way Her Majesty decided on her own to come home to Chisholm after the assassination attempt, for example. That was exactly what I felt needed to be done. In fact, it was what I advised rather strongly that very morning, but it had never occurred to me that she might actually do it so promptly. Now I understand how the two of you have managed it."

"In fairness to Cayleb and Sharleyan, Your Highness, they didn't have the advantage of instant communication until *after* the assassination attempt," Merlin pointed out, and Nahrmahn nodded thoughtfully.

"You're right," he agreed. "And they were operating almost that smoothly even before that, weren't they?"

"Yes 'they' were," Cayleb said rather dryly. "Which brings me back to my original question, Your Highness."

"I won't say it doesn't come as a considerable surprise, Your Grace," Nahrmahn acknowledged. "Of course, I suspect you'd be a bit disappointed if it hadn't! The odd thing, though, is that I don't think it's really *shocked* me."

"It hasn't?"

There was a faint but distinct tremor in his wife's voice. He looked at her quickly, and she gave a slightly shaky smile at the concern in his eyes.

"I can safely say it shocked *me*," she continued. "And"—she turned her eyes to Cayleb and Sharleyan—"I have to admit it disturbs me, as well. Even with all of *Seijin* Merlin's evidence, you're asking us to believe a great deal. Or perhaps I should say to *disbelieve* a great deal. You're not talking about just the Group of Four anymore. Not just about corruption in the Church, or about evil men twisting God's message. You're telling us the message *itself* is a lie. That the faith to which we've trusted our souls—the souls of our *children*—is nothing more than one enormous falsehood."

*There's steel in that woman's soul,* Merlin thought respectfully. *She's telling the truth when she says she's shocked, but she's cutting straight to the core of the entire story, what really* matters *to her.*

"That's exactly what Merlin is telling you, in part," Staynair responded before anyone else could. She looked at the archbishop, and he smiled sadly at her. "The Church of God Awaiting *is* a lie, the 'enormous falsehood' you just called it," he said. "But the men and women who created that lie built it out of fragments of genuine belief in God. They stole pieces of the truth to build a lie, and that's what's made it so damnably—and I choose my adverb with care, Your Highness—believable for so long. But as Merlin said when he began, there really isn't that much difference between Eric Langhorne and the Group of Four. Aside from the fact that, whether we agree with him or not, Langhorne truly could argue that the very survival of the human race depended upon the success of *his* lie."

Ohlyvya's eyes narrowed, and Staynair shrugged.

"I won't dispute a single thing Merlin's had to say about Langhorne and Bédard and the rest of the 'Archangels.' They were mass murderers and, clearly, megalomaniacs, and what they created was a monster and an abomination before God. I'm a Bédardist myself, and discovering the truth about the patron of my order was one of the more unpleasant experiences of my life. But having said that, the Order of Bédard's done an enormous amount of good over the centuries. I believe it's grown into something quite different from what Adorée Bédard had in mind when she was busy 'reprogramming' the minds of helpless, sleeping people to make them believe the lie, but I've also been forced to admit I might be wrong about that. We know *what* she and Langhorne did; we will never know what they were truly *thinking* when they did it. I'm not proposing that the nobility of their motives, assuming they actually possessed any such thing, justifies their acts. I'm simply saying that we, as human beings, have a tendency to judge on the basis of what *we* understand, what *we* see, even when we know intellectually that there are almost certainly things we *don't* under-stand and haven't yet seen. We do that with other humans. We do it even with ourselves, when you come right down to it. I think we ought to recognize that, Your Highness. And, just perhaps, that we might try to avoid doing the same thing to God."

She gazed at him for several moments, then nodded slowly. It wasn't really a gesture of agreement—not yet at least. But it was a concession of under-standing. Or perhaps of a *beginning* of understanding.

"In time, Ohlyvya," Sharleyan said, "every human being is going to have to decide how to respond to the lie for himself or herself. I know how I've re-sponded, but no one can predict how everyone else will. That's one reason we've been so cautious when it comes to deciding who we can reveal the truth to."

"And if it turns out you were *wrong* to reveal it to someone, Your Majesty?" Ohlyvya asked very softly. "What happens then?"

"The fact that you've asked means you already know the answer," Sharleyan replied, her voice equally soft yet unflinching. "We can't—and won't—pretend about that. God alone knows how many people are going to die before this struggle ends, and the information Merlin's shared with you and Nahrmahn to-night would be devastating in the hands of the Temple Loyalists. If you were in our place, what would *you* be willing to do to prevent it from reaching them?"

Silence hovered once more, tense and brittle. Then, surprisingly, Ohlyvya Baytz smiled. It was a small smile, but genuine, Merlin realized.

"I've been married to Nahrmahn almost as long as you've been alive, Your Majesty," she said. "During all those years, he's done his best to 'shelter me' from the harsh realities of the 'great game.' I'm afraid, though, that he never re-ally succeeded in that quite as well as he thought he had, even if I didn't have the heart to tell him he hadn't."

She turned her head, her smile growing broader and warmer as her eyes met her husband's and she squeezed his hand. Then she looked back at Sharleyan and Cayleb, and her expression had sobered once more.

"But after all that, of course I know what you would have done, and I don't doubt for a moment that Nahrmahn would have done exactly the same thing in your place. For that matter," she looked Sharleyan in the eye levelly, "so would I. So I suppose it's a good thing, for all our sakes, that you won't have to."

"We won't?" Cayleb asked quietly, and Ohlyvya shook her head.

"Your Grace, if Nahrmahn had been inclined to denounce you as heretics and demon worshippers, he would have done that the moment you told him *Seijin* Merlin sees 'visions.' You didn't need to tell him the *seijin* also flies through the air, and doesn't need to do little things like, oh, breathe, for him to have realized there was more at work in him than the Group of Four guesses. He knew from that moment that Merlin was an 'unnatural creature,' and I don't doubt the *Writ*'s warning that such things serve Shan-wei passed through his mind. It's a very *active* mind, you know."

She smiled again, shaking her head at Nahrmahn yet managing simultaneously to keep her gaze on Cayleb as she continued.

"I know my husband," she said simply, "and while I don't doubt the *seijin* would have been able to keep him under continuous observation, I think he would have succeeded in betraying you, if he'd decided you and Merlin *did* serve Shan-wei. He might not have survived the experience, but he would have *succeeded*. And I think, now that you've come to know him, you probably realize he would have done it *knowing* he wouldn't survive, if he'd truly believed you intended to betray the entire world to the Dark."

Nahrmahn's face had turned an interesting shade of pink, Merlin observed, but the rotund little prince didn't flinch.

*And she's right about him, too, by God,* Merlin thought, and shook his head mentally. *I wouldn't have thought it myself, when I first met him, but she's right. If he'd thought that, he would have done exactly what she's just said.*

"As it happens," Ohlyvya continued, "I have considerable faith in his judgment. It's not infallible, and he's made his share of mistakes. But it's a somewhat smaller share than that of quite a few other princes I could mention. And in this case, I think my judgment agrees with his."

She looked at Staynair.

"Your Eminence, I'd really like the opportunity to examine some of those other holy writs you've mentioned. I'm sure that when I do, they'll create plenty of questions of their own. But I was prepared to trust you against the Temple when your rejection of Mother Church's interpretation of the only *Writ* I knew of was based on nothing but faith. Perhaps you are asking us to believe even more, now, but you're also offering us a lot more in the way of evidence and proof." She shrugged. "No doubt someone like Clyntahn will still find all sorts of reasons to reject it. I've already made up my mind that he doesn't worship the same God I do, though, so that's not a problem for me."

Merlin felt himself relaxing as he realized she meant every word of it. He looked around the table and saw his own reaction mirrored, to greater or lesser extent, in each of the other faces. Except Nahrmahn's, perhaps.

The Prince of Emerald wasn't looking at Merlin Athrawes. Nor even at his emperor and empress. No, he was looking at someone far more important than either of those august individuals.

He was looking at his *wife,* and for once, as his eyes clung to hers, there was no guard on his expression or his emotions at all.

.VI.

### Prince Nahrmahn's Sitting Room,<br>Imperial Palace,<br>Cherayth,<br>Kingdom of Chisholm

G ood morning, Your Highness."

"Yes it is, isn't it? *Morning,* I mean." Nahrmahn Baytz looked out the palace window at a winter-gray Chisholmian day, and shuddered.

It wasn't actually all *that* early, Merlin reflected, but then again, Cherayth was four time zones farther east than Eraystor. Of course, Nahrmahn had enjoyed quite a lengthy voyage, so there'd been plenty of time for his internal clock to reset. Which led Merlin to the sad conclusion that Prince Nahrmahn simply wasn't what deplorably perky people back on Old Earth had persisted in calling "a morning person."

*Fair enough,* Merlin thought, suppressing a temptation to smile. *After all, I was never a "morning person" if I could avoid it, either.*

"And what may I do for you at this ungodly, frigid hour?" Nahrmahn inquired, stepping closer to the fire crackling on the guest sitting chamber's hearth. He held out his hands to the flames, although, to be perfectly fair, it wasn't especially freezing in the sitting chamber. Or not by Chisholmian standards, at any rate.

"Actually, I need to discuss a few things with you, Your Highness," Merlin said, and Nahrmahn's eyes narrowed, his expression turning rather more serious as he looked at the *seijin.*

"In my role as Their Majesties' imperial councilor for intelligence?" he asked. "Or in my role as new initiate into the 'inner circle'?"

"Both, actually." Merlin shrugged slightly. "I'm sure you've already realized, at least theoretically, how your ability to analyze intelligence is going to shift once we get you properly instructed in the use of your com. I doubt you're *fully* prepared for it, though. I mean no offense when I say that, but, frankly, I don't see how anyone who hasn't already experienced it *could* be fully prepared."

"Somehow, I don't doubt that at all." Nahrmahn's tone was dry and he shook his head. "I've been remembering all those neatly written 'summaries' you and . . . Owl have provided and trying to visualize what it must have been like to actually *watch* the things you reported in such detail." He shook his head again. "The one conclusion I've positively come to is that no matter how hard I try to imagine it, the reality's going to be even more . . . impressive, shall we say?"

"I think that's probably a safe estimate. Still, I also think you'll get accustomed faster than you expect right now." Merlin smiled. Then his expression sobered a bit. "But another thing you'll discover, unfortunately, is something called 'information overload.' " It was his turn to shake his head. "That's how Sharleyan almost ended up assassinated despite all of my SNARCs and parasites. There was simply too much data coming at me, even with Owl to help, for me to keep track of everything. And unlike you, Your Highness, I really can go without sleep virtually indefinitely when I need to."

"I imagine that's true enough," Nahrmahn said thoughtfully. "For that matter, I've been thinking about how difficult it must be for Their Majesties simply to find the time—and privacy—to sit down and 'look' at all the material you've been describing. It's not as if they can just sit around in the throne room ignoring everyone else while they listen to voices no one else can hear, now is it? Sooner or later, people would start to talk."

"Believe me, it's even worse than you may've been thinking." Merlin rolled his eyes. "I imagine it's going to be at least as bad with you, for that matter."

" 'At least as bad'?" Nahrmahn repeated, arching both eyebrows.

"You've got access to Owl's computer files now, Your Highness, and I know where your older children got their taste for reading. I shudder to think what's going to happen when you find Owl's history banks. And God help us all when you get your hands on a copy of Machiavelli!"

"Machiavelli," Nahrmahn repeated the bizarre-sounding name slowly, wrapping his tongue carefully around the odd syllables. "What a peculiar name." He cocked his head. "Is that the name of the book, or the author?"

"I'll let you find that out for yourself, Your Highness." Merlin did shudder, delicately. "I probably shouldn't have mentioned it to you at all, but I've told Owl to help all system users figure out how to do data searches, and knowing you, you'd have turned up all sorts of references to it on your own soon enough."

"You realize you're only making me even more curious," Nahrmahn pointed out.

"Yes, I guess I am." Merlin crossed to the window and stood looking out across the winter-dulled countryside beyond. "I think part of it's finally having someone I can talk to about this at all," he said slowly. "It's almost . . . almost as if human history isn't really dead anymore, and I hadn't truly realized how much I missed it until I discovered other people I can actually dare to share it with."

Nahrmahn's expression softened, and he laid one hand lightly on the *seijin*'s shoulder.

"There's a proverb," he said quietly. "I imagine they had something like it back on 'Old Earth.' It says, 'Lonely is the head that wears a crown.'" He shook his own head, looking out the window beside Merlin. "I realized years ago just how true that was, but it never occurred to me that there could be someone who was as lonely as *you* must have been when you woke up in that cave of yours."

Merlin turned his head, looking down and across at the pudgy little Emeraldian for a moment, then nodded slowly.

"You know, Your Highness," he said in a deliberately lighter tone, "I'm happier every day that we managed to settle that unpleasantness between Charis and Emerald without making anyone a foot or so shorter than he used to be."

"Especially those of us who had so few inches to spare to begin with," Nahrmahn agreed wryly, looking up at the towering *seijin*.

"To be sure." Merlin smiled. Then he gave himself a shake.

"But I suppose I ought to be getting back to the real reason I came to see you this morning," he said more briskly.

"By all means," Nahrmahn invited.

"The thing is that I'm leaving for Maikelberg as soon as you and I finish this chat. I have an errand there for Their Majesties—one that actually does have a little something to do with our present conversation. Because I'm going to be away, I won't be able to walk you and Princess Ohlyvya through the familiarization with your coms the way I would otherwise. Cayleb and Sharleyan can do that just fine, though, and I believe they're going to invite you—and Archbishop Maikel—to supper again tonight to do exactly that."

He paused, eyebrows raised, until Nahrmahn nodded in understanding, then went on.

"Once we've got you up to speed and you're comfortable using the interface with Owl, we'll ask you to help take some of the information load off the rest of us. Cayleb and Sharleyan already have aspects of Owl's total intelligence take that they're responsible for vetting every day. The hard part where you're concerned is going to be avoiding the temptation to really load you down. To be honest, Your Highness, I believe you're the best analyst we have. You're certainly better at it than I am, and I think you're actually better at it than Wave Thunder, for that matter. So we need to strike the right balance between having you screening raw data yourself and looking at all the more important things someone else—someone who's not as good an analyst—has turned up for you to consider."

"I can see that," Nahrmahn mused. If he was embarrassed by Merlin's compliments about his analytical ability, he hid it well, the *seijin* reflected wryly.

"There are some areas, however, where we are going to want you to take the first look at the data itself," he said out loud. "Which brings me to my trip to Maikelberg."

"In what way?" Nahrmahn asked when Merlin paused.

"Certain people," the *seijin* chose his words with care, "are either already talking to people they shouldn't be talking to or else *looking* for people they shouldn't be talking to. Some of them are quite highly placed."

"I'm not surprised," Nahrmahn said sourly. "In fact, I could probably hazard a guess at some of the 'highly placed' people in question. Those summaries you used to hand me contained a few of those names, for that matter. Should I assume someone in Maikelberg falls into that category?"

"There are several people in Maikelberg who fall into that category, as a matter of fact, Your Highness." Merlin grimaced. "Fortunately, there are a lot more who might have fallen into it who don't. Duke Eastshare, for example."

"Really?" Nahrmahn gazed at Merlin intently, then nodded slowly. "Good. Good!" He nodded more firmly. "I thought that was probably the case, but I'm *delighted* to have it confirmed!"

"You're not exactly alone in that," Merlin said feelingly, then shrugged. "For obvious reasons, we can't go around arresting people when we can't possibly present the evidence—the proof—of their treason in an open court. We *can* use what we know to steer people out of particularly sensitive positions when we know we can't trust them, and we do. But there are a relatively small handful who we know are traitors who we either can't ease aside without some ironclad justification or who, for various reasons, we don't *want* to ease aside."

"Knowing who the traitor is allows you to control the information flow," Nahrmahn said.

"Exactly." Merlin nodded vigorously. "That's the thinking behind most of Cayleb and Sharleyan's decisions to leave people in those sorts of positions, and they're going to ask you to take over on monitoring that information flow."

Nahrmahn nodded again, still gazing thoughtfully up at Merlin.

"In addition, though, there are a very few people—just a handful, actually—who have been left in place for very specific reasons. Reasons that don't really have much to do with controlling the information they're passing to someone else. Cayleb calls them our 'Master Traynyr Specials.'"

He watched Nahrmahn's expression expectantly. The prince frowned for a moment, then found himself nodding yet again at the reference to the legendary director of Safeholdian puppet theater.

"So your journey to Maikelberg has something to do with one of those puppets." His tone was thoughtfully speculative. "Someone you're maneuvering into doing something himself? Or someone you're using to maneuver someone *else* into doing something?"

"Your Highness, watching you in action is one of my guilty pleasures," Merlin told him with a grin. "For that matter, it was one of my guilty pleasures even when you were on the other side!"

"I'm enchanted to discover I've given you so many hours of amusement, *Seijin* Merlin." Nahrmahn's tone was dry, but his eyes twinkled, and Merlin snorted.

"Let me tell you about the noble Earl of Swayle," he said. "He's quite an interesting fellow. He has even more interesting friends, too, and Cayleb and Sharleyan—and I—would appreciate your perspective on him. And, for that matter, on exactly how I should go about . . . presenting myself in the course of that errand I mentioned a few minutes ago. You see—"

## .VII.
## Archbishop's Palace,
## City of Tairys,
## Province of Glacierheart,
## Republic of Siddarmark

Are you certain about this, Your Eminence?"

Father Gharth Gorjah couldn't quite keep his own reservations out of his tone, and Zhasyn Cahnyr smiled. Gorjah was little more than half Cahnyr's own age, and he'd been with the archbishop literally since leaving seminary. He was adept at all the skills a proper secretary required, and Cahnyr had no doubt any number of other bishops or archbishops would cheerfully have hired the younger man away from him. Gorjah had never shown the least interest in any of the offers which had come his way, however. Cahnyr hoped and believed much of that was because Gorjah enjoyed working for him. He certainly treasured the under-priest's services, although he supposed it was selfish of him not to have nudged the boy into taking one of those competing offers. An archbishop with more powerful alliances could probably have moved Gorjah's career along more rapidly, after all. By now, he would undoubtedly have been at least an upper-priest if he'd been in the service of one of those better connected prelates.

But another aspect of his secretary's loyalty, as Cahnyr was well aware, was the fact that he'd been born and raised right here in Glacierheart. His father and older brothers had all gone into the mines in late boyhood, but his parents had decided young Gharth would aspire to greater things, and his entire family had shouldered the sacrifices to make it so.

The Church provided five years of schooling to all God's children at no charge (as well she should, Cahnyr thought now, sourly, thinking of how many marks the tithe squeezed out of them every year), but it was a rare Glacierheart family who could spare a potential laborer long enough for a child to acquire anything greater than basic literacy. Gharth's parents had been determined to do better than that, and, somehow, they'd managed to keep him out of the mines and in school. Their local priest had seen something in the lad, as well, which had earned Gharth more attention from his instructors, who, in turn, had discovered that this short, stocky coal miner's son had a first-rate mind.

From there, the youngster's path had been pretty much preordained. Mother Church always needed talent, and it had become apparent early on that Gharth had a true vocation. That had brought him to the attention of Cahnyr's predecessor in Glacierheart, and with his archbishop's sponsorship, he'd attended seminary in Zion itself. The previous archbishop had intended to employ the young seminarian on his staff, and when Cahnyr was elevated to his see following his unexpected death, the new archbishop had taken an instant liking to newly ordained Father Gharth.

*Which probably explains why the young sprout feels qualified to look at me as if I were a slightly addled uncle,* that archbishop reflected now.

"If you mean am I certain this is a good idea," he said out loud, his tone thoughtful, "the answer is yes. If you mean am I certain this is going to be the most pleasant time of the year for a retreat, the answer is no. If you mean am I certain the instructions I just gave you were the ones I *meant* to give you, then, again, the answer is yes."

He scratched his chin in obvious rumination for a moment, then gave the younger man a glower. It was fierce, that glower, a thing of majesty and power . . . slightly flawed by the humor gleaming in his eyes.

"Over all, I believe the 'yesses' have it. Don't you?"

"Of course, Your Eminence!" Gorjah actually blushed a bit, but he also shook his head with true Glacierheart stubbornness. "It's just that, as you say, this isn't the best time of the year for a retreat. Especially not to Summit House. I don't even know what shape the house is in, and it's entirely likely we'll get a blizzard through here with little warning. If you're up there with no one but Fraidmyn to look after you and the weather turns really bad. . . ."

He let his voice trickle off, and Cahnyr smiled.

"I appreciate your concern, Gharth—really I do. But I'm fairly confident even a pair of old dodderers like Fraidmyn and me can survive a few days of isolation. And Summit House has been perched on that peak for over a hundred years, so I doubt any storm is likely to knock it down around our ears. And, finally, if conditions are going to be a little austere, that's scarcely a minus for a spiritual retreat, now is it?"

"No, Your Eminence. Of course not. It's just—"

"Just that you don't want me out of your sight where I might get myself into trouble?" Cahnyr finished dryly, one eyebrow cocked.

Gorjah blushed again, then laughed.

"Guilty, Your Eminence—guilty!" he confessed with a smile. But then his expression sobered, and his eyes looked searchingly into his superior's.

Cahnyr returned that look levelly, steadily, but without answering the questions it asked. He couldn't—wouldn't—give Gorjah those answers. Not now. He'd decided long ago that the less young Gharth knew about his archbishop's riskier activities, the better. It hadn't been easy keeping the under-priest outside so much of his life, but he'd been active in the Circle long before Gorjah entered his service. His conduits to the Wylsynns and the Circle had already been in place, and he'd simply declined to make his new secretary aware of them.

There'd been times he'd questioned that decision, and not just because of how it made his own life more difficult than it might have been. He'd recognized the kindred spirit inside Gharth Gorjah, and he'd had little concern—not *no* concern; no man could ever be absolutely certain of anything before the test—that the young man would have betrayed him or the Circle. For that matter, he'd been confident his secretary would have promptly agreed to join the Circle's activities. But he'd declined to allow the youngster to make that decision at such an early stage in his own life. It wasn't the sort of thing a man could simply walk away from if he later decided he'd made a mistake, and he'd been more than half-afraid Gorjah would have agreed at least in large part simply because of his respect and liking for Cahnyr himself.

By the time a few years had passed, and he'd been more confident Gorjah would have made an informed decision for the right reasons, there'd been other factors. Clyntahn had become Grand Inquisitor, which had raised the stakes starkly. The Circle itself had decided it would henceforth restrict all knowledge of its activities and its very existence to the ranks of the episcopate. Only a limited number of junior clergy already knew about those things, and the Circle had judged it best to keep it that way, both for security and to protect their juniors. And, finally, Gorjah had married his childhood sweetheart and the first of their (currently) three children had already been on the way.

Given all of that, Cahnyr had decided it was his duty to keep Gorjah away from that part of his life. In fact, for the last five years, Gorjah hadn't even accompanied him back to the Temple between pastoral visits. Cahnyr had engaged another secretary—one he was confident was an Inquisition informant, in fact—in Zion while he delegated more and more of the routine duties here in Glacierheart to Gorjah. When Bishop Executor Wyllys Haimltahn's secretary, who'd been much more elderly, died of pneumonia three years before, Gorjah had slipped into the secretary's role for Haimltahn, as well, so it had never been as if there weren't plenty of legitimate duties to keep him fully occupied here in Tairys.

There'd been times, especially over the past few months, when Cahnyr had felt profoundly guilty over not telling Gorjah about the Circle. He was far from certain Clyntahn would believe Gorjah had known nothing about his superior's activities. Worse, he suspected Clyntahn wouldn't *care* whether or not Gorjah had been actively involved. The Grand Inquisitor might well decide that, guilty or not, Gorjah would make another excellent pointed example, and it wasn't as if there weren't plenty of under-priests to replace him, after all.

Yet, in the end, the archbishop had held fast to his resolve against entangling the younger priest in his own fate. His Zion secretary saw every bit of his correspondence with Gorjah, which was one reason Cahnyr had kept him on even after he'd become confident the man was making regular reports to the Inquisition. That correspondence had never so much as hinted at anything concerning the Circle or its activities, and his only real hope was that its routine nature, coupled with Gorjah's genuine ignorance of his superior's "disloyal" activities, would be his secretary's best defense.

*Poor as it may prove in the end, Gharth,* the archbishop thought, *it's the best I can do for you.* He smiled a bit sadly. *I can't even invite you to run with me— assuming I ever actually* get *the chance to run. A desperate flight through the teeth of a mountain winter with three small children and a pregnant wife is the* last *thing you need.*

"Very well, Your Eminence," Gorjah said finally. "I won't say I think you're being foolish, since I'm far too dutiful to ever harbor such disrespectful motions. And perish the thought that a pair of . . . esteemed gentlemen, neither of whom will ever see sixty again, aren't perfectly capable of looking after themselves under even the most primitive of conditions." He gave Cahnyr a stern look, then sighed and shook his head when the archbishop returned it blandly. "I'll make the arrangements. And if you'll give me a five-day, I'll see to it the coal bins are full and the pantry's properly stocked, as well."

"Thank you, Gharth." Cahnyr patted the younger man gently on the shoulder. "That's very thoughtful of you. I appreciate it."

Which was true, he thought. And even better, the delay the secretary had asked for would be almost exactly the right length.

I f he'd still been a flesh-and-blood human being, Merlin Athrawes reflected as his most recent remount trotted briskly along under him, he'd really be getting tired of this particular exercise. Or of making this particular trip, at any rate.

The city of Maikelberg had been built by Sharleyan's father, King Sailys. It lay just under a hundred and fifty miles north of Cherayth on the narrow neck of land between Lake Morgan and Cherry Bay, and it had been intended from the outset as a fortress city.

The three true keys to King Sailys' success in breaking the power of the nobles who had marginalized his father and grandfather had been, first, the Royal Army, which had been commanded by his brother-in-law, the Duke of Halbrook Hollow; second, the Crown's alliance with the Commons, which had been arranged and orchestrated by his boyhood friend, Mahrak Sahndyrs, Baron Green Mountain; and, third, geography. Well, geography coupled with more of Green Mountain's astute diplomacy.

Green Mountain had been very careful to enlist the support of the Duke of Lakeshore, the Duke of Broken Rock, and the Earl of Helena, although he'd had to do rather more dragon-trading than he'd really liked, especially in Broken Rock's case. Coupled with the fervent support of the free city of Port Charlz (which had been renamed Port Royal by its citizens as a token of its enthusiasm for the Crown), their backing had given Sailys (who was himself the Duke of Cherayth) a solid territorial base of his own. Protected by Lake Morgan and Lake Megan, to the west, and by the sea to the east and south, he had commanded the kingdom's best ports and most productive artisans, which had constituted a major advantage over his fractious, internally bickering opposition.

Maikelberg had been built on the territory of the then-Duke of Eastshare, who had not been one of Sailys' greater admirers, to protect that advantage. It had been designed to keep Eastshare on his own side of Lake Morgan, thus freeing Sailys to concentrate on the more dangerous, broader approaches across the Duchies of Lakeshore and Windshore. And the king had been careful to extend his control gradually, working westward, without ever uncovering his back.

The old Duke of Eastshare had been considerate enough to get himself killed in battle before producing an heir of his own body. At that point, the title had passed to a collateral line, and the new duke—the current duke's father—recognizing which way the wind was setting, had become one of the Crown's loyal adherents. Despite that, Sailys had kept the walls of Maikelberg in excellent repair, and Sharleyan had followed suit. Of course, Sharleyan had also completed her father's plans for Lake Morgan and Lake Megan, linking Lake Morgan to Cherry Bay by way of the King Sailys Canal and Lake Megan to Lake Morgan via the Edymynd Canal. The canals had stimulated the economy of the area around Cherayth still further, and it was no coincidence that the King Sailys Canal had been placed in a perfect location for Maikelberg to protect.

Maikelberg's proximity to Cherry Bay and to Lake Morgan gave it excellent waterborne communications, which had made it a logical place for the present Duke of Eastshare to go about organizing the new Imperial Army. It was also connected to Cherayth by a carefully maintained high road, and as a member of Emperor Cayleb's personal guard, Captain Athrawes had priority for fresh horses from the posting stations the Crown maintained along the way. All of which meant he could make the journey between the two cities by horseback in about two of Safehold's long days. If he pushed the pace a bit, he could have made the same trip in a day and a half, or even a little less.

*Of course, if I were able to use the* skimmer, *I could make it in about* ten minutes, *couldn't I?* he reflected dryly as he (finally) saw the walls of Maikelberg rising before him. He grimaced only half-humorously at the thought.

*At least it's not as if the time is wasted,* he reminded himself.

Nimue Alban had been an indifferent equestrienne, at best. She'd learned to ride, more or less, as a little girl, only because her wealthy father—himself a world-class polo player—had insisted. Her own interests had lain elsewhere . . . a point which had obviously perplexed her father, who had been firmly convinced that every girl child ever born idolized horses. Maybe every *other* girl child ever born had, but Nimue had been much more interested in sailboats.

As a consequence, however, Merlin Athrawes' riding skills had been less than stellar, as well. Fortunately, the preferred style on Safehold was what had been called "Western-style" (in remarkably disapproving tones) by young Nimue's riding instructors. Also fortunately, Merlin had a PICA's reactions, strength, and ability to literally program his artificial body with "muscle memory" skills. With those advantages, his performance on horseback had improved dramatically, which had been fortunate for his *seijin*'s reputation.

By now, Merlin was capable of setting himself on autopilot once he climbed into the saddle and performing there with a polished skill few breathing humans could have bettered. In fact, with the situational awareness provided by his artificially enhanced senses, and the reaction speed provided by his fiber-optic nervous system, he could readily afford to multitask during the lengthy rides between Cherayth and Maikelberg, which gave him the opportunity to catch up on some of the unending data dumps coming to him from Owl's remotes.

That was precisely what he'd been doing ever since he'd left the palace, and as usually happened when he had uninterrupted opportunities to examine the data, he'd discovered a few previously unsuspected alligators crawling out of the swamp. Most of those alligators had not yet reached the potentially disastrous stage, but at least one of them was likely to lead to an "interesting" conversation with Archbishop Maikel.

*Under the circumstances, I think I'd better postpone that until I can get home and have it in person, though.*

That reflection carried Merlin and his present mount to Maikel's Bridge, the largest of the three drawbridges across the King Sailys Canal. Iron-shod hooves sounded with a dull hollowness on the bridge's timbers, and Merlin shifted mental gears as he shook himself fully back into the moment. Conversations with Staynair could wait until he got back to Cherayth; the one he was here to have with Duke Eastshare was likely to prove quite "interesting" enough to be going on with.

▼   ▼   ▼

"*Seijin* Merlin."

Ruhsyl Thairis, the Duke of Eastshare, was forty-five years old, brown-haired and brown-eyed, a couple of inches under six feet tall, and stocky for his height. Although he was one of the Kingdom of Chisholm's highest-born noblemen, he came to his feet as Merlin was ushered into his office.

"Your Grace," Merlin replied, and bowed deeply.

"It's good to see you again," Eastshare continued, extending his hand. They clasped forearms, and the duke smiled a bit crookedly.

"It's good to see you," he repeated, "but I can't help wondering exactly *why* I'm seeing you. Or, rather, seeing you again this soon."

"Actually, Your Grace, there are several reasons, but one of them is more important than any of the others." Merlin's answering smile was rather more crooked than his host's had been. "In particular, Their Majesties have a message for you which they thought should probably be delivered in person."

"Ah?" Eastshare raised one eyebrow.

"And, to be honest, Your Grace, it's also a bit . . . complicated. I think it's going to take me a little time to explain things properly."

"I see."

Eastshare regarded his visitor thoughtfully. Despite his own loyalty to the Crown and, specifically, to Sharleyan Tayt Ahrmahk, the duke was every inch a Chisholmian noble. Since the Duke of Halbrook Hollow's treason, Merlin had satisfied himself (both from personal contact and from the recordings of Owl's

SNARCs) that Eastshare's allegiance to the Empire—and, despite a few initial reservations, to the Church of Charis, as well—was genuine. Despite that, Eastshare was one of those people who had trouble truly grasping the concept that the majority of commoners were just as much people as he was. It wasn't even arrogance, in his case; it was simply incomprehension. The natural and innate superiority of the nobly born was so much a part of the world in which he had been raised that it was literally impossible for him to make that leap on anything except a purely intellectual basis.

Yet there was one area in which that was clearly not the case, for he had no difficulty at all accepting commoners who also happened to be Army officers as the equals of their more aristocratic fellows. In fact, he was well known for ruthlessly quashing any efforts to establish "old boy" networks of aristocratic patronage when it came to promotions and assignments.

Some of that, Merlin suspected, was because Eastshare regarded "all" his officers, including the common-born ones, as members of his own extended family. Another part, however, was probably institutional, given the fact that the Army had been specifically created to break the aristocracy's grip on Chisholm. It had been created around commoners, not aristocrats, and despite the towering nobility of his own birth, Eastshare had no problem maintaining that tradition. In the *Army*, at least; *outside* the Army, he seemed perfectly comfortable with the patronage-backed ascendancy of his fellow aristocrats.

In Merlin's case, Eastshare had obviously decided he fell under the "soldier" heading, even if he had had the bad taste to be born somewhere besides Chisholm, and related to him accordingly. And although Merlin's official rank was still only "captain," Eastshare—who was no dummy—clearly realized some captains were more equal than others. In particular, a captain of the Imperial Guard, assigned to head the emperor's personal detail, who'd first introduced himself to the emperor by foiling an assassination attempt when the emperor in question had been a mere crown prince, and who was routinely used by both the emperor and the empress as their personal messenger and troubleshooter, was one hell of a lot more equal than other captains. That, Merlin had decided some time ago, was the reason Eastshare habitually addressed him as *"seijin"* rather than using his official rank. And it was probably also the reason he treated a commoner—and a *foreign-born* commoner, at that—as something very close to an equal. Not quite, of course. But close.

"If Their Majesties think I need to hear something from you personally, why don't you join me for supper?" the duke asked now. "Lady Eastshare is off visiting our newest grandchild, and she won't be back until sometime late tomorrow, so I was planning on dining at headquarters, anyway, then turning in in my quarters here instead of riding all the way home. I'd intended to ask some of my staff to join me. Should I assume the nature of your message would make it more advisable for you and me to dine privately?"

"Actually, Your Grace," Merlin murmured, "I think that might be a very good idea."

▼    ▼    ▼

"So, *Seijin* Merlin," Eastshare said three hours later. "About that message?"

"Of course, Your Grace."

Eastshare's orderly had overseen the servants who had removed the dishes, then poured the wine, set the decanter on the table at Eastshare's elbow, and withdrawn from the private dining room adjacent to the duke's quarters here in the Maikelberg citadel. It had been an excellent dinner, Merlin thought appreciatively, and the wine was quite good, too. Fusion-powered PICAs didn't require nourishment, although his internal arrangements were designed to scavenge the material he needed to produce his "naturally growing" hair and beard from the food he ingested. Most of that food simply had to be disposed of later, but PICAs had been designed to allow their owners to do anything they could have done in their own biological bodies. Merlin's tastebuds were fully functional, although any Safeholdian healer would have gone off in gibbering madness if Merlin had tried to explain to him exactly *how* they functioned. He'd enjoyed the meal, and aside from a certain degree of tunnel vision resulting from that single blind spot where commoners were concerned, Eastshare was an incisive observer, with a trenchant wit. The table conversation had been just as enjoyable as the meal, and Merlin hoped that wasn't going to change.

*It'll be interesting to see whether or not he goes ballistic,* the *seijin* thought. Cayleb and Sharleyan had a side bet going, and he suspected the two of them were watching through one of the SNARCs to see which of them had been right. *For that matter, Nahrmahn's probably looking in, too,* he reflected.

Eastshare was looking at him across the table, he realized, and there was more than a hint of impatience in the duke's steady regard.

*Stop dithering, Merlin,* he told himself firmly, and cleared his throat.

"I'm sure you're aware, Your Grace," he began, "that there have to have been some . . . concerns about conflicting loyalties in the Army's officer corps."

"You mean I'm aware Their Majesties have to have wondered how many of the rest of their officers are going to go the way Halbrook Hollow went," Eastshare said flatly. Merlin's eyebrows rose involuntarily at the bluntness of the duke's comment, and Eastshare chuckled a bit harshly.

"You've always been the soul of courtesy, *Seijin* Merlin," he said, "but only an idiot—which, I assure you, I'm not—could have failed to realize that one reason you've paid so many visits to Maikelberg on Their Majesties' behalf was to look into that very concern. And, frankly, I've assumed from the beginning that you had to be looking more closely at me than at anyone else, given that Byrtrym was married to my sister and how long he and I were friends even before that. Not to mention the fact that I inherited my present post directly from him. I've also assumed, however, since I haven't been *removed* from that post, and since Their Majesties have always treated me with courtesy and frankness, that your reports to them must have been at least generally favorable."

Merlin looked at him silently for a moment or two, then shrugged.

"I hope I wasn't *too* obvious about it, Your Grace," he said a bit wryly, and Eastshare gave another, slightly less harsh chuckle.

"As a matter of fact, when I said you were the soul of courtesy, I meant it. And to be honest, I'd have been disappointed if Sharleyan and Cayleb hadn't had reservations." It was his turn to shrug. "I've watched Her Majesty, in particular, since she was twelve, *Seijin* Merlin. She didn't survive in Queen Ysabel's shadow by being stupid. She didn't do it by being so clumsy as to rub people's noses in the fact that she had to regard them as untrustworthy until they proved otherwise, either, though. I'd say you've served her quite admirably in both those regards."

"Thank you." Merlin bobbed a half bow across the table, then smiled. "And, yes, Your Grace, the verdict in your case was entirely favorable. And while it may not really be my place to add this, my impression is that Her Majesty was as pleased by that on a personal level as she was in her official persona. I don't believe she regards—or values—you solely as a vassal, or even as the commander of her army."

"Good." Eastshare's expression softened. "I couldn't blame her for worrying, but I won't pretend it didn't bother me, anyway." Sadness touched his brown eyes. "I suppose a lot of that was because of the reason she had to worry in the first place." He shook his head. "I wondered how Byrtrym was going to deal with that conflict of loyalties. I knew it was going to be hard for him, but—"

The duke broke off, shaking his head again, harder. There was something about the motion, almost like a prize fighter trying to shake off the effects of a powerful left jab, and his eyes were distant, looking at something only he could see. Then he gave his shoulders a small twitch, took a sip of wine, and turned back to Merlin with a brisker air.

"And now, about that message—?"

"Well, discarding all the courteous euphemisms and circumlocutions I was going to employ, Your Grace, the short version is that Their Majesties and Prince Nahrmahn have determined that, unlike you, one of the officers on your staff most definitely does have divided loyalties. In fact, the evidence available to Prince Nahrmahn suggests the officer in question is actively involved in treason."

*And every word I just said is completely true,* he reflected, *even if Sharleyan and Cayleb—and Nahrmahn—have made that determination on the basis of information I provided.*

Eastshare snapped upright in his chair, and his expression hardened abruptly. The adjective that came to mind, Merlin decided, was "thunderous."

"Who is the bastard?!" the duke demanded, and his tone was even harsher than his expression. "I'll roast his fucking balls over a low fire! And that'll be the *gentlest* thing that happens to him!"

*Well, so far it looks like Cayleb's going to win the bet,* Merlin thought dryly.

"Please, Your Grace!" Merlin raised both hands and made gentle, patting "go-slow" motions. "I warned you this is going to be complicated. I doubt Their Majesties would have any problem with your doing exactly that . . . eventually."

" '*Eventually*'?!" Eastshare's expression transformed into one of disbelief. "Langhorne, *Seijin*! You just said he's on my own *staff*! Do you realize what sort of information that means he has *access* to? How much *damage* he can do?"

"That's the reason—or one of the reasons, at least—Their Majesties sent me to discuss this with you." Merlin grimaced. "To be perfectly frank, Your Grace, I think there was some concern about how well you'd be able to dissemble if you knew the officer in question was a traitor. I hesitate to say this, but you're not . . . exactly known for personal subtlety."

For a heartbeat, it looked as if Eastshare literally couldn't believe what he'd just heard. Merlin looked back calmly, wondering whether or not the duke was going to explode, but then, instead, Eastshare astounded him with a sharp, barking laugh.

"Not known for *subtlety,* is it?" The duke jabbed an index finger at his dinner guest. "Subtlety!"

"Only on a *personal* basis, Your Grace," Merlin said earnestly. "When it comes to *politics,* Her Majesty believes you can lie, deceive, and dissemble with the best!"

Eastshare laughed again, then shook his head and gave Merlin a moderately severe glare.

"All right, *Seijin*. Point taken. But"—his expression sobered once more, and he leaned slightly forward—"I stand by my original observation. Anyone on my staff knows entirely too much about the new weapons, the new tactics, our strategic thinking and planning, our troop strengths." He shook his head again. "If someone's passing on that kind of information, even just to our own Temple Loyalists, it's damned well ending *up* in the Temple!"

"Agreed." Merlin nodded, and his own expression was much more serious than it had been. "On the other hand, I think part of the decision-making process was that with the Church's semaphore systems in the Empire now in our hands, and not the Group of Four's, any information from Chisholm will take months getting to Zion. By the time it does, it's going to be thoroughly obsolete and out-of-date. It's not going to have any immediate tactical value to them, at any rate."

"But it could have quite a lot of value in terms of doctrine and how the new weapons work," Eastshare countered. "The longer it takes them to start figuring out that kind of crap, the better I'll like it."

"Your Grace, much as I might wish it were otherwise, not all the people serving Clyntahn and Maigwair are idiots, and the Inquisition's intelligence services have always been among the best in the world. It could hardly be any other way, given the Inquisition's responsibilities, now could it?"

Merlin held Eastshare's eyes until the duke nodded slightly, then shrugged.

"That being the case, I think we have to assume more information than we'd like, especially about the new weapons, is going to find its way into the Temple's hands, no matter what we do. For that matter, by this time, someone's almost certainly managed to divert actual examples of them into Temple Loyalist hands. I'd be extremely surprised if they don't already have at least a few of our rifles in Zion by now, for example. And I think we have to take it as a given that anything Corisande had figured out before our actual invasion had been transmitted to the Temple, as well. So even though our staff officer–traitor may be able to do some damage in that regard, Their Majesties are of the opinion that the damage he can do is outweighed by . . . other considerations."

" 'Other considerations,' " Eastshare repeated, his eyes narrowing. "Should I assume from that, *Seijin* Merlin, that Their Majesties—oh, and let's not forget Prince Nahrmahn—have concocted some strategy to *use* this traitorous bastard?"

"Oh, I think you can take that as a given, Your Grace." Merlin smiled nastily. "In fact, if you can restrain your impulse—completely natural and fully understandable though it is—to cut off his testicles and roast them, I think we may be able to use one relatively minor 'traitorous bastard' to set a little trap for a very *major* 'traitorous bastard.' "

"Did I say something to make you think I intended to cut them off *before* I fried them?" Eastshare inquired acidly, and despite the fact that Nimue Alban had been born a woman, Merlin winced slightly as he realized the duke meant it.

"My error, Your Grace," he apologized. "Nonetheless, my point stands."

"I see."

Eastshare settled back in his chair again, right hand toying with the stem of his wineglass while the fingers of his left hand drummed slowly, rhythmically, on the linen tablecloth.

"It occurs to me," he said finally, "given what you've just said about my 'subtlety,' or lack thereof, that Their Majesties wouldn't have sent you to tell me about this unless they need me to make this strategy of theirs work. I mean, they would have preferred not to tell me a thing about it and give me the opportunity—in my own inimitably unsubtle fashion—to warn him he's under suspicion." The duke showed his teeth briefly. "I imagine, for example, that squeezing his head like a pimple the next time I saw him might be just a *tiny* giveaway."

"Indeed." Merlin decided not to respond directly to that last comment and contented himself with another nod, then went on a bit more briskly. "Actually, there are two things they need you to do. First, they wanted to be certain you knew about him—and about their plans—before you became aware of his activities on your own. They were pretty sure that if that happened, you'd arrest him immediately, then inform them of what you'd discovered."

He paused briefly, and Eastshare nodded in understanding.

"Secondly," Merlin continued, "they want you to actually help his treason along a little bit."

The duke's facial muscles tightened ever so slightly, and he looked, for a moment, as if he were going to protest. He didn't, though.

*Thinking that if someone else notices you "helping his treason along" they're likely to assume you're a traitor, too, aren't you, Your Grace?* he thought. *Well, I don't blame you. And, frankly, the fact that the thought occurred to you and you didn't automatically object only makes me think still better of you.*

"Who is this fellow?" Eastshare asked instead.

"Earl Swayle, Your Grace," Merlin replied quietly.

The duke grimaced. There was pain in that expression—not surprisingly, given how long the Thairis and Rahskail families had known one another. But there was less surprise than there might have been.

"I wondered about that. Or perhaps I should say I was *afraid* of that." Eastshare's voice was even quieter than Merlin's, and he shook his head sadly. "He's shut up about it lately—especially since that business at Saint Agtha's—but his initial reaction to the marriage proposal was . . . unhappy." The duke shook his head again. "I think he blamed the Emperor for 'luring' the Queen into apostasy. If he did, it was stupid of him. I can't remember the last time—or, for that matter, the *first* time—anyone managed to 'lure' Sharleyan into anything she didn't want to do all along! Still, I wouldn't be surprised if that's what drew him into active treason. Assuming Prince Nahrmahn's evidence is valid."

"If it turns out Their Majesties' suspicions are baseless, then what they have in mind will do no harm, Your Grace. If their suspicions are *valid,* however, we may accomplish several very useful things."

"All right, *Seijin* Merlin," Eastshare said with a trace of sorrow. "I'll accept, tentatively, at least, that he's gone rogue. And I'll not only keep my hands off him but pretend he's still one of my trusted officers . . . and friends. Now, please be good enough to tell me exactly what it is Their Majesties have in mind."

"Of course, Your Grace. The main thing is—"

.IX.
Saint Kathryn's Church,
Candlemaker Street,
and
a Warehouse,
City of Manchyr,
Princedom of Corisande,
and
Captain Merlin Athrawes' Room,
Imperial Army Barracks,
Maikelberg,
Duchy of Eastshare,
Kingdom of Chisholm

S o, *there* you are!"

Tymahn Hahskans twitched, then looked up with a visibly guilty expression. Dailohrs Hahskans stood at the top of the narrow stair in her nightgown, looking down at him, arms folded while the toes of one bare foot tapped ever so gently on the landing. She was a tallish, slender woman, eight years younger than her husband, with auburn hair just starting to go gray and blue-green eyes. At the moment, those eyes were sternly narrowed, Hahskans noted. He considered—briefly—prevaricating, but after the next best thing to thirty years of marriage, that would have been an exercise in futility. So, since he'd been caught anyway, he decided his best course was to manfully own up to his misdeeds.

"I was discussing this five-day's sermon with Zhaif Laityr."

"Swilling down beer with Zhaif Laityr until all hours, don't you mean?" she demanded.

"We might, perhaps, have partaken of a tankard or two. Strictly as a source of desperately needed sustenance while we contemplated weighty matters of theology," he replied with immense dignity, and the corners of her mouth twitched. It was barely a shadow of the broad grin he would normally have seen at this point in their familiar, well-worn exchange, yet his heart eased—a little, at least—when he saw it.

Father Zhaif Laityr was the senior priest at the Church of the Holy Archangels Triumphant in Gray Lizard Square, two parishes over from Hahskans' own Saint Kathryn's, and the two of them had been friends for many years. Despite the fact that Hahskans was a Bédardist while Laityr was a Pasqualate, they saw eye to eye on quite a few issues . . . including several they'd both been forbidden to speak about.

Which was why Dailohrs' eyes were worried and she found it so difficult to smile.

"Desperately needed sustenance, is it?" She cocked her head, deliberately seeking the reassurance of comforting routine. "Should I assume from the fact that you were forced to resort to *liquid* sustenance that Mistress Dahnzai was somehow incapable of providing you and your crony with sandwiches?"

Lyzbyt Dahnzai had been the housekeeper in charge of Holy Archangels Triumphant's rectory even longer than Ezmelda Dobyns had held the same post at Saint Kathryn's. Over the years, she'd become adroit at the care and feeding of Father Zhaif, and probably almost as good at bullying him into taking care of himself as Dailohrs and Mistress Dobyns were at chivying Hahskans into doing the same thing.

"As a matter of fact, we did supplement our liquid intake with a wyvern breast sandwich or two," Hahskans acknowledged.

"Good. In that case perhaps the two of you stayed sober enough to actually get something worthwhile done," his wife observed, and he chuckled as he climbed the stairs and folded her into his arms.

She was stiff, for just a moment, and he felt another spasm of sorrow as he recognized the tension which had tightened her muscles. Then she relaxed, leaning her cheek against his chest and putting her arms around him in a tight hug whose strength said all the things she hadn't allowed herself to voice.

He bent over her, tucking the top of her head under his chin and raising his right hand to stroke her hair ever so gently. After so long together, he knew there was no need for him to apologize or explain—that she knew exactly what had impelled him, *driven* him, to the stance he'd taken. She didn't like it. In fact, she'd argued with him when he'd first told her he intended to acknowledge Archbishop Klairmant's and Bishop Kaisi's authority. Not because she'd had any great love for Manchyr's previous bishop or for Bishop Executor Thomys, because she hadn't. But she *had* been afraid of where Hahskans' inner anger at the Church's corruption was likely to take him. And she'd been more than a little afraid his decision would find him branded a traitor to Corisande as well as to Mother Church.

Yet despite her concerns, despite her very real fear for the husband she loved, she'd argued neither long nor hard. Perhaps that had been because she'd recognized argument was futile. That, in the end, he was going to do what faith and conscience demanded of him, no matter what. He thought it was more than that, though. Her concern was for his safety, not the product of any rejection of his beliefs, for she shared those beliefs. She might be less passionate than he, more willing to work by increments rather than confront the whole mass of the Church's corruption head-on, but she *recognized* that corruption. She knew as well as he did what a travesty of God's original intent the Church had become.

Which didn't make her one bit happier at the thought that he and Zhaif Laityr, whose Reformist zeal was every bit as deep as his own, had been coordinating their sermons for the coming Wednesday.

"I'm sorry, love," he murmured into her ear now, and her embrace tightened further. "I don't mean to distress you, but—"

"But you're a stubborn, determined, passionate, pigheaded lunatic of a Bédardist," she interrupted, never lifting her cheek from his chest, and produced a laugh that was only slightly wavery around the edges. She stayed where she was for another moment or two, then leaned back just far enough to rise on her toes and kiss his bearded cheek.

"I can't pretend I didn't know that when you proposed. Although, now that I think about it, the pigheadedness, at least, has probably gotten a bit more pronounced over the last few decades."

"I imagine it has," he said softly, his lively brown eyes warm with affectionate gratitude.

"Oh, I'm *sure* it has!" She looked back at him, gave him one last, affectionate squeeze, and then let him go. "I assume that despite your present drink-befuddled condition you'll want to transcribe your sermon notes before you come to bed?"

"I'm afraid so," he agreed.

"Well, I can't say I'm surprised. And Ezmelda left a plate of ham sandwiches in your study. Just in case hunger should threaten to overcome you again, you understand."

"And a tankard of beer to go with it?" he asked hopefully, eyes laughing at her.

"And a pitcher of cold *water* to go with it," she responded severely. "She and I were of the opinion that you'd probably have had sufficient beer while 'contemplating weighty matters of theology' with Zhaif."

"Alas, you were probably right," he told her, reaching out to touch her cheek lightly.

"Then go—go!" She made shooing motions with both hands. "And don't stay up all night," she admonished as he started down the stairs once more.

▼   ▼   ▼

The better part of two hours later, Hahskans leaned back in his chair and rubbed his eyes lightly. Those eyes were no longer as young as they'd once been, and although Ezmelda Dobyns kept the lamps' reflectors brightly polished, their illumination was a poor substitute for daylight.

*And it's not exactly as if you had the best handwriting in the world, either, Tymahn,* he reminded himself.

Which was true enough. Fortunately, he was just about finished. He wanted to let the thoughts roll around in his brain for another day or so before he put it into final form. And there were a couple of scriptural passages he needed to consider inserting. As a general rule, he tried to avoid weighting his sermons with too *much* scripture, yet—

His thoughts chopped off abruptly as the heavy cloth bag descended over his head from behind.

Total shock immobilized him for a single heartbeat . . . which was just long enough for whoever had managed to creep so silently into the study behind him that he'd never heard a thing to jerk the throat of the bag tight around his neck. He started to reach up and back, arching to fling himself out of the chair, then stopped as cold, sharp steel touched his throat just below the edge of the bag.

"Make one sound," a voice hissed in his ear, "and I cut your fucking throat right now!"

He froze, heart racing, and someone laughed quietly. It was an ugly, hungry sound.

"Better," the voice said, and he knew now that there were at least two of them, because it didn't belong to the man who'd laughed. "Now you're coming with us," the voice continued.

"No." Hahskans was surprised by how calmly, how firmly, the word came out. "Go ahead and cut, if that's what you're here to do," he continued.

"If that's what you want," the voice said. "Of course, if that *is* what you want, we'll have to cut the throat of that bitch upstairs, too, won't we?"

Hahskans' heart froze.

"Didn't think about *that,* did you?" the voice sneered. "Not so cocky now, are you, you fucking *traitor*?"

"I've been many things in my life," Hahskans replied as levelly as he could with a knife at his throat and terror for his wife in his heart, "but never a traitor."

"I see you're a liar, too," the voice grated. "Now *there's* a surprise! But either way, you're coming with us—now." The knife pressed harder. "Aren't you?"

Hahskans was silent for a moment, and then he made himself nod.

▼   ▼   ▼

Tymahn Hahskans had no idea how long he'd sat bound to the chair.

He had only the vaguest notion of where he might be. They'd brought him here in a freighter's cart, hidden under its canvas cover with the blinding bag still over his head. He didn't think they'd hauled him around long enough to actually leave the city, although he couldn't be certain of that. He'd thought about crying out, despite the fact that it was unlikely anyone would have been wandering about the capital's streets to hear him at such a late hour, but his captors had gagged him after they'd bound him, and the voice with the knife had squatted beside his head the entire time.

From the sound the cart's wheels had made when they finally reached their destination, and the noise of what had sounded like heavy sliding doors, he suspected he was in a warehouse somewhere. There were enough of those still standing idle and empty in the wake of the Charisian siege, and this one had seemed quite large. Large enough, he felt confident, that no one outside its walls was likely to hear anything that went on *inside* it.

He'd spent his time silently reciting scripture. The familiar passages helped, yet not even they could dissolve the cold, frozen lump in his belly. The nature of his abduction, and the threat against Dailohrs, told him entirely too much about the men behind it, and he was only mortal. There were limits to the amount of fear even the strongest faith could nullify.

No doubt they were leaving him here, abandoned and alone, to let that fear work upon him. He wished he could say the strategy wasn't working, but—

A door opened suddenly behind him. He stiffened, muscles tensing, then blinked painfully against the light as the bag was snatched off of his head at last.

The light, he realized a moment later, wasn't actually as bright as it had seemed to his darkness-accustomed eyes. It took them a few seconds to adjust, and then his gaze focused on the wiry, brown-haired, brown-eyed man standing facing him with his forearms folded across his chest. The man was probably at least twenty years younger than Hahskans, with a severely scarred cheek. It looked like an old burn, and even now Hahskans felt a twinge of sympathy for whatever sort of injury could have produced that deep and disfiguring a scar.

"So," the scar-faced man said, and Hahskans' sympathy evaporated abruptly as he recognized the voice from his study, "have you been enjoying a quiet little meditation, *Father?*"

His sneer turned the clerical title into an obscenity, and Hahskans felt his own eyes hardening in response.

"As a matter of fact," he forced himself to say calmly, "I have. You might try it someday yourself, my son."

"I'm not *your* 'son,' you fucking traitor!" the scar-faced man snarled. His arms unfolded abruptly, his right hand falling to the hilt of the ugly-looking knife sheathed at his belt.

"Perhaps not," Hahskans said. "But any man is a son of Mother Church and God . . . unless he chooses not to be."

"Like *you,*" the scar-faced man hissed.

"I've chosen nothing of the sort." Hahskans met the other man's ugly, hating eyes as steadily as he could.

"Don't lie to me, you bastard!" The scar-faced man drew a quarter inch of blade out of the sheath. "I've sat in your fucking church myself. I've *heard* you spewing filth against Mother Church! I've *seen* you licking the arse of the Shan-wei-damned Charisians and those gutless wonders on the '*Regency Council*'!"

" 'None are so blind as they who refuse to see,' " Hahskans quoted quietly.

"Don't you *dare* quote the *Writ* to me!" The scar-faced man's voice rose sharply, but Hahskans simply shrugged as well as he could, given how tightly bound to the chair he was.

"That's why it was given to us," he replied. "And if you hadn't stopped up your ears and closed your eyes, exactly as Langhorne had in mind when he gave us *that* passage, you'd know I've never 'spewed' a single word of 'filth' against Mother Church. I've spoken only the truth about her enemies."

The knife hissed out of its scabbard, and the scar-faced man twisted the fingers of his left hand in Hahskans' hair, yanking his head back. Keen-edged steel pressed his arched throat once more, and the other man's lips drew back in an ugly, animal-like snarl.

"You *are* her enemy!" he half whispered, eyes blazing with hatred. "Every time you open your mouth you *prove* it! And you drag others with you into heresy and apostasy and treason!"

" 'For it will come to pass that the wise man will speak wisdom to the fool, and the fool will not recognize it.' "

Hahskans had no idea how he managed to get the words out as he stared up into that hate-filled glare. It was part of the same passage from *The Book of Langhorne* he'd already cited, and for an instant, he thought his captor was going to slash his throat then and there. In fact, a part of the priest hoped he would.

But the scar-faced man made himself stop. He twisted the hair in his left hand hard enough to make Hahskans hiss with anguish despite all he could do, then threw the captive's head to one side and stepped back.

"I told them you wouldn't have anything worthwhile to say," he said then, calmly, almost caressingly. "They thought you might, but I knew. I've listened to you *preach,* you worthless son-of-a-bitch. I know exactly what kind of—"

"That's enough, Rahn."

Hahskans hadn't heard the door open again behind him, but now he turned his head and saw another man. This one wore the purple habit of the Order of Schueler and a priest's cap with the brown cockade of an under-priest, and Hahskans' stomach muscles clenched as he saw him.

The newcomer looked at Hahskans in silence for several seconds, then shook his head.

"Young Rahn can be a bit impetuous, and his language is often intemperate, Father Tymahn," he said. "Nonetheless, he does have a way of cutting to the heart of things. And, deep in your own heart, I'm sure, you realize even now that everything he's said is true."

"No, it's not," Hahskans replied, and there was an odd serenity in his voice now. "You—and he—can shut your eyes if you choose. God gave you freedom of will; He won't stop you from exercising it, no matter how you may have perverted your own understanding of His truth. But the fact that you choose not to see the sun makes it no less bright."

"At least you remember the *words* of the *Holy Writ,* I see." The Schuelerite's smile was thin. "It's a pity you've chosen to turn your back on its *meaning.* 'I have established His Holy Church as He has commanded me, and I give it now into your care, and the care of your fellows, chosen of God. Govern it well, and know that you are my chosen inheritors and the shepherds of God's flock in the world.' Langhorne gave that charge to the vicarate, not to me, and most assuredly not to *you.* When you raise your voice in impious attacks on the vicarate, you attack Langhorne and God Himself!"

"I do not," Hahskans said flatly, the words measured and cold. "In the very next verse, Langhorne said, 'See that you fail not in this charge, for an accounting shall be demanded of you, and every sheep that is lost will weigh in the balance of your stewardship.' Vicar Zhaspahr and his *friends* should have remembered that, because somehow I doubt *God* will forget it when their time comes to face Him. I am not He, to demand that accounting, but I *am* a priest. I, too, am a shepherd. I, too, must one day give my accounting, and I will lose none of *my* sheep for a 'Grand Inquisitor' so lost to corruption and ambition that he casts entire realms to fire and destruction on a *whim*!"

The Schuelerite's eyes glittered, yet he was more disciplined than the scar-faced man. His nostrils might flare, and anger might darken his face, but he made himself draw a deep breath.

"Shan-wei can entrap men in many ways," he said coldly. "And arrogance of spirit, the sheer vanity that sets your own intellect higher than God's holy word, is one of the most seductive. But Mother Church is always prepared to welcome home even the worst of sinners, if their repentance and contrition are genuine."

"Or if the Inquisition tortures them long enough," Hahskans returned grimly.

"Sparing the flesh and losing the soul is scarcely the path of godly love," the Schuelerite said. "And in your own case, Father, you've done enormous damage to Mother Church. We cannot permit that. So we offer you a choice. Renounce your heresy, your lies, your false accusations and vile assault on the very foundations of God's creation in this world, and Mother Church will once again embrace you."

"You mean you want me to stand in my pulpit once more and lie." Hahskans shook his head. "I won't. You and I both know I've spoken nothing but the truth. I won't renounce it at the command of someone who continues to serve the filth and corruption festering at the heart of the Temple."

"Schueler knows how to deal with Mother Church's enemies," the Schuelerite said ominously, and Hahskans surprised both of them with a short, sharp bark of laughter. It was a sound of contempt, not humor.

"Do you think I didn't already realize where you were headed?" He shook his head again, his eyes defiant. "I know what your master in Zion did to Archbishop Erayk, and I know the true reason he did it. For myself, I have no love for the *Empire* of Charis, but the *Church* of Charis knows God's enemies when it sees them. So do I. And I know who I choose to stand with."

"You speak bravely now," the Schuelerite said coldly, softly. "You'll change your tune soon enough when you realize Shan-wei will not stretch forth her hand to save you from God's just wrath."

"I may." Hahskans made no effort to hide the fear both of them knew was coiled at his core like some frozen serpent, yet his voice was steady. "I'm only a man, not an Archangel, and the flesh is weak. But whatever may be about to happen to my flesh, I will face God unafraid. I've done only what He commanded all of His priests to do. I'm sure I've made mistakes along the way. All men do that, even those called to His service. But in this much, at least, I've made no mistake, and you and I both know that's the true reason I'm here. You have to shut me up before I do even more damage to that whoremonger Clyntahn."

*"Silence!"*

The Schuelerite lost his temper at last, and his open palm smashed across Hahskans' face. His arm came back the other way, backhanding the bound priest, and Hahskans grunted in anguish as he tasted blood and more blood erupted from his nostrils. Only the cords binding him to the chair kept him in it.

The Schuelerite stepped back abruptly, rigid arms straight down at his sides, and Hahskans spat a thick gobbet of blood on the warehouse floor.

"So telling the truth about Clyntahn is a worse crime than 'betraying' Mother Church, is it?" he asked then, his voice thicker as he was forced to breathe through his mouth.

"You profane God's very air with every word you speak," the Schuelerite told him flatly. "We cast you out. We commit you to the outer darkness, to the corner of Hell reserved for your dark mistress. We expunge your name from the children of God, and strike you forever from the company of redeemed souls."

Hahskans' stomach muscles were a solid lump of curdled lead as he heard the formal words of condemnation. They came as no surprise—not after what had already passed—yet he discovered that actually hearing them carried a terror, a sense of finality, he hadn't anticipated even now. Perhaps, a corner of his mind suggested, that was because he hadn't realized he could feel any more terrified than he'd already felt.

Yet there was more than simple fear, more than panic. There was an awareness that the moment had come for him to repay all the joys God had granted him. He watched the scar-faced man slowly, mockingly, drawing his knife once again, and despite his fear, he breathed a silent prayer of thanks. He never doubted that what was about to happen would be worse—*far* worse—than anything he could truly have imagined, but at least his captors lacked the full array of implements of torture *The Book of Schueler* prescribed for Mother Church's enemies. Whatever happened to him, he would be spared the full horror the Inquisition had inflicted upon Erayk Dynnys. And as he watched that knife being drawn, even as a hand jerked his head back once more and another hand ripped his cassock down around his waist, he prayed that he would find the same courage, the same faith, Dynnys had found.

▼     ▼     ▼

Merlin Athrawes' eyes snapped open.

Nimue Alban had always slept deeply, restfully. She'd never really liked waking up, and the process of getting her brain stirred into full wakefulness had usually taken at least a minute or two. Merlin wasn't like that. For him, the shift between "sleeping" as Cayleb had demanded that he do each night and coming totally awake was as abrupt as turning a switch.

Which, after all, was exactly what happened.

So when those sapphire eyes opened, he was fully aware of his surroundings, of the hour. Which meant he was also fully aware that his internal clock should not have awakened him for another hour and twelve minutes.

"Lieutenant Commander Alban."

Merlin's eyes, faithful to the involuntary reflexes of their human prototype, widened in surprise as the voice spoke silently in his electronic brain.

"*Owl?*" he blurted, so astonished he actually spoke out loud. "Is that you, Owl?" he went on, thus (he realized an instant later) confirming his astonishment, since there was no way he could have failed to recognize the distant AI's voice. At least he'd managed to subvocalize this time, though. A not insignificant consideration, given that his guest bedchamber's walls here in Duke Eastshare's Maikelberg headquarters were scarcely anything one could have called soundproof.

"Yes, Lieutenant Commander Alban," the computer confirmed.

"What is it?" Merlin demanded, widened eyes narrowing once more in speculation.

"A situation not covered by my instructions has arisen and I require your direction to resolve it, Lieutenant Commander Alban."

"In what way?" Merlin's voice was taut. This was the first time the AI had initiated contact with him without specific instructions to do so. As such, it was evidence that the fully realized self-awareness the manual had promised Owl would gradually develop might actually be starting to turn up. But the fact that the computer had awakened him suggested that whatever had impelled him to reveal his developing capabilities wasn't going to come under the heading of good news.

"I have just receipted a routine upload from SNARC remote Charlie-Bravo-Seven-Niner-One-Three," Owl replied to his question. "Analysis of its content suggests you would wish it called to your attention."

"What kind of content?" Merlin asked. The two-letter initial designator for the SNARC indicated that it was one of the Corisandian recon platforms, but although his own memory was as perfect as Owl's, these days, he hadn't attempted to "remember" the full designation on any of them.

"The subject Hahskans, Father Tymahn, has been abducted," Owl said.

*"What?"* Merlin sat bolt upright on his bed.

"The subject Hahskans, Father Tymahn, has been abducted," Owl repeated, and developing self-awareness or no, the AI's electronic voice sounded far too calm. Disinterested.

"When?" Merlin demanded, swinging his body around to put his feet on the floor and already reaching for his clothes.

"He was abducted approximately five hours, nineteen minutes, and thirty-one seconds ago, Lieutenant Commander," Owl responded.

"And you're only telling me about it *now?*" Merlin knew the question was unfair even as he asked it. The fact that Owl had decided on his own to mention it at all was the next best thing to a miracle, yet even so—

"I had no specific instructions to monitor for abductions, Lieutenant Commander," Owl told him calmly. "Absent such instructions, my filters did not call the event immediately to my attention. I discovered the situation only as the result of a routine data dump from Charlie-Bravo-Seven-Niner-One-Three. When I downloaded the data I immediately contacted you."

Merlin stood, dragging on his breeches and reaching for his tunic.

"What's Hahskans' current situation? Give me a real-time from the SNARC!"

"Of course, Lieutenant Commander."

The AI obeyed the instruction almost instantly, and Merlin Athrawes grunted in shock as the imagery appeared suddenly in his electronic brain.

*Dear God,* a stunned corner of his mind thought numbly. *Dear God!*

He flinched as the SNARC's audio sensors faithfully filled his senses with a throat-tearing scream. The bloody horror of the scene hammered in on him, and that same numb, distant corner of his mind knew that if he'd still been a being of flesh and blood his stomach would have heaved in automatic protest.

It froze him, that horror, and he'd seen horror enough for a dozen normal lifetimes by now. He started to order Owl to ready the recon skimmer, but the order died ungiven. He was almost three thousand miles from Manchyr. It would take him forty minutes to make the flight, even at Mach five, and another fifteen minutes just to get the recon skimmer here and himself aboard it. For that matter, however cautious he might be, there was always the possibility someone might spot the skimmer picking him up. From the hideous damage which had already been inflicted upon the priest, there was no way Hahskans would survive long enough for Merlin to get there. And given the limitations of Safeholdian medicine, his brutal wounds were undoubtedly already mortal.

Even if Merlin chose to risk betraying his own "demonic" capabilities, Tymahn Hahskans was already a dead man.

*And, God help me, the sooner he dies, the better,* Merlin thought sickly.

He sank back down on the bed, sapphire eyes blind as the sights and sounds ripped through his direct feed from the SNARC. He should shut it down, he told himself. There was nothing he could do, not now. It was too late. And there was no need—no reason—for him to subject himself to the horror of Hahskans' death.

But there *was* a need, and a reason. He understood Adorai Dynnys now, better than he ever had before. Understood why she hadn't been able to turn away, refuse to witness what the Inquisition had done to her husband.

Someone had to know. Someone had to bear witness.

And, he told himself grimly, someone had to *remember.*

.X.
## Priory of Saint Zhustyn,
## City of Manchyr,
## Princedom of Corisande

Aidryn Waimyn leaned back in his chair and rubbed weary eyes. The messages and reports in front of him were beginning to blur when he tried to read them, and common sense was trying to insist it was time he took himself off to bed. He could still get a couple of hours sleep before dawn, and Langhorne knew he needed them.

There never seemed to be enough hours in a day. That was true for any intendant, even when he operated openly from his office in his archbishop's palace. When he was forced to discharge his duties from hiding, skulking about lest the very secular authorities who were supposed to obey his instructions find him and drag him before an apostate "archbishop," the situation could only get worse.

*Still,* he reflected wryly, lowering his hand, *there are at least some compensating factors, aren't there? The loss of the semaphore, for example.* He snorted. *I may have to worry about little things like the damnation of lost souls, being captured and tried for treason, being executed—minor concerns like that. But at least the damned message traffic's been cut way down!*

His lips twitched at his own feeble attempt at humor, yet there was more than a little truth to it. He was as secure here at Saint Zhustyn's as he could have been anywhere in conquered Corisande, and the truth was that he had little fear of being betrayed to the authorities. That wasn't quite the same thing as *no* fear, yet it came close. And as the resistance movement spread here in the city, his feelers and information channels continued to spread and grow with it. Yet even though that meant a steadily increasing flow of messages and reports, his lost access to Mother Church's semaphore stations had completely cut him off from events in the rest of the princedom.

The handful of dispatches which had reached him here from Bishop Executor Thomys Shylair, smuggled in by trusted couriers, were both short and cryptic. Compared to the smooth, almost instant communication he'd been accustomed to before the Charisian invasion, it was like being rendered deaf and blind. He didn't like it at all, and he especially didn't like it because of how little he knew about what was truly happening outside Manchyr.

*What you mean,* he told himself, *is that you worry about it because you don't really trust Bishop Thomys' ability to manage something like this. He's not the sharpest bishop you've ever served, is he? But at least he's determined to do something, instead of selling himself to the Charisians, and that's nothing to sneeze at, Aidryn!*

Indeed it wasn't, and to be fair to the deposed bishop executor, the contacts he'd apparently established with people like Earl Storm Keep, Earl Deep Hollow, and Baron Larchros sounded far more promising than Waimyn would have anticipated even a few months earlier. Of course, Waimyn didn't have any real details on just how Bishop Executor Thomys and his secular allies were coming, or exactly what it was they had in mind, and he'd been excruciatingly careful not to record a single word about them in writing, even here. It didn't really matter, though. His own instructions had come from the Grand Inquisitor himself, issued as a precaution well before the Charisian invasion. Shylair knew—roughly—what those instructions were, and Waimyn didn't doubt he was factoring that knowledge into his and his new allies' plans, but whatever they might be up to didn't change Waimyn's mission.

*And Vicar Zhaspahr was right,* the intendant reminded himself yet again. *What happens up north is important, maybe even critical, but what happens right here in Manchyr is even more important. It's not just the capital, it's the biggest city in the entire Princedom, and every other city and town is watching to see what happens here. If this "Regency Council" and Cayleb's "Viceroy General" can't maintain their control here,* then the rest of the Princedom's going to be a lot more willing to challenge them.

He sat forward once again, and reached for the next report. In some ways, he hated writing *any* of this down, even though he was careful to use codenames known only to him to identify most of his agents. Written records weren't the safest thing for a conspirator to keep lying around, but without them, he would quickly have lost the ability to keep track of his own operations. It was a matter of striking the best balance he could between security and efficiency.

He frowned as he read through the memo which had worked its way to the top of the current pile. It was from Ahlbair Cahmmyng, and Aidryn Waimyn was very much in two minds where Cahmmyng was concerned. The man was undoubtedly capable, and he'd proved extraordinarily useful in the past. Unfortunately, one reason he'd proved so useful was that so far as Waimyn could tell, he was completely untrammeled by anything remotely like a scruple. He was, quite simply, a professional assassin. One of the best assassins money could buy . . . which was the very reason Waimyn was ambivalent where he was concerned. Money had bought him Cahmmyng's services; it was always possible that *more* money, from another source, would buy Cahmmyng's betrayal.

And if Ahlbair Cahmmyng chose to betray Waimyn, the consequences could be catastrophic, since only Cahmmyng knew the true identity of the man who'd actually bought and paid for Prince Hektor's assassination.

Waimyn had considered having Cahmmyng quietly eliminated. In fact, he'd considered it quite often, but he never had. First, because Cahmmyng continued to prove so useful and energetic. Indeed, Waimyn was tempted to conclude that Cahmmyng cherished a genuine (if somewhat anemic) devotion to Mother Church, although the intendant wouldn't have been prepared to wager any enormous sum on the probability. But the second reason Waimyn had so far refrained from arranging the assassin's permanent disappearance was the suspicion that Cahmmyng had made his own arrangements to protect himself. It would have been just like the man to tuck away evidence linking Waimyn—and, by extension, the Grand Inquisitor himself—to Hektor's murder. Waimyn could think of several ways Cahmmyng could have arranged things so that any such evidence would find its way into the hands of the occupation if he himself should suffer a mischief. And the intendant was certain Cahmmyng was more than sufficiently inventive to have come up with quite a few approaches which hadn't even occurred to him.

*On the other hand, the fact that he was involved in Hektor's assassination cuts both ways,* the intendant thought. *He can't afford for me to be taken and forced to talk any more than I can afford for him to be taken. So the two of us have an excellent reason to look after one another, don't we? And that, ironically, makes him the most reliable agent I have.*

And there were certain advantages to relying on a professional. Whatever his other faults, Cahmmyng was scarcely going to be betrayed into a fatal misstep by zealotry, and that was more than could be said for some of Waimyn's more recently recruited agents. People like Paitryk Hainree had plenty of enthusiasm, fueled all too often by bitter resentment and hatred. But that same enthusiasm could make them hard to control, which was the main reason Waimyn had been so careful to maintain his own anonymity where they were concerned. Hainree was one of the few exceptions to the rule, but he also thought the intendant had long since "escaped" from the city. That was one of the reasons Waimyn had put Cahmmyng in charge of managing his contacts with Hainree's group.

It was also one of the reasons he'd decided to trust Cahmmyng to decide who to use for the current operation. The intendant had selected the Inquisitor to be entrusted with the mission, but he'd left it to Cahmmyng to choose who would provide what the assassin called "the muscle" to actually accomplish it. Cahmmyng was far more familiar with the individual agents he'd recruited—with their capabilities *and* their personalities and motivations—than Waimyn was. And Waimyn was confident Cahmmyng had used every one of his considerable talents to make sure none of those agents were in a position to lead the authorities back to him. Which, in turn, meant they weren't in a position to lead those same authorities back to Waimyn, either.

*And that's not a minor consideration where* this *one is concerned,* the intendant reflected grimly.

The truth was that at least a tiny part of him regretted having ordered Father Tymahn's kidnapping and execution. Of course, it was *only* a tiny part, given how utterly the priest's own actions had condemned him. He was scarcely the only member of the clergy to have damned himself by deserting to the "Church of Charis," yet despite his relatively junior ecclesiastic rank, he'd emerged as a clear leader of the "Reformist" traitors here in Corisande. For himself, Waimyn had frequently enjoyed Father Tymahn's sermons, back before the Charisian invasion. The priest had always been an inspired preacher, with a genuine gift for reaching his congregation—for reaching out *beyond* his own congregation, in fact. Even before the invasion, on the other hand, Waimyn had been aware of how Hahskans chafed under Bishop Executor Thomys' discipline. Indeed, his righteous indignation, his burning desire to denounce the "corrupters" in the Temple, had brought him to the Inquisition's attention more than once. He'd found himself in Waimyn's office on several occasions, and Waimyn doubted Hahskans could have been in any doubt about how Corisande's intendant felt about his arrogance in daring to judge the actions of the vicarate. Only the fact that he'd discharged all his other priestly duties so well—and been wise enough to keep his mouth shut about those private concerns of his—had prevented him from being removed from Saint Kathryn's on at least two occasions.

So Waimyn had been less than surprised when Hahskans betrayed his vows to Mother Church and gave his allegiance to the Charis-spawned abomination. What *had* surprised him, however, was the vigor and the eloquence Hahskans had brought to his betrayal . . . and how effective a traitor he'd proven. He'd become the core of the small but steadily growing clique of churchmen who'd labeled themselves "Reformists" and openly attacked Mother Church at every step. That was bad enough. Even worse, however, was the way in which those "Reformists" were concentrated here in Manchyr. Their churches, by and large, ministered to the city's common folk, and that made them dangerous. By legitimizing the *Church* of Charis among the capital's commoners, they lent legitimacy to the *Empire* of Charis, as well, and the people who were listening to them were the very people *Waimyn* needed to reach if he was going to effectively challenge the occupation's control of the capital.

Despite his own bitter fury at Hahskans' actions, Waimyn had never believed the priest had betrayed his vows out of personal ambition or greed. No, it was even worse than that, unfortunately. Ambition might have been worked with, and greed might have been appealed to. But the arrogance of self-justified indignation, the sheer effrontery of a man who could set his own faith—his own isolated interpretation of the *Writ*—against the might and the majesty of God's own Church, those were something else again. Hahskans didn't give a damn about personal power, or wealth, or luxury; that was precisely what had made him so effective—so dangerous. Yet however he might dress it up for his congregation's consumption, however skillfully he might twist the *Writ* to make it seem to support his own apostasy, and however the first breach in his own faith might have pierced the defenses of his soul, the man had given himself wholly over into Shan-wei's service now. He had turned his back upon God and the vicarate, and that was why Waimyn could scarcely pretend he felt any true regret at having ordered that the traitor be eliminated.

*And eliminated in a fashion that's going to give the rest of his "Reformist" . . . colleagues reason to reconsider their apostasy.* The intendant's jaw tightened. *From Cahmmyng's report, we can count on this Aimayl to do just that, and he doesn't have any idea at all that I gave the order. For that matter, neither does Father Daishan.*

Unlike Aimayl, Father Daishan Zahcho knew exactly who Aidryn Waimyn was, since he'd worked directly for him for over six years. But Zahcho had excellent reason to believe Waimyn had gotten out of Manchyr with Bishop Executor Thomys, since Waimyn had specifically told Zahcho he was going to do exactly that. So even in the unlikely event that he and Aimayl were both taken by the authorities, Zahcho couldn't lead those authorities back to Saint Zhustyn's. And of all the Inquisitors who had been assigned to Corisande, Zahcho was the least likely to hesitate for a moment over the execution of an apostate priest.

*I can't pretend I'm sorry it had to be done,* the ex-intendant admitted, *and at least I had the right people in place to see to it.*

He finished Cahmmyng's report, then found himself yawning hugely as he set it aside.

*Enough! I'm going to start making mistakes out of simple fatigue if I keep this up. Time to get some sleep.* He yawned again. *Tomorrow's another day.*

*For some of us, at least.*

.XI.
Gray Lizard Square,
Sir Koryn Gharvai's Townhouse,
and
Priory of Saint Zhustyn,
City of Manchyr,
Princedom of Corisande

A sharp, stabbing gesture brought Sir Koryn Gahrvai's escort to an abrupt, clattering halt on the cobblestones. The anger in Gahrvai's overly controlled, clenched-fist hand signal was highly unusual. There were men in his escort who'd been with him at the Battle of Haryl's Crossing and served with him throughout the Talbor Pass campaign. They'd seen him in the midst of battle, seen him visiting his wounded and comforting his dying, even seen him riding out to surrender his army to Cayleb of Charis. They'd seen him angry, seen him worried, seen him grieving, seen him bitterly determined.

They'd never seen him like this.

The escort reined in its horses more like anxious children, creeping about in the shadow of a father's poorly understood anger, than like the elite, picked troops they actually were. They looked around the buildings surrounding Gray Lizard Square, washed with early morning sunlight under a deep blue sky. The air was crisp and cool, warning of heat still to come, yet even more pleasant because its present coolness must be so fleeting. Windows, gay awnings, and the booths and kiosks of the Gray Lizard Market, normally one of the largest and busiest in the city, gleamed in the golden wash of the sun.

Those booths and kiosks were empty, though. The people who should have crowded the square, bargaining and chaffering, stood hushed, crowded back around its edges, held there by grim-faced armsmen of the City Guard. The stillness and silence of that crowd of people was profound, so absolute that the faint yet clear whistle of wyverns high overhead sounded almost shocking.

Gahrvai dismounted. Yairman Uhlstyn, his personal armsman, swung down from the saddle beside him, but a chopping hand warned Uhlstyn that even his presence was not welcome this day. He clearly didn't like it, but the dark-haired armsman had served the Gahrvai family since he was fifteen, and he'd been assigned to Sir Koryn since the general had been a boy. He probably knew Sir Koryn's moods better than any other living man, and so he simply accepted the order, took his master's reins, and stood watching as Gahrvai strode across to the red-stained white sheet.

*I'd not like to be the ones behind this.* Uhlstyn's thoughts were harsh with anger of his own. *I've served the General and his father, man and boy, and I've never seen either of them like this. He'll find whoever did this, and when he does. . . .*

▼    ▼    ▼

Sir Koryn Gahrvai walked across the cobbles like a man marching into battle, feeling the stillness around him, acutely aware of the contrast between the cool morning air and the white-hot fury roiling inside him. He forced his face into a mask of calm, but that mask was a lie, for there was no calm in him.

*Slowly, Koryn. Slowly,* he reminded himself. *Remember all those watching eyes. Remember you're a general, the Regency Council's personal representative, not just a man. Remember.*

He reached the red-splotched sheet. A priest knelt beside it, a fair-haired man, going to gray, with a full beard. He wore the green habit and caduceus of a brother of the Order of Pasquale, and his priest's cap bore the green cockade of an upper-priest.

The clergyman looked up as Gahrvai reached him, and the general saw the tears in the older man's gray eyes, yet the priest's expression was composed, almost serene.

"Father." Gahrvai knew his single-word greeting had come out harsher than he'd intended, and he tried to make his brief bow of greeting less curt. He rather doubted he'd succeeded.

"General," the priest returned. He reached out and laid one gentle hand on the sheet. "I'm sorry you've been called here for this," he said.

"So am I, Father." Gahrvai inhaled deeply. "Forgive me," he said then. "I'm afraid I'm feeling just a bit *angry* this morning, but that's a poor excuse for discourtesy. You are—?"

"Father Zhaif Laityr. I'm the rector at Holy Archangels Triumphant." The priest twitched his head at the stone spire of a church at the nearer end of the square, and his expression tightened. "I'm reasonably sure they left him here at least partly as a message to me," he said.

Gahrvai's eyes narrowed for a moment, but then he nodded in understanding as he recognized Laityr's name. Sir Charlz Doyal, who'd commanded his artillery at the beginning of the Talbor Pass campaign, was now his chief of staff. In addition, Doyal fulfilled the role of Gahrvai's chief intelligence analyst, and the words of his reports on the growing Reformist movement here in Manchyr replayed themselves in Gahrvai's memory.

*Yes. The bastards who did this would want to make sure Laityr gets the "message,"* he thought.

"I'm afraid you're probably right about that, Father," he said out loud. "On the other hand, I imagine they intended this as a 'message' for *all* of us." He bared his teeth for an instant. "And when we figure out who they are, I'm going to have a little *message* for them, as well."

"Pasquale is an Archangel of healing, General," Laityr said, looking back down at the sheet-covered form. "Just this once, though, I think, he'll forgive me for wishing you every success." His hand moved on the sheet, stroking it, and he shook his head. "They didn't have to do *this* to him." His voice was so low even Gahrvai could scarcely hear him. "They didn't *have* to do it; they *wanted* to do it."

"I think you're right about that, too, Father," Gahrvai replied, equally quietly. Laityr looked back up at him, and he shrugged very slightly. "So far, I've seen very little hatred out of the Church of Charis, or your own Reformists. I've seen quite a lot coming out of the Temple Loyalists, though."

"As have I," Laityr acknowledged. "And it's in my mind that one reason they did this is to ignite that hate among us, as well." He looked back down at the covered body. "Tymahn never hated anyone, except perhaps for those corrupt men in Zion, and no one could ever listen to him preach without realizing that. I think that's why he was so effective. And that's why the Loyalists want us to hate as hotly as they do. They want us to lash out at them—to let our own anger fuel the conflict between us, drive the breach still wider and deeper. Let our intemperance justify their own."

"You may be right about that, Father," Gahrvai said grimly. "And as a son of Mother Church, I hope you and the other priests who have spoken out can resist that hatred, that anger. But I represent the *secular* authorities, and it's not my job to forgive things like this."

"No. No, I suppose it's not."

Laityr looked down for a few more moments, then rose. From the stiffness of his movement, Gahrvai suspected he'd been kneeling there on those unyielding cobblestones since the body was first discovered, and the general reached out a steadying hand. The older man took it gratefully, then shook himself and nodded once again in the direction of his church.

"I know we had to leave him here until you could examine the scene yourself, General. I understand that. But his wife is in the rectory there, with my housekeeper. I offered to stay with her, but she insisted I stay with Tymahn, instead. It was all I could do to talk her into letting me keep him company until you arrived, instead of her. I don't think I'd have succeeded if she were in any state to think clearly or argue. Now, though . . ." Laityr shook his head. "Please, General. I . . . don't want her to see him. Not like this."

"I understand." Gahrvai met the priest's eyes levelly. "When you go back to her, tell her we have to take the body for our own healers to examine for their reports. Keep her there, until we've gone. Tell her it's my request, as part of the investigation. I'll have my people do what they can before we release the body to her." His lips tightened. "From the preliminary reports, I don't expect to be able to do a lot. But if you could have clothing for him delivered to my headquarters, I'll have him decently dressed when the healers are finished. Hopefully that should hide the worst of it, at least."

"Thank you, General." The priest laid one hand on Gahrvai's forearm and squeezed lightly. "I'm afraid she already knows from my reaction that it's ugly, but there's a difference between that and actually having to see what those butchers did."

Laityr's voice thickened on the last phrase, and he squeezed Gahrvai's forearm again. Then he cleared his throat a bit noisily.

"I've already said my farewells," he said softly. "And I've already asked God if Tymahn can wait a little, until the rest of us catch up. So, if you'll excuse me, I have a dear friend's widow to comfort."

"Of course, Father," Gahrvai said gently. He bowed again, more deeply, and Laityr sketched the sign of Langhorne's Scepter, then turned and walked slowly towards his church and the rectory next door.

Gahrvai watched him go, reading the combined outrage, grief, and determination in the set of the priest's shoulders. There was a courage in Laityr's steady stride, as well. One Gahrvai envied. For himself, he would rather have faced a charge of heavy cavalry—or even a line of Charisian riflemen—than what Laityr was about to face. He wondered for a moment exactly what that said about the difference between physical courage and moral courage. Then he drew another deep breath, went down on one knee, reached for a corner of the sheet, and steeled himself for what he was about to see.

▼    ▼    ▼

Much later that evening, Gahrvai sat behind the desk in his townhouse study. He was alone, with no watching eyes, and so he permitted his expression to show the bitter anger and frustration no one else was ever allowed to see.

He leaned back in his expensive swivel chair, rubbing his eyes. They felt dry and scratchy, partly from fatigue, but mostly, he suspected, from how much reading he'd been doing lately. The reports were piling up, and he didn't much care for the trends he saw developing.

The savagery of Father Tymahn's murder—and Gahrvai's healers confirmed that the priest had probably not actually died until close to the very end of the catalog of atrocities and mutilations which had been visited upon him—dwarfed anything else which had yet happened, yet attacks on the Church of Charis' clergy and laity were slowly but steadily mounting. The majority were still relatively minor—fistfights, vandalized homes and property, anonymous threats nailed to church doors or wrapped around stones thrown through windows.

Most of those incidents, he thought—and Doyal agreed—were genuinely spontaneous, the result of personal anger or frustration, and they'd arrested, jailed, and fined several of the people responsible for them. Personally, Gahrvai would have preferred a punishment that was rather more severe, but Viceroy General Chermyn had strongly supported Archbishop Klairmant's view that the authorities' response had to balance severity with restraint. Chermyn had made it clear that so long as there were no riots or large-scale violence, he intended to allow Gahrvai and the Regency Council to set policy in such matters, yet he'd also emphasized his own instructions from Emperor Cayleb and Empress Sharleyan to be no more repressive than he absolutely had to be.

Most of the time, Gahrvai appreciated that restraint on Chermyn's part. For that matter, *most* of the time he agreed with the viceroy general and the archbishop. But there'd been a handful—a steadily growing trickle—of uglier, more violent attacks, and he rather doubted *those* incidents were spontaneous and unplanned. He'd been concerned by the pattern he'd seen emerging over the past several five-days, and now there was this. There was no way to pretend Father Tymahn's abduction, torture, and murder had been the impulsive act of some individual hothead. This had been carefully planned and executed, and it had been intended as much as a challenge to the secular and temporal authorities as as a warning to other Reformist-minded priests.

*There's restraint, and then there's weakness,* Gahrvai thought grimly. *When they chose Father Tymahn they deliberately chose one of the most beloved men in this entire city. They chose to kill the focus of all that love, all that trust, and they did it, at least in part, to prove they could do it. To enhearten the Loyalists—who probably hated him as much as everyone else loved him—and to demonstrate that we can't even find them, much less stop them from doing it again, whenever they choose to. I don't think even the Archbishop is going to be arguing in favor of a great deal of "restraint" when we find the butchers who did this. But that's the rub, isn't it, Koryn? First you've got to find them, and you don't even know where to start looking!*

He hated—*hated*—admitting that, yet it was pointless to pretend otherwise. Oh, he and Doyal had their own agents, and a surprising number of individuals had been coming forward, generally to speak quietly with their own parish priests about things they'd seen or heard. Aided by those hints, Doyal's agents had penetrated at least a dozen individual groups—"cells," as Doyal called them, likening them to the individual cells in a honeycomb—but all of them, so far, had been relatively low level. In fact, most had been little more than groups of drinking buddies with thuggish mentalities. Yet even some of them had operated with more . . . sophistication than they should have been capable of. It was obvious to Doyal—and Gahrvai—that there was a far more tightly organized and centrally directed authority operating behind the scenes, one which was directing and using those low-level groups without ever identifying itself to them, and Doyal had come to the conclusion that it had actually been organized and set up, at least in part, well before the Charisian invasion. Which, considering the membership of the previous Church hierarchy here in Corisande, suggested it had probably been the work of Father Aidryn Waimyn, Bishop Executor Thomys' intendant.

Given certain suspicions both Gahrvai and Doyal had come to nourish about just who had actually been responsible for Prince Hektor's murder, the general longed for the opportunity to . . . discuss a few matters face-to-face with Father Aidryn.

*But it's not going to happen. He's gone too deeply to ground for that,* Gahrvai thought bitterly. *I know the bastard is somewhere inside the city. I know* it! *but I don't have a clue where, and without that—*

*CRRRRRRRaaassssshhhhh!*

The sudden sound of shattering glass yanked Gahrvai up out of his thoughts. He came to his feet, right hand reaching instinctively for the hilt of the dagger he'd taken off when he entered the study. He spun towards the study windows which looked out over the landscaped garden in the townhouse's square central plaza, half-crouched, and his heart raced.

He waited, muscles taut, wondering how someone had gotten past his sentries. But nothing else happened. It was so quiet he could hear the ticking of the clock in one corner, actually hear the quiet "swish-click" sound of the pendulum as it swung steadily, monotonously. After a few moments, he felt himself relaxing—a little, at least—and straightened from his semi-crouch.

There was no light beyond the windows, and he stepped cautiously around the end of the desk, eyes sweeping back and forth, then stopped once more.

There was a rock on his carpet, lying in a halo of glass fragments. It wasn't a large rock, but his eyes narrowed as he realized someone had wrapped something around it before launching it through his study window.

He walked across to it, hearing broken glass crunch under his boots, and picked it up a bit gingerly. It was wrapped in paper, tied with twine, and he held it in his left hand, using the fingers of his right hand to brush away the slivers of glass which clung to it.

His brow furrowed, and he walked the rest of the way to the broken window, looking out through the shattered panes. Moonlight spilled down over the garden. The pools of silver and inky black were enough to confuse the eye, but not so badly that he couldn't tell that the garden was empty. No one larger than a midget could have hidden behind its shrubbery or flower beds. So whoever had thrown this through the window obviously hadn't hung about to see how Gahrvai was going to react. But how had they gotten into the garden in the first place? And having gotten there, how had they gotten back *out* unseen? Gahrvai knew the quality of the troopers assigned to guard his residence. If any of them had seen or heard *anything*—including the sound of breaking glass— his study would be full of armed, angry, alert men at this very moment.

Which, manifestly, it was not.

He walked back across the glass-crunching carpet and sat back down behind his desk, laying the paper-wrapped rock on the blotter in front of him. He gazed down at it for several seconds, then used a penknife to cut the twine and unwrapped it.

The paper was an envelope, he realized, and his own name was written on the outside. He wasn't particularly surprised by the fact that, to the best of his knowledge, he'd never before seen the handwriting, but he felt a tingle of odd excitement as he weighed the envelope in his fingers and realized it must contain several sheets of paper. He had no idea why his unknown correspondent had chosen to deliver his mail in so unconventional a fashion, but he doubted that it would have taken more than a single sheet to express even the most passionate of death threats, which suggested this must be something quite different from what he'd initially assumed it must be.

He used the same penknife to slit the envelope and extracted its contents. There were eight sheets of paper—thin and expensive, covered with closely spaced lines written in the same neat, precise hand as the address on the outside of the envelope. He laid them on the blotter and adjusted his desk lamp, then bent over the letter curiously.

▼    ▼    ▼

*"Open! Open in the name of the Crown and Holy Mother Church!"*

The stentorian bellow was punctuated by a sudden, deafening crash as sixteen men carrying a ten-foot, iron-headed ram slammed it into the closed gate. Whoever had issued the demand clearly wasn't waiting for a response.

"What?!" another voice cried in obvious confusion. "What d'you think you're *doing!?* This is a house of *God!*"

The monk assigned as the night gatekeeper dashed out of his little gate-side cubicle, wringing his hands, running for the priory's gate even as the ram crashed into it a second time. He'd almost reached the closed portal when both halves of the gate flew abruptly open. A piece of shattered gate bar hit him in the shoulder, knocking him off his feet, and then he grunted in anguish as a large, heavy boot slammed down on his chest. He started to shout some protest, then froze abruptly, mouth half-open, as he found himself looking up at the point of a very sharp, very steady bayonet perhaps eighteen inches from his nose.

It wasn't alone, that boot on his chest. In fact, it was only one of scores of boots as an entire company of grim-faced infantrymen stormed through the gate. More bayonets glittered, voices shouted harsh commands, and more doorways slammed open as musket butts and shoulders crashed into them.

More of the priory's brethren came tumbling out of their cells, blinking in confusion, shouting questions. They got precious few answers. Instead, their eyes went wide in disbelief as impious hands seized them, spun them around, slammed them face-first into stone walls and columns. None of them had ever imagined such a brutal, direct assault upon monks of Mother Church, and especially not upon brothers of the Order of Schueler. Sheer, stupefied shock at such incredible impiety possessed them. They were the Inquisitors of Mother Church, the guardians and keepers of her law. How *dared* someone violate the sanctity of one of *their* priories?! Here and there, one or two started to struggle, to resist, only to cry out as waiting musket butts hammered them to their knees.

"How *dare* y—?!" one of them shouted, starting back to his feet, only to break off with a choked scream as a musket's brass buttplate crashed into his mouth this time, not his shoulder. He went down, spitting teeth and blood, and only the quick shout of a sergeant kept that musket from hammering down on the back of his skull with lethal force.

More hands yanked the disbelieving Schuelerites' arms behind them, rough-toothed rope bound wrists tightly, and then they were dragged—none too gently—back into the priory's courtyard. Hard-eyed soldiers slammed them down on their knees, and they found themselves kneeling on the cobblestones, surrounded by bayonets that gleamed faintly but murderously in the moonlight while they stared up fearfully, numbed brains fighting to comprehend what was happening.

Sir Koryn Gahrvai left that to the infantry company's experienced noncoms. His own headquarters lay just outside Saint Kathryn's Parish, and Father Tymahn had been just as popular with many of his troops as with the majority of people who'd ever heard him preach. Even the ones who hadn't fully agreed with him had respected him, and his sermons had been energetically discussed by Gharvai's headquarters company. After what had happened to him, the general rather suspected those noncoms were going to find it more difficult to restrain their men than to motivate them, and he had other matters to attend to.

His boot heels rang on the stone floor as he marched purposefully down the corridor with Yairman Uhlstyn and Captain Frahnklyn Naiklos, the company's commander, at his heels. They were accompanied by one of Naiklos' squads, and Uhlstyn and two of the squad's troopers carried sledgehammers, not muskets.

Gahrvai turned a corner, then looked down, consulting a handwritten sheet of paper.

"There," he said flatly, pointing at a wall mosaic.

"Stand back, Sir," Uhlstyn replied grimly, then nodded to one of the sledgehammer-equipped soldiers. "Over there, Zhock," he said, twitching his head, and the soldier nodded back. He and Uhlstyn stood side by side, facing the mosaic's peaceful pastoral scene, and then the hammers swung in almost perfect unison.

The iron heads crunched into the mosaic, shattering tiles. The sound of breaking stone filled the corridor, and through it, Gahrvai could dimly hear voices from the streets beyond the priory's walls. Saint Zhustyn's was one of the oldest, largest priories inside the city of Manchyr proper, located in a well-to-do neighborhood less than ten blocks from Manchyr Cathedral, and the brethren's neighbors were clearly stunned and not a little frightened by the sudden eruption of midnight violence.

*Well, they'll just have to* deal *with it,* he thought harshly, watching the hammers rise once more. *And it looks like we really did surprise the bastards, too. So maybe the rats I'm looking for are still in their holes. Or*—his teeth flashed in a fierce, predatory grin—*maybe they're busy dashing down their escape tunnel. I'd almost prefer that, even if I'm not there to see their expressions when they run right into Charlz's arms!*

The sledgehammers thudded into the wall again. More bits and pieces of mosaic flew, but there was another sound, as well. A hollow sound which didn't sound quite right coming from one of the priory's ancient, solid stone walls.

The hammers swung a third time, and Sir Koryn Gahrvai's grin grew broader—and more cruel—as holes suddenly appeared in what had been supposed to be a solid wall. Not dark holes battered into the masonry, either. No, these were illuminated from the other side, and he heard a voice saying something frantic as the hammers pounded into the wall again, and again, and again.

The holes in the wall grew bigger, spreading, merging into one, and then an entire section of thin stone blocks tumbled away. Something exploded thunderously, a muzzle flash belched a choking cloud of powder smoke, and one of Naiklos' infantryman cried out as a musket ball slammed into his left leg. Before Gahrvai could say a thing, one of the wounded man's squad mates had his own musket at his shoulder, and a second shot hammered ears already cringing from the first one. Fresh smoke billowed, thick and vile-smelling, and someone shrieked from the other side of it.

"In!" Captain Naiklos barked. "And remember, we want the bastards alive!"

"Aye, Sir!" the squad's sergeant acknowledged grimly. Then—"You heard the Cap'n! *Hop it!*"

The squad's unwounded members shouldered their way through the hole, the passage of their bodies widening it as they went. The room on the other side was as large as the precise directions from Gahrvai's mysterious correspondent had indicated. And according to those same directions, it was also only the first of a half-dozen rooms which had been hidden by the priory's original architect better than five centuries ago. Unlike some priories and monasteries or convents which had changed hands and religious affiliations more than once over the years, Saint Zhustyn's had always been a Schuelerite house, and Gahrvai found himself wondering how many other concealed rooms might have been tucked away in the order's other religious houses and manors.

*No telling,* he thought as he ducked his head to follow Uhlstyn and Naiklos through the hole in the wall. *This is the first I've ever heard of any of them. For that matter, neither Archbishop Klairmant nor Bishop Kaisi had ever heard about anything like this. Or I don't* think *they had, at any rate.* He grimaced mentally. *Damn. Now I'm starting to wonder if even the bishops I* trust *are holding back information I need!*

He heard raised voices—angry, threatening voices. They were coming from the next room, and he coughed on a fresh cloud of smoke as he stepped through the door into it. Not powder smoke, this time, he observed. Instead, it was the smoke of burning paper, and his eyes smarted as he saw the overturned brazier. Obviously, someone had been burning documents when his men arrived, and even as he watched, Uhlstyn was stamping out the last flickers of flame from the pile of paper he'd dumped on the floor.

Two men, both in nightclothes, stood with their backs against a wall, pale faces strained as they faced the points of his soldiers' bayonets. He recognized one of them without difficulty.

"Father Aidryn Waimyn," he said in a voice of stone, "I arrest you in the name of the Crown and of Mother Church, on the authority of Prince Daivyn's Regency Council and Archbishop Klairmant, on charges of sedition, treason, and murder."

"You have no authority to arrest me!" Waimyn spat back. He was obviously shaken, and there seemed to be as much disbelief as anger in his expression. "You and your apostate masters have no authority over God's true Church!"

"Perhaps not," Gahrvai replied in that same stony voice. "But they have enough authority for *me,* Priest. And I advise you to recall what happened to the Inquisitors of Ferayd."

Fear flickered behind the outrage and fury in Waimyn's eyes, and Gahrvai smiled thinly.

"More of my troops are calling on Master Aimayl even as we speak," he told the ex-intendant. "And Master Hainree is being visited about now, as well."

Waimyn twitched visibly when he heard those names, and Gahrvai's smile broadened without becoming a single degree warmer.

"Somehow I suspect one of those fine gentlemen is going to confirm what we already know," he said. "It won't even take the sort of torture you're so fond of. Which, in my personal opinion, is a great pity." He looked deep into Waimyn's eyes and saw the fear-flicker dancing higher. "There's a part of me that regrets the fact that the Emperor and Empress and Archbishop Maikel have specifically renounced your own Book's penalties for the murder of priests. On the other hand, it's probably as well for the state of my own soul. I'd hate to find myself damned to the same coals as *you,* so I suppose I'll just have to settle for a rope."

"You wouldn't dare!" Waimyn got out.

"I'm sure that's what the Inquisitors at Ferayd thought, too," Gahrvai observed. He examined the ex-intendant coldly for another moment, then turned to Naiklos.

"Your men have done well here tonight, Captain, and so have you," he said. "Now I want all of these prisoners transported to Kahsimahr Prison." He gave Waimyn another icy smile. "I understand they're expected."

.XII.
A Private Council Chamber,
Imperial Palace,
Cherayth,
Kingdom of Chisholm

Y our Majesties."
Prince Nahrmahn of Emerald bowed as he stepped past the guardsmen outside the door in answer to the pre-breakfast summons. Cayleb and Sharleyan sat at a table beside one of the chamber's windows. It was still dark, and the moonless, starless winter sky was cloudy enough no one should expect to see the sun even when it finally deigned to rise. The hour was a bit early, even for vigorous, youthful monarchs, Nahrmahn reflected. It was somewhat more than "a bit early" for him, on the other hand, given that he preferred a rather more leisurely schedule, and he hadn't really expected to be summoned to a conference even before breakfast.

The chamber had been fitted with one of the Howsmyn foundries' new cast-iron stoves, its chimney ducted into the flue of an enormous but old-fashioned and rather less efficient fireplace, and it was actually comfortably warm, even by Nahrmahn's semi-tropical Emeraldian standards. A tall, steaming carafe of hot chocolate sat beside an equally steaming pot of tea, and both were accompanied by cups, plates, and a tray well provided with scones and muffins. Before his arrival here in Cherayth, Nahrmahn had never encountered the scones, laced with nuts and sweetbriar berries, but they were a local specialty and he approved of them enthusiastically. Especially when they were still hot from the oven and there was plenty of fresh butter available.

He brightened visibly as he saw them, and not simply because he hadn't eaten yet. That was rather central to his reaction, but there *were* other factors. Specifically, since he and Ohlyvya had acquired their own coms and access to Owl's computer files, his wife had begun to fuss over his eating habits. Nahrmahn himself had spent many hours now poring over those same files with delight, yet he'd been interested in significantly different portions of them. He supposed he was glad they had access to information which told them the truth about health issues the *Holy Writ* had demoted to rote obedience to "religious law," but he could have wished that information had not contained words like "cholesterol" and "arteriosclerosis." It had been quite bad enough, in his opinion, when Pasqualate-trained healers had fussed at him about what he ate without any knowledge of the actual reasons behind Pasquale's dietary suggestions.

He smiled at the thought, but then his smile faded as he saw the emperor's and empress' expressions.

"Good morning, Nahrmahn," Sharleyan replied to his greeting. Her voice was courteous, but there was something hard, angry, about her tone. Whatever it was, though, at least it didn't appear to be directed at him, for which the prince was grateful. "Please, join us."

"Of course, Your Majesty."

Nahrmahn crossed to the indicated chair, facing Cayleb and Sharleyan across the table and looking out through the window behind them. He sat, and Sharleyan poured hot chocolate and handed it to him. He accepted the cup with a murmured thanks, sipped, then set it on the table before him, folding his hands around it, while he considered possible reasons for his unanticipated summons. His first thought had been that it had something to do with Merlin's mission to Maikelberg, but he'd watched the "imagery" of Merlin's conversation with Duke Eastshare himself. It didn't seem likely anything had gone wrong there, yet if not that, then—?

"Forgive me, Your Majesty," he said, looking at Sharleyan, "but from your tone, something's happened of which I'm not aware."

His own tone and raised eyebrows made the statement a question, and Cayleb gave a harsh, ugly little bark of a laugh. Nahrmahn transferred his attention to the emperor and cocked his head.

"You might say that," Cayleb said. "When I woke up this morning, I touched base with Owl. I usually do, and I usually have a couple of things I've got him keeping track of—specific things I'm particularly interested in." He shrugged. "Most of them, frankly, aren't particularly earthshaking. You might even call them purely selfish. Things like the baseball scores and standings back in Old Charis, for example. Or keeping track of Hektor and *Destiny*. That sort of thing."

He paused, and Nahrmahn nodded in understanding.

"Well, one of the things I've had him keeping track of was Father Tymahn's sermons down in Manchyr. Not so much because of their political implications, but because I've enjoyed them so much on a personal level. So this morning I asked him how Father Tymahn was coming on this Wednesday's sermon." The emperor's face tightened, and his voice went harsh and flat. "Unfortunately, he won't be preaching this five-day after all. Those bastards of Waimyn's murdered him night before last. As a matter of fact, they tortured him to death and then dumped his naked body in Gray Lizard Square yesterday morning."

Nahrmahn stiffened, and his eyes darted to Sharleyan. He understood the rage glittering in her eyes now. The empress had been looking forward to the day she would finally get to meet the priest who had emerged as the spiritual leader of the Corisandian Reformists. He knew how much she'd come to respect Hahskans, and he suspected that the priest's murder, especially at Waimyn's direct orders, must resonate with the memory of how so many of her own guardsmen had been killed as the result of another high churchman's plans to murder *her*.

"Owl is positive Waimyn personally ordered it, Your Grace?" He asked in as neutral tone as he could manage, choosing to direct the question to Cayleb, and the emperor made a sound midway between a growl and a snarl.

"Oh, he's positive, all right. The bastard passed the order through Hainree to Aimayl."

"I see." Nahrmahn's expression was simply thoughtful, but something harder and colder glittered at the backs of his habitually mild brown eyes. "I must admit I'm a bit surprised by his decision to escalate matters this way," the rotund prince continued after a moment. "I realize his communications with Bishop Executor Thomys and the 'Northern Conspiracy' are roundabout and limited, but surely he must be aware their plans are far too incomplete for any sort of direct confrontation with the Regency Council and General Chermyn."

"Obviously we've all believed that," Sharleyan said. Now that Nahrmahn knew what had happened, he recognized that cold, hard tone as an echo of the hard-won self-discipline a child queen had learned so long ago. It was painfully evident that it required quite a lot of that self-discipline to control the rage deep inside her.

"Whatever we believed, though," she continued, "we were wrong."

"I don't think that's exactly what happened," Cayleb said. She looked at him, her eyes considerably colder and flatter than usual, and he shook his head. "What I mean is that I think he's perfectly well aware the Bishop Executor and his secular cronies aren't ready to move yet, and we know he's been trying to coordinate things in Manchyr to bring the city to a boil gradually. To touch off the fuse at the moment the Northern Conspiracy *is* ready. That suggests to me that something must have happened to change his plans."

"I believe I agree with His Grace, Your Majesty," Nahrmahn told Sharleyan after a moment. He reached out and began absently buttering a still-warm scone. "Of course, Waimyn's always had the problem of those poor communications. Any sort of fine coordination with Shylair, Storm Keep, and the rest has been out of the question. Still, it's been obvious he recognizes the need to orchestrate his own efforts with theirs in so far as he *can,* so I'm strongly inclined to believe that some purely local factor—a tactical one, one might say, and not a fundamental shift in his strategic thinking—produced this decision on his part."

From Sharleyan's expression, it was obvious Nahrmahn's apparent detachment irritated her. The prince wasn't too concerned about that, though. She and Cayleb had come to know him well enough by now that she had to recognize the manner in which he normally approached this sort of analysis. It was her own pain and anger which woke her irritation, and Sharleyan Tayt Ahrmahk, for all her youth, was more than wise enough to recognize that, as well.

"I've had a little longer to think about it than you have, Nahrmahn," Cayleb said, reaching for his own chocolate cup, "and I imagine it was actually a combination of things. If I had to guess, I'd say Father Tymahn was proving more effective in unifying support for the Church of Charis than Waimyn had expected. And while I don't think it was what Father Tymahn truly had in mind, that's been spilling over into an at least grudging acceptance of the *Empire* of Charis among a significant segment of the capital's population, as well. I'm positive Waimyn saw that, whether Tymahn and the rest of the Reformists did or not, and I doubt he cared for the impact it was having on his own plans and organization. For that matter, we *know* he's been concerned about the number of people who have begun quietly passing on bits and pieces of information about his operations to priests like Tymahn. So my theory is that he reached the point of deciding Tymahn was proving an unacceptable hindrance and had to go. And the way he had him killed, and where he had the body dumped, was intended to . . . discourage not only Tymahn's fellow Reformist clergy, but also any members of the laity who might have been inclined to 'collaborate' with them."

"All of that makes sense, Your Grace," Nahrmahn allowed after a moment. He took a bite of buttered scone, chewed slowly and thoroughly, his eyes thoughtful, then swallowed.

"All of that makes sense," he repeated, "and I'm inclined to agree with your analysis. At the same time, however, I believe you've overlooked another factor."

"I'm sure I've overlooked dozens of other factors!" Cayleb snorted. "Which one, in particular, were you thinking about?"

"Waimyn's temper, Your Grace," Nahrmahn said flatly. "There's not much question that he deeply and personally hated Father Tymahn for his 'treachery' and 'apostasy.' And the man's a Schuelerite. For him, this wouldn't be simply a matter of passing a message, important though that must definitely be. It would also be a matter of appropriately punishing a priest for heresy and the betrayal of his vows of obedience to the Grand Vicar."

"In other words," Sharleyan's voice was even flatter than Nahrmahn's had been, "it was personal."

"Your Majesty, it's almost always 'personal' to at least some extent,"

Nahrmahn said a bit sadly. "If I had a mark for every prince or vicar who's let personal anger push him into some truly, outstandingly, monumentally *stupid* catastrophe, I could buy the Temple from Duchairn and we could all go home and live happily ever after. When you come down to it, this entire war is the result of Zhaspahr Clyntahn doing exactly that, after all."

"That's true enough," she agreed after a moment.

"What has Merlin said about it?" Nahrmahn asked, looking back at Cayleb.

"We haven't discussed it yet." Nahrmahn's eyebrows rose again, and Cayleb shrugged. "It was hard enough for me to get him to take the 'downtime' he needs every night, and events persist in throwing up entirely too many good, legitimate reasons for me to yank him back out of it. I'm not going to get into the habit of doing that unless it's really an emergency, and Father Tymahn was already dead." The emperor waved one hand in a choppy gesture of dismissal. "Waking Merlin up couldn't have changed anything, and he'll be coming back 'online' in another fifteen minutes or so, anyway. We can wait that much longer before we com him."

"I see."

Despite his own shock and anger over what had happened to Hahskans, Nahrmahn felt his lips trying to twitch into an inappropriate smile. He knew he shouldn't have found it amusing, but Cayleb's fierce protectiveness—and Sharleyan's, for that matter—where a millennium-old, immortal, virtually indestructible PICA was concerned was far more evident than either of them probably suspected. And rather touching, too, for that matter.

"In the meantime, though," Sharleyan said, "I think we need to reconsider how wise it would be to allow Maikel to continue on to Corisande the way he's planned. If Waimyn's come far enough out into the open—or, at least, been willing to escalate things far enough—to kill Father Tymahn, I think we have to assume he'll be perfectly willing to attempt Maikel's assassination, as well. I know Gahrvai's been doing a surprisingly good job of protecting the Church in Corisande so far, but there've still been those acts of vandalism, and now they've gotten to Father Tymahn, too. Unless we're willing to send Merlin along to personally protect Maikel, I don't think we can afford to risk the possibility that they might get lucky again. Especially when we don't have *anyone* in Corisande with whom we can communicate directly using the SNARCs."

"Your Majesty, there are some challenges I'm more willing to undertake than others," Nahrmahn said dryly. "Having sailed all the way from Emerald to Chisholm in company with the Archbishop, it's my opinion you'd have better luck forbidding snow to fall or the tide to rise than telling him he can't go to Corisande because you're concerned about his physical safety."

Despite the somberness of their collective mood, both Cayleb and Sharleyan smiled unwillingly. Then the empress reached for one of the muffins, as if yielding to the prince's example. Her pregnancy—and her morning sickness—were far enough advanced that she was extraordinarily careful about what she ate, however, especially early in the morning. The state of her stomach was also the reason she was drinking tea, instead of the rich, dark chocolate, and she looked rather wistfully at Nahrmahn's scone, with its chopped nuts and mixed berries, dripping with melted butter, then bit into the plain, dry, unbuttered corn muffin.

"I realize he's likely to be . . . stubborn about it—" she began, her voice a bit indistinct as she chewed, but Cayleb interrupted her with a rueful laugh. She looked a question at him, and he shrugged.

"I was just thinking about an officer's evaluation Bryahn showed me several years ago. It was about a certain Master Midshipman Ahrmahk . . . otherwise known, at least on social occasions, as Crown Prince Cayleb."

"It was?" Sharleyan's eyes narrowed, then their darkness lightened with just a touch of true humor. "And may one ask why High Admiral Lock Island shared this no doubt fascinating document with you?"

"He was making a point, actually."

"Excuse me, Your Grace," Nahrmahn put in, "but this is the first I've heard about 'officer's evaluations.' Is this a standard part of your Navy's procedures? Or was there a particular reason one was written about . . . ah, the midshipman in question?"

"Oh, they've been part of our regular practice for thirty or forty years now," Cayleb replied. "Grandfather instituted them when he was a serving officer himself. Every commanding officer is responsible for writing an evaluation of each officer under his immediate command every year. They go into the personnel files of the officers in question to be available for future promotion boards." He shrugged again. "In my case, obviously, promotion boards weren't going to be a factor, since Father had already decided he needed me understudying him in Tellesberg more than he needed me serving in the Navy somewhere. Still, I *was* a midshipman, and evaluations get written on every midshipman, so one got written on me."

"I see. And who was the officer who produced this document, my love?" Sharleyan asked.

"A fellow by the name of Dunkyn Yairley," Cayleb replied. Sharleyan's eyebrows flew up in genuine surprise, and the emperor chuckled. "He was only a lieutenant at the time, but, yes, that's one reason I had Hektor assigned to *Destiny*. And I specifically told Captain Yairley I didn't want Hektor told that I'd been a midshipman under him. I doubt he would have anyway, but I just thought I'd make sure."

"Under the circumstances, then, should I assume Lieutenant Yairley produced a glowing testimonial to your own sterling character, Your Grace?" Nahrmahn inquired with a slight smile as he raised his chocolate cup once more.

"Well, that depends on your definition of glowing testimonials." Cayleb smiled back. "What he actually said was, 'His Highness possesses a superabundance of that quality which, in myself, I should characterize as tenacity and maintenance of aim, but which, in His Highness' case, I can describe only as sheer bloody-minded obstinacy.'"

Nahrmahn, who'd been unwise enough to be sipping chocolate at that particular moment, spluttered into his cup. Sharleyan surprised all of them—and herself most of all, probably—by giving a sudden, delighted giggle, and Cayleb shook his head at both of them.

"I can see why you wouldn't be overly concerned by his ability to deal with a midshipman of Duke Darcos' sudden seniority, Your Grace," Nahrmahn said, blotting his lips with a napkin.

"No, I'm not," Cayleb agreed. Then his expression sobered slightly. "On the other hand, his description of me at thirteen is only a pale reflection of Maikel Staynair at seventy-two. He can out-stubborn a dragon. For that matter, he can probably even out-stubborn a *cat-lizard*, much less a mere emperor or empress!"

"I'm afraid you're right about that, Your Grace." Nahrmahn laid his napkin on the table and pursed his lips for a moment. "And while I understand your concerns, Your Majesty," he continued then, looking at Sharleyan, "I'm afraid that on a purely intellectual basis, I'd have to agree with the Archbishop."

"I beg your pardon?" Sharleyan seemed too surprised by his statement to be angry over it, and in light of her general mood, Nahrmahn continued just a bit quickly, before that could change.

"Your Grace, his visit has already been announced, in Manchyr as well as here. Everyone in Corisande knows he's coming, and they know he's coming specifically to make a pastoral visit and show his support for the local Church. If he suddenly decides to cancel that trip, people are going to wonder why. If he announces its cancellation now—immediately—before news of Father Tymahn's murder has had time to reach us here by normal means, we *could* argue his decision had nothing to do with any specific concerns about his safety. The problem is that I doubt very much he'd be willing to . . . prevaricate in that fashion. And, even if he were, there would be plenty of people—the majority of them, in fact—who would never believe the actual sequence. Whatever we might say, and whatever proof we might offer, it would be generally believed that he'd made the decision only *after* he learned about Father Tymahn's murder."

"He's right about that, Sharley," Cayleb said with a grimace.

"And if they do believe that, it will be child's play for the Group of Four and the Temple Loyalists to portray his decision as cowardice," Nahrmahn went on with implacable logic. "For that matter, let's be honest—that's what it would be, in some ways. Oh," he waved his hand gently before Sharleyan could object, "I agree a better word for it would be 'prudence,' Your Majesty. In fact, I'll go further and call it *simple* prudence, or even sanity. And all three of us know it would be prudence on *our* part, not his. That we'd have to have Merlin in here to arm wrestle him into submission before he'd agree. But the impression in Corisande, and probably even in Chisholm and Emerald, would be that he'd stayed away in order to avoid the threat of assassination. I'm sure a lot of people who already support the Church of Charis would be delighted if he did just that; unfortunately, even more people who *oppose* the Church of Charis would be just as delighted by it. They'd hammer away at the point that not even the Church's own Archbishop has enough genuine faith to risk death in support of his beliefs. And if they can do that successfully, Your Majesty," the plump little prince met Sharleyan's eyes very levelly, "then everything Archbishop Maikel has already achieved, and everything Father Tymahn died trying to achieve in Corisande, would be for nothing."

The quiet in the council chamber was deafening. The quiet crackle of coal in the stove seemed almost deafening by contrast, and outside the windows a few dry flakes of snow began to dust down out of the clouds, brushing against the windowpanes like silent ghosts. The stillness lasted for several seconds, and then, grudgingly, Sharleyan nodded.

"You're right," she said with manifest unhappiness. "That's exactly what Maikel would argue . . . and he'd be *right,* damn it." She looked down at the muffin in her right hand and discovered she'd been picking it to pieces with the fingers of her left hand. "Worse, I know it, too. And, worse yet, all I'd do if I tried to argue him out of it would be to make him even more stubborn."

She continued the muffin's gradual destruction for another minute or so, then looked back up, and her eyes were fierce.

"But if that's the case, then we are *damned* well going to send Merlin along with him! I think we could justify that on the basis of what happened to Father Tymahn without anyone deciding Maikel lacks the courage of his convictions. And if there's anyone—outside me—Cayleb would be willing to send Merlin to look after, it would have to be him! And it's not as if we have to actually have Merlin right here in Cherayth so we can confer with him when we need to, either."

"No, that's true." Cayleb's eyes were thoughtful. "It never occurred to me, but you're right. We've already been sending him off on little errands for us here in Chisholm, like his current visit to Eastshare. So we could—"

Someone knocked gently on the council chamber door, and all three of them turned to face it. Then it opened, and their eyes went wide in astonishment when Merlin Athrawes stepped through it, as if the mere mention of his name had magically summoned him back from Maikelberg. His boots were thick with mud, more mud had spattered his breeches and the hooded coat he wore over his breastplate and hauberk, and his shoulders were dusted with melting snow.

"Your Majesties." He bowed to Cayleb and Sharleyan, then to Nahrmahn. "Your Highness."

The door closed behind him, and he straightened.

"And good morning to *you,* too," Cayleb said, his head cocked quizzically, as the closing door provided them with privacy once more. "Forgive me for asking this, but aren't you still supposed to be in Eastshare discussing things with Green Valley and the Duke?"

"I am," Merlin agreed. "Something's come up, though. I thought it would be better to discuss it with you face-to-face rather than over the com, so I headed home yesterday." He grimaced and looked down at his muddy boots. "I'm afraid I didn't put in my downtime last night." He raised his head once more. "I changed horses a dozen times or so, and I hoped I was going to make it in time to speak to you and Sharleyan first thing this morning." He grimaced again, this time with a ghost of humor. "I hadn't expected the two of you to be up quite this early."

"That was because you failed to consider my regularly scheduled bout of morning sickness, I imagine," Sharleyan said wryly. "Admittedly, it doesn't usually get us out of the bedchamber this early, but, I assure you, we're usually *awake* by now."

Nahrmahn took another bite of buttered scone as the simplest means of suppressing his smile.

"You're right, Your Majesty. I did somehow manage to forget about that. I apologize." The *seijin* bowed to her again, a bit more deeply than before.

"You said you meant to talk to us 'first thing in the morning,' " Cayleb said as Merlin straightened once more. The emperor's eyes were intent. "Should I assume you intended to discuss certain events in Corisande?"

"I see you already know about that." Merlin's tone was just a bit odd, Nahrmahn thought. Almost—not quite, but *almost*—uncomfortable.

"You might say that," Cayleb replied grimly. "I've been asking Owl to keep an eye on Father Tymahn's sermons. When I asked him for an update this morning, he told me."

"I see."

Merlin's voice still seemed just a little off normal, Nahrmahn thought, and felt his own curiosity perk.

"We've just been discussing with Nahrmahn whether or not we should allow Maikel to continue with his pastoral visit," Sharleyan said. "Obviously, Cayleb and I aren't especially overjoyed at the prospect in light of all this. So we've been thinking we should send *you* along to make sure Waimyn and his butchers don't take a shot at him, as well."

"That Wai—?" Merlin began, then stopped.

He looked back and forth between Cayleb and Sharleyan for a moment, his expression most peculiar, then cleared his throat. All three flesh-and-blood members of his audience knew a PICA had absolutely no reason ever to do anything of the sort, just as all three of them had long since realized it served

Merlin as a sort of time-buying mannerism. Which explained why all three of them found themselves looking back at him in various degrees of confusion, puzzlement, and speculation.

"Merlin?" Cayleb asked with the stern, slightly rising inflection of a parent who suspects his offspring has Been Up To Something. Merlin looked back at him, then did another thing a PICA never really had to do and sighed.

"You said Owl told you Father Tymahn had been murdered," he said just a bit obliquely. "I assumed from that that you meant you'd asked him for a complete report on the situation."

"What was there to ask about?" Cayleb retorted. "Tymahn was already dead, and it's not as if anything we decide this morning is going to have any immediate effect in Corisande. For that matter, it isn't even dawn yet in Manchyr."

"Actually," Merlin corrected with scrupulous accuracy, "it *is* dawn in Manchyr. And they're having lovely, clear weather down there, too, I might add."

"And just what *else* is happening in Manchyr, Captain Athrawes?" Sharleyan demanded, regarding him with pronounced suspicion.

"Well, as a matter of fact, it happens that at this particular moment Koryn Gahrvai and his father, Charlz Doyal, General Chermyn, Bishop Kaisi, and Archbishop Klairmant are having their first interview with Aidryn Waimyn."

"They're *what?!*" Cayleb actually rose an inch or two out of his chair, and Sharleyan's eyes widened in astonishment. Nahrmahn, on the other hand, simply sat back with his chocolate cup in hand.

"I'm sorry, Cayleb," Merlin said. "When you told me Owl had told you what had happened, I thought you meant he'd told you everything."

"Well," Cayleb said with commendable restraint as he sat back down again, "obviously, you were in error."

"So I've just realized," Merlin replied a bit dryly. Then he shook his head. "Actually, Owl's finally starting to show signs of real autonomous self-awareness. He became aware of what was happening and realized I'd want to know about it, so he woke me up." The *seijin*'s artificial face muscles tightened. "Unfortunately, he'd picked up on it too late. Even if I'd dared to go to Manchyr to intervene, I'd never have gotten there in time. So all I could do was sit there and watch him die."

Merlin's face was a grim, harsh mask now. Sharleyan had never seen it quite that way before, even after the assassination attempt at Saint Agtha's. Cayleb had . . . on the quarterdeck of the galley *Royal Charis* when Merlin realized he hadn't been in time to save King Haarahld, after all.

"It was ugly," Merlin said quietly. "Very ugly. And I couldn't do one single damn thing to stop it." His right fist clenched at his side, and he looked down at it, as if it belonged to someone else. "I didn't see any reason to com you two and wake you up in the middle of the night to see something like that when none of us could do anything about it, anyway." He looked back up again. "So

I decided I'd wait until I could get back here in person, *then* tell you—preferably not until after you'd had breakfast, since I didn't expect you to have a lot of appetite afterward. But when I reached the palace, Franz Ahstyn told me you were already up and that you'd summoned Nahrmahn. I was afraid I knew why."

"All right," Cayleb said slowly. "I understand that much. But what's this business about Waimyn?"

"I couldn't keep them from murdering Father Tymahn," Merlin replied. "But I decided I could keep them from murdering anyone else. And that I'd damned well *better,* if I didn't want even more of the Reformists butchered and dumped on street corners somewhere. So I used one of Owl's remotes to write a little note, then toss it through Koryn Gahrvai's window." He smiled faintly, despite his grim mood. "I think it got his attention. And when he'd read it—"

▼    ▼    ▼

"—so that's about the size of it," Merlin finished several minutes later. "Gahrvai's men got Aimayl and at least three-quarters of the rest of Waimyn's top cell leaders. Hainree heard them coming, though, and he managed to evade them. And so did that nasty piece of work Cahmmyng. But Gahrvai's confiscated all four of their main weapons caches, and he's got more than enough people to interrogate." Merlin grimaced. "They're not being any too gentle about how they ask questions, either. They're being scrupulous about staying away from *The Book of Schueler,* but that's not stopping them from being pretty damned . . . insistent. I imagine he and Doyal will be coming up with all sorts of 'normal' leads to help keep what's left of Waimyn's organization in Manchyr on the run."

"My God, Merlin." Cayleb had sat silent during Merlin's recital. Now he shook his head. "Forgive me for asking, but hadn't we all pretty much decided we needed to leave those people *alone?* Keep an eye on them and build up that 'database' of yours?"

"We had," Merlin agreed. "But when they murdered Father Tymahn they escalated things to an entirely different level." His sapphire eyes were grim and hard. "Bad enough if they'd only kidnapped him, held him as a hostage while they made demands or something like that. But they intended to kill him from the outset, and they did it in a way which was a deliberate challenge to Archbishop Klairmant, to Gahrvai's authority, to the Regency Council, and even to Chermyn. I couldn't let that stand—not when Tymahn and the other Reformists have been making so much ground in the capital."

"*You* couldn't let it stand?" Sharleyan said in a careful tone, and Merlin nodded.

"*I* couldn't," he confirmed flatly.

There was silence in the council chamber again. Snow was falling more heavily outside the window, and Nahrmahn rather imagined he could feel the day's chill even from where he sat. Except that the cold breeze blowing down his spine at the moment had nothing at all to do with the weather.

*We tend to forget that Merlin—Nimue Alban—has his own agenda,* the Emeraldian prince thought quietly. *We work together with him so closely, and the success of Charis is so important to his mission, that we forget he isn't really a Charisian himself. Not even a* Safeholdian, *when you come to it. I suspect this is the first time since Cayleb learned the truth about him that Merlin hasn't even consulted the Emperor before making a decision of such magnitude. I wonder how Cayleb and Sharleyan—especially Cayleb—are going to react to that?*

"And the reason you didn't tell us all this yesterday?" Cayleb asked quietly.

"Because, as I said, I wanted to tell you in person. I hoped you wouldn't have heard about Father Tymahn's murder before I got back here, since I'm the one who normally monitors what's going on in Manchyr. I wanted to give you that news personally, not over the com. And I wanted to tell you personally what I'd done about it."

"Because you expected us to be angry that you didn't even consult with us before standing our entire strategy for Manchyr on its head? Was that it?" It was impossible to read Cayleb's tone, but his eyes were very intent.

"Not so much because I expected you and Sharleyan to be angry, no," Merlin replied steadily. "I did think, though, that since I'd already gone ahead and acted—since it was what we used to call a 'fait accompli' back on Old Earth—I at least owed you the courtesy of a personal explanation of what I'd done and why."

Cayleb sat back in his chair on his side of the table, gazing at the tall, blue-eyed man in the blackened armor, badged with the gold, blue, and silver of the Empire of Charis, standing on its other side. Nahrmahn wondered which Cayleb was seeing in that moment: the Imperial Guardsman, or the PICA with the soul of a dead woman?

Then the emperor glanced at Sharleyan for a moment and shrugged.

"First, Merlin, let me say—and I imagine I speak for Sharley in this, as well—that, under the circumstances, I wholeheartedly approve of your decision."

He lifted one eyebrow at his wife, who nodded in firm agreement, then turned his attention back to Merlin.

"Second, however, I'd like to remind you of a conversation you had, once upon a time, with my father. 'I respect you, and in many ways I admire you,' you said to him. 'But my true loyalty? That belongs not to you, or to Cayleb, but to the future. I *will* use you, if I can, Your Majesty.' "

The council chamber was silent once more, and Cayleb smiled thinly.

"Are you surprised I knew what you said to him?" the emperor asked.

"A bit," Merlin admitted after a moment. "I didn't realize he'd told you about that."

"He didn't. Charlz Gahrdaner did. Father hadn't told him not to, and when he saw how close you and I were getting, he thought I should know. It wasn't that he distrusted you, Merlin. It's just that *his* loyalty was first, last, and always to Charis. To the House of Ahrmahk."

"And are you angry that mine isn't?" Merlin asked softly.

"Merlin." Cayleb shook his head with a sudden, unexpected smile. It was a bit crooked, that smile, but it was definitely a *smile*. "Merlin, I've *always* known that. Even if Charlz hadn't told me, you have, often enough and openly. It hasn't kept you from offering Sharley and me your friendship—even your service. For God's sake, you flew halfway around the planet to save her *life*! Of course I could wish—hope—we'll always find ourselves in general agreement. And I'll admit that I would have preferred to have at least a little input before you sicced Gahrvai on Waimyn. In that regard, please feel as free to wake me up in the middle of the night as I've always felt about waking *you* up. But don't think I expect you to do one inch less than whatever it is you believe your duty requires of you. I'm not that stupid. And I'm not that *selfish*, either, Merlin." He shook his head again. "There's a phrase you used to me once, about someone else. You said he'd 'paid cash' for the right to make up his own mind about something. Well, so have you."

There was another moment of silence, then Merlin chuckled.

"I hoped you'd take it that way," he said. "I'd be lying if I said I'd been certain you would, though."

"And would it have made one bit of difference to your future actions if I'd decided to pitch an imperial tantrum about your having had the sheer effrontery to make a decision without consulting me and Sharley?"

"No," Merlin told him a bit wryly. "No, not really."

"That's what I thought, too," Cayleb said.

M aikel Staynair looked up from the book in his lap as someone rapped lightly on his chamber door.

The morning had been as quiet as only a winter morning could be. He'd stationed himself by his chamber's eastern-facing window in order to take advantage of the morning light for his reading, but it had also let him look out across the snowy Chisholmian landscape. He hadn't been in Cherayth long enough for the novelty of snow to fade, and he found the graceful, floating descent of the snowflakes endlessly fascinating. Ahrdyn, on the other hand, had decided snow was a terrible idea. Fortunately for the cat-lizard's peace of mind, his basket was large enough to accommodate a truly luxurious, incredibly soft blanket—a gift from Empress Sharleyan, in fact—and he was currently burrowed down under it, with only the very tip of his nose exposed.

Whoever their visitor was rapped again, a bit more loudly.

"Yes?" Staynair called, and the door eased open just far enough to admit a human head. The head in question belonged to Father Bryahn Ushyr, his personal secretary and most closely trusted aide.

"I'm sorry to disturb you, Your Eminence, but *Seijin* Merlin wonders if he might have a moment of your time?"

Staynair's snowy eyebrows rose. He sat there for a moment, then slipped a bookmark into the volume in his lap and closed it.

"Of course, Bryahn. Ask the *seijin* to come in, please."

"Certainly, Your Eminence," Ushyr murmured, and his head disappeared once more.

The door opened again—wider—a few seconds later, and Merlin Athrawes stepped through it. Staynair was surprised to see him for several reasons. For one thing, he'd understood Merlin would be remaining in Maikelberg for at least another day or so. For another, he was a little perplexed as to why Merlin might have come to see him in person rather than simply using their coms, since the *seijin*'s SNARCs must have told him Staynair was alone in his chamber, which meant no one would have noticed him talking to himself.

"Thank you for seeing me on such short notice, Your Eminence," Merlin said as Ushyr closed the door once more behind him.

"You're always welcome," Staynair replied with a smile. "All the same, I must admit I'm a little surprised by your visit."

"I'm sure you are." Merlin smiled back, but then the smile faded. "I've just come from a meeting with Cayleb, Sharleyan, and Nahrmahn, though. Well," he corrected himself, "I've just come by way of a bath and a clean uniform."

"What sort of meeting?"

"There've been some . . . unexpected developments in Manchyr." Staynair's eyes narrowed as Merlin's voice turned unexpectedly grim. "In fact, one reason I'm here is to ask you to join the three of them to discuss those developments. They wanted to wait until after you'd had breakfast. For several reasons."

"Should I assume the 'unexpected developments' in question are less than happy ones?" Staynair asked quietly.

"I'm afraid so. And, frankly, I'm also afraid they're going to have some implications for your own visit."

"I see." Staynair laid his book aside and started to climb out of his comfortable armchair.

"Just a moment, Your Eminence. Please."

The archbishop's eyebrows rose once more as Merlin gestured for him to remain seated. He settled back, cocking his head to one side.

"Yes?" he invited.

"I said that *one* reason I'd come was to extend their invitation," Merlin said. "I have another one, though. One I really need to discuss with *you* before I bring the matter to their attention."

"This has something to do with what's happened in Manchyr?"

"No, Your Eminence. Or, not directly, at any rate. It has to do with a discussion you had with Baron Wave Thunder before you departed for Emerald."

"I beg your pardon?" Staynair blinked, and Merlin gave him an off-center smile.

"Before you left Tellesberg, Your Eminence, you arranged for Father Bryahn to deliver several cases of documents to the Baron. Documents which had been sent to you from Zion . . . by way of Madame Dynnys."

Staynair stiffened. For a moment, simple surprise—and shock—held him motionless in his chair, his eyes widening in astonishment. Then his normally gentle face darkened. The eyes which had gone wide narrowed, and his entire body seemed to quiver as a bolt of outrage went through him.

"*Merlin—!*" he began in a hard, angry voice.

"Please, Your Eminence!" Merlin said quickly, raising one hand in a pacific gesture. "I have no intention of violating your confidence in any way!"

"You already have!" Staynair was as furious as Merlin had ever seen him. "I realize the entire 'Church of God Awaiting' is only a farce, and not a good one," he said sharply, "but you know perfectly well that I still take my priestly responsibilities seriously! And you obviously *also* know Madame Dynnys came to me under the seal of the confessional!"

"Yes, I do," Merlin agreed, keeping his own voice deliberately calm. "And I became aware of it only because Owl gave me the information in a routine data dump. I'm sorry to say it hadn't occurred to me—then—to put in place a filter which would respect the privacy and confidentiality of your pastoral discussions with individual members of the Church. Since that incident, I have."

Staynair glared at him, and Merlin looked back levelly.

"You're perfectly welcome to check with Owl about that, Your Eminence," he said very quietly.

A tense, brittle silence hovered for a moment. Then Staynair's nostrils flared as he inhaled deeply.

"That won't be necessary." His voice was as quiet as Merlin's had been. "Your word is more than good enough for me, *Seijin* Merlin. It always has been."

"Thank you," Merlin said sincerely.

"I must assume, however," Staynair continued with the air of a man deliberately stepping back from a brink, "that there's a reason you brought your . . . awareness of this particular situation to my attention?"

"There is."

Merlin crossed to the window and stood gazing out into the snow. He said nothing more for several seconds, then turned his head to look at the archbishop.

"Your Eminence, I became aware of the existence of Mistress Ahnzhelyk's files purely by chance, and I understand exactly why Madame Dynnys wants to protect her identity—and her—from accidental betrayal. What I don't know, because of those filters I had Owl put in place since your original conversation with her, is whether or not Madame Dynnys ever did tell you the identities of those within the Temple who have been working with Ahnzhelyk?"

Staynair considered the question for a moment, then shrugged.

"No, she hasn't."

"I'm not really surprised." Merlin turned back to the window. "However, ever since I became aware of your conversation, I've been . . . keeping an eye on Mistress Ahnzhelyk."

"What?" Alarm tinged Staynair's tone. "I thought you said—"

"What I've said," Merlin interrupted, never looking away from the window, "is that I don't dare operate the SNARCs or their remotes *inside* the Temple proper." He shrugged. "I still don't have any idea what all those power sources under the Temple are. Obviously, quite a lot of them have to be associated with the Temple's environmental services and the automated remotes that keep all its 'mystic' features up and running. I think there's more than would be needed just for that, though, and I'm not going to risk tripping any close-in sensors. But Ahnzhelyk's townhouse is far enough from the Temple that I can keep an eye on it. Cautiously, of course. In fact," he looked back at the archbishop with a strange, flickering little smile, "I've actually been to Zion, you know."

"You've *been* to Zion?" Staynair couldn't quite hide his surprise, and Merlin chuckled.

"That was before I'd been able to tell any of you the truth. Tell me, didn't you ever wonder exactly how Archbishop Erayk came to take that extremely convenient tumble on Ahnzhelyk's steps?"

Staynair's eyes widened once more, and Merlin nodded.

"Wasn't that just a bit risky?" the archbishop asked after a moment. "From what you've said, I'd have thought it would constitute a considerable risk of detection."

"It did," Merlin agreed. "Unfortunately, it was the only way I could think of to head off his pastoral visit, and we needed the time."

"That's true enough," Staynair acknowledged feelingly, and Merlin shrugged.

"At any rate, as I say, I've been keeping my eye on her. And, to be honest, I'm getting more and more concerned about her safety."

"Concerned? Why? What's happening?" Staynair asked quickly.

"I'm not entirely certain," Merlin admitted, "but she's been making some unusual contacts. And she's been doing some other . . . peculiar things. Among other things, she's got several groups of people hidden away in different places scattered across Zion. I haven't been able to identify most of them, but I do know who at least some of them are."

"Who?" Staynair asked when he paused.

"They're family groups. I'm sure of that much. And unless I'm badly mistaken, they're the families of senior churchmen. Vicars and archbishops."

Brown eyes met eyes of sapphire, and Staynair's chamber was very, very quiet for several breaths.

"Those 'reformers' of Adorai's," Staynair said, then, very softly.

"That's what I think—what I'm afraid of." Merlin shook his head. "The more I've seen of Ahnzhelyk, the more I've come to admire her. That's a *very* capable lady, Your Eminence, and I'm sure she's prepared her own escape route, even though I haven't managed to catch her at it. That's probably a good sign, not a bad one; if Owl and I haven't stumbled across any clues, it seems unlikely the Inquisition would have. On the other hand, there's no way to be sure of that, especially since I don't dare insert remotes directly into the Temple. And however good her arrangements may be, the sheer number of people she's trying to get out is going to work against her. I'm sure Clyntahn and Rayno are already trying to figure out where quite a few of those people have gotten to, and if there's one thing Inquisitors are good at, it's finding people."

"I see."

Staynair leaned back in his chair, his eyes worried, one hand playing with the pectoral scepter of his office. He sat that way for several seconds, then looked back up at Merlin.

"Exactly where are you heading, Merlin?"

"To Zion, I think," Merlin replied.

This time, Staynair's eyes didn't even flicker. He clearly didn't like where this seemed to be bound, but it was equally clear he wasn't surprised.

"How?" he asked simply.

"What I have in mind isn't really all that complicated. A bit risky, perhaps, but not complicated."

"You fill me with dread," Staynair said dryly, and Merlin chuckled.

"Actually, what started me thinking about it was something Sharleyan said earlier this morning. She and Cayleb are planning on sending me to Corisande with you to keep an eye on you. As she pointed out to Cayleb, we can stay in communication now wherever I am, and it would actually make sense for Cayleb to send his personal armsman to protect the Archbishop of Charis. But if they can send me to Corisande and stay in touch, then I could send myself to Zion without dropping out of contact, as well."

"And just go strolling around the city? In your Imperial Guard uniform, no doubt?"

"Not quite." Merlin smiled slightly. "In fact, I can reconfigure my PICA, Your Eminence. There are limits to the amount of change I can crank in on things like height, but I can alter the color of my hair, the color of my eyes, my complexion." He shrugged. "Trust me, I'm a true master of disguise. Or perhaps I should say *mistress*."

Staynair nodded. He'd seen file imagery of Nimue Alban now, and he had to admit that no one would ever have recognized her in Merlin Athrawes. There was an obvious—and certainly understandable—"family resemblance" between them, but Merlin was unmistakably a *man*.

"I won't pretend getting me and all the electronics tucked away inside me—not to mention my power plant—that close to the Temple doesn't make me nervous," Merlin continued, "but no one who sees or meets me is going to associate me with Merlin Athrawes. Not even if they later *meet* Merlin."

"All right, I can see that," Staynair conceded.

"Well, while I'm admitting things, I suppose I should also admit I'll be pretty much playing things by ear once I get there." Merlin shrugged. "It can't be any other way. But I'll have several advantages Ahnzhelyk *doesn't* have, and I can always explain that I'm another *seijin*—a friend of *Seijin* Merlin's who's rallied around to help him out, for example. That should help account for some of those 'advantages' if I have to call on them in front of witnesses."

"And just exactly where is '*Seijin* Merlin' going to be while all of this is going on?" Staynair shook his head. "You're going to have to be gone at least several days—more probably for five-days."

"That's one of the reasons I came to see you," Merlin said. "I think we can probably cover at least a short absence on my part by using the stories about *sei-jins*. According to at least some of the tales, they need to 'withdraw from the world' to meditate from time to time. *Seijin* Merlin, on the other hand, has been continually 'on-duty' ever since he first arrived in Charis. No doubt he's long overdue for that sort of withdrawal. Call it a 'spiritual retreat.' Given the fact that Cayleb and Sharleyan want to send me to Corisande with you, and that all they're going to be doing themselves for the immediate future is to stay parked here in the palace with oodles of guardsmen to keep an eye on them for me, I think we could get away with explaining to anyone who asks that I'm taking this opportunity for the aforesaid spiritual retreat before you and I depart."

"I imagine we could do that," Staynair agreed slowly, his eyes thoughtful.

"The problem is that we have to convince Cayleb and Sharleyan to go along with all this." Merlin's lips twitched in something halfway between a smile and a grimace. "I don't think either of them's going to be happy with the notion, but I'm not about to set out on something like this without keeping them fully informed. We just, ah, had a little conversation about exactly that point, as a matter of fact." His expression turned into a true smile for a moment, then smoothed. "However, I can't tell them where I want to go and why without telling them about Ahnzhelyk, Your Eminence. And I can't do that if it would violate your confidence and the sanctity of the confessional."

"I see," Staynair said again.

He sat for well over two minutes, thinking hard, then his eyes refocused on Merlin.

"This is an awkward situation," he said. "First, you're already party to the information covered by the confessional seal. Technically, that means you don't need my permission to share that information—information which came into your possession through no intentional violation of the confessional—with Cayleb and Sharleyan. For that matter, you're not even a churchman, so the seal of the confessional wouldn't apply to you in the first place. You and I both know that that's simply a legalistic argument, though."

Merlin nodded silently, and Staynair drew a deep breath.

"As Archbishop, I have the authority to release the seal of the confessional under certain clearly delineated circumstances. Frankly, I wouldn't even consider violating it for most of the justifications the Church of God Awaiting recognizes, since they mostly have to do with turning people over to the Inquisition. However, even the Church of Langhorne recognizes that there are instances in which the immediate safety of others must be considered. That's obviously true in this case! And, unfortunately, there's no possible way for me to consult with Adorai and ask her permission in time to do any good. At the same time, I have to tell you that if it were not for the imminence of the threat to Madame Ahnzhelyk and the innocent people you say she's trying to help escape, I wouldn't even consider this. You understand that?"

Merlin simply nodded once more, and Staynair sighed.

"All right, Merlin. Given the situation, I'll support you with Cayleb and Sharleyan."

.XIV.
## Madame Ahnzhelyk Phonda's Townhouse,
## City of Zion,
## The Temple Lands

Soft music drifted through the luxuriously appointed sitting room. Richly attired men, most in cotton silk and steel thistle silk cassocks, several in the orange of vicars, sat or stood around the room, holding wineglasses or snifters of brandy. Business was always good at Madame Ahnzhelyk's, and never better than during the winter months, when the citizens of Zion turned inevitably to inside occupations. Young women—of all casts of complexion, but uniformly lovely—sat or stood with their guests, chatting easily, laughing. All of them were tastefully dressed, most with elegantly understated cosmetics. Anything less like the popular concept of prostitutes would have been difficult to imagine.

Which was precisely why Madame Ahnzhelyk had always been so successful.

No vulgarians among *her* young ladies! No common, or crude, or coarse conversation. No lowbrow humor. Madame Ahnzhelyk's courtesans were all intelligent, lively, well educated. They were encouraged to read, to follow the latest news, to discuss any subject which might arise with combined wit and tact. They attracted only the very highest quality clients, and it was known throughout the Temple hierarchy that Madame Ahnzhelyk's ladies were unfailingly discreet.

Ahnzhelyk's standards were high, but no higher than the ones she'd met during her own "working girl" days, and it was astounding how many members of the vicarate stood on . . . intimate terms with her, even today. Now she made her way across the room, pausing for a brief word here and there with those she knew particularly well. A graceful, caressing touch upon a shoulder. A chaste kiss on a cheek, for the more favored. A laughing smile, a jest, for others. No one looking at her could have guessed she felt the least concern about anything.

Of course, one of the very first requirements of a successful courtesan was acting ability.

Her head turned as she caught movement out of the corner of one eye, and then an eyebrow rose as a well-dressed man she'd never before seen entered the room.

He was tall, clean-shaven, with hazel eyes. His brown hair was a bit longer than current Zion fashion dictated, pulled back in a simple ponytail confined by a jeweled clasp, and the heavy, snow-dusted overcoat he'd just handed to the porter was trimmed with a mountain slash lizard's white winter pelt. A heavy golden chain around his neck, and equally golden rings on his well-manicured fingers, were additional indications of affluence, and Ahnzhelyk's still lovely brow furrowed slightly in speculative interest.

"Excuse me," she murmured to her current conversational partner. "I believe I see someone I should be greeting, Your Eminence."

"Certainly, my dear," the archbishop to whom she'd been speaking replied.

"Thank you," she said, smiling warmly at him.

She drifted gracefully towards the newcomer, who was looking about him, not obtrusively but with obvious interest. He spotted her approach, and she smiled once again, more broadly, as she extended a slim hand.

"Welcome," she said simply.

"Thank you," he replied in a pleasant tenor voice. He lifted her hand gallantly to his lips, and kissed it. "I have the pleasure of addressing Madame Ahnzhelyk herself, I hope?" he asked.

"Indeed you do, Sir," she acknowledged. "And you are?"

"Ahbraim Zhevons." He bowed slightly, and she nodded. He spoke with a slight but recognizable Desnairian accent, she thought.

"Are you a visitor to our city, Master Zhevons?"

"Please, call me Ahbraim." White teeth flashed in a charming smile, and his hazel eyes smiled at her, as well. "Indeed I am. Has my accent given me away? Do I sound *too* rustic?"

"Oh, hardly *rustic* . . . Ahbraim!" Her silvery laugh was as charming as all the rest of her. "But I did seem to detect at least a little accent. Desnairian?"

"Almost." His smile turned just a bit impish. "Silkiahan, actually."

"Oh, forgive me!" Her laugh was a little louder, this time. Many citizens of the Grand Duchy of Silkiah resented being identified as Desnairians.

"There's nothing to forgive," he assured her. "And if there were, it would be my pleasure to extend that forgiveness to someone as charming as yourself."

"You don't seem to have been stinted on charm yourself, Ahbraim," she observed.

"My parents would like to think not, at any rate."

"May I ask what brings you to Zion at this time of year?" Ahnzhelyk grimaced delicately. "While I would never question the Archangels' judgment,

I've sometimes wondered what they were thinking to place the Temple some-where with Zion's winter climate!"

"It does make travel to the city a bit arduous at this time of year," he ac-knowledged with a slight shrug. "Unfortunately, business required my presence here. And however arduous the journey, the company waiting at the other end of the trip has certainly made it worthwhile."

"I'm glad you think so. Shall I introduce you to one of my young ladies?"

Ahnzhelyk's tone was as courteous and gracious as ever, yet somehow it contrived to make it perfectly clear that her own "working days" were behind her. Zhevons seemed amused by the implication.

"I think that would be a very good idea," he said. "I do trust, however, that we'll have the opportunity for at least a little more conversation?"

"Oh, I'm sure we will," she assured him, taking his hand and tucking it into her own elbow with a proprietary air as she led him across the sitting room towards a stunningly attractive blue-eyed, golden-haired young woman.

"Ahbraim, allow me to introduce Mahrlys," Ahnzhelyk said. "Mahrlys, this is Ahbraim. He's just arrived from Silkiah."

"Really?" Mahrlys gave Zhevons a dazzling smile. "Oh, I know why Madame introduced you to *me*, Ahbraim!"

"So do I," Zhevons replied as he recognized her own, considerably stronger accent. "Do I detect the accent of Silk Town itself?"

"You do, indeed," Ahnzhelyk assured him, passing his captive hand across to Mahrlys. "I thought you might find it comforting this far from home."

"Oh"—Zhevons smiled broadly—"I'm sure I'll find it *very* comforting."

▼    ▼    ▼

Several hours later, the sitting room was virtually deserted when Ahbraim Zhevons reentered it. Mahrlys Fahrno accompanied him, and the smile on her face was more than merely professional, Ahnzhelyk thought as they approached her. That was good. Mahrlys was one of her favorites, and she'd hoped the young woman would find Zhevons pleasant company. First impressions could always be misleading, however, and she was glad this one apparently had not been.

"Are you leaving us, Ahbraim?"

"I'm afraid I must," he replied. "I have a meeting tomorrow morning to discuss one of the shipbuilding contracts. I need to be rested before I match wits with Vicar Rhobair's minions."

"A very wise attitude!"

"So I've been told." He smiled at her. "Before I leave, however, I wondered if I might have a word in private?"

"In private?" Her eyebrows arched.

"I have a request to make . . . for a friend."

"I see." Ahnzhelyk's expression was only politely attentive, but mental ears pricked at something about her guest's tone. It was very slight, whatever it was—almost more imagined than heard. Yet it was there. She was oddly certain of that.

"Of course," she invited after the very briefest of hesitations, and gestured gracefully at one of the small side rooms. "Will that be sufficiently private?"

"Perfectly," he assured her, and offered her his arm.

They strolled across the all but deserted room, chatting easily, and Zhevons casually closed the smaller chamber's door behind them. Then he turned to face Ahnzhelyk.

"And now, Ahbraim," she said, "about this 'request' of yours . . . ?"

"It's really quite simple," he told her. "Adorai would appreciate your joining her in Charis."

Despite literally decades of hard-won experience and discipline, Ahnzhelyk's eyes flew wide. She stared at him for a fleeting instant, then paled as she realized how she had betrayed herself. One slim hand rose to her throat, and her fingers closed on a locket she wore about her neck on a silken riband.

"Don't," Zhevons said gently. She stared at him, eyes huge, and he shook his head. "I don't think Adorai would be very happy if you swallowed that cyanide tablet . . . Nynian."

She froze, scarcely breathing, and he smiled crookedly at her.

"I know what you're thinking, but think a bit harder. If Clyntahn and Rayno suspected you—if they knew enough to know the name your aunt and uncle gave you—they'd have no reason to entrap you. You'd already be in custody."

She gazed at him, color slowly creeping back into her face, but she didn't take her hand from the locket.

"That depends," she said after another long pause, and her voice was astonishingly steady, under the circumstances. "I can think of a few scenarios in which tricking me into trusting you could be more useful—advantageous, at least—than simply arresting me and putting me to the Question."

"I'm sure you can." He nodded. "At the same time, I think you know Clyntahn better than that. Rayno"—he shrugged slightly—"might be subtle enough to attempt something like that. But Clyntahn?" He shook his head. "Not in your case. Not if he began even to suspect all of the documentary evidence you sent to Adorai in Tellesberg. Or, for that matter, that you were the one who got her and the boys out of the Temple Lands in the first place."

Her eyes narrowed at the further evidence of how much he knew about her.

*And he's right*, she thought with an inner shiver she didn't allow to touch her eyes. *If that pig Clyntahn had any idea of how much damage I've done, I'd be screaming in one of the Inquisition's "questioning chambers" this very instant. And I'd go on screaming for a very long time.*

"All right," she said finally, although her fingers remained in contact with the locket. "I'll assume you're really from Adorai. There doesn't"—she smiled very crookedly—"seem to be a great deal of point in pretending I don't know what you're talking about, at any rate. But why did she send you? Why now?"

"To be perfectly honest," he said carefully, "she didn't send me. She doesn't even know I'm here."

"But you said—" Her hand tightened around the locket again.

"Gently!"

His own hand shot out with blinding speed, more quickly than she'd ever seen—or imagined!—a human hand could move. It closed on her wrist, and her eyes flew wide. Its grip was almost absurdly gentle, yet it might as well have been a steel vise. She jerked against it with all of her strength, hard enough she actually staggered half a step forward, and it didn't move a fraction of an inch.

"I said she doesn't know I'm here, Ahnzhelyk," he said quietly. "I also said she'd like you to join her in Tellesberg. Both of those statements were accurate."

"What do you mean?"

She abandoned her useless effort to pull free of his grip, and her eyes narrowed once more, speculatively.

"I'm sure that even here in Zion you've heard stories about 'Seijin Merlin' and his service to Charis." Zhevons' tone made the statement a question, and she nodded. He shrugged. "Well, you might say I'm cut from the same cloth as the seijin, and Archbishop Maikel and Merlin . . . became aware of certain events transpiring here in Zion. On the basis of what they'd learned, the two of them decided it would be wise to send me here. Unfortunately, there wasn't time for them to explain their fears to Adorai or consult with her about it before they did. That's why I know a great deal about you, but not everything."

"So you claim to be a seijin, as well?" Ahnzhelyk sounded more than a little skeptical, and Zhevons smiled.

"Like Merlin himself, I simply say I possess some of the abilities legend ascribes to seijins." He shrugged. "Still, it's a convenient label." He paused, regarding her levelly. "If I let go of your wrist, will you promise to leave yourself unpoisoned long enough for us to talk?" he asked her then, with a ghost of a smile.

"Yes," she said. "But only if you let go of my wrist . . . and step back a bit."

She held his gaze, her own unwavering, and he spent a second or two obviously contemplating her requirement. Then he nodded.

"Very well." He released her wrist and stepped back three strides. It was about as far as he could go in the small chamber, and he smiled again, sardonically, as he folded his arms in a manifestly unthreatening gesture. "Is this sufficient, My Lady?" he inquired.

"I suppose it will have to do, won't it?" she replied, although, having seen how quickly he could move, she suspected he was still more than close enough to stop her before she actually got the poison into her mouth. "Now, you were saying?"

▼　　▼　　▼

Ahnzhelyk Phonda sat up in bed, propped against a luxurious stack of pillows, breakfast tray across her lap, and gazed out her frosty window through the wisps of steam rising from the fresh cup of chocolate clasped between her slim hands. The sun was just rising, touching the frost crystals on the windowpanes with iridescent gold and red, and her expression was serenely pensive.

She frequently started her mornings this way, although she was seldom up quite so early, given the late-night hours she tended to keep. But although no one would have guessed it from her expression, she'd slept very little during the night just past, and her thoughts were far more anxious than her well-schooled expression might have suggested.

Someone rapped very gently at her bedroom door, and she looked away from the window.

"Yes?"

"Mahrlys is here, Mistress," Sandaria Ghatfryd, Ahnzhelyk's personal maid, replied from the other side of the closed door.

"Come in, then—both of you."

The door opened, and Sandaria stepped through it, followed by Mahrlys. The contrast between the two women was noteworthy, and not simply because Sandaria was as neatly and soberly dressed as always, while Mahrlys wore an embroidered robe over her nightgown and her hair tumbled loosely over her shoulders. Sandaria was a good twenty-five years older than Mahrlys, with slightly mousy brown hair, brown eyes, and an almost swarthy complexion from her Harchongese mother. She was also at least four inches shorter than the golden-haired Silkiahan. Yet there was abundant intelligence behind both women's eyes, and although Sandaria would never have passed the beauty requirements for one of Ahnzhelyk's young ladies, she'd been in her mistress' service for close to twenty years. Indeed, although no one else knew it, Sandaria had known Ahnzhelyk far longer even than that.

"Yes, Mistress?" Sandaria asked now. Although Ahnzhelyk employed an official steward who doubled as her butler and majordomo, everyone in her household knew Sandaria was the true manager of that household.

"I have a few things you and I need to discuss, Sandaria," Ahnzhelyk replied. "But first, I wanted to ask you, Mahrlys—what was your impression of Master Zhevons?"

Mahrlys frowned thoughtfully. Not in surprise, because Madame Ahnzhelyk was very protective of her young ladies. Most of her clients were well known to her, or had been vouched for by someone who was. On the occasions when someone about whom she knew nothing turned up, she generally quizzed whichever of her young ladies had spent time with him. All of them expected that . . . just as they knew a couple of the sturdy young armsmen Madame Ahnzhelyk employed as "footmen" were always close at hand whenever they were in the company of someone with whom Madame Ahnzhelyk was not already acquainted.

"I liked him, Madame," she said simply, after a moment. "He was courteous, witty, generous, and a gentleman." She wrinkled her nose charmingly. "He didn't have any peculiar requests, and he was actually quite gentle. One of those men who seem as concerned with giving pleasure as receiving it. And"— she smiled even more charmingly—"quite good at it, too."

"I take it the two of you actually spent a little bit of time talking, as well?" Ahnzhelyk inquired with a smile of her own, and Mahrlys chuckled.

"A little bit," she admitted.

"It must have been nice to have the opportunity to talk to someone from home."

"Actually, Madame, I've never really missed Silkiah that much." Mahrlys grimaced. "I don't think my mother's family approved of me after Father died—even before they figured out that if I had a 'vocation,' it certainly wasn't with Mother Church!" She smiled again, considerably more tartly this time. "Still, I have to admit I rather enjoyed being brought up to date on events in Silk Town. And Ahbraim knew *all* the current scandals!"

Mahrlys rolled her blue eyes, and Ahnzhelyk chuckled.

"So I take it you wouldn't be unhappy if he should visit us again?"

"Oh, I think you could take that as a given, Madame!"

"Good." Ahnzhelyk nodded. "I think that answers all of my questions, Mahrlys. Why don't you go and find your own breakfast now?"

"Of course, Madame. Thank you."

Mahrlys gave an abbreviated curtsy and withdrew, and Ahnzhelyk cocked her head at Sandaria as the door closed behind the younger woman.

"Yes, Mistress?" Sandaria was the only member of Ahnzhelyk's household who habitually addressed her by that title rather than "Madame."

"Our Silkiahan visitor last night was rather more interesting than Mahrlys realizes," Ahnzhelyk told her. Sandaria quirked one eyebrow, and Ahnzhelyk snorted. "As a matter of fact, if he's telling the truth—and I rather think he is—he's not a Silkiahan at all. Or, at least, he's not here on any of Silkiah's affairs."

"No, Mistress?" Sandaria asked calmly when Ahnzhelyk paused.

"He says, and I'm inclined to believe him, that he's here as a representative of the Charisians," Ahnzhelyk said flatly.

"May I ask why you believe him, Mistress?"

"Because he knows a great deal about me," Ahnzhelyk replied. "He knows about the material I sent Adorai. He knows about Nynian." Her eyes met Sandaria's. "And, most disturbing of all, he knows about at least some of our . . . guests."

"I see." If Sandaria was alarmed, she showed no sign of it. She simply frowned thoughtfully, eyes half-closed for a moment, then looked back at her mistress. "I'm sure you've considered the possibility that he's being less than truthful with you."

"Of course I have." Ahnzhelyk shrugged. "In fact, I raised that very point with him, in a manner of speaking. And he pointed out in return that if he were an agent of Clyntahn's, they wouldn't be wasting time trying to entrap me."

"Unless they want you to lead them to those 'guests,' Mistress."

"I know." Ahnzhelyk sighed, returning her gaze to the fire-struck frost on the bedroom window. "I think he's probably right, though, that Clyntahn would simply have ordered me arrested and put to the Question."

There was the ghost of a tremor in her voice. No one who didn't know her extremely well would ever have noticed it, but Sandaria *did* know her well, and the maid's eyes narrowed slightly as she castigated herself for not noticing the locket around Ahnzhelyk's neck. It did not constitute part of her mistress' regular sleeping attire.

"But even granting that he's right about Clyntahn," Ahnzhelyk continued, oblivious to Sandaria's reaction to the locket, "it's always possible he's working for *Rayno,* instead. We've seen Rayno keep things from Clyntahn until he's investigated them to his own satisfaction in the past."

"True, Mistress." Sandaria nodded. "On the other hand, is it really likely he'd do something like that under the present circumstances?"

"I . . . think not," Ahnzhelyk said slowly. She shook her head—slightly, at first, then more firmly. "Given how urgently Clyntahn's been looking for them, I don't think Rayno would sit on any clues as to their whereabouts that might come his way. That's one of the reasons I'm inclined to believe 'Master Zhevons.' "

"*One* of the reasons?" Sandaria repeated, raising an eyebrow once more.

"One," Ahnzhelyk said, her smile going a bit off center as she remembered Zhevons' blinding speed and the impossible strength of his gentle grasp.

"Very well, Mistress." Sandaria nodded, her complete trust in Ahnzhelyk's judgment evident. "What do you wish to do?"

"I'm worried about the Circle," Ahnzhelyk said flatly. "To be honest, I'm astonished Clyntahn has waited this long, assuming Samyl's right about his plans." Her lovely eyes darkened, shadowed with the premonition of a long-anticipated grief. "He won't wait much longer, though—I'm positive of that much. And when he moves, you know everyone he takes will be put to the Question . . . at least."

Sandaria nodded again. Both of them knew exactly how efficient the Inquisition was at torturing information out of its prisoners. When the prisoners in question were the Grand Inquisitor's personal enemies, the interrogators could be counted upon to be even more ruthless than usual.

"Samyl and Hauwerd are the only two who know about us," Ahnzhelyk continued. "Or that's what I hope and believe, at any rate. And I trust their courage completely. But if they're taken, we have to assume that, eventually, they'll reveal my—*our*—involvement, however courageous they may be. And I'm afraid we can't be entirely certain none of our guests have communicated with their husbands, so it's entirely possible someone else could be broken and lead the Inquisition at least to his own family. Which, in turn—"

She shrugged, and her maid nodded.

"Under the circumstances, Sandaria," Ahnzhelyk said, "I think we have to assume this man is who he says he is. And if he is, then we have to accept his warning that it's time to smuggle our guests out of Zion. Now."

"Yes, Mistress." Sandaria bent her head in an oddly formal bow, like an armsman acknowledging his liege's orders.

"I'm afraid you're going to have to go shopping, this afternoon." Ahnzhelyk smiled faintly. "See if you can find me some blue steel thistle silk."

"Of course, Mistress."


.XV.
The Temple
and
Hahriman and Market Streets,
City of Zion,
Temple Lands


I don't suppose you have any *good* news for me, Wyllym?"

Vicar Zhaspahr Clyntahn, Bishop General of the Order of Schueler and Grand Inquisitor of the Church of God Awaiting, regarded the Archbishop of Chiang-wu with cold, unhappy eyes. His expression was no more cheerful than his eyes, and most members of the Order of Schueler would have felt a cold, solid lump of panic, resting in their bellies like a frozen round shot, had Clyntahn turned those eyes and that expression upon *them*.

If Wyllym Rayno felt any panic, however, he concealed it well.

"Not, I'm afraid, on the front you're inquiring about, Your Grace," he said with remarkable calm. "The latest reports from Corisande do indicate that things may be taking a turn in Mother Church's favor there, but they're very preliminary, and like every message from Corisande these days, rather badly out-of-date. The shipbuilding programs—in the ice-free ports, at least—seem to be proceeding fairly well, although there are still bottlenecks and delays. Earl Thirsk seems to be making excellent progress with his training efforts, and Tarot has finally begun its share of the building program. And, of course, I've shared Seablanket's reports on the Earl of Coris' . . . suitability to Mother Church's ends." He smiled faintly. "None of which touches upon the matter about which you were inquiring, does it, Your Grace?"

"No, Wyllym. It doesn't." There might have been a glimmer of respect for Rayno's calm demeanor in the backs of Clyntahn's eyes. On the other hand, there might not have been, too. "So why don't you address the point I *was* raising?"

"Very well, Your Grace." Rayno bowed slightly. "We've had no success since my last report in locating the traitors' families. They appear to have vanished from the face of the world."

"I see." Clyntahn seemed unsurprised by Rayno's admission. He leaned back in his chair, gazing across his desk at the Adjutant General of the Order of Schueler, and folded his hands across his belly. "I imagine you've figured out that I'm not very happy about this, Wyllym," he said with a thin, cold smile.

"Of course I'm aware of that, Your Grace. In fact, I would imagine I'm probably almost as unhappy about it as you are. Would you prefer that I promise you we're making progress on finding them when, in fact, I know we're not?"

Clyntahn's eyes glittered for a moment, but then his nostrils flared as he inhaled deeply.

"No, I wouldn't prefer that," he acknowledged, and it was true.

One of the reasons he valued Rayno so highly was that the adjutant general wouldn't lie in an effort to cover his own posterior . . . or failures. Clyntahn was certain there had been occasions upon which Rayno had "managed" news by refraining from bringing things to his attention at an inopportune moment. That was quite a different matter, however, from lying outright, and Clyntahn had encountered more than enough people who were stupid enough to do just that. They didn't seem to consider the fact that, sooner or later, the Grand Inquisitor would discover the lie, at which point the consequences would be even worse.

He had additional reasons for valuing Rayno, though. Among them was the fact that the archbishop had amply demonstrated his own loyalty. More than that, Clyntahn knew Rayno was well aware he himself could never aspire to the Grand Inquisitor's chair. He had too many enemies, and not enough leverage to overcome them, which meant his present position was as high as he could hope to go . . . and that he would certainly lose the one he had if Clyntahn fell from power or withdrew his support. Which meant Rayno had every reason to serve his superior with steadfast loyalty.

Besides, the adjutant general was extremely good at what he did. True, Samyl Wylsynn's family had slipped through his fingers on the very doorstep of Zion, but that wasn't Rayno's fault. He'd had the woman and her brats under surveillance by no less than three of his most trusted Inquisitors . . . all of whom had *also* disappeared that same evening. Clyntahn had come to the conclusion that at least one of those Inquisitors must, in fact, have been a traitor. Preposterous though that might be, it was the only answer to Lysbet Wylsynn's successful disappearance he could come up with, yet he had personally reviewed the records of all three of the missing men. If one of them *had* turned traitor, nothing anywhere in his file would have suggested that possibility in advance. Clyntahn certainly hadn't seen anything which suggested to *him* that Rayno should have seen it coming, at any rate. And the adjutant general's current failure to locate the families of no less than three vicars and two archbishops who *had* made it to Zion—families they *knew* were almost certainly somewhere under their very noses, even now—was extremely unusual. In fact, the Grand Inquisitor could think of only one other occasion in which Rayno had suffered a similar failure.

"So there's been no progress at all?"

"None, I regret to say, Your Grace." Rayno shook his head. "There's been no communication between any of them since they disappeared, and our agents throughout the city haven't turned up a single trace." He paused a moment, then cocked his head. "We could always have Stantyn inquire about them."

"No." Clyntahn shook his own head instantly. "We might as well go ahead and ask them ourselves! For that matter, given the fact that we can't find their families, we have to at least consider the possibility that they might slip through our fingers themselves if they thought we were about to pounce."

Rayno nodded, although he wasn't positive he agreed with his superior in this case. Nyklas Stantyn, the Archbishop of Hankey, was Clyntahn's mole within the group of reform-minded vicars who called themselves "the Circle." In fact, it was Stantyn who'd first revealed the Circle's existence to the Grand Inquisitor. It seemed obvious to Rayno that the other members of the Circle— or its leadership, at least—must realize one of their number had betrayed them, although they obviously didn't know who. Personally, Rayno was at least half-inclined to stake Stantyn out. There were a couple of members of the Circle— Hauwerd Wylsynn came to mind—who Rayno rather suspected would come out into the open to cut Stantyn's throat. It wouldn't save them in the end, but they'd probably take a certain satisfaction out of it anyway. And when they did, it would be conclusive proof of their own guilt which could be readily displayed for the remainder of the vicarate. It would be a bit hard on Stantyn, but his value would disappear anyway the moment the Circle was broken. In Rayno's opinion, he'd be far more useful at that point as a martyr whose death would have underscored the Circle's treason.

And if it didn't underscore that treason, Stantyn would be no great loss, anyway.

As far as the renegades' realizing Clyntahn was simply biding his time before having them arrested, Rayno was certain they must have already recognized what was coming. At least one vicar who'd been a member of the Circle for over ten years, according to Stantyn, had committed suicide the month before. Two more had perished in what looked like accidental deaths, although Rayno was confident appearances were deceiving.

*No, all three of them killed themselves,* he thought again. *They decided that would be an easier end than the one* The Book of Schueler *lays down for heretics. And they probably decided it was the only way to keep the Inquisition from going after the remaining members of their families, as well.*

He didn't know if they'd been right about that last point, or not. That would be Clyntahn's decision, and while the Grand Inquisitor's first inclination would undoubtedly be to make examples out of the traitors' families, as well, he might choose not to. If he held his hand in that regard, it might encourage future enemies to take the same escape—remove themselves from the vicar's path without putting him to the bother of having them removed. It would be interesting to see which approach Clyntahn chose in the end.

*And for now,* Rayno thought dispassionately, *he's enjoying the knowledge that the others* have *realized what's coming. It's not as if they could get far in the coldest month of a Zion winter even if they tried to run, and in the meantime, they have to see him every day and know what's going to happen to them. And so does everyone else in the vicarate, whether they're willing to admit it or not.*

That was the real reason Clyntahn had waited so long, Rayno was certain. It wasn't something the Grand Inquisitor was going to discuss in detail even with him, but Rayno hadn't served Clyntahn so long and so well without realizing how the vicar thought.

Clyntahn had deliberately stoked the steadily growing fear within the vicarate, but not out of simple sadism, or even out of a simple desire to punish those who'd dared to challenge the Group of Four's control. No. He'd used the gnawing terror to hone the internal, factional tensions which always afflicted the Temple during the winter months to an even sharper, more dangerous edge. He'd wanted to force decisions, to drive even those who'd traditionally attempted to stand aloof from the vicarate's internal political struggles to choose sides. To commit themselves. And he'd wanted them to do it under circumstances *he* controlled. His own command of the Inquisition, and Allayn Maigwair's command of the Temple Guard, gave the Group of Four an absolute monopoly on force within the Temple and Zion, and the winter had trapped all of Mother Church's highest hierarchy right here. There was, quite literally, no countervailing force, which meant everyone knew Clyntahn was in a position to bring the full, sledgehammer repressive power of his office down on anyone who marked himself out as the Group of Four's enemy.

In the face of that sort of threat, it was scarcely surprising that even many who nursed serious doubts as to the Group of Four's handling of the crisis had found themselves looking for ways to prove their loyalty. To curry favor like a frightened dog, licking the hand which threatened to beat it in the hope of buying some sort of mercy. Or, at least, of securing short-term survival. Because even the dimmest dullard had to recognize that without *short-term* survival, there could be no *long-term* survival.

No doubt it did amuse Clyntahn to use enemies and rivals to serve his own political ends. In fact, Rayno never doubted it did, and he supposed the streak of cruelty, even sadism, that demonstrated was a serious flaw. Yet he'd come to the conclusion long ago that all men had flaws, and that the greater the man, the greater the flaw tended to be. And the fact that Clyntahn *enjoyed* making his enemies suffer made his strategy no less effective. Besides, it wasn't as if any other strategy had ever truly been possible, for there could be no rapprochement between Samyl Wylsynn and Zhaspahr Clyntahn. It simply couldn't happen—if for no other reason, because Clyntahn would expect other potential adversaries to see it as an act of weakness on his own part. As an accommodation he'd sought because he doubted the strength of his iron fist. It was essential he prove he entertained no such doubt . . . and that he would not tolerate that doubt's existence in any other vicar's mind.

To do that, he must *use* that strength. He *had* to crush his enemies, openly and utterly, and so he would. He might delay the moment, might stretch out the agonizing anticipation, in order to force others to offer him their submission, but the ultimate outcome had never been in doubt. It *could* never have been in doubt, lest it be seen as hesitation or timidity on his part.

Rayno understood that, and his own estimate was that Clyntahn had accomplished virtually all of his goals. Further delay would achieve very little in terms of the internal dynamic of the members of the vicarate likely to survive the coming purge. Which meant that, at this point, Clyntahn was holding his hand for purely personal reasons. Having achieved his political objectives in all their essentials, he was treating himself to the predatory satisfaction of watching his doomed foes suffering all the anguish of anticipation.

*And if anyone else realizes that's what he's doing, it will only make them even more terrified of crossing him in the future. So even now, he's still killing two wyverns with a single stone, as it were.*

The only flaw in the Grand Inquisitor's satisfaction was the possibility that some of his enemies' families might escape him after all, but neither he nor Rayno were concerned by the possibility that anyone who hadn't already disappeared might do the same. Rayno still hadn't figured out how the missing family members—and especially the Wylsynns—had managed to vanish so thoroughly, although he'd come to suspect there was an additional player in the game. One Stantyn didn't know about and so had been unable to betray. There was a sense of . . . craftsmanship to the families' disappearances which reminded Rayno strongly of the disappearance of Archbishop Erayk Dynnys' family. He still hadn't been able to figure out how *that* had happened, either, but he'd developed a grudging respect for whoever had managed to get them out of the Temple Lands and into Charis without leaving a single footprint behind. The adjutant general would cheerfully officiate over the fellow's execution, whoever he might be, but he did respect the quality of his opponent.

However good that opponent might be, however, none of the other families were going to disappear. All of them were under constant surveillance, and he'd handpicked the Inquisitors responsible for keeping them that way. Of course, he'd done that in the Wylsynns' case, as well, but this time he'd assigned double teams to each family, and it struck him as extraordinaily unlikely that he could have *that* many traitors (if that was truly what had happened in the Wylsynns' case) in his own ranks. No, the *other* families weren't going anywhere without his knowledge. In fact, he rather wished some of them would make the attempt. If they did, they might yet lead his Inquisitors to the others, and he'd become privately convinced that that was the only way he was going to find those others at this point.

Not that he had any intention of giving up the hunt. And meantime . . .

"Have you given any more thought to exactly when you wish to have them arrested, Your Grace?" he asked after a moment.

"I think we can give them another five-day or so, don't you, Wyllym?" The adjutant general's question seemed to have restored the Grand Inquisitor's humor, and he smiled jovially. "There's no need to cut the others' time with their families short, now is there?"

"I suppose not, Your Grace." Rayno returned his superior's smile with rather more restraint.

Unlike Clyntahn, Rayno would take no personal satisfaction from the Grand Inquisitor's enemies' destruction. Nor was he particularly looking forward to having the members of their families put to the Question in front of them. It was, he acknowledged, one of the most effective of the Schuelerites' techniques for extracting information, and their inability to apply it to the family members who had escaped probably helped explain at least some of Clyntahn's frustration. For himself, however, Rayno would be just as happy to avoid as much of that sort of thing as he could. It was unlikely to be necessary, in any case. They had plenty of evidence already, they could count upon the accused to confess in the end (the accused always *did* confess in the end, didn't they?), and aside from a few junior bishops and archbishops who'd managed to get out of the city before winter closed in, they could put their hands upon the guilty parties anytime they chose.

Even those who'd contrived to get out of Zion had only delayed the inevitable. They were all being watched by trusted Inquisitors who were simply waiting for the semaphore message to take them into custody.

*I suppose it's remotely possible one or two of them might manage to escape, at least briefly. But not more than one or two . . . and anyone who does run won't get far.*

▼    ▼    ▼

No one who knew Lysbet Wylsynn would have recognized her in "Chantahal Blahndai's" warm, but extremely plain, Harchong-style poncho, worn over an equally utilitarian hooded, woolen coat. At least, Lysbet thought, as she tucked her mittened hands into her armpits under the poncho, burrowed her chin deeper into her woven muffler, and hunched her head against the wind, she devoutly hoped they wouldn't have.

She'd always hated Zion in the winter. Her husband's estates lay in the southern Temple Lands, just across the border from the Princedom of Tanshar. Lysbet's own family, although it had connections to quite a few of the great Church dynasties, was Tansharan, and while winter could be cold enough along the Gulf of Tanshar, it was never as bitterly frigid as winter in Zion. Her husband had been born barely five miles on the Temple Lands' side of the border, and he fully understood—and shared—her distaste for Zion winters. He seldom insisted that she join him here for the winter months.

He hadn't planned on her joining him this winter, either, and for considerably more weighty reasons than her dislike for snow. In fact, he'd sent her word (very discreetly) that he thought it would be wise for her to make alternate travel plans. Unfortunately, she'd become aware, even before his message arrived, of the fact that she and the children were being watched.

It hadn't been anything most people would have noticed, but Lysbet Wylsynn wasn't "most people." She was a smart, observant woman who'd recognized when she accepted Samyl Wylsynn's proposal that wedding a husband from that particular dynasty was inevitably going to embroil her in Temple politics. The notion had repelled her, but despite the differences in their ages, Samyl most definitely had *not*—her lips twitched in bittersweet memory—and she'd shared his outrage over what Mother Church had become.

She hadn't expected things to get this bad. Not really. No one ever *really* expected the end of their world, even when they genuinely thought they were prepared for it. Yet she'd always been at least intellectually prepared for the possibility of disaster, and over the last couple of years—especially since the Group of Four's disastrous assault on the Kingdom of Charis—she'd been quietly taking precautions of her own. And unlike the other members of Samyl's Circle within the vicarate, Lysbet had known who the true hub for the Reformists' communications had been. When Adorai Dynnys had been forced to flee to Charis following her husband's arrest, she'd passed her own responsibilities on to Lysbet. In the process, she'd had to give Lysbet certain information only Adorai and Samyl had possessed, which meant Lysbet had become aware of Ahnzhelyk Phonda's importance to the Circle . . . even though almost no one else *in* the Circle had entertained the least suspicion of that importance.

So far as Lysbet knew, she and Samyl—and Samyl's brother, Hauwerd—were now the only people in the Temple Lands who knew about Ahnzhelyk's connection to the Circle at all. So when she'd realized she and the children were being watched, that any effort to flee would be instantly intercepted, she'd decided on a plan of her own. Instead of staying away from Zion, she'd written—openly, using her privileges as a senior vicar's wife to send it over the Church semaphore—to tell Samyl she'd be joining him there this winter, after all. And she'd made arrangements to do just that.

Then she'd made rather *different* (and much quieter) arrangements with Ahnzhelyk. She hadn't expected all three of the Inquisitors who'd been spying on her to end up dead in the process, but she hadn't shed any hypocritical tears over their demises, either. Unfortunately, Ahnzhelyk's initial plan to immediately get her and the children out of the Temple Lands had proved unworkable in light of the clandestine but intense search for them which Wyllym Rayno had instigated. The open hunt for her family's "abductors" would have been a serious obstacle under the best of circumstances, yet it was Rayno's ruthlessly efficient *secret* hunt which had inspired Ahnzhelyk's caution.

*And her determination to get as many other families out of the city as she can,* Lysbet reminded herself now. The selfish mother in her—the mother who wanted *her* children in safety, and Shan-wei with anyone *else's* children!—bitterly resented that decision on Ahnzhelyk's part. Most of her, though, agreed entirely. Despite her terror for her own family's safety, she knew that simply abandoning anyone else they could have saved would have been a betrayal of everything the Circle had ever stood for.

And since her husband, and her brother-in-law, and most of their dearest friends in the vicarate were going to *die* for what the Circle had stood for, Lysbet Wylsynn could no more have betrayed their cause than Ahnzhelyk could.

None of which had made the nerve-racking five-days hiding here in Zion, the city which had become the heart of the beast itself, any easier to endure. The good news was that Chantahal Blahndai didn't look at all like Lysbet Wylsynn. She was older, her hair was a different color, she had a prominent mole on her chin, and she was at least thirty pounds heavier than slender, youthful Madame Wylsynn. Not only that, but whereas Madame Wylsynn had been accompanied by both of her sons and her daughter when she disappeared, Chantahal had only a single son.

It was amazing how skilled someone who'd followed Ahnzhelyk's vocation became when it came to matters of cosmetics and hair dye, and winter clothing made it far easier to pad one's figure without anyone noticing. And while most mothers wouldn't normally have wanted their twelve-year-old daughters and eight-year-old sons spending the winter in what was, however elegant it might be, a "house of ill repute," Lysbet had no concern in Zhanayt's or Archbahld's case. In fact, she couldn't think of anyplace they might have been safer, and her greatest concern had been that one of them—especially Archbahld, in view of his youth—might inadvertently betray them all to the Inquisition.

Her older son, Tohmys, on the other hand, was fourteen now—a serious boy who already shared his father's sorrow (and anger) over what Mother Church had become. He was his uncle's nephew, as well, however. Like Hauwerd, he'd been headed for a career in the Temple Guard, and despite his youth, he was a skilled swordsman and an excellent shot, whether with a matchlock musket, an arbalest, or a standard bow. He was also fiercely protective of his mother, and he'd flatly refused to join his younger brother and sister in hiding.

Truth to tell, Lysbet hadn't tried all that hard to convince him to do so. Partly because she recognized his father's son and knew a futile endeavor when she saw one. But mostly because as much as she trusted Ahnzhelyk, and as effective as Ahnzhelyk had always proved herself to be, Lysbet hadn't quite been able to bring herself to put all of her eggs in one basket. Which was also the reason Ahnzhelyk had made completely different arrangements to whisk Lysbet's oldest daughter (well, stepdaughter, technically, although she was the only mother Erais had ever actually known) and her husband and son out from under the Inquisition's nose. Lysbet suspected that her own willingness to come to Zion had been a factor in Ahnzhelyk's ability to do just that. She'd been so clearly willing to walk directly into the spider's web that the Inquisition's vigilance over Sir Fraihman Zhardeau and his wife and son had lapsed, at least a little.

She'd rejoiced in quiet, fervent gratitude when Ahnzhelyk got her word that Fraihman, Erais, and young Samyl had made good their escape . . . at least for the present. But now, under a wind-polished sky of frozen blue, as she made her way along an icy sidewalk half-blocked by overnight snowdrifts, their centers trampled down by the feet of earlier traffic, she felt the familiar weight of despair. Not for her own safety, and not really for the safety of her children and grandchild—although that was a much sharper, more bitter-edged anxiety than any she might feel for herself. She had no intention of becoming careless, yet she'd come to the conclusion that if the Inquisition had been going to find her or her children, they would have done so by now. No, the despair she felt was not for herself, but for her husband and all he'd striven for so long to accomplish. For the friends and trusted colleagues who'd given him their allegiance and their assistance . . . and who were going to share in his agonizing death when the moment came.

*It's not as if he tricked or deceived any of them into supporting him,* she thought, hugging herself more tightly under her poncho as the keen-toothed wind whistled between the tenements on either side of the street. *All of them were as angry and determined as he was, and all of them knew this could happen. Yet to know it is going to happen, that someone like that greedy, bloody-minded bastard Clyntahn is going to win after all . . .*

Lysbet had no way of knowing how her own thoughts, her own anger at God for allowing this to happen, mirrored her brother-in-law's reaction. If she had known, it wouldn't have surprised her; she'd known Hauwerd as long as she'd known Samyl, and in many ways, she and Hauwerd were more alike than she and Samyl. Which was probably the reason she'd been so much more strongly attracted to Samyl from the very beginning than she'd ever been drawn to Hauwerd—as a husband and a lover, at least. As a brother-in-law, he'd always been her favorite. Dearer to her, in fact (though she would never have admitted it), than either of her birth brothers. There was a reason she'd been so content to see Tohmys taking so strongly after his uncle, for she couldn't imagine a better pattern he could have chosen for himself.

She reached the corner where Hahriman Street met Market Street, halfway between her cheap, spartanly furnished tenement apartment and Zion's third largest market, and glanced across the street at the milliner's.

She didn't even pause as she turned the corner, and her stride never hesitated, but her eyes first widened, then narrowed, as she saw the shop window. A bolt of blue fabric—steel thistle silk, she thought—was displayed in that window, and the shop's coal heaver must have spilled a couple of large lumps of coal just on the other side of the barred delivery gate when he made the morning's delivery. Someone had spilled them there, at least. Lysbet could see the glittering black chunks, starkly visible against the dirty snow, just far enough inside the gate that none of the city's desperate poor could glean them.

It took only a single glance to note the silk and the coal, and she bent her head a little more deeply as she found herself walking directly into the wind, now.

She would continue to the market, she thought. It was Chantahal's regular shopping day, and she would chaffer for the ruinously expensive potatoes and winter-woody carrots she'd come to purchase. She might even pick up a few onions, assuming they weren't *too* pricey this late in the winter, before she headed back to her tenement once more.

Whatever she did, however, she would give no sign, and no indication at all, that she'd seen that blue silk or those lumps of coal.

That she'd recognized in them Ahnzhelyk's warning to be ready to move on an instant's notice.

.XVI.

Madame Ahnzhelyk's Townhouse
and
The Temple,
City of Zion,
The Temple Lands

Ahbraim Zhevons gazed into the mirror at his hazel eyes and brown hair. There was a faint—very faint—"family resemblance" to Merlin Athrawes and Nimue Alban, he thought. Something about the lips that he hadn't managed to randomize as much as he'd intended. He wondered if his subconscious had been responsible for that, or if it was simply a quirk in the PICA software which had carried over. Prior to her cybernetic reincarnation, Nimue had never been particularly interested in the software which allowed a PICA's appearance to be modified at will. She'd been more interested in its applications for extreme sports. For that matter, she'd never really *wanted* a PICA at all; it had been a gift from her wealthy father she simply hadn't had the heart to turn down. So she was nowhere near as well versed in the "cosmetic" aspects of her current physical avatar as she might have been, and it *was* possible something in its software might have been responsible for the carryover.

*Sure it could have been,* "Ahbraim" thought sardonically. *But it wasn't. You know that perfectly well, Merlin.*

It was odd, he thought, turning away from the mirror. He still thought of himself as "Merlin," rather than as Nimue or Ahbraim. Probably because that was who he'd been for the last few years. Or, possibly, because he'd finally accepted that Nimue was dead and he was someone else, entirely. Or, possibly again, simply because he needed a single identity upon which to hang his sense of personhood if he wasn't going to go completely off the deep end. Which might also explain that little glitch about the lips.

*Well, no one's going to notice anyway, even if they've seen both Ahbraim and Merlin,* he told himself. *Not once Merlin regrows his mustache and his beard, at any rate.*

He looked out the window of his hotel room. It was snowing again. It did a lot of that here in Zion, and he wondered once more if the "Archangels'" choice of the city's site had been made solely to make the "mystically maintained" internal comfort of the Temple even more impressive to those who beheld it. More probably, though, he'd decided, the original decision to put the colony's planetary HQ in this particular spot had been made because the climate was so bad it was likely to discourage the low-tech colonists and their descendants from settling in the area. Back before the destruction of the

Alexandria Enclave (and Commodore Pei's retaliatory attack on Langhorne and Bédard), there'd *been* no Temple. Merlin had come to suspect that Langhorne and Bédard had seen the site of their headquarters as something along the lines of a barely accessible Mount Olympus—somewhere beyond the normal reach of mere mortals, yet with sufficient proximity to those mortals' world to provide a sense of Archangels hovering permanently just over the horizon. The climate wouldn't have been a problem for *them,* after all, and the "fabulous palaces of the Archangels" would have helped bolster the command crew's divine status for any colonists who did visit here.

He had no proof of that, of course. On the other hand, a couple of references in Commodore Pei's download had hinted at that sort of thinking, and it was entirely probable that Chihiro and Schueler (who'd apparently emerged as the "Archangels'" leaders after Commodore Pei's vest-pocket nuke destroyed the original HQ) had followed the same line of thought. And it was also distinctly probable that they'd deliberately rebuilt on the same spot to emphasize the victory of "the powers of Light" over "Shan-wei's Dark legions from Hell," as well. Just as they'd built the entire Temple as a tangible reminder of the "Archangels'" power.

*It would've made sense, in a way,* Merlin thought again, watching snowflakes dance on the sharp-edged, steadily rising wind. *After so many of Langhorne's people went up in the Commodore's fireball, they'd need something to remind the colonists the "Archangels" had won after all. Might've been a bit hard to convince everyone of that, given the casualties they'd taken, without something pretty drastic to drive the point home.*

Whatever the logic behind it, it was a thoroughly miserable place to put the planet Safehold's biggest city—in the winter, at least. In the summer, it was quite a different matter. On the other hand, "summer" in Zion was a fleeting experience. One that wouldn't be around again for quite some time, which had unfortunate implications for "Ahbraim's" immediate future plans.

As he'd told Maikel Staynair, he'd kept a surreptitious eye on Ahnzhelyk Phonda ever since Adorai Dynnys' astounding revelations had suggested just how much more Ahnzhelyk was than Merlin had originally assumed. He'd taken extraordinary precautions, using remotes that recorded their data and were then physically retrieved, rather than transmitting—however stealthily—to his orbital communications arrays. That had bottlenecked his surveillance badly, but it had also provided an additional level of security which, given those power sources under the Temple, had seemed highly advisable.

It had also, unfortunately, made it impossible for him—or Owl—to reposition those remotes "on-the-fly" the way they could elsewhere. In Zion, he couldn't move his pickups to independently track individuals the way he could anywhere else on the planet, which meant he had far less complete information than he could wish he had. Despite that, however, he'd realized over the last five-day that Ahnzhelyk had been at her dangerous game even longer than he'd assumed after Adorai's revelations. In fact, he'd come to the conclusion that Ahnzhelyk had probably contacted Samyl Wylsynn, rather than the reverse.

Merlin had resisted that possibility when he first became aware of it. Not because of any doubts about Ahnzhelyk's capabilities, but because she'd obviously been "only" the communications relay for Wylsynn's organization. Given what Merlin had seen of young Paityr Wylsynn in Charis, and what he'd been able to glean from what his Tellesberg remotes had been able to examine—once Staynair had agreed to permit it—of the documents Adorai had delivered to the archbishop, it was apparent that the Wylsynn family's involvement in efforts to reform the Vicarate had been a multigenerational affair. On that basis, it had been obvious Samyl must have recruited Ahnzhelyk.

*But that isn't what happened at all,* he mused. *Unless I'm mistaken, what really happened is that Ahnzhelyk became aware of his organization and put herself at his service to manage his communications. But she had her own organization, already up and running, before she ever contacted him, and she never combined the two. That's why she was able to get Adorai and her boys out of the Temple Lands so smoothly. And it's how she managed to "disappear" Lysbet Wylsynn and the others.*

They were still quite a lot of things about Ahnzhelyk Phonda that he *hadn't* figured out. Of course, the fact that *he* couldn't figure them out, even with all of the advantages he enjoyed—even here in Zion, despite his limitations compared to other realms—probably helped explain how she'd managed to avoid the Inquisition's notice for so long. It also meant he had absolutely no idea how she'd contacted the other five families she'd hidden away right here in Zion. The one thing he *had* decided upon, where that was concerned, was that, once more, she was the one who'd done the contacting.

He'd finally managed to locate Lysbet and Tohmys Wylsynn, and studying the take from the bugs he'd planted on Lysbet, he'd realized Samyl Wylsynn must have seen what was coming but been unwilling—or unable—to inform the rest of the Circle. Merlin found it difficult to conceive of what could have kept a man of Wylsynn's obvious integrity from passing that information on, but he was fairly confident that was what had happened. Yet it was equally apparent that *Ahnzhelyk* had been aware of it. From all indications, it was she who'd initiated her original contact with the other families and who'd smuggled them into hiding without ever discussing it with their husbands and fathers.

*Those poor bastards are probably wondering whether their wives and children have managed to evade Clyntahn—so far, at least—or whether the bastard has them in custody somewhere already,* Merlin thought grimly. *God, I hadn't realized how sadistic he really is. If the Circle—or Wylsynn, at least—has seen this coming for as long as I think, then that sick, twisted son-of-a-bitch has been watching them squirm for months. And from everything I've been able to see, he's been enjoying the hell out of it.*

Zhaspahr Clyntahn had no idea how fortunate he was that he never left the Temple's precincts. If he ever did—if he ever once strayed into an area where Merlin could get at him without risking triggering some unidentified sensor system or automated response in the Temple—he was a dead man. There was no question, no hesitation, about that on Merlin's part.

But it also wasn't something that was going to happen. Not anytime soon, at any rate. Not soon enough to save any of Clyntahn's present list of victims. Merlin had been forced to accept that, and his focus now was on getting those family members—and as much of the rest of Ahnzhelyk's organization, however large or small it was, as he could—out of the Temple Lands.

Which was rather the point of this evening's visit, he reminded himself, and reached for Zhevons' coat.

▼     ▼     ▼

"Good evening, Ahbraim," Ahnzhelyk Phonda said with a welcoming smile.

"Good evening, my dear!" Merlin bent over her hand once again, kissing it gallantly. *Maybe one reason I think of myself as "Merlin" instead of Nimue,* he thought, *is that Nimue was never interested in other women. Merlin, on the other hand . . .*

He set that consideration aside once more, although he really wasn't sure whether it was legitimately a case of Merlin being interested in "other women," or of Merlin being interested in the "opposite sex" (whichever sex that happened to be at the moment), or of Merlin having discovered something about himself that Nimue had never suspected about *herself,* or simply of Merlin finding something else to worry about that wouldn't have mattered to anyone else on the entire planet.

"I'm glad you could join us this evening," Ahnzhelyk continued. "Although I'm afraid company's going to be a bit sparse on a night like this."

"I'm not surprised." Merlin cocked his head, listening to the wind-howl keen around the eves of Ahnzhelyk's townhouse.

The temperature outside was eight degrees below zero—eight *Fahrenheit* degrees below zero—and still falling. The wind was gusting to speeds of almost forty miles per hour, too, and Merlin was grimly aware that even as he stood in the comfortable warmth of Ahnzhelyk's townhouse, men and women—yes, and their children—were freezing to death, literally, outside it. He knew about the gardener's shed on Ahnzhelyk's grounds, and about the four poor families who had moved into it this winter. He knew how she'd weatherproofed it, the way she did every winter. How she'd made sure there was enough coal for the ceramic stove she'd had installed. And he knew how, despite her best efforts, the members of those families were huddled together, sharing body warmth as well as the life-giving heat of that stove. They would be cold, stiff, and miserable, and he doubted any of them would really sleep, as violently as they were shivering. Yet in the morning, unlike all too many of the poor huddled for warmth around the waste heat vents of the Temple's environmental system, they'd be alive.

*And she knows exactly what's going on out there,* Merlin thought, looking at his hostess' smiling face. *The same woman who's gone to such lengths to give them the chance to survive, who's organized Wylsynn's communications and hidden those families of refugees somewhere here in Zion, is smiling and laughing as if she doesn't have a care in the world.*

He felt his admiration click up another notch, and he tucked her hand into the bend of his elbow, and escorted her across the sitting room to one of the buffet tables. A servant offered him a plate piled high with choice delicacies— rolls of ham, thin slivers of rare beef, breast of wyvern and chicken, spider shrimp, olives, deviled eggs, pickles, cheese, bread. . . . There was enough food on the table to feed the people huddled in Ahnzhelyk's gardener's shed for at least a month, he reflected. And on any given morning, he knew, that was precisely where the "leftovers" from the previous evening's buffet went. There and to one of the soup kitchens operated by the Order of Bédard.

*And there's another thing that pisses me off,* he reflected. *If any of the other original "Archangels" was Langhorne's enabler, it was Bédard. And—I know it's stupid, damn it!—but I'd really prefer for "her" order to be as sick and twisted as the Order of Schueler, and it's not. Not anymore, anyway. Why can't the original villains of the piece still be the villains?*

"I believe Mahrlys has kept her schedule clear for you this evening, Ah-braim," Ahnzhelyk told him with a smile, and he smiled back.

"Actually," he said quietly, turning to survey the all but deserted sitting room, "charming as Mahrlys is, and as much as I've enjoyed her company, I came to speak with you tonight."

"Ah?" She cocked an eyebrow at him, and he smiled faintly.

"I'm not sure," his expression was that of a man exchanging inconsequential small talk with his beautiful hostess, "but I think time is running out."

He met her eyes for a moment, then looked back out across the room.

"Yes, I'm afraid it is." She smiled up at him, obviously amused by whatever he'd just said, but her soft voice was ineffably sad. "I'd hoped I could get a few more people out," she went on. "Unfortunately, I can't. There's no time."

"No?" It was his turn to raise an eyebrow, and she shook her head.

"I have a source inside the Inquisition. Clyntahn is moving tomorrow."

"Against you?" Despite himself, despite even the fact that he was a PICA, and not a creature of flesh and blood, Merlin couldn't quite keep the concern out of his voice and eyes.

"I don't think so," she replied. "Not immediately, at any rate. But when he starts putting people to the Question . . ."

She let her voice trail off, and he nodded slightly, but his thoughts were racing. Unlike Ahnzhelyk, he had access to an entire network of weather satellites. He knew this evening's howling wind and plunging temperatures would ease somewhat over the next couple of days, but there was another winter storm coming behind the thaw. One which was going to be at least this bad.

"Is there someplace here in the city where you can go to ground for a five-day or two?"

"If I have to," she said, and then smiled faintly. "Why? Is one of those 'seijin-like' skills of yours telling you something I don't know, Ahbraim?"

"Something like that," he told her with an answering smile. "The weather's going to be unusually severe for the next few days." She looked the slightest bit skeptical, and he patted her hand with his free hand. "Just trust me, Ahnzhelyk. If we can avoid it, we don't want you—or any of the others—trying to travel."

She regarded him thoughtfully for a moment, then shrugged.

"It's going to take a day or so for me to get the actual movement out of the city organized, anyway," she said. "And, to be honest, it probably won't hurt to have a few more days to work with. Assuming I've been as successful as I think I have in building my bolt-holes!"

"I think you have," he assured her.

"Well." She looked around the sitting room for a moment, then shrugged again. "I'll miss this place," she said, almost wistfully. "I've accomplished at least a few useful things here. I only wish I hadn't failed so completely in the end."

"You haven't failed," he told her quietly. She looked back up at him, and he shook his head. "Trust me, the Group of Four's days—the *Temple's* days—are numbered. It's going to take longer than you or I would like, but it's going to happen, and people like you and Adorai Dynnys are one of the reasons it is."

"But how many are going to die, first, Ahbraim?" she asked sadly, her expression still that of a woman chatting idly with a favored guest. "How many people are going to die, first?"

"Too many," he said, unflinchingly. "But it's not your doing, or your fault, and there are going to be a lot fewer of them, thanks to you, than there would have been otherwise. So, if you don't mind, instead of worrying about how completely you've 'failed,' let's just see about getting you and as many of those other people out of this alive as we can, all right?"

▼ ▼ ▼

Captain Khanstahnzo Phandys of the Temple Guard walked swiftly down the Temple hallway. He wore the polished steel cuirass and scarlet tunic of the Guard over a heavy woolen sweater that was just a bit too warm here inside the Temple proper. His sword was sheathed at his hip, his gloves were tucked under his belt, and although he'd shed his heavy coat at the cloakroom when he entered the

Temple, his tall boots and the legs of his breeches were dotted with the wet spots left by melted snow.

Captain Phandys' expression was not a happy one, but he was scarcely alone in that, these days. In fact, he'd discovered that quite a few of his fellow Guard officers were obviously on edge this morning, as well, and there was something invisible in the air—something unseen, scentless, impossible to touch, yet all-pervasive.

It was scarcely the first time that had been true over the three years since the cataclysmic failure of the attack on the heretical Kingdom of Charis. That had been the sort of earthquake which came along perhaps once in a hundred years, Phandys thought now. It wasn't the sort of thing a mere Guard captain was supposed to be thinking, but there was no point pretending he didn't know it was true. Just as there was no point pretending that the tremors which the subsequent defection of Chisholm, Emerald, and Zebediah and the conquest of Corisande had sent through the Temple and the ranks of the vicarate hadn't been even more deadly, in their own way.

For most subjects of the mainland realms, all of those distant lands were unimportant, lost beyond the periphery of their own interests. Besides, while Charis' wealth might be the stuff of fabulous (and envious) legend, the island kingdom's population was surely too small to pose any threat to the power of such great realms as Desnair, Dohlar, Harchong, even the Republic of Siddarmark. The very notion was ridiculous . . . and that completely overlooked the fact that God, in His wisdom, would never permit the aggression of such apostate and heretical lands to prosper!

Yet those who wore Mother Church's orange had a somewhat different view of things. Little though they might care to admit it—and, indeed, many flatly *refused* to admit it—they knew the rebellion of the "Church of Charis" had found frightening echoes in the other lands of the newborn Charisian Empire. They had begun to realize, however dimly, that people like Samyl and Hauwerd Wylsynn might have had a point all along. That the luxurious lifestyles and personal power to which they had become accustomed might not actually be quite so universally beloved and approved of as they'd told one another.

That in its attack on Charis, the Group of Four might just have unleashed forces which could destroy them all.

Such considerations were the business of those who far outranked Captain Phandys, and he knew it. He wasn't an idiot, however, and his assignment to the Courier Service had put him in an ideal position to recognize what was going on, since so many of the messages about world events passed through his hands. And even if that hadn't been true, he'd been stationed here in the Temple for over two years now. During those years—and especially this past winter—he'd seen how things had changed since his last Temple tour. He'd seen what others had seen, recognized what others recognized, and there was no doubt in his mind that Grand Inquisitor Zhaspahr and Phandys' own ultimate superior, Captain General Maigwair, had decided they could not afford to be threatened on more than one front at a time.

Which was precisely what brought Phandys here today, when he was supposed to be in his own office down in the Courier Service's lakeside annex.

He reached a cross hallway and turned left. A pair of vicars stood by one of the windows, gazing out into the frozen early morning. Their heads popped up, like startled wyverns, as Phandys appeared. They actually flinched, visibly, before they got themselves back under control, and the captain wondered what they'd been talking about so quietly. Given the way they'd reacted to the appearance of a mere Guard captain, it was probably something they *shouldn't* have been discussing . . . as far as the Group of Four was concerned, at least, he reflected grimly. There'd been a lot of that going around lately.

Khanstahnzo Phandys had served in the Temple Guard for over fifteen years, and this was his fourth tour here in the Temple itself. In all those years, however, he'd never seen a winter like this one. Never seen the most senior ranks of the episcopate and the vicarate itself broken up into such ragged knots of apprehensive, all too often half-terrified men, all watching their own backs, frightened to reveal their true inner thoughts even among their closest intimates.

He saluted the vicars courteously as he strode past them. Neither acknowledged his salute. They only stared at him the way an ice wyvern perched on the edge of an ice flow might watch a circling kraken glide past.

He continued down the hall, turned another corner, descended a short, broad flight of steps, and found himself outside a closed door. He paused very briefly—a hesitation that was felt, more than seen—then rapped sharply.

"Yes?" a voice inquired.

"May I speak with you for a moment, Major Kahrnaikys?" Phandys replied. "I'm afraid it's fairly important, Sir."

The voice didn't reply immediately. Then—

"Enter," it said curtly, and the mystically powered doors slid silently open as someone waved a hand above the magic eye which commanded them.

Major Zhaphar Kahrnaikys was a tallish man, with red-brown hair, bushy brows, and dark eyes. He was a bit unusual in that he held rank simultaneously in both the Temple Guard proper and in the Order of Schueler, and Phandys felt his pulse quicken slightly as he saw Kahrnaikys' sheathed sword lying on his desk instead of being racked on the wall in his inner office.

"What is it, Phandys?" the major said with an edge of impatience. He had the air of a man who was preoccupied. Phandys recognized that impatience, but he still took a moment to glance at the orderly sitting at his own desk in the outer office. Kahrnaikys followed his eyes. The major's mouth tightened, obviously irritated at the implication, but then he grimaced and shook his head.

"Give us a minute, Sergeant," he said sharply.

The noncom looked up, then rose quickly.

"Yes, Sir!" He managed to keep most of the curiosity out of his eyes as he stepped past Phandys, but some of it leaked out anyway. As did an undeniable flicker of relief as the doors closed behind him, shielding him from whatever had brought Phandys to visit Kahrnaikys.

The major watched the doors close, then looked back at Phandys.

"Well?" he said brusquely, and the captain drew a deep breath.

"Sir," he said, his voice more than a little troubled, "I've just become aware of something that . . . disturbs me. Something I thought should be drawn to the proper person's attention."

"You have, hey?" Kahrnaikys' eyes narrowed, and he cocked his head to one side. "And from the fact that you're standing in my office, should I assume you've decided I'm that 'proper person,' Captain?"

"In a way," Phandys agreed. "At any rate, you're the first one I thought of." He let his eyes stray briefly to Kahrnaikys' sword-and-flame Schuelerite badge.

"I see." Kahrnaikys leaned back and crossed his arms. "Very well, Phandys. Tell me about it."

"Sir, I'm the duty officer for the Courier Service this morning," Phandys began, "and—"

"If you're the Courier duty officer, what are you doing here instead of in your office in the Annex?" Kahrnaikys interrupted harshly. He had a reputation as a demanding disciplinarian.

"Sir, I was at my post when I discovered an order that . . . looked odd to me," Phandys said, clearly choosing his words with care. "Given the nature of that order, I felt I had no choice but to hand the duty over to Lieutenant Vyrnahn while I came and reported it to you."

"What sort of order?" Kahrnaikys obviously doubted Phandys' judgment, which could bode poorly for the captain's future, but he was committed now.

"Sir, it was an order booking passage on the morning iceboat to Lakeview." Kahrnaikys frowned, and Phandys hurried on. "The authorization had been logged in last night, and I probably wouldn't have noticed it if I hadn't been catching up on some of my own routine paperwork. But the reason it seemed odd to me was that there was no name listed for the passage; the space was supposed to be reserved, but there was no notation as to who the passengers were going to be. So I checked it against the order book, and there was no name listed for the officer who'd signed in the initial authorization, either. Sir, as far as I can tell, the order just *appeared,* without anyone having officially authorized it."

"What?" Kahrnaikys' frown had deepened. "That doesn't make any sense."

"No, Sir, that's what I thought, too." Phandys' relief at the major's reaction was obvious. "So I did some more checking around. And as nearly as I can tell from the form numbers, the order got inserted into the queue sometime after Langhorne's Watch this morning. You know how quiet things are then?"

"Yes, yes!" Kahrnaikys said, unfolding his arms to wave one hand impatiently. "Of course I do. Go on!"

"Well, Sir, about that time, the night-duty officer logged in a long message from one of the vicars. In fact, it was long enough—and apparently important enough—that the vicar sending it *personally* brought it down to the Annex . . . despite how miserable the weather was." Phandys shrugged. "I know the weather is *always* miserable this time of year, but last night was especially bad. He must've been half-frozen by the time he crossed the Colonnade all the way to the Annex. And since the message receiving room is usually closed at that time of night, the duty officer had to roust someone out to open it for him."

"Are you suggesting, Captain, that while he was opening the receiving room and logging in this message, someone was slipping this anonymous iceboat reservation into the queue?" Kahrnaikys didn't sound as incredulous as he might have, Phandys noticed.

"Sir, I think that's exactly what happened," the captain admitted. He shook his head, his own expression manifestly unhappy. "Major, I know we're not supposed to officially know everything that's going on. And, Sir, Langhorne knows I don't want to be poking my nose in somewhere it's not supposed to be! But this just doesn't make sense to me, not the way it seems to've happened, and, well . . . under the circumstances. . . ."

His voice trailed off, and Kahrnaikys gave him a thin smile. Yet for all its thinness, there was at least a little approval in it, Phandys thought.

"I understand, Captain. And I . . . appreciate the delicacy of your situation. But, tell me—which vicar had this lengthy message to send at such an ungodly hour?"

Silence hovered for an instant, as if Phandys realized he stood upon the brink of a precipice. That there could be no going back from this moment. Yet the truth was that he'd known that before he ever opened his mouth the first time, and so he simply squared his shoulders and looked Kahrnaikys square in the eye.

"It was Vicar Hauwerd, Sir," he said softly, and Kahrnaikys' eyes flashed with dark fire.

"I see." He looked at Phandys for a seemingly endless moment, then nodded sharply, pushed back his chair, and surged to his feet, reaching for his swordbelt as he rose.

"Captain, if I've seemed to doubt your judgment in bringing this to me, I apologize. You did exactly the right thing. Now, come with me!"

▼    ▼    ▼

Samyl Wylsynn picked up his chocolate cup, cradled it in both hands, and gazed across it at his brother, sitting on the other side of the breakfast table. Samyl's eyes were speculative, and he tilted his head to one side as he contemplated Hauwerd's expression.

"Are you ready to tell me why you invited me to breakfast this morning?" he asked. Hauwerd looked up from the breakfast sausage he'd been pushing aimlessly around his plate for the last ten minutes, and Samyl smiled gently. "I'm always happy to share a meal with my favorite brother, Hauwerd. My only brother, now that I think about it. But you're not exactly a big fan of early rising at the best of times, and I practically have to stand over you with a club to get you to join *me* for breakfast. For that matter," he nodded at the fork-herded sausage making yet another perambulation around his brother's plate, "I don't think you've managed to actually eat a single thing this morning. So I have to admit to a fair amount of curiosity."

"Was I that obvious?" Hauwerd's answering smile was crooked.

"Actually, yes," Samyl said. He paused for a moment, sipping chocolate, then drew a deep breath. "Would it happen your contacts have suggested something to you that indicates we may not have a great many more breakfasts to share?"

Hauwerd's powerful shoulders stiffened. He started to respond quickly, but then he stopped himself and gazed back at his older brother for several seconds.

"Yes," he said then. He grimaced. "I still have a few friends in the Guard, you know. One of them—I'd rather not say who, even to you—warned me we're running out of time, Samyl. I think . . . I want you to reconsider what we discussed last five-day. Please."

"No." Samyl's tone was gentle, almost regretful, but firm.

"Samyl, you *know*—" Hauwerd began, but Samyl raised one hand and shook his head.

"Yes, Hauwerd. I *do* know. And I won't pretend I'm not terrified—that your suggestion isn't tempting. Very tempting. But I can't. Whatever else may happen, whatever else I may be, I'm still a vicar of Mother Church. And I'm still a priest."

"Samyl, even *The Book of Schueler* makes it clear that when a situation is truly hopeless, there's no sin in—"

"I said it was tempting," Samyl interrupted, his tone a bit sterner. "But you know that the passages in *Schueler* you're talking about have a lot more to do with illnesses than with matters of faith."

"You're splitting hairs!" Hauwerd's voice was harder, ribbed with frustration and concern. "Damn it, Samyl! You *know* what Clyntahn's going to do to you—to *you,* especially, of all people!—if he gets his hands on you!"

"There's a point where it doesn't matter anymore," Samyl replied. "It's only a matter of degree, Hauwerd—and he's going to do exactly the same thing to men we've known and loved for years. Brothers, even if you and I don't share our parents with them. Should I abandon them? I'm the one who got them involved with the Circle in the first place. I've been their *leader* for years. Now you want me to take the easy path out and leave *them* to reap the whirlwind?"

"Oh, for Langhorne's sake!" Hauwerd snapped, his eyes flashing. "It's going to happen to them whatever you do, Samyl! And don't pretend you got them into this all by yourself—that they didn't know *exactly* what they were doing! You aren't the only grown-up in the vicarate, damn it, and don't you take that away from them. Away from *me!*" Hauwerd glared at his brother. "Yes, all of us followed your lead. And I'm pretty sure at least some of the others did it for the same reasons I did—including the fact that I love you. But we also did it because you were *right*! Because we owed God at least an attempt to reclaim His Church from bastards like Clyntahn. Even from bastards like Trynair, who's never been the outright sadist Clyntahn is! That was *our* choice, and we *made* it, and don't you *dare* take that away from us now!"

"Hauwerd, I—"

Samyl's voice was husky, and he broke off, gazing out at the snowy morning and blinking rapidly. Then he cleared his throat and looked back at his brother.

"I'm sorry," he said humbly. "I didn't mean to imply—"

"Oh, shut up." The words were harsh, but Hauwerd's voice was soft, the hard edges gentled by love, and he shook his head. "I didn't mean that the way it sounded. And I know that's not what you meant, too. But that doesn't change anything. I guess that's what really pisses me off. You know as well as I do that it won't change a thing. All you're doing is being stubborn, and that's stupid."

"Maybe it is," Samyl acknowledged. "You could well be right. But I'm not going to give Clyntahn that particular satisfaction. I'm not going to face God and the Archangels with someone like him thinking I killed myself because I was so terrified of what he intended to do to me."

"So instead of giving him *that* satisfaction you're going to give him the satisfaction of actually torturing you to death?!" Hauwerd shook his head harder. "Samyl, that's the dictionary definition of 'stupid'!"

"Probably." Samyl's smile was twisted, yet there was a shadow of real amusement in it. Then the smile faded, and it was his turn to shake his head. "Erayk Dynnys found the moral courage and faith to speak the truth when he'd been given the chance to buy an easy death with a lie, Hauwerd. Can I do less? And can I give Zhaspahr Clyntahn the weapon of my own suicide? Give him the opportunity to shout to all the world that the members of the Circle lacked the faith, in the end, to face the Question and the Punishment of Schueler for what we truly believed in? Let him reduce our commitment to the level of his own ambition and greed? You know he'd never have the courage to face something like this for *his* faith, for what *he* believes in. Am I supposed to tell the rest of the vicarate, the rest of God's Church, the rest of God's *children,* that this was really only one more power struggle? One more contest over who was going to wrest political power from whom? If I do that, what happens to the *next* Circle? To the next group of men and women who might have *successfully* opposed Zhaspahr Clyntahn? Or his successor? Or his *successor's* successor?"

Hauwerd Wylsynn looked at his brother, and for just a moment, as he heard the passion still glowing in Samyl's voice, saw the absolute, unyielding commitment still burning in Samyl's eyes, he saw something else, as well. A memory of another day, when he'd been . . . what? Six years old? Something like that, he thought, remembering the day in the boat, remembering watching his older brother—the older brother he longed with all his heart to emulate—bait his hook for him.

It was odd. He hadn't thought about that day literally in years, but now he did, and he remembered it with such utter clarity. The Tanshar sunlight warm on his shoulders, the way he'd watched Samyl's fingers, admiring their dexterity and wishing it were his. The desultory conversation which had gone with their long, lazy fishing expedition—with the coolness radiating up off the water and chilling the boat under their bare feet even while the thwarts grew uncomfortably hot under the honey-thick sunlight pouring down from above and the breeze blew pollen dust and the scent of spike thorn from the shore to tickle their nostrils like rich, golden incense.

They hadn't caught much, he remembered. Not that day. Certainly not enough for dinner for everyone, although their mother had loyally had their meager catch cleaned and broiled for the two of them—and for her, the parent whose courageous hunters and fishermen had managed to feed her after all—while their father had tried hard—so *hard!*—not to laugh.

But if Hauwerd Wylsynn hadn't caught many fish that day, he'd caught something else. He'd caught the great prize, the doomwhale of prizes, the joyous, leviathan prize to which he had given his entire life. For while they'd fished and the languid conversation had drifted like another breeze above the lake, Samyl had retold the stories. The wonderful stories, about the Archangels, and about their responsibilities. About the charge Schueler had given the Wylsynn family. About the whispered legends that they were . . . might be . . . *could* be descended from Schueler himself. About the price their ancestors had paid to serve Mother Church and the solemn, joy-filled weight of duty.

It hadn't been the first time Samyl had told him those tales, but that day had been different. He hadn't realized that, then. Not really. In fact, he thought wonderingly, he hadn't *truly* realized how different it had been until this very moment. Hadn't realized, that day when he'd seen the glow in Samyl's eyes and felt its twin in his own, where those tales were going to lead them both.

Now he did. And he felt a bittersweet smile hover just behind his lips as that realization touched him at last.

Silly, really, he thought. That was the only word for it. *Silly* for two boys—even Samyl couldn't have been more than fifteen—to be thinking such solemn thoughts. To recognize their priestly vocations in the incense of lakewater and pollen, the smell of the bait jar, the paint and varnish of the rowboat. To realize, as the years passed, that *that* had been the day they'd truly given themselves to the task God had set for their family so many centuries before. Yet that was precisely what they had done. That golden jewel of a day, he knew now, had been the true beginning of their decision to take up the task God had sent them.

And now they had come to this, and the joy of giving themselves had been touched by the terrible ice of fear. By the bitter knowledge that they'd failed. By the horror of the fate they were about to suffer in the name of the very Archangel from whom those boys had decided they really must be descended. It changed everything, that fear. Transmuted joy into sorrow and hope into despair. Not despair for their own souls' ultimate fates, for neither of them questioned *that* for an instant, but for their failure. The *Writ* said that all God truly asked of a man was the best he could do, and they'd done that, but it hadn't been good enough in the end, and that knowledge prickled the backs of Hauwerd's eyes with tears.

Yet as he looked into Samyl's eyes this morning, he saw the same determination still burning there. The same passion for the cause to which they had given themselves. And the same love for the younger brother who had followed his lead for so many weary years, shouldered his own share of their task's weight without protest or hesitation. There'd been times Hauwerd had thought Samyl was hopelessly idealistic, times the younger brother had . . . modified their plans without mentioning it to the older. Yet he'd never wavered in his own commitment or doubted, for one single, fleeting moment, the constancy of Samyl's unwavering love for him.

Their parents were gone now, thank God. Lysbet and the children had managed—somehow—to disappear after all. And Hauwerd himself had no wife, no children. Aside from a handful of distant cousins, they were alone once more—just the two of them, drifting again in that fishing boat. God had given them that much grace, despite their failure, and—despite their failure—they were still committed. Even now. Foolish as it undoubtedly was, it was also the truth, and Hauwerd Wylsynn would not have changed that truth even if he had known from the very first day exactly where it must lead them.

And neither would Samyl.

In those eyes across the table, Hauwerd recognized the same argument he'd been trying to win for five-days . . . and he knew, now, that it was one he wasn't *going* to win. There were other points he could have raised—other points he *had* raised, more than once. Like the fact that, whatever Samyl actually did, Zhaspahr Clyntahn would proclaim whatever story, whatever version of the "facts," best served his own purposes. Or the fact that, in the end, even someone with Samyl's powerful faith and determination might well be brought to "confess" to sins he'd never committed, to renounce the things he'd fought for all his life. Or the fact that even if he later recanted his "confession," Clyntahn would wave it in triumph anyway, once Samyl was safely dead and unable to dispute the Grand Inquisitor's claim that it proved the Inquisition's victory over the forces of Shan-wei.

Or the fact that, of the entire Circle, only Samyl and Hauwerd knew the truth about Ahnzhelyk's involvement. That if either of them was truly broken, they could lead Clyntahn's Inquisitors to Ahnzhelyk, to all of her own contacts . . . to Lysbet, Zhanayt, and the boys.

*It's too much, Samyl,* he thought, eyes burning as he remembered that rowboat. *Too much. God may demand our willingness to die for our faith, but you always insisted He's a loving God, and you're right. And a* loving *God doesn't—can't— demand everything else you're willing to pay. But I can't convince you of that, can I? Which is the real reason I invited you to breakfast this morning.* He felt his lips twitch in a brief, totally unanticipated smile and shook his head mentally. *Eternity's a long time,* he told himself. *Probably long enough for you to forgive me . . . eventually.*

"Samyl—" he began out loud, then stiffened as a heavy hand pounded on the door to his suite and he realized that, however long eternity might be, he'd just run out of time to convince his brother.

Samyl's head whipped around towards the sound of that pounding fist. His face tightened, and he inhaled deeply, but his hand was steady as he set his chocolate cup aside.

"I'm afraid it's time, Hauwerd," he said in a remarkably calm voice, never looking away from the archway into the suite's vestibule as the fist pounded yet again. "I love y—"

"And I love *you,* too, Samyl," Hauwerd Wylsynn whispered through his tears as the sword he'd hidden under the breakfast table severed his older brother's spinal cord.

The force of the blow hurled Samyl's corpse out of his chair. And it *was* only his corpse. Samyl Wylsynn was dead before his body reached the floor; the powerful, well-trained, loving guardsman's hand behind that blow had seen to that.

"I'm sorry," Hauwerd told his brother as the pounding was replaced by the high-pitched whine of one of the Inquisition's wands. Hauwerd didn't need the sequence of warning notes from his suite's door to tell him the lock was being overridden, but he took one more moment to kneel beside Samyl and close the startled eyes. "Couldn't let you do it," he said huskily, remembering lakewater and sunlight, solemn joy, and the smell of God's own love for the world He'd made in the pollen and the flowering spike thorn. "If that's murder, I'll take my chances arguing the case with God."

He traced the sign of the Scepter on his brother's forehead, then brushed tears from his eyes with a hand stained with his brother's blood, stood, and stepped into the archway just as the first armored guardsman came charging towards it.

"Hauwerd Wylsynn, I arrest you in—" a voice he recognized only too well bellowed from behind the charging guardsman, only to break off as Hauwerd's first deadly thrust drove home above the first man's protective breastplate and blood fountained from a severed throat.

"Oh, *fuck* you, Kahrnaikys!" Hauwerd snapped almost gaily across the tumbling body. "You always were a prick!"

A second guardsman backpedaled suddenly, trying to stop as he found himself facing not a startled, panicked, unarmed vicar but a trained soldier with a weapon in his hand. Unfortunately, he didn't have time to adjust to the unexpected situation.

"And fuck *Clyntahn,* too!" Hauwerd said, as the tip of his sword drove past the guardsman's frantically interposed forearm and took the man cleanly through the right eye.

The luxurious vestibule was suddenly filled with the stink of blood and voided bowels. Voices were raised in consternation, and Hauwerd bounded forward. There were at least two dozen guardsmen in Kahrnaikys' party, but no more than four could crowd into the vestibule at once. Hauwerd had counted on that when he'd laid his plans against this day, and he bared his teeth as he charged his foes. A third guardsman went down before the others finally got their own weapons drawn. Steel rang on steel, and yet another guardsman staggered backwards. This one was only wounded, not dead—or not *yet* at least; that might change, Hauwerd thought, watching blood pump from the deep wound in the other man's thigh—and two of his companions split to come at the vicar from either side.

Hauwerd gave ground, retreating, stooping to snatch a dagger from the belt of the first guardsman he'd killed. He reached the archway, where no one could flank him, and stopped, sword in one hand, dagger in the other, and a deadly, deadly smile on his lips.

"Come on, boys!" he invited.

Both guardsmen attacked simultaneously. The dagger in Hauwerd's left hand parried the first thrust, driving it out and to the side, and his own sword licked out once more. His other opponent's breastplate was no protection against a swordpoint which went home a hand's breadth above it, and Hauwerd turned on the sudden corpse's companion. A lightning flurry of feints and thrusts, and another guardsman was down.

Hauwerd staggered back a half step, feeling the sudden pulse of blood.

*I guess armor does help,* a corner of his brain thought as his left elbow pressed in against the deep wound the fifth guardsman's sword had opened in his ribs before he died.

The wounded vicar shook his head, blinking to clear his eyes, and saw yet another guardsman coming at him. This one wore the insignia of a captain, and Hauwerd just managed to parry the first blinding thrust.

"*Yield!*" Captain Phandys shouted, parrying the vicar's counterthrust in turn.

"Go fuck yourself!" Hauwerd gasped back, and steel grated on steel as the captain's breastplate turned a powerful thrust from the dagger in the vicar's left hand.

The two men clashed in a swirl of edged metal. Swords rang—not like bells, but like the insane clangor of Shan-wei's own anvil—and Hauwerd was taller and stronger than Phandys, and more experienced, to boot. But he was also older, already wounded . . . and unarmored.

None of Kahrnaikys' guardsmen had ever seen a fight like it. Had ever imagined they might watch one of Mother Church's vicars and a member of the Temple's own Guard clash in an explosion of deadly swordplay here on the Temple's own sacred ground. Hauwerd's orange cassock was a deeper, darker color as blood pulsed from his wound, but there was nothing weakened about his sword arm or the cold, focused light in his eyes. He drove Phandys back— one stride, then another. Another. The captain gave ground, then stopped and counterattacked, and there was something beautiful in the brutal violence of that exchange. Something fierce, predatory. Something . . . clean.

Major Kahrnaikys was shouting, but no one could make out his words over the clash of swords. And no one was really listening, either. Not really. They were all watching. Watching a bleeding vicar reject the distortion of the Inquisition's power. Watching a single wounded man—a man who *knew* he was doomed, that the corrupt enemy he despised with all his heart was about to crush every voice of opposition in God's own Church—defy a score of armed and armored foes . . . and *smile* as he did it.

It was something they knew they would never forget. Something they knew they would never be allowed to share with others . . . and which they already knew they would share anyway, in whispers so soft not even Zhasphar Clyntahn would ever hear them. Whatever else Hauwerd Wylsynn might be, he had been one of their own, commanded some of those same men—men like Khanstahnzo Phandys himself—now forcing their way into his suite, and as they watched his hopeless battle, his refusal to yield, they knew that whatever the Inquisition's warrant of arrest might say, he had been worthy of their obedience.

That he was *still* worthy of it.

And then, suddenly, Hauwerd rose on his toes, spine arching, as Captain

Phandys' sword drove into his chest. It caught the vicar as he was closing, and the weight and momentum of his own body combined with the power of the thrust itself to drive the blade entirely through him.

He grunted and dropped the dagger, clutching at the guard of Phandys' sword as he thudded to his knees. The guardsman released the hilt almost automatically, and Wylsynn bent forward, folding around the agony of his death wound. But then the fallen vicar managed to straighten. Somehow he found the strength to raise his head once more. Blood bubbled from his lips, yet his eyes found Phandys', and there was something in them. Something like . . . gratitude.

Then Hauwerd Wylsynn's eyes closed forever, and he toppled forward over the sword which had killed him.

.XVII.

Bruhstair & Sons Warehouse
and
The Temple,
City of Zion,
and
The Northern High Road,
The Temple Lands

The travel arrangements were going to be . . . unique.

The man who was currently Ahbraim Zhevons (and he was beginning to think he really needed a program listing the team's entire roster to help him keep his identity straight on a moment-to-moment basis) had wondered exactly how Ahnzhelyk intended to transport a couple of dozen people, all of them fugitives from the Inquisition, out of what amounted to the Church of God Awaiting's capital city, in the middle of winter, without seeing every one of them spotted, stopped, and arrested. In fact, however, he'd discovered, she didn't intend to transport "a couple of dozen people" at all; she meant to move twice that many of them.

A bit more than that, actually. In fact, the exact total was fifty-seven.

He'd gawked at her when she first informed him of that minor point. Yet it had quickly become evident that he'd (yet again) underestimated the sheer scope of her operations, and this time around, he decided, he'd had even less of an excuse. It had been clear from the moment he first arrived in Zion that Ahnzhelyk was planning on leaving the city herself, not just smuggling out the families of a few highly placed churchmen. That being the case, it should have been equally evident to him that her plans would include the escape of any members of her own organization who might have been exposed (or to whom her own disappearance might have led the Inquisition), as well. He supposed that one reason it hadn't occurred to him was the sheer scale of the thing. It must have required a massive dose of what had once been called chutzpah to even contemplate an evacuation (especially in a single effort) on the scale of the one Ahnzhelyk had in mind.

"You're joking," he said now, quietly, standing beside her in the icy, echoing emptiness of the warehouse.

Ahnzhelyk had abandoned the expensive, beautifully tailored, exquisitely fashionable garments she'd worn for so many years. She'd also abandoned her long, elaborately coiffured hair, the elegant cosmetics, the jewelry, the flawlessly manicured hands. The smallish woman standing beside Zhevons, her breath steaming gently in the warehouse's cold, wore quilted trousers, sensible, sueded boots, and a thick but utilitarian and deplorably drab woolen sweater. She was slender, true, yet she radiated a sort of compact solidness sadly at odds with the fashionably languid, slightly fluttery, somehow ethereal Ahnzhelyk. At the moment, she also wore an unbuttoned coat that looked remarkably like one of the Imperial Charisian Navy's winter-weather watch coats. The thing had to weigh as much as Merlin Athrawes' cuirass, but it was undoubtedly impervious to anything as minor as a subzero blizzard.

"Joking?" Ahnzhelyk looked up at him and used one hand to smooth her now short-cropped hair. "Why should you think that, Ahbraim?"

"You're telling me you actually managed to arrange all of this"—"Zhevons" waved his hands around the warehouse—"right under Clyntahn's nose?"

"No, not really."

Ahnzhelyk gazed around the warehouse herself. Like many such buildings in Zion, the solidly built structure had been packed to the rafters at the beginning of winter. Mostly with bulk foodstuffs, in this warehouse's case, although at least a quarter of its floor space had been given over to bagged Glacierheart coal, while well over half of the storage yard outside it had been covered in huge piles of the gleaming black stuff from the Mountains of Light's deep mines. This late in the season, over two-thirds of the warehouse's contents had been disposed of (undoubtedly at a tidy profit), and its staff had been reduced accordingly.

"As a matter of fact," she continued, returning her attention to her guest, "I made most of these arrangements well before Clyntahn was ever confirmed as Grand Inquisitor." She grimaced, her expressive eyes going bleak and far colder than the warehouse's interior, at the mention of that name. "I've always believed in planning ahead, Ahbraim. Even in the days when I was foolish enough to believe not even the vicarate could be so corrupt—so *stupid*—as to name someone like Clyntahn Inquisitor. Now—"

She shrugged quickly, angrily, and Zhevons nodded. In the wake of her own disappearance, Ahnzhelyk's information net had been largely shut down, but they scarcely needed it to confirm that her worst estimates of Clyntahn's intentions had been horrifyingly accurate. Not a single member of Samyl Wylsynn's Circle in the Temple or here in Zion had escaped. The handful of lower-ranked bishops and archbishops who'd managed to get out of the city before winter might still have some faint chance of evading the Inquisitors, but no one else— aside from the family members Ahnzhelyk had gotten to in time—had pulled it off.

It had taken three days to confirm Samyl and Hauwerd Wylsynn's deaths, and Ahnzhelyk had withdrawn to the tiny cubbyhole here in the warehouse which had replaced her luxurious townhouse. She'd closed the door very quietly behind her, and only a PICA's exquisite hearing could have detected the soft, stifled, disciplined, infinitely bitter, brokenhearted sobs which had been her companions in that dark little room. When she'd reemerged an hour later, her eyes might have been the tiniest bit swollen, but if they were, that was the only sign of her bottomless grief.

Nor were the Wylsynns the only people she had to mourn. They were the only members of the Circle who had truly known about Ahnzhelyk's activities, but many of the others had known "Madame Ahnzhelyk," and many of those others had grown to be close personal friends over the years. Very few of them had held Ahnzhelyk's profession against her, and most of them had learned, gradually, of her charitable activities and, especially, her contributions to the winter soup kitchens and shelters. If Samyl and Hauwerd were lost to her forever, at least they were already dead; her other friends, less fortunate, were in Clyntahn's power, and she had no illusions about what was happening to them at this very moment.

And gathered together here in this warehouse were six families, all of them forced to live with that same knowledge.

*At least they won't be "gathered here" much longer,* Zhevons thought. *Thank God. This city's been bad enough from the moment I got here. Now, it's ten times worse.*

The news of the Circle's arrest had hit Zion like a hammer. Like Ahnzhelyk herself, the majority of the Circle's members had been active in the city's charitable activities. Many had been Bédardists or Pasqualates, affiliated with the Church shelters those orders maintained. Inadequate, underfunded, understaffed, and largely ignored by their mother orders though those shelters might be, they were still the difference—literally—between life and death for many of the city's poor, and the high churchmen who had deigned to support them— who, in some cases, had actually *served* in them on a regular basis—had been deeply beloved by those same poor citizens of Zion. Others had worked with individual churches who took their obligation to care for their less fortunate brothers and sisters seriously, and they, too, had been known and loved by the needy in Zion.

Quite aside from the citizens those vicars and archbishops had helped directly, the sincerity of their faith and compassion had been evident to the junior clergy and laymen who'd worked with them. The news that they'd been arrested for treason and heresy, that they were to be condemned—effectively already had *been* condemned—as "secret heretics" affiliated with the "Charisian apostasy" (not to mention all manner of unspeakable personal perversions), had stunned all of those people. It seemed impossible on the face of it, an obvious mistake. Yet the rumors of arrest turned out to have been true, and the "confessions" were already beginning to surface as the Inquisitors "reasoned" with their prisoners.

Zion was in very quiet, very secretive tumult. No one dared say so out loud, but there were plenty of people who suspected what had truly happened. People who saw in the Circle's destruction a ruthless, coldly planned and executed maneuver to silence anything which could be construed as dissent. It was the eradication of toleration. The official endorsement of fanatical loyalty not simply to Mother Church but to the vicarate and—especially—to the Group of Four.

Zhaspahr Clyntahn had closed an iron fist about the Temple and the very heart of the Church of God Awaiting, and the city of Zion held its breath, trembling, while it waited to discover the cost of his triumph.

*It's not going to be long before the denunciations begin,* Zhevons told himself sadly. *The Inquisition's always had its informants and its spy networks all over Safehold. Here in Zion and the Temple, more than anywhere else, and for damned good reasons. But now people are going to start looking for someone—anyone—they can turn in to prove their own orthodoxy, their own loyalty and reliability. People they can throw to the krakens to protect themselves and their own families.*

"I have to admit," Ahnzhelyk continued with bleak, bitter satisfaction, "that even though I started planning for this long before Clyntahn came to power, it pleases me immensely to *use* that pig to get all these people out of Zion."

Zhevons nodded again, although if *she* had to admit that, *he* had to confess that the sheer audacity of her plan made him more than a little nervous. But that bold effrontery was probably the very thing that was going to make it work, he reminded himself.

He'd already realized Ahnzhelyk Phonda was a shrewd businesswoman, as well as a skilled conspirator. He hadn't realized quite how wealthy she'd become, however. He supposed it shouldn't surprise him that someone who'd been able to hide her activities from the Inquisition for so long had been equally successful at hiding her various business enterprises from the city and Church tax collectors, as well. Although, to be fair, he was pretty sure she'd actually paid all her taxes and business licensing fees—and probably a few reasonably generous bribes, on the side, as well. She just hadn't paid them in her own name. In fact, now that he knew what to look for, he'd managed to identify no less than nine completely false business identities she'd set up and maintained—in one case, for almost twenty-six years—and he was positive he still hadn't found all of them. She'd been wired into the Zion business community, including its less than fully legal aspects, since well before Cayleb Ahrmahk was born, and almost all her various ventures had shown a profit. The level of profits had varied from case to case—from "just-better-than-breakeven" to "license-to-mint-money" levels, as a matter of fact—but the cumulative total and variety of her assets had been amazing.

Including this warehouse and Bruhstair & Sons, the perfectly legitimate—and *highly* profitable—warehousing and freight-hauling business which officially owned it. Of course, like many such operations, especially here in Zion, Bruhstair & Sons made its own contributions to the "gray economy." Rather large contributions in Bruhstair's case, as a matter of fact. Bruhstair Freight Haulers, Bruhstair & Sons actual drayage unit, had been fifty-seven years old, with a workforce of over two hundred, when Ahnzhelyk acquired it (through suitably anonymous and/or fictitious intermediaries) from the last of the original "& Sons," and it had grown substantially under her management. A transportation company that big and that profitable (it had shown a clear profit of almost eighty thousand marks last year, which was a staggering return for a mainlander warehousing firm) didn't last that long in Zion without having reached the appropriate accommodations with members of the vicarate and the Church hierarchy in general. It was amazing, for example, how few import duties actually got paid on freight destined for someone like, say, Vicar Zhaspahr Clyntahn.

There'd always been some of that, but it had grown steadily worse over the last century or so. By now, no one even bothered to insist on *good* forged paperwork. Customs agents and tax collectors knew better than to look closely at anything consigned to senior members of the Church, and Langhorne help the occasional—*very* occasional—agent or collector naïve enough (or stupid enough) to make the mistake of noticing something he shouldn't have noticed!

Of course, there weren't very many of those. According to Ahnzhelyk, when he'd raised that concern with her, the last confirmed sighting of an honest customs agent in Zion had been just over thirty-seven years ago. It wasn't that the present crop of officials weren't efficient or capable; it was simply that they understood very clearly that a significant portion (Zhevons' current estimate ran as high as twenty-five percent, and even that might be low) of the city's commerce—especially in high-priced luxury items—was actually being carried out by or for vicars or archbishops or bishops who were effectively tax exempt. And since no one had ever gotten around to making that tax exemption legal, even the most dedicated of customs agents recognized that he was winking at an unlawful trade.

*And once you realize you're doing that, you have to start wondering why you shouldn't be building up a little nest egg of your own,* he thought harshly, comparing the local situation and the rampant corruption it promoted to anything which would have been tolerated for a moment in the Empire of Charis.

Not that he had any intention of complaining. And especially not given that Ahnzhelyk Phonda had possessed both the talents to make that corruption work so well for her . . . and the chilled-steel nerve to enlist none other than Zhaspahr Clyntahn's own bailiff as a silent partner in Bruhstair & Sons.

The brazen audacity of it awed "*Seijin* Zhevons." What tax agent, what customs inspector, in his right mind was going to meddle with *Zhaspahr Clyntahn's* illegal smuggling trade even at the best of times? The very idea was ridiculous! And, at *this* moment, when Clyntahn was establishing his very own reign of terror throughout the city, *no one* was going to take the slightest chance of calling himself to the attention of an irritated Grand Inquisitor. Which made his involvement with Bruhstair Ahnzhelyk's best and most effective protection against his own vengeful search for the people she was protecting.

The exquisite irony of her solution was beautiful to behold, despite the tension quotient, he thought admiringly.

"We'll be ready to leave in the morning," Ahnzhelyk said now. "What do your '*seijin*-like abilities' tell you about the weather, Ahbraim?"

"Indications are that it should be clear and cold pretty much for the rest of the month, now," he replied. "We'll get another day or so of snowfall around the middle of next five-day, but nothing like the blizzards we've been seeing. Probably not more than another ten inches to a foot or so, where you'll be traveling."

She gave him a speculative look, which he returned with the blandest of smiles. He no longer doubted that very soon after getting her charges to Old Charis, Ahnzhelyk Phonda was going to find herself admitted to another circle. In the meantime, he rather enjoyed watching the razor-edged brain behind that thoughtful expression trying to figure out just how he managed such incredibly accurate weather predictions.

Among other things.

"I'm glad to hear it," she said after a moment. Then she looked around the cavernous warehouse again and shook her head. "I'm actually going to miss this place," she sighed.

"May I ask what sort of arrangements you've made for your enterprises here in Zion after you, ah, depart?" he inquired, and she shrugged.

"I was tempted to leave them all up and running, actually," she confessed. "I spent so long putting them together in the first place that giving them up is almost like an amputation. I hadn't expected to feel that way about it, but I have to admit I do. And once I finally admitted that to myself, I also discovered I was trying to convince myself that maintaining them long-distance would provide me with a valuable operational base here in Zion. One that might come in handy for . . . doing Clyntahn and his cronies a mischief some fine day."

She shook her head, her jaw tightening, and he saw bleak hatred flicker deep in her eyes as she gazed at something only she could see.

"But—?" he prompted after a moment when she paused.

"What?" She gave herself a shake, blinked, and refocused on him. "Oh. Sorry. I was just . . . thinking."

"I realize that. But from what you were saying, it sounds like you've decided *against* trying to keep them in operation?"

"Yes." She shrugged. "The way I have things arranged right now, all of my Zion business interests will either be quietly liquidated or else transferred to the ownership of the people who've managed them for me all along. I decided a long time ago that it would be better to quietly fold my tent and bury my tracks than to have a dozen or so businesses suddenly and mysteriously go *out* of business about the same time Ahnzhelyk Phonda disappeared into thin air. Besides, most of the people who have worked for me—even if most of them never realized they were working for *me,* if you understand my meaning—have done their jobs well." She shrugged again. "I think of this as a sort of retirement settlement."

"I can see that." He nodded. "On the other hand, I suspect that rewarding them for their loyalty and hard work isn't the only thing on your mind."

"It isn't." She looked up at him. "If any single thing under heaven is certain, Ahbraim, it's that Clyntahn's going to tighten his grip throughout all the mainland realms. He probably won't be able to wrap Siddarmark up as tightly as he'd like to; or not until he's done a lot more preparation work in the Republic, at any rate. But the other kingdoms, the empires—those he's going to rule with an iron fist in Mother Church's name. And if he's going to be doing that anywhere, you know his control is going to be tighter and even more restrictive here in Zion than anywhere else. So, tempting though it was to hang on to a toehold here, I can't possibly justify exposing all of these people to potential punishment as 'agents of Shan-wei.' I've been very careful to avoid traceable connections between any of my operations here in Zion and the Circle. I'm not going to endanger people who have worked for me for so long by tying them into active operations against the Temple now that Clyntahn's so obviously out for blood."

"I see. Of course," he smiled thinly at her, "that does rather imply that you intend to maintain those 'active operations against the Temple' once you're safely out of Zion yourself, now doesn't it?"

"Oh, I think you can *rely* on that, Ahbraim," she said very softly, and no one would ever have mistaken the tight flash of her white teeth for a smile. "I'm a very wealthy woman, you know," she continued. "Even after giving up all of my affairs here in Zion, I'm still going to find myself quite well off. You'd be amazed—well, *you* might not be, but most people would—by the amounts I've got stashed away in accounts in Tellesberg or with the House of Qwentyn in Siddarmark. From what you and Adorai have both said, I think I can probably count on Emperor Cayleb and Empress Sharleyan to keep a roof over my head, too. In which case all of that money—and all of my mainland contacts—will be available to help me do my very best to make Zhaspahr Clyntahn's life a living hell . . . and"—her dark eyes flashed with hungry fire—"as short as humanly possible."

▼　　▼　　▼

"Is that the last of it, Rhobair?" the Earl of Coris asked, watching as Rhobair Seablanket finished closing and strapping up one final trunk.

"It is, My Lord." Seablanket rested one hand on the trunk as he turned to meet his employer's gaze, and although his tone was as matter of fact as ever, it would've taken someone far stupider and less observant than Phylyp Ahzgood to miss the relief in his valet's eyes.

"In that case, let's get them down to *Hornet*." Coris smiled without a great deal of humor, but with a degree of relief which was even greater than Seablanket's. "Father Hahlys is expecting us, and I'd prefer not to disappoint him by being late."

"No, My Lord," Seablanket agreed fervently. "I'll have them aboard within the hour."

"Good, Rhobair. Good."

Coris patted his valet on the shoulder, then turned and walked across to stand gazing out through his window across the city of Zion.

*God, I can't wait to get back across the lake!* He shook his head. *I thought on my way here that things couldn't get a whole hell of a lot worse. How little did I know . . .*

His own meetings with Zahmsyn Trynair and Zhaspahr Clyntahn had been bad enough. He'd come to the conclusion he'd actually underestimated Clyntahn's cynicism . . . and ruthlessness. Frankly, he wouldn't have believed Clyntahn *could* be even more ruthless and calculating than he'd initially assumed, but he'd learned better. And if he might somehow have managed to cling to any tiny fragment of an illusion in that regard, Clyntahn's vicious purge of any opposition within the vicarate would have disabused him of it.

Coris folded his hands behind him, gripping them tightly together. He'd never actually met Samyl or Hauwerd Wylsynn, but he had met Vicar Chiyan Hysin, of the Harching Hysins, and anyone less like a ravening heretic who molested little girls would have been impossible to imagine. Yet those were the crimes of which Hysin stood accused . . . and to which, according to the "shocked and stunned" Inquisitors, he had already confessed.

There was no doubt in Coris' mind that Hysin's true crime—just like the true crime of everyone else who had been arrested, or killed resisting arrest, or simply died under mysterious circumstances, in the last three five-days—had been to oppose, or threaten to oppose, or even to remotely *seem* to oppose—the Group of Four. There did appear to be at least some genuine evidence of . . . clandestine activities on Hysin's part. Coris had to admit that much. But even though he'd been unable to establish anything like the sort of intelligence network he could have put together elsewhere, under more favorable circumstances, he'd managed to get at least a few feelers threaded through the Temple and the city. And those feelers all agreed—quietly, cautiously, in whispers designed to avoid anyone else's attention—that any "secret activities" on the part of Hysin and the rest of the vicars and prelates who'd been labeled the "Charisian Circle" had been directed at the Group of Four and the rampant abuses within the clergy, not designed to somehow betray the Temple and God into the hands of the apostate.

*Of course that's what they were doing,* the earl thought coldly. *The fools. Oh, the* fools! *How could they—?* He shook his head. *Be fair to them, Phylyp. Before this whole business with Charis exploded in everyone's face, opposing Clyntahn was only insanely risky, not automatically suicidal. They didn't just decide to start doing this the day before yesterday . . . and Clyntahn hasn't been licking his chops in anticipation of this moment because he genuinely thinks they had any immediate plans to stage some sort of coup inside the vicarate, either. This is just a case of his killing two wyverns with a single stone . . . and enjoying the hell out of it when he does it.*

He closed his eyes for a moment, leaning his forehead against the icy windowpane in a brief, silent prayer for the men who were undoubtedly at that very moment undergoing the tortures of the damned at the Inquisition's hands. The men who were going to face the same hideous death Erayk Dynnys had already faced . . . unless Clyntahn could come up with ones which were still worse.

And the men whose *families* had been arrested right along with them.

*You've got to get back to Talkyra,* he told himself flatly, almost desperately. *You've got to get back to Irys and Daivyn.* He shook his head, eyes still closed. *If Clyntahn's willing to do this, willing to arrest one-in-ten of the vicarate itself and condemn them to death just to secure his own position, then it's for* damned *sure he'll throw Daivyn away in a heartbeat.*

Coris shook his head. The only member of the Group of Four who'd seemed to give a genuine damn about Daivyn's well-being had been Rhobair Duchairn. He'd met with the Treasurer only twice, yet he hadn't *had* to meet with him even once. Those meetings—officially to discuss Daivyn's financial needs and the proper amount of the Church subsidy to support his court in exile—had been arranged from Duchairn's side, and it was obvious to Coris that it had been the vicar himself who had done the arranging specifically so that he and Coris might meet face to face.

The earl appreciated that, although he'd been careful about showing it. He was almost certain—but only *almost,* unfortunately—that Duchairn's concern for Daivyn was sincere. It fitted with his own earlier assessments of Duchairn's attitudes, at any rate, and the sorrow hiding behind the vicar's eyes had looked genuine enough. There'd been no way to be positive about that, however, and it had always been possible Duchairn was simply testing Coris' suitability as the Group of Four's tool in a rather more subtle fashion than would have occurred to Clyntahn. Walking the tightrope between doing his best for Daivyn's future interests and maintaining his own persona as a properly corruptible henchman hadn't been the easiest thing Coris had ever done, although a lifelong career as a spy had helped.

But however real (or feigned) Duchairn's concern might have been, there was no doubt at all where the *rest* of the Group of Four stood. Coris' present ability to follow the news from Corisande was limited, especially at such a vast distance, yet his sources here in the Temple, fragmentary though they were, all suggested things weren't going outstandingly well for the Temple's interests in Corisande. The tone of his more recent conversations with Trynair suggested the same thing, as well. Although the Chancellor had done his best to downplay any concern he might personally be feeling, the situation in the capital, in particular, seemed to be tilting towards a genuine accommodation with Cayleb and Sharleyan—or with the Church of Charis, at least. And the moment Zhaspahr Clyntahn decided the Corisandian fire needed another kick, that another dastardly Charisian assassination might tilt Manchyr back the other way . . .

*I've* got *to get back to Talkyra.*

▼   ▼   ▼

*She's actually pulled it off,* Ahbraim Zhevons thought. *My God, she's actually pulled it off!*

Or, at least, she had so far, he reminded himself. It was still possible the wheels would come off, but as he'd watched the caravan of massive, snow lizard-drawn sleighs sliding over the icy high road, it had become obvious that his initial concerns about Ahnzhelyk Phonda's safety had been just a trifle premature.

In many respects, the timing on Ahnzhelyk's escape from Zion could hardly have been better. This late in the winter, with the roads and ground frozen iron-hard, it was actually easier to move heavy loads overland over snow and ice aboard properly designed sleighs (assuming the availability of draft animals like Safeholdian snow lizards) than to move them aboard wheeled wagons during the fall or early winter . . . and *much* easier than it would be once the spring thaw began, in another month or so. In fact, in some ways it was easier even than it would have been in summer. And it was a damned good thing that was true, too. Despite the existence of scores of warehouses, granaries, and supply depots in Zion, by this point in the winter, the city was always in desperate need of resupply. Regular freight shipments were always bound into Zion and the Temple, except for the month or so each year when weather completely isolated the city. Now that the freeze had set hard enough and deep enough, the delivery tempo had been steadily increasing for several five-days, despite the winter storms which had recently howled their way across the northern Temple Lands.

And just as movement *into* the city had picked up, so had movement *out* of the city, including a large convoy from Bruhstair Freight Haulers. There was a fair amount of general merchandise in it, including several hundred bottles of fine brandies and whiskeys. Personally, Zhevons found the Chisholmian whiskeys superior to anything coming out of Zion, but there was no denying the prestige of the Zion and Temple distilleries. Whether they were actually the finest spirits available or not (which they definitely were *not,* in his humble opinion), they commanded exorbitant prices purely on the strength of their labels.

In addition to the spirits, however, there were also crates of books from Zion's publishing houses, somewhere around a quarter-million marks' worth of religious art, and a consignment of fine jewelry which was probably at least equally valuable. Most of the other freight consisted of relatively low-weight (though often quite bulky) items—like an impressive assortment of tapestries, fine carpets, and woven luxury goods from the Church's flocks of sheep and mountain lizards—but even many of those were high-value commodities, and security was always a significant concern in cases like that. Which explained why so many of Bruhstair Freight Haulers' sleighs were built around large, sturdy, thickly planked cargo boxes. They were almost as large, in some cases, as freight containers Nimue Alban had seen loaded aboard starships during her naval career. And, of course, they had been locked—and securely sealed—by gimlet-eyed customs agents before they ever departed Zion. Every item aboard them had been meticulously checked . . . according to the paperwork, at least. And, in fact, they had been checked just as thoroughly as they always were. Which was to say the customs agents had examined the manifests, found Zhaspahr Clyntahn's bailiff listed as one of the shippers, and promptly sealed the sleighs' cargo boxes just as officially as anyone could possibly have asked.

In their doubtless commendable zeal to speed Vicar Zhaspahr's property on its way, however, a few small . . . irregularities appeared to have escaped their alert attention. Specifically, it would seem they'd failed to note that six of the larger sleighs were equipped, in addition to the carefully locked and sealed hatches through which their valuable cargoes had been loaded, with small, oddly unobtrusive *belly* hatches, as well. Cargo doors which, for some unknown (but undoubtedly sound) reason, had been designed so that they could be reached only by someone who actually got down on his hands and knees (or, for most adults, on his belly) and crawled under the sleighs, between the runners.

The hatches through which over fifty fugitives from the Inquisition had entered those sleighs.

It wasn't the most convenient mode of travel ever invented, but the sleighs' cargo boxes were thick-walled and weathertight. The passenger-carrying cubbies hidden away inside them were large enough to accommodate mattresses and bedrolls and allow at least some movement, and they were surrounded and thoroughly concealed by rugs and tapestries, by piles of expensive, Zion-made blankets and other big-ticket textiles. In fact, the people hidden away inside those cubbyholes were warmer than anyone else in the entire convoy. And once they were at least a couple of days away from Zion, they'd been allowed to leave their hiding places, after the sleighs had halted for the night, and mingle unobtrusively—*very* unobtrusively—with the Bruhstair drovers and wagoneers. Who, alas, were not unaccustomed to seeing the occasional unmanifested face turn up on journeys such as this one.

The trip would not be brief. In fact, the sleighs would follow the southern shore of Hsing-wu's Passage all the way from Zion to the shores of the Icewind Sea. Along the way, they would drop off at least some of their cargo in various towns and small cities strung out along the Passage, but the real reason for taking that particular route was that it avoided the extraordinarily difficult terrain of the Mountains of Light.

To help them do that, Mother Church, the Temple Lands, and the Republic of Siddarmark had cooperated over the centuries to build and maintain the high road which paralleled the Passage. When the seagoing route was navigable, grass grew—literally—on the high road; when winter closed Hsing-wu's Passage, the high road came into its own once more. By now, Ahnzhelyk and her refugees were almost a third of the way to Siddarmark and the galleons which would ultimately carry them to Tellesberg and—hopefully—safety. Unless something went dreadfully wrong, they should be aboard ship within two months . . . and in Tellesberg seven or eight five-days after that.

*By the end of June at the latest. I can't* believe *how easy she's made all this look.*

Zhevons shook his head wonderingly as he crossed to the sleigh assigned to "Mistress Frahncyn Tahlbaht," who, oddly enough, didn't look a thing like dainty, fragile, lovely Ahnzhelyk Phonda. No, Mistress Tahlbaht was pleasant-looking enough, but she was also clearly the experienced, professional, sensibly dressed senior clerk Bruhstair & Sons had assigned to ride herd on this particular convoy's more valuable items.

He rapped lightly on the sleigh's side door, then opened it and climbed the short boarding step when a voice invited him to do so.

"Good morning, Ahbraim," Mistress Tahlbaht said with a smile. "What can I do for you today?"

"Actually, I've just come to bid you farewell," he replied. She sat back in her seat at the small, built-in desk, eyebrows rising, and he shrugged. "As nearly as I can tell, you've gotten away clean," he said. "We could both be wrong about that, but I don't think so. And now that I've figured out your evacuation route, I can arrange to have some of *Seijin* Merlin's other friends keep an eye out for you." He chuckled suddenly. "After all, the Mountains of Light are the traditional training grounds for *seijins,* aren't they?"

"So I've heard," she acknowledged, then turned her floor-mounted swivel chair to the side and stood. "I'll miss you, you know," she said, taking the two steps required to cross her tiny mobile office and hold out her hand. This time he simply took it in both of his, squeezing it without kissing it, and she smiled. "Will I be seeing you again?"

There was an odd note in her voice, he thought. An almost whimsical one. Or wistful, perhaps. They'd known one another for less than a month, yet he was confident she'd realized as well as he that they were kindred souls.

*Another of those capable, uppity females,* he reflected. *She and Sharleyan are going to get along like a house on fire—I can already see that. And I suppose I still come under that "capable, uppity female" label, too. In a somewhat convoluted manner of speaking, at least.*

"Oh, I think you can count on that," he said out loud. "I've been told I'm a bit like a bad habit or a cold." Her eyebrows rose higher, and he chuckled. "Almost impossible to get rid of once you've got me, I mean."

"Good." She smiled and squeezed his hand back. "I'll look forward to it."

"So will I," he assured her. "So will I."


## .XVIII.
## Royal Palace,
## City of Tranjyr,
## Kingdom of Tarot

King Gorjah III was in a foul mood.

That had become unfortunately common over the last couple of years. Since the effectively total destruction of his fleet at the Battle of Rock Point, which had occurred almost precisely two years ago, as a matter of fact, if anyone had been marking his calendar to keep track.

Gorjah didn't need to mark any calendars, but he'd definitely been keeping track. He'd been rather strongly motivated in that regard.

At the moment, he stood gazing northwest out of his palace window up the length of Thol Bay. Seven hundred–plus miles, Thol Bay reached from the city of Tranjyr to Cape Thol and North Head and, beyond that, the Gulf of Tarot and the continent of East Haven. It was a magnificent stretch of saltwater. It might be a bit shallow, in places, its shoals a bit treacherous, here and there, but over all it offered Tranjyr splendid access to the seas of the world, and the broad sweep of the city's wharves and warehouses was ample proof of the way in which the world's commerce had taken advantage of that access.

*Once upon a time,* he thought grumpily.

He ran a hand over his kercheef, the traditional bright, colorful headwear of the Kingdom of Tarot, and his foul mood deepened as he contemplated the absence of merchant shipping in that anchorage. The dearth of lighters plying between those nonexistent merchant vessels and the city's wharves. The peculiar paucity of longshoremen and stevedores who'd once been employed loading and unloading the cargoes which no longer filled those extensive warehouses.

There was a reason for those absences, for that dearth. A reason which had something to do with the squadron of the Imperial Charisian Navy—no more than a handful of schooners, supported by a single division of galleons—who'd taken up residence in Thol Bay. Who'd had the sheer effrontery to actually set up their own anchorage in Holme Reach, well inside the Bay's protective headlands. To send parties of seamen and Marines ashore on Hourglass Island to plant and tend *garden plots* to provide their crews with fresh vegetables and salads! Somehow, for some reason Gorjah really didn't understand himself, that particular bit of Charisian brashness was especially infuriating.

Perhaps, he'd occasionally thought, because he knew he'd brought it on himself. Mostly, at least; he still didn't see any way he could have said no to the "offer."

*Not that you* tried *all that hard,* he thought moodily now. *It seemed like such a* good *idea at the time, after all. Which probably should have reminded you that things which seem too good to be true usually are. Which was the reason Edmynd argued against it from the outset.*

The king grimaced as he recalled the diplomatic language in which Edmynd Rustmyn, the Baron of Stonekeep, had attempted to restrain his own enthusiastic response to the bait which had been trolled in front of him.

Gorjah's grimace deepened at the memory.

*I'd like to say it was all the Church's fault—well, the Group of Four's, anyway. And I suppose it was. But be honest, Gorjah. Edmynd was dead right to try to . . . moderate your enthusiasm, wasn't he? And* you *wouldn't listen, would you? They'd figured out exactly the right lever to pull in your case, hadn't they? You resented the hell out of the treaty—never mind the fact that it had its good sides, as well—and you figured it was a chance to get your own back. And why did you think that way? Because you were a frigging* idiot, *that's why!*

His grimace turned briefly into something like a snarl. Then it vanished, and he folded his hands behind himself, turned his back on the window, and crossed to the lavishly carved, not-quite-a-throne chair at the head of the brilliantly polished table. Summer sunlight from the window bounced off the imperfect mirror of the tabletop, throwing a spot of brightness on the council chamber's ceiling, as he seated himself. The chair had been custom-built for his father, who'd been considerably taller and stockier than the slender, dark-haired Gorjah. The king favored his mother—physically, at least—far more closely than he ever had his father, and he contemplated (not for the first time) the desirability of having a new one—one that made him look less like a child sitting in his parent's chair—commissioned. From the viewpoint of political psychology, of his ability to dominate meetings, the notion probably had much to recommend it, but the chair was almost sinfully comfortable. Besides, as a boy then-Prince Gorjah had spent quite a few hours sitting in his father's lap in this very chair. Those memories came back to him every time he sat in it, and especially over the last couple of years when his infant son, Rholynd, had been cuddled in his own lap.

*I wonder if* he'll *ever get to sit in it?* the king thought moodily. *For that matter, I wonder how much longer* I'll *get to sit in it!*

They were both valid questions, and he didn't much care for the answers which tended to suggest themselves.

Cayleb of Charis had obvious reasons to want his blood, given the way Tarot had betrayed the terms of their treaty. Simply adding Tarot's fleet to the onslaught on Charis would have been bad enough, but Gorjah hadn't stopped there. Oh, no! He'd followed Chancellor Trynair's orders, like a good little henchman, and lied to King Haarahld, as well. Promised to honor his treaty obligations even as he was ordering Baron White Ford to rendezvous with the Royal Dohlaran Navy. The fact that Haarahld had been subsequently killed only made bad worse in that respect, although Gorjah could at least reflect that none of his ships had been involved in the Battle of Darcos Sound. So he could argue that he personally hadn't contributed to Haarahld's death . . . not that he expected that particular fine distinction to cut much ice with Haarahld's son.

Unfortunately, Cayleb wasn't the only person Gorjah had to worry about. In fact, if Cayleb *had* been his only concern, he'd have been considerably happier. But despite his very best efforts, the Group of Four seemed to feel he'd proved just a tad inept as a traitor, scoundrel, and general all around backstabber. And, to be honest, Gorjah couldn't really disagree. He'd tried—he really had—yet someone in his Court had leaked the "Knights of the Temple Lands'" plans to Haarahld, thus neatly undoing all of his own efforts in that direction.

He still didn't know who'd done that, and not for lack of trying to find out.

The ruthless, meticulous investigation had turned up all sorts of interesting things—from minor peccadilloes, to bribery, to extortion—on the parts of his nobles and officials. That had undoubtedly been useful, he thought. At least he'd hammered his nobility and bureaucrats so hard the survivors were deeply dedicated to doing their jobs efficiently—and, above all, honestly—in a fashion Tarot hadn't seen in decades. Probably in *generations,* really. Yet all his efforts had failed to unearth a single clue as to how the Group of Four's plans had reached Charis.

Gorjah had respectfully pointed out in his correspondence with Vicar Zhasyn that his investigations had been personally assisted by Bishop Executor Tyrnyr and by Father Frahnklyn Sumyr, his intendant. For that matter, the full resources of the Inquisition here in Tarot had been thrown into the task, and none of that effort had found even a trace of whoever had done the leaking. Perhaps, the king had suggested as diplomatically as possible, that indicated the security failure hadn't, in fact, occurred in Tarot after all?

As far as Gorjah could tell, Failyx Gahrbor, the kingdom's archbishop in far distant Zion, supported his argument. Gahrbor certainly had plenty of personal reasons to do so, at any rate. And officially—*officially*—Chancellor Trynair had cleared Gorjah himself of any wrongdoing. It had been a grudging clearance, however. Gorjah couldn't say that surprised him. For that matter, if he'd been in the Chancellor's cassock, he probably wouldn't have gone even that far. Because the damning truth was that the only royal court which *could* have leaked the information upon which Haarahld of Charis had acted so decisively was Gorjah's own. There simply hadn't been time for the information to reach Charis from anywhere else speedily enough.

Given that, he supposed, and especially in light of how devastating the Charisian ambush off Armageddon Reef had been, it wasn't surprising it had taken Trynair over a year to go even as far as he had. During that year, unfortunately, Gorjah and his entire kingdom had languished under Mother Church's disapproval. His shipyards had been deliberately and pointedly excluded from the Church's original building program, for example. Which, given the fact that virtually the entire Royal Tarotisian Navy had been destroyed, had made Gorjah even more unhappy than he might have been otherwise. He'd *needed* new ships, and almost as badly as he'd needed *them,* he'd needed access to the rivers of gold the Church had poured into its new galley fleet.

As a matter of fact, he'd needed the money even more badly, given the ruinous economic consequences his ill-advised decision to betray Charis had produced. At the time, everything had seemed extremely simple. The Group of Four had decreed Charis' destruction, and so Charis was going to *be* destroyed. The possibility that the Church might fail of its purpose had never crossed his mind. And why should it have? *No one*—well, no one outside of Haarahld of Charis, perhaps—could have seriously entertained such a preposterous notion for a moment! And with Charis destroyed, Tarot would almost inevitably have absorbed a comfortable chunk of the onetime Charisian maritime monopoly.

That rosy road to the future, unfortunately, had encountered a minor pothole when Charis declined to perish on schedule. Not only had the pestiferous kingdom been gauche enough to survive, but its navy had emerged even more powerful than it had ever been, and a plague of Charisian privateers had amused itself eliminating all the rest of the world's merchant shipping for fun and profit. Tarot's merchant marine had come in for special and loving attention, and the privateers' depredations had been followed up by coastal raids by Charisian Marines, under the cover of Imperial Charisian Navy galleons. And then, to make bad worse, Empress Sharleyan had ordered the official ICN blockade of Thol Bay.

Rather than improving its position, the Tarotisian merchant marine had become extinct, with catastrophic consequences for the kingdom's revenues. Even that wasn't the worst of it, however, because there was still a substantial flow of Charisian goods into Tarot, although Gorjah had been careful to ensure that he had no official knowledge of that state of affairs. None of it was legal, of course. Charis had declared a blockade, and Mother Church—or, at least, the office of the Grand Inquisitor—had officially closed all of the world's ports to Charisian merchant ships. Obviously, therefore, no one could possibly be delivering the products of Charisian manufactories to a law-abiding kingdom like Tarot!

Unfortunately, Tarot *needed* those products. No one in the kingdom could produce them in sufficient quantity—or cheaply enough—to meet the needs of Gorjah's subjects, and the last thing he needed was the resentment of subjects who couldn't provide their families the necessities of life because their king was worrying about pettifogging legal technicalities about closed ports and embargoed goods. And so he winked at the bustling clandestine commerce of the smugglers landing cargoes all along the southeastern coast of the Duchy of Tranjyr.

But, in many ways, the smuggling only made things worse. None of the smugglers were especially interested in charity. They demanded—and got—cold, hard cash for their wares. Which meant Tarot's limited (and dwindling) supply of hard currency was steadily hemorrhaging its way into the very pockets of the kingdom's enemies! The Temple's refusal to extend its largess to Gorjah had been a particularly painful blow under those circumstances.

*And things aren't a lot better now,* he thought moodily. *Not that I can blame all of it on the Group of Four.*

After Trynair officially absolved Gorjah of having betrayed the Group of Four's plans, the kingdom had finally been grudgingly included in the Church's building plans. Probably even that had happened only because of how much revision those plans required once that incomparable military genius Allayn Maigwair finally figured out that they should have been building *galleons* all along. Gahvyn Mahrtyn, the Baron of White Ford, had made that point rather strongly in his own initial report on the Armageddon Reef campaign. That report had been summarily ignored, of course. In fact, there'd been some pointed comment about defeated, incompetent admirals offering up excuses for their own failures. There was a certain bitter satisfaction in seeing White Ford vindicated, although Gorjah wasn't especially surprised when no one in Zion bothered to make that vindication official. And there was no doubt that the change in the Church's plans, with the sudden need for even more shipyard capacity, had quite a lot to do with the fact that it had finally begun placing orders even in Tarot.

The grudging nature of Tarot's inclusion was evident in the number of ships the kingdom had been assigned, however. Of the two hundred forty-plus new-build war galleons the Church had ordered laid down, only twenty-two had been ordered from Tarot, despite the fact that Tranjyr, alone, could have built half again that many. And the kingdom had been directed to convert less than twenty merchant galleons for naval purposes, as well. Even the Desnairian Empire, which had never really *had* a navy before, had been assigned twice as many vessels . . . and paid the absurdly inflated prices the Desnairian yards had demanded. For that matter, the Church had helped build their damned yards in the first place!

Unfortunately, Gorjah couldn't pretend the Church's decision to throw such a small piece of the pie in Tarot's direction had been motivated solely by pique. The unhappy truth was that Tarot was the only one of the Church's building sites which wasn't connected to the mainland. Charisian privateers and cruisers had stung, hampered, and pillaged the coastal shipping carrying naval materials to the mainland yards badly enough; their ability to dominate the Tarot Channel between Tarot and Siddarmark's Windmoor Province had put a virtual stranglehold on any effort to get those same materials to Tranjyr. Timbers could be cut domestically and dragged, if slowly and laboriously, overland to the shipyards. Hulls could be built. Sails could even be woven, and rigging could be set up. But no foundry in Tarot had the expertise to produce naval artillery. All of the Royal Tarotisian Navy's pre-war guns had come from *Charisian* foundries, which—for some peculiar reason—seemed moderately disinclined to deliver their wares to Tranjyr just at the moment.

In many ways, Charis had been ironmaster to the world, for not even Siddarmark or the Harchong Empire had truly rivaled the output of her foundries. Not only had it been far cheaper to buy ironwork, including artillery, from Charis, but the *expertise,* as well as the foundries' physical plant, had been overwhelmingly concentrated in Charis, as well. So even if Gorjah had possessed unlimited financial resources (which he most definitely did *not*), he had no experienced foundry masters who knew how to build cannon that didn't blow up the second or third time they were fired. A couple of small domestic foundries were making some progress in acquiring the needed skills, but it was frustratingly difficult and agonizingly slow.

*And as White Ford's pointed out, it's probably not totally unreasonable for crews to be just a tad leery of guns that have demonstrated such a pronounced tendency to kill or mangle their gunners,* he thought disgustedly.

Well, perhaps this morning's meeting might usher in some improvement in that situation. It was unlikely, but a man could always hope.

"All right," he said as he settled himself more comfortably into the cushions of his father's chair, turning his head to look at the chamberlain standing just inside the council chamber's door. "Tell Sir Ryk he may come in now."

"Of course, Your Majesty."

The chamberlain bowed, opened the door, and stepped out into the hallway. A moment later, a stout, stocky man somewhere in his late sixties entered the chamber. He was mostly bald, and his remaining fringe of hair had gone entirely gray, but his eyebrows remained bushy and black, and his full beard was only lightly streaked with silver. His eyes were a very dark gray, and his nose was decidedly crooked, having been broken in a shipboard brawl in his youth. He also walked with a pronounced limp, courtesy of the fall from aloft which had ended his career at sea and sent him into an apprenticeship in a Charisian foundry. In the decades since, Sir Ryk Fharmyn had become one of the wealthier foundry masters of Tarot . . . until the majority of his wealth—like that of quite a few other Tarotisian subjects—had been largely destroyed as a consequence of the Charisian blockade.

Fharmyn was still much better off than most of those other subjects of Gorjah's. In fact, he was in a position to recoup much of what he'd lost, because he was also one of the handful of people in the entire kingdom who had any experience at all in casting and boring artillery.

"Your Majesty," the foundry owner said, bowing respectfully.

"Sir Ryk." Gorjah acknowledged the courtesy with a nod, then waved for the older man to straighten up once more. Fharmyn obeyed the gesture, and Gorjah leaned back in his oversized chair. "Tell me," the king said, "to what do I owe the pleasure of your company this morning?"

"First, Your Majesty, let me thank you for agreeing to see me. I realize I made the request for an audience on rather short notice."

Gorjah's left hand made a waving-away motion, and Fharmyn dipped his head slightly to acknowledge the king's graciousness.

"Second, Your Majesty," Fharmyn continued, "I've come to invite you to join Baron White Ford at the foundry in a couple of days—Tuesday, I think— for the proof firing of our latest attempt to produce a satisfactory thirty-six-pounder." The ironmaster's lips twitched a bit sourly. "I hope this one will go a little better than the last. Having said that, though, I'm not about to let you— or Baron White Ford—get anywhere near the thing when it's actually loaded, Your Majesty."

"I'm sure Queen Maiyl will appreciate that," Gorjah murmured with a slight, whimsical smile.

"I always try to stay on the Queen's good side, Your Majesty," Fharmyn assured him, and there was a gleam of answering humor in his gray eyes.

"A wise decision, trust me," Gorjah replied. Then he cocked his head. "And were those your only reasons for asking to see me this morning?"

His tone was still pleasant, yet it carried a distinct edge of hardness, as well. Not anger, but an indication that he was fairly certain those *weren't* the only reasons for Fharmyn's request . . . and a suggestion the foundry owner get on to his other, and presumably more important, motivations.

"No, Your Highness," Fharmyn acknowledged, and his tone had shifted a bit, as well. In fact, to Gorjah's surprise, it had taken on a hint of . . . tentativeness. That wasn't the exact word the king was looking for, and he knew it, but it came closer than anything else he could think of.

The foundry owner paused—one might almost have said he hesitated—for an instant, then shrugged ever so slightly.

"As I'm sure you know, Your Majesty," he went on then, a bit obliquely, "I was originally trained in Charis. Over the years, I've done quite a bit of business with Charisian manufactories, as well. Or, perhaps I should say that I *did* do quite a bit of business with them before the present . . . unpleasantness."

He paused again, watching the king's expression, and Gorjah nodded.

"Of course I'm aware of all that, Sir Ryk," he said just a little impatiently. "And you're scarcely alone in having had financial relationships—or, for that matter, *personal* relationships—with Charis! I don't imagine there's anyone involved in our current building programs who didn't, if that's what you're concerned about."

"I'm not *concerned* about it, precisely, Your Majesty, but it does have a certain bearing on the reason I asked to see you this morning." Fharmyn looked at the king levelly. "It happens, Your Majesty, that a letter was recently delivered to me by someone who, alas, I suspect acquired it from a Charisian smuggler."

Gorjah's eyebrows rose, and Fharmyn coughed delicately into a raised hand.

"I don't say he acquired it *directly* from a smuggler, Your Majesty," he said then. "I only say I believe that was how the letter in question originally entered the Kingdom. It was, however, addressed to *me,* which—as I'm sure Your Majesty will appreciate—caused me quite a bit of anxiety." He shrugged again. "My first thought was to deliver it directly to Father Frahnklyn, although I will readily confess to Your Majesty that I wasn't at all happy about the prospect of directing the Inquisition's attention to the man who had handed me the letter."

*Well, I'm not surprised to hear that, Sir Ryk,* Gorjah thought dryly. *And not simply because you didn't want to get the other fellow—whoever he may be—into trouble. Oh, I'll do you the courtesy of believing you thought about that, but I'm certain keeping yourself out of the Inquisition's sights wasn't exactly a minor factor in your decision not to go pestering the Intendant, as well!*

But Fharmyn wasn't quite finished yet.

"Nor was I happy about the prospect of directing the Inquisition's attention to the addressee of the letter which was enclosed in the one to me," the older man went on. "Because that addressee, Your Majesty, was *you*."

Gorjah's eyes went wide, and he leaned forward in his chair.

"I beg your pardon?" he said in a very careful tone, and Fharmyn smiled humorlessly.

"That was rather my own reaction, Your Majesty. I opened my own letter only because I've known the man who sent it to me for so long and because, frankly, I wanted to judge the extent to which it might compromise me in the Inquisition's eyes." He made the admission calmly. "So far as I was aware, I'd done or said nothing which might have created a legitimate problem for me, but one can never be too careful about things like that in times like these."

He held the king's gaze unflinchingly, and Gorjah nodded slowly as the other man's implication sank in. The king could think of quite a few possible consequences of the Inquisition's discovering that anyone in Charis was addressing correspondence directly to *him*, as well. Oddly enough, not one of those consequences would have been pleasant.

"Once I found the enclosure," Fharmyn continued, "I seriously considered burning both letters. On more mature consideration, however, I realized I had no way of knowing if additional letters would be sent if this one didn't produce whatever outcome its sender had in mind. The idea of having an unknown number of Charisian letters addressed to me—and, quite possibly, to Your Majesty—floating around the Kingdom didn't appeal to me. And, frankly, the thought that the letter-sender might attempt to reach you through a different channel—one which could end up bringing all of this to the Inquisition's notice after all—was even less appealing."

The foundry owner hadn't mentioned the probability that "a different channel" wouldn't have known the initial letter had come by way of Fharmyn. Which would have meant, presumably, that the other man wouldn't have been implicated, so far as the Inquisition knew, in the effort to set up some sort of clandestine communication with the king. Fharmyn was far too astute not to have thought of that, and the fact that he hadn't chosen to say a word about it suggested many things to King Gorjah of Tarot.

"Should I assume, Sir Ryk," he said, carefully, after a trickle of seconds, "that you've brought that letter to me?"

"I have, Your Majesty."

Fharmyn bowed gravely, then extracted a large envelope from inside his tunic. Gorjah held out his hand when he saw it, and Fharmyn limped around the table to lay it in his palm. But he paused before he handed it to his king.

"Your Majesty, I've brought you *both* letters," he said, looking Gorjah in the eye. "Obviously, I haven't opened the one addressed to you. I have no idea what it contains. If you choose to place all of this in the Inquisition's hands, I will cooperate in any way they—or you—require. Indeed, if you wish it, I'll take both of them to Father Frahnklyn immediately, without ever mentioning this meeting."

"I appreciate the generosity of your offer, Sir Ryk," Gorjah replied, and he meant it. "Nonetheless, as yourself, I believe it behooves me to see what this letter contains first." He showed a flash of white teeth, and his dark eyes glinted with genuine, if sardonic, humor. "I can think of quite a few ways in which a letter could be crafted to create all manner of suspicion in someone's mind."

"I considered that, Your Majesty," Fharmyn acknowledged. "At the same time, though, it occurred to me that if the idea was to plant false information, false suspicion, in the mind of the Inquisition, there were probably simpler and more reliable ways for Earl Gray Harbor or Baron Wave Thunder to 'acciden-tally' allow their correspondence to 'fall' into the Inquisition's hands."

Gorjah's eyes narrowed thoughtfully. There'd been no need for Fharmyn to offer that last observation, and the king wondered why he had.

*Is that simply your way of suggesting that you think whatever this damned thing says is genuine? Or is it your way of suggesting that I ought to read it . . . and possibly give some serious thought to whatever it* does *say?*

He considered asking the question out loud, but only briefly. Either way, it really didn't matter . . . except that—again, either way—the foundry owner obviously did think he should read it.

"That's an excellent point," he said instead, and waggled the fingers of his outstretched hand very slightly.

Fharmyn took the hint and laid the envelope in his palm. Gorjah let it lie there for a moment while he gazed down at it, feeling its weight, wondering what it said. Then he looked back up at Fharmyn.

"Sir Ryk, I'm well aware that bringing this to me was no easy decision. I appreciate your courage in doing so, and the frankness of your explanation. And, for that matter, the wisdom of your analysis. Now, however, I think it would be best for you to return to your home while I examine this and think about it."

"Of course, Your Majesty." Fharmyn began to back away from the table, avoiding the social solecism of turning his back upon his monarch, but Gorjah raised the index finger of his free hand, and the foundry owner paused.

"If it should happen I decide the Inquisition needs to be informed about this, Sir Ryk," the king said quietly, "I'll have word sent to you first. Before I contact Father Frahnklyn." He saw Fharmyn's face tighten slightly. "I believe I owe you that courtesy. And, whatever happens, I promise you that I won't for-get your service in bringing it to *me*."

He emphasized the final pronoun very slightly, but deliberately, and Fharmyn nodded.

"Thank you, Your Majesty. And, now, with Your Majesty's permission—?" He gestured in the door's direction, and Gorjah nodded.

"By all means, Sir Ryk," he agreed, then watched while the foundry owner eased out of the council chamber and the door closed quietly behind him.

The King of Tarot gazed at that closed door for the better part of two minutes. Then, finally, he laid the envelope on the table in front of him, opened it, and extracted its contents. He paid no immediate attention to the cover letter to Fharmyn. Instead, he slowly unfolded the second envelope which had been enclosed in the first one, and his eyes widened as he saw the handwriting. He paused for just a moment, then flattened it on the table, holding it down for a moment with both hands, the way a man might restrain a small, unknown animal he wasn't certain wasn't going to bite.

*Well, I don't suppose* that's *a surprise,* a corner of his brain reflected as he studied the handwritten address. *Or, maybe it is. I'm sure he has a secretary somewhere he could trust with almost any correspondence. On the other hand, I imagine he could be fairly confident this would be one way to get my attention.* The king surprised himself with a snort of humor. *Not that his rather dramatic way of getting it delivered didn't already take care of that!*

King Gorjah shook his head, looking down at the envelope an extraordinarily busy and powerful man had addressed himself. There was no question in the king's mind that the man who'd done that had expected his addressee to recognize his handwriting, know it had truly come from *him.*

Now it only remained to see exactly what Rayjhis Yowance, the Earl of Gray Harbor and, effectively, the first councilor of the Charisian Empire, had to say to him.

# MARCH, YEAR OF GOD 894

It was cool on deck, despite the bright sunlight, as the brisk easterly wind pushed HMS *Dancer* steadily westward in a wind-hum of rigging and the wash and bubble of water around the hull. The galleon was on very nearly her best point of sailing, with the wind coming in just abaft the starboard quarter, and with all sail set to the royals, she was making almost ten knots. That was a very respectable turn of speed for any galleon, even one only two months out of port. Of course, like every galleon in the Imperial Charisian Navy, *Dancer* was copper-sheathed below the waterline. It protected her from both the borers which all too often devoured a ship's timbers without anyone noticing (until her bottom fell out, that was) and from the weed which killed her speed, as well. Nothing could *completely* stop a ship's bottom from growing steadily fouler, but *Dancer's* copper gave her a tremendous advantage. It was going to make her faster than most ships she might meet, even as far away from home as the Gulf of Dohlar.

Still, she could have done a bit better than her present speed if she'd been sailing by herself, Admiral Sir Gwylym Manthyr thought as he paced steadily back and forth along the railed walkway which stretched the full width of her stern. Ships sailing in company were always slower than they might have been sailing alone, because every sailing vessel was unique, each had her own best point of sail. Even sister ships from the same dockyard, as alike as two peas to the human eye, took wave and wind differently, made their best speeds under slightly different conditions. A captain who knew his ship as well as Captain Raif Mahgail knew *Dancer* could wring the very best performance out of his command in any given wind and sea, but when ships sailed in company, they were limited to the best speed of the *slowest* vessel under whatever conditions currently applied.

That thought was one which had been largely academic when Manthyr had commanded HMS *Dreadnought,* then-Prince Cayleb's flagship. Despite the fact that *Dreadnought* had been a fleet flagship, Manthyr's responsibilities hadn't included deciding what that fleet was going to do next, or worrying about how long it was going to take *all* of its ships to get from one point to another.

Of course, he wasn't a mere flag captain any longer.

He'd lost *Dreadnought* at Darcos Sound, a memory which still brought him intense pain, and not simply because of how much he'd loved that ship. He'd lost her, in the end, because he'd deliberately rammed her into a Corisandian galley under all the sail she could carry. Even though she'd struck bows-on, she'd been traveling too fast at the moment of impact, and he'd split her seams wide open. He'd managed to stave in a good twenty feet of her hull planking, as well, inflicting far too much damage below the waterline for her crew to save her, desperately though they'd tried. He'd known well before she struck that he was going to do potentially fatal damage, too. But that wasn't the reason the memory hurt so much. No. No, it hurt so much because, even so, he'd been too late. Because despite all he and his crew had been able to do—and he knew, without doubt, that they'd done everything humanly possible—they'd been ten minutes too late to save their king's life.

Gwylym Manthyr would have sent a dozen galleons to the bottom in return for those ten minutes.

He realized he'd stopped pacing, that he was standing with his hands on the sternwalk rail, staring back across *Dancer*'s wake. He looked out over the vast expanse of the Southern Ocean and gave himself a shake. The only person in the world who blamed him for being too late was himself, and he knew that, too. His knighthood, and his promotion from captain to admiral, would have been proof enough of that, even without his current assignment.

His was the most distant of all of Charis' far-flung squadrons. He was two months out from the great naval base at Lock Island, with eighteen war galleons, six schooners, and no less than thirty transports, and wind and weather had favored him quite unreasonably. Indeed, he was the better part of two five-days ahead of his originally projected passage time, some hundred miles south of the Thairmahn Peninsula, rounding up around the southern end of the continent of Howard to pass through the Gosset Passage between Westbreak Island and the western tip of the enormously larger island called The Barren Lands into the Harthian Sea. That put him nine thousand miles from Lock Island, but that was in a straight line, and ships couldn't just fly through the air. To reach this point, Manthyr's squadron had been forced to sail over *fifteen* thousand miles, and they still had almost five thousand to go. At such a vast distance from any of his superiors, Manthyr was entirely on his own, which was a pretty conclusive statement of those superiors' trust in him and his judgment, however he looked at it. After all, he had only the resources aboard his own ships—plus whatever he could "liberate"—and no one to turn to for orders or directions.

In some ways, that made him no different from the captain of any warship on independent duty. Ultimately, every captain in that situation was always on his own when it came to the decision point. And whatever that captain decided, someone else was likely to decide he'd been wrong and say so—loudly. But that was part of the price for commanding a king's (or, now, an emperor's) ship.

*Still,* he thought, gazing out over that enormous spread of dark blue water, *I have to admit that I never really appreciated, as a mere captain, how much . . . nastier the whole thing gets as a flag officer.*

His lips twitched wryly. One thing he'd learned long ago was that the perspective was always different. As a midshipman, he'd thought captains were God and lieutenants were Archangels. As a lieutenant, he'd started to recognize that captains were only masters *after* God, but they'd still been at least equal to the Archangels in their godlike authority and power. As a captain, he'd come to recognize—fully recognize, for the first time—the full crushing weight of the responsibilities a captain shouldered in return for his all-powerful authority at sea. But now that he was an admiral himself, he realized that, in many ways, flag officers had the worst of all worlds. For all their lordly authority, they commanded squadrons and fleets, not *ships.* They directed, they administered, they devised strategies, and the full weight of responsibility for success or failure rested upon *them,* but they were forced to rely on *others* to execute their plans, carry out their orders. They might even get to direct the movements of their squadrons up to the moment battle was actually joined, yet once the ships under their command finally came into action, they were spectators. Passengers. For all their lordly power to direct the movement of *other* ships, they would never again command their own, and he hadn't realized just how much that was going to hurt.

*Oh, stop it, Gwylym!* He chuckled harshly. *If that's the way you feel, you can always ask them to take the nice admiral's streamer back! Or you could have asked them not to give it to you in the first place. There's a price for everything, and you learned that a long time before you got your captain's commission. Do you really think you could convince anyone—including yourself!—that you don't want to be out here doing what you're doing?*

Probably not, he reflected, and then, in response to a certain rumbling sensation from the direction of his stomach, pulled his watch from his pocket.

No wonder he was feeling peckish. Lunchtime had arrived ten minutes ago, and he had no doubt Captain Mahgail and the rest of his officers were already seated around the large table in his dining cabin, waiting for him.

*Yet another proof rank has its privileges,* he thought wryly, closing the watch. He straightened and inhaled another deep lungful of the clean ocean smell. *They're all sitting there waiting for me while I stand here in lordly splendor and isolation. I wonder how much longer they'll be willing to give me before Dahnyld comes ever so respectfully looking for me?*

He had to admit that a tiny, nasty part of him was half tempted to wait and see how long it would take for Dahnyld Rahzmahn, his highly efficient flag lieutenant, to overcome his natural deference and oh-so-diplomatically remind his admiral that he had luncheon guests waiting for him. But it was only *half* a temptation. Maybe even only a *quarter* temptation, he reflected judiciously. No, it was at least a *third* of a temptation, he decided. Which probably said less than complimentary things about his own nature.

He grinned broadly and shook his head.

*It's good to be the Admiral, Gwylym,* he told himself. *It might be a good idea not to let it go to your head, though. I think Admiral Lock Island said something in that general vein when he gave you your orders, didn't he? In his own inimitably diplomatic fashion, of course.*

That thought transformed the grin into a deep, rolling laugh. He gave his head another shake, then turned and stepped through the windowed door from the sternwalk into his day cabin.

## .II.
## Summit House Lodge,
## Province of Glacierheart,
## Republic of Siddarmark

"Your Eminence, how long have I been your valet?"

Zhasyn Cahnyr turned to look at Fraidmyn Tohmys speculatively. He knew that long-suffering tone entirely too well.

"For quite some time," he said mildly, at which Tohmys folded his arms and gave him a very stern look indeed.

At the moment, the Archbishop of Glacierheart sat in front of a fire barely short of roaring. Summit House Lodge, the name some long-ago archbishop had bestowed upon his summer retreat, lay considerably higher up the mountain behind the city of Tairys than the city itself. The relatively modest lodge was also, despite the steep-pitched, snow-shedding roof all buildings required in these mountains, intended as a *summer* residence. A place for the archbishop and his favored guests to withdraw into rustic seclusion and relax. (Cahnyr suspected that at least one of his predecessors had also seen Summit House as a secluded venue for drunken parties and the occasional orgy far enough away from his parishioners' disapproving eyes to avoid any official scandal.) The fact that it had been viewed primarily as a summer residence, however, also meant that even though it was weathertight, it hadn't really been designed for occupancy in the coldest month of an East Haven winter. Despite the high-piled coal fire on the drawing room's hearth, the air temperature left much to be desired. Which was why Cahnyr wore a thick sweater over his heavy woolen winter-weight cassock.

Despite which he felt a certain sympathy for a ham hung up in an ice-house.

"For forty-three years, Your Eminence," Tohmys told him now. "*That's* how long I've been your valet."

"Really?" Cahnyr canted his head to the side. "I do believe you're right. Odd. I thought it had been longer than that somehow."

Something glinted in Tohmys' eyes, and his sternly set lips might have twitched ever so slightly. It was possible, at any rate.

"Well, Your Eminence, saving your pardon and all, I hope you'll not take it the wrong way if I tell you that of all the addle-brained flights you've gotten up to—and, yes, I *do* remember that 'party' of yours when you near as nothing got tossed out of seminary—this one is the worst."

"It's not as if I really have much choice at this point, Fraidmyn," Cahnyr replied in a much more sober tone. "And I deeply regret having gotten *you* involved in all of this. But—"

He shrugged, and Tohmys snorted.

"The way *I* recall it, Your Eminence, I was as enthusiastic about it as ever you were. I'd not go taking all the credit, were I you."

"No, that's fair enough, I suppose. But I'm the archbishop around here. It's not right that you should suffer for my actions. Or that you should be stuck up here with me hoping whoever wrote that letter meant what he said."

"And where else should I be?" Tohmys demanded. "I've no more chick nor child than you do, Your Eminence, and you need someone to look after you. I've gotten into the habit of doing that." He shrugged. "Look at it how you will, there's little point in regretting and even less in trying to change what's done."

"Well," Cahnyr smiled, feeling his eyes burn slightly, "if that's the way you feel, then why this sudden criticism of my plans?"

"Why, as to that, if it were to happen you *had* any 'plans' to speak of, then I'd not have opened my mouth." Somehow, Cahnyr found *that* a bit difficult to believe. "As it happens, howsomesoever, as near as I can see, your 'plans' consist of turning up in the middle of the night in the middle of the mountains in the middle of the winter in nought but the clothes on your back and *hoping* someone as you've never met and don't even know the name of will be waiting there for you. Would it be I've got that more or less straight, Your Eminence?"

"Actually, I think that's a fairly masterly summation," the archbishop conceded.

"And you think all of that's a good idea, do you?" Tohmys demanded.

"No, I simply think it's the best idea available to us," Cahnyr replied. "Why? Have you thought of a better one?"

"No, and it's not my business to be thinking of better ones, either." If Tohmys had been fazed by Cahnyr's challenge, he gave no sign of it. Besides, as both of them understood perfectly well, his was the duty to sound the voice of gloom and doom, not to suggest how his dismal prophecies might be evaded. "It's just that I was wishful of being certain I had all that straight in my head."

"I'd say you do," Cahnyr said judiciously.

"Well, in that case, and seeing as how your mind's made up, I'd best see about finishing packing, hadn't I?"

▼    ▼    ▼

Much later that afternoon, Zhasyn Cahnyr stood, gazing out of his Summit House bedchamber window. This late in the day, especially here on the eastern side of Mount Tairys, the tallest peak of the Tairys Range, evening would already have been settling into night, under even the best of conditions. Under the current conditions, he could see very little beyond the flakes of hard-driven snow being blown through the feeble illumination of the window's own light.

Wind howled around Summit House's eves, and despite the fires on the hearths, his breath steamed. It would be an excellent night for freezing to death, he reflected.

He turned back to survey the bedchamber in which he would not be sleeping tonight after all. He understood why his decision to make a retreat up here had dismayed Gharth Gorjah. Summit House's primitive facilities, its isolation, and the possibility of weather exactly like this night promised had been more than enough to make his secretary worry about his well-being. For that matter, Cahnyr was forced to admit he shared some of Gorjah's concerns. On the other hand, he knew something about Summit House which he doubted his secretary had even considered while he was thinking of things to worry about. There was no reason he should have thought about it, given how carefully Cahnyr had kept the younger man ignorant of the worries crushing down upon him. And the very things which had made Gorjah worry about Cahnyr's spending a couple of five-days up on the mountain had actively reassured Bryahn Teagmahn . . . who very definitely did not know about Summit House's special features.

It was possible Bishop Executor Wyllys *did* know the aspect of Summit House which had made it so suitable to Cahnyr's present purposes, despite the season and the weather. He'd served the last Archbishop of Glacierheart for over eight years even before Cahnyr had been confirmed as archbishop, and he'd used the residence frequently himself, during the hottest five-days of the summer. As such, it was possible he'd made the same discovery Cahnyr had. Of course, even if he had, it probably wouldn't have occurred to him to worry about it.

Probably.

Cahnyr didn't know if the bishop executor had been actively recruited by the Inquisition. He doubted it, yet he was also aware that he *wanted* to doubt it because of how much he liked Wyllys Haimltahn. The bishop executor was hardworking, dedicated to the well-being of the archbishopric and its people, and remarkably restrained in the graft he skimmed. He wasn't *immune* to the peculation which had infected the Church, but that would have been a bit much to expect. In fact, it was expected he *would* find the odd way to slip a few less-than-legal marks into his purse. However much it might sadden the archbishop to admit it, that practice had become so accepted that the Treasury allowed for it when establishing a bishop executor's official remuneration.

And the fact that Haimltahn was part of that system was the only real criticism of him Cahnyr could have levied. Unfortunately, he'd never evinced any particular awareness of, or zeal to attack, the far greater and uglier corruption at the heart of the Temple. It wasn't that he *approved* of it. Cahnyr was certain of that much, at least. But Wyllys Haimltahn was a provincial bishop executor assigned to one of the poorest archbishoprics in all of East Haven. He was never going to find himself serving in Zion or the Temple, whatever happened, and so he'd resolutely set his focus on *his* world and his responsibilities in it, leaving the concerns of the greater and more powerful *to* the greater and more powerful.

Cahnyr couldn't really fault him for that, but it was the reason he'd never approached the bishop executor about his own activities. Which meant he could hardly have asked Haimltahn whether or not he did know Cahnyr's true motive for "retreating" to Summit House.

*Oh, stop it,* he told himself. *First, you're probably doing Wyllys a profound disservice even considering the possibility that he's been conspiring with Teagmahn. Secondly, even if he is, Teagmahn obviously didn't object to your coming up here. So either he doesn't know about your little secret, or else he doesn't see how it could have any bearing on the current situation.*

Despite the seriousness of the moment, Cahnyr snorted in dry amusement. From Teagmahn's reaction to his decision to spend several days up at Summit House, the intendant had clearly decided exactly what Cahnyr had hoped he would decide: that having the archbishop safely tucked away in an isolated vacation lodge reached only by a single, narrow road (little more than a trail, really, in many places) suited the Inquisition's needs perfectly. There was no way Cahnyr could possibly sneak back down from Summit House and creep through Tairys without Teagmahn's knowledge.

All of which, Cahnyr thought, was quite true . . . and completely irrelevant to his own plans. Such as they were and what there was of them, at any rate.

Knuckles rapped on his bedchamber door, scarcely audible over the storm howl raging about Summit House, and Cahnyr turned from the window as the door opened.

"It's time, Your Eminence," Fraidmyn Tohmys said, and held out the heavy parka.

▼　　▼　　▼

Glacierheart was mining country, and always had been. No man living had any clear idea of the full extent of shafts, galleries, and excavations which had been sunk into the bones of the world by generation upon generation of miners. There were charts and maps, yet no one was foolish enough to believe they were anything like comprehensive. Or, for that matter, accurate.

The mine which had been run under what eventually became Summit House was on none of those charts, none of those maps. It was very old, and Cahnyr had often wondered who'd driven it. It was obvious that it had been following a thick bed of coal, but it was equally obvious that the coal had been playing out by the time the mine reached this point, and Summit House was literally miles away from the Graywater or the Tairys Canal. For that matter, Cahnyr suspected this particular mine had been abandoned long before the canal had been built or the river's locks had been constructed. So even when it had been productive, just getting the coal to market must have been a back-breaking task.

What mattered at the moment, however, was that one long-ago summer, Zhasyn Cahnyr had fallen through the well-rotted timbers covering one of the mine's escape shafts.

The shaft had been driven very near the end of the gallery directly under the lodge, with the result that it had been no more than thirty or forty feet long. More importantly for Cahnyr, it was steep, but not vertical. He'd been bruised and winded by the fall, but he'd also been younger at the time, and curiosity had quickly displaced the urge to sit in the dark nursing a barked shin and muttering words of which Mother Church would not have approved. So he'd gotten back to his feet, returned to Summit House, and commandeered Gharth Gorjah and Fraidmyn Tohmys (both of whom had already discovered his passion for spelunking), a bagful of candles, a piece of chalk, and a ball of string.

He still didn't know why he'd never mentioned his discovery to anyone else. It wasn't that he'd ever decided he'd best keep it secret against some desperate future need to escape from the Inquisition. And, to be honest, he *should* have mentioned it to someone else, especially if he intended to go on poking around inside the mountain. He hadn't grown up here in Glacierheart, but as an experienced cave-crawler, he'd been only too well aware of the dangers of cave-in, gas, water, accidental falls—all of the manifold ways the world could crush the life out of men rash enough to seek to steal its treasures. He'd been careful, and he'd never been so foolish as to go by himself (although, to be fair, neither he nor Tohmys would ever again be able to claim the adjective "spry"), but he'd steadfastly kept the discovery to himself.

Part of it, he'd later realized, was the quiet down in the mine. The stillness.

The hush. The old coal mine was a far cry from the natural caves and caverns which had first drawn him into spelunking. It wasn't even very interesting, when one came right down to it. It was simply a very long, very deep, very dark hole in the ground.

Yet it was a very old hole, and one which had been made by the hands of man, and not the patient wash of water. There was that sense of stepping into the past, of touching the lives of the miners who'd labored here scores—hundreds— of years before Cahnyr's own birth. In an odd sort of way, that mine had become a cathedral. Its hushed, *listening* stillness had become a perfect place for him to simply sit, and contemplate, and *feel* the presence of God. It had become, in many ways, his true spiritual retreat, and he'd shared it with no one except his secretary, his valet, and God. He'd never actually ordered the other two not to mention their discoveries to anyone else, but he'd realized long ago that both of them had recognized his desire to keep it to himself.

He hadn't spent all of his time in the mine in meditation, however. In fact, he'd spent many an hour exploring, rambling through the galleries and shafts. The mountain was solid here, and he'd discovered little of the timbering which could yield to rot and age and create death traps. There was one gallery he'd assiduously avoided after one look at its roof, and he'd encountered several flooded sections which had, obviously, ended exploration in those directions. Still, he'd hiked more than a few miles under the earth's surface, marking the walls as he went, always trailing his string behind him in case of disaster.

Now he paused, just inside the shaft he'd discovered so many years before, brushing matted snow off the front of his parka with mittened hands. The short hike from Summit House to the shaft entrance had been enormously harder than he'd let himself expect. The wind was even more violent than he'd thought, lis- tening to it howl around the lodge, and the temperature was still falling. He and Tohmys had transported a small stack of essential supplies to the shaft the day af- ter they arrived at the lodge, and it was just as well they hadn't waited. Just the knapsacks each of them wore had been burdensome enough under the current conditions.

He finished slapping off as much as he could of the thick skim of snow, then tugged off one mitten and dragged out his fire-striker. It was cold enough, and his hand was shivering enough, that it took him longer than usual to get the bull's-eye lantern lit, but its glow once he got the wick alight was ample com- pensation for his efforts. Most people might have been excused for thinking that the bare, cold rock of the escape shaft's walls could be considered a welcoming sight, but "most people" weren't Zhasyn Cahnyr and didn't know the Inquisi- tion was simply biding its time before it pounced.

"Well, so far so good!" he said cheerfully.

"Aye?" Tohmys regarded him skeptically in the lantern glow. "And how far would 'so far' be being, Your Eminence?"

"The *Writ* tells us the longest journey begins with the first step," Cahnyr replied serenely.

"So it does, Your Eminence, and I'm not one to be arguing with the Archangels. Still and all, though, it occurs to me we've quite a few other steps to be taking."

"Now *that*, Fraidmyn, is a very sound doctrinal point." Cahnyr picked up the lantern and lifted his pole of the two-man, two-wheeled cart on which their supplies were stacked. "Shall we go?" he invited.

▼    ▼    ▼

Several hours later, Cahnyr's legs felt about as tired as they'd ever felt.

It had been some time since he'd been this deep in the mine, and he'd forgotten how far it was. Or, rather, he'd been younger the last time he'd been here, so he hadn't allowed for how much longer it had become in the interim. And it was going to be a great deal longer before they came out on the other side. In fact, it was going to be evening again by the time they could get there.

He smiled wearily at the thought, sitting on the edge of the cart, gnawing on the sandwich Tohmys had offered him. The bread was thick-sliced, and the meat, cheese, and onions were delicious. He'd have liked a little lettuce, as well, but lettuce wasn't something one saw a lot of in Glacierheart in the winter. He'd considered for years having a greenhouse added to the archbishop's palace, and he'd always meant to get around to it. Now, though . . .

He brushed that thought aside, dug out his watch, and tilted it enough to make out its face in the lantern light. It was always easy to become disconnected from the world's time down here deep in the earth. With no sight of sun or sky, no contact with weather, it was more difficult to estimate the passing hours than someone who'd never made the attempt might have guessed. At least the mine maintained a constant, unwavering temperature, although he would never have made the mistake of calling it "warm," and despite the need to weave their way through the complex pattern of underground passages, they'd made much better time than they would have made into the teeth of the blizzard howling around the outside of the mountain. Still, they had to reach their destination within the "window of time" his mysterious letter writer had defined.

"We need to move on," he said after swallowing a mouthful of sandwich.

"No doubt." Tohmys handed him a deep mug filled with beer. "And as soon as you've finished that sandwich, it's moving on we'll be."

"I can chew and walk at the same time," Cahnyr said mildly, putting his watch back into his pocket in order to free up his hand and accept the mug. "For that matter, I can *swallow* and walk at the same time, if I concentrate hard."

"The fact that you *can* do it isn't to say as how you do it *well*, Your Eminence," his unimpressed henchman responded. "Now eat."

Cahnyr looked at him for a moment, then shook his head—but meekly, *meekly!*—and ate.

▼　　▼　　▼

"And did stopping to eat put us behind schedule after all, Your Eminence?"

There was only the merest trace of satisfaction, by Fraidmyn Tohmys' standards, in the question, and Cahnyr shook his head in resignation. The only thing worse than Tohmys' being right about something like this were the almost unheard of occasions when he was *wrong*. At which point, he could become extremely difficult for a mere archbishop to put up with.

"No, Fraidmyn, we're actually a bit early," he admitted.

"Fancy that, now," Tohmys murmured. Cahnyr very carefully failed to hear the comment.

"So now what do we do, Your Eminence?" the valet asked after a moment.

"We poke our heads outside and see what the weather looks like," Tannyr said, gathering up the bull's-eye lantern, and proceeded to do just that.

He had to crouch as he approached the mouth of the tunnel. As nearly as he'd been able to determine from his explorations, the tunnel through which he was now making his way had been driven—probably—many years after the main mine had been abandoned. It had come from the outside, and he wondered how the people digging it had reacted when they'd broken through and discovered that someone else had already dug out the coal they'd hoped to discover.

Fortunately, they hadn't had to go all that far to make the discovery. The tunnel was barely a hundred yards long, and it had never been more than a rough-edged shaft. He had to pick his way with a certain degree of care, especially since he didn't want to get too close to the tunnel mouth with a lit lantern. About fifteen yards from the end of the tunnel, he closed the lantern's slide and proceeded slowly and cautiously, one hand feeling along the wall.

He felt the cold intensifying as he got closer and closer to the mountainside, and he wondered, once again, what had inspired the letter writer to pick the spot for which he and Tohmys were bound as one of the rendezvous he'd set up. It was a logical enough choice, in a lot of ways: a modest, backcountry posting house at a crossroads. Not on the main high road, but where two country roads—*mountain* country roads—met and nodded to one another in passing before they continued on their ways. One of those roads, although it was very little used in the winter, linked two minor cities, just over a hundred miles apart. The twisting, turning, climbing, and diving nature of mountain roads explained why people usually chose to use the high road which skirted the central mass of the Tairys Range and, while longer, traveled through what passed for bottomlands in Glacierheart.

The second road was even less heavily used in winter. It headed generally southwest, towards the southern edge of the Tairys Range and the city of Mountain Lake on the shore of Glacierborn Lake.

This time of year, there wouldn't be much traffic for the posting house to serve. The owners would be delighted to see any customers they could get, and it was isolated enough to make it unlikely that news that a stranger was hanging about would reach Tairys before the "time window" closed and he was gone. On the other hand, it wasn't exactly conveniently located from the perspective of the archbishop's palace. In fact, it was almost eighty miles from Tairys as a wyvern might have flown, and over three hundred by road. Assuming there'd been a road from Summit House to the crossroads, Cahnyr would still have to have crossed the better part of forty-five miles of winter mountainside. Of course, thanks to the abandoned coal mine, he and Tohmys would emerge from their subterranean passage little more than fifteen miles from their destination, but someone writing from what had to be Zion could scarcely have counted on that. From that distant a perspective, this was clearly the *least* convenient of the three rendezvous points the letter writer had proposed, and the archbishop suspected it was actually little more than a last-hope fallback position. It seemed unlikely anyone could have genuinely expected Cahnyr to somehow reach the posting house.

*And now that we're here,* Cahnyr thought, picking his way cautiously through the blackness, *I still don't know how I'm supposed to walk into the posting house and make contact. It's not exactly as if I'm the least well known man in Glacierheart! I can always* hope *no one will recognize me this far from Tairys, but somehow I think* counting *on it might not be the smartest thing I could possibly do. So how do I discreetly—*

His thoughts chopped off, and he froze as his dark-accustomed eyes suddenly widened. Light! There was *light* ahead, and—

"Actually, Your Eminence," a voice said from ahead of him, "I rather expected you *last* night."

Cahnyr's eyes went wider than ever. It couldn't be!

*"Gharth?!"* he heard his own voice say hoarsely.

"Well," his secretary said, emerging around the bend in the tunnel with his own bull's-eye lantern and smiling broadly, "having me involved *did* make delivering that letter a bit easier, now didn't it, Your Eminence?"

▼　　▼　　▼

"You're mad, Gharth," Zhasyn Cahnyr said with soft, firm emphasis several minutes later. "God knows I've spent *years* keeping you clear of all this! And you're a father—and Sahmantha's *pregnant,* for Pasquale's sake!"

"Yes," Gharth Gorjah agreed with a remarkably calm nod. "Clyntahn's timing on all of this could have been much more considerate, don't you think?" He gave his superior a decidedly stern look, his youthful face older in the lantern's shadows. "And if you truly thought you'd managed to keep me ignorant of your activities all this time, Your Eminence, I can only say I am astonished that such an inept conspirator managed to get away with it this long."

"But—" Cahnyr began.

"Your Eminence, we can argue about this as long as you want," Gorjah interrupted, "but I really think we ought to get underway while we do it. Unless you want to turn around, climb all the way back up through that mountain, and simply forget about it. I wouldn't recommend that, though. I'm pretty sure that offal-lizard Teagmahn expects orders to arrest you any day now."

Cahnyr closed his mouth, and Gorjah reached out to touch his arm gently.

"Your Eminence, you didn't recruit me. Whatever I'm doing, I'm doing because I choose to do it, and Sahmantha had a pretty fair idea of how I think, what I believe in, before I ever asked her to marry me. I haven't done anything without consulting with her, and she's supported me every step of the way. Trust me, she agrees with you about Clyntahn's timing, and I'm not saying she's not—that we both aren't—scared to our marrow thinking about what could happen to us and, especially, to the kids. But it's not as if we never saw this coming, either."

"But what is it you *are* doing, Gharth?" Cahnyr asked. "Somehow I don't think you've simply been sitting around keeping an eye on me just in case I got into trouble. And if you haven't been actively involved in what *I've* been doing, then what *have* you been involved in?"

"The truth is, Your Eminence, that I *have* been basically 'sitting around keeping an eye' on you." Gorjah shrugged. "I'll tell you all about it as soon as I can—as soon as I have permission to. For right now, though, just accept that someone else knew about you and your friends in the Temple. I don't know who those others are, and I don't know everything you've been up to. I do know, now, why you had me doing some of the research in the archbishopric's records. Why you were looking for proof of corruption, or of directives from the Temple that were . . . less than appropriate for one of God's vicars or archbishops to be issuing, shall we say. And I understand now why you've taken some of the stances you've taken, despite the fact that you knew they were going to be wildly unpopular with other members of the episcopate.

"I'll admit it hurt, at first, when I realized there was something deep and dangerous going on that you weren't telling me about. I thought, at the beginning, that you didn't trust me. Or, even worse, you didn't think I felt the same things you felt when I looked at how Mother Church was falling so far short of what she ought to have been. Then I realized you were doing it to protect me and, later, to protect Sahmantha and the kids, and I loved you for that."

His hand tightened on Cahnyr's arm, and his voice hoarsened for a moment. He paused and cleared his throat, then continued.

"I loved you for it, and I realized you were right. I did have other people to worry about—'hostages to fortune,' as Bédard put it. So I let you go ahead and exclude me. But when I was contacted by someone else who knew about your activities, and when that someone else convinced me he wasn't the Inquisition in disguise, and that all he wanted me to do was to stay right here in Glacierheart to coordinate ways to get you out if whatever you were doing finally blew up in your face, I was delighted. *Delighted,* Your Eminence.

"Whoever your friend in Zion is, he sent me word months ago that this was coming, and I've been making my arrangements ever since. Teagmahn never even noticed. As a matter of fact, I've been one of his informants for the last couple of years now." The secretary smiled nastily. "That was one of the things your friend in Zion suggested as a way to make certain there was no suspicion pointed in *my* direction. I can't pretend I've enjoyed having him believe I actually think the same way *he* does, but your friend was right about what a perfect cover it made. Every single word I've ever reported to him has been true, too, so I'm sure I'm considered a very reliable source. With the added advantage that he's been so busy watching *you* that I'm sure he never even glanced in *my* direction."

The under-priest shrugged.

"So, Your Eminence, the upshot is that Sahmantha and the kids are waiting at the posting house, the owner of which happens to be a cousin of hers. He doesn't know exactly what we're doing, but he does know you're in trouble, and like quite an amazing number of people here in Glacierheart, he loves you. All he has to do is not mention ever seeing us, because I don't think it's going to occur to the Inquisition that you somehow managed to get from Summit House clear around to the other side of Mount Tairys during one of the worst blizzards in the last thirty years. I don't think they're going to believe you could have gotten back down the mountain and escaped through Tairys itself, either, but that's going to seem a lot more reasonable to them than *this* does. So I expect they're going to concentrate their efforts on traffic in and out of Tairys. In fact, this time of year, I think they're almost going to have to concentrate their main efforts on the Graywater and the river road to Mountain Lake and then on to Siddar City. In the meantime, though, we're going to be heading west into Cliff Peak, then swinging south across the South March into Silkiah."

Cahnyr stared at him. He had no idea who his mysterious benefactor might be, or how anyone could have had the foresight to arrange something like this so long in advance. And despite everything Gorjah had just said, there was a part of him which railed against involving his secretary—and especially the under-priest's *family*—in his own dangers. But it was evident that things were out of his hands, at least for the moment.

*The* Writ *says God works in mysterious ways, Zhasyn,* he reminded himself. *And remember what you were thinking when you first got that letter, how it proved there were others who saw what you'd seen and recognized what you and the Circle had recognized.* His lips twitched wryly. *And who seem to have organized themselves just a bit more effectively, when it comes down to it. If there are still people who can put something like this together, without even me noticing a thing along the way, and actually pull it off, then it looks as if Clyntahn and Trynair's neat little house may have more spider-rats in the foundations than I'd ever imagined. I think Samyl's right—that real change, real reform, is going to depend on the external threat of the Church of Charis. But maybe, just maybe, there are going to be more people inside Mother Church prepared to act than Clyntahn ever suspected or I ever hoped.*

He felt a brief burn of shame with the last thought. Shame for the arrogance which had kept him from suspecting that those other people were there. For having excluded Gharth Gorjah, however noble his motives, from something the young priest obviously had wanted so badly to be part of. For having doubted that God could find the hearts and souls He needed whenever He decided to call them.

He reached out and laid one palm against the side of the younger man's head, cupping his cheek, and smiled at him in the lantern light.

"I still think you're mad," he said softly, "but if you are, so am I. And sometimes, a madman is exactly what God needs."

.III.<br>
HMS Chihiro, 50<br>
Gorath Bay,<br>
Kingdom of Dohlar

M y Lord, Bishop Staiphan and Admiral Hahlynd are about to come alongside."

The Earl of Thirsk looked up from the report on his desk as the rather dashing young man with coal-black hair stuck his head respectfully into the day cabin with the announcement. Lieutenant Ahbail Bahrdailahn—*Sir* Ahbail Bahrdailahn, on social occasions—was the youngest brother of the Baron of Westbar. His brother's barony was located in the southwestern corner of the Duchy of Windborne, which happened to be completely landlocked. Despite that, Bahrdailahn had made his preference for a naval career clear at an early age. In fact, according to his somewhat exasperated brother, his very first sentence had been "Avast there, you nanny!" Most people considered that a likely exaggeration, but his family, which had provided officers to the Royal Army since time out of mind, truly had done its best to dissuade him from such an unnatural step. Stubbornness, however, was one of young Bahrdailahn's most pronounced characteristics, and his various brothers, sisters, cousins, aunts, and uncles had given up the task before he turned twenty. (His parents had been wise enough to abandon the effort much sooner than that.)

Now, about five years later, young Bahrdailahn had found himself assigned as Thirsk's flag lieutenant. He had not, to put it mildly, thought much of the assignment when it was first offered to him. He would vastly have preferred the command of one of the Navy's new brigs or, failing that, a first-lieutenancy on one of the galleons. And, to be fair, he would have been qualified for either. True, he wasn't the seaman many of the Navy's old sailing masters were, yet unlike altogether too many of the "old navy's" officers, he'd made a conscientious effort to acquire at least the rudiments of seamanship, and there'd never been anything wrong with his courage or fighting ability.

Despite that, he'd resigned himself to his new post with a minimum of complaint. He'd later admitted to Thirsk that his original intention had been to do his best "brainless noble fop" imitation to convince Thirsk to replace him, but he'd gotten over that quickly as he found himself plunged into the enormous task of building a brand-new navy—a navy based on the professional Charisian model—from the waterline up. Unlike too many "old navy" officers, he'd not only understood what Thirsk wanted to accomplish but actually approved wholeheartedly. He was also astute enough to recognize the enemies Thirsk was making along the way, and the earl's unflinching willingness to do just that had won Bahrdailahn's admiration. Admiration which had transmuted into devotion over the past strenuous five-days and months.

Which probably explained the trepidation hovering behind his eyes. It was well hidden, that trepidation, but Thirsk knew him too well not to see it.

"Thanks for the warning, Ahbail," the earl said now, mildly, as he heard the bosun's pipes and the rush of feet across the deck. Captain Baiket had obviously spotted the approaching barge and called away the proper side party.

"Please go and make certain Mahrtyn's prepared to join us," Thirsk continued. "And tell Paiair to break out a bottle of my best whiskey. Then stand by to escort our guests aft."

"Yes, My Lord." Bahrdailahn started to withdraw, but Thirsk's raised finger stopped him. "Yes, My Lord?"

"I've known Admiral Hahlynd for a great many years, Ahbail, and so far, at least, I've heard that Bishop Staiphan is fairly reasonable. I don't anticipate finding myself locked in a death struggle with either of them in the next few hours." He smiled ever so slightly. "I trust I make myself clear?"

"Yes, My Lord. Of course!" Bahrdailahn might have colored just a bit, although it was difficult to tell against his dark (and darkly tanned) complexion. Then the young man smiled a bit sheepishly. "Sorry about that, My Lord," he said in a more natural tone. "It's just—"

He broke off with a quick little headshake, and Thirsk's smile broadened.

"Trust me, Ahbail, I know *exactly* what it is. And I appreciate your . . . loyally supportive attitude, shall we say?" His eyes glinted wickedly as Bahrdailahn raised one hand in the gesture of a fencer acknowledging a touch. "I think it's fairly evident no one could be moving the shipyards along any faster than we are, though," the earl continued, his smile fading into a more sober expression, "and Duke Thorast and his friends are just going to have to put up with my little training missions, I'm afraid."

Bahrdailahn looked very much as if he would have liked to argue about that last statement. Although his older brother was a mere baron, Bahrdailahn was a distant cousin of Duke Windborne's, and he'd absorbed the realities of the deadly infighting between the Kingdom of Dohlar's great nobles with his mother's milk. He was well aware that the Duke of Thorast and his allies, however deeply they might protest their loyalty in public, never missed an opportunity to slide another dagger into Thirsk's back. At the moment, they were concentrating on the "disgraceful slothfulness" with which the fleet was being built, on the one hand, and on the earl's "ill-considered and manifestly dangerous" training exercises, on the other. Both of which (whether or not the earl chose to admit it worried him) obviously had a little something to do with this morning's meeting.

"Go on, now." Thirsk made shooing motions with one hand.

Bahrdailahn gave him a quick smile, nodded, and disappeared, and Thirsk gathered up the report he'd been reading and jogged the pages neatly together. He put them into a folder, slid the folder into his desk drawer, and climbed out of his chair to walk across to the cabin's great stern windows.

He folded his hands behind him, gazing out through the salt-mottled glass at Gorath Bay. It was cold, with a brisk wind raising a wicked chop, and he hoped Bishop Staiphan Maik and Admiral Pawal Hahlynd hadn't gotten themselves too badly soaked during the long row out to *Chihiro*. Whether they'd managed to stay dry or not, they were undoubtedly going to be thoroughly chilled, and he looked over his shoulder as Paiair Sahbrahan, his valet, quietly entered the cabin.

Sahbrahan was a smallish man, even shorter than Thirsk, with quick, deft hands, who was extraordinarily efficient, and not at all shy about bullying his admiral into remembering to do little things like eat or sleep. He was also an excellent cook, who could probably have earned a lucrative living as a chef, if he'd chosen to, and Thirsk had total confidence in his ability to manage the earl's wine cellar and spirits.

Despite that, the valet had never been popular with the other members of Thirsk's staff, domestic or naval. They appreciated his good qualities, but they were also only too well—one might say *painfully* well—aware of his vanity and secondhand arrogance. Sahbrahan was far more concerned with the deference due to someone of Thirsk's birth and rank than the earl himself had ever been. He'd been known to drive the staffs of inns and hotels to the edge of sanity with demands for fresh linens, clean towels, hot water *now,* and no excuses, if you please! He was completely capable of doing the same thing aboard ship, and he had a well-earned reputation for browbeating the valets and stewards of mere ships' captains mercilessly. None of which even considered his legendary rows with the cooks and pursers of various flagships over the years.

Thirsk was as well aware of his valet's foibles as anyone, and Sahbrahan knew better than to try anything of the sort in the earl's presence. At the same time, Thirsk was also aware of how difficult it would have been to find an equally capable replacement. Besides, Sahbrahan had been with him for almost eight years.

Now the valet pattered quickly across the thick carpet covering the deck, set a large silver tray with two decanters of whiskey and one of brandy on a side table, and turned to face Thirsk.

"I've brought the Stahlmyn, the Waykhan, and the Tharistan, My Lord," he said, indicating the decanters. "Will that be satisfactory?"

"Eminently," Thirsk agreed.

"I've also informed the galley that you will be requiring hot chocolate for your guests, should they so desire," Sahbrahan continued. "And, as you instructed, luncheon will be ready to serve at fourteen o'clock, promptly."

"Good." Thirsk bobbed his head, then looked past the valet as Mahrtyn Vahnwyk, his personal secretary and senior clerk, entered the day cabin.

The secretary was considerably taller than Sahbrahan, despite the slight stoop of his shoulders, and he was a bit nearsighted. Nevertheless, he was one of the best secretaries Thirsk had ever been fortunate enough to possess . . . and he and Sahbrahan hated one another cordially.

*Well, fair's fair,* the earl thought dryly as he watched the two of them very carefully not glaring at one another in his presence. *I think just about* everyone *hates Paiair, really. And much as I hate to admit it, he gives them plenty of justification.*

"If you're satisfied, My Lord, I shall withdraw and attend to the arrangements," the valet said. Thirsk nodded in agreement, and Sahbrahan drew himself up, bowed slightly, and withdrew with stately majesty . . . somehow managing to completely ignore Vahnwyk's existence in the process.

*Langhorne!* Thirsk thought. *And I thought the blood between me and* Thorast *was bad!*

He was still chuckling at the thought when Lieutenant Bahrdailahn knocked on his cabin door once more.

"Enter!" Thirsk said, and crossed the cabin quickly to greet his visitors.

Pawal Hahlynd was about Thirsk's age, a foot or so taller, and considerably less weatherworn-looking. Auxiliary Bishop Staiphan Maik was about midway between Thirsk and Hahlynd in height, with thick silver hair and lively brown eyes. He was a vigorous man, radiating a sense of leashed energy, although Thirsk had been told the bishop had a serious weakness for sweetbreads. According to the earl's sources, that weakness for sweets was one reason Maik was so fanatical about exercising. Those same sources said Maik did his best to conceal that weakness, apparently in the belief that it went poorly with the Order of Schueler's reputation for austerity and self-discipline. For himself, Thirsk found it rather reassuring, an indication that Schuelerite or not, official intendant of the fleet or not, the bishop was also a human being.

"My Lord." The earl greeted Maik first, bending over his extended hand to lightly kiss the bishop's ring of office. Then he straightened and held out his hand to Hahlynd, who smiled broadly as he took it. "Pawal."

"Admiral," Maik responded with a smile. "It's good to see you, although I must confess that the trip across the harbor was somewhat more . . . brisk than I had allowed myself to hope it might be."

"I'm sorry to hear that, My Lord. As you know—"

"Please, My Lord!" the bishop said, raising his left hand, index finger extended. "I'm perfectly well aware of the reasons—the official reasons—for our meeting out here."

"My Lord?" Thirsk said a bit cautiously, and the bishop chuckled. It was not a particularly amused sound, however, and those lively brown eyes were narrow.

"I said I'm aware of the official reasons we're meeting aboard your flagship rather than in a comfortable office somewhere ashore," he said now. "And I'm also aware of the *unofficial* reasons. Such as the list of who else might have been attending any meeting in the aforesaid comfortable office ashore."

"I see." Thirsk faced the bishop, his own eyes calm, and Maik studied his expression for a long moment. Then the churchman smiled again, a bit crookedly.

"By an odd turn of chance, My Lord Admiral, I happen to agree with your strategy in this instance. I realize I shouldn't say that. For that matter, I suppose I really shouldn't admit I'm aware of the bad blood between you and Duke Thorast at all. Unfortunately, it serves no one's purposes for me to do anything of the sort."

"My Lord, I regret the . . . 'bad blood' you've mentioned," Thirsk said levelly. "I agree that it exists, however. And I'm very much afraid things have been made still worse by the decisions I've been forced to make. Or, rather, by the Duke's resistance to and resentment of those decisions."

"The truth, Earl Thirsk," Maik said, walking across the cabin to seat himself in one of the armchairs facing Thirsk's desk, "is that Thorast hates you. It's true he resents your decisions, but his resistance to them stems far more from the fact that they're *your* decisions than anything having the least bit to do with their actual merit. Which, considering that you're the one who made them, I very much doubt he's bothered to consider at all."

Despite himself, Thirsk's eyes widened slightly at the bishop's bluntness, and Maik chuckled again, this time with genuine humor. *Sour* humor, perhaps, but genuine.

"Of course I'm aware of the situation," he said. "I'd be a poor choice for the Navy's Intendant if I weren't! Unfortunately, I don't see an easy solution to the problem." He paused and waved at the armchair beside his own and at Thirsk's desk chair. "Please, gentlemen—be seated."

Both admirals obeyed, although Thirsk found himself concealing a slight smile at how effortlessly Maik had assumed at least temporary ownership of his day cabin. The bishop glanced across at Vahnwyk, but he'd apparently already assessed the secretary's discretion, and he turned his attention back to the earl.

"The fact of the matter is," he said, "that I don't believe anything you could possibly do would compensate in Thorast's view for the fact that you were entirely right before Armageddon Reef and his brother-in-law was entirely wrong. He's never going to forgive you for the incredible insult of having proved Duke Malikai was a complete, feckless incompetent."

Thirsk felt himself settling back in his chair, and the bishop showed a flash of teeth in a tight, fleeting smile.

"There are limits to the amount of open resistance Thorast is prepared to demonstrate," he continued in an almost clinical tone. "At the moment, King Rahnyld has made it clear to him that attacking you too openly would be . . . inadvisable. I've also made that point to him, in my own rather more subtle fashion, and so has Bishop Executor Ahrain. So, at the moment, he's going to restrict himself to the sort of innuendo it's almost impossible for even the Inquisition to positively trace back to its source. And he's going to obey any order you give, although—as I'm sure you're aware—he isn't missing the opportunity to append his own carefully reasoned reservations to many of those orders in his reports to me." Maik grimaced. "That, unfortunately, is his right and privilege."

"My Lord," Thirsk said, "I won't pretend I'm not aware of everything you've just said. I have to admit, however, that I never expected you to approach those points quite so . . . forthrightly."

"The truth is, Admiral," Maik said somberly, "that Thorast's alliances are ultimately far stronger, and reach far higher, than yours do, and he's been playing this sort of game all his life. All you have on your side are virtue, intelligence, courage, skill, experience, and integrity which, alas, are of far more value on the field of battle than in the dagger-prone atmosphere of council chambers and salons. Ultimately, unless something changes radically, he *will* succeed in destroying you. And the fact that you've committed the unforgivable sin of being right when all of his cronies were just as wrong as he was will only make it easier for him when the present emergency passes."

Thirsk simply looked at him across the desk, and the bishop studied the admiral's expression. Then he nodded slowly.

"I see I truly haven't said anything that surprises you, My Lord. That only strengthens my already high regard for you. And I give you my word that so long as I remain the Navy Intendant, I will bear Duke Thorast's attitude—and the reasons for it—fully in mind. At the moment, you have my full support, and, frankly, I foresee no circumstances which would be likely to change that. As I'm sure you also know, however, and as I'm not supposed to admit, Mother Church is far from free from the pernicious effects of politics and cliques. Duke Thorast has long-standing relationships with several powerful members of the clergy. It's entirely possible . . . no, let's be honest, it's virtually *certain* that he's prepared to use those relationships to undermine me, as well as you, once he becomes aware of how unlikely I am to support him in any clash between the two of you.

"I mention this because the only means I see of keeping you where you are, doing what so badly needs to be done, is for the two of us to produce success while everyone is still worried enough to give us—or, rather, *you*—your head. Not just minor successes, either. Not just getting the fleet built and manned. That's obviously the first essential, but to truly blunt the Duke's attacks, it's essential that we demonstrate we can produce *victories*. You were right before Rock Point and Crag Hook, but we lost both of those battles anyway. Now, you must prove not only that you're right once again, but that listening to you leads to victory."

It was very quiet in the day cabin for several seconds, then Thirsk exhaled sharply and cocked his head at Maik.

"I can't promise victory, My Lord," he said quietly. "First, because no man can ever *promise* victory, but second, because no matter how well we build and how hard we train, we'll still confront the Charisian Navy. Call it the Imperial Navy or the Royal Navy—it's still the same fleet, with the same admirals, the same captains, and the same crews. They aren't supermen. They *can* be defeated. But at this moment in time, they are the best trained, most experienced battle fleet on the seas of Safehold. Quite possibly the best trained and most experienced battle fleet *ever* to sail the seas of Safehold, in fact. I'm not arguing against facing them at sea, and I'm willing to do so. Yet the truth is that we're likely to suffer more reverses before we achieve many victories. We're in the process of learning our trade, and altogether too many of our officers and our seamen are terrified, whether they're willing to admit it or not, of the Charisians' reputation. And they're right to be concerned, because that reputation was fully earned even before Rock Point, Crag Reach, and Darcos Sound. We'll have to demonstrate to our own people that they *can* beat Charisians before they *will* be able to beat them in pitched battle."

The bishop looked back at him, his expression thoughtful.

"Well, that's certainly candid," he said dryly.

"I refuse to be anything else," Thirsk said flatly.

"So I've noticed." Maik leaned back in his armchair, fingertips steepled to-gether in front of his chest, lips pursed. "What I seem to hear you saying, Ad-miral," he said after a moment, "is that you believe you can build a navy which will eventually be able to meet the Charisians on an even footing, but that you believe it's going to be necessary to blood our officers and men first? And that in the blooding process, we're likely to see at least some additional defeats?"

"I think it's very likely that's exactly what will happen," Thirsk replied. "I could be wrong, and I'd like to be. It's possible we'll be given an opportunity to bring our numbers to bear sooner than I expect. And I assure you, My Lord, that I intend for any squadron of ours that goes into action to do so planning on *winning,* not expecting even before the first shot is fired that defeat is in-evitable. Moreover, wind and wave play no favorites, and the Charisians' re-sources are stretched to the limit. They can't be strong everywhere, and if we can pounce on a few detachments, cut them up in a few local engagements be-fore we commit to a full-fledged battle, the situation is likely to change in our favor. I simply can't promise that will happen, and absent some set of circum-stances like that, we're going to take more losses before we hand the enemy a significant loss of his own.

"If I can complete my training programs, and if I can get our current flag officers and our current ship captains to start thinking in terms of galleon tac-tics and galleon-based strategy, then ultimately I expect us to win. We have the numbers and we have the resources. The plain, cold fact is that we don't have to be as good as they are on a ship-for-ship basis as long as we can build enough more ships and be *almost* as good as they are. That's what I think I can give you . . . whether I'm still around to command or not."

The day cabin was even quieter as the earl admitted that out loud to some-one at last, and Maik regarded him with a long, steady gaze.

"I understand," the bishop said finally, "and my respect for you has just in-creased still further. I hope you're wrong, that *you'll* have the opportunity to win those victories for us in command of the navy you're building. At the same time, I think I now more fully understand exactly what it is you're trying to accomplish. The reason, for example, why you've been so adamant about building squadrons, not just single ship's companies, and then sending those squadrons to drill at sea, despite weather damage."

Maik glanced at Hahlynd, who still hadn't said a word. Yet it was evident from the other admiral's expression that he hadn't kept silent because he *dis-agreed* with Thirsk, and the bishop nodded slowly as he recognized Hahlynd's support for the earl's position.

"You realize, My Lord," he said, turning back to Thirsk, "that Thorast has been criticizing your operations on that very basis." The bishop grimaced. "He can scarcely criticize the way in which you've accelerated the building and manning aspects of your duties, so he's reserved his fire for the way in which you're organizing the ships as they come forward . . . and how hard you're driving them. In essence, his position is that since it will be some time still before the bulk of our construction is ready to be placed in commission, it makes little sense to send such small forces to sea—especially in the winter, and especially when they keep returning with damage that requires repairs and diverts yard workers from the new construction. Better to conserve our strength here in port, where we can carry out gun drill and sail drill in safety, until all of it is ready to deploy. After all, what's the point in losing hard-to-replace spars and masts and sails to winter gales when there's not a single Charisian galleon within two thousand miles of Gorath Bay?"

"We're not losing just spars and masts, My Lord. We're also losing *men,*" Thirsk admitted unflinchingly. "But that's because the only place to learn seamanship is at sea, and saltwater is a harsh teacher. Whether we like to admit it or not, Charisian seamen are the finest in the world, and Charis has a far greater pool of trained seamen to draw upon. A huge percentage of our crews, on the other hand, are made up of landsmen, and if they haven't learned the *sea*man's trade by the time they cross swords with a Charisian squadron, then we might as well prepare them to haul down their colors right now."

The earl grimaced and shook his head.

"Of course I realize Duke Thorast has been criticizing me for my 'pennypacket' deployments and the cost of repairing damaged ships. And, of course, he's been hammering away at the way in which I'm 'throwing away' the lives of our seamen, as well. And the truth is that if we had the time to do this any other way, I'd actually agree with a great deal of what he's saying.

"But I don't think we *do* have the time. The Charisians know we're building a navy, and it's not going to be so very much longer before they start dispatching squadrons of their own to do something about that. I realize we're thousands of miles away from Charis here in Dohlar, and they've got plenty of things to worry about much closer to home. But they've already demonstrated that they'd send every single galleon they had as far from home as Armageddon Reef when they couldn't even be certain exactly where *our* ships were. I see no reason to believe they wouldn't send a powerful detachment of their present, much larger galleon fleet to our own waters to harass us when they do know exactly where to find us, and it's not as if Gorath Bay moves around very much. When that happens, I'll need at least a few squadrons that are ready for the test of battle. It won't help us to have an enormous fleet that *isn't* ready—we already saw that at Rock Point and Darcos Sound. It *will* help us to have a battle-ready core of ships, even if it's relatively small, with some chance of meeting the Charisians on an equal basis."

"I understand, Admiral Thirsk," Maik said quietly. "And I agree. I'll do all in my power to support you, both with Mother Church and with His Majesty. Of course, I may have to be a little . . . indirect in some instances. As

I've already pointed out, the Duke has powerful connections and allies of his own. The longer I can keep him from realizing I've decided to throw you my full support, the slower he'll be to start using those connections and allies effectively."

Thirsk nodded, and the bishop smiled thinly.

"I can already think of a few ways to blunt some of his objections, at least in the short term, and probably without his realizing I'm doing it deliberately. And I think it's going to be important that you and I stay discreetly—*discreetly*, Admiral—in communication outside official channels." He shook his head. "It shouldn't be necessary for Mother Church's defenders to creep around, hiding what they're up to, simply in order to defend her *effectively*. Unfortunately, God gave man free will, and not all of us exercise it wisely. In fact, some of us are horses' asses."

Thirsk surprised himself with a laugh, and the bishop smiled at him.

"Well, there's no point pretending an onion is a rose, now is there? Although in the case of a certain nobleman we've been discussing this morning, I think it's rather more a case of a pile of dragon shit smelling like a rose. So, for what it's worth, and as long as I'm in a position to do it, I'll see what I can do about sweeping as much as possible of that shit out of your path. Beyond that"—the bishop looked directly into Thirsk's eyes, his expression suddenly sober—"it's going to be up to you and Admiral Hahlynd."

.IV.
### Kahsimahr Prison,
### City of Manchyr,
### and
### Crag House,
### City of Vahlainah,
### Earldom of Craggy Hill

Father Aidryn Waimyn stood gazing out the barred window at the gallows in the prison courtyard. Those gallows had been busy over the last few five-days, and he'd been able to recognize the faces of at least a quarter of the condemned men as they were marched up the steep wooden stairs to the waiting nooses.

*I suppose I should be flattered they've let me wait till last,* he thought. *The bastards!*

His face tightened, and his nostrils flared as he ran his hand over the plain, scratchy prison tunic which had replaced his silken cassock. They'd *graciously* allowed him to retain his scepter, and his fingers sought the familiar, comforting weight hanging around his neck, but that was as far as they were prepared to go. He held the scepter tight, leaning his forehead against the bars, and remembered fury—and, little though he cared to admit it, terror—flowed through him.

He still had no idea who had betrayed him. Someone had to have. Worse, it had to have been someone from within his own order, and that was bitter as gall on his tongue. Yet as much as it sickened him to confront the truth, that was the only way they could have known where to find him at Saint Zhustyn's. Only the Order of Schueler had known about the concealed rooms, the secret entrance at the far end of the carefully hidden tunnel. And it had to have been someone close to him, someone he'd trusted, because that eternally damned traitor Gahrvai had known exactly who to scoop up. In that single disastrous night, he and the other traitors on the Regency Council had completely decapitated—no, completely *destroyed*—the resistance organization Waimyn had so carefully and laboriously constructed. It turned his stomach—literally; he could feel the nausea churning in his belly even now—to know that native-born Corisandians, men who *claimed* to love God, had knowingly and deliberately shattered the only organized resistance in Manchyr to the filth and poison and lies of the accursed, apostate heretics who served the "Church of Charis."

He choked the nausea down and forced himself to inhale deeply, opening his eyes and staring at the gallows once again.

Tomorrow, it would be his turn to mount those stairs. He felt fear flutter at the base of his throat at that thought, but once again, anger dominated fear. He was willing to die for God, and he made no apologies for defending God's true will, His plan for all men, against the impious lies and perversions of others. But he was an ordained, consecrated priest. He was no common felon, no casual criminal, to be hanged by the unconsecrated hands of secular authority—even if he'd acknowledged for one heartbeat the legitimacy of that authority! The *Writ* itself made that blindingly clear. Only Mother Church held authority over her clergy. Only *she* could decree their punishment, and only she could carry it out.

*But they've got an answer for* that, *too, don't they?* His lips drew back in a snarl, and his grip on his pectoral scepter went white-knuckled. *The civil authorities can't hang a priest? Very well, just strip him of his priesthood!*

And that was precisely what they'd done. The excommunicate traitors had dared—*dared!*—to defrock a priest made by the Grand Vicar's hands in the Temple itself. They'd set their Shan-wei-accursed pride and arrogance above all else, above the Archangels and even God Himself, and told him he was no longer God's priest. That they—*they*—had judged him a criminal not simply against the secular puppets of Charis, but against the law of God. They had declared that the execution of the traitor Hahskans had been not the Inquisition's justice, but simple murder. And that even greater traitor, Gairlyng—"Archbishop

Klairmant"—had actually stood in judgment and declared that *he*, Waimyn, as the one who had ordered that execution, had violated the sanctity of the priesthood by his actions. Gairlyng, the foresworn, *excommunicated* apostate, had passed *judgment* on the legitimate Intendant of Corisande and in profane and heretical violation of every ecclesiastic law, expelled Waimyn from the priesthood of the Church for the "torture and murder of a fellow priest, brother, and innocent child of God."

Waimyn had been unable to believe anyone could have the sheer effrontery, the insolence before God, to claim authority to do any such thing. Yet the "archbishop" had done precisely that, and the secular authorities had accepted his judgment. Indeed, they had *applauded* it.

He realized his teeth were grinding once again, and made himself stop. It wasn't easy. He'd gotten into the habit over the five-days of his imprisonment, and he smiled bleakly, without humor, as he reflected that at least he wouldn't have to worry about that particular problem very much longer.

He pushed away from the window and paced slowly back and forth across his cell. It was better than some cells, he supposed, but, once again, it was the cell of a common criminal. Ten feet on a side, with a narrow cot, one table, a chair, a pitcher of water, a washbasin, a battered cup, and a chamber pot. That was all, aside from the copy of the *Holy Writ* they'd oh-so-graciously permitted him. The austerity had been yet one more calculated insult, a way to underscore their contempt for the man who was Mother Church's chosen champion.

In the end, though, they hadn't had the courage—or the insolence—to truly carry through on the beliefs they proclaimed so loudly. Aidryn Waimyn was only too well aware of the penalties *The Book of Schueler* prescribed for anyone guilty of the crimes for which they had convicted him. Indeed, what had been done to the traitor Hahskans had been well short of the fullness of those penalties; it had simply been the best that could be done in the time and with the tools available.

Waimyn was a Schuelerite. If anyone knew that, he did, and he wasn't going to pretend, even to himself, that he wasn't prayerfully grateful they'd been too cowardly to put him to the Question or decree the Punishment of Schueler. The thought of the wheel, the rack, the white-hot irons—of castration and blinding, of having his belly slit and his intestines drawn forth living, and then the fire—was enough to terrify any man, and rightly so. Schueler had instituted those penalties as much to deter such crimes as to punish them. Yet had "Archbishop Klairmant" and his lapdog Regency Council truly possessed the courage of their convictions, they would have decreed the full Punishment of Schueler for his alleged crimes, not settled for a simple hanging.

His lips twitched with contempt as he recalled what the "Church of

Charis" called an interrogation. They'd refused to employ even the most gentle of the Inquisition's techniques. Sleep deprivation, yes, and endless relays of interrogators, hammering away, hammering away, hammering away. And he had to admit they'd gotten more out of him than he'd expected. That had been mostly because they already knew so much, though. It had proven far harder than he'd ever anticipated not to answer their questions when they'd already demonstrated they knew at least two-thirds of the answers before they ever asked. And as the fatigue mounted, it had become harder and harder to prevent little bits and pieces from dribbling out.

*But they didn't get the big admission out of me,* he thought grimly. *They came closer than they ever guessed more than once, but they never got it. That secret held, at least. They knew—or they sure as Shan-wei suspected—who gave the order, but they obviously don't have any evidence of it, and Cahmmyng, at least, must have gotten away. That bastard would've betrayed me in a minute, if the offer was right. But they never got me to admit it—not once!* His eyes flickered with grim, hating triumph—and contempt for his enemies—at the thought. *The fools. Anyone can be made to confess with the proper persuasion, an Inquisitor knows that if anyone does! If they'd been willing to put the Question, they'd have gotten it out of me, however hard I tried to resist, but the cowards wouldn't do it.*

The secular authorities had been more willing to accept . . . rigorous techniques. Indeed, Waimyn had been shocked by the readiness of common soldiers to lay violent, impious hands on his person. It seemed the traitor Hahskans had been even more popular with Gahrvai's troops than with the bulk of Manchyr's citizens. The sheer, blazing hatred in their eyes when they learned Waimyn had ordered the priest's kidnapping and execution had stunned the intendant, and the fists and boots which followed had been even worse. He'd been battered, bruised, bleeding, half-naked, and less than half-conscious when a captain, two lieutenants, and a quartet of leather-lunged sergeants rescued him. And there'd been a time or two here, in the prison, when one of his jailers had helped him "fall" or a pair of them had administered a brutally skilled, methodical beating that left no bruises where anyone was likely to see them.

At first, he'd thought the soldiers responsible for those actions had actually been acting under orders. That they were the true face of the "Church of Charis'" pious public disavowal of the Inquisition's methods. But he'd gradually decided he was wrong. First, because it was so haphazard, so uncoordinated and inefficient. Any Inquisitor worth his salt would have managed the whole thing far better, far more effectively, without ever *officially* Questioning the prisoner. Waimyn had done precisely that at least a dozen times during his own novitiate, after all.

But second, and probably even more conclusive, at least three jailers who'd been responsible for giving him "special treatment" had been severely disciplined by their own superiors. It hadn't stopped the occasional abuse, yet he was convinced their punishment had been genuine.

When he'd finally accepted that, he'd felt two conflicting emotions. One was an even deeper contempt for his captors, for their craven refusal to interrogate him effectively even under the cover of "spontaneous" actions by common soldiers. But the other, the one which still shocked and confused him, was the realization that the soldiers *were* doing it on their own. That the troopers were so furious over Hahskans' death that they were actually *defying* orders to beat and abuse a consecrated *priest*.

And worse, far worse, was the crushing realization that the soldiers weren't alone in their anger.

Despite everything else they'd done, his captors had at least permitted him access to clergy. He had no doubt their willingness to allow that was just as much a thing of cynical calculation as everything else they'd done, but he couldn't pretend he wasn't grateful. They'd even allowed him a *true* priest—one of God's servants who'd had the integrity and moral and spiritual courage to remain an openly observant "Temple Loyalist"—rather than giving him the opportunity to reject their own false and faithless clergy. He'd been permitted to make confession, but as a condemned murderer, he was not permitted to speak privately even with his confessor. A priest of the "Church of Charis" was always present, sworn (of course) to respect the sanctity of the confessional (not that Waimyn believed for a moment he actually would) even as he enforced the legal restrictions *upon* the confessional. That had prevented Waimyn from using it to pass messages to anyone outside the prison via the confessor. On the other hand, he hadn't had anyone left to pass messages *to,* either, given the clean sweep Gahrvai had made.

But the confessor's thrice-a-five-day visits had given him at least a limited window on events beyond Kahsimahr Prison's walls, and that window had confirmed his captors' version of events in Manchyr. The other priest hadn't wanted to tell him that—out of pity and compassion, Waimyn suspected. He hadn't wanted the intendant to discover how completely and utterly he'd failed. Yet in the end, the bits and pieces he'd been willing to admit had convinced Waimyn the stories of his interrogators, the taunts of his jailers and the jeers of the common soldiers, had been only too true.

So now he was to hang, his great work in God's name completely undone by the stupid credulity and gushing sentimentality of the ignorant, unwashed cretins who had allowed themselves to slobber over a single provincial upperpriest and the justified fate his betrayal of God and his own vows had brought upon him.

Aidryn Waimyn closed his eyes again, pacing, pacing, pacing, while the smoking lava of hatred, failure, and despair flowed through him.

▼　　▼　　▼

"It's confirmed, Your Eminence," Wahlys Hillkeeper, the Earl of Craggy Hill, said grimly. "I've just had a runner from the semaphore station. They hanged him this morning."

"May God and the Archangels welcome him as their own," Bishop Executor Thomys Shylair murmured, tracing Langhorne's Scepter.

There was a moment of silence, a stillness, in the luxuriously appointed chamber. It was so quiet they could hear the distant voices of the city of Vahlainah from beyond the walls of the earl's palatial residence. Crag House was more mansion than castle, although it was surrounded by a twenty-foot wall. It was also large enough, and possessed of enough . . . unobtrusive entrances and exits, that Shylair felt reasonably safe visiting it. It wasn't as remote and as secure as the tiny monastery outside Serabor where he'd been the guest of Amilain Gahrnaht, the legitimate Bishop of Larchros, but it was secure enough. Especially now that Craggy Hill, like the Earl of Storm Keep and Baron Larchros, had quietly increased his own strength of armsmen.

*And, to be honest,* Shylair thought now, *I feel a lot more secure here than I felt in Sardor.*

The bishop executor's well-trained face showed no sign of his mental grimace. He and Mahrak Hahlynd, his secretary and aide, had been the "guests" of Mailvyn Nohrcross, the Bishop of Barcor, for almost a month before they moved on to Larchros. Nohrcross was one of the senior clergymen who'd sworn obedience to the "Church of Charis" in order to retain his see, and he'd offered what seemed the most promising port in the storm when Shylair fled Manchyr. In the event, however, Nohrcross' palace in Sardor, the capital of the Barony of Barcor, had proved less suitable than he'd hoped.

The fact that Nohrcross had sworn to obey and follow directives from "Archbishop Klairmant" had bothered neither him nor Shylair, since no one could swear a valid oath to someone Mother Church had excommunicated. And Shylair was confident of Nohrcross' loyalty to the legitimate Church. His outrage and anger over the heresy of the "Church of Charis" certainly seemed genuine, even if a bishop who'd officially pledged his loyalty to that church had to be careful about where he allowed them to show. And, if nothing else, the Bishop of Barcor was in too deep to back out now. But that hadn't made Shylair any happier about being dependent upon the *Baron* of Barcor for his security.

He'd come to the conclusion that Sir Zher Sumyrs, the current baron, was much better at bluster and promises than at action. His efforts to increase his force of personal armsmen were pathetic compared to those of men like Craggy Hill and Baron Larchros, and he was far more willing to make extravagant guarantees in private conversation than to run the slightest risk to bring those guarantees to fruition. In fact, Shylair had concluded that for all of Barcor's undoubted hatred for Sir Koryn Gahrvai and the members of the Regency

Council, he was far too timid to do anything likely to draw attention his way. He was willing enough to talk, even to shovel substantial sums of money in the resistance's direction, but not to risk coming out into the open.

*He's covering his arse, is what he's doing,* Shylair thought coldly. *If we win—when we win—he'll remind us all that he was on our side from the very beginning, and he'll expect his share of Mother Church's reward to her loyal sons. And if it should happen that we* don't *win, he'll go back into hiding and pretend he didn't know anything about it. Not him! Why, he's always been a loyal and faithful subject of Prince Daivyn! One who'd never dream of defying the legitimate orders of Daivyn's regents! And as for ecclesiastic matters,* he's *certainly not qualified to make such judgments! Who is* he *to set his judgment above the confirmed and consecrated archbishop sitting in Manchyr? The very notion never entered his head.*

But thinking of Barcor left a bad taste in the bishop executor's mouth, and he didn't need any more bad tastes on top of Craggy Hill's news. He pushed the absent baron resolutely to the back of his mind and considered the men sitting around the table with him.

Craggy Hill, as their host and the senior noble of their strategy council, sat at the head of the table. They'd been joined by Earl Storm Keep and Baron Larchros, and Bishop Amilain and Larchros' chaplain, Father Airwain Yair, were also present. Bryahn Selkyr, the Earl of Deep Hollow, and Sir Adulfo Lynkyn, the Duke of Black Water, unfortunately, had been unable to be present, which was the real reason Hahlynd was taking notes. It wasn't the same as actually having them there would have been, but at least it would allow them to be brought up-to-date on any decisions which were actually made today.

And whether they liked it or not, it was the only way coordination could be maintained, really. None of them cared for the notion of committing their plans and hopes to paper, even in the most secure cipher Mother Church could contrive, yet it was less risky to rely on written messages than it would have been for all the members of their conspiracy to gather in one place and mark themselves out for the informants Anvil Rock and his son had undoubtedly put in place by now. For that matter, the Earl of Windshare had stationed thirty of his "mounted constables" here in Vahlainah itself. They weren't getting much cooperation out of Craggy Hill's subjects, who were as insular and stubbornly loyal to their earl as anyone could have asked, but simply hiding Craggy Hill's steadily growing number of armsmen was a problem. At the moment, he had them distributed among half a dozen manors scattered across his earldom's hinterlands, where, hopefully, no one would realize each group was only one small part of the total force he was raising. It was easier to hide a few dozen, or even a few hundred, armsmen out in the countryside than it was to hide the comings and goings of great feudal lords, however.

"Was there any indication of unrest in Manchyr following Father Aidryn's execution, My Lord?" Shylair asked now, looking across the table at Craggy Hill.

"None, Your Eminence," the tall, powerfully built earl replied unflinchingly.

"That doesn't necessarily mean there wasn't any, Your Eminence," Mahrak Hahlynd pointed out diffidently, looking up from his notes. Shylair's secretary had been close to Waimyn, and there was a stubborn light in his eyes. "This came over the *official* semaphore," he reminded his superior now. "You don't think Anvil Rock, or Gahrvai, or—especially—Gairlyng would *admit* to any such thing in an official communiqué, do you?"

"I'd like to think you might have a point, Father Mahrak," Craggy Hill said before Shylair could respond. The secretary looked at him, and the earl shrugged. "The message wasn't sent for general dissemination, Father," he explained almost gently. "It was sent to me, for my information as a member of the Regency Council, and it specifically reported that the capital was calm following the execution."

Hahlynd's face tightened, and Shylair felt his own trying to do the same thing.

"So," Earl Storm Keep said after a moment. "It sounds as if they've managed to turn the situation around, at least in Manchyr."

"I'm afraid they have," Craggy Hill confirmed. He was the only member of the Regency Council who was an active party to the resistance, and all of the others watched his expression carefully.

"I don't think Anvil Rock and Tartarian really trust me," he began, "and I *know* that bastard Gahrvai and his arse-licker Doyal don't. On the other hand, if they had any concrete evidence against me, they would've acted on it by now. And whatever else we can say, Anvil Rock and Tartarian have been scrupulous about keeping all the members of the Council fully informed when we can't be personally in Manchyr." He grimaced. "They don't have much choice, given the terms of their authority under Parliament's grant, but I have to admit they've been more forthcoming in their reports than I would have anticipated. Because of that, I'm pretty sure they aren't lying, or even misrepresenting their view of the situation, when they say the arrest of Father Aidryn and his associates seems to have broken the back of any effective resistance in Manchyr itself."

The earl paused for just a moment, gazing at Shylair with oddly opaque brown eyes, then shrugged.

"The truth is, Your Eminence, that Father Aidryn seems to have badly underestimated Father Tymahn's popularity in Manchyr. We knew he'd always been popular with the riffraff, the common city trash, but it would appear a sizable percentage of the better sort were listening to him, too. I don't say they *agreed* with him, but it seems pretty evident that his . . . execution has inspired a general sense of outrage. And when Gahrvai followed that up by arresting Father Aidryn and virtually his entire leadership group—and when he managed to turn up so much evidence, completely exclusive of any confessions, of all they'd already accomplished and of their future plans, as well—it was fairly decisive."

"Wahlys is right about that, Your Eminence, I'm afraid," Storm Keep said heavily. The bishop executor raised an eyebrow at him, and the earl shook his head. "Having the arrests follow so quickly on Hahskans' execution, especially when there'd been so *few* arrests prior to that, made Gahrvai look not simply decisive, but *effective*. A lot of people who'd been trying to decide where their true loyalties lay were wavering in large part because of uncertainty, the question of whether or not the Regency Council could provide stability. Whether its legs had the strength to stand. Well," he raised his right hand, palm uppermost, "the verdict seems to be in, now. At least as far as Manchyr is concerned. And, to be brutally honest, the restraint Gairlyng's shown is working in favor of a general acceptance of the authority of both the Regency Council and the 'Church of Charis.'"

" '*Restraint*'!" Amilain Gahrnaht repeated, gazing incredulously at Storm Keep. "He's had five priests of Mother Church, including the archbishopric's *legal* Intendant, and twenty-one brothers from Saint Zhustyn's *hanged*, My Lord. Hanged by the *secular* authorities, in direct contravention of the *Writ*! Another twenty-five or thirty priests and brothers are still in custody—*secular* custody—to serve prison terms. *Prison terms* for consecrated priests of God!"

"That's true, Bishop Amilain." Storm Keep's voice was rather colder than the one in which he usually spoke to the bishop. "On the other hand, assuming he's serious about claiming authority in the name of the Church in Corisande, Gairlyng could just as easily have had all of them put to the Question and sentenced to the full Punishment of Schueler. As it happens, there's no evidence any of them, including Father Aidryn, were even interrogated under duress. You and I may be aware of the enormity of Gairlyng's offense against Mother Church and God," from his tone, Shylair thought, the earl was rather less impressed with the gravity of that offense than Gahrnaht was, "but the majority of the common folk aren't. They regard Church law as the Church's business, and what *they* see is that 'Archbishop Klairmant' could have had every single one of his prisoners put to the Question for the murder of a priest before they were executed themselves. They may not be aware of everything *else The Book of Schueler* prescribes for that sort of an offense, but they know that much, and they know Gairlyng didn't do it. And the rest of the clergy, at the very least, *do* know that *Schueler* decrees the Punishment for anyone convicted of priest-killing. As far as the people who see those things are concerned, My Lord, that *is* restraint, and there's no point pretending otherwise. We have to deal with what *is*, not what we'd like to be, and deceiving ourselves is the best way I can think of to fail in our efforts to undo this entire abomination."

Gahrnaht started to reply hotly, but Shylair held up a restraining hand.

"Peace, Amilain," he said, quietly but firmly. "Earl Storm Keep's spoken nothing but the truth, I'm afraid. And he's right about the common folk leaving matters of Church law to the Church. For that matter, that's exactly what they *ought* to do. It's simply . . . unfortunate that, in this case, the men claiming to speak for Mother Church actually serve Shan-wei."

Gahrnaht's expression was manifestly unhappy, but he settled back in his chair, obedient to Shylair's gesture. The bishop executor gazed at him for a moment, then turned his attention back to Craggy Hill.

"It would seem from what you've said, and what Sahlahmn's said," he nodded at Storm Keep, "that for now, at least, we have no choice but to abandon any hope of a popular rising in Manchyr. Would you agree?"

"I'm afraid so, Your Eminence." Craggy Hill leaned back in his own chair, tugging at an earlobe. "It was always going to be difficult to coordinate Father Aidryn's efforts with our own. And, to be frank, the southeastern part of the Princedom seems increasingly inclined to follow the capital's example. I tried to talk Anvil Rock and the others out of concentrating their efforts south of the Barcors, but I couldn't push too hard, and, unfortunately, they were too smart to spread their forces and their efforts as thinly as I wanted them to." He shrugged. "As a result, they've been able to build themselves what amounts to a secure base extending outward from the capital. I'm not trying to say they're *entirely* secure, but they do have Rochair, Tartarian, Airyth, Coris, Dairwyn, and Manchyr itself pretty much in their pockets. The northwest and west are more of a toss-up—they could go either way. Wind Daughter would probably break for the Regency Council at this point in any open confrontation, but the islanders don't have very much population. And that leaves us, up here in the north, where at the moment Anvil Rock's and Tartarian's authority is shaky, to say the very least."

"So what do you think they're planning, My Lord?" Shylair asked.

"I know exactly what they're planning, Your Eminence. I've sat in on enough of their meetings for that! In essence, their strategy is to continue to gradually expand their area of control, working outward from Manchyr. It's not going to be quick, but they've decided that steady—and successful—is more important than quick, and they're not about to overreach themselves."

"Which gives us at least a little more time," Baron Larchros observed.

"Yes, but we can't afford to squander it," Storm Keep said forcefully.

Heads nodded around the table. Things had moved with frustrating slowness, despite their very best efforts, and every one of them was acutely aware of the hours and days trickling away.

"Well, the good news is that we may be able to begin moving after all,"

Craggy Hill said. The others looked at him, and he smiled sourly. "Zebediah's finally ready to stop dancing around. Oh, he's still holding out for our guarantee of the recognition of complete Zebediahan independence—under him, of course—but I think it's a formality at this point. At any rate, he's committed himself to providing us with the new-model muskets we need. Or some of them, at least."

"He has?" Shylair straightened in his chair, eyes brightening.

Although his secular associates had been steadily increasing their manpower, they were all only too conscious of their lack of weapons. They were too ill-supplied in that regard to arm the men they'd already raised even with swords and pikes, and all of them combined had less than four hundred muskets—all of them old-fashioned smoothbore matchlocks. Against Gahrvai's forces, alone, they would be totally outclassed; once Viceroy General Chermyn put his Marines, with their rifles and artillery, into the field in support, any form of armed uprising would be futile. It could result in nothing but a bloodbath for the resistance, especially now that the southeastern portion of the princedom was accepting the Regency Council's authority, and the bishop executor knew it.

But now. . . .

"Is it just the rifles, Wahlys?" Storm Keep asked.

"Let's not pooh-pooh rifles, Sahlahmn," Craggy Hill replied with a sour smile. Storm Keep nodded in acknowledgment, and Craggy Hill shrugged. "At the moment, he's promising only the rifles. He says we can have the first four or five hundred within a month or so of reaching an actual agreement. Artillery's going to be harder, because Cayleb's being so coy about making it available to Zebediah. Apparently, for some strange reason, he doesn't quite *trust* Zebediah."

From the expressions of his fellow conspirators, that didn't exactly come as a stunning revelation.

"That raises an interesting point, My Lord," Gahrnaht observed. "If Cayleb's watching Zebediah, will he actually be able to divert enough rifles to make a difference?"

"I don't know," Craggy Hill said frankly. "I do know that, according to his envoy, he's already creatively 'lost' somewhere around two hundred rifles which were passing through Zebediah. Apparently, no one in Cayleb's quartermaster's corps even noticed. However, the majority of the arms he's proposing to deliver to us will never officially enter Zebediah at all."

"I beg your pardon, My Lord?" Gahrnaht's eyebrows rose, and Craggy Hill snorted.

"I don't know how he's planning to manage it, either, Bishop Amilain, but his envoy seems confident. Apparently, Zebediah hasn't lost any of his penchant for sneakiness. As nearly as I can put it together from what his envoy's let slip, he's got a contact in Chisholm who's in a position to divert arms and material from their new 'Imperial Army.' As fast as they're expanding, and with everything that has to be going on while they worry about the Church's counterattack, I wouldn't be surprised if someone with big enough balls—if you'll pardon the language—could manage to 'lose' quite a few rifles, or even artillery pieces, if he were in the right position. And from what Zebediah's envoy is saying, it sounds like his contact in Chisholm *is* in the right position."

Once again, heads nodded all around the table, this time with varying degrees of profound satisfaction. If Craggy Hill was right, then they were finally in a position to begin serious planning. If they had the weapons and the firepower to stand up to Gahrvai long enough, there were plenty of Temple Loyalists who'd rally to their colors, and for the first time in far too long, they shared a sense of actual confidence.

None of those nodding heads, however, were aware of the tiny, almost microscopic, sensor remote clinging to the underside of one of the chamber's ceiling beams while it eavesdropped on their entire conversation.

.V.
Imperial Palace,
City of Cherayth,
Kingdom of Chisholm

M erlin!"
An Empress Sharleyan whose pregnancy was just beginning to show leapt to her feet as the tall, black-haired guardsman stepped through the door. It wasn't the way a crowned head of state normally greeted a mere captain of the Imperial Guard, but no one in the council chamber appeared conscious of any irregularity.

Edwyrd Seahamper, Sharleyan's personal armsman, had the duty inside the chamber. His face looked as if it were about to split in two around the fracture line of his enormous grin, and Emperor Cayleb was no more than a step or two behind his wife as the two of them closed in on Captain Athrawes. Prince Nahrmahn of Emerald sat back in his own chair with a smile of welcome whose genuine warmth would have astounded even Nahrmahn as recently as a few months ago, and Archbishop Maikel's smile was almost as broad as Seahamper's.

"Your Majesty," Merlin replied as Sharleyan threw her arms around him in a hug which would have threatened the structural integrity of a mere flesh-and-blood rib cage, even if he *was* wearing a cuirass. His tone was matter of fact, almost bland, but it didn't fool any of those present, and he hugged her back carefully.

"Took you long enough," Cayleb observed, reaching out to clasp forearms with Merlin as Sharleyan moved aside to give him room.

"It *did* take longer than I anticipated," Merlin confessed. "On the other hand, Ahnzhelyk turned out to be a lot more impressive than I'd anticipated, too."

"We want to hear all about it," Sharleyan said. Merlin's need to maintain the lowest profile possible, electronically speaking, had precluded the sort of daily conversations to which they'd become accustomed. He'd passed along enough information to keep them generally informed, but they knew little of the details.

"We want to hear all about it," Sharleyan continued, "but we don't have time for a full report right this minute. Mahrak and Mother will be here anytime now. So anything that they're not cleared for is going to have to wait until later. Except for what you can squeeze in before they arrive, of course."

"Understood, Your Majesty," Merlin said, and bowed slightly.

Baron Green Mountain and Queen Mother Alahnah had been as surprised as almost everyone else when it had been announced Captain Athrawes would be withdrawing from court for an overdue period of meditation. They'd been less happy than some, too, given how handy Merlin had proved when it came to stopping assassination attempts. Still, they'd also recognized that Cayleb and Sharleyan's confinement to the palace—which the weather would have enforced, even if there'd been no other factors to consider—provided an opportune window for him to do just that without jeopardizing their security. They also knew, better than most, how close he was to Sharleyan and Cayleb, however. Now that he was back, they would probably give the emperor and empress at least a little time to welcome him home. On the other hand, this was supposed to be a working meeting, and there were a great many details to settle before Cayleb and Sharleyan departed for their scheduled return to Tellesberg at the end of the month.

Under the circumstances, Merlin felt sure they'd be along shortly. Fortunately, Lieutenant Franz Ahstyn, Merlin's second-in-command from Cayleb's personal detail, had the duty section outside the council chamber. Ahstyn knew about Merlin's "visions," and also knew Green Mountain and Alahnah hadn't been cleared for that knowledge. He could be relied upon to knock on the door and announce the first councilor and queen mother's arrival instead of simply opening it and ushering them through.

In the meantime—

"The short version is that unless something goes incredibly wrong, Ahnzhelyk is going to get herself and all her people—and, trust me, there are more of them than we ever suspected—safely out of the Temple Lands to Siddar City. I've managed to figure out her arrangements for getting from there to Tellesberg, as well, and I think they should work fine. It's going to be a bit ticklish, in some ways, but she has an excellent relationship with the House of Qwentyn, and she's already booked passage on one of those 'Siddarmarkian' ships with Charisian crews which the Qwentyns appear to have acquired."

He smiled broadly in remembered admiration, but then he sobered.

"The other good news is that she managed something quite extraordinary. She has Samyl Wylsynn's family and the families of four other vicars who were members of Wylsynn's 'Circle' with her. That's astonishing enough to be going on with, but she's managed to pull out *thirteen* other vicars' families, as well, from all over the Temple Lands. And she's managed to get Archbishop Zhasyn out of Glacierheart and sixteen more of the 'Circle's' bishops and bishops executor . . . *and their families*." He shook his head. "That's over *two hundred* men, women, and children Clyntahn and the Inquisition are searching everywhere for. When word gets out that they came up short on that kind of scale, it's not going to do a thing for Clyntahn's aura of omnipotence."

"My God." Cayleb sounded almost reverent. "How in the name of all that's truly holy did she *manage* it?"

"Obviously I haven't been able to ask her for the details, since I didn't even realize everything she was up to until I was already on my way back here. For that matter, I doubt I've actually found *everything*, even now. But from what I've seen of the way she operates, it probably didn't take anywhere near the manpower Clyntahn's going to assume it did. I'd guess she was probably the only person outside the 'Circle' itself to whom Wylsynn had trusted the names of every member of his group, and if I had to pick the single most dangerous thing about her, from Clyntahn's perspective, it's that she plans ahead—with a vengeance.

"I'd been keeping tabs on Cahnyr myself, so I've got a pretty good feel for what she did in his case, and I'd guess she used the same technique with most of the others. With variations, of course. But, put most simply, she identified the people most at risk because of their association with the 'Circle,' and she arranged—years ago in Cahnyr's case, at least—a network to get them out quickly and quietly in an emergency. Her idea of how to maintain operational security makes anyone else we've seen yet—even you, Your Highness," he smiled at Nahrmahn, "look positively garrulous, too. I'll guarantee you that not one of the people she was arranging to rescue knew any more about her plans than Cahnyr himself did. That way if one of them was taken, he couldn't expose the existence of the network to anyone else. And I'm just about as certain that the people she'd contacted to do the rescuing had no idea who *she* was or how to initiate contact with her. It was a cellular system—'sleeper cells,' they used to call them back on Old Earth—that was already in place and waiting long before Clyntahn discovered the 'Circle's' existence. All she had to do was get the prearranged execution orders to her . . . extraction teams."

"It sounds like we need to hire her to work for *you,* Nahrmahn," Cayleb said, looking over at the rotund little Emeraldian with a flickering smile.

"It sounds to *me,* Your Grace, as if we need to create her own special bureau and put her in charge of clandestine operations," Nahrmahn replied very seriously indeed. "I've never attempted anything on the scale Merlin's describing, and certainly not right under the Inquisition's nose, but I think I have a feel for the difficulties. And for the degree of forethought and planning involved. I realize she had years—decades—to put all this in place, but I'm still deeply impressed."

"Well," Merlin's expression had been sober; now it went positively grim, "I agree with you that I'm impressed, Your Highness, but don't expect *her* to be." He inhaled deeply. "She may have gotten two hundred people out; from what Owl's picked up, though, Clyntahn's arrested almost two thousand."

"Two *thousand?*" Sharleyan repeated very softly and carefully, her tone stricken, and Merlin nodded slowly.

"Wylsynn's 'Circle' was larger than we suspected," he said heavily. "In addition to him and his brother, there were at least twenty other vicars—there may well have been more; at this point, according to the remotes Owl left in Zion, he's arrested over thirty. In addition, he's arrested the families of all of the accused vicars—aside from the ones Ahnzhelyk got out—as well as every member of the vicars' personal staffs and *their* families. And they've arrested fifty bishops and archbishops, and all of their immediate families, as well."

"*Thirty* vicars?" Staynair shook his head, his expression as shocked as Merlin had ever seen it. "That's a tenth part of the entire vicarate!"

"I'm aware of that, Your Eminence. And I don't think he's done yet. It's obvious he's taking this opportunity to purge the vicarate of everyone he thinks might have the courage to oppose him. And"—Merlin's PICA's face was carved granite—"the Inquisition has already announced it intends to apply the full rigor of *The Book of Schueler* to any 'vile, forsworn, and damnable traitor who has betrayed his vows to God, the Archangels, and Mother Church, no matter who he may be or what office he may have attained' and to their families, as well."

Sharleyan's hand rose to cover her mouth, and Cayleb swore viciously in a savage undertone. Nahrmahn's expression didn't actually change at all, and yet there was a peculiar hardening—an icy thing, more sensed than seen—in his eyes, and Seahamper's expression was a fitting mirror for Cayleb's fury. But Staynair's was, in many ways, the most frightening of all.

Maikel Staynair was a gentle, compassionate, and loving man. Anyone who'd ever met him realized that. But there was another side to that gentleness and compassion—a fiercely protective side. The side which had made him truly a shepherd. And at that moment, when Merlin looked at the Archbishop of Charis, what he saw was a shepherd standing between his flock and one of

Safehold's six-legged 'catamounts' with a hunting spear in his hands and murder in his heart.

"Will he really do it, do you think, Merlin?" Nahrmahn's tone of clinical detachment fooled none of them. All of them looked at him, and the Emeraldian
shrugged. "What I mean is, do you think Trynair, Maigwair, and Duchairn will
let him do something so stupid?"

"I don't know," Merlin replied frankly. "Ahnzhelyk has a far better feel for
what's been happening inside the vicarate and the Group of Four than we did.
From what she's said, I think Duchairn would stop Clyntahn, if he could, but
Maigwair's basically a nonentity. Worse, in Ahnzhelyk's opinion, he probably
agrees with Clyntahn about the need to crush any possible opposition. And I
doubt he has either the moral courage or sufficient stature within the Group of
Four to stop it, even if he wanted to. Trynair's *smart* enough to recognize the
damage this sort of excess could do, but I'm afraid he's desperate enough in the
short term to go along. The question in my mind is whether or not Duchairn
is going to try to stop Clyntahn . . . or recognize that he *can't*. That all he
could accomplish would be to add another victim—this one from the Group
of Four itself—to the list."

"And I hate to say it, Nahrmahn," Cayleb said harshly, "but from their perspective, it may not seem stupid at all. Their fleets are getting close enough to
completion that they'll be ready to at least begin their counterattack soon. At
the same time, the Group of Four's prestige and authority have been badly
damaged by all the reverses they've suffered to date. Not to mention the fact
that the rest of the vicarate knows the entire war started solely because the
Group of Four fucked up. I don't know about Duchairn, but Clyntahn, for
sure, and Trynair and Maigwair, almost as certainly, see this as an opportunity to
reestablish an iron grip on the vicarate. They're going to crush any possible internal voice of opposition—especially any voice that might have counseled
moderation in victory—before they turn that new navy of theirs loose on us.
And if they win, they're going to do exactly the same sorts of things to all *our*
people. They think they're going to create so much terror, so much fear, no one
will ever again dare to argue with *their* interpretation of God's will and their
own power."

The emperor's brown eyes were dark with the vision of the thing of horror the Church of God Awaiting would become if the Group of Four won.

"In the long run, it will destroy them, and possibly even the Church," he
went on, his voice still bitter and cold. "The kind of atrocity they're talking
about, visited on so many men and women—and *children*, damn their black
hearts to hell—who're all known to the rest of the vicarate? Who are cousins
and aunts and uncles of the rest of the vicarate?" He shook his head with the
grim assurance of a prophet. "In the end, even those who are most terrified of

them at this moment are going to remember. There may not be one of them with the guts and the moral courage to stand up to them *now,* but in the end, they'll remember even carrion lizards can pull down a great dragon . . . if there are enough of them and it's distracted.

"So you're right, Nahrmahn. It would be a stupid thing for them to do, ultimately. In the long term. In the fullness of time. But they aren't thinking about the long term. They're thinking about the present, right now, and possibly next month, or next year. That's as far as their vision extends, and so I'm telling you, as surely as I'm standing here in this council chamber at this moment, they are going to do this. God help us all," his voice fell to a whisper, "they *are* going to do this!"

.VI.
### Rhobair Duchairn's Private Chapel,
### The Temple,
### City of Zion,
### The Temple Lands

Rhobair Duchairn knelt before the tiny altar, hands locked around a simple wooden scepter, his eyes fixed upon the icon of Langhorne with its golden, upraised echo of the scepter he held in his own merely mortal hands, and felt the tears running down his face.

*Help me,* he prayed. *Holy Langhorne—God—help* me! *I can't let this happen. I can't, not on top of everything else! This* can't *be what You want done in Your name. Tell me how to* stop *it! Show me a way!*

But the icon was silent. It returned no answer, and strain the ears of his soul though he might, he heard no whisper of God's voice in his heart.

He closed his eyes, face twisted with anguish, squeezing the scepter he held so hard he was amazed the carved wood didn't shatter in his grip. He'd thought he'd known what Clyntahn was going to do, and dreaded it, tried frantically to think of some way to stop it—even warned the intended victims. Yet his worst nightmares had fallen short of what was actually happening.

Duchairn was the only member of the Group of Four Samyl Wylsynn had ever dared approach directly. So when Clyntahn started dropping his mysterious, smirking little hints last fall, Duchairn had been sinkingly certain who his targets were. But neither Trynair nor Maigwair had picked up on those hints. They'd known *something* was in the air, just as everyone else had, yet they'd been as surprised as any other members of the vicarate when Clyntahn and his Inquisitors actually struck. At first, they'd been inclined to be incredulous, to think Clyntahn must have overreacted. He wasn't known for his moderation, after all. But Clyntahn had been prepared for that, and Duchairn's grip on the scepter tightened still farther as he recalled the scene. . . .

▼    ▼    ▼

"What's the meaning of this, Zhaspahr?" Zahmsyn Trynair demanded. The normally urbane and controlled Chancellor's voice was harsh, his expression tight with mingled anger and an undeniable edge of fear, as he confronted the Grand Inquisitor across the council table.

"I think that's plain enough," Clyntahn replied in a cold, dangerously level tone. "I've been telling all of you for some time that we had traitors right here in the vicarate. I realize the three of you have been discounting my warnings. That you've gone your way comfortably assuming it's just a case of me once again seeing enemies in every shadow. Well, I won't say that hasn't happened in the past. I won't apologize for it, either; it's better to be overly suspicious rather than blindly oblivious in the service of God and Schueler.

"But not this time. Oh, no, not *this* time! These bastards have been conspiring against Mother Church, against the Grand Vicar's authority, against our struggle with the heretics in Charis, and against God Himself. They can dress it up any way they want, try to justify it any way they choose, but the truth will come out. Trust me. The truth . . . *will* . . . come out."

Rhobair Duchairn could not recall ever having seen Zhaspahr Clyntahn's expression so armored in assurance and so ribbed with iron determination. He radiated a terrifying power as he glowered at his three colleagues, crouched forward like a jowly, hot-eyed, furious great dragon about to open its vast maw and charge with a bellow of killing rage.

The Treasurer started to open his mouth, although he had absolutely no idea what he was going to say. While he hesitated, searching for words, Trynair sat back in his chair, his eyes intent, and spoke first.

"What truth, Zhaspahr?" he asked. "I know Wylsynn and his brother were always critics, always pains in the arse. And I know they were dangerous—to *us*, at least. But there's a world of difference between that and what you're accusing them of now. And all of these arrests, midnight seizures of women and children . . . Langhorne, man! Can't you see what this is going to do? D'you think all those people aren't related to other families throughout the Temple Lands? Some of them are related to *me*, for God's sake! How do you think the *rest* of the vicarate's going to react if they think *their* families are going to be threatened with something like this just because we think they're opposing our policies?"

"Is *that* what you think this is?" Clyntahn stared at Trynair in disbelief. "Oh, it would have given me immense pleasure to take that sanctimonious bastard and his brother down, don't think for a moment that it wouldn't have. But this isn't something I've manufactured just to quash an enemy, Zahmsyn. This is something that came to *me*. It's a conspiracy that extends far beyond Wylsynn and his brother, and it's only God's own mercy I found out about it at all."

"What kind of conspiracy? And just how *did* you 'find out about it'?" Trynair demanded, his skepticism eroding slightly before Clyntahn's tone of steely certitude.

"They've been conspiring to overthrow the Inquisition and its God-given authority as the first step in their plan to recognize the *legitimacy* of the 'Church of Charis,'" Clyntahn said flatly. "They've been gathering material they believed they could use to blackmail other vicars, extort their support against us and the Grand Vicar, as a means to do just that. They've been working steadily to undermine fundamental Church doctrines, including the doctrine of the Grand Vicar's infallibility when he speaks in Langhorne's name, and planning to undermine Mother Church's central authority by actually supporting the demands of people like Staynair and his so-called 'Reformists' for the local election of bishops. I think all of that constitutes a fairly significant threat to Mother Church and God's plan for Safehold, Zahmsyn. And it doesn't even begin to get into some of the things we've discovered about their *personal* degeneracy."

Duchairn felt a sudden surge of nausea at hearing someone like *Clyntahn,* of all people, accuse someone else of "degeneracy." Yet even he was a bit taken aback by the catalog of the Grand Inquisitor's other accusations. He never doubted that Clyntahn had twisted and misconstrued everything Samyl and Hauwerd Wylsynn had been trying to accomplish—the Treasurer had that terrifying note Hauwerd had slipped him as evidence—but he was frighteningly confident that Clyntahn could sell his interpretation of their intentions to a lot, possibly even a majority, of the other vicars. Those other vicars were already terrified of the consequences of the war with Charis, and the reports of more and more Reformist-inclined clergy going over to the Church of Charis in places like Emerald and Corisande would only make them even more suspicious of, more frightened by, the specter of betrayal from within.

"Those are serious accusations," Trynair said, and this time the Chancellor sounded shaken, even a little frightened. "And you still haven't told us how you came to 'discover' all of this? And why you didn't tell all of *us* about it at the time?"

"I didn't tell the rest of you about it, first, because it was the Inquisition's business, not yours," Clyntahn said bluntly. "Langhorne and Schueler established the Inquisition expressly to deal with this sort of internal rot. I didn't need to consult with anyone else to recognize what my office and my own vows required of me. Second, I didn't tell the rest of you—or anyone, outside of Wyllym Rayno and a handful of senior Inquisitors whose ability to keep their mouths shut I unreservedly trusted—because it was essential the conspirators not know I'd become aware of their actions until winter trapped them here in Zion and I'd had time to complete my preliminary investigations and arrange to seize all the guilty parties simultaneously. I'm not saying any of you would have deliberately warned someone capable of this sort of damnable treason," his eyes flipped briefly to Rhobair Duchairn's face, and those eyes had gone cold, instead of hot, "but even a single incautious word in the wrong spot could have warned them before I was ready. You have no idea how far their nets extended, how deeply into the staffs of other vicars and other archbishops their corruption had spread.

"As for how I discovered it, I wish I could take credit for that, but I can't." Duchairn's eyes weren't the only ones that widened in astonishment as Zhaspahr Clyntahn disavowed the credit for discovering a conspiracy on the scale of the one he'd just described. "As it happens," he continued, "someone who'd been recruited by the conspirators and recognized where they were actually headed brought it to my attention."

"Who?" Duchairn heard his own voice demand.

Clyntahn gazed at him silently, almost thoughtfully for a moment, then nodded. He pushed back his chair with a little grunt of effort, stalked to the chamber's door, and opened it.

"Yes, Your Grace?" the purple-cassocked Inquisitor outside the door said.

"Fetch him," Clyntahn said flatly.

"At once, Your Grace."

The Inquisitor bowed, then turned and walked swiftly down the corridor while Clyntahn returned to his place at the table. He sat back down, folded his arms across his chest, and sat silent, waiting.

The wait wasn't as long as it felt—Duchairn was certain of that—yet it seemed forever before the door opened once more and the Inquisitor returned. He was accompanied by another man, this one in the orange-trimmed white cassock of an archbishop.

"I believe all of you know the Archbishop of Hankey," Clyntahn said.

Duchairn's eyes narrowed. He did, indeed, know Nyklas Stantyn, the Archbishop of Hankey, although not well. Their paths had crossed on several occasions, especially where the details of Hankey's finances were concerned, but he'd never actually gotten to know Stantyn. Now he considered the obviously frightened man in front of him, wondering what lay behind that exquisitely tailored façade. There was something dark in Stantyn's brown eyes, and his hands trembled visibly before he concealed them in the sleeves of his cassock.

"Nyklas came to me last May," Clyntahn continued. "He sought me out because he had become aware of a truly horrendous plot by so-called men of God right here in the vicarate. They'd approached him, and for some time, as he will freely confess, he allowed himself to be deceived and taken in by their lies. They convinced him their goal was simply to 'reform' certain 'abuses' within Mother Church." The Grand Inquisitor smiled thinly. "Does that sound like what we're hearing from other lands about 'Reformists' trampling all over one another in their eagerness to betray Mother Church to Staynair and his heretics?"

Duchairn felt his heart sink as he realized how that question was going to resonate with other frightened vicars. Indeed, he saw a flicker in *Trynair's* eyes, and it was obvious from Maigwair's expression that he was prepared to embrace whatever expedient was required to crush any "Reformist plot" coming from *inside* the Temple.

"At first, Nyklas was so impressed by their apparent sincerity and devoutness that he allowed himself to be taken in," Clyntahn went on after letting his question sink fully home. "In time, however, he came to realize their actual objectives were rather more sinister. Then this business with Charis erupted. In their eagerness to seize the opportunity they believed it presented, they made the mistake of coming a bit too far out into the open, and he began to see things he hadn't seen before, including the evidence of deeply hidden *personal* corruption. He was, I think, understandably frightened—both by what he was discovering, and by how Mother Church and the Office of Inquisition might respond to his own involvement. It took him some time, and a great deal of prayer, to realize it was his duty to bring all this to my attention. To lay it before me, so Mother Church might defend herself against this attack out of the night. He recognized the personal risk he ran in informing me of it, yet he was resolved to do so, and he did."

*He was so terrified of what you'd do to all of them if you found out on your own that he came to you to sell the others out and buy the best personal terms he could, you mean,* Duchairn thought coldly.

"May we hear this from Archbishop Nyklas himself?" Trynair asked in a painfully neutral tone.

"Of course you may." Clyntahn sounded almost exasperated, as if he couldn't believe there'd ever been any question in Trynair's mind, and glanced at the waiting, silent archbishop. "Tell them, Nyklas."

"Yes, Your Grace," Stantyn replied.

He looked at the other three vicars, cleared his throat, and swallowed hard. Then he drew a deep breath.

"It's as the Grand Inquisitor has already described, Your Graces." His voice quivered slightly, yet he met their eyes squarely. "At first, I genuinely believed Vicar Samyl and Vicar Hauwerd had only Mother Church's best interests at heart. In fact, I believed that for several *years*. It was only gradually that certain parts of what they said began to sound as if they were contradicting other parts, and even then, I was able to convince myself I'd simply misunderstood. But they had me . . . doing things which made me uncomfortable. Spying on my fellow bishops and archbishops. Gathering information about members of the vicarate—even the Grand Vicar himself. Looking, especially, for evidence which might have been used to blackmail or pressure members of the Inquisition. And, in addition, for anything which might have been used as a weapon against the Chancellor, the Grand Inquisitor, and the Treasurer."

He paused, as if gathering his thoughts, then continued.

"I began to realize that what they were gathering was information which might be used against personal enemies in the vicarate. That concerned me deeply, especially when I began to discover certain . . . unpleasant aspects of their own lives." His mouth twisted briefly in what might have been a grimace of distaste . . . or, perhaps, fear. "I've found that behind the virtuous façade they strove to present, they were actually dedicated to a personal licentiousness that shocked me. Your Graces, I'm no prude, and no stranger to reality. I know bishops, archbishops, even vicars are still men, that all of us are still prone to the temptations of the flesh, and that, too often, we succumb to them. I'm not prepared to condemn any of my brothers in God for being weak, because all mortals are weak and fallible. But there are perversions at which I must draw a line. Unnatural lusts, and the abuse of children, are more than I could endure."

Duchairn's eyes widened. Surely Clyntahn didn't think he could sell *that* to the rest of the vicarate? Not about Samyl and Hauwerd Wylsynn, of all men!

Yet even as he thought that, he was struck by how damnably sincere and convincing Stantyn sounded. By the way men already eager to justify the destruction of someone they'd been convinced was their enemy would seize upon such additional charges.

*Well, now I know what terms you made when you sold your soul, Stantyn,* he thought coldly.

"As my eyes were opened," Stantyn continued, "I began to see even more things I'd sought not to see. And then came the war with Charis, and suddenly they were all excited, all eager, over the opportunity—the opening—our initial defeats offered them. I became aware that they didn't care if Mother Church shattered, so long as they were able to assert their own control over whatever remained in the wreckage. They were perfectly prepared for the 'Church of Charis' to grow and prosper, if that would allow them to impose their own 'doctrinal reform' here in Zion and appoint themselves the rulers of Mother Church."

The Archbishop of Hankey shook his head sadly, his expression that of a man who had been betrayed by those he had trusted . . . rather than a man who was busy betraying those who had trusted *him.*

"Once I realized the truth, Your Graces, I decided I had no choice but to take my knowledge and suspicions to the Grand Inquisitor. Which I did. And after he'd heard my confession, he said—"

▼   ▼   ▼

Rhobair Duchairn returned to the present, opened his eyes, and stared once again, imploringly, at the icon on the altar. But still, the icon made no answer to his silent, anguished plea.

Stantyn had turned the trick, he thought hopelessly. Duchairn didn't know if Trynair really believed a single word about the supposed "perversions" of the Wylsynns' inner circle, but he suspected Maigwair had convinced himself it was the truth. Yet what he knew Trynair *did* believe was that Samyl and Hauwerd Wylsynn and their . . . associates had been determined to wrest control of the Temple from the Group of Four. And, Duchairn thought, the Chancellor also believed the Wylsynns truly had been prepared to entertain a negotiated settlement with the Church of Charis. One which would have recognized that heretical church's right to exist. It was debatable which of those would have appeared as the greater treason, the greater threat, to Zahmsyn Trynair. Either would probably have been enough to incline him to support Clyntahn; both of them together had definitely done the trick.

And so Rhobair Duchairn found himself the only member of the Group of Four who recognized—or would admit, even to himself, at any rate—what Zhaspahr Clyntahn really intended. The only possible voice which could be raised against the madness. Yet he was an *isolated* voice, and not just within the Group of Four. All the rest of the vicarate was aware of the way in which he had turned his focus back to his personal faith, and in the process, he'd spent a great deal of time in the same circles as Samuel and Hauwerd Wylsynn. The same circles as several— indeed, the majority—of the vicars who had been seized as conspirators with the Wylsynn brothers.

The shock of what had happened to the Wylsynns when the Inquisition sought to arrest them had gone through the vicarate like a thunderbolt. One vicar killed by another, by his own *brother*, to prevent his arrest? The murderer slain in pitched combat against the Temple Guard itself? And *why* had Hauwerd killed Samyl? To spare his brother from the Question and the Punishment . . . or to silence a voice which might have condemned *him* under interrogation?

Duchairn's eyes burned. He knew exactly why Hauwerd had done what he'd done, and he remembered the way Hauwerd had looked into his own eyes on the day he passed him that note. He knew what Hauwerd had expected of him on that day. But he could also hear the mob rising behind Clyntahn, the voices driven by panic into shrill denunciations, into fevered pledges of loyalty, into passionate demands for vengeance upon those who would betray Mother Church—*anything* to keep Clyntahn and the Inquisition pointed away from them and *their* families.

He couldn't stop it.

The thought burned through him suddenly, cold and clear, as he stared at the icon of Langhorne.

He *couldn't* stop it. Not now. No one could. If he tried, he would simply be added to the list of victims, and it was entirely probable that his own family—his brothers, his sister, and *their* families—would be delivered to the

Inquisition with him. He shrank from the thought of what would happen to them there, of the accusation in their eyes as they suffered all the horrors Schueler had prescribed and knew it was all because *he* had sacrificed them in his vain attempt to assuage his own conscience by opposing Clyntahn.

*That wouldn't be what actually happened,* he thought despairingly, his mind filled with the terror and the accusation and the betrayal in his nieces' and nephews' eyes, *but it's what they would think, what they would* feel . . . *what they would suffer. I have the right to destroy* myself; *do I have the right to destroy them right along with me?*

Yet even if he had that right, it would accomplish nothing. Nothing accept the removal of the one voice within the Group of Four which might have opposed it.

*It doesn't matter. It shouldn't* matter. *I may not always know what's right, but I know what's* wrong, *and I'm a* vicar. *I'm a priest. I'm a* shepherd. *Langhorne himself says, "The good shepherd sacrifices his life for the sheep." It doesn't get any plainer than that. And yet . . . and yet. . . .*

He closed his eyes, thinking once more of the note Hauwerd Wylsynn had handed him. Of the demand it made, the hope it offered, and the promise it had required of him. If he sacrificed himself now, at this moment, the way his priestly office demanded, that hope would die with him and the promise would wither unfulfilled.

He remembered the passion in Hauwerd's eyes that morning, remembered Samyl Wylsynn's gentle smile and his delight in doing God's will, remembered his love for his own family, remembered the baying hounds gathering at Clyntahn's heels, and pressed his forehead against the scepter in his hands.

# APRIL, YEAR OF GOD 894

I s it as bad as the reports all say it is, Phylyp?" Irys Daykyn asked somberly. She and Earl Coris stood in one of her favorite spots, looking out across Lake Erdan from the window of a small hanging turret. One reason it was one of her favorite spots was the view of the enormous lake, especially at this time of day, with the sun setting in red and gold splendor beyond its farther shore. Another reason was its convenience, since it gave directly onto the sitting room of the small suite she'd been assigned in the central keep of King Zhames' castle. But the most important reason was that this particular spot was immune to eavesdropping.

She only wished there were another spot somewhere in the entire castle where that was equally true.

At the moment, a bald-headed man in his forties, with a thick version of what had once been called a "walrus mustache" on a planet called Old Earth and a nose which had obviously been broken more than once, stood outside her suite to ensure she and her "guardian" were not disturbed. His name was To-bys Raimair—*Sergeant* Tobys Raimair, recently retired (in a manner of speaking) from the Royal Corisandian Army. Raimair hadn't been part of her original entourage, but Captain Zhoel Harys, who'd managed to get her and her brother out of Corisande in one piece, had recommended Raimair to Coris. He was, the captain had said, not only loyal and stubborn but also "good with his hands," so perhaps he might be of service to His Highness during his . . . visit to Delferahk.

In the months since, both Coris and Irys had concluded that Captain Harys had known what he was talking about, and Raimair had quietly assembled a small, competent, and completely unofficial "royal guard" for their nine-year-old prince. Only one of them was a Delferahkan, and all of them were paid directly by Irys, using "discretionary funds" Coris had hidden away in various mainland accounts for the use of her father's spy networks. As a result, their primary loyalty was to her—and Daivyn—and *not* to King Zhames. Zhames had put up with it so far, undoubtedly because (assuming he was even aware Daivyn's "guard" existed in the first place) it was so small. There were only twelve men in it, after all.

At the moment, Coris wished there were twelve *hundred*.

He gazed at the princess, considering her question. She would be eighteen in another two months, yet she looked ten years older, and her hazel eyes were intent, dark with a worry she was careful to let very few see. Those were not the eyes of a young woman—a girl—her age, Coris thought sadly. But they *were* the eyes of someone to whom he owed the truth.

"Actually, I'm afraid it's probably *worse* than the reports say," he said quietly. He looked away for a moment, gazing out across the crimson sheet of lake water. "What we've seen so far are the official reports," he continued. "The *preliminary* reports. They're still setting the stage, I'm afraid." His lips tightened. "When Clyntahn's ready, the reports are going to get a lot worse."

"May God and Langhorne have mercy on their souls," Irys murmured. It was her turn to stare unseeingly at the lake for several seconds.

"How much truth do you think there is to the charges?" she asked even more quietly, then, and Coris inhaled deeply.

That was a dangerous question. Not just for her to be asking, even here, where he was virtually certain there were no unfriendly ears to hear, but for her even to be thinking.

*And you think she's not* already *thinking them, Phylyp?* he asked himself sarcastically.

"Do you really want my honest answer, Irys?" he asked softly. She met his eyes levelly, and nodded. "Very well," he sighed. "Obviously, we can't really *know* from this far away, but in my opinion there's no truth to at least ninety percent of Clyntahn's accusations. In fact, there may well not be *any* truth to them."

"Then why?" Her tone was almost pleading. "If it isn't true, then why arrest them? Why accuse them of something that carries such a horrible penalty?"

"Because—" Coris began, then paused. Irys Daikyn was a highly intelligent young woman, and one who understood political maneuvers. If she truly couldn't answer those questions for herself, he would have preferred—preferred more than almost anything else in the world—to leave her in that state of ignorance.

*But the truth is, she already knows,* he told himself sadly. *She just hasn't wanted to believe it. In fact, she's probably wanted so badly* not *to believe that she's half convinced herself her suspicions are wrong. But only half.*

"Your Highness—Irys," he said, "I don't doubt Vicar Samyl and Vicar Hauwerd were doing something *Clyntahn* considered treasonous. The truth, unfortunately," he met her eyes unflinchingly, "is that Clyntahn's definition of 'treason' has very little to do these days with treachery against Mother Church or God and a great deal to do with opposition to *him*.

"My own reports and analyses of the vicarate's internal politics make it clear Samyl Wylsynn was Clyntahn's only real rival for the post of Grand Inquisitor, and he's—he *was*—a very different man from Clyntahn. I have no doubt he was horrified by many of the Group of Four's actions over the last couple of years. Given what's been reported to me about his personality, I'd be very surprised if he *hadn't* been trying to do something to at least moderate Clyntahn's . . . excesses. And that, I'm afraid, would have been more than enough justification—in Clyntahn's mind—for having him and any of his . . . associates arrested."

Irys' eyes had flinched very slightly at the word "excesses." It was the first time he'd used that particular word, his most open statement of disagreement with the official keeper of Mother Church's soul. Yet her only surprise was that he'd finally used it, not that he felt that way.

"But to order his arrest—*their* arrest—on charges like *these*," she said. "Charges which will condemn them to such horrible punishment. And to arrest entire *families,* as well." She shook her head, and Coris grimaced.

"Irys," he said as gently as he could, "Clyntahn chose those charges *because* of the penalty they carry. Oh, he needed alleged crimes serious enough to justify the arrest and removal of members of the vicarate itself, but his real reasons—his true reasons—are, first, to find charges which permanently and completely discredit his critics, and, second, to punish those critics so severely no one will dare to take their places when they're gone. He's trying to deter *anyone* from opposing him or the Group of Four's policies and strategy, and this is his way of warning any of those would-be opponents of exactly how . . . unwise of them it would be to even hint at criticizing them."

He saw something flicker in her eyes. It puzzled him, for a moment, but then he realized what it had been.

*You're thinking about your father, aren't you?* he thought. *Thinking about how he sometimes punished someone more harshly in order to deter others from committing the same offense. And you really are smart, Irys. Little though you might want to think that about your own father, you know there were other things he did—things he never discussed with you—that had very little to do with "justice" and quite a lot to do with deterrence.*

"So you think he really will inflict the Punishment of Schueler on them?"

"I'm afraid the only real question is whether or not he'll inflict the Punishment on their families, as well," Coris said sadly. Irys inhaled sharply, fresh horror filling her eyes, and he reached out and touched her cheek gently, something he almost never did.

"But the *children,* Phylyp," she said pleadingly, raising her own hand and cupping it over the hand on her cheek. Her voice was barely a whisper. "Surely he'll spare—"

She broke off as Coris shook his head sadly, gently.

"They're not children to him, Irys. Not anymore. At best, they're the 'spawn of traitors and heretics.' Worse, they're pawns. They'll be more useful to Mother Church—and him—as warnings to future 'traitors.'" He shook his head again. "No, I think the only question is whether he'll settle for simply having the children executed rather than subjecting them to the Punishment of Schueler, as well."

Irys looked physically ill, and Coris didn't blame her. Some of those children would be mere infants, in some cases still babes in arms. And it wouldn't matter one bit to Zhaspahr Clyntahn. Not any more than—

He chopped that thought off quickly. Irys, he knew, remained convinced Cayleb Ahrmahk had ordered her father's and her brother's assassinations. In many ways, he wished her mind were more open to other possibilities—especially the one which had begun to look to him more and more like a certainty where Zhaspahr Clyntahn was concerned. But as he saw the worry, the sickness, in those hazel eyes, he felt a familiar hesitation.

She was already deeply concerned for her little brother's safety. Did he want to add to that concern? Fill her with even more worry and fear? For that matter, her own best defense against Clyntahn might well reside in her obvious, ongoing ignorance of the part Coris had become certain the Grand Inquisitor had played in Hektor's and his son's murders. As long as she remained passionately and openly convinced of Cayleb's guilt, she was useful to Clyntahn—another voice, a highly *visible* voice, condemning Cayleb and Sharleyan and all of Charis for the crime. Yet another source of legitimacy for anyone in Corisande tempted to resist the Charisian annexation of that princedom. But if she ever once openly *questioned* Cayleb's guilt, she would go instantly from the category of "mildly useful" to the category of "liability" in Clyntahn's mind. And if that happened. . . .

"They got in his way," the Earl of Coris said, instead of what he'd been thinking about saying. "And he's not going to overlook the fact that so many of the people who might oppose him are also fathers and mothers. Can you think of a single threat which could be more effective than that?"

He asked the question quietly, and, after a moment, she shook her head in mute reply.

"Of course you can't." Coris' lips worked like a man who wanted to spit out something rotten, and he looked back out the window at the lake. At the pure, cold water of the lake. "Of course you can't," he said softly, "and neither can Zhaspahr Clyntahn. Which is why he'll do it, Irys. Never doubt it for a moment. He *will* do it."

R hobair, you can't keep doing this," Zahmsyn Trynair said flatly.
"Doing what?" Rhobair Duchairn asked calmly, almost coldly, looking up from the endless sea of paperwork which flowed across his desk daily.

"You know perfectly well *what*."

Trynair closed the door of Duchairn's private office behind himself and crossed to stand before the other vicar's desk.

"Do you think Zhaspahr is the only one who's noticed what you're doing—or *not* doing?" he demanded.

Duchairn sat back in his chair, elbows on the armrests, and gazed at the Chancellor of the Church of God Awaiting. As always, the office was perfectly, restfully lit and exactly the right temperature. The chair—as always—was almost unbelievably comfortable under him. The walls—as always—bore a slowly, almost imperceptibly changing mosaic of fresh green trees, growing against the backdrop of distant blue mountains. And the air—as always—was filled with the gentle sound of background music.

It was all a jarring, almost—no, not *almost*—obscene contrast to the horrors Zhaspahr Clyntahn's Inquisition was even then visiting upon men, women, and children in God's name.

"What is it, precisely, I'm not doing, Zahmsyn?" he asked. "Tell me. Am I failing to participate in the judicial murder of my fellow vicars? Failing to applaud the torture of women, wives, who probably didn't even know what their husbands were doing . . . assuming their husbands were actually *doing* anything at all? Failing to lend the seal of my approval to the decision to have sixteen-year-old girls burned to death because their fathers pissed Zhaspahr off? Is *that* what I'm failing to do, Zahmsyn?"

Trynair's eyes widened at Duchairn's cold, biting contempt. He gazed at the other vicar for a long moment, then his own eyes fell and he stood looking at Duchairn's desktop until, finally, he raised his eyes once again.

"It's not that simple, Rhobair, and you know it," he said.

"On the contrary, it's *exactly* that simple," Duchairn responded. "You may argue that there are other factors involved, other considerations, but that doesn't make a single question I just asked you any less valid or less pertinent. You can lie to yourself about that if you want, but I won't. Not anymore."

"Don't you understand how Zhaspahr's going to react if you start saying things like that to someone else?" Trynair's eyes were almost pleading. "If he even *thinks* you're trying to inspire some sort of resistance to the Inquisition. . . ."

The Chancellor's voice trailed off, and Duchairn shrugged.

"To my own shame," he said flatly, "I'm doing nothing of the sort. I'm keeping my mouth shut . . . and may God forgive me for it. Because, believe me, Zahmsyn, if I thought for one single moment that I *could* inspire some effective resistance—that I could stop this . . . this *atrocity*, I would do it. I would do it if I knew I would die tomorrow myself for the doing."

He met Trynair's gaze flatly, unflinchingly, and tension hummed between them, singing in the depths of the office's silence.

Something deep inside Zahmsyn Trynair quailed before Duchairn's unwavering eyes. Something which had once believed it, too, was a true vocation to serve God's will.

He'd always thought that, in many ways, Rhobair Duchairn was the weakest of the Group of Four. Far smarter—and more principled—than Allayn Maigwair, perhaps, but ultimately flawed. Unwilling to face what had to be done in the service of maintaining Mother Church's authority. He was the sort of man prepared to look the other way, to *acquiesce* when someone else was willing to do what must be done, so long as it was not required of *him*.

Most of the Chancellor still thought that. But not all of him . . . not that something in himself which had once believed.

*Maybe he is still like that,* he thought. *Maybe all this "regenerated faith" of his is only another way to avoid doing the unpleasant things. But I don't think it is. Not really. If that were all it was, he wouldn't antagonize Zhaspahr this way. And he sure as Shan-wei wouldn't antagonize* me *when I'm the only potential ally against Zhaspahr he can possibly hope to find!*

"If Zhaspahr ever hears you say something like that," Trynair heard his own voice saying almost conversationally, "the fact that you're a member of the 'Group of Four' won't save you. You do realize that, don't you? That you might as well go ahead and oppose him openly?"

"I could find myself in far worse company," Duchairn replied levelly.

"But not in any *deader* company."

"Probably not. Which is why you're the only one I've said it to. Of course, you can always go and tell him what I said, couldn't you? On the other hand, if you do that, and he does to me what he's already done to so many other men and women we've known all our lives, then you'll be all alone with him and Allayn, won't you? How long do you think you'll last—especially when you're the one the Grand Vicar listens to, the only person with a source of authority which might rival that of the Inquisition—once he starts worrying about traitors in our own ranks?"

Trynair felt his jaw trying to drop. He restrained the impulse with the experience of decades of political infighting, yet the acuity of what Duchairn had just said shocked him.

*And he's right, damn him. I can't afford to have Zhaspahr thinking that way. And I can't afford to let Rhobair go down, either. Because as long as he's still here, I can always divert Zhaspahr into going after* him *if I have to. Once he's gone. . . .*

"All right. I won't deny—I *can't* deny—your point," Trynair admitted out loud. "I *don't* want to be the only potential voice of opposition, now that he's got the bit between his teeth. But that's not going to keep you alive and in one piece if you antagonize him badly enough. I may have selfish reasons to not want to see . . . anything happen to you. But it won't do you any good if I go down with you, either, and I'm not willing to do that."

It was Duchairn's turn to gaze thoughtfully at Trynair. That was the frankest admission he'd ever heard out of the Chancellor.

"Tell me, Zahmsyn," the Church Treasurer said finally, "do you really believe *any* of the testimony being presented? Be honest—with me, at least. You know how the Inquisition goes about extracting 'confessions,' so tell me. Do you think Samyl and Hauwerd Wylsynn—*Samyl and Hauwerd,* of all people— were molesting *children*? That they were practicing Shan-wei worship, right here in the Temple? That they were in treasonous communication with the Church of Charis? That they were planning to cooperate with the Charisians, recognize the 'legitimacy' of the schism in return for Charis' support in putting one of *them* on the Grand Vicar's throne here in the Temple?"

Trynair looked away. He stood staring unseeing at the wall mosaics for almost a full minute, then drew a deep breath and looked back at Duchairn.

"No," he said softly. "No, I don't believe that. But I do believe they were conspiring against Zhaspahr. And, by extension, that means against you and me, as well. *You* may be sufficiently confident in your faith to take something like that calmly. I'm not. I'll admit it—I'm not. But it's not just my own security, my own power and comfort I'm thinking about, either. Whether they were planning to conspire with the Charisians or not is really beside the point, in at least one way. If they'd succeeded in bringing down Zhaspahr, it would have created a huge power vacuum in the Temple and the vicarate. God only knows how that would have worked out, what it would have meant for Mother Church's cohesiveness at this moment. But even worse, they might have *tried* to bring him down . . . and failed.

"You think what's happening now is terrible? Well, I can't really disagree. But how much worse would it be if they'd managed to provoke a genuine revolt against Zhaspahr? Managed to stir up enough of the vicarate to support them? Managed to fracture Mother Church—fracture Mother Church's *vicars,* with all of the implications that would have for the faith and support of the ordinary people? Do you think that *wouldn't* have opened the door wide to the Charisians, whether that was what they wanted or not? And do you think, for one moment, that Rayno and Zhaspahr's other handpicked appointments in the Inquisition and the Schuelerite hierarchies wouldn't have stayed loyal to him? What do you think would have happened if the Wylsynns had created a genuine civil war inside Mother Church's most senior vicars? You think the cost wouldn't have been immensely worse even than what we're already seeing?"

"I've thought about that," Duchairn admitted. "I'm not sure it could be 'immensely worse.' For that matter, I'm not sure it could be *worse,* at all. But I can't know that it wouldn't be, either. And I have to admit that at this moment, I don't see anybody who could possibly stand up to the Inquisition and the hysteria Zhaspahr's created. Without something, anything, with a realistic hope of actually *stopping* him—and we both know he'd have to be stopped by force at this point—*trying* to stop him would only make things worse. I know that. Which is the reason I *haven't* tried. The reason I'm not planning on trying."

"But—" Trynair began.

"I won't try to stop him, but I'm not going to give him the imprimatur of my support, either. Maybe it's sanctimonious, but I'm not going to attend these ghastly murder fests of his. I'm not going to sign any warrants of execution. Not going to approve the murders of any children or give him one single ounce of cover or justification he can't create for himself. He's the Grand Inquisitor. Can you even begin to *count* the number of times he's told us that? All right, let him *be* the Grand Inquisitor. Let him take the responsibility—and claim the *credit,* if there is any—for defeating this vile effort to betray Mother Church to her enemies."

Duchairn's irony was withering, and Trynair frowned.

"What are you saying you're going to do, then, Rhobair?" he asked after a moment. "If you're not going to oppose him, and you're not going to support him . . . what? Are you planning on retiring to a monastery somewhere?"

"Oh, I've considered it," Duchairn said very, very softly. "Believe me, Zahmsyn, you cannot *imagine* how I've considered doing exactly that. But I can't. It would be running away, hiding from my own responsibilities."

"Then tell me what you *are* going to do!" Trynair snapped, and his tone was so exasperated that Duchairn surprised them both with a twisted ghost of a smile.

"All right, I will." He let his chair come forward again, folding his arms before him on the desk, leaning over them while he gazed up at Trynair. "I'm going to do my job as Mother Church's Treasurer. I'm going to maintain her fiscal health—as well as I can, in the face of how much this insane war is costing. And somehow, at the same time, I'm going to see to it that the Bédardists, and the Pasqualates, and the other charitable orders actually get the funding and support they're *supposed* to have. I'm going to see to it, next winter, that there are soup kitchens all over Zion, Zahmsyn. I'm going to throw up bar-racks for the poor to survive the snow and the ice outside our front door. I'm going to build hospitals to care for all of the maimed this war is going to pro-duce, and orphanages to care for all of the orphans it's going to leave. I am fi-nally going to use my position as a vicar of the Church of God Awaiting to do exactly what Maikel Staynair and Cayleb and Sharleyan Ahrmahk have accused us—rightly—of *not* doing."

Trynair stared at him. Then he gave a sharp, barking crack of laughter.

"What's this, Rhobair? Trying to buy the Archangels' forgiveness? Is this your bribe? What you're promising God as compensation for your failure to oppose Zhaspahr's 'excesses' openly?"

"In some ways, yes," Duchairn said unflinchingly. "That's one way to put it. Another way to put it would be that I'm going to accomplish all I can *de-spite* Zhaspahr's 'excesses,' though, wouldn't it? And since it would be so . . . inexpedient for you to allow me to disappear from the equation, you have my permission to present it to Zhaspahr in exactly those terms. Consider it my own personal bargain with Shan-wei."

"What do you mean?" Trynair frowned, and Duchairn's eyes glittered.

"I thought it was clear enough." He leaned back again, crossing his legs. "Go ahead, tell Zhaspahr you and I talked about this. Tell him I can't support his deci-sions as Grand Inquisitor, but I recognize that they *are* his decisions as Grand In-quisitor. That I won't openly oppose him, but that in return, he won't stand in my way of seeing to it that the charitable orders—which come under the general control of the Exchequer, anyway—receive the support they require. Tell him you think it's my way of buying off my own conscience. Langhorne, you might even be right! But I also suggest you remind him about the dragon drover who found out he needed a carrot to go with the stick. He can leave all that saccharine fawn-ing, all that slobbering concern 'for the masses,' to me. Let me handle it—God knows I'll be better at it than *he* ever would! And as long as I'm still a member of the 'Group of Four,' it will be the 'Group of Four'—including Zhaspahr—who get the credit. He's proven he can terrorize people into obedience. Now all he has to do is let me *buy* their obedience, as well, and he'll be happy, I'll be . . . satisfied, and the end result will be to *strengthen* his position, not weaken it."

Trynair frowned, once again taken by surprise by Duchairn's political per-spicacity. That was precisely the right way to present the Treasurer's argument to the Grand Inquisitor. Not only that, it actually made sense.

He considered the other man narrowly, wondering exactly what had changed inside Rhobair Duchairn. There was something, he could *sense* it, but he couldn't quite put his finger on what it was. It wasn't that any of the Trea-surer's reborn faith had disappeared. Not that he was suddenly comfortable with Clyntahn's brutality. Not even that he'd made his peace with it. It was something . . . else.

*Maybe it's just that Zhaspahr's finally proven he can't be controlled. Maybe it's just a dose of realism, acceptance tempering all that idealism of his. And maybe it isn't, either. Maybe it's something else entirely. But that doesn't mean he's wrong about the best way to sell it to Zhaspahr. And there's no way he's wrong about the importance of finding some motivator besides simple terror, either! That's always been Zhaspahr's blind spot. If I can only convince him to let Rhobair be our . . . our kinder, gentler face, then maybe I can actually undo some of the damage he's busy doing.*

He gazed into Duchairn's eyes once more, then, finally, he shrugged.

"All right, Rhobair. If my brokering some kind of deal between you and Zhaspahr will satisfy you, if you'll give Zhaspahr your assurance you'll leave inquisitorial matters up to the Inquisition if he'll give you free rein where your charitable activities are concerned, I'll try. And I think I'll probably succeed . . . as long as you're serious about this. But don't lie to me. If this will satisfy you, I'll do my damnedest to sell it to Zhaspahr. But if I ever find out later that you aren't prepared to live up to your end of the . . . understanding, I'll wash my hands of whatever finally becomes of you. Is that understood?"

"Of course it is," Duchairn said, and surprised Trynair yet again—this time with an oddly gentle smile. "You know, in many ways, Zhaspahr's always been his own worst enemy. And one reason is that he's forgotten—and I have to admit, I'd forgotten the same thing—that sometimes kindness, gentleness, is just as strong a weapon as any terror or punishment. Of course, it's not the sort of weapon he's constitutionally suited to wielding, I suppose. So I'm sure it will be best for us—for *all* of us—if he lets me take care of it for him."

.III.
### Father Paityr Wylsynn's Office,
### Gold Mark Street,
### City of Tellesberg,
### Kingdom of Old Charis

Father Paityr Wylsynn stared sightlessly out his office windows.

The Tellesberg sun was bright, shining down on the broad street beyond the deep, green shade of the trees growing around the ex-Exchequer building in which that office was housed. It was late morning, and, as always, Tellesberg was a bustling stir of energy. Wylsynn's office was far enough from the harbor and the warehouse district which served it for the local traffic to be relatively free of the heavy freight wagons which spent so much time rumbling through much of the rest of the city. This was primarily a financial district, home to bankers and law masters, stock traders and counting houses, and aside from the regularly scheduled lizard-drawn trolleys, most of the traffic here consisted of pedestrians interspersed with only an occasional carriage or horseman. A few sidewalk vendors were spotted about, their carts and small wagons shaded by colorful awnings. Most of them were food sellers, serving the office workers employed in the vicinity, and an occasional tantalizing wisp of aroma drifted through his open windows.

Wylsynn didn't notice. Not any more than he noticed the contrast between brilliant sunlight and dark shade, or than he heard the vendors' raised voices, or actually saw the passing pedestrians. No. His attention was elsewhere, focused on the remembered words of the letter which lay folded on the desk before him.

*So it's finally happened.* He felt a fresh burning sensation at the backs of his blue eyes. *After all these years.*

He didn't know how the letter had reached him. Oh, he was sure he could have tracked it back through at least the last two or three sets of hands, but after that, it would have disappeared untraceably into the anonymity its sender had required, and he was glad it was so.

He leaned his head against the tall back of his chair, closing his eyes, and remembered every step of the journey which had carried him to this office, on this street. He remembered his own realization that he had a true vocation as a priest. He remembered choosing to follow his father into the Order of Schueler because that was what Wylsynns did, and because he shared his father's commitment to reforming what that order had become. And he remembered the day his father had urged him to take the position as Archbishop Erayk Dynnys' intendant.

"Clyntahn's becoming obsessed with the Charisians," his father had told him somberly, a vicar speaking to a young priest he trusted as much as a father speaking to a son. "They desperately need an *honest* intendant, someone who'll apply the Proscriptions fairly and not pander to Clyntahn's paranoia. And, frankly," the father had come to the fore, "I want you out of Zion. I don't like the direction things are heading, and you've already made yourself just a bit too visible for my peace of mind."

Paityr had felt his eyebrows rising, and his father had snorted harshly.

"Oh, I know. I know! The pot and the kettle and all that. But at least I'm a senior vicar, not a mere upper-priest! Besides—"

He'd started to say something else, then stopped and simply shaken his head. But Paityr had understood what his father *hadn't* said, as well. If Samyl Wylsynn didn't "like the direction things were heading," then at least part of the reason he wanted Paityr in Tellesberg was to get him as close to out of Zhaspahr Clyntahn's reach as was physically possible.

In the long run, it probably wouldn't make any difference. When it came down to it, no place on Safehold was truly beyond Clyntahn's reach, for the

Grand Inquisitor's reach was that of Mother Church herself. But Paityr had understood the logic, and however little he'd liked the thought of "deserting" his father and the rest of Samyl Wylsynn's circle of reformers, he'd realized his father was also right about the Charisians' need for an honest intendant. And honest intendants, unfortunately, were an ever-scarcer commodity.

And so he'd taken his father's advice and accepted the post.

In the years since, he'd been glad he had. He'd understood exactly why Charisians would have alarmed and infuriated someone like Clyntahn, yet the better he'd come to know them, the more groundless he'd realized Clyntahn's fears were. Perhaps Charisians were more innovative than they ought to be, but there was no taint of the Dark among them. He was certain of that. And none of the innovations he'd been called upon to evaluate had even approached an actual violation of the Proscriptions. But Clyntahn had been unprepared to accept that conclusion—not because he had any concrete evidence to the contrary, but because any hint of "unorthodoxy" among the citizens of Charis was an offense against his own power as God's enforcer. Worse, it potentially threatened the Inquisition's cozy little empire.

Even so, Paityr had been unprepared for the sudden eruption of outright warfare between the Kingdom of Charis and "the Knights of the Temple Lands." The abrupt escalation had taken him as much by surprise as anyone else, and he'd found himself forced to choose between his vows of obedience to the Grand Inquisitor who headed the Order of Schueler and his vows of obedience to God.

In the end, it had been no contest. He couldn't pretend he'd been comfortable—that he was truly comfortable, even now, for that matter—with his current position. He'd agreed to serve Maikel Staynair as *his* intendant, yet he hadn't expected to end up running the new Royal and then Imperial Patent Office! He was no longer simply making certain new innovations didn't violate the Proscriptions. Oh, no! Now he was involved in actively *encouraging* innovations . . . *as long as* they didn't violate the Proscriptions.

As he'd feared from the beginning, the tension between those two sets of responsibilities was pushing him steadily farther and farther into a "Charisian" mindset. He was moving from an understanding that they *had* to innovate if they were going to survive the attack upon them to regarding innovation as a worthy end in itself. That was a dangerous perspective for any man, but especially for the priest charged with protecting the Proscriptions. Still, he'd managed to live with that . . . so far, at least. It had helped that he'd come so deeply to admire Emperor Cayleb and Empress Sharleyan and—especially—Maikel Staynair. The "heretical" Archbishop of Charis was as godly as any man Paityr Wylsynn had ever known, including any of his father's colleagues, and Paityr had become deeply and personally devoted to his new archbishop.

But now this.

His mind ran back over the letter. It had been sent in the special cipher he and his father had devised before his departure for Tellesberg, and he never doubted for a moment that it had come from the person who'd signed it.

*. . . so your father wanted me and the children to stay home. I'm afraid for him, Paityr, but we won't be remaining home, after all. I don't know what you'll hear out of the Temple and Zion in the next few months. I don't expect it to be good. But if all goes according to plan, the children and I won't be there. Someone I know—and trust—will arrange that, and also for Erais, Fraihman, and young Samyl to join us eventually. I don't know exactly how, and if I did know, I would not commit it to writing, even to you. But know that I will do everything—anything—in my power to protect your brothers and your sisters and to bring them safe to you. And know also that your father loves you and is very, very proud of you.*

*Lysbet*

He knew what that letter meant. He didn't know if it had happened yet, but he knew what it meant for his father and his uncle and all the other men who had joined their struggle to redeem the Order of Schueler and Mother Church herself.

He'd wept when he opened that letter the evening before. Wept for his father and his friends, and for Mother Church . . . and for himself. Not for his father's death—*all* men died—but for the manner of the death his father would die. For the fact that his father would die with the great task of his life unfinished.

And for the fact that with his father's death, that great task fell to Paityr Wylsynn, who was exiled forever to a land far from the Temple. He was the only living man on Safehold—or would be, all too soon—who held the Key, and he would never be in a position to use it unless, somehow, the Church of Charis could actually defeat Mother Church and all the vast power she wielded in the world.

He'd spent the long sleepless night praying and meditating. Begging God to show him his path, lead him where he must go. And he'd spent just as many hours praying for the woman who had written that letter.

*You never let me call you mother, Lysbet,* he thought. *You always insisted that I remember my "real" mother. And I do, and I thank you for that, but I was only four when she died giving birth to Erais, and whatever you've allowed me to call you, you are my mother, too.*

He hadn't always felt that way. In fact, he remembered all too clearly (and with more than a little shame) how his fourteen-year-old adolescent ego had bristled with outraged propriety when his elderly father—he'd been all of forty-one at the time—had brought home a new "wife" barely seven years older than his own motherless son. For that matter, less than eleven years older than his own *daughter!* Disgraceful! What business did his father have sniffing around someone so much younger than he was? It was obvious he'd simply been smitten by her physical beauty and her youth, wasn't it?

It had taken Lysbet the better part of a year to lay those outraged bristles. To this day, an older (and hopefully wiser) Paityr Wylsynn knew it was, indeed, her physical attractiveness which had first drawn Samyl Wylsynn to her. And the fact that her slender brunette beauty was so different from his first red-haired, blue-eyed wife had probably helped. Yet whatever the reason he might first have noticed her, simple beauty and youth weren't the reasons he'd wedded her. And as Paityr had come to know her, as she coaxed those bristles down, he'd come to love her himself, as deeply as he loved the younger brothers and baby sister with whom she had gifted him.

And now she was in hiding somewhere . . . if she'd been lucky. She and those brothers and a sister he loved so much were fleeing for their lives, desperately hiding from members of the same order whose colors and badge Paityr Wylsynn wore even now. If they were found, if they were captured, she might see not simply her husband but her *children* put to the Question before her very eyes. And yet, facing all of that terror, all of that potential horror, she'd taken the time to remind him of his father's love. To remind *him,* to comfort *him.*

*Please, God,* Father Paityr Wylsynn prayed now. *Let them be safe. Protect them. Put Your Hand over them and bring them here, to safety.*

## .IV.
## The Lock,
## Lock Island,
## The Throat,
## Kingdom of Old Charis

So how bad is it this time?" High Admiral Bryahn Lock Island, the Earl of Lock Island, asked in less than cheerful tones.

At the moment, he stood on an iron balcony, bolted to the face of the tallest tower in the city-fortress known simply as The Lock. Despite the fact that it was a wealthy city, as well as the Kingdom of Old Charis' most important single naval base, and that it stood on Lock Island, the critically important island which constituted his entire earldom, he'd always thought that was a particularly unimaginative name for a city. Oh, it was descriptive enough, since it sat squarely in the center of The Throat, the only avenue by which any invader could reach Howell Bay, the true heart and vital center of Old Charis. As long as Charis held The Lock, its control of Howell Bay was absolute; *lose*

The Lock, or let someone force it open, and Old Charis lay open and vulnerable.

As he gazed out across the waters of The Throat, sparkling and flurried with white caps in the late-morning light, he was unusually well aware of both the value and the vulnerabilities of The Lock.

Over the centuries, Old Charis had poured a fortune into fortifying The Lock and the two fortresses, known as the Keys, on either shore of The Throat. Yet for all the care and expense lavished upon stone and catapults, and then cannon, the fortresses' real purpose had been only to free up the kingdom's *true* defenses. The fortifications had been the kingdom's shield; the *Navy* had been its sword.

"The fortress of Charis is the wooden walls of her fleet."

Old King Zhan II had said that, better than a hundred and fifty years ago. At the time, it had been more boast than fact, of course. The Royal Charisian Navy of Zhan II's time had been just beginning its rise to prominence. But he'd known precisely what he had in mind, and he and his inheritors had worked steadily ever since to raise Safeholdian sea power to a pinnacle no one else could challenge. And as long as the fleet stood watch on her coasts, Old Charis was a fortress in her own right.

"This fortress made by God Himself, this Charis," as Zhan II had also said, Lock Island thought. The earl had always been quietly amused by the number of fortresses the old king had apparently envisioned, but that didn't mean the old codger hadn't had a perfect grasp of the strategic realities of the kingdom his dynasty had still been in the process of building.

In Lock Island's opinion, it was Zhan II who'd truly created the concept of Charisians as *Charisians,* their sense of identity with one another which extended throughout the entire huge island.

*I wonder what he'd make of our current situation?* the high admiral thought mordantly, and turned his back on the sunlit seawater. He leaned back, propping his spine against the balcony's waist-high railing and reaching back to grasp that railing with both hands as he braced himself and faced his three "guests."

Rayjhis Yowance, the Earl of Gray Harbor, was a small, dapper man. He was considerably shorter than Lock Island, and built more for speed and wiry endurance than brute power. Always immaculately groomed and always at the height of fashion, some particularly unwary souls had written him off as a fop. People had a tendency not to make that mistake twice, however. Lock Island was willing to concede that there probably was at least a *trace* of foppishness in the earl's makeup, but although Gray Harbor was getting on in years now, he'd been a king's officer—and a good one—in his younger days. He was also probably one of the two or three best first councilors the Kingdom of Old Charis had ever boasted, as well as directly related to Emperor Cayleb—and, for that matter, to Bryahn Lock Island—by marriage.

Sir Domynyk Staynair, the Baron of Rock Point, on the other hand, would never be mistaken by anyone for anything except a naval officer. He strongly favored his older brother, the archbishop, but he was considerably younger and had quite a reputation with the ladies. The loss of his leg at the Battle of Darcos Sound didn't seem to have slowed him up a bit in that department, either, Lock Island thought dryly.

And then there was Bynzhamyn Raice, Baron Wave Thunder, about as solidly, stolidly, archetypically *Charisian* as they came. Bald-headed, weathered-looking, plainly (if expensively) dressed, deliberately displaying all the breathless flamboyance of a lump of rock.

"Well, Bynzhamyn?" Lock Island invited now. "How bad *is* it?"

"Probably about as bad as you think," Wave Thunder replied calmly. "But you know even better than I do that there are no magical shortcuts when it comes to building warships, Bryahn. They aren't going to suddenly astound us with a completed, fully manned, fully armed, fully trained fleet off East Cape tomorrow."

"I'm sure that's very reassuring," Lock Island said just a bit tartly. "I'm also sure you'll understand, though, that as the man responsible for recommending what to do with the Navy while Cayleb and Sharleyan are away, I do appreciate the occasional update on their progress."

The high admiral, Rock Point thought, was clearly more anxious than he wanted to appear. It was scarcely unreasonable of him, under the circumstances, but it was a sobering sign of just how serious those circumstances were.

There were those who mistook Lock Island's habitually cheerful demeanor and fondness for (admittedly) bad practical jokes for buffoonery. Even those who ought to have known better occasionally made the mistake of assuming that someone as staggeringly wealthy as he was simply playing at his naval responsibilities for something to do while the marks rolled in. Lock Island was not a particularly large earldom, but every single ship which passed through The Throat paid the Earl of Lock Island a passage fee. It wasn't very high, and no single ship ever really missed it, but an enormous number of ships passed through that waterway every single five-day, and every one of them put its small contribution into Lock Island's purse. Given that one of the earls' traditional responsibilities was to see to it that The Throat *stayed* open, and that they'd done the job so well for so long, very few people were inclined to object to the arrangement.

Which ought, perhaps, to have suggested to those souls who took the high admiral lightly that his own and his family's history required a second look at that comfortable assumption. Because the truth was that Bryahn Lock Island was about as intellectually tough as they came, and a driving energy and powerful sense of responsibility resided behind that jovial exterior. When *he* started to get irritable, it was usually a sign the situation was serious . . . and getting worse.

"I'm inclined to agree with Bryahn, Bynzhamyn," Gray Harbor said in a considerably milder tone. Wave Thunder glanced at him, and the first councilor shrugged. "It won't change anything, I'm sure, but any naval commander wants the best information he can get, as early as he can get it. The sooner you've got it, the sooner you can begin planning how to respond to it."

His eyes darkened briefly as all three of them recalled what King Haarahld had accomplished with the information *he'd* had prior to the Group of Four's assault on Charis.

"I understand, and I agree," Wave Thunder said. He returned his gaze to Lock Island. "Obviously, with Merlin out of the Kingdom, we've been thrown back onto other means of keeping track," he said, and Lock Island nodded. All four of them were aware of *Seijin* Merlin's visions, although only Rock Point and Wave Thunder knew the full truth about him. So far, at least.

"All right, with that proviso, and bearing in mind that all of my information is considerably older than it might have been," that statement wasn't precisely accurate, Rock Point reflected, given Wave Thunder's personal access to Owl's SNARCs, although neither of them had any intention of explaining that to Lock Island or Gray Harbor, "it would appear Earl Thirsk is moving the Dohlaran units ahead rapidly. I'm not positive yet, but I think he's probably going to get them completed ahead of our original projections, and Dohlar's foundries are doing a much better job than the others when it comes to producing the new guns, as well. Not as well as *we* are, but better than the rest of the Group of Four's mercenaries. I wouldn't be surprised"—he glanced briefly at Rock Point—"if he didn't have the majority of his merchant conversions already fitted out for sea, although, like all of their shipyards, they're still trying to get back on track with the new construction after shifting from galleys to galleons.

"Desnair is about where we expected them to be. Like Dohlar, they have the advantage that they can build year-round, but they're still figuring out how to do it. Their supply of trained shipwrights is low, and, frankly, the 'experts' Maigwair's shipped in from Harchong to 'advise' them have only made matters worse. Desnairians aren't Charisians, but they aren't Harchongese, either, and they don't appreciate being treated like serfs." Wave Thunder's teeth flashed in a humorless smile. "My best estimates give them roughly all ninety of the galleys they built under Maigwair's *first* plan, and probably fifty-five or sixty-five—call it two-thirds—of the galleons they're responsible for building under the new dispensation. I doubt if even half those galleons have completed fitting out, yet, though. They're bottlenecked for guns, of course, but also for crews. It's going to be at least another couple of months before the ships they've already built are really ready for sea."

"Could they cut that interval by pulling men off the galleys, Bynzhamyn?" Gray Harbor asked, his eyes intent, and Wave Thunder shrugged.

"At the moment, they seem unwilling to give up the galleys," he replied. "I don't know how many of them have really accepted the primacy of the galleon—deep inside, I mean. When Yairley captured Commodore Wailahr back in November, he threw a rock into the gears, I think."

"Dunkyn is good at that sort of thing," Lock Island observed with a grin, and Rock Point snorted.

"That's been my own impression," Wave Thunder agreed. "But my point was that Wailahr, at least, seems flexible enough to grasp the way the equation has shifted, even if he is basically an army officer. Even more importantly, perhaps, he was one of the few Desnairian flag officers who I'd call truly offensive-minded. From my agents' reports and what Merlin had to say in his last message to me, most of the rest of the Desnairian commodores and admirals are . . . less than eager to cross swords with us on blue water. And what happened to Wailahr probably hasn't made the rest of them any more eager to emulate his exploits."

"Harchong and the Temple Lands?" Lock Island asked, and Wave Thunder chuckled sourly.

"Without access to Merlin, I can't really tell a thing about what's happening that far away, Bryahn," he pointed out. "I will say that most of the reports I *have* received indicate it's been a particularly hard winter up there. They were already behind schedule, and I don't expect all that ice and snow helped things any. Harchong, at least, isn't quite as badly strapped for foundries as Desnair is. Still, they're having a lot more trouble coming up with the artillery they need than we are, now that Ehdwyrd Howsmyn's really hit his stride in Delthak. So even assuming they've got all their shipwrights back to work, it's still going to be a while before they're able to arm two hundred galleons. I doubt they'll have them ready to go until late next spring or early next summer, to be honest."

"And Tarot?" Rock Point asked.

"And Tarot—and our good friend King Gorjah—are still up the proverbial creek full of krakens without a paddle," Wave Thunder said with a wolfish smile. "He's actually doing quite well when it comes to *building* the ships, but he's completely and utterly screwed when it comes to *arming* them. And even with all of the Church's subsidies, he's having an awful time finding the funding to help what foundries he actually has expand their capacity to produce artillery."

"That's good," Lock Island said with undisguised satisfaction, and Gray Harbor laughed.

"As a matter of fact, Bryahn, it's considerably better than 'good,'" the first councilor told him. Lock Island quirked an eyebrow, and Gray Harbor shrugged. "I suppose I can share this little tidbit with you, if I can share it with anyone, but

I've established communications with Gorjah. As Her Majesty suggested before she departed for Chisholm, he realizes he's caught between the doomwhale and the deep blue sea, and he doesn't like it a bit. He's being coy at the moment, not committing himself to anything. In fact, all he's done basically is send a message back asking me what we have in mind while professing his own eternal loyalty to Mother Church. I imagine most of that is to cover his arse in case this should fall into the Church's hands . . . not that it would be likely to do him much good in the end. Still, the fact that he's gone even that far says a lot to me about just how desperate—and frustrated, I'd guess—he's feeling about now."

"Do you really think you can trust him to turn his coat back the other way—and stay turned?" Lock Island sounded skeptical, and Gray Harbor shrugged.

"All the evidence, including Merlin's visions, suggests that Gorjah was more guilty of opportunism—and, of course, obeying the Group of Four's orders—than a fundamental enemy, like Hektor. Oh," the first councilor shrugged again, waving one hand, "we've always known he resented that treaty his father signed, so I'm not suggesting he participated as reluctantly as Her Majesty did. For that matter, I'm not pretending he was *reluctant* at all, once he realized what the Group of Four was promising him. But I don't think his malice ran anywhere near as deep as Hektor's did. Or King Rahnyld's, for that matter. And whatever he may have been thinking then, at this point he's a sadder, wiser man."

"Another Nahrmahn?" Lock Island sounded even more skeptical, if possible.

"No." Gray Harbor shook his head. "I think we'd all underestimated just how seriously Nahrmahn took his responsibilities to Emerald. I don't think Gorjah is anywhere near that selfless—for example, I don't see him sending Pine Hollow to negotiate with us, even realizing Cayleb might have demanded his own head as the price of any peace treaty. But he's not as frivolous as, say, Rahnyld or Emperor Waisu, either. Or, God help us all, Zebediah!"

For a moment, the dapper first councilor looked like he was going to spit on the balcony's floor. Instead, he settled for a sound that was half growl and half snarl, then gave himself a shake.

"My point is that I'm pretty sure he realizes his position is hopeless if we decide to move against him. By the time Cayleb and Sharleyan get home, I think our friend Gorjah will be just about ripe for a little pointed negotiating."

"But in the meantime, I assume, you need Domynyk and me to keep the pressure on him?"

"Definitely!" Gray Harbor nodded vigorously. "We especially need to keep the Tarot Channel closed, not just blockade Thol Bay. I don't want Emperor Mahrys being able to ship in troops to reinforce Gorjah's own army."

"You really think Gorjah would ask for that?" Rock Point asked dubiously, and Gray Harbor's raised hand made a back and forth so-so motion.

"I doubt he'd make the request willingly, given how much effort previous

Desnairian emperors have invested in attempts to add Tarot to their empire. On the other hand, he might feel he has no choice, especially if he's scared enough of the Group of Four. For that matter, the Group of Four might 'suggest' the same thing any day now. More to the point, though, I want to crank up the pressure. I want him to realize that even if he *wanted* to call in Desnairian support, it couldn't get there. The Channel's less than four hundred miles wide. I want him thinking about the fact Desnair can't get transports across even that piddling distance."

"You want him feeling even more isolated," Rock Point said, and Gray Harbor nodded again.

"Exactly. And I also don't want some clever soul in Siddarmark deciding he can sneak small, fast coasters across the Channel to run our blockade with any of the goods Tarot needs. I want that blockade to *hurt*, not leak."

"So what we're really saying here," Lock Island mused, "is that our current dispositions only need a little adjustment."

He gazed back out across The Throat for a few moments, then looked at Rock Point.

"How comfortable would you be shifting your anchorage from Hanth Town to Holme Reach?"

Rock Point's eyebrows rose at the question. He started to respond quickly, then stopped and examined the possibility more carefully.

"I hadn't really considered it," he said slowly. "But now that you've asked, I don't see any reason we couldn't. Yairley already has his squadron based there, after all, and so far there's been damn-all Gorjah—or White Ford—can do about it. Be a bit . . . audacious, though. Or maybe the word I'm looking for is 'insolent.'"

"Perfect!" Gray Harbor chortled. "Oh, that's *perfect*, Bryahn! Gorjah will burst a blood vessel! And when *Clyntahn* hears about it—!"

Rock Point understood the first councilor's glee. Having a single small squadron occasionally visit your home waters without invitation was one thing; moving in with an entire hostile fleet and daring you to do something about it was quite another. Gorjah would, indeed, as Gray Harbor had so inelegantly put it, "burst a blood vessel" at the news.

And, the admiral thought, there *wouldn't* be anything he could do about it, either. Holme Reach measured a hundred and sixty miles, north to south, and a good hundred miles, east to west, and the water off the east coast of Hourglass Island was shallow enough, and the bottom was sandy enough, to offer a good anchorage. That far from the mainland of Tarot, nothing but another fleet could possibly threaten them, and Gorjah of Tarot didn't *have* a fleet anymore.

It still wouldn't be perfect, although Hourglass would offer shelter against the occasional westerly that could turn the reach into one of the most treacherous bodies of water on the face of Safehold. The one real drawback—aside

from the fact that every bit of the reach's coastline was controlled by the Kingdom of Tarot—was what a sufficiently powerful *south*westerly could do. Any
ships in the reach could probably find shelter behind Hourglass or Sprout Island even with the wind dead out of the southwest, but working a galleon out
of the reach against a southwesterly would be a slow and laborious process, at
best. Still, it was unlikely he'd find himself actually trapped inside it.

*Especially,* he thought, *since, unlike Dunkyn, I'll have Owl for reconnaissance and
weather forecasts.*

"I wouldn't suggest it if Gorjah still had a navy," Lock Island said, obviously following Rock Point's own thoughts (or most of them, at any rate). "In
those waters, even a galley fleet could make things tricky. But I'm confident
you'd have the firepower to handle anything he could throw at you out of his
present resources."

"I agree." Rock Point nodded crisply. "And it would put me in a lot better
position to cover the Tarot Channel. For that matter, I'd be better placed to
meet any Desnairian attempt to get a squadron or two from the Gulf of Jahras
to Tarot. It wouldn't be perfect, but I'd be three thousand miles closer than I am
now. Which would also put me between any effort to combine the Desnairian
and Temple Lands squadrons by sneaking along the Haven coast."

"But you'd be a lot farther from Margaret Bay," Wave Thunder pointed
out.

"Unless the Temple Lands are much further along than your reports are
suggesting, that won't be a problem," Lock Island replied. "What we're talking
about right now is what Desnair and Tarot have, and Domynyk could hold his
own against both of them combined—at this point—if he had to. And we
need a base closer to Tranjyr if we're going to make Rayjhis' point to Gorjah."

"I agree," the first councilor said firmly.

"Very well, then, Domynyk. Once you've finished your little face-to-face
conversation with Ahlfryd and Dr. Mahklyn, I want you to go ahead and
arrange the movement. I'll pry loose a couple of battalions of Marines and
some artillery, too. If we're going to base you in Holme Reach, let's go ahead
and put in a couple of defensive batteries and make Dunkyn's little vegetable
patches on Hourglass permanent." He smiled nastily. "I imagine that will *really*
piss Gorjah off."

From Baron Seamount's office window, looking down from the citadel across the anchorage, Admiral Rock Point's flagship looked like a child's toy. Or, better, like a perfectly detailed model. HMS *Destroyer* lay to her anchor, awnings spread above her decks against the sun's heat, and he saw one of her boats pulling steadily about her in a circle. Rock Point recognized Captain Tymythy Darys' barge, and his lips twitched on the edge of a smile. Darys loved his galleon, but he was never *quite* satisfied with her trim. He never missed the opportunity to study her when she lay still, considering whether he should shift ballast to bring her up an inch or two by the bow or, conversely, to increase her draft forward.

He shook his head, then turned back from the window to face Sir Ahlfryd Hyndryk. The commodore sat behind his desk, in front of the expanse of chalk-covered slate with which he'd had his office paneled. As always, the diagrams and calculations sprawling across that slate—and the notes he'd jotted there to remind himself of various things—were fascinating, but Rock Point kept his attention resolutely focused on the baron himself.

At the moment, another naval officer stood at one end of Seamount's desk. Commander Urvyn Mahndrayn was about eight years younger than Rock Point himself and thin as a ferret. In fact, even though he had only four limbs, instead of six, and black hair, instead of a ferret's scaled hide, a ferret was what Mahndrayn had always reminded him of. He had that same almost frightening abundance of energy, and he was an equally relentless hunter. True, his quarry tended to be ideas, not spider-rats, but once he got his teeth into his prey, there was no getting him to back off until he was victorious.

That made him the almost perfect assistant for Seamount. Unfortunately, he was just as eager to get Seamount's concepts into service as the commodore himself, which meant. . . .

*Bryahn, you coward,* Rock Point thought at the absent high admiral. *"Can't spare the time away from the fleet," my arse! The real reason you sent me to drop Rayjhis off in Tellesberg instead of doing it yourself was that you didn't want to face Ahlfryd. So you dumped it on me.* He snorted. *Don't think I'm going to forget it, either. Somehow, some way, you'll pay. Trust me, you'll pay!*

"The High Admiral and I have read your reports with a great deal of interest, Ahlfryd," he said now. "We've been impressed, as always. And"—he nodded in Mahndrayn's direction—"with the Commander's contributions, as well."

"Good! I'm glad to hear it." Seamount beamed, although Rock Point had the impression he was even more pleased at having Mahndrayn singled out for praise.

"Dr. Mahklyn"—Rock Point glanced at the head of the Royal College, who'd accompanied him to Helen Island—"has been keeping us up-to-date on his own evaluation of your work, as well. Of course, he's been more interested in placing what you're accomplishing in context with everything else than in individual, specific ideas, but in some ways, that's been even more useful."

This time Seamount only nodded, and Rock Point smiled and turned his attention to Mahndrayn.

"I was particularly struck by your conclusions from the artillery tests, Commander. I have to say that when Commodore Seamount first described your proposals to us, I hadn't realized just how exhaustive you intended to be."

Which, Rock Point admitted to himself, was an understatement. He had no idea how many rounds Mahndrayn had fired off in his various tests, but he knew it had run to literally thousands of round shot and charges of grape, as well as over a hundred of the new shells Seamount was about ready to put into production. The commander's tests had considered ballistics; differences in powder quality; the effectiveness of large, heavy shot compared to smaller, faster moving shot; the effects of humidity; better carriage designs; ways to increase rate of fire; how many shots a given gun of a given weight was good for before the barrel simply wore out or broke; how to prevent round shot from rusting; the best ways to store cartridges at sea; how far windage could be reduced before it reached a point at which fouling *reduced* rate of fire. . . . He'd even had life-size sections of hull built on land—sections of everything from a traditional galley to one of the Navy's schooners to standard merchantmen to the Navy's heaviest galleons—and then methodically blown them to bits, stopping after each discharge to examine and evaluate the damage that shot had inflicted. And instead of the straw-stuffed dummies which had been used in Seamount's original demonstration firings, Mahndrayn had hung sides of meat from cattle and hogs inside the targets to evaluate the wounding effects of the various combinations of ammunition.

According to Merlin, no one had gotten around to conducting such exhaustive trials back on Old Earth until artillery had been in service literally for centuries, and the amount of information the commander had accumulated was astounding.

"I have to admit I'd already suspected that we were overgunning," he said now, "although it's good to have confirmation of it." He grimaced. "It would be even better if there were a quick fix, of course."

"I agree, Sir." Mahndrayn's voice was a melodious tenor. "We actually need to give each of them about a foot more clearance on either side. As it is, we're too crowded for the maximum rate of fire—people are getting in each other's way. About a foot." He grimaced. "I know it doesn't sound like much, but—"

"Oh, I believe you!" Rock Point waved one hand. "In fact, the main reason I stuck with *Gale* as my flagship all the way through the Armageddon Reef and Darcos Sound campaigns, despite the fact that she mounted only thirty-six guns, was that her gunnery drill always seemed just a tiny bit sharper than anyone else's. Which, as your report points out, was probably because she had almost thirteen feet of gundeck per gun, instead of ten and a half, like *Destroyer*."

"Exactly, Sir!" Mahndrayn grinned. "She had that extra foot, but we squeezed it down in the new designs to mount the most guns we could." His grin turned into something more like a grimace. "I suppose it would've been silly to assume we'd get everything right when we were making such radical changes in our armament and how we mount it."

"Of course," Rock Point agreed, "and Sir Dustyn's already altered the plans for *Sword of Charis* and her sisters. It's just unfortunate that it's so much easier to alter the port spacing on a ship that hasn't been built yet than to do the same thing on ships that are already in commission!" He frowned. "One point you didn't address, though, Commander, was whether or not it would help to go to lighter guns. Would reducing the *size* of the guns have the same effect—or some of the same effect—as spacing them farther apart?"

"We did think about that, Sir," Seamount put in. "The problem is that the *carriage* dimensions are effectively identical, unless you want to go to *much* smaller and lighter pieces. Given the difference in effectiveness of heavy shot versus light shot, it seemed better to us to continue with the slightly less than optimum rate of fire. The difference in rate is measurable, especially in sustained firing, but not great enough to justify going to guns which are going to inflict so much less damage with each hit actually scored."

Rock Point nodded. He'd been fairly confident that was what they were going to say before he'd asked the question, so he moved on to the next point.

"I was also struck by your observation that a uniform armament of shell-firing guns would be much more effective than a mixed battery, firing round shot *and* shell."

He cocked an eyebrow at Mahndrayn, inviting the commander to expand upon that point, and Mahndrayn shrugged ever so slightly.

"As our report indicates, Sir, we discovered fairly early on that the most effective combination of shot weight and velocity was that which would *just* breach the vessel's hull. As I'm sure you've discovered from your own experience, it's much harder to sink a ship outright than we'd originally hoped." He shrugged again, a bit harder. "I suppose that was inevitable, too. After all, we didn't have very much experience with *trying* to sink ships with artillery, since no one's guns had been good enough to make them the primary weapon.

"Now that we've had an opportunity to evaluate combat reports and conduct our own experiments, it's obvious—and should have been obvious to us *ahead* of time, if we'd bothered to really think about it—that round shot punch relatively small holes. Not only that, wood is . . . elastic. It tends to let the shot through, then tries to snap back into its initial shape. So the holes aren't very large, which makes it relatively easy for the ship's carpenter to plug them. Even worse, from the perspective of sinking somebody, most of the holes are above the waterline, since that's the part of the other ship we can actually hit. We managed to sink several galleys with gunfire at Rock Point and Crag Reach, but it took the fire of up to a dozen galleons to do it, and they were Dohlaran ships. Their planking and *framing* were a lot lighter than ours or the Tarotisians, and from my own evaluations, I think what happened was that the frames themselves broke up under the pounding, which resulted in much larger hull breaches.

"But what our captains' reports make clear is that defeating an enemy vessel depended much more on destroying its *crew* than on destroying the fabric of the ship itself." Mahndrayn's eyes were intent, and he leaned forward slightly, hands moving in eloquent (if unconscious) gestures. "It was casualties which rendered a ship unable to continue to fight or maneuver, more often than not, Sir. Galleons are going to be more vulnerable to damage aloft than galleys, but galleys are more vulnerable to personnel losses among their rowers, and neither of them can *fight* effectively if they lose too much of their crews. *That* was the decisive factor in almost every combat report I've been able to examine.

"So, instead of trying to sink the ship, it's more effective to concentrate on using the ship's *hull* to inflict casualties on the ship's *crew*." He raised both hands, palm uppermost. "Our tests indicate that a large, heavy shot, moving just fast enough to punch through the scantlings on one side of the hull but *not* fast enough to continue clear across and punch out through the other side, or simply embed itself, will produce the most casualties. It will produce the most *splinters* on its way through, and clouds of splinters, spreading outward from the shot hole, are going to produce maximum casualties. And if the ball doesn't continue clear out of the ship or embed itself in its timbers, it will be available to ricochet around the gundeck and inflict additional direct casualties."

Rock Point nodded slowly. A part of him couldn't help being just a little appalled at Mahndrayn's cold-blooded approach to the best way to inflict the maximum number of casualties—how to kill or maim the most human beings possible—per shot. At the same time, he knew that was foolish of him. The object of any commander worthy of his men had to be finding ways to kill as many of their enemies in exchange for as few of *them* as possible.

"On the basis of our tests," Mahndrayn continued, "mounting the heaviest possible guns, taking into consideration factors such as how quickly they can be served and the effect their weight has on the ship's structure, should provide the most effective armament. Fewer hits would be scored, but each individual hit would be far more effective.

"That's true for round shot, but our tests also indicate it's even more true for shell-firing guns." The commander shook his head, his eyes intent, as if gazing at something Rock Point couldn't see. "We haven't had many shells to experiment with—we're still basically manufacturing them one at a time as needed for the tests, and Master Howsmyn tells me it's going to be several months before we could go to any sort of volume production. But even with the relative handful we've been able to test, the difference between a single hit from a thirty-pounder firing a solid shot and a thirty-pounder firing a *shell* is . . . profound, Sir. As I say, a round shot punches a relatively small hole in the hull; a shell, especially if it lodges in the ship's timbers, blows a *huge* hole. By our measure, the holes a thirty-pounder's solid shot produces are only about five inches in diameter. Actually, they're a little less than that, allowing for the wood's elasticity. The holes a shell *blows* through the same hull are up to three and even six *feet* in diameter. One of those below the waterline, or even simply between wind and water, would be almost impossible for a carpenter to patch. One or two might be survivable, if the ship could fother a sail across the hole quickly enough, but several of them would send the biggest galleon in the world to the bottom.

"In addition, shells are far more destructive to a ship's *upper* works, as well. Not only do they tear holes in the side, they also produce more splinters in the process and destroy the ship's structural integrity far more rapidly and effectively than round shot, as well. *And* they have a powerful incendiary effect." The commander shook his head again. "By any standard, Admiral, a shell-firing armament is going to be enormously more destructive than one firing round shot."

"I see." Rock Point gazed at Mahndrayn for a moment, then walked back across to the window and gazed down upon his flagship once more. "And what about the manufacturing problems your report mentioned?"

"We're working on those, Sir," Seamount responded. "As Urvyn says, Master Howsmyn is making progress—in fact, he's building an entirely new facility at his main foundry expressly to make them. We don't want to interrupt the production of our existing, standard projectiles, and casting a *hollow* shot is going to be both more complicated and more time-consuming than casting *solid* shot. That means we won't be able to produce shells as rapidly as round shot even when he has his new facility up and running, especially since we need to produce fuses for them, as well. Each shell for Commander Mahndrayn's evaluation was basically special-made for him. If we're going to produce them in adequate numbers, we need to get them up to a production rate which is at least half, let's say, the rate for round shot, and we're still a long way from that. As I say, Master Howsmyn's making progress, though, and I think he'll be able to begin large-scale production, if not at the rate we'd prefer, by, say, October. After that, it will take us several months—more likely at least a half year—to produce enough of them to replace our magazine allotments of round shot on a one-for-one basis."

"I see," Rock Point repeated, never taking his eyes from *Destroyer*. He tried to imagine what a deluge of explosive shells would do to his flagship and her crew. Then he decided he didn't want to imagine that, after all.

He shook himself, glanced at Mahklyn out of the corner of one eye, and turned back to Seamount and Mahndrayn.

"Obviously, you're authorized to proceed, Ahlfryd. And I'm sure I don't need to remind you or any of your people about the need for absolute secrecy. Our best estimate right now is that sometime next spring or early next summer, the Group of Four's navy will be ready—or as close to 'ready' as it's ever going to be—to come after us. When that happens, we're going to need every advantage we can get to even the odds. Including your infernal exploding shells. And we need those advantages to come as surprises to the other side."

"Yes, Sir. Understood." Seamount nodded soberly, and Rock Point nodded back. Then he inhaled deeply.

"Which brings us," he said, "to your rifled artillery pieces."

"Yes, Sir!" Seamount's eyes brightened visibly.

"Ahlfryd and Commodore Mahndrayn have accomplished some really remarkably accurate shooting, Sir Domynyk," Rahzhyr Mahklyn put in helpfully.

"Indeed we have, Admiral!" Seamount beamed. "In fact, Urvyn and his crews, firing a rifled thirty-pounder, have been able to score hits regularly at ranges of over six thousand yards. In one test, they registered eight hits out of ten shots fired at a measured range of sixty-five hundred yards on a target the same length and height as one of our schooners!"

Rock Point nodded, and he was just as impressed as his expression indicated. One of the new-model thirty-pounder smoothbores could throw a ball six thousand yards, given enough elevation, but the probability of hitting anything as small as a ship at that range was essentially nonexistent. And that was true even when the gun was firing from solid land, as Mahndrayn's crew had been doing in the test-firing Seamount had just described.

*Which is rather the point,* the admiral thought wryly.

"I expect we'll be able to extend the range still farther once Master Howsmyn begins producing his 'wire-built' guns," Seamount continued enthusiastically. "Of course, that's still going to take some time. Not as much as I was afraid it would, though. His mechanics' designs for the wire-drawing equipment have been completed and tested now. It's coming up with a way to turn the gun and wrap the wire with sufficient precision and accuracy that's taking the time at this point. Well, that and the power of the machinery we need. You see—"

"Ahlfryd."

Seamount closed his mouth, and his eyes narrowed as he recognized the gentleness—and something very like . . . regret—in Rock Point's tone.

"Yes, Admiral?"

"Correct me if I'm wrong, but you've just said Commander Mahndrayn's gun crews scored eighty percent hits at a range of over three miles. Is that accurate?"

"Yes, Sir," Seamount confirmed just a bit warily.

"I assume this required favorable circumstances. I mean, clear weather for good visibility? A stable gun platform?"

"Well, yes, Sir. Of course. But even under less than ideal conditions, accuracy would obviously be greatly enhanced, and—"

"I realize that," Rock Point said. "But, here's the thing, Ahlfryd. We're not going to have those ideal conditions at sea. Even under the best of conditions, both the ship and the target are going to be moving. In fact, they're going to be moving in several different directions at once."

"Of course, Sir. But as I was saying, even if conditions are less than perfect, we'd still—"

"Ahlfryd, who's going to be more likely to have conditions favorable for long-range engagements with these rifled guns of yours? A fleet at sea—like, say, *ours*—or a nice stable, unmoving, solid stone fortress—like, say, one that belongs to the Group of Four? One that our ships might be *attacking*?"

Seamount sat very still for a moment. Then his shoulders slumped. He shook his head, rubbing his eyes with one hand. At the end of his desk, Commander Mahndrayn looked equally crestfallen. If the subject matter had been even a little less deadly serious, Rock Point was fairly certain he would have found it very difficult not to laugh at their expressions.

"I suppose we should have thought of that, shouldn't we?" Seamount said finally, his tone chagrined. "Obviously, this is something that's going to favor the defense more than the offense, isn't it?"

"I don't know that that's true in every case," Rock Point demurred. "As you just pointed out, and as Dr. Mahklyn pointed out when he and High Admiral Lock Island and I first discussed this, your rifled guns are going to be more accurate at all ranges, including the ones at which naval artillery is already effective. That's nothing to sneer at. The problem is that in order to deal effectively with this new navy the Church is building, we're more likely to be attacking their anchorages than they are to be attacking ours. Or, to put it another way, if they *are* in a position to attack our anchorages, we're probably already completely screwed. This is obviously something we want to pursue, but we've come to the conclusion that it's not something we want to actually put aboard ship. Not yet."

"I see." Seamount's disappointment was still obvious, but he gave himself a shake and managed to smile. "So what do you and High Admiral Lock Island—and Dr. Mahklyn, I'm assuming—want us to do with this, Sir?"

"We want you to continue to develop it," Rock Point said crisply. "From what you've been saying, we wouldn't be in a position to put these new guns into production for some time, anyway. It seems more likely to us from your reports that we'll be able to provide shells for the smoothbores much more quickly. So our thinking at this point is that we press ahead as quickly as possible with the smoothbores. In fact, it's been suggested that we look into producing Commander Mahndrayn's proposed heavy shell guns, possibly something with an eight- or nine-inch bore, specifically to fire the most destructive shells possible. That should give us a decisive advantage at *sea* even without rifled artillery.

"At the same time, and under conditions of as much secrecy as possible, press the development of Master Howsmyn's rifled pieces—hard. Go ahead and test them here, at King's Harbor, where you can keep curious eyes at bay. Once you've come up with a workable model, we'll go ahead and put it into production as a shore-defense weapon. If the gun proves practical as a seagoing weapon, as well, we'll develop a naval carriage for it, too. But we'll hold it in reserve until either we know we're going to need it to defend ourselves, or we're in a position of such strength that revealing it to the enemy isn't going to be critical."

"Yes, Sir."

"And in the *meantime,* Commander," Rock Point went on with a flashing smile as he turned his attention to Mahndrayn, "High Admiral Lock Island and I have another little challenge for you and your purveyors of destruction."

"Yes, Admiral?"

If Seamount had sounded a *bit* wary a few moments before, there was downright trepidation in Mahndrayn's tone, and Rock Point's smile broadened.

"Oh, it's nothing *too* complicated, Commander," he assured the younger man. "It's just that, as your tests have so thoroughly demonstrated, explosive shells are going to be extremely destructive. That being the case, and since your tests were so thorough and so professionally executed, it seems to the High Admiral and myself that you're the perfect man for our next project—figuring out how to protect or armor a ship's hull so that shells *don't* tear it apart."

His smile turned positively beatific at Mahndrayn's expression.

"I'm sure you'll find it no challenge at all, Commander."

S ir Koryn Gahrvai stood as the organ prelude soared like the wings of the
Archangels themselves and the vast doors of Manchyr Cathedral swung
open. The procession started up the aisle behind the scepter-bearer and the thurifer. Ropes of sweet-smelling smoke trailed the jeweled thurible as it swung
on its golden chain, and the thurifer was followed by a half-dozen candle-
bearers, then a solid phalanx of acolytes and under-priests. Behind that, however,
came the true reason the cathedral was so densely packed on this particular
Wednesday.

Archbishop Maikel Staynair, Primate of the Church of Charis, followed
those acolytes, those under-priests. As the cathedral choir's massed voices rose
in glorious song, those close enough to the archbishop could see his lips moving as he sang along with them. The rubies of his crown glittered like fresh
hearts of blood in the morning sunlight spilling through the cathedral's stained
glass, and he was a full head taller than Klairmant Gairlyng, who walked at his
side.

They paced steadily through the tumultuous waves of music and voices,
and Gahrvai wondered how hard it was to do that. Despite the serenity of the
archbishop's expression, the memory of the Temple Loyalists who'd attempted
to assassinate him in his own cathedral had to be floating about in his mind, especially in light of what had happened to Tymahn Hahskans.

If it was, there was no sign of it in Staynair's demeanor, and Gahrvai discovered he wasn't really surprised by that.

His lips twitched as he remembered Staynair's initial meeting with his own
father and the rest of the Regency Council—minus Earl Craggy Hill, who'd
been rather conveniently (in Gahrvai's opinion) recalled to Vahlainah by some
purely local affair. Although he supposed it was undutiful of him, Gahrvai had
decided his father's attitude towards the archbishop had been remarkably similar to a stiff-legged hunting hound whose keen sense of smell suggested he was
about to come face-to-face with a slash lizard. Tartarian had been less overtly
stiff, though even his manner had been more than a bit wary, and the rest of the
Regency Council's reactions had ranged downward from there.

Yet there was something about Maikel Staynair. . . .

Sir Koryn Gahrvai couldn't put a label on that "something," but whatever it was, it was potent stuff. It was less what the archbishop had said than

how he'd said it, Gahrvai decided. He'd obviously simply decided to assume the members of the council were men of goodwill. That, despite the fact of Cayleb's—and, for that matter, his own—excommunication, they'd given their oaths in good faith. That he understood their first concern must be the welfare of the Corisandians who looked to them for protection. That he took it for granted that when men of goodwill recognized a problem, they would seek its solution.

And it had been equally evident that if there was a single intolerant, bigoted, zealotry-ridden bone anywhere in his entire body he was a wizard at concealing it.

*That's his real secret weapon,* Gahrvai thought now. *He genuinely is a man of God. I don't think there's an ounce of weakness anywhere in him, yet it's obvious—to me, at least—that it's gentleness that drives him. Outraged gentleness, perhaps, but still gentleness. No one can spend twenty minutes in his presence without realizing that. He may be* wrong, *but there's no question that he's motivated by genuine love for God and his fellow man. And what makes that "secret weapon" so effective is that it's not a weapon at all. It's simply the way he is. Of course, there's also. . . .*

The general's eyes drifted upward to the royal box. As in every cathedral, it was close enough to the sanctuary to be certain its occupants saw and heard everything clearly. With Prince Daivyn and Princess Irys in exile in Delferahk, the box was rather conspicuously unoccupied. Which only made the single Imperial Guardsman standing in front of its closed wicket gate even more noticeable.

He wore the black armor and the black, gold, blue, and silver of the Charisian Empire, but what everyone seemed to notice about him first were those strange sapphire eyes. Unlike the vast majority of Corisandians, Gahrvai had met *Seijin* Merlin Athrawes before. Indeed, every member of the Regency Council had met him, in passing, at least, and the Earls of Anvil Rock and Tartarian had spent quite a bit of time in his company, since he'd been the only armsman Cayleb had allowed to be present during the surrender negotiations. Sir Alyk Ahrthyr knew him even better, in some ways—or knew the *seijin*'s handiwork better, at any rate, since it was the only thing that had kept him alive at the Battle of Green Valley.

But everyone in the entire princedom knew his reputation. Knew he was the most deadly warrior in the entire world . . . and that he'd personally killed all three of the assassins who'd attacked Staynair in Tellesberg Cathedral. So knowing he was there, alert eyes sweeping back and forth constantly over the packed cathedral, probably contributed at least a little bit to the archbishop's serenity.

The opening hymn carried Staynair and Gairlyng to the sanctuary, and Gahrvai settled back in his own pew once both archbishops had seated themselves in their waiting thrones and the congregation was free to sit, as well.

The service flowed smoothly. There'd been virtually no changes to the long-standing and much beloved liturgy. Indeed, the only substantive change was the omission of the pledge of loyalty to the Grand Vicar as the head of God's Church on Safehold. Which, Gahrvai suspected, probably struck the Group of Four as a *very* "substantive change."

But, eventually, they reached the point for which every person in that cathedral had been waiting, and the enormous structure was hushed, so silent the faint sounds of Staynair's footsteps were clear and distinct as he crossed to the pulpit.

He stood for a moment, gazing out across the cathedral, then traced the sign of the scepter over the enormous bound volume of the *Writ* before he opened it. The sound of the turning pages whispered through the cathedral's listening silence, and when he cleared his throat gently, it seemed almost shockingly loud.

"Today's scripture," he said, his deep voice carrying to every ear, "is taken from *The Book of Chihiro,* Chapter Nine, verses eleven through fourteen.

"Then said the Lord to the Archangel Langhorne, 'Behold I have created my Holy Church to be the mother of all men and women on the face of this the world I have made. See to it that she nurtures all of My children. That she teaches the young, supports the footsteps and wisdom of those who are grown, cares for the elderly. And, above all, that she trains up all of My children in the way they should go.

"'Find men worthy of this great charge among My priests. Instruct them in all of their duties, examine them and measure their souls, weigh them in the scales of My balance, fire them in the furnace of My discipline, hammer them upon the anvil of My love.

"'And when you have done these things, when you are confident that *these* are the priests fit to lead and feed My sheep, set them in places of authority. Give them that which they need to do My will, and remind them, and the priests who will come after them, and all the priests who shall follow them, that their purpose, and their charge, and their duty is to *do* My will and always and everywhere, in every way, to serve My people.'

"And the Archangel Langhorne listened to all of these instructions from the Most High and Holiest, and the Archangel bowed his face to the earth, and he said unto the Lord his God, 'Truly, it shall be as You have commanded.'"

The archbishop laid his hand on the opened book, looking out across the cathedral.

"This is the Word of God, for the Children of God," he told them.

"Thanks be to God, and to the Archangels who are His Servants," the congregation replied, and there was an edge of tension in that response. A sort of breathless wonder as to how Staynair proposed to address those verses.

"Be seated, my children," he invited, and feet scraped and clothing rustled in a great sighing murmur as they obeyed him.

He waited the better part of another full minute, hands clasped lightly on the *Writ*. He gazed out at them, his eyes sweeping the entire cathedral, letting them see his examination and giving them time to examine him, in turn. There was no sign of any notes, not even a single note card, and he smiled.

It was a thing of wonder, that smile. Gentle and warm, welcoming, and—above all—real. It was no actor's trained smile. It came from somewhere deep inside the man, and Gahrvai felt an odd little stir, more sensed than heard, sweep through the cathedral as the worshippers saw it.

"I picked today's scripture deliberately," he told them then. "But I bet most of you had already figured that out," he added, with a perfect sense of timing, and somehow that smile had turned impish.

A soft mutter of laughter—laughter which had surprised itself—gusted through the cathedral, and his smile grew even more dazzling for a moment.

"Of course I selected it deliberately." His smile faded, and his voice turned serious, dropping a bit lower, so that they had to listen just a bit harder. "All of you have heard that passage time and time again. In fact, it has a name, doesn't it? 'The Great Charge,' we call it. And we call it that because that was what the *Archangels* called it, and because it *is* the Great Charge. This passage, *this* scripture, is the fundamental basis of Mother Church, God's own warrant for her creation and birth. His instruction to Holy Langhorne contains not only His command for Mother Church's creation, but also the description of her duties. The end—the *purpose*—for which He ordained her creation. It tells us what she is supposed to do in simple, straightforward words."

He paused, allowing his own words to settle into his listeners' minds and thoughts, then continued.

"Of course, 'simple and straightforward' isn't the same as *easy*. No great task, however straightforward, is *ever* 'easy,' and what task could be greater than the one God Himself assigned to Mother Church? And what other institution of this world could command the devotion, the respect, and the love of God's children more strongly than His own Church? We are enjoined again and again, over and over, in every book of the *Holy Writ*, to love God, to keep His laws, to do His will, to live in fulfillment of His plan, and to honor and obey His Church."

The stillness in the cathedral had grown tighter, more focused, and he smiled again, sadly, as if he felt that physical pressure bearing down upon him.

"Of course that's what He said," the schismatic archbishop told them all calmly. "There's no 'wiggle room' in God's instructions on this matter, my children. No gray theological areas where scholars and theologians can argue and debate and parse the language. It's not a suggestion, not an invitation, not a proposal—it's a *command*. It's *God's* command, just as surely as He has commanded us to keep Wednesdays holy or to love one another as much as we love ourselves."

He shook his head.

"And yet the very fact that I stand here before you in this cathedral is proof the Church of Charis is *not* obeying the Church's decrees." His voice was hard, now. Not angry, not denouncing, not even challenging, but unflinching as a sword.

"I have been excommunicated by the Grand Vicar," he continued, and tension ratcheted upward in the cathedral as he met that fact head-on. "I have been stripped—by him—of my priestly status. I have been condemned, in absentia, for heresy, apostasy, and treason and sentenced to suffer the Punishment of Schueler for my manifold crimes and sins. The 'Church of Charis' has risen in revolt against the decrees of the vicarate, of the Grand Inquisitor—of the Grand Vicar, himself. We have rejected instructions from the Temple. We have defrocked and hanged for murder priests acting in the Grand Inquisitor's name. We have created our own bishops and archbishops, ordained our own priests, and in every *corner* of the Empire of Charis, we have defied Mother Church and dared her to do her worst. We have met her proxies in battle, and we have conquered other lands—even this Princedom of Corisande—by force of arms in spite of Mother Church's declared will. And I tell you now, it is only a matter of time, and not a great deal of it, before Mother Church declares Holy War against the Church of Charis, the Empire of Charis, and any human being—any child of God—who has been so lost to his obedience to Mother Church as to support her enemies. We did not come to you here bearing peace, my children, and I will not pretend we did. No, we come bearing a *sword*, and that sword is in our hand just as surely as defiance is in our hearts."

The stillness was so intense now that Gahrvai was distantly astounded that it didn't shatter when he inhaled. Staynair let that stillness linger, let it roar in the worshippers' ears. He stood in the stained-glass sunlight, wreathed in tendrils of incense, like a lump of stone at the bottom of a deep, cold well of silence.

"Yes," he said at last, "we have rejected our obedience to Mother Church, despite God's own order. But there is a *reason* we've done that, my children. Despite anything you may have heard, the Kingdom of Charis and the Church *within* Charis did not declare war upon Mother Church."

Feet and bodies stirred in protest, but he shook his head sharply, and the stirrings ceased.

"Mother Church declared war upon *us,* my children. She decreed the destruction of Charis, and she used your prince and your navy and your husbands and fathers and sons and brothers to bring that destruction to pass. She launched her attack without warning or declaration. She did not remonstrate with us, never told us we had fallen into doctrinal error, never instructed us in what we might have done better, more obediently. She simply decreed our destruction. That we be broken and shattered and wiped from the record of Safehold's history. That our people be murdered in their own homes, and that those homes be burned above their heads. And so we defended ourselves, protected our homes—our *families*—from that destruction . . . and for that—for *that*—we were pronounced heretics and excommunicate."

He shook his head again, his expression grim.

"And in the thirteenth verse of this morning's scripture, you will find our defense. The Lord said to Langhorne, 'When you are confident that *these* are the priests fit to lead and feed My sheep, set them in places of authority. Give them that which they need to do My will.' But He also said to Langhorne, 'Remind them, and the priests who will come after them, and all the priests who shall follow them, that their purpose, and their charge, and their duty is to *do* My will and always and everywhere, in every way, to serve My people.' He instructed Langhorne that it was their charge, the very reason he had brought the vicarate into existence, to nurture and teach and guide and protect and *serve* His people. There is no—can *be* no—calling higher than that one. No deeper obligation, no more solemn duty.

"But Mother Church failed that obligation, ignored that duty. Mother Church, my children, is governed by *men*. They are enjoined to govern her in accordance with God's will, but they are still *men*. And the men who currently control Mother Church, who have turned the Grand Vicar himself into their puppet and mouthpiece—men like Allayn Maigwair, Rhobair Duchairn, Zahmsyn Trynair, and, above all, Zhaspahr Clyntahn—are as corrupt and venal and evil and *foul* as any *men* who ever walked God's world."

The gentle archbishop's voice was the very sword he'd told them the Church of Charis had brought to Corisande, and it was as keen-edged and as merciless as any blade ever forged.

"It is our duty to obey Mother Church, but it is also our duty to recognize when the orders we are given come not from Mother Church—not from the Archangels, and *never* from God Himself—but from corrupt powermongers. From men who have chosen to turn God's holy Church into a prostitute. Who sell the power of their high offices. Who sell Mother Church herself. Who decree the murders of entire kingdoms. Who use the power of the Inquisition to terrify any thought of opposition to their corruption. Who have Mother Church's own priests tortured to death on the very steps of the Temple for failing to be corrupt enough.

"God's instruction to obey Mother Church is as simple and straightforward as the words of this morning's scripture, but so is His great charge to the *priesthood* of Mother Church. To the men called to wear the orange of vicars. To the Grand Vicar, and the Grand Inquisitor. And those men in Zion . . . have . . . *failed* . . . His . . . charge.*"

That last, measured sentence rang in his listeners' ears like an iron gauntlet, hitting a stone floor in challenge.

"Obedience to instructions to commit sin becomes *complicity* in sin, no matter the source of those instructions. Schueler tells us that in his Book. *'No matter the source'*—those are the Archangel Schueler's very words, my children! I know you've heard Temple Loyalists here in Manchyr quoting that passage. And the Church of Charis will not tell them to be silent. Will not seek to dictate to their souls. But the Church of Charis believes we cannot give *godly* obedience to sinful men *claiming* to speak in His most holy name when they have long since forfeited that claim by their own actions."

He drew himself up to his full height, facing the packed pews of Manchyr Cathedral.

"We cannot, we have not, and we *will* not," he said. "We dictate to no man or woman's conscience. We will not compel. We will not torture and kill those who simply disagree with us. But neither will we *yield*. Let it be known throughout Corisande that any who wish to join us in our effort to reclaim Mother Church's soul from the corrupt men who have defiled it will be welcome. That we will greet you as our brothers and our sisters and our fellow children of God. And that we will go forward to the end of this great task to which we have been called. We will not falter, we will not be swayed, and we will never—*ever*—surrender. Let Clyntahn and Trynair and their flunkies be warned. In the fullness of time, the Church of Charis *will* come for them. Come for them in that day when it comes to Mother Church's rescue and liberates her from the servants of the Dark who have profaned her for far too long."

.VII.
Crag House,
City of Vahlainah,
Earldom of Craggy Hill,
Princedom of Corisande

Bishop Executor Thomys Shylair looked up from his conversation with Mahrak Hahlynd as someone rapped sharply on the chamber door. Despite the fact that he knew—intellectually—that he was perfectly safe here in his Crag House office, a spasm of alarm flashed through him. There were no scheduled visitors or conferences this morning, and for a hunted fugitive (especially a fugitive bishop executor whose intendant had been impiously murdered), "unexpected" translated itself into "threatening."

*Oh, don't be silly, Thomys!* he scolded himself. *I doubt armed minions of the Regency Council or the "Church of Charis" could break this far into an earl's townhouse without at least some alarm preceding them. For that matter, I tend to doubt the present authorities would knock politely once they got this far! They didn't bother to "knock" on* Aidryn's *door, at any rate.*

His face tightened briefly at that thought. Then he cleared his throat.

"Enter!" he called, and the Earl of Craggy Hill stepped through the door.

"Good morning, My Lord." Shylair heard the surprise in his own voice. "I didn't expect to see you this morning."

"I didn't expect to *be* here, Your Eminence."

Something in Craggy Hill's manner, something glittering in his brown eyes, brought Shylair a bit more upright in his chair. He glanced quickly at Hahlynd, catching a glimpse of an echoing speculative curiosity in his secretary's expression, then returned his full attention to Craggy Hill.

"May I ask what changed your plans, then, My Lord?" the bishop executor inquired, gesturing at the comfortable armchair before his desk as he spoke.

"You most certainly may, Your Eminence."

Craggy Hill flashed a brief, tight smile before he settled into the armchair. Hahlynd started to rise, but the earl waved him back into his own chair.

"Stay, Father," the nobleman said. "I'm sure you and His Eminence will be preparing quite a bit of correspondence in the next few five-days, so you might as well here my news now."

"Of course, My Lord," Hahlynd murmured.

The secretary sat back down after glancing at his superior for confirmation, and Craggy Hill returned his full attention to Shylair.

"I realize the reports from Manchyr have been fairly disappointing ever since Staynair arrived in the Princedom, Your Eminence," he said then, which, Shylair reflected, was one of the best examples of understatement he'd heard in the last several years. Calling the semaphore summaries from Manchyr "fairly disappointing" was about the same as calling Carter's Ocean "fairly deep."

It was obvious, however little the bishop executor cared to admit it, that not simply the city of Manchyr but the entire duchy was largely lost. Aidryn's order for Hahskans' execution had backfired badly. Shylair was astounded that the fully justified death of a single apostate priest could have spawned such seething anger and outrage. It was as if the citizens of Manchyr had deliberately chosen not to understand the depravity of Hahskans' attack upon Mother Church. As if they'd actually *sympathized* with him, simply because he was capable of occasional bursts of eloquence in the service of God's enemies.

Yet it would have been foolish to underestimate the strength of that furious anger . . . or the severity of its consequences. Staynair certainly hadn't. His very first sermon from the stolen pulpit of Manchyr Cathedral had capitalized upon that anger as he'd set forth his attempts to justify his own betrayal of Mother Church and the creation of the "Church of Charis." Nothing *could* possibly justify such an abortion, yet angry minds were not reasonable ones, and Staynair's sermons had fallen upon fertile ground. Even many of those who continued to bitterly resent the Empire of Charis were weakening in their opposition to the "*Church* of Charis." For that matter, any residual anger in the capital over the fashion in which Aidryn Waimyn and the other slain priests had been martyred was increasingly directed towards the *secular* authorities, rather than Staynair . . . or Gairlyng. Any idiot ought to recognize that neither the Regency Council nor Viceroy General Chermyn would have dared act in such a fashion except at the direct orders of the Church to which they had given their allegiance. Yet a dangerous degree of separation between the Charisian church and the Charisian crown had crept into the minds of all too many. And Staynair's other sermons, with their emphasis on "freedom of conscience," their renunciation of the Question and the Punishment of Schueler, their specific guarantees that "Temple Loyalists" who abided by the law might continue to worship using the liturgy and even the priests they chose, had won him still more support. Even worse, perhaps, it was winning him *toleration* even among those who thought they were remaining loyal to Mother Church. There were reports that even many of the "Temple Loyalists" had come to respect him—even if grudgingly—for his "integrity."

That erosion of faith was what most worried Shylair, yet he knew his secular allies—like Craggy Hill—were just as worried by the fact that despite the separation some still drew between empire and church, the acceptance of the "Church of Charis" was slowly but steadily eroding resistance to the empire, as well. Primary loyalty to Prince Daivyn clearly remained high, many Corisandians continued to distinguish between their exiled prince and the Regency Council acting in his name, and the people of Corisande were a long, long way from forgiving Cayleb for Prince Hektor's murder. Yet there was a vast difference between rejecting the current regime's legitimacy and actively *resisting* it. That was where the overflow of the creeping acceptance of the "Church of Charis" was gradually eating away at the foundations of the resistance's secular support.

And, just to make things worse, the capital's population seemed to have come to the conclusion that the resistance—their *liberators*—were the true enemy. Intellectually, Shylair could grasp the crude physical factors involved in that process, yet he was constitutionally incapable of truly sympathizing with anyone who could entertain such a bizarre notion. It involved such a profound rejection of God's will in favor of such purely selfish, material considerations of this world that he literally *could not* understand it.

Yet whether he could understand it or not, he'd still been forced to admit its existence and factor it into his own increasingly depressing thinking.

Under Charisian protection, trade was beginning to flourish once more in southeastern Corisande. Goods were flooding the ports, businesses were open, Prince Hektor's tariffs and import duties (many of which had been heavily increased as he prepared to resist the Charisian invasion) had been slashed, and Charisian investors were clearly on the lookout for opportunities. The capital's economy had not yet recovered to pre-invasion levels, but it was approaching them quickly, and at a rate which suggested it would soon *exceed* them.

At the same time, the devastating blow Gahrvai had dealt to Waimyn's organization had brought all coordinated, centrally managed resistance to an end. A handful of his people might have escaped, but they were too scattered, driven too deeply into hiding, to accomplish much. That had brought the "spontaneous incidents" Waimyn had been carefully nursing to a sudden, knee-buckling halt. What was left were far more often than not outbreaks of pure thuggery, however little Shylair liked admitting that. They were no longer carefully targeted. Indeed, they were so *poorly* targeted they were virtually random, almost as likely to inflict damage on Temple Loyalists as on the traitors. That was turning a steady trickle of those Temple Loyalists against the people responsible for their own losses. And those responsible for it were also being dealt with ruthlessly by the authorities. Which meant those attempting to resist the occupation were increasingly seen as the source of violence and destruction, while those *supporting* the occupation were seen as the citizenry's *protection* from acts of violence.

It would have taken a Bédardist to explain *that* chain of logic to Shylair. Surely anyone ought to be able to understand that it was the occupiers' presence which was *provoking* the violent response. That being the case, what twisted chain of reasoning could possibly give them credit for *suppressing* the violence rather than assigning them the blame for having *caused* it in the first place?

Yet however bizarre he might find the thought, he couldn't deny that it was happening. And, even more discouragingly, the Regency Council was actually garnering an increasing degree of respect, even among the capital's Temple Loyalists, for its "restraint." No one was simply being arrested and tossed into prison "just in case." Gahrvai's guardsmen weren't particularly gentle with those who resisted arrest, but anyone who was arrested was also charged. And no one who'd been charged was punished without a trial. And while they were in prison awaiting trial, they were permitted access to Temple Loyalist clergy and to family members . . . which just happened to knock any rumors about prisoners being secretly tortured neatly on the head.

There'd been quite a few executions, and everyone in Manchyr knew there were going to be more, but the Regency Council had been scrupulous about maintaining at least the semblance of justice.

It had become depressingly clear that there would be no general uprising—not on the scale they needed—in the southeast. There would still be some support, some knots of resistance, and it was probable a substantial portion of the people would exhibit at least *passive* resistance when the moment came. But none of that could disguise the fact that when they finally launched their own uprising, beginning here in the north, they would be initiating not a general insurrection, but a *civil war,* right here in Corisande, between those willing to lick the Charisian hand and those still loyal to Mother Church and Prince Daivyn.

*And every day only tilts the odds a little more against us,* Shylair thought bitterly. *Anvil Rock and Tartarian are already moving to expand their tidy little citadel down there in the southeast, and from the sounds of things, Baron Black Cliff is about to sign his soul away and publicly support them.*

He shook free of his depressing reflections and nodded to Craggy Hill.

"I think 'disappointing' would be one way to describe those reports, My Lord, yes," he said dryly.

"Well, I have a bit of news which is considerably more encouraging, I think," the earl told him. "It doesn't have anything to do with anything going on down there in the south, I'm afraid. But Zebediah has finally stopped dancing around."

"He has?" Shylair sat up straighter, expression suddenly intent, and Craggy Hill smiled. It was not, the prelate thought, an especially pleasant expression.

"Oh, he has, Your Eminence. In fact, I think the dance may have come to more of a complete halt than he realizes."

"In what way?"

"He's been very careful to communicate only verbally, by way of personal representatives he trusts," Craggy Hill said. "Oh, I've been in correspondence with him, but none of our letters have contained anything incriminating. We've both had excellent reasons to avoid *that.*"

The earl grimaced, and Shylair snorted. Treachery came as naturally as breathing to Tohmys Symmyns, Grand Duke of Zebediah. If Craggy Hill had been so incautious as to include any open reference to "treason" in a letter to Zebediah, the grand duke would have sold it to Cayleb and Sharleyan the moment it offered him any advantage.

"But," the earl continued, "he's finally committed to a definite schedule for supplying us with the new rifled muskets. And he's said as much in writing."

"You're joking!"

"Oh, no." Craggy Hill's smile was thinner than ever. "Of course, he didn't realize he was committing that to *me.* His correspondence to me is still the very soul of discretion, but he's had to be a bit more . . . frank in his instructions to those envoys of his. I've been aware of that for some time, and I'm afraid his current envoy was brutally set upon and robbed last night."

The earl clasped his hands in front of him and raised his eyes piously towards heaven for a moment.

"Obviously, I'm investigating, and the envoy—who suffered only minor injuries and the loss of all of his jewels and money—is torn between mentioning the fact that his stolen money belt contained his most recent instructions and hoping to Shan-wei we never catch up with the thieves in question."

"You think he truly doesn't realize you already have it—which you clearly do, My Lord?" Shylair asked, his eyes narrowing.

"Oh, he has to recognize it as a possibility, Your Eminence. But it was a very *convincing* robbery, if I do say so myself. And the thieves were clearly planning to cut his throat to make sure there were no witnesses when he managed to 'escape,' which should make him at least a little doubtful about my involvement. He knows I have to know that if I'd had him *killed,* Zebediah would instantly have smelled a spider-rat and backed away. What he *doesn't* know is that I knew—or, rather, strongly suspected—he had those instructions on his person. I don't think he realized my agents had been able to identify the factor here in Vahlainah who's been passing Zebediah's mail back and forth. So he doesn't know the 'thieves' followed from picking up his latest dispatch. As a matter of fact, I'm not positive he'd had time to read it himself, although from some of the things he's said it's pretty evident he's at least generally aware of its contents. Given all that, there's got to be a huge question mark in his mind where the possibility of my involvement is concerned, but he can't be certain either way. So he's probably hoping it really was thieves who'll be interested only in his money and jewels and simply throw the correspondence away. Or, failing that, that they'll be bright enough to realize just how dangerous it is and burn it before it can get them killed. The *last* thing he wants is for my guardsmen to lay the thieves by the heels, find Zebediah's letter to him, and hand it over to me.

"But the critical point is that even if Zebediah thinks I arranged it, even if he decides he wants to back away, he can't now. I have a letter in his own hand, telling his envoy to tell 'our friends in Corisande' he's prepared to supply weapons for the purpose of resisting the Charisian occupation. Specifically, with rifled muskets diverted from the Imperial Army in Chisholm. Neither I nor anyone else in Corisande is identified in the letter, but *his* intentions are spelled out quite clearly, over his own signature."

The bishop executor decided he could easily have shaved with Craggy Hill's smile, and he felt himself smiling back.

"That letter's going into my personal strongbox, Your Eminence," the earl said in a tone of intense satisfaction. "And if Zebediah should happen to prove . . . difficult, I can always gently inform him that I have it. And, of course, that should he *continue* to prove difficult, it just might find its way into Gahrvai's—or Chermyn's—hands."

Shylair leaned back in his chair once more, and his smile faded into a more sober expression of gratitude.

*Thank you, God,* he thought. *Forgive me for having doubted, for having permitted myself to feel despair. The* Writ *says You will deliver Your enemies to justice, using even the hand of the ungodly themselves. I can scarcely pretend the Grand Duke is a godly man, but You've given him into our hands, and in the end, we will use that to bring Your enemies to justice.*

He closed his eyes briefly, as he made that promise. But even if he'd kept them open, he would never have noticed the tiny remote, perched upon his ceiling, which had just transmitted every word of his conversation with Craggy Hill to a far distant artificial intelligence named Owl.

# MAY, YEAR OF GOD 894

# HMS *Chihiro*, 50,
## Gorath Bay,
## Kingdom of Dohlar

E xcuse me, My Lord, but I think you'd better see this."
  The Earl of Thirsk turned from *Chihiro*'s stern windows and his contemplation of the ships of his slowly growing fleet. The commander who'd just entered his day cabin was about thirty, with brown eyes, a dark complexion and dark hair, and a particularly luxurious mustache.

"And what, precisely, might 'this' be, Ahlvyn?" Thirsk asked mildly.

"Sorry, My Lord." Commander Ahlvyn Khapahr smiled wryly. "It's a dispatch from the Governor of Queiroz. It was marked 'urgent,' so the semaphore station sent it over immediately instead of waiting for the regular afternoon boat."

"The Governor of Queiroz?" Thirsk frowned. He could think of a handful of reasons the governor of a province of the Harchong Empire might be sending him an urgent dispatch. There was only one that seemed particularly likely, however, and he felt his nerves tightening.

"Very well, Ahlvyn."

The earl extended his hand, and Khapahr handed him the heavy envelope. Then the commander bowed slightly and withdrew from the admiral's cabin.

Thirsk watched him go with a smile. One of these days, Ahlvyn Khapahr was going to make a very fine galleon captain. At the moment, however, he was busy creating a position which was something entirely new in the Royal Dohlaran Navy. Thirsk hadn't yet come up with a term for that "something new," but back on a planet called Old Earth, it would have been "chief of staff." One of the things the earl had realized was that he needed a group of assistants to help him handle the immense task of rebuilding the navy which had been destroyed off Armageddon Reef. Khapahr was one of those assistants, and very good he was at his job, too.

*Almost as good as he is at inveigling young ladies into spending copious quantities of time in his own charming company.* Thirsk shook his head. *That young man is going to go far . . . assuming he manages to avoid getting himself killed in a duel somewhere!*

He put that thought aside and opened the envelope. He scanned its contents quickly, and his smile vanished.

He refolded the single sheet of paper and turned back to the windows, gazing out across the bay, but his unfocused eyes didn't really see it, now. They were looking at mental images of remembered charts, while his mind whirred.

He stayed that way for several minutes, then gave himself a shake, walked across to the cabin door, and poked his head out.

"My Lord?" the sentry stationed there (he was an army corporal detailed to naval service; Thirsk was still trying to get Thorast to agree to form a dedicated marine corps like the Charisian Marines) asked, coming to attention quickly.

"Pass the word for Lieutenant Bahrdailahn and Master Vahnwyk to report to me immediately, please," Thirsk instructed.

"At once, My Lord!"

Thirsk nodded and turned back into the cabin while he heard the message being passed. He was looking out the stern windows again when Mahrtyn Vahnwyk and Ahbail Bahrdailahn arrived.

"You sent for us, My Lord?" the flag lieutenant said.

"Indeed I did, Ahbail." Thirsk gazed out across the bay for a moment longer, then swung to face them.

"We need to send some messages," he said crisply. "We'll need letters to Duke Fern and Duke Thorast, Mahrtyn, with copies to Bishop Staiphan and Admiral Hahlynd, for their information."

"At once, My Lord." The secretary crossed to a side table set up as a writing desk, pulled a sheet of paper towards him, and dipped a pen. "I'm ready, My Lord."

"Good." Thirsk smiled in approval, then glanced at Bahrdailahn. "Once we've gotten the letters off, I'll also want you to collect Commander Khapahr and the others—and Captain Baiket—for an immediate meeting here, Ahbail." The earl pointed at the carpet under his feet, and the flag lieutenant nodded.

"I'll see to it, My Lord."

"Good," Thirsk repeated. Then he inhaled deeply, turned back to Vahnwyk, and began to dictate.

" 'My Lords'—put in all the proper salutations, Mahrtyn—'I have the duty to inform you that I have received a dispatch from the Governor of Queiroz informing me that an imperial dispatch boat has sighted Charisian warships and transports passing through the Straits of Queiroz on a northerly heading. The Governor states in his message that he has high confidence in the officer making the report, but that it was impossible for him to obtain a definite count before he was forced to withdraw to evade pursuit by a Charisian schooner. The schooner in question was positively identified as a cruiser of the Imperial Charisian Navy, and not a privateer vessel.' Underline both 'positively' and 'not,' Mahrtyn."

"Of course, My Lord."

If the secretary was dismayed by the letter's content, his voice showed no sign of it, and Thirsk smiled approvingly at the crown of his bent head before he resumed.

" 'The Harchongese dispatch boat captain reports that he counted a minimum of eight Charisian war galleons and what appeared to be at least that many transport or cargo vessels. It would seem unlikely that imperial Charisian warships have been dispatched this far afield as mere convoy escorts. I believe, therefore, that we must assume the merchant galleons the Governor sighted are, in fact, transports, and that this represents an operation directed against us here in Dohlar or against the Harchong Empire. Given the more advanced state of our naval preparations, I feel this Kingdom is the more probable target, although the possibility of operations against both realms clearly cannot be ruled out.

" 'The presence of transports suggests to me that the Charisian intention is to seize a suitable base somewhere in the Sea of Harchong or in the Dohlaran Gulf proper. Obviously, at this point we cannot possibly say which of those possibilities is their actual intention, but I am inclined to believe their most probable destination is Claw Island. It is virtually uninhabited, it is far enough from our own naval bases or those of the Empire to discourage any hasty counterattack upon it, and it would be well placed to threaten the coasts of Queiroz, Kyznetsov, Tiegelkamp, Stene, and even Shwei Bay, in addition to interfering with our own commerce and shipping in the Gulf of Dohlar.

" 'The actual distance from Claw Island to Gorath is, of course, in excess of four thousand miles, but I believe it is entirely possible that having secured and fortified Claw Island, an audacious Charisian commander might well seize an unfortified anchorage much closer to us, purely as a forward operating base. I have pointed out in the past the desirability of fortifying the islands of the Dohlar Bank chain.' " *That* was going to piss off Thorast, who'd rejected his recommendations in that respect, Thirsk thought, but it still had to be said. " 'As things now stand, I cannot guarantee the Navy's ability to prevent a sufficiently powerful Charisian squadron from seizing such an anchorage on Trove Island or any one of the Trios.

" 'It will, obviously, be some time before any warships as far distant as the Straits of Queiroz can pose any threat in home waters. I believe, however, that it behooves us to be as beforehand as possible in dealing with this incursion. I therefore humbly request that we immediately consult with the Harchong ambassador about the possible coordination of our efforts in this regard. In the meantime, Bishop Staiphan and I will consult on how best we may prepare our own forces. I will report to you as soon as he, Admiral Hahlynd, and I have completed our preliminary evaluation of our capabilities and how they might best be utilized in the face of the threat I anticipate.

" 'I have the honor to be, et cetera, et cetera, et cetera.' "

The earl looked back out the windows for a moment, thinking, then shrugged.

"Read that back, please, Mahrtyn."

"Of course, My Lord." The secretary cleared his throat. " 'My Lords, I have the duty to inform you that I have received . . .' "

Sir Gwylym Manthyr watched the schooner *Messenger*'s topsails as she cleared the mouth of Snake Channel and altered course. He couldn't see her hull from here, but he could track the white flaw of her sails against the looming brown mountains of Claw Island, and he frowned as he contemplated them.

His greatest concern over Hardship Bay's suitability as an anchorage was what an easterly wind would do to it. Even a schooner would have a terrible time trying to claw her way out against an east wind. Snake Channel, the bay's southern entrance, would be usable with the wind out of the northeast-by-east, and North Channel would be usable with the wind out of the southeast-by-east, but a galleon would have trouble making it out of either channel even under those conditions. At the moment, however, the wind (such as there was and what there was of it) was out of the south-south*west,* and *Messenger* settled down on the starboard tack, with the wind almost broad on the beam, and headed for his flagship.

All the rest of his command—fifty-three ships—lay hove-to in Shell Sound, the broad body of water between Green Island and Hardship Shoal. It was oppressively hot, even by Charisian standards. He'd left his tunic in his cabin, yet sweat glued his shirt to his skin, and when he held his hand an inch or so above one of the black-painted quarterdeck carronades, the heat radiated back up against his palm as if from the top of a stove. The awnings rigged above the deck to give the crew some little shade helped, but in Manthyr's opinion, it was basically the difference between being slowly baked in an oven or broiled over an open flame.

He'd expected heat, but he hadn't been prepared for heat *this* hot, and the fact that the wind had dropped to no more than a gentle breeze didn't help. Nor was it going to speed *Messenger* to *Dancer* anytime soon. In this wind, even the fleet little schooner was doing well to make two or three knots with all sail set, and she had the better part of fifteen miles to cover to reach the flagship.

Manthyr looked up at the sun and pursed his lips. Call it five hours—more likely six—and it was already past eleven. He grimaced and stepped back into the quarterdeck awning's shade. It wasn't a particularly dense shade, but after the unfiltered, eye-searing sunlight beyond it, it felt like stepping into a cave.

A very *hot* cave.

"Dahnyld?" he said, turning his head and blinking as he looked for his flag lieutenant before his eyes had really adjusted to the relative dimness.

"Yes, Sir?" Lieutenant Dahnyld Rahzmahn responded from somewhere behind him, and he turned towards the voice.

"Ah, there you are!" The admiral shook his head, smiling in wry sympathy. "I was afraid you'd finally been rendered down."

"Not quite yet, Sir." Rahzmahn returned his admiral's smile, although, truth be told, Manthyr's jest cut entirely too close to reality, in the lieutenant's opinion. Rahzmahn was a Chisholmian, one of the growing number of Chisholmians being integrated into the Imperial Navy, with exotic (by Charisian standards) auburn hair and gray eyes . . . and a fair complexion that was perfectly happy to burn angry red, blister, or even peel painfully but flatly refused to tan.

"Well, there's time yet, I suppose," Manthyr chuckled. It wasn't that he didn't sympathize; it was simply that there wasn't anything either of them could do about it *except* laugh.

"No, Sir," Rahzmahn agreed. "In the meantime, though, was there something you needed me to do?"

"As a matter of fact, yes." Manthyr waved in *Messenger*'s direction. "I imagine it's going to take five or six hours for her to reach us. Under the circumstances, I thought we might move supper forward and invite Commander Grahzaial to join us this evening. It seems the least we can do after sending him all the way in to talk to these people."

"Of course, Sir. Do you wish Captain Mahgail to join you?"

"The Captain, Master Seasmoke, and Lieutenant Krughair—no, Krughair will have the watch, won't he?" Manthyr thought for a moment, then shrugged. "Make it Lieutenant Wahldair and young Svairsmahn. And you, of course."

"So . . . six guests, including me?" Rahzmahn said, mentally counting up the names. "I'll go and tell Naiklos, Sir." The flag lieutenant smiled again, faintly. "He's still going to complain that we didn't give him enough notice, you realize."

"Of course he is. It's what he does."

Manthyr's answering smile held just a bit of resignation. Raiyhan Hahlmyn, his servant of many years, had been killed at Darcos Sound, and Manthyr missed him badly. Not just because they'd been together for so long, although that was definitely part of it, but also because Hahlmyn had suited him so well. Manthyr's birth had been as common as even a future Charisian seaman's came, and Hahlmyn had been a Howell Bay fisherman before he joined the Navy. Personally, Manthyr suspected "Raiyhan Hahlmyn" hadn't always been the man's name. There'd been any number of men like that in the Royal Charisian Navy, and that hadn't changed now that it was the *Imperial* Charisian Navy. As long as a man did his duty and didn't get into fresh trouble, the Navy was willing to overlook any indiscretions in his previous life. In Hahlmyn's case, Manthyr had observed that he never voluntarily went ashore in Tellesberg.

Whatever might have lurked in Hahlmyn's past, young Lieutenant Manthyr had always found him a reliable hand and a skilled coxswain. When Lieutenant Commander Manthyr got his first command, he'd taken Hahlmyn with him, first as his personal coxswain and then, later, as his cabin servant. Calling him a "valet" would have stretched a perfectly serviceable noun far beyond its acceptable limits. Still, he'd been loyal, tough, hardworking, and remarkably good with a cutlass, which had done perfectly well for Gwylym Manthyr.

Yet he was gone now, and *Sir* Gwylym Manthyr had required a replacement. Enter Naiklos Vahlain, who clearly considered Manthyr a work in progress. The dapper, dark-haired valet was about ten years older than Manthyr, and he'd been highly recommended by Domynyk Staynair.

"He'll fuss and fidget you to death," Staynair had said, "but he'll also manage to feed you hot soup in the middle of a howling gale. No matter how long you give him to prepare for a formal dinner, he'll swear it's not long enough . . . then come up with a five-course meal and somehow conjure up fresh vegetables when you're stuck in the middle of The Anvil. And, to be honest, Gwylym, I think he's exactly what you're going to need now that you've got your streamer."

There hadn't been much doubt in Manthyr's mind what Rock Point had been getting at. Captains might not have to worry overmuch about appearances; admirals did. And the unvarnished truth was that Manthyr's life and career had made him a consummate professional as a seaman but didn't seem to have gotten him around to matters of etiquette, the proper choice of wines, or all those other little details admirals were supposed to know about.

Vahlain was fixing that, and there were times Manthyr felt a certain kinship with a white-hot piece of bar stock being hammered into a horseshoe. He was deeply grateful, but that didn't necessarily mean he enjoyed the process, and Vahlain was just as persnickety, finicky, precise, and downright fussy as Rock Point had warned him the man would be.

Which, the admiral reflected, watching his flag lieutenant head below, was why he'd sent Rahzmahn to beard Vahlain in his den. Rank, after all, had its privileges.

▼    ▼    ▼

In the end, they didn't have to move supper forward after all . . . much to Vahlain's long-suffering (if unvoiced) disgust. The wind had continued to drop, falling to a complete calm with *Messenger* still two miles short of the flagship, and Lieutenant Commander Grahzaial had covered the final distance in his quarter boat. At the moment, his oarsmen were enjoying a well-deserved rest in *Dancer*'s crew's mess while Grahzaial apologized to his admiral for the delay.

Like Rahzmahn, Grahzaial was a Chisholmian, although he was as dark-haired and -eyed as any Charisian. He tanned better than Rahzmahn, too, Manthyr thought with a certain amusement, watching them stand almost side by side. In fact, Grahzaial had darkened to a deep, coppery bronze which, combined with his rather worn tunic (like most of the Navy's junior ship commanders, he didn't appear overly long in the purse), gave him a distinctly piratical look. Or, rather, the look pirates were supposed to have according to bad novels. Manthyr had read a novel, once. The fact that it had been about pirates might have been one reason he'd never read another. After all, he'd met *real* pirates, and anything less like the jolly, good-hearted-but-misunderstood characters in that particular literary abortion would have been difficult to imagine.

He shook that thought aside and waved away Grahzaial's apologies.

"Don't worry about it, Commander. No one can issue orders to the wind—well, not and have them *obeyed,* anyway! Frankly, you did well to get here this promptly. I understand from my valet, however," he very carefully did not cock a wary eye in Naiklos Vahlain's direction, "that supper is ready. I suggest we all sit down and eat before it spoils. We can discuss such minor things as reports after we have that safely out of the way."

The sniff of satisfaction he thought he heard from the direction of Vahlain's pantry was probably only his imagination.

▼    ▼    ▼

Sometime later, when Vahlain and the wardroom steward he'd pressed into service had cleared the table, poured the wine, and put Manthyr's tobacco humidor in the center of the table, the admiral leaned back in his chair with a sigh of content.

The wind had picked back up a bit, and the canvas wind scoop rigged for the skylight funneled some of it through the dining cabin. It brought with it a welcome breath of coolness, blowing back out through the stern and quarter windows. Fussy as Vahlain might be, he'd done his usual outstanding job, and two of the wyverns he'd acquired when the fleet paid a brief call at Westbreak Island to take on water and fresh vegetables had made the ultimate sacrifice. The vegetables which had been purchased at the same time were mostly gone, but the hens were laying well enough to provide mayonnaise, and Vahlain had contrived a potato salad—heavy on pickles and onions and short on celery and bell pepper, unfortunately, but still tasty—to accompany the roasted, rice-stuffed wyverns. Fresh-baked bread and butter (which, alas, had been somewhat less fresh than the bread) and spiced bread pudding had completed the menu.

Now the admiral lit his pipe and waited patiently while everyone but young Master Svairsmahn, *Dancer's* signal midshipman, followed his example. Once all pipes were drawing nicely, Manthyr cocked an eyebrow at Mahshal Grahzaial.

"And now that the evening's *serious* business is out of the way, Commander," he said around his pipe stem, "suppose you tell us how your mission ashore went?"

"Of course, Sir." Grahzaial straightened and cleared his throat. "As you instructed, I carried your message to Claw Keep." He grimaced. "Calling it a 'keep' is a definite overstatement, in my opinion, Sir Gwylym. It does have a curtain wall, but I imagine we could knock it down with a fourteen-pounder in an afternoon, and there's no real *keep* at all. Just a couple of dozen buildings—mostly houses, of a sort, but at least three saloons—sort of huddled together inside the wall."

"Not too surprising, Sir," Captain Raif Mahgail put in. Manthyr's flag captain was a wiry, black-haired man with extremely dark brown eyes. He was eight years younger than his admiral, and his promotion to captain's rank was relatively recent—there was a lot of that going around—but he'd been at sea since he was twelve, and there was very little he hadn't seen.

"That 'curtain wall' of Mahshal's would be intended to discourage pirates—or, *other* pirates, I should say—rather than provide any serious defense." The flag captain sniffed disdainfully. "I may not think much of the Harchongese Navy, but if these people were ever foolish enough to make themselves a *serious* nuisance to the Empire, all the walls in the world wouldn't save their arses, and they know it."

"That was my impression, Captain," Grahzaial agreed with a nod. "And, Admiral," he returned his gaze to Manthyr, "they've got a *lot* of fishing boats for such a small town. Some of them are damned near as big as *Messenger,* too. And they've got brackets for swivel wolves. Captain Lahfat—he's the fellow in charge—seemed just a bit eager to keep me from noticing that little detail."

"Point taken, Master Grahzaial," Manthyr said.

"Wolf" was a generic term for artillery pieces with a bore of less than two inches and a shot which weighed one pound or less. "Swivel wolves" were at the small end of the range—whether they were very light cannon or extremely heavy muskets was mostly a matter of semantics. They had little effect on the hull of a ship, but they were portable, easily mounted on a ship's rail (or dismounted and hidden when a cruiser came along), and effective antipersonnel weapons . . . just the thing for a crew of pirates who wanted to swarm over a lightly manned, weakly armed merchant vessel.

"So your impression is that this—Lahfat, was it?—might occasionally fish for something besides forktail or hake?" he went on, and Grahzaial nodded again.

"I'd say that's exactly what he does, Sir," the lieutenant commander replied. "Mind you, from the look of things it doesn't seem to pay very well." Manthyr snorted. He'd never yet met a pirate who couldn't have earned more, over the long run, doing *honest* work. Not to mention living longer, into the bargain. "And I don't doubt for a moment that 'Captain' Lahfat's rank was entirely . . . self-bestowed. I couldn't decide where he's from originally, but I'm pretty sure he's not Harchongese. He's too tall, among other things. And I don't think he's at all pleased with the notion of having us move in."

"Now, I wonder why that might be?" Yairman Seasmoke, *Dancer*'s first lieutenant, murmured, earning an even harsher snort from his admiral.

"Should I assume from that that he told you to pound sand, Commander?" Manthyr asked dryly, and Grahzaial laughed.

"I think that's exactly what he wished he could do, Sir. Unfortunately, one of those fishing boats of his apparently got a fairly accurate count on the squadron before it ran for harbor. I don't think he thinks all those transports are empty."

This time, a general mutter of laughter ran around the dining table.

"Lahfat—if that's even his real name—has obviously decided he doesn't want to lock horns with you, Sir Gwylym," Grahzaial continued. "He tried to argue that the island's wells don't produce enough water to support this many extra mouths. I think he's exaggerating his concerns, but I don't think he's making them up entirely, either. In the end, though, he agreed to open his gates to us. I imagine everyone in Claw Keep is busy hiding evidence before the Marines come ashore."

"I imagine that's exactly what they're doing," Manthyr agreed. "Well, that and trying to get a messenger out to report us to the Governor of Queiroz— or maybe Tiegelkamp, depending on the wind. I suppose he promised faith- fully that no such action would ever so much as cross his mind, Commander?"

"Something of that sort, Sir. Yes."

"Good." Manthyr smiled nastily. "It's not as if the Harchongese aren't go- ing to figure out we're here pretty damned quick, if they didn't already guess this was where we were headed. But when the good 'Captain's' messenger runs into *Lance* lying in the middle of North Channel, it'll give me a little more leverage with him. Or, a bigger club to beat him with, at any rate."

The admiral considered for several moments, then nodded to himself.

"You did well, Master Grahzaial," he said. "I'll see to it that my reports in- dicate as much."

The young Chisholmian smiled with obvious pleasure but said nothing, and Manthyr turned to his flag captain.

"With any luck, we'll have a south or southeast wind tomorrow morning, Raif. Assuming we've got one we can work with, I want the entire fleet inside Hardship Bay by evening. I doubt 'Captain Lahfat' is stupid enough to try anything foolish, but let's not take any chances. We'll use a couple of the schooners to lead the squadron, and tell Brigadier Tyotayn that I want two or three companies of his Marines to go ashore and secure the 'keep' before we anchor."

"Yes, Sir."

"In that case, Gentlemen," the admiral said, reaching for the whiskey decanter, "I think we can safely lift a glass to a job well done by Commander Grahzaial."

.III.
## HMS *Dancer*, 56,
## Off Trove Island,
## Gulf of Dohlar

Green, Sir Gwylym Manthyr thought, was a remarkably nice color. It was particularly nice after spending two entire five-days on rocky, barren, sun-blasted, thoroughly miserable Claw Island.

The green which prompted that particular consideration was found in the trees and grass covering Trove Island, off the Dohlar Bank. Technically, the island's inhabitants—of which, thankfully, there were not many—were subjects of King Rahnyld of Dohlar. Trove Island, however, did not belong to King Rahnyld. Emperor Waisu VI's ministers had made that point abundantly clear. Actually, the present emperor's father, who had also happened to be named Waisu, had made it clear to King Rahnyld's father (who had also happened to be named Rahnyld), and the current Waisu had simply expressed his intention to keep things that way.

The current Rahnyld didn't much care for it, since he had pretensions of extending Dohlaran sway throughout the entire Gulf of Dohlar. Despite the money he'd poured into the fleet which had been destroyed at Rock Point and Crag Reach, however, he'd never had the military strength to survive a serious disagreement with Harchong. It was, admittedly, unlikely Harchong would put itself to the trouble and expense of squashing Dohlaran posturing, but "unlikely" wasn't the same thing as "never going to happen," and provoking Harchong to military action was the sort of mistake one normally only got to make once.

On the other hand, he'd managed to get Harchong to agree that the Dohlar Bank and the islands around Whale Island Shoal, farther west, would be unclaimed by either realm. Waisu—or, rather, his ministers; it was entirely possible Waisu hadn't made a single policymaking decision during his entire twelve years on the throne—hadn't cared enough to argue. All they'd wanted was to make certain Dohlar didn't fortify any of the islands' harbors and that Rahnyld's expansionist ambitions were held more or less in check. Well, they'd also wanted to be sure the lucrative smuggling traffic which passed through the islands (and deposited sizable sums in their purses) continued unabated, of course.

Manthyr had been pleasantly surprised to discover that that state of affairs continued unchanged. He'd expected the Dohlarans and Harchongese to have patched up some sort of understanding, now that the Group of Four had more or less married them at swordpoint. From a Charisian perspective, leaving nice, convenient island bases less than five hundred miles off the coast of Dohlar (and even closer than that to Harchong's Province of Erech) wide open to enemy occupation was an act of lunacy. It would no more have occurred to Emperor Cayleb to do such a thing than it would have occurred to him to go swimming with krakens with a fresh steak tied to his back. If anything had been wanting to convince Manchyr that neither Dohlarans nor Harchongese had even the ghost of a whisper of a clue where the realities of naval strategy were concerned, finding these islands completely unfortified and unprotected provided it.

He watched boatloads of Marines pulling for the shore and shook his head. Disgusted as he was, he was also grateful. Chelm Bay, on Trove's northeastern coast, was too small for his entire force. It measured barely eight miles in width, and it was totally open to any northerly wind, but the water was relatively deep, the bottom was good holding ground, and it was practically impervious to wind from any other direction, thanks to the island's rocky height. As a temporary anchorage for minor repairs or resupply, it would do very well, indeed. And it was the island's *only* really good deep-water anchorage, so once Major Brainahk Wyndayl's battalion of Colonel Vahsag Pahraiha's Fourteenth Marine Regiment was ensconced ashore, taking the island back again would present a major military challenge. Especially with the battery of thirty-pounders which had been thoughtfully brought along specifically to make King Rahnyld's and Emperor Waisu's lives difficult.

He was just as happy Chelmsport, the island's largest town, had less than two hundred inhabitants. It decreased the probability of anyone's doing anything foolish, although he couldn't quite rule the possibility out, especially with the religious component to consider. Still, it seemed unlikely, and Chelmsport had reliable sources of water, which was always the greatest potential weakness of a warship. Assuming the locals were inclined to be reasonable, it might also be another source of fresh food, which wasn't anything to sneeze at.

Brigadier Tyotayn's Fifth Brigade (and the second battalion of Colonel Pahraiha's independent regiment) had laboriously broken ground for crops back at Claw Island, and the water supply there was nowhere near as limited as "Captain Lahfat" had suggested. It had taken quite a bit of ingenuity to rig an aqueduct and a wind-powered pump to feed it to provide adequate irrigation, but one thing the island had in plenty was seabird and wyvern guano. That provided lots of fertilizer, and at least half Tyotayn's Marines had been farm boys before they enlisted. Still, it would be an arduous task to grow enough food for the expedition. He expected to get at least some supplies from the prizes he was shortly going to be taking, but having an additional source would be more than simply convenient.

*And if the Trove Islanders will sell us food, then we can probably convince the other islands in the area to do the same thing, if we're willing to be discreet about it. Another thing the naval geniuses who left them wide open this way obviously didn't consider.*

He shook his head wonderingly one more time over his opponents' stupidity, then turned away from the rail. It was time he and his captains got down to the business of making the other side's lives as miserable as possible.

*And it serves the idiots right, too,* he thought.

.IV.
### HMS *Chihiro*, 50,
### Gorath Bay,
### Kingdom of Dohlar

"M y son, you should sit down and count to one thousand slowly. If not in the interest of your spiritual serenity, in the interest of avoiding apoplexy."

Earl Thirsk's head whipped around. Had the speaker been anyone besides Staiphan Maik, the earl's response would probably have been both pungent and profane. Under the circumstances, however, both those options were denied him, although he couldn't *quite* keep the heat out of his gaze.

Maik simply gazed at him serenely, and, after a moment, Thirsk felt his own lips twitch unwillingly. After all, the bishop had a point.

"Seriously, Lywys," Maik said, pointing at the earl's desk chair. "Stop pacing around like a slash lizard with its tail cut off. I understand exactly why you're so furious. But, in the long run, I think this may actually work out in our favor."

Thirsk blinked in surprise. He looked at the bishop for several seconds, then walked slowly around the desk, seated himself as directed, and cocked his head.

"I would be very interested to hear how you reached that conclusion, My Lord," he said politely.

"Think about it," Maik replied. "They've done exactly what you predicted. And they got away with it because neither Thorast nor the Harchongese did what you've been recommending for months. So, the Charisians now have their forward bases, exactly where you said they'd want them. For that matter, exactly where you told Thorast they'd *put* them after you got the Governor of Queiroz's dispatch! And I don't doubt they're going to make their presence very unpleasantly felt. Which, in turn, is going to increase the pressure on you—and on me, once Chancellor Trynair and his colleagues"—Maik was far too cautious to use the term "the Group of Four" even with someone he'd come to trust as much as he trusted Thirsk—"hear about this. Agreed?"

"Oh, I can safely say I concur with *that* much," Thirsk said, and the bishop shrugged.

"Well, when they start screaming at you to do something—*anything*—I, for one, am going to point out to them—quite forcefully—that if they'd listened to you in the beginning, you wouldn't have to do the aforesaid something—*anything*—to get their arses out of the crack they've wedged themselves so tightly into."

Thirsk's eyebrows rose. He and Maik had found themselves working more and more closely together, and his respect for the Schuelerite had grown steadily. He had to admit that his willingness to *trust* Maik had taken a severe blow as the reports coming out of the Temple had mounted, however. He knew perfectly well that Maik hadn't had a thing to do with that . . . that . . . *madness*, but the bishop *was* a Schuelerite, and Thirsk had found that hard to forgive.

*Probably because I spent so much time under "official displeasure" myself after Crag Reach,* he thought now. *For a while there, I was fairly certain Fern was going to hand me over to either Thorast or the Inquisition as the Kingdom's scapegoat. So I suppose I've got a better feel for the sheer cynicism involved in all this. But to think that even Clyntahn* would *go this far. . . . Just slaughtering so many of his fellow vicars, and so many bishops and archbishops, would have been bad enough, especially this way! But their* families? *Madness!*

He knew he wasn't the only Dohlaran who felt that way, although very few of those who did were stupid enough to say so. And he suspected Bishop Staiphan came very close to sharing his own feelings. On the other hand, Clyntahn had made his point crystal clear. Treachery would be punished as severely as heresy . . . and anything short of complete and total loyalty was, by definition, treachery.

*And I don't doubt military defeat will be defined as "treachery," too,* he thought grimly. *Especially if someone's been unfortunate enough to have suffered defeat once before. I suppose I should think of it as an additional incentive to do well.*

That last thought woke at least a flicker of amusement, and he was grateful for it. Humorous thoughts had been hard to come by lately.

"I hadn't thought of it from exactly that perspective, My Lord," he said with a wintry smile. "My previous experience with being right when everyone else was wrong hasn't precisely filled me with boundless confidence in how they're going to react when it all happens again. My observation is that powerful men get even more vengeful if you insist on proving they're *always* wrong."

"Ah, but this time, *you're* going to keep your mouth shut. You're not going to say one word about Claw Island, or Trove Island. You're just going to provide your normal, well reasoned, cogent arguments about how we should respond. *I'll* rub all the salt into the wounds. At least something good should come of—"

The bishop paused suddenly. For an instant his mouth tightened, then he shrugged.

"At least something good should come of your being right yet again," he finished.

Thirsk nodded silently, but his eyes were very intent. He knew what Maik had started to say, though it was the closest he'd yet come to anything which could be construed as remotely critical of the head of his own order. Yet there was a certain grim truth to it, Thirsk reflected. After Clyntahn's brutal demonstration, no layman, and precious few bishops or archbishops, were going to so much as *look* like they were arguing with a *Schuelerite* bishop.

"I hope you're right about that, My Lord," Thirsk said, addressing what the bishop had said, rather than what he had *not* said. Their eyes met, and he saw the understanding in Maik's gaze. Then the bishop shook himself.

"So! What *do* you recommend?" he asked.

"Actually, My Lord, if you're serious about the latitude I'm likely to enjoy, I think we may be able to turn this into an opportunity, as well as a problem."

"Indeed?" Maik's eyes narrowed. "How so?"

"Well, I don't doubt the Charisians are going to raise Shan-wei's own hell with our coastal shipping," Thirsk said frankly. "The escorts I've been attaching to the local convoys have been enough to encourage *privateers*—even Charisian ones—to go hunting elsewhere. Of course, I have to admit that having the Temple lean on the Governor of Shwei didn't exactly hurt, either." The earl grimaced. "Distance is our best protection against privateers, to be honest, as long as there's no local port where they can dispose of their prizes.

"This is a *naval* squadron, though. Unless they come across something extraordinarily valuable to their war effort, they're not going to care about getting prizes home for disposal. They're going to be sinking and burning anything they can take, and their galleons are powerful enough to brush aside my escorts. Or perhaps I should say my *present* escorts."

He paused, and Maik pursed his lips. Then his eyebrows arched.

"You're thinking about the *training* opportunity, aren't you, My Lord?" There was a note of respect in his voice, and Thirsk shrugged.

"If I were commanding this little expedition," he said, "I'd have several objectives in mind. I'd want to do everything I could to hamper our naval buildup, which would mean coming as close as possible to shutting down our coastal traffic. I'd want to draw as much as possible of our attention to my activities here in order to discourage us from planning more offensive actions of our own somewhere else. And I'd want to prune back our strength. I'd want to suck Dohlaran and possibly Harchongese galleys and galleons into combat with *my* galleons on *my* terms so I could defeat them in detail and whittle them down. And, frankly, I'd want to impress on those inexperienced Dohlarans and Harchongese the fact that they really, truly don't want to confront *Charisian* seamen on blue water."

Maik was nodding, and Thirsk shrugged.

"Well, I'm not ready to take the ships we have off to Trove Island—or, even worse, *Claw* Island—to try to take it back. The best estimate we've got right now is that they have somewhere between fifteen and twenty galleons, and we have less than half our projected strength actually in commission." He shrugged again. "Oh, we've got forty-three theoretically ready for sea, but only about thirty have crews I'd consider fully worked up. And, let's be honest, even with all the training we've been able to give them, they're not going to be the equal of Charisian crews. Not yet. So if they've got twenty galleons, they'd probably still have the advantage against thirty of ours. I wouldn't be surprised if at least part of their thinking in taking the islands isn't a hope of drawing us into action in an effort to *retake* them."

"I hadn't thought about it that way," the bishop mused. "Take something we need to take back, then wait for us to come to them on their terms, you mean?"

"Something like that, yes." Thirsk nodded. "But if we decline to do that, they'll simply go ahead and begin raiding our shipping. At that point, they'll discover we're using convoys, and they won't be able to cover enough water just to locate something as elusive as a convoy unless they split up their own strength. I doubt their admiral's going to be willing to send out anything much smaller than four or five galleons, with one or two of their schooners to scout for them, even so. I wish he'd be that foolish, give *us* the opportunity to do the pouncing and the defeating in detail, but I doubt he will.

"On the other hand, he *will* have to come to us to raid our shipping. In that sense, the convoys are lodestones. They'll *attract* the Charisians, and the Charisians are a long way from home. I'm sure they brought a lot of naval stores—replacement canvas, extra spars, things like that—with them, but that's not remotely the same as having dockyard support. The same thing holds true for their manpower; what they have with them is all they're *going* to have. So even if the loss rate in an engagement is in their favor, strategically, it will be in *our* favor, because we *can* make our losses good. And, let's face it, in the long term, every ship Charis loses is going to hurt the Charisians worse than losing the same ship would hurt us, because, ultimately, our resources are so much deeper than theirs."

"So you're saying this is an opportunity to grind them down?"

"Yes, it is. And, even more importantly, if we do this the right way, we'll have the opportunity to blood some of our ships' companies. If our convoy escorts are strong enough to beat off a few attacks, even if we lose some merchant ships—or even a war galleon or two—the warships we *don't* lose will be steadily gaining experience. And confidence. As long as we don't simply get our arses kicked up between our ears, of course."

"Oh, of course."

Maik smiled, then leaned back while he thought. He stayed that way for several moments, then inhaled sharply, and nodded.

"I understand your points, Lywys, and I think they're all good ones. You'll certainly have my support with Duke Thorast and—if necessary—with Duke Fern, as well. Of course, if it turns out that they don't cooperate with you, we'll have to think of something else." He grimaced. "Doing *nothing*, unfortunately, is not an option."

"Nor should it be," Thirsk agreed. "Obviously, I don't think I'm wrong, but the possibility always exists. And if, as you say, they decline to cooperate with me, I'll just have to come up with something to change their minds, won't I?"

.V.

**HMS *Squall*, 36,
Hankey Sound,
Kingdom of Dohlar**

S tand by the starboard battery!"

Captain Ahrnahld Stywyrt watched the gap of gray-green water narrow as HMS *Squall* drove hard to the north-northeast, closing in on the Harchongese coaster. The small, lubberly fugitive had done its limping best to stay away from *Squall* when she and her consorts swooped down on the straggling cluster of brigs and sloops, but there'd never been much chance of that. The tubby little brig trying to evade destruction was less than half *Squall*'s size, with a correspondingly smaller sail plan and far less ability to carry sail in blustery conditions.

*And "blustery,"* Stywyrt thought, *pretty much sums up the day, doesn't it, Ahrnahld?*

Not that he had any urge to complain. The wind had risen steadily since dawn. By now, it was blowing a stiff topsail breeze out of the southwest, with wind speeds approaching thirty miles per hour and ten-foot waves. *Squall* was leaning heavily to the quartering wind, foaming towards her prey on the larboard tack, and she was making good just under nine knots. The poor little brig was making six, at best, and her desperate break for shallow water had come too late. Besides, *Squall* was one of the ICN's converted merchantmen; she drew little more than two-thirds as much water as a proper war galleon like Admiral Manthyr's flagship.

Stywyrt could see the merchant ship's captain standing by the taffrail, staring helplessly at the oncoming galleon, and wondered what was going through the other man's mind. Ships like the runty little coaster tended to be family affairs, with small crews who were mostly related to each other. There wouldn't be more than ten or twelve men aboard her—fifteen at the most— and a single accurate broadside from *Squall* would reduce her to a wrecked slaughterhouse. Her skipper had to know that, too. In fact, Stywyrt was more than a little surprised the man hadn't already hauled down his Church pennant and hove-to.

*Probably has something to do with the reports coming out of Zion,* he thought grimly. *If Clyntahn's willing to do that to vicars and archbishops, God only knows what he'd do to some poor bastard of a merchant captain for surrendering too quickly!*

Ahrnahld Stywyrt wasn't the sort to waste a lot of pity on the enemies of his Empire and his Church, yet he couldn't avoid a sort of disgusted compassion for the captain he was overtaking. The disgust wasn't for the hapless seaman, either.

*Well, I'll sympathize with him all day long, but I'll also send his sorry, ragged arse to the krakens, along with all his friends and relations, if he doesn't haul his wind pretty damned quick,* the captain told himself testily, and raised the leather speaking trumpet in his right hand.

"Master Mahldyn!"

"Aye, Sir?"

Lieutenant Zhames Mahldyn, *Squall*'s tall, thin first lieutenant, was well forward, standing beside the starboard chaser with his reddish-brown hair blowing in the wind. Now he looked back at his commanding officer, and Stywyrt pointed at the brig with his free hand.

"Encourage that fellow to see reason, Master Mahldyn!"

"Aye, aye, Sir!"

Stywyrt could see Mahldyn's huge, white grin all the way from the quarterdeck, and the lanky lieutenant bent over the fourteen-pounder's breech. He fussed for a moment, waving hand commands while the gun captain stood to one side, arms crossed, watching with a sort of resigned amusement. Despite the fact that Mahldyn was the officer responsible for ensuring the discipline of the ship's company (and his notion of appropriate punishment could be stiff), he'd always been popular with the men. Probably because he was ruthlessly equitable in the penalties he awarded. It was well known, however, that he'd always really wanted to be a gunner. He was fanatical about gun drill, insisting that every crew ought to consist solely of qualified gun captains, and he took every opportunity to work one of the guns himself.

Which meant the gun captain he'd so carefully trained got to stand there, watching the first lieutenant play.

Now Mahldyn took one more look along the barrel, waved the rest of the crew back, took tension on the firing lanyard, waited for exactly the right moment in *Squall's* movement, and pulled.

The fourteen-pounder bellowed, gun trucks squealing as it recoiled across the planking until the breeching ropes brought it up short. A huge gush of flame-cored smoke belched from the muzzle, and Stywyrt's eyebrows rose as the very first shot scored a direct hit.

The round shot punched through the brig's bulwark, slammed into the boat stowed atop the main hatch, tearing it in half and sending splinters hissing, then punched through the opposite bulwark and plunged into the sea well beyond the merchant vessel. At least one member of the Harchong crew was down, writhing around on the deck with both hands locked around his right thigh. *A splinter wound,* Stywyrt thought. They could be far nastier than they first looked, especially with their tendency to become infected.

He hadn't really expected Mahldyn to actually *hit* the brig. In fact, what he'd wanted was for the first lieutenant to fire across her bow. He started to say something sharp, then stopped and mentally replayed his own instructions.

*Damn. I didn't say "across the bow," did I? And I know how . . . enthusiastic Zhames is, too.*

He grimaced, but at least the single shot had produced the desired effect. The brig had let fly her sheets, spilling the wind from her sails in token of surrender, and Stywyrt looked up at his own sails.

"Back the main topsail!" he commanded, and feet pattered across the deck.

The main topsail yard swung around, taking the wind aback, the sail pressing against the mast, and *Squall* lost speed rapidly. She drifted slowly to leeward, coming down upon her prize while canvas flapped and the bosun marshaled a party to lower the starboard quarter boat while Stywyrt turned to Captain Bahrnabai Kaits, the commanding officer of *Squall's* Marine detachment.

"No nonsense out of them, Bahrnabai," he said. "We're closer to the shore than I like. Get their wounded man aboard the boat first, then check the cargo. Unless you find something interesting, make sure you've got everyone off and you've got her papers—assuming she's got any!—then burn her."

"Aye, Sir." Kaits touched his chest in salute, then jerked his head at his first sergeant. "You heard the Captain, Sergeant!"

"Aye, aye, Sir!"

Stywyrt watched a half-dozen Marines climbing into the boat along with the midshipman detailed to command it and the seamen told off as oarsmen.

The swinging davits were another new innovation of Sir Dustyn Olyvyr's, and Stywyrt heartily approved of the concept. They made it far easier—and safer— to drop a boat, and stowing a ship's boats on davits cleared a lot of precious deck space.

The boat hit the water in the galleon's lee, the oars dug in, and the boat went swooping across the steep-sided waves in a cloud of spray and wind. Stywyrt remembered his own midshipman days and boat trips just like that one, although most of his had been made in what was at least technically a time of peace.

*Well, the lad better get used to it now,* the captain thought soberly, turning and looking back to the south where two columns of smoke climbed into the heavens, announcing that two of the brig's fellow coasters had already been put to the torch. *Unless I miss my guess, he's going to be* my *age—at least—before* this *war's over. But in the meantime . . .*

He turned his attention back to his own prize, watching his boat go alongside, and shook his head. He felt a solid sense of satisfaction at depriving the Group of Four and its lackeys of the brig's cargo, yet he took no pleasure in the thought of destroying the little ship's crew's livelihoods.

*Nothing I can do about that, except see to it they're treated as well as we can until we put them ashore somewhere.*

He drew a deep breath, clasped his hands behind him, and began to pace slowly up and down the weather side of the deck.

# JUNE, YEAR OF GOD 894

S o, Koryn, what do you think this is all about?"
      "Father, if I knew that, I'd also know how to read minds, predict weather, choose the winning horse, and figure out where my left sock's gone," Sir Koryn Gahrvai replied, and Earl Anvil Rock laughed.

"I think we can probably make at least a few guesses, Rysel," Sir Taryl Lektor offered. The Earl of Tartarian sat at one end of the conference table, cleaning his fingernails with the tip of a penknife while he leaned back comfortably with the heels of his boots propped on the seat of the chair normally assigned to the Earl of Craggy Hill. Personally, Gahrvai suspected Tartarian hadn't exactly chosen that particular chair at random.

"Well, in that case, Taryl, guess away," Anvil Rock invited.

"First," Tartarian said. "Captain Athrawes asked to speak to just the four of us—not to the entire Council. Second, we all know how close the *seijin* is to the Emperor, and—unless I miss my guess—the Empress, as well. Third, Archbishop Maikel *isn't* going to be present."

He paused, holding up his left hand to admire his nails, and Anvil Rock snorted.

"And those three considerations suggest exactly what to your powerful intellect?"

"I strongly suspect the good Captain is going to deliver a message to us," Tartarian replied, looking across his hand at his old friend. "Given the Archbishop's absence, I would also suspect it's a seriously secular message. Possibly the sort of thing the Church doesn't want to know about."

"Why do you think he's waited so long to deliver it, in that case?"

"That's a bit harder," Tartarian conceded. "On the other hand, we know they've been receiving a steady stream of messages. So it seems most likely this is something he didn't know about until Cayleb sent him a dispatch."

"Except, My Lord," Sir Charlz Doyal put in respectfully from his place beside Gahrvai, "that Cayleb and Sharleyan left for Tellesberg over a month ago. Which means they're at sea right now, which would make sending any dispatches to *Seijin* Merlin a bit difficult."

"Rash and impetuous youngsters who point out holes in their elders' logic come to bad ends," Tartarian observed to no one in particular, and Doyal (who wasn't all that many years younger than the earl) chuckled.

"Still, Taryl, he has a point," Anvil Rock said.

"Of course he does. If he didn't, I'd simply annihilate him with the deadly force of my own logic and be done with it. As it is, I'm forced to admit I have no idea why the *seijin* has waited this long to discuss whatever it is with us. There!" He began working on the nails of his other hand. "I've admitted it. I'm fallible."

"Be still my beating heart," Anvil Rock said tartly, and it was Gahrvai's turn to laugh.

The truth was that *none* of them had any idea what Captain Athrawes wanted to speak to them about. Except, of course, that Tartarian was almost certainly correct about who the *seijin* would be speaking *for*. On the other hand, the atmosphere in the council chamber was enormously more relaxed—and confident—than it had been only a few months ago.

Gahrvai still bitterly regretted Father Tymahn's murder, yet Waimyn's decision to have him killed had clearly been the turning point here in Manchyr. Gahrvai wasn't about to issue any overly optimistic proclamations of triumph, but the incidence of violence had plummeted following Waimyn's arrest, and the ex-intendant's execution had evoked not protests and riots, but something much closer to a huge sigh of relief. Anti-Charis broadsides were still being tacked up on doors throughout the city. Temple Loyalists continued to gather in their own churches, following their own priests. Parties of Charisian Marines continued to draw glowers, even the occasional catcall, but no one actually threw dead cat-lizards any longer. In fact, they didn't even throw overripe tomatoes.

The Charisian occupation was still a source of resentment, yet most Corisandians—in the southeast, at least—seemed prepared to accept, if only grudgingly, that the Charisians were doing their best to avoid walking all over them.

The fact that Viceroy General Chermyn had been scrupulous about observing both local law and customary usages wherever possible hadn't hurt. And the fact that the Charisians obviously trusted Gahrvai's guardsmen to serve as the princedom's primary peacekeeping force hadn't been lost on Corisandians, either. The acid test, in many ways, had come when three Charisian Marines raped a young farm girl. Gahrvai had gone straight to Chermyn, and the viceroy general's response had been quick and decisive. He'd ordered the suspected rapists' arrest, impaneled a court-martial, and had Gahrvai's guardsmen bring in the Corisandian witnesses. The defense counsel's questioning had been sharp, but those witnesses had been given full credence, and the court's verdict had been swift. The Articles of War set only one penalty for forcible rape, and the guilty parties had been marched to the very farm where the crime had taken place for execution.

That hadn't been the only incident of swift, impartial justice, either. To be fair, there'd been far fewer such incidents than Gahrvai would have expected. In fact, he was unhappily aware that his own army, when he'd been resisting the Charisian invasion, had committed more crimes against Prince Hektor's subjects than the invaders had. There'd been additional infractions, of course—Charisians might be well behaved, but they were scarcely saints! Theft, looting, the occasional fistfight or beating, and at least two deaths, one of which had clearly been a matter of self-defense on the Charisian's part. Yet the princedom's subjects had been forced, many against their will, to concede that "the occupation" truly was determined to enforce *justice* and not just Charisian authority.

*And then there's Staynair,* Gahrvai thought. *That man is* scary. *It's just not natural. He's a Charisian and a heretic . . . and I think he could probably talk a slash lizard into eating out of his hand.*

His lips twitched a half-smile, yet he wasn't certain the thought was entirely hyperbole. Maikel Staynair had never once apologized for the Church of Charis' schismatic fervor. He'd drawn the line between the Church of Charis and the Temple Loyalists as unflinchingly in every sermon he'd given as in the very first, and no one who'd seen and heard him preach could doubt his unswerving devotion to that schism for a single moment. And yet, for all the adamantine power of his personal faith and bitter defiance of the vicarate and the Group of Four, he radiated a gentleness, a kindliness, only the most bigoted could deny.

Many of those bigots did just that, but Gahrvai had watched Staynair walk down the nave of cathedrals and churches throughout the capital. He'd seen the "foreign Archbishop," the "apostate heretic" and "servant of Shan-wei," pause to lay his hand on children's heads, speak to those children's parents, stop entire processions for a word here, a blessing there. It must have been a living nightmare for the people responsible for keeping him alive, because there was no way anyone could have guaranteed there were no hidden daggers in those houses of God.

Yet he'd done it anyway. He'd reached out, embraced, welcomed. And everyone in each of those cathedrals and churches had heard the tale of what had happened to him in Tellesberg Cathedral. They knew that *he* knew, from direct and personal experience, how easy it would have been for someone to repeat that attack. And, knowing that, still he chose to walk among them, risk exactly that.

Archbishops weren't supposed to be like that. They were supposed to be regal. They were supposed to visit their archbishoprics once a year. They might celebrate mass in the cathedrals adjacent to their palaces, but they didn't go to small churches—like Saint Kathryn's, or the Holy Archangels Triumphant. They passed through congregants like the princes of Mother Church they were, not stopping to bounce a baby in their arms, or lay a soothing hand on an ailing toddler, or bestow a gentle blessing on a bereaved widow. They dispensed Mother Church's rulings and justice, and they governed, but they didn't scoop a grubby six-year-old up in their arms, laughing and tickling, heedless of their exquisitely tailored cassocks, when they went to visit one of Mother Church's orphanages.

Corisande had no idea what to make of him. For that matter, Gahrvai wasn't certain what to make of Staynair himself. He wasn't accustomed to encountering saints . . . *especially*, he thought more grimly, in an archbishop's vestments.

*Of course, he's not a saint—he'd be the very first to insist on that! But until something better comes along . . . .*

The sound of an opening door pulled him up out of his reflections, and his eyes narrowed as Merlin Athrawes stepped into the council chamber.

The *seijin* crossed to the conference table and bowed courteously.

"My Lords, thank you for allowing me to speak to you," he said.

"I don't really think there was ever much probability that we wouldn't 'allow' you to speak with us," Anvil Rock said dryly.

"Perhaps not." Merlin smiled. "Still, there *are* appearances to maintain."

"Indeed there are." Anvil Rock cocked his head thoughtfully. "I'm sure you won't be surprised to discover that we've been speculating amongst ourselves on exactly why it was you wished to speak with us, *Seijin* Merlin. Am I correct in assuming you're here on the Emperor and the Empress's business?"

"You are, of course."

"In that case, I suppose we ought to invite you to sit down," the earl said, pointing at an unoccupied chair across the table from his son and Doyal.

"Thank you, My Lord."

Merlin unhooked the scabbard of his katana, laying it on the table in front of him, then sat and folded his hands on the tabletop.

"Very well, *Seijin*," Anvil Rock invited. "You have our attention."

"Thank you," Merlin repeated, then smiled slightly.

"My Lords," he began, "by this time, I'm sure, the entire world knows the Emperor has his own personal *seijin* bodyguard. As you may have heard, however, I've never actually claimed to be a *seijin*. The truth, so far as I know, is that there *are* no true *seijins* in the sense of all the old fables and folktales."

He made the admission calmly, and his audience stirred. Anvil Rock leaned forward, one elbow propped on his chair arm, and Tartarian frowned thoughtfully.

"If you go back to the tales of *Seijin* Kohdy, for example," Merlin continued, "you'll find he's capable of all sorts of magical, mystical feats, from mind reading to levitation to talking to great lizards. And let's not forget his magic sword and his ability to walk through walls, either." He smiled crookedly.

"Trust me, My Lords, there have been quite a few times I've wished I *could* walk through walls. Unfortunately, I can't.

"Yet that isn't to say that there's not a certain core of truth in those fairy tales." His smile vanished. "And, while I've never actually claimed to be a *seijin*, I have to admit I do have *some* of the capabilities ascribed to *seijins*. As such, the label has a certain applicability, and it provides a convenient . . . handle. Or perhaps it would be better to say a mental pigeonhole people can tuck me into."

He paused for a moment, studying his audience, then shrugged.

"The reason I've brought this up, My Lords, is because I may not be so unique as you've assumed. Or, to put it another way, there may be more '*seijins*' around than you might have guessed."

All of his listeners stiffened. They looked at one another quickly, then leaned towards him as one, and his smile was back, a bit fainter and even more crooked than before.

"When I first offered my services to King Haarahld, and then, later, to Emperor Cayleb, it wasn't on a whim, My Lords," he told them flatly. "I won't pretend I foresaw everything that's happened since, but I did see which way the wind was setting, and I knew where I stood. Yet when I offered Charis my sword, that wasn't all I brought to Tellesberg with me, nor did I truly come alone. If it's accurate to call me a *seijin* at all, because of the abilities I possess, then I'm not the only *seijin* on the face of Safehold."

"You're not?" Anvil Rock said quietly, when Merlin paused once more.

"Of course not, My Lord." Merlin shook his head. "Of course, even the fables insist not all *seijins* are warriors. They may also be councilors, teachers, mentors, even spies."

"Yes, they do say that," Doyal said slowly, and Merlin smiled at him.

"Indeed, they do, Sir Charlz. And it happens there are quite a few '*seijins*' right here in Corisande."

"There are?" Anvil Rock sat up very straight, and Merlin nodded.

"Yes, My Lord. In fact, Sir Koryn's already had evidence of that."

"I have, have I?" Gahrvai considered Merlin across the table.

"Assuredly." The *seijin*'s smile turned into something remarkably like a grin. "It came in the form of a rock tossed through your study window."

"That was a *seijin*?" Gahrvai's eyebrows rose, and Merlin chuckled.

"If *I'm* a *seijin*, that was most definitely a *seijin*, too, General. This entire Princedom's been under observation, My Lords—starting even before the Emperor invaded." He shrugged at their incredulous expressions. "Obviously, not even our network can see everything. If it could, we'd know who ordered Prince Hektor's assassination, and we don't."

His unearthly sapphire eyes hardened as he made that admission. Then he inhaled deeply.

"We can't see everything, but we see a great deal, and as Sir Koryn can attest, we're quite good at getting information into the hands of the authorities when it seems appropriate. Which is the reason I asked to speak to you today. I've received several reports while here in Corisande confirming something Their Majesties have expected for some time. Since Archbishop Maikel is scheduled to leave the Princedom at the end of next five-day, and I'll be leaving with him, my . . . contacts here in Corisande will probably need to provide information directly to you after I've left. Specifically, to Sir Charlz and Sir Koryn. Since those contacts' effectiveness depends on their anonymity and unobtrusiveness, any reports from them will be in written form, and they'll find their own ways into your hands."

"By flying through windows?" Gahrvai asked sardonically, and Merlin chuckled.

"We'll try to be a bit less destructive than that," he said.

"I hope none of your fellow *seijins* come to grief trying to creep through our sentries," Anvil Rock said a bit tartly. The earl clearly found the concept of overly clever spies sneaking about in black, hooded cloaks less than amusing.

"I think that's . . . unlikely to happen, My Lord."

"You mentioned you've received reports confirming something the Emperor and Empress have been expecting?" Doyal said slowly, and Merlin nodded, his expression sobering.

"I have, indeed," he said. "Specifically, I've received this."

He produced an envelope, laying it on the table in front of him.

"All jesting aside, My Lords, our agents here in Corisande have confirmed that Earl Craggy Hill, among others, is engaged in an active conspiracy against both the Empire and this Council."

Every face around the table tightened, less in surprise than with tension.

"That's a serious charge, *Seijin* Merlin," Tartarian said after a moment. "It would be a serious charge against *anyone*; against someone of Craggy Hill's stature—not to mention his membership on this Council—it becomes extraordinarily so."

"Trust me, My Lords, Their Majesties are fully aware of that. Just as they're aware Craggy Hill isn't acting alone. In fact, he's coordinating with Earl Storm Keep, Earl Deep Hollow, Duke Black Water, Baron Larchros, Baron Barcor, and at least a dozen other minor knights and landowners, not to mention quite a few bankers and merchants in northern Corisande." His audience was staring at him now, their expressions fixed. "In addition, Bishop Mailvyn in Barcor, Bishop Executor Thomys, and Amilain Gahrnaht, the ex-Bishop of Larchros, as well as several dozen other Temple Loyalist clergy are involved . . . the majority in violation of their vows to Archbishop Klairmant."

The others stared at him for several heartbeats, then exchanged quick glances.

"I won't pretend I haven't nourished my own suspicions about some of the people you've just named, *Seijin* Merlin," Tartarian said then. "Coupling them all together, though . . ." He shook his head. "That's a pretty hard mouthful to swallow. And, to be blunt, it's going to take some extremely solid evidence to convince me to accept it."

"I'm sure it will, My Lord. And, to be honest, I'm *relieved* it will."

"'Relieved?'" Anvil Rock's expression contained more than a hint of suspicion. "And why might that be, *Seijin* Merlin? I'd think that if such a serious conspiracy were truly underway you'd want us to act immediately!"

"My Lord, Their Majesties have known about this conspiracy literally for months now. Their agents have amassed quite a lot of evidence over that time, and that evidence will be made available to you. However, Their Majesties have no desire for you to act precipitously or ill-advisedly."

"No?" Anvil Rock's eyes narrowed.

"The truth is, My Lord, that Their Majesties have deliberately allowed this to go forward without drawing it to your attention. First, because they feared you'd act as immediately and vigorously as is your wont. Normally, that would be a good thing. In this case, however, Their Majesties, with Prince Nahrmahn's advice, preferred to allow the conspirators to fully commit themselves so that when we *do* act, there will be no question about their guilt. No room for anyone to legitimately suggest that Their Majesties—or the Regency Council—have trumped up the charges as a means of purging the Princedom of personal enemies. Second, however, there was another factor, another conspirator whose commitment Their Majesties have been awaiting."

"Should we assume the 'conspirator' in question is now committed, then, *Seijin* Merlin?" Doyal asked.

"You should, Sir Charlz," Merlin said calmly. "According to our agents, Grand Duke Zebediah has now pledged to provide modern, rifled muskets to the conspirators. Moreover, we have evidence that the rifled muskets in question will be provided by a traitor attached to the Duke of Eastshare's headquarters."

If their expressions had been incredulous before, they were far more disbelieving—and shocked, this time.

"*Rifled muskets?*" Anvil Rock got out in a half-strangled voice, rearing back in his seat in astonishment. "From Eastshare's own *headquarters*? Are you telling us the *Duke* is—?"

"Of course not, My Lord!" Merlin waved one hand. "I've personally discussed this matter with Duke Eastshare on Their Majesties' behalf. His immediate impulse was to order the traitor's immediate arrest. As Their Majesties' envoy, however, I was able to talk him out of that."

"You were able—" Gahrvai began, then stopped abruptly, his eyes lighting with speculation. Merlin simply gazed at him for several seconds, until Gahrvai began shaking his head and leaned back in his chair once more.

"So you think they've got enough rope now, do you?" he asked softly.

"Something along those lines," Merlin acknowledged, with a slight, seated bow. The other Corisandians looked at Gahrvai, and then Tartarian began to nod.

"So the Emperor and Empress have decided to cut off the kraken's head, is that it?" the earl said, and there was a hint—faint, but unmistakable—of something very like admiration in his tone.

"Precisely, My Lord." Merlin shrugged. "Grand Duke Zebediah's agent in Duke Eastshare's headquarters is unaware we've been very carefully tracking the rifles he thinks he's managed to 'lose.' We've followed them every step of the way from the manufactories in Old Charis to Chisholm, and we can establish—with both witnesses and written testimony—the exact point at which he diverted them from the Imperial Army depots for which they were bound.

"Other of our agents have been tracking his correspondence with Grand Duke Zebediah, just as we've become aware of certain documentary evidence in Earl Craggy Hill's possession proving Zebediah's involvement. It's Their Majesties' intention to allow those rifled muskets to be *delivered* here, in Corisande. When that happens, you'll be informed—as will Viceroy General Chermyn. At that time, the Viceroy General, on Their Majesties' behalf, will request your assistance in moving against the conspirators. The Imperial Navy will provide sealift to transport your forces, supported by the Viceroy General's Marines, to arrest the conspirators and seize the weapons and other evidence."

"Langhorne," Anvil Rock said softly. He looked more than moderately stunned. Tartarian, on the other hand, wore a remarkably evil-looking smile.

"I never did like Zebediah," he remarked. "And Craggy Hill's been a pain in the arse from the instant Prince Hektor was assassinated."

"And I can't say it breaks *my* heart that Barcor's up to his cowardly arse in all this," Gahrvai observed almost dreamily.

"Mine, either," Doyal said rather more grimly, reaching down to massage the leg which had been half-crippled at Haryl's Crossing.

The four Corisandians looked at one another, and Merlin sat back in his own chair to let them think. After several minutes of silent introspection, their attention returned, one by one, to him.

"May I ask how long Their Majesties—and let's not forget Prince Nahrmahn—have been allowing this little plot to simmer?" Tartarian asked finally.

"From the moment they found out about it," Merlin replied. "I suppose I should admit, though, that we've been keeping an especially sharp eye on Grand Duke Zebediah from the very beginning."

"Of course you have!" Anvil Rock snorted. "Anybody but a blind, drooling idiot—which, by the way, Emperor Cayleb has amply demonstrated he *isn't*—would be watching him with *both* eyes!"

"Why do I have the distinct feeling, *Seijin* Merlin, that this proof of Zebediah's treason didn't exactly devastate Their Majesties?" Tartarian inquired.

"Partly, I suppose, because it scarcely came as a surprise, My Lord," Merlin said. "And also, I suspect, because they're rather relieved to get it out of the way as soon as possible." He shrugged. "The way the Emperor put it, the question was never whether or not Zebediah would betray his oaths, but simply a matter of when. That being the case, Their Majesties are quite happy to have unambiguous, demonstrable *proof* of his treachery."

"And the same thing's true here in Corisande, isn't it?" Anvil Rock's eyes were shrewd.

"And the same thing is true here in Corisande, yes, My Lord." Merlin met the earl's gaze levelly. "I realize many of the people who have been party to this conspiracy consider themselves patriots. In their position, I might feel the same way. Not all of them do, however, and whether they do or not, Their Majesties propose to levy the most severe penalties only upon those who have betrayed their own sworn oaths. I'm not suggesting everyone else involved will get off scot free, because they won't. But I believe you've seen in Viceroy General Chermyn's approach to the disturbances here in Manchyr and the surrounding lands the proof that Their Majesties have no desire to be bloody despots. Punishment will be meted out only in accord with law, and where practical, compassion will have a voice in sentencing.

"Hopefully, at the end of the day, we'll be able to—as Earl Tartarian put it—cut off the kraken's head in a single blow, without a pitched battle and with a minimum of bloodshed. Their Majesties want *all* of the traitors, My Lords, but one reason they want them is to ensure we won't have to do this again and again."

Merlin looked back at the Corisandians, his blue eyes steady.

"Cayleb and Sharleyan aren't Zhaspahr Clyntahn. They take no pleasure in cruelty or blood. But they are determined to put an *end* to this business, once and for all, because you may be certain men like Craggy Hill and Zebediah and Barcor aren't planning on shedding *their* blood in the name of Corisandian independence. They're planning on shedding *other* people's blood in the name of their own power, and Their Majesties have no intention of letting them do that."

*W*ell, at least we *found* them, Captain Ahrnahld Stywyrt told himself. *Of course, figuring out what to do with them now that we have is another problem.*

Stywyrt smiled thinly, then grimaced as the leading Dohlaran galleon fired another broadside. His own *Squall*, bringing up the rear of the abbreviated—very abbreviated—Charisian battleline, had yet to engage, and it was going to be a while yet, unfortunately, before she could.

The late-morning sun was hot, burning down on the blue waters of Hankey Sound, the southern lobe of the Gulf of Dohlar, and the green slopes of Dragon Island, to the east, but the stiff breeze out of the northwest was brisk, almost chill. It piled up nine- or ten-foot waves, and the copper-bottomed *Squall* forged along on her southeasterly heading at almost seven knots under topgallants and single-reefed topsails with the wind fine on her larboard quarter. The Dohlaran ships, holding their course to the southwest on the starboard tack as the two forces slowly converged, had the wind nearly abeam. It was close to their best point of sailing, yet they were making no more than six knots. Unfortunately, they were between the Charisians and their intended prey, and there were five of them.

Three of the Dohlarans were already in action with HMS *Dart*, leading the Charisian formation. Captain Zhon Pawal, *Dart*'s skipper and the senior officer present, was a veteran of Rock Point, Crag Reach, and Darcos Sound, and his ship was one of Sir Gwylym Manthyr's newest vessels. *Dart* was actually five and a half feet longer than *Empress of Charis*, Emperor Cayleb's preferred flagship, yet she mounted ten fewer guns. Sir Dustyn Olyvyr had come to the conclusion that *Empress of Charis* was going to be overgunned, too heavily laden for her displacement, even before she'd been completed. The fact that she'd quickly begun to hog after she came into service, her keel bending upward amidships because of the heavy weights bearing down on the ends of her hull, had only confirmed his initial fears. Her powerful broadside had made her a fearsome foe, yet once it became obvious his concerns had been well placed, there'd been little choice but to reduce her armament. Having seen the problem coming, however, he'd taken pains to avoid it when he designed the *Sword of Charis*–class ships, and, in addition to reducing weights and increasing displacement, he'd experimented with diagonal planking as a means of further increasing her longitudinal strength.

As a result, *Dart* carried her designed armament with ease. She mounted the same number of thirty-pounders as *Empress of Charis*, but only twenty carronades, and the additional length on the gundeck seemed to have produced a higher rate of fire. And although she carrried fewer of them, her carronades threw *fifty-seven*-pound round shot, instead of thirty-pound shot, which actually increased her weight of broadside. She also carried her guns slightly higher, and her scantlings were thicker. All of that made her the ideal ship to be leading the Charisian line at this particular moment, but it didn't change the fact that she was engaged against three enemy vessels.

HMS *Shield*, *Dart*'s next astern, would be able to come to her assistance in the next ten or fifteen minutes, but *Squall* had been detached up to windward when the enemy was spotted. Her merchant ship origins also made her, little though Stywyrt liked admitting it, the slowest sailor of the three, and she'd lost ground on her consorts during the pursuit. It was evident she was still faster than the Dohlaran galleons, yet on their present courses, she was at least forty minutes—more likely an hour—from any range at which *she* could engage. On the other hand, the two rearmost vessels in the Dohlaran formation lagged almost as badly.

*But they're not supposed to be keeping formation this well.* Stywyrt realized his own thoughts sounded plaintive, almost petulant. *Sir Gwylym told us Thirsk was the most dangerous fellow on the other side, but this is ridiculous!*

It was mostly a fluke that they'd encountered this convoy in the first place. Captain Pawal's detachment had been cruising off the northeast coast of Shwei Province's Harris Peninsula, looking for shipping in the waters between Parrot Point, to the north, and Sandy Head, to the south. They'd had reports that foundries in Shwei were shipping guns to the Dohlaran yards in Gorath, and Sir Gwylym had posted Pawal to intercept that traffic.

They'd intercepted five small brigs which had, indeed, been laden with Harchong-cast bronze artillery, and Captain Pawal had found prize crews to send them back to Claw Island. He'd disliked giving up the men for those crews, but their cargo of guns had been too potentially valuable not to send them in. After that, though, there'd been almost a full five-day of boring inactivity before Lieutenant Commander Showail, in the ten-gun schooner *Flash*, on the eastern flank of Pawal's formation, had spotted topsails farther to the east. That had been the evening before, and they'd gone in pursuit, chasing all through the night by moonlight . . . and with *Squall* slowly falling yet farther astern. Now, the better part of thirty hours later, they'd finally overtaken the convoy, and the Dohlaran galleons had peeled off and turned to place themselves between the pursuers and the merchantmen.

*Showail never would've spotted them if not for the escorts,* Stywyrt thought now. *The merchant ships' masts were too short to sight until we got closer.*

The fact that the galleons had betrayed the convoy's presence might turn out to have been something of a mixed blessing, however. All the Dohlaran warships were larger than *Squall*. None were as large as *Dart* or *Shield*, perhaps, yet Stywyrt's best estimate was that they carried at least two hundred guns to the truncated Charisian squadron's hundred and forty-four. The Dohlaran weapons were probably lighter, yet that was still a considerable disparity.

At the moment, *Flash* and her slightly larger sister, *Mace*, were both off sliding around the Dohlaran galleons' rear. The pair of galleys assigned to the coasters' close protection were new, bigger, and more powerful than anything Dohlar had taken to Armageddon Reef, but Stywyrt doubted they'd be any match for the nimble, well-handled schooners' carronade broadsides. Unfortunately, between the galleys and the galleons, it was likely most of the coasters would escape if they scattered soon enough. Each schooner might be able to run down two of them—possibly even three, if they disposed of the galleys quickly enough—but there were fourteen of them. If *Squall* and her galleon consorts had been able to lend a hand, the entire convoy would undoubtedly have been obliterated.

Which wasn't going to happen now.

▼　　▼　　▼

Captain Caitahno Raisahndo smiled in fierce satisfaction as HMS *Rakurai*'s starboard broadside thundered again. His gunners probably weren't being as accurate as he might have liked, but they were maintaining an impressive rate of fire, especially for a ship's company which had never before seen battle.

He could have wished he had the weather gauge, instead of being forced to engage from leeward, but at least he was to windward of the *convoy*. He'd been tempted to detach HMS *Prince of Dohlar*, his rearmost galleon, to assist the galleys assigned to the coasters' close escort. Unfortunately, *Prince of Dohlar* couldn't have gotten there before the infernally fast, Shan-wei-damned Charisian schooners. By the same token, however, all five of Raisahndo's ships were between the Charisian *galleons* and the convoy, and he was satisfied none of them were going to break past him to assist in the merchant ships' massacre. Not without fighting their way through, at any rate.

*And the truth is, even if I am never going to admit it to a single soul, that pounding two or three Charisian galleons into driftwood would be worth the loss of the entire convoy.*

As a converted merchantman, *Rakurai* lacked the poop deck of the Dohlaran Navy's purpose-built galleons. As a result, her wheel, quarterdeck guns, and officers were completely exposed to overhead fire. On the other hand, it meant Raisahndo had (at least in theory) a clear view as he stood by the starboard rail, gazing towards the enemy. Unfortunately, he was also staring directly into the choking bank of evil-smelling powder smoke rolling back across *Rakurai*'s decks on the wind. That was another problem with being to leeward. Not only did his gunners have to cope with their own smoke, blowing straight back into their faces, but the Charisian artillery's smoke came driving down across them, as well. The wind was brisk enough to clear their own smoke quickly, actually, but there were always fresh clouds of *Charisian* smoke to replace it. All they could really make out were their target's masts above the seething, stinking fog bank, and that couldn't contribute to their accuracy.

Another Charisian broadside came smashing back. They seemed to be firing a bit more slowly, but they were scoring an unpleasant number of hits. And each of those hits did substantially more damage than Raisahndo estimated his own, lighter pieces were accomplishing. He'd expected thirty-pounders, even thirty-five-pounders, from Earl Thirsk's reports of Crag Reach, and he hadn't looked forward to the disparity in weight of metal. Unfortunately, at least some of his present opponent's guns were even heavier than that, and he winced as one of his own quarterdeck twelve-pounders took a direct hit.

The round shot came screaming in through the bulwark gunport at just enough of an angle to chew a perfectly rounded half-moon out of the forward edge of the open port's frame. It slammed into the gun carriage, apparently at a slightly rising angle, and struck the underside of the twelve-pounder's barrel. The ton-and-a-half bronze gun tube erupted upward, leaping out of the explosion of splintered carriage timbers and shattered ringbolts like a sounding doomwhale. Half the eight-man crew was killed as the enormous round shot slashed directly through them; two of the four survivors were crushed and broken as the barrel of their own weapon crashed back down on top of them.

Something—probably a splinter; possibly a broken iron bolt—hissed by Raisahndo's right ear, close enough to make his head ring as if someone had just slapped him . . . hard.

*Another inch or two, and I wouldn't have to worry about anything ever again,* he thought, then brushed the thought aside as he contemplated the carnage that single hit had left in its wake.

*Probably one of those damned "carronades,"* he reflected grimly. At least they knew what the Charisians *called* the shorter, stubbier guns, but that didn't help a lot when the Temple had decreed that all of *Mother Church's* galleons would be equipped solely with long guns.

In some ways, Raisahndo actually agreed with Vicar Allayn's logic. The "carronades" clearly had a shorter maximum range than a long gun of the same bore, and the ability to pound the enemy (and kill his crews) before he got into range to return the compliment had a great deal to recommend it. There were, unfortunately, a few flaws in that logic.

For one thing, Earl Thirsk was right about the two sides' relative seamanship. Much though Raisahndo hated to admit it, a Corisandian admiral was far more likely to achieve the engagement range he wanted than a Dohlaran admiral was to prevent him from doing so. Even ignoring that, however, Vicar Allayn seemed to be still thinking in terms of conventional boarding actions, despite the logical disconnect between them and the greater range he wanted from his longer guns. He seemed more interested in larger numbers of lighter guns, suitable for sweeping an opponent's decks just before closing to board, than in smaller numbers of *heavier* guns, capable of smashing their way through an enemy ship's timbers at longer ranges. Killing the other fellow's crewmen was all well and good, in Raisahndo's opinion, but boarding actions had clearly become secondary (at best) to artillery duels. And, in an artillery duel, if the other fellow's gunners were protected by heavy bulwarks your artillery couldn't penetrate, he was going to be far better placed to kill your personnel than you were to kill his.

*Oh, stop complaining, Caitahno!* he scolded himself. *You've still got more guns than they do, and more ships than they do, and it's time you concentrated on what you're going to do to* them *instead of what* they're *going to do to* you!

"Let her fall off a quarter point!" he shouted to the helmsmen.

▼　　▼　　▼

Captain Zhon Pawal watched the leading Dohlaran galleon's masts as the other ship altered course slightly. He was turning a bit further away, and Pawal would have liked to think that meant he'd had enough. Unfortunately . . . .

*He's just giving himself a little more range until his friends get here,* Pawal thought harshly. *Not exactly what I expected. They were* supposed *to either run the hell away or come in as a mob, like they did at Rock Point and Darcos Sound.*

Pawal began to pace slowly up and down, well clear of the recoiling carronades. The range had fallen to a bit over two hundred yards, well within the fifty-seven-pounders' effective range, and he bared his teeth as he contemplated what those massive shots must be doing to their targets.

But the fierce grin faded slightly as the enemy's fire continued slamming back. They weren't especially accurate, those gunners over there, but they were damnably persistent. It was the first time Pawal had faced an actual broadside, and he was frankly astonished by how steadily the Dohlarans were standing up. The sheer weight of Charisian fire had broken the morale of ship after ship at Rock Point and Darcos Sound, but it wasn't doing that this time.

*Or not from this* range, *at least,* he told himself, and looked astern, where Harys Aiwain's *Shield* was coming up fast. With all the smoke, he could no longer see *Squall's* sails, but she had to be somewhere behind *Shield.* He *hoped* she was, at any rate! The two leading Dohlarans continued to pound away at *Dart,* but the third and fourth enemy galleons were beginning to fire on *Shield.* Aiwain wasn't firing back yet, though. He was clearly reserving his own first broadside until he reached the range he wanted . . . assuming he got there.

"Bring her a point to larboard!" Captain Pawal snapped.

▼　　▼　　▼

Captain Stywyrt watched the mast tops poking up out of the boil of smoke as *Dart*'s head came a bit farther north, moving the wind around to almost dead astern as Pawal moved to prevent the enemy from holding the range open. Stywyrt approved, although he wished the other captain had waited a bit longer and let *Squall* get closer before he'd done it.

*Shield* foamed steadily along in her consorts' wake, and he still had a clear view of Captain Aiwain's ship through his spyglass. As a result, he could see the white feathers leaping from the wave slopes like sudden fountains as the Dohlarans began to fire at *Shield*. From the scattered appearance of those feathers, the enemy's gunners weren't overly blessed with accuracy, but there were obviously a *lot* of them.

Even as that thought crossed his mind, a hole punched itself abruptly through *Shield*'s main topsail. The range from *Shield* to the closest Dohlaran galleon was down to two hundred yards, at the most, Stywyrt thought, and wondered how much longer Aiwain was going to wait.

▼    ▼    ▼

Harys Aiwain looked up as the round shot punched through *Shield*'s main topsail with the sound of a giant, slapping fist. She'd taken at least three more hits on her way in, but so far, there was no report of casualties. *Shield* was a shorter, stubbier ship than *Dart*, a sister of HMS *Dreadnought*, the very first galleon designed as a warship from the keel up. She carried the same number of guns as *Dart*, although her battery was more cramped than the later, larger ship's and her carronades were only thirty-pounders, and she was a bit slower under most conditions. Her frames and timbers, though, were heavier than those of any converted merchantman, and they'd stood up well to the handful of hits the Dohlarans had so far achieved.

*Looks like Commodore Seamount was right about their powder being weaker than ours,* Aiwain thought. *Of course, it doesn't hurt that their guns are lighter, to boot!*

He knew at least some of the Dohlaran artillery was lighter, at any rate; all he had to do was peek over the hammock nettings and look down at the twelve-pound shot standing half-buried in his ship's side just forward of her number twenty-seven gunport. He doubted any of his own thirty-pound shot would fail to penetrate when the time came.

*Of course, as we get closer,* they'll *start punching through, too,* he reflected. *That will be unpleasant.*

He looked across at the nearest Dohlaran. The range was coming down on a hundred yards, and he heard a sudden scream from below decks as at least one Dohlaran shot finally got through. He didn't know whether it had penetrated *Shield*'s timbers or come through an open gunport, but whichever it had done, he didn't doubt he was going to start taking more casualties very soon.

"Stand to, the larboard battery!" he shouted to Mohtohkai Daikhar, his first lieutenant.

▼    ▼    ▼

Sir Dahrand Rohsail glowered into the blinding smoke as it cascaded back across HMS *Grand Vicar Mahrys*. He stood on the starboard poop deck ladder, three feet above the level of his quarterdeck, trying to see across the netted hammocks which formed a (hopefully) musket-proof barrier along the rail. At the moment, the stinking tide of smoke that spewed out with each broadside rendered his efforts to see anything more or less useless.

Rohsail's fifty-gun ship was one of the first of the Royal Dohlaran Navy's new-construction galleons, and he'd been more than a little surprised when he received command of her. He'd never made any secret of his personal allegiance to Duke Thorast, and he shared the duke's dislike for the Earl of Thirsk to the full, if not for all the same reasons. Although Rohsail was never going to forget all he owed to Thorast's patronage, he couldn't deny—in the privacy of his own thoughts—that Thirsk had clearly been right and Duke Malikai had obviously been *wrong* before Rock Point. Anyone with the least awareness of how court politics worked knew it would have been foolish to expect Thorast to commit the disastrous folly of *admitting* his brother-in-law's stupidity had pissed away almost the entire peacetime navy, yet even the duke must know it was true. *Rohsail* did, at any rate!

For that matter, the captain was willing to admit the advantages of the signal flags Thirsk had copied from the damned Charisians. The degree of control—of the ability to communicate between ships—they provided was priceless, and he shuddered to think of how things might have worked out if it had remained a Charisian monopoly. In fact, he'd been forced to concede Thirsk had a clearer, more realistic view than Thorast, in almost every respect, of the kinds of ships and tactics needed to knock those arrogant Charisian bastards back on their heels.

All that was true, and Rohsail knew it. But he also knew the earl was systematically gutting the Navy in the process. He was promoting *commoners* over nobles, insisting *gentlemen* had to accept "schooling" from uncouth, low-born *merchant seamen*, like Ahndair Krahl, of the *Bedard*. He was undermining discipline with his foolish restrictions on how it could be enforced. And this madness of his, requiring a seaman's wage be paid directly to his family, if that was his choice, when he was at sea. And that it had to be paid in full and on time!

Rohsail had no objection to paying the men their wages . . . eventually. But money was always tight. Sometimes decisions had to be made about where to spend limited funds, and seamen aboard a warship didn't have anything to spend money *on*, which made not paying them until the end of the commission a reasonable way to husband scanty funds. Of course, sometimes they couldn't be paid immediately after a ship paid off, anyway, but there were always brokers willing to buy up their delayed wages for a twenty percent commission or so. And if a man got himself killed at sea—which was bound to happen fairly frequently—the Navy didn't have to pay *anyone*, now did it? But not according to Thirsk!

Even without the insanity of lifetime pensions for widows and orphans, insisting wages be paid immediately to a man's family was going to play hell with the Navy's finances in the fullness of time. *Mother Church* might be able to afford it, but there was no way the Kingdom of Dohlar could continue the practice once the heretics were crushed. And who was going to end up being blamed and hated by the common lower-deck scum when it had to be abandoned? Not Earl Thirsk, that was for certain! No, it would be left to Duke Thorast to clean up the mess, and they'd be lucky if they avoided mutinies in the process.

*And when that happens, the way Thirsk's cut the balls off navy discipline isn't going to help one bit, either,* Rohsail thought grimly. "The lash can't make a bad seaman good, but it *can* make a good seaman bad," indeed! *The lash is all most of them* really *understand! The way Thirsk's sucking up to them is going to leave all of us even deeper in the shit when it comes time to clean up behind him.*

But this wasn't the time to pick fights with the man Vicar Allayn and Vicar Zhaspahr had selected to command the Dohlaran Navy. That time would come once the disastrous consequences of Thirsk's more outlandish policies became apparent, and Rohsail was rather looking forward to that day of comeuppance. In the meantime, though, there was a war to fight, and as insane as Earl Thirsk might be in altogether too many ways, at least he understood what had to be done if that war was going to be won.

*Grand Vicar Mahrys* heaved as she blasted yet another broadside into the smoke, and Rohsail smiled thinly as he pictured what that torrent of iron must be doing to its target.

*I wish I could see the damned thing,* he admitted to himself. *Still, I can see the* masts, *and the rest of the frigging ship has to be somewhere under them!*

He snorted in harsh amusement at the thought and climbed the rest of the way up the ladder to the poop deck. He'd be more exposed from there, but maybe he could actually *see* something up to windward.

▼　　▼　　▼

A fresh Dohlaran broadside came howling in. This one was better aimed, and Harys Aiwain watched a round shot carve its way through the midships bulwark. Splinters of shattered planking, some of them three feet long or more, went hissing across the deck, and tatters of shredded canvas flapped wildly as the shot tore through the tightly rolled hammocks standing on end and netted between the stanchions atop the bulwark. Two men went down on the number five carronade. One of them hit the sanded deck limply in a splattered spiderweb of blood, but the other screamed, clutching at the jagged splinter standing out of his right shoulder. Someone dragged the wounded man clear, and two men from the starboard battery—one each from number six and number eight carronades—moved quickly to replace the casualties.

The captain absorbed all those details, as well as the fresh holes appearing in his fore topsail and a length of shrouds blowing sideways in the wind as it was clipped off by yet another round shot. But he absorbed them with only a corner of his brain; the rest of his attention was focused on the third ship in the Dohlaran line. She was almost directly opposite *Shield* now, and no more than fifty yards away. He waited a moment longer, and then his sword slashed downward.

"*Fire!*"

▼　　▼　　▼

*Shield* fired on the downroll.

In point of fact, Captain Aiwain's range estimate had been slightly off; the actual distance to *Grand Vicar Mahrys* was only forty yards, and the avalanche of *Shield*'s fire crashed into Rohsail's ship with devastating effectiveness. Despite the fact that *Grand Vicar Mahrys* had been designed and built as a warship, her frames and timbers weren't as heavy as *Shield*'s, and the thirty-pound Charisian round shot sledgehammered through them with contemptuous ease, slamming across the Dohlaran's gundeck in butchering fans of splinters.

Aiwain's gunners were far more experienced than Rohsail's. They could see their target more clearly, and they were better judges of their own ship's motion, as well, and they timed *Shield*'s roll almost perfectly. Despite the short range, despite their experience, a great many of their shots managed to miss, anyway. Only someone who'd actually fired a smoothbore cannon in the midst of the smoke and thunder and howling chaos of a naval battle could truly realize just how difficult it actually was to hit something the size of an enemy warship under those circumstances, even at relatively short range. But far *fewer* of *Shield*'s gun crews missed their target, and none of their fire went high. Every hit smashed into their target's hull, and they were close enough to hear the screams.

▼　　▼　　▼

Captain Raisahndo grimaced as the second Charisian ship came into action. There was no mistaking the sound of that single, massive broadside—or, for that matter, the sudden eruption of fresh smoke. He peered aft, trying to decide which ship the Charisian had targeted. It was hard to make out details. In fact, he could barely see HMS *Bedard*'s headsails as she sailed along in *Rakurai*'s wake. It didn't look as if Ahndair Krahl's ship had been hit, though, and Raisahndo was unpleasantly confident that a Charisian broadside fired at such short range wasn't going to completely miss its target.

*Must've been* Grand Vicar Mahrys, he decided.

The thought evoked mixed emotions. Personally, Raisahndo hated Sir Dahrand Rohsail right down to his oh-so-nobly-born toenails. The man was an arrogant, aristocratic prig who'd never bothered to hide the fact that he was a member in good standing of the officers sucking up around the Duke of Thorast. Or, for that matter, to hide his disagreement with Earl Thirsk's notions of shipboard discipline. On the other hand, he'd *complied* with Thirsk's restrictions on the use of the lash, whether he agreed with them or not, and he had guts. He'd actually been willing to learn at least the rudiments of seamanship (however much he'd hated taking lessons from commoners), for that matter, and no man who lived could question his willingness to come to grips with the enemy.

*I may hate the bastard, but the bloody-minded son-of-a-bitch is in the right place right now!*

▼　　▼　　▼

Rohsail staggered as a section of rail five feet to his left disintegrated. Something slammed into his shoulder with brutal force, nearly knocking him to his knees, and he heard shrieks from the waist of the ship, where the bulk of the broadside had gone home. His right hand clutched convulsively at the undamaged rail in front of him, keeping him on his feet somehow, and he turned forward.

His left shoulder felt broken, his arm dangling uselessly at his side, but there was no sign of blood, and a corner of his brain wondered what had hit him. There was no time to worry about that, however, and he stumbled forward to lean on the poop deck rail, staring toward the bow.

Most of the enemy's fire had gone in low, punching into *Grand Vicar Mahrys'* gundeck. From the screams, it must have inflicted Shan-wei's own lot of casualties, he thought, then reminded himself not to assume the worst. A wounded man's shrieks could be loud enough for two or three, after all.

But at least some of those round shot had plowed across the upper deck. Unlike Charisian ships, *Grand Vicar Mahrys* mounted no guns on her forecastle, but she did mount ten on the upper deck in the waist, five in either broadside.

Now there were only *two* in action to starboard.

Rohsail's jaw tightened. One of the three silenced twelve-pounders was permanently disabled, dismounted by a direct hit; the other two appeared to be intact, but most of the sixteen men who'd manned them were down, either dead or wounded. Of the forty men who'd crewed all five pieces, no more than a dozen were on their feet, and they were all busy dragging dead and wounded crewmates away from the still serviceable guns.

*Grand Vicar Mahrys* was barely a hundred and sixty feet long, yet billowing smoke—most of it rolling down from the enemy's guns, now—made it difficult to pick out details forward of the waist. From what he *could* see, though, at least another half dozen or so seamen and soldiers serving as shipboard infantry were down, as well. And that was only the upper deck; there was no telling how many men had been killed or wounded on the *gundeck*.

Yet, despite the screams and the blood, Rohsail's other gunners were still in action. They were firing independently now, as quickly as each crew could reload, without the disciplined unanimity of controlled broadsides. The cannon's thunder was a hellish cacophony, an almost uninterrupted succession of bellowing discharges. Accuracy had to be suffering as each gun captain fired blindly into the smoke at whatever *he* thought was the appropriate point in the ship's roll, but they were *firing*, and even through the bedlam, he heard shouts—of encouragement from officers and petty officers, and of defiance from sailors and soldiers.

He looked up. There were holes in several sails, severed sheets and halyards blew on the wind here and there, and at least four or five dead men sprawled over the edge of the maintop where they'd been marked down by the spitefully cracking rifles of Charisian Marines. Nothing critical seemed to have carried away, though, and even as he watched, topmen were swarming through the rigging, heedless of round shot and bullets alike, to repair the ship's running rigging.

They'd never be anything but common-born scum, Rohsail thought—all too many of them the sweepings of Gorath's gutters. Yet as he watched them dragging dead and wounded messmates towards the center of the deck, making repairs in the teeth of the Charisian fire, tossing broken bits of railing and fallen blocks off the breeches of their guns, reloading and firing again and again, he felt a fierce stab of pride in them.

"Lay it to them, lads!" he heard himself shouting. "*Lay it to them!*"

▼    ▼    ▼

Captain Stywyrt swore under his breath, restraining a most uncaptainly temptation to pound a fist on the binnacle, as the fury of the artillery exchange mounted. From his own position, astern and still up to windward, he could see *Dart*'s and *Shield*'s masts clearly as their course folded together with the Dohlarans. They were in action with three of the five Dohlaran galleons now, and the fourth enemy ship was about to pile in.

So far, all of *Dart*'s and *Shield*'s rigging seemed intact; both ships were still under control, and unlike the Dohlarans, still firing controlled broadsides. That told Stywyrt a great deal. Despite the fury of the engagement, despite the fact that they were about to find themselves fighting at two-to-one odds, both Pawal and Aiwain were still firing *broadsides*, rather than going to independent fire. He suspected each of them was also engaging only a single enemy ship, as well, preferring to methodically smash one target at a time rather than split their fire between two targets and inflict lighter damage on both. That took cool nerves, since it meant at least one of their opponents was left undisturbed, her gunners free to load and fire without worrying about round shot or grapeshot screaming into their own faces. By the same token, it gave them a far better chance of completely disabling one of their foes relatively quickly.

He turned his own attention to the last galleon in the Dohlaran line. She seemed to be smaller than the others, little larger than his own undersized *Squall*. Despite that, though, her captain was crowding on more sail as Stywyrt watched, resetting his courses to get more speed. Obviously, he intended to pile onto *Dart* and *Shield* as quickly as possible.

*More gutsy and determined than smart,* Stywyrt thought. *Dart and Shield are both faster than any of them are. He may be able to overtake them with his courses set, but he's only going to cramp their own formation once he gets there. He certainly won't be able to get up to windward of Zhon and Harys whatever he does! In fact, he'll have to haul out of line or run into one of his own consorts!*

It was a mistake, although as mistakes went, it was preferable to a lot of others. At least that other captain was determined to get *into* action, rather than hold back to *avoid* it, and that said unpleasant things about the degree to which the Royal Dohlaran Navy's morale must have recovered since Rock Point and Crag Reach.

*Well, we'll just have to see what we can do about that, won't we, Ahrnahld?* he thought grimly.

▼      ▼      ▼

Captain Raisahndo was in no position to see what Captain Mahrtyn Zhermain's *Prince of Dohlar* was doing. The dense smoke made that impossible from deck level, and the men aloft, including those detailed as lookouts, were (understandably) more focused on the Charisian ships alongside than on their own consorts. If Raisahndo *had* been able to watch *Prince of Dohlar's* maneuvers, however, he would have fully endorsed Ahrnahld Stywyrt's analysis of Zhermain's actions. At the same time, little though he would have liked what Zhermain was doing, he would also have agreed with Stywyrt that too much aggressiveness was a far better problem to have than too much timidity.

Just at the moment, however, Raisahndo had rather more pressing things to worry about. The leading Charisian galleon was slowly closing the range, despite Raisahndo's own turn away, and her fire was both unpleasantly heavy and dismayingly accurate. The steady, measured bellow of her guns—obviously still firing in controlled broadsides—was like the rhythmic concussion of some giant's spiked boots, tramping relentlessly across *Rakurai's* decks. He was confident he was scoring more hits of his own, now that the range had dropped, but Charisian round shot were beating in *Rakurai's* bulwarks and side like the remorseless blows of that same giant's club.

A half dozen of *Rakurai's* guns—a quarter of her entire larboard battery—were out of action now, and the pile of bodies along the centerline of the deck was growing thicker. Wounded men were being dragged below to the healers and surgeons, making it hard to form any detailed estimate, but Raisahndo suspected that he'd taken at least forty or fifty casualties. That was almost one in eight of his entire company, yet the crew—experienced seamen and pressed landsmen alike—stood steadily to their guns, firing back as quickly as they could reload.

The Charisian continued to fire low, smashing broadside after broadside into *Rakurai*'s hull, slaughtering her crewmen steadily, while the marksmen in *Dart*'s tops fired across at their Dohlaran counterparts or down into the smoke below. At least a few Charisian shot had gone high, though, and *Rakurai*'s deck was littered with fallen blocks and lengths of cordage. Raisahndo had seen two or three men felled by those heavy, plunging blocks, and he castigated himself for not having thought of the protective rope nets he'd observed aboard the Charisian galleons before fire was opened. Obviously, they'd been rigged above the enemy's decks to catch debris—and bodies—falling from overhead, and he made a mental note to suggest that Dohlar adopt the same practice in his report to Earl Thirsk.

Of course, first he had to get back to *make* that report.

▼　　▼　　▼

Zhon Pawal's head jerked up as something cracked thunderously overhead. For a moment, he didn't know what it had been, but then his eyes widened as he saw the entire main topmast beginning to topple.

*Oh, shit*, he heard a mental voice say almost calmly, and then he was dodging as the wreckage began to plummet.

▼　　▼　　▼

"*Yes!*"

Captain Ahndair Krahl of HMS *Bedard* realized the voice shouting that single word was his own. It probably wasn't a properly heroic thing for the captain of a king's ship to be doing, but at the moment, he didn't much care. His gun crews had been pounding away at the lead Charisian for what seemed like hours, whatever his lying pocket watch said, without any apparent effect. He hadn't even been able to convince the bastard to divert any of his fire to *Bedard*. Instead, the enemy had continued to hammer mercilessly at *Rakurai*. Krahl couldn't see the flagship clearly, but he *could* see Raisahndo's sails becoming more and more tattered, and, difficult as it was to form any accurate judgment in such a bedlam, it sounded to him as if *Rakurai*'s fire had begun to drop.

Now he watched his target's main topmast, topgallant, and royal pitch slowly to larboard like some falling forest giant. The mizzen royal went with it, and for a moment, he hoped the foremast might go, as well. He was disappointed in that, but the Charisian galleon seemed to stagger as over half her set canvas went thundering over the side.

Now *what, you bastards?* he thought.

▼    ▼    ▼

*Dart* slowed precipitously with the abrupt loss of power. Captain Pawal was astounded that the fore royal and topgallant didn't go, as well, but he felt the sudden drag of the wreckage landing in the water alongside, still tethered to the ship by shrouds and stays, only too clearly. The overhead nettings—still more or less intact, although they'd snapped like cobwebs where the butt of the main topmast had fallen across the larboard bulwark—were littered with broken wood, fallen blocks, and long snakes of cordage.

Somehow, the men on the wheel managed to maintain control, and axes and even cutlasses were flashing amid the tangled-snake chaos of fallen rigging as the bosun and his mates led parties of seamen to cut away the wreckage. Until they could, though, almost half of *Dart*'s larboard guns were blocked by the debris lying across their ports. That was bad enough, but the lost speed meant the Dohlarans would begin drawing ahead. They were going to be able to bring all five of their ships into action against the head of Pawal's own line.

He'd lost his speaking trumpet in the scramble to avoid the plummeting wreckage, so he cupped his hands around his mouth in an improvised substitute.

"*Master Daikhar!*"

*Dart*'s first lieutenant managed to hear him despite the tumult, and Pawal pointed urgently at the suddenly stubby-looking mainmast.

"Get the course on her!" he shouted.

Daikhar looked at him for a moment, then nodded in obvious understanding. The course wasn't part of the ship's normal fighting sail. It was too big, too cumbersome, and too close to the upper deck when it was set. The loss of the main topsail and topgallant sail had to be compensated for somehow, though, and the first lieutenant started dragging men out of the damage control parties and off of the disengaged guns and starting them aloft.

Pawal left him to it, turning his own attention back to the enemy, and his jaw tightened as he saw the Dohlaran sails beginning to move ahead, exactly as he'd feared.

▼    ▼    ▼

Harys Aiwain swore vigorously as *Dart* slowed. He had no choice but to reduce sail himself if he was going to keep station on the flagship. Part of him wanted to overtake *Dart*, instead, and get around in front of her. But if he did, his own guns would be masked by *Dart*'s hull as he passed along her disengaged side, preventing him from firing a shot until he'd cleared Pawal's ship.

His mind worked feverishly, considering alternatives. At the moment, he didn't know whether or not the Dohlarans meant to push the engagement fully home. If they wanted to break off, satisfied they'd protected their convoy, the damage to *Dart*'s rigging offered them the perfect opportunity to do just that.

If, on the other hand, they wanted to stay and fight it out, that same damage would give them a pronounced maneuvering advantage.

There was no doubt in Aiwain's mind what a *Charisian* squadron would do, but Dohlarans weren't Charisians. They might decide to content themselves with the knowledge that they'd already done far better against Charisian war galleons than anyone else had managed, and the convoy—currently under attack by *Flash* and *Mace*—was their primary responsibility.

*Best stay where we are and pound their trailers as hard as we can,* he decided, but he also beckoned one of his midshipmen to his side.

"Get forward, Master Walkyr," he told the white-faced twelve-year-old flatly. "I want you at the fore topgallant crosstrees. You watch the flagship—don't take your eyes off her! If she alters course or you see one of these bastards working around ahead of her, you get your arse back down here and *tell* me! Got it?"

"Aye, aye, Sir!" the youngster replied, and went scampering off through the smoke and the thunder.

▼    ▼    ▼

Ahndair Krahl's ship crept steadily farther forward, running broadside-to-broadside with the bigger, more powerful, but lamed Charisian galleon. Round shot hammered back and forth, and despite her damage aloft and the growing number of shot holes Krahl could see in her bulwarks and side, the Charisian was still giving as good as she got.

And her guns were still heavier than anything he had, a point driven home as a Charisian round shot crashed through *Bedard*'s side, killing a dozen men and shattering the carriage of one of her gundeck twenty-five-pounders.

He looked aft, to where *Grand Vicar Mahrys* was finally beginning to draw clear of her duel with the second Charisian. Krahl was no fonder of Sir Dahrand Rohsail than Rohsail was of him. Despite that, he had to admit the arrogant, aristocratic prick was no slouch. *Grand Vicar Mahrys* had taken a severe hammering from her opponent's more powerful artillery. Krahl wasn't positive, but he thought he could actually see blood trickling from the scuppers of Rohsail's ship. Despite that, her guns were still in action, and as he watched, they switched targets and began pounding the leading Charisian along with *Bedard* while Mahrdai Saigahn's *Guardsman* took up the second Charisian's challenge.

▼    ▼    ▼

Ahrnahld Stywyrt made himself stand motionless, hands clasped behind him, face expressionless, as the Dohlarans crowded in on *Shield* and *Dart*. The smoke was so dense now that he could see only the upper masts of the enemy galleons, but it was obvious what was happening. With *Dart* slowed and *Shield* trapped behind her, the lead Dohlaran galleon was forging steadily ahead of the two Charisian ships. It wouldn't be long before she was in a position to swing farther to the west, trying to head the Dohlaran line, possibly even get into a position to rake *Dart* from ahead.

*And I'm* still *not in a position to engage!*

He glared up at his own sails, then made his decision.

"Shake out the topsail reefs, Master Mahldyn!" he said crisply. "And after that, we'll have the royals on her, if you please."

▼  ▼  ▼

*Oh, you bastard,* Zhon Pawal thought grimly.

*Dart*'s deck was heaped with dead and wounded. The wreckage of masts, sails, and spars had been cleared away and the ship was under complete command once more, but even with the main course set, she was losing ground to her opponents. The lead Dohlaran was two ship's lengths ahead of her, and the second ship in the Dohlaran line was starting to range ahead, as well. The third galleon had moved up to batter away at her, although that ship seemed to have been pretty well battered herself. Astern, he could hear *Shield* still in furious action—with the fourth ship in the Dohlaran line, now—and Pawal's eyes were set and hard as he watched the angle of the first Dohlaran's masts begin to shift.

She was making her move to cut across *Dart*'s course, and he turned to his own helmsmen.

"Bring her two points to starboard!" he ordered.

▼  ▼  ▼

"Sir! *Sir!*"

Harys Aiwain turned towards the high-pitched voice. Midshipman Walkyr ran towards him, barely even hesitating as a seaman staggered back. Both of the wounded man's hands flew up to clutch at the blood-splashed ruin where his face had been, and he fell to the deck directly in front of Walkyr. The boy simply hurtled over the body and slid to a stop, gasping for breath.

"What?" Aiwain demanded.

"Sir," Walkyr panted, "*Dart*'s altering to starboard! About two points, I think! And . . . and I couldn't see for sure, but I think it's because the enemy's trying to get round in front of her!"

"Good lad!"

Aiwain slapped the boy on the back, then wheeled to his helmsmen.

"Three points to starboard!" he snapped, then raised his speaking trumpet.

"Hands aloft! Shake out the reefs and prepare to loose courses!"

▼  ▼  ▼

*Dart* swung to starboard, altering course to take the wind on her starboard beam, as *Rakurai* tried to get around in front of her. *Dart* was turning inside the smaller ship, giving her a shorter distance to travel, but *Rakurai* was considerably faster now, and the duel between them redoubled in ferocity. *Bedard*, keeping station on *Rakurai*, continued to fire furiously, pounding away at *Dart's* quarter, and Pawal was devoutly grateful that the Dohlarans' accuracy matched neither their discipline nor their determination.

Despite that, his ship was badly hit, and he knew it. He'd lost five guns out of his larboard broadside, and his starboard gun crews had been badly thinned by the need to replace killed and wounded in the other battery. He'd never had enough gunners to completely man both broadsides simultaneously; at this rate, he wouldn't have anybody at all on the starboard guns entirely too quickly.

Someone cheered suddenly, and he wheeled back around just in time to see *Grand Vicar Mahrys'* mizzenmast pitch over the side. The Dohlaran galleon slowed abruptly, and it was obvious the wreckage was hampering her steering. As Pawal watched, her main topgallant followed the mizzen and the battered Dohlaran fell off before the wind, drifting down to leeward.

Something loomed in the corner of his vision, and he looked to starboard just as *Shield* came forging up on his disengaged side, leaning hard to the wind with the reefs shaken out of her topsails and her courses set below them. Her lee gunports were barely two feet above the wave tops as she heeled heavily, and he knew instantly what Aiwain had in mind,

He snatched off his hat, waving it at the other ship.

"Look at that, boys!" he shouted. "*Shield's* going to bloody those bastards' nose for them!"

At least some of his men heard him, and he heard them raise a cheer in reply. It wasn't much of a cheer, not with so many of them already down, but it was far from defeated, and he bared his teeth in a fierce grin.

*Of course, there's still the two bastards Aiwain was fighting before*, he thought harshly. *I'm sure* they'll *be alongside us soon enough. But let the lads cheer for now.*

▾     ▾     ▾

Even with her increased sail, *Shield* had needed a good fifteen minutes to overtake and pass *Dart*. She'd been out of action that entire time, and Harys Aiwain had felt the dull ache of his clenched jaw muscles as he heard the renewed thunder of artillery from behind him. He knew the fourth and fifth Dohlaran galleons were crowding in on *Dart*, battering away at the badly wounded flagship with fresh fury, yet there was nothing he could do about that. Pawal was just going to have to hang on while *Shield* dealt with *Rakurai* and *Bedard*.

At least the respite had given time for him to reorganize his gun crews, reload carefully, and carry out some of the most essential rigging repairs while *Shield* forged ahead, leaning to the pressure on her canvas. He felt himself urging her along as she crept steadily ahead of *Dart*, and his brain clicked like one of the newfangled abacuses, calculating ranges and bearings.

"Brail up the courses!" he shouted as the abacus in his head came together with a glimpse of the lead Dohlaran's mastheads above the thinning smoke. Hands dashed to sheets and tacks and clewlines, and the sails began rising like huge curtains drawn by invisible hands.

The smoke was even thinner now. *Shield* was well ahead of *Dart* and still traveling considerably faster, and . . .

There!

"On the *uproll!*" he barked, then paused a moment and—

"Fire as you bear!"

▼    ▼    ▼

Caitahno Raisahndo stood drumming the fingers of his right hand on the binnacle and squinting against the omnipresent, choking smoke as *Rakurai* crept slowly but steadily ahead. Another ten minutes, fifteen at the outside, and he'd be far enough ahead to come still farther up to windward. With the Charisian's rigging damaged, *Rakurai* was certain to be able to get closer to the wind. With just a very little luck, he was going to cross *Dart*'s bows and—

Another ship's bowsprit and headsails pushed suddenly clear of the smoke, and Raisahndo's squinted eyes flew wide. It was the second Dohlaran galleon, and she'd set her courses without his noticing through the smoke and the confusion.

*And through my concentration on their lead ship*, he admitted, and cursed himself for letting it happen. He shouldn't have permitted his attention to narrow, but it was too late for that now.

The Dohlaran captain was running a risk carrying that much canvas in the middle of a battle. The wind pressure on the additional sail area increased the strain on his rigging badly—even a normally minor hit aloft could produce serious damage to masts or spars under those conditions—and too much heel could drive his opened gunports under, flooding his ship. But he'd accomplished what he wanted, and his untouched courses, already disappearing as he cleared the obstacle of his flagship, looked impossibly white and pure against the dirty gray walls of smoke and the torn and stained canvas above them.

Raisahndo didn't have long to contemplate their beauty, however. Even as he began to bark orders of his own, fire flashed in *Shield*'s gunports.

▼    ▼    ▼

The range was just under two hundred yards. That was long range for a naval engagement, but *Shield* had been given time to get ready for it, and for the first time, she was firing on the uproll, *not* the downroll. The carefully aimed and prepared broadside scorched across the water between her and *Rakurai*, and the Dohlaran ship's foremast disintegrated.

▼    ▼    ▼

"*Damn it!*" Raisahndo swore viciously as his foremast went over the side. His main topgallant mast went with it, and *Rakurai* wallowed at the sudden loss of sail area. The abrupt disappearance of the headsails made bad infinitely worse. Their most important function was to counterbalance her rudder and mizzen during maneuvers; with them gone, she fell off even more quickly than *Grand Vicar Mahrys* had.

*Shield* altered course as well, preparing to swoop down on *Rakurai* and fin-ish her off, but *Bedard* charged forward to intercept her as Captain Krahl inter-posed his ship between her and his own damaged flagship.

▼    ▼    ▼

Zhon Pawal staggered, all but knocked off his feet as one of his quarterdeck Marines slammed into him. For a moment he thought the corporal had been hit, but *only* for a moment. Just long enough for the Marine to shove him out of the way of the toppling mizzen.

The falling mast crushed at least three other members of *Dart*'s crew, and the galleon staggered almost as badly as her captain had. Like the upper sections of the mainmast before it, the mizzen plunged over the side, dragging at the crippled ship, and once more axes and cutlasses flashed amid the wreckage.

Pawal took one heartbeat to slap the Marine on the shoulder in acknow-ledgment and thanks, then turned back to the battle as HMS *Guardsman* and HMS *Prince of Dohlar* charged up to complete *Dart*'s destruction.

▼    ▼    ▼

Captain Mahrtyn Zhermain couldn't see what was happening ahead of the Dohlaran flagship. In fact, he couldn't see much of *anything* through the chok-ing smother of gunsmoke. It was everywhere, blinding watering eyes, tearing at noses and lungs. Despite frequent gunnery practices, he truly hadn't realized until this moment just how thick and totally obscuring the smoke from so many cannon was going to be. But he could still make out the ghost-like, foggy shape of the target he'd been closing in upon for so long.

"*Fire!*" he shouted, and *Prince of Dohlar*'s first broadside ripped into *Dart*.

▼    ▼    ▼

An entire section of *Dart*'s midships bulwark disintegrated. Two of her car-ronades were dismounted, and another twenty-three of her crew were killed or wounded. Captain Pawal staggered into the carnage, shouting orders through a throat that felt ripped raw, lending his own hands to clear away the wreckage.

*She can't take a lot more*, he thought. *She just can't.*

"Stand to your guns, boys!" he heard himself shouting. "*Hammer* the bas-tards!"

▼   ▼   ▼

The enemy's fire was finally beginning to falter, Mahrdai Saigahn thought, and about damned time, too. Now that his own *Guardsman* and *Prince of Dohlar* had gotten to grips with her, the Charisian galleon had been engaged against all *five* members of Captain Raisahndo's squadron . . . and she'd given as good as she'd gotten to all of them.

*They may be frigging heretics,* Saigahn thought harshly, *but they've got Chihiro's own guts! Not that it's going to do them much good very much longer.*

"Pound her!" he shouted. "Pound the bitch!"

▼   ▼   ▼

Zhermain watched *Dart's* mizzen crumple and, like Saigahn, he realized it was only a matter of time, now. He still didn't know what was going on at the head of the line, but with three Dohlaran galleons against a single Charisian, he wasn't too concerned about that. No, that was up to Raisahndo, Krahl, and Rohsail. He and Saigahn had their own kraken to land, and—

▼   ▼   ▼

"*Fire as you bear!*"

It had taken far too long, but Ahrnahld Stywyrt felt his lips draw back in a hunting dragon's grin. The smoke and the Dohlarans' concentration on *Dart* and *Shield* had concealed *Squall's* approach. He hadn't been able to see the enemy much better than they could have seen him—assuming they'd been looking—but he'd steered by what he could see of their mastheads. Now, leaning dangerously to the wind with all sail set to the royals, *Squall* came charging out of the smoke, erupting almost directly across *Prince of Dohlar's* stern at a range of barely thirty yards.

Gunport by gunport, all down her starboard side, double-shotted new-model krakens and thirty-pounder carronades bellowed. There were eighteen guns in that broadside. They hurled thirty-six carefully-aimed iron balls, each six inches in diameter, down the full length of *Prince of Dohlar's* decks. The Dohlaran galleon's stern windows disintegrated, and round shot screamed the full length of her gundeck, killing gunners, dismounting weapons.

Mahrtyn Zhermain never had time to realize what had happened before one of those round shot tore him in half. Another dismounted three of *Prince of Dohlar's* quarterdeck guns. That single broadside killed or wounded a third of the galleon's entire crew, and, even worse, one shot smashed into her tiller head, and her wheel spun loosely as her rudder flapped freely.

With no way to steer, she fell off, pivoting to point her bow straight downwind.

▼　　▼　　▼

"Hard a larboard!" Stywyrt snapped. "In royals and courses!"

Acknowledgments came back, and the wheel spun to the left as the top-men poised aloft started fisting in the canvas.

*Squall*'s rudder kicked to the right, and the ship turned sharp to starboard. Her speed had carried her past *Prince of Dohlar*, and her new heading brought her swinging back around onto a southwesterly heading.

"Hands to sheets and braces! Back the main topsail!"

With so many men tending to her sails, *Squall* had only enough men to man a single broadside, but she slowed abruptly as the main topsail was thrown aback. It reduced her speed even more quickly, steadying her up just as *Prince of Dohlar* fell completely off the wind and pointed her bow into *Squall*'s starboard broadside.

"Fire!"

Another broadside ripped into the staggering Dohlaran. There was no way for Stywyrt to know how devastating his two broadsides had been. *Prince of Dohlar* was obviously badly hurt, yet there was no time to finish her off. *Guardsman* was still furiously engaged against *Dart*—Stywyrt couldn't even tell if the Dohlaran galleon realized what had just happened to her consort—and *Dart*'s fire was beginning to falter.

"Larboard your helm!" he commanded once more, and *Squall* came sweeping still farther around, taking the wind on her starboard bow. "Brace round the main topsail, Master Mahldyn! Hands to the larboard battery, there!"

▼　　▼　　▼

Mahrdai Saigahn wheeled around in shock at the sudden eruption of cannon fire astern of him. For just a moment, his mind was completely blank, unable to grasp what it could be. Then, like the flash of Langhorne's own *rakurai*, understanding struck, and he swore vilely.

Damn it! *Damn* it! He'd *known* there were three of them all along, and he'd let himself forget. Let himself get so focused, so concentrated on the ship alongside, that he'd completely ignored the threat of its second consort!

Even through the blinding banks of gunsmoke, he could see *Prince of Dohlar*'s masts swinging around as she fell downwind. Despite the fact that her rigging appeared intact, it was obvious she was no longer under control, which meant either her wheel or her rudder must have carried away. In either case, she was no longer able to maneuver, and Saigahn swore again as the third Charisian, main topsail briefly backed to slow her as she charged along under an insane press of canvas, poured a second raking broadside into *Prince of Dohlar*'s bows.

Even as he watched, the Charisian galleon was slicing up to lay herself between *Guardsman* and her current opponent, and Saigahn felt his belly knot at the thought of suddenly finding himself engaged at two-to-one odds. Especially two-to-one odds half of which was the completely untouched galleon which had just effectively knocked *Prince of Dohlar* out of action with just two broadsides.

"Starboard your helm!" he commanded, and *Guardsman* fell quickly off to larboard. She swung downwind, momentarily offering her stern to *Squall*, as she broke away to leeward.

▼     ▼     ▼

It was Ahrnahld Stywyrt's turn to swear.

*Squall* was still moving faster than either *Dart* or *Guardsman* as he used her momentum to drive between the other two galleons. Even his well-drilled crew was frantically busy as gunners thundered across the deck from right to left and *Guardsman*'s abrupt turn exposed her stern. It would have been the perfect, lethal opening to rake his second opponent . . . if *Squall*'s own heading hadn't robbed him of the opportunity. His larboard battery was loaded and ready, his starboard guncrews had gotten there in time to man the guns, but the two ships' relative motion carried *Guardsman* outside the arc of *Squall*'s fire until she'd swung far enough to come almost parallel to her. Instead of the rake he'd *almost* achieved, the two ships passed in opposite directions, larboard-to-larboard on what amounted to reverse headings, with *Guardsman* to leeward of *Squall*. Stywyrt's gunners were as disappointed as their captain by the lost opportunity, but they recovered quickly and poured a destructive broadside into their foe as they passed.

*Guardsman* was unable to reply. She'd been engaged against *Dart* with her *starboard* battery. Her larboard guns had never been loaded or run out, and her crew was still frantically casting off lashings when *Squall* fired.

The range was much longer than the range to *Prince of Dohlar* had been, and double-shotted guns were notoriously inaccurate at anything above half-pistol shot. On the other hand, *Squall*'s gunners were very good, and *Guardsman* staggered amid a chorus of screams as a fresh hurricane of iron blasted into her.

▼     ▼     ▼

Mahrdai Saigahn was no coward, or he would never have been handpicked by the Earl of Thirsk as one of his first galleon commanders. Yet he was no more immune to the effects of surprise than the next man, and he felt something entirely too much like panic as the Charisian broadside crashed into his ship.

*Stop it!* he commanded himself fiercely. *Yes, you let the bastards sneak up on you. Accept that—and deal with it!*

He shook his head, like a man shaking off a punch to the jaw, then drew a deep breath and looked around, assessing the situation.

*How did it go to shit so quickly?* he wondered a moment later.

*Prince of Dohlar* was drifting on the wind, completely out of control. She'd cleared the worst of the smoke, as had *Guardsman* on her present course, and

Saigahn could see her clearly now. Not that it was much comfort; judging from the chaos on her decks and the bodies hanging in her tops and draped over her hammock nettings, she must have been hit extraordinarily hard by the Charisian's two broadsides. Worse, there was no evidence of any organized response to her difficulties, and Captain Zhermain was too good, too competent, for things to be . . . drifting that way if he were still on his feet.

That was bad enough, but *Grand Vicar Mahrys* was even farther downwind than *Prince of Dohlar* or *Guardsman* herself. Unlike Zhermain's ship, Rohsail clearly had *Grand Vicar Mahrys* under command, but her rigging had been severely damaged. It looked as if even Rohsail had had enough, and as Saigahn saw the streams of red oozing down her sides, human blood literally running from her scuppers, he didn't blame the other captain one bit. And, just to make Saigahn's day complete, *Rakurai* was making clumsily off to leeward, as best she could without foremast or headsails, as well.

Which meant that, in effect, his own *Guardsman* and Krahl's *Bedard* were the only effective Dohlaran galleons left.

He looked back astern, where *Squall* had altered course yet again, coming up alongside *Dart*. Even as Saigahn watched, the Charisian flagship's fore topgallant and fore royal seemed to bend forward slowly, buckling into the smoke in a welter of snapping shrouds and stays. No one had been firing at her at the moment, so it had to be the result of cumulative damage, but Saigahn wasn't about to complain.

More guns thundered from the southwest, and he turned his attention that way to see *Bedard* breaking off, as well. Ahndair Krahl was maintaining a brisk fire on his larger opponent, but his true purpose was clearly to cover his own wounded flagship until she could get clear.

*And what the hell do we do?* Mahrdai Saigahn asked himself harshly.

▼    ▼    ▼

Harys Aiwain watched *Bedard* veering away. Instinct urged him to follow up, crowding the smaller ship and pounding her into submission. Or at least driving her off while he finished his business with the Dohlaran flagship.

Unfortunately, he still didn't know what was happening astern of him. What he *could* see was that *Dart*'s fore topgallant and fore royal had gone by the board, leaving the flagship all but dismasted. Combined with the heavy casualties he already knew Pawal's company had suffered, *Dart* would be all but helpless if anyone managed to get to grips with her. And while it was obvious Stywyrt had finally been able to bring *Squall* into action—apparently with crushing effectiveness—Aiwain had no idea how badly damaged *Guardsman* or *Prince of Dohlar* might actually be.

He looked farther down to leeward and saw several columns of smoke rising from the sea. It looked as if *Flash* and *Mace* had managed to get to grips with the convoy, after all. He doubted they'd managed to pick off more than a few of the coasters before the others scattered, but some was better than none.

*Yes, it is*, he thought. *And, yes, you'd really like to finish at least one of the bastards off. But* Dart's *been shot to shit; you've got more than enough dead and wounded of your own; we're the better part of a thousand miles even from Trove Island; and there's no telling when* another *squadron of these bloody-minded bastards is going to turn up.*

He grimaced unhappily at his unpalatable conclusion. Unfortunately, he couldn't dispute his own logic.

▼   ▼   ▼

Stywyrt watched *Guardsman* making more sail.

She was clearly running, and under the circumstances, much as he might have liked to, Stywyrt couldn't really fault her skipper's thinking. At the very least, he needed to get clear while he figured out what was going on.

*And when he does, they're going to go on running*, Stywyrt decided.

Two of their ships had suffered heavy damage aloft, whereas *Squall*'s and *Shield*'s rigging was still effectively intact. They'd want to protect their cripples, and Stywyrt had no idea how close Dohlaran reinforcements might be. It was possible this wasn't the only squadron Thirsk had sent to sea. In which case, their "fleeing" opponents might "just happen" to lead them straight into an ambush.

Under the circumstances, he was willing to let them run if they were willing to do the running. Besides, he had *Dart* to worry about, and then there was *Prince of Dohlar*. She still hadn't been brought back under control, which suggested *Squall*'s fire had been even more effective than Stywyrt had been prepared to assume. That didn't mean she wasn't going to recover at any moment, though, and if she did, she could well pose a serious threat to the crippled Charisian flagship.

*Best to make sure of her*, he decided. *She's our wyvern, after all!*

He grinned at the thought, then gave himself a shake.

"Very well, Master Mahldyn," he said. "Prepare to put the ship about, if you please." He twitched his head in *Prince of Dohlar*'s direction. "I believe we have a prize to collect."

HMS *Empress of Charis* was no longer the most powerfully armed warship in the world. In fact, eighteen of her sixty-eight gunports were empty, leaving her with only twenty-eight long thirty-pounders on the gundeck and four long fourteens and eighteen thirty-pounder carronades on her spar deck. Despite the reduced armament, she remained *one* of the most powerfully armed warships in the world, however, and she also remained Emperor Cayleb's favorite flagship.

Which was why she was currently ghosting towards the oared galleys off the Tellesberg seawall. There was very little wind, barely enough to raise a light swell, and with every stitch of canvas set she was making no more than two knots. In fact, probably less. The breeze barely sufficed to occasionally flap the banner at her mizzen peak, but that was enough to display—fitfully, perhaps—the golden Ahrmahk kraken swimming across the silver-and-blue checkerboard of Chisholm quartered with the black of Charis. But this banner was different from any other imperial Charisian banner, for it displayed both a gold and a silver crown above the kraken, indicating that both of the Empire of Charis' monarchs were aboard.

Which, in turn, had something to do with the hordes of light craft swarming out to meet her and the deafening cheers rising from them. Almost a full year had passed since Empress Sharleyan's departure for Chisholm, and it had been a year and a *half* since Emperor Cayleb had sailed for Corisande. In fact, they'd been officially supposed to return to Tellesberg a full month earlier, and more than one Old Charisian had waxed grumpy—eloquently so, in some cases—over the delay.

Of course, half the delay was due solely to contrary winds on the voyage home, which not even an emperor or an empress could expect to do anything about. Still, they had been supposed to leave Cherayth a full three five-days earlier than they had, and there was no denying that a certain rivalry had already arisen between the Charisian Empire's twin capitals. Overall, it was a remarkably friendly rivalry, but that made it no less real, and the more persnickety Old Charisians had taken exception to their monarchs' decision to extend their stay in Cherayth.

For the most part, those who complained found scant sympathy from their fellows. For one thing, their youthful monarchs were remarkably popular with their subjects (aside, of course, from the Temple Loyalists, most of whom would have liked nothing better than to see them dead, but one couldn't have everything). For a second thing, most of their subjects understood that the rulers of an empire fighting for its life against the other seventy or eighty percent of the world might, upon occasion, find themselves involuntarily forced to alter schedules. And for a third thing, as a direct consequence of that need to occasionally alter schedules, Sharleyan had spent three extra months in Tellesberg before she ever left for Cherayth.

Yet the true reason the complainers were rather brusquely told to shut their mouths was the news that not only was Empress Sharleyan pregnant, but that the heir to the imperial throne would be born right here, in Tellesberg. The child would be not just a Charisian, but an *Old* Charisian by birth. Doubtless the royal family would be far too tactful ever to *say* so, but everyone who mattered would *know*. Hence the wild tide of cheering sweeping over those hundreds of small craft as *Empress of Charis* furled her canvas and the towing hawsers went across to the galleys waiting to shepherd her to quayside.

Take *that*, Cherayth!

▼   ▼   ▼

"You know, if all our Old Charisians don't stop gloating, we're likely to have a civil war," Rayjhis Yowance said whimsically.

The Earl of Gray Harbor sat at the foot of the dining table, looking up its length at Cayleb. Sharleyan sat to Cayleb's right, facing Bishop Hainryk Waignair across the table, and Bynzhamyn Raice sat to the bishop's right. Rahzhyr Mahklyn, to the empress' left, completed the dinner party.

Which seemed—especially to Wave Thunder and Gray Harbor— inescapably incomplete without Merlin Athrawes standing at the emperor's back.

"Oh, surely not, Rayjhis," Waignair responded to Gray Harbor's statement serenely. He was approaching eighty years of age, with snow-white hair and brown eyes surrounded by smile wrinkles. His slender frame, stooped posture, and the prominent veins on the backs of his hands gave an impression of frailty, but his health was actually excellent, and there was nothing at all wrong with his mind.

"Oh, no, My Lord?" Gray Harbor smiled. "Perhaps you haven't been listening to what *I've* been hearing?"

"I've heard as much gloating—excuse me, excessively joyous celebratory comment—as you have," Waignair replied. "I'm certain, however, that Her Grace's Chisholmians will never take undue offense. After all," it was his turn to smile, "the heir may be be born here in Tellesberg, but where was the child *conceived*?"

Gray Harbor's eyes widened and he sat back in his chair, gazing at the bishop for a long moment. Then he shook his head.

"Do you know, that never even occurred to me." He shook his head again, his expression bemused. "My, my! They *are* going to gloat over that, aren't they?"

"As a matter of fact, they already are," Cayleb said in a resigned tone. "Gloating, I mean. And talking about mysterious 'things' in Chisholmian water or air." He smiled crookedly. "I know everyone in the Empire has a legitimate interest in securing the succession. I *understand* that. I even sympathize with it. But I have to tell you, I'm beginning to feel like some prized racehorse or dragon stud."

"Which makes *me* precisely what, if I may inquire?" Sharleyan asked, resting one hand on her swollen abdomen.

"The other half of the equation?" Cayleb suggested innocently, and she whacked him across the knuckles with her other hand.

"You see what I have to put up with?" she asked the table in general, and a chorus of laughs answered.

"Actually, Your Grace," Gray Harbor said then, his expression more serious, "having your child conceived in Chisholm and born in Old Charis is probably the very best thing that could have happened. With all due respect for His Majesty's delicate feelings—and your own, of course—this has to be the most widely discussed pregnancy in the history of both kingdoms. And"—his smile turned suddenly gentle—"the vast majority of your subjects are delighted for you."

"That, Your Grace, is absolutely true," Waignair said softly. "We've offered Thanksgiving masses every Wednesday afternoon in Tellesberg Cathedral since we received news of your pregnancy. Attendance has been high. And a lot of your subjects have been quietly leaving small offertory gifts—a few coins here or there, sometimes just a spray of flowers or a little note telling you how hard they're praying for you and your child." He shook his head. "I very much doubt that any prospective mother in Charisian history has ever been the recipient of as many prayers and blessings as you have."

Sharleyan colored slightly, but she met his gaze steadily across the table, then gave a small nod of acceptance.

"Actually," Wave Thunder's brisk tone was that of a man deliberately changing the mood, "the one thing that seems just plain *wrong* to me is having both Maikel and Merlin someplace else."

Heads nodded soberly as someone finally said it out loud. Gray Harbor, the only person present who didn't know the true story of a young woman named Nimue Alban, still knew about *Seijin* Merlin's "visions." He also knew how close to both Cayleb and Sharleyan Merlin had become. So he wasn't surprised to hear Wave Thunder include the *seijin* right along with the archbishop.

"I agree," Sharleyan said after a moment, her voice soft. But then she shrugged. "I agree, but we all knew Maikel probably couldn't get back from

Corisande in time, and there was no way we were letting him go there without Merlin. Not after what happened to Father Tymahn."

"I don't see how anyone could fault your priorities, Your Grace." Waignair's voice had turned grim. "The murder of any child of God is a thing of grief and horror. To murder anyone—especially a priest—in so hideous a fashion simply to terrify others into obedience goes beyond grief and horror to abomination."

There were no smiles now, for no one could miss the bishop's implication.

Reports had amply confirmed what had happened to Zhaspahr Clyntahn's enemies in the Temple and Zion, and, as Waignair had just said, it went beyond grief and horror to atrocity.

Thirty-one vicars had been arrested, put to the Question, and suffered the Punishment of Schueler. Including Samyl and Hauwerd Wylsynn, thirty-three of the three hundred vicars of the Church of God Awaiting had died. Eight of the Wylsynns' fellow Reformists had been fortunate enough to die under the Question; twenty-three had been delivered to the full, hideous catalog of barbarisms the Punishment demanded before their final death by fire. Only sixteen had actually lived long enough to be burned, which seemed a scant enough mercy.

Fifty-two bishops and archbishops had joined them. As had the personal staffs of almost every one of the condemned prelates. Wives had been put to the Question, as well, and every one of them had been executed, although Clyntahn had extended the "mercy" of merely having them hanged. Children over the age of twelve had been rigorously "interrogated." Most over the age of fifteen had joined their parents. The Questionings and the Punishments had taken over two months to complete, and the city of Zion was in shock.

All told, almost twenty-five hundred had been arrested, and over fourteen hundred men, women, and children had died. Surviving infants and babes in arms had been "graciously spared by Mother Church" and consigned to other members of the vicarate to be reared. Children over the age of four—those whose lives had been spared—had been remanded to monastic communities (most in Harchong, the citadel of orthodoxy) with traditions of severe asceticism and discipline.

Nor had Clyntahn missed the opportunity to trot out the handful of Charisian survivors of the Ferayd Massacre. There weren't many of them—only seven, in fact—and every one of them had been a tottering physical wreck, eager to "confess" to anything, even knowing they were to be burned, if only that would end the horror their lives had become. And so they had—confessed to every conceivable heresy and perversion. Proclaimed their worship of Shan-wei, their hatred of God, the pacts in which they had knowingly sold their souls to the Dark.

Against the backdrop of that "evidence" of how deeply the Charisian apostasy had penetrated, that self-confessed "proof" of the Church of Charis' heretical abominations and the way in which it had sold itself to evil, the Grand Vicar's long anticipated declaration of Holy War had been almost an afterthought. No one had questioned it, just as there was no voice raised against Clyntahn and the Group of Four in the Temple Lands. Not any longer. There was no one left who would have dared to raise one.

Yet if there were no raised voices, there *were* rumors, whispers, that the Grand Inquisitor's sweep had been less complete than he'd intended. Several of the condemned vicars' families had mysteriously vanished, and dozens of bishops' and archbishops' families had done the same. No one knew how many had escaped the Inquisition's net, yet the fact that *any* had managed it chipped away, if only slightly, at the omnipotent aura of Clyntahn's iron fist.

There were counterrumors, of course—whispers that the missing families' miraculous escape was proof of Shan-wei's influence, proof they'd been her minions in very truth. That only the Mother of Darkness could possibly have whisked them out of the Inquisition's grasp. There was no doubt in the minds of the people around Cayleb and Sharleyan's supper table who was responsible for those whispers. Nor did anyone doubt that one reason they'd been crafted was to discredit any testimony those escapees might offer if ever they reached safety in the Charisian Empire.

"Forgive me," Waignair said softly, after a moment. "This dinner is supposed to be a celebration. I apologize for darkening it."

"My Lord, you're not the one who darkened it," Sharleyan told him. "We all know who did that, and I fear thoughts of what's happened in Zion are never far from any of us."

"Nor should they be," Cayleb said harshly. They looked at him, and he shook his head fiercely. "Those bastards have a great deal to answer for, and we owe it to all their victims to remember that it's not just what they've done—or tried to do—to *us*. It's what they've done to *anyone* who dares to get in their way!"

"Yes, Your Majesty, it is." Waignair shook his head sadly. "All our priests are reporting they've been approached by parishioners trying desperately to understand how even the Group of Four could commit such acts 'in God's name.' We try to comfort them, but the truth is that none of us really understand it ourselves." He shook his head again. "Oh, intellectually, yes. But inside? Emotionally? Where our own faith in the goodness and love of God resides? No."

"That's because you *do* believe in God's love and goodness, Hainryk," Gray Harbor said. "I don't know what—if anything—Trynair and Maigwair truly believe in, but I think we've all seen what *Clyntahn* believes. At best, he believes solely in his own power; at worst, he truly believes in some monstrous perversion of God. And in either case, he's willing to do *anything at all* to accomplish his ends."

"I'm afraid you're right." Waignair sighed. "But that doesn't give much scope for comforting those who are frightened and confused. All we can do is urge them to pray, trust God, and remember the duty of all good and godly people to resist evil wherever it may be found . . . even in the orange of a vicar's cassock. I'm afraid that can be scant comfort, no matter how strong someone's faith is. And especially for those who remain ignorant of loved ones' fates . . . like Father Paityr."

He looked across the table at Sharleyan, his eyes dark, and she nodded slightly in understanding. She knew how dreadfully tempted Waignair must have been to reassure Paityr Wylsynn that his stepmother and his brothers and sister had escaped. She was more than a little awed by the way the young in-tendant had managed to continue discharging his responsibilities in the wake of his father's and his uncle's confirmed deaths . . . and the total silence where the rest of his family was concerned. She also knew how much Waignair, like everyone else who had ever worked with the young Schuelerite, respected and admired and even loved him. Watching him deal with his grief and fear would have been hard enough under any circumstances. Watching him go through all of that when Waignair could have told him the rest of his family would be joining him in Tellesberg only made it even worse.

*But they're going to be here within another two or three five-days,* she reminded herself. *Their ship's already halfway across The Anvil. He'll know then, God bless him . . . and them.*

"I understand exactly what you're saying, Hainryk," she said out loud, meeting those dark eyes head-on. "And I agree. I wish there were a way to comfort all of those fears and concerns."

"If you'll forgive me, Your Grace," Gray Harbor said quietly, "I think you're about to do just that for a great many of your subjects."

She cocked an eyebrow at him, and he glanced at Waignair.

"You apologized for bringing the subject up, Hainryk, but the truth is, re-minding us of what's transpired in Zion may not be that bad a thing, especially at a moment like this. I think it helps us here in Old Charis, and throughout the Empire, to realize how blessed we truly are. We, at least, know precisely what we're fighting for—that God has given us the opportunity to put an end to the butchery of someone like Clyntahn. How often are men and women given the chance to accomplish something that important? I think all our people, even those frightened and confused souls seeking comfort you just mentioned, realize that deep down inside. And that, Your Grace," he returned his gaze to Sharleyan, "is why your child is so important to all of them. Because they genuinely love you and Cayleb, yes. I believe that, too. But this child represents more than just the securing of an imperial succession. He—or she—is also the symbol of the struggle that empire was forged to fight."

The Earl of Thirsk turned away from the stern windows as Lieutenant Bahrdailahn ushered his visitors into *Chihiro*'s great cabin.

"Gentlemen," the earl said quietly.

"My Lord," Caitahno Raisahndo, as the senior officer, replied for all four of them.

"Please," Thirsk gestured at the four chairs facing his desk. "Be seated."

They obeyed the politely phrased command, and he stood for a moment longer, considering them, before crossing to sit behind the desk.

All of them—especially Raisahndo and Rohsail—looked exhausted. In addition, Rohsail was in obvious discomfort, despite a determined effort to hide it. His left elbow had brushed the arm of his chair in sitting, and the fingers of his left hand had twitched in an automatic pain reaction where they protruded from the sling.

There was more than simple exhaustion, or even pain, in the shadowed eyes gazing back at him, however, and he folded his hands on the desk before him.

"I've read your reports, and those of your first officers—your acting first officer, in your case, Captain Krahl. There are, of course, certain inconsistencies. Given the confusion of a sea action, it's scarcely surprising none of you observed exactly the same things. Despite that, however, I believe a clear and consistent picture emerges, and I have so advised Bishop Staiphan and Duke Thorast."

He paused, and the tension in the quiet cabin could have been sawn into chunks.

"I have also advised them," he continued after a moment, in the same calm voice, "that I fully approve of your actions. That, in fact, I believe they reflect great credit upon all four of you and upon your ships' companies."

No one actually so much as moved a muscle, but it was as if four sets of lungs had simultaneously exhaled, and the earl permitted himself a small smile. Then he leaned forward slightly over the desk.

"Don't mistake me, Gentlemen. I would have been even happier if you'd managed to take one or two of the Charisians. Or, for that matter, if we hadn't lost five ships out of the convoy and both galleys of the close escort, as well." He smiled again, a bit more thinly. "Which completely leaves aside the little matter of *Prince of Dohlar*."

None of the captains facing him replied. Which didn't exactly surprise him.

"I'm sure it comes as no surprise to any of you that I should feel that way," he continued. "For that matter, I'm confident each of you agree with me. But whatever we might wish, no one can simply snap his fingers and magically produce victory in a sea fight. True, you had the enemy outnumbered, and I won't pretend I haven't heard a few comments—all of them from individuals who weren't there, I might observe—to that effect. In every case, however, I have reminded those making the comments that your vessels were individually smaller, your guns were lighter, and that Cayleb of Charis would have hand-picked his most experienced captains for a deployment this far from Charis. In other words, Gentlemen, in your very first battle, you were up against the other side's very best.

"Obviously, we don't want to get into the habit of assuming we'll always need a numerical advantage of two-to-one. Nor, for that matter, do I think that situation will obtain indefinitely. For the moment, however, given the relative inexperience of your ships' companies and your officers, and how new all of us are to this style of naval warfare, I think you did extremely well. For the first time, a Charisian naval squadron has been turned back short of its objective. Yes, you lost one of your own vessels. And your casualties—especially yours, Sir Dahrand—were severe. But at no time did you allow the engagement to degenerate into a rout, and your crews fought well from beginning to end. I see no evidence of defeatism on anyone's part, unlike the complete collapse of morale we suffered the *first* time we encountered Charisian galleons."

His bared teeth bore very little resemblance to a smile.

"Trust me, Gentlemen. What I saw in Crag Reach when Cayleb came sailing out of the teeth of a gale in the middle of the night was just that—a complete and total moral collapse. I saw ships under my command run themselves on shore, set themselves on fire, rather than face the Charisians in combat. I understand why that happened, and the shock of their firepower came as just as great a surprise to me as to anyone else. But what strikes me most strongly about *your* engagement is that no one panicked. You didn't, your officers didn't, and your crews didn't.

"I'm sure you also learned a great deal. That experience is going to stand the entire Navy in extremely good stead, and I'll be asking all of you to share it with your fellow captains. From a long-term strategic perspective, that will be a priceless advantage.

"As for our relative losses, while I'm sure all of us regret *Prince of Dohlar*'s loss, we need to remember how far from home the Charisians are. It's evident that at least one of their galleons was severely hammered. Their casualties may well be as severe as your own, and they, unlike you, are thousands of miles from replacements. By the same token, we have fully equipped dockyards and shipyards to deal with the damages to your vessels; they don't. At best, they have Claw Island, and I would hardly call Hardship Bay an ideal place to make repairs. Not to mention the fact that first they have to get there. Under those circumstances, I believe any impartial judge would be forced to consider the outcome of your battle as a draw, at the very worst. In my own opinion, it was in fact a strategic victory."

He shook his head.

"I'm sure some might conclude I'm simply trying to find a bright side to look upon. If anyone should decide that, however, they'll be in error. I'm not saying all your decisions were perfect, because they weren't, and in a few minutes we'll begin discussing where mistakes were made, what lessons can be drawn from them, and how they can be corrected. But you fought and fought hard, and completely irrespective of the casualties and damage you inflicted, the enemy's going to think two or three times before he divides his forces into such small squadrons again. That's going to have a significant impact on his ability to interdict our shipping.

"I've made those same points to Bishop Staiphan, to Duke Thorast, to Duke Fern, and in my own written report to His Majesty. And I've also made the point that our strength is steadily increasing. I intend, shortly, to take the offensive, Gentlemen, and when I do"—he looked them in the eyes—"you and your ships will be in the van."

All four of the captains, even Rohsail, were sitting straight in their chairs now. They were still weary and worn, but their eyes glowed, and he nodded in satisfaction. He'd meant every word he said. Oh, he'd dressed it up a bit, glossed over a few parts, but in the main, he'd been completely sincere.

*Because they* did *do well—*damned *well,* he thought. *Even allowing for honest overestimates on their part—hell, even allowing for a certain amount of* deliberate *exaggeration on their part!—they hammered the crap out of at least one of the Charisians. And the Charisians know that as well as I do. It's going to affect the way they think, how willing they are to take risks. And it's going to do the same thing for our own crews. We're not going to magically turn into the scourge of the seas overnight, but this action is the first step in convincing ourselves—and the* Charisians—*that Cayleb's navy isn't really invincible. And that, my friends, is worth every man you lost. Yes, and* Prince of Dohlar *into the bargain.*

"And now, Gentlemen," he said with a smile, "since I've reassured you of my approval, let's start examining those mistakes. But don't worry. I promise"—his smile grew a bit broader—"to be gentle."

Sir Gwylym Manthyr glowered across the dark, blue-black waters of Chelm Bay. The sun had disappeared beyond the bulk of Trove Island behind him, and shadows had stretched themselves across the bay, turning its surface into ink, but the upper yards of *Squall* and *Shield* were gilded by the last level rays of sunset, reaching across Trove's heights.

HMS *Dart*'s weren't, since she didn't *have* any upper yards.

Work parties labored steadily on Captain Pawal's ship. They'd already set up a new mizzenmast and a new main topmast, and given the ingenuity and skill of Charisian seamen, Manthyr was confident they'd make the damage to her rigging good before Thirsk could react by sending a more powerful squadron to evict the squatters on Trove Island.

*On the other hand, I think we can take it as a given that he'll be* sending *that squadron.* Manthyr shook his head. *And before he does, I'm going to have to rethink my estimate of his combat capability.*

He let his eyes rest on the fourth galleon lying to anchor in the small bay. Repairs to *Prince of Dohlar* had actually been faster and easier to make, and although working parties still labored on her, as well, she was essentially ready for sea. In most ways, Manthyr was glad to see her. Her guns didn't match those of any of his other vessels, and all the ammunition he had for them was what was already in her shot lockers. Still, she represented a useful boost to his overall strength, and her capture was evidence of what Manthyr's captains and crews could accomplish even at three-to-five odds.

As were the fifty percent casualties Captain Stywyrt had inflicted upon her Dohlaran company.

Manthyr scowled as that thought reminded him of his *own* casualties . . . and why his gratitude at seeing the captured galleon wasn't unalloyed. His eyes moved back to *Dart*, and his scowl deepened.

Eighty-four of Pawal's crew had been killed or wounded in the battle. *Squall* had escaped with only three wounded, but *Shield* had suffered another thirty-two casualties. That was a hundred and nineteen sailors and Marines out of action, and seventy-one of them were dead. It was likely a third of the survivors would be permanently disabled, as well. Even if they weren't, it would be a long time before they returned to duty. But the pressing point was that those casualties represented a third of a galleon's total complement, and his supply of replacements was limited.

*Very* limited.

The admiral crossed his arms across his chest, leaning one shoulder moodily into the window frame as he contemplated that unpalatable fact.

He'd anticipated personnel losses. Even aboard a Charisian ship, there were always ways a man could be killed or injured. Falls from aloft, accidents at gunnery practice, hands or feet accidentally crushed moving any of the myriad heavy weights aboard a warship . . . .

Unlike some navies, at least drunkenness was seldom a factor in the ICN. Other navies—the pre-conquest Corisandian navy and, especially, the Imperial Harchongese Navy came forcibly to mind—provided daily issues of rum to their crews. The men in those navies looked forward to their daily "tots" as a palliative for the boredom, drudgery, and (especially aboard Harchongese ships) misery of their lives, and more than a few spent as much of their time in an alcohol-induced fog as possible.

Manthyr was a naturally abstemious man, yet he had had nothing against alcohol. Nor did he begrudge his men whatever small pleasures they could find. The Charisian Navy's position for over a hundred years, however, had been that drunkenness on duty was unacceptable. It was one of the few offenses for which the Navy still prescribed flogging for an enlisted man; in an officer's case, it cost him his commission. Fortunately, conditions aboard Charisian warships were far better than most of those other navies could boast. Charisian seamen seldom felt the need to escape into a drunken haze, and even if they had, opportunities would have been few. Not that alcohol was completely banned aboard Charisian warships. Their crews were issued beer (and *good* beer, at that) every day, usually for their midday meal; for supper, at other times. And rum was often issued for medicinal purposes or on celebratory occasions. But it was kept under lock and key between such instances and was nowhere near as available as in other navies.

As a consequence, the accident rate aboard Charisian warships was barely a tenth as high as that aboard, say, a Harchongese galley.

Accidents still happened, though, and despite all the Order of Pasquale could do about diet and hygiene, the packed living conditions aboard any warship, with its manpower-intensive crew and inescapably damp environment, too often became breeding grounds for disease. So, yes, he'd allowed for a certain number of casualties even exclusive of any which might be inflicted by enemy action.

Unfortunately, it was evident his estimates had been low. The battle off Dragon Island represented the first true test case for what was likely to happen when the Imperial Charisian Navy confronted equally determined, properly designed enemy galleons, and it was clear to him that he'd been overconfident. Pawal's small squadron had triumphed despite a significant numerical disadvantage, and Manthyr strongly suspected his ships had inflicted heavier casualties than they'd taken. Yet from the squadron's reports, he also suspected that if the Dohlaran commander had been prepared to haul off to make repairs, then renew the action, the result might have been much less satisfactory.

*And whatever happened here, I'm down half a galleon's crew—probably more than that, by now, in the squadron as a whole, allowing for accidents and disease—and I've just added an additional ship. So where, exactly, do I find the men to man them?*

The question had a certain pertinency, yet at the moment it actually came second to a more pressing concern. The Earl of Thirsk was a tough-minded professional. He'd draw much the same conclusions Manthyr had. And, unlike Manthyr, Thirsk was in a position of steadily *increasing* strength. It was unlikely a man like that, with the evidence of how well his captains had done at Dragon Island, wouldn't be looking for ways to use that growing strength.

*We should have brought more schooners*, Manthyr thought. *What I really need to do is to send a couple of dozen of them out to operate independently and raise Shan-wei's own mischief. Let them pounce on Dohlaran and Harchongese shipping in as many places as possible. That would force Thirsk to spread his galleons out, and he'd play hell running down any of the schooners. But I don't have enough of them to be everywhere they'd need to be, which means he's going to be able to cover his most important shipping in convoys, like he did at Dragon Island, and still free up the strength— if not now, soon enough—to try something a bit more offensive. And the only way I'm going to have the strength to stop him is going to be to keep my own galleons concentrated.*

He didn't care for that conclusion. He was supposed to be whittling down the Church's naval forces, and his new appreciation of the Dohlaran Navy's combat worthiness was going to make that more difficult. He knew he'd already imposed a significant delay on the Dohlaran building program. He'd captured or sunk too many cannon-laden coasters and shipments of turpentine, pitch, spars, and every other variety of naval stores imaginable for any other result. And he was confident he could inflict still more delay, still more damage. But he was going to have to operate more defensively, and the less aggressive he could be, the less effective he was going to become.

*And if Thirsk is willing to commit to offensive operations of his own, the first item on his list is going to be Trove Island. And even if Major Wyndayl's Marines had enough heavy artillery to hold the anchorage forever—which they don't—there's a limit to how long a siege they could stand. If Thirsk has the galleon strength to drive us off, he could isolate the island with just a handful of old-style galleys. And if I don't have the strength to break through and lift Wyndayl out, Thirsk will eventually starve him and his men into surrender, however willing to hold out they might be.*

He sighed as he admitted that.

*Well, it's not the end of the world, Gwylym*, he told himself philosophically. *Trove's been convenient and useful as hell, but it's not essential. You've got the transports*

*Wyndayl arrived on, so it's time you pulled him out and sent him back to Claw Island. That's a lot more defensible, anyway, and by the time Thirsk starts getting any ambitious ideas about Claw, he's going to be a hell of a long way from his own ports. And in the meantime, you can probably raise quite a bit of hell with the Harchongese.*

He nodded sharply, turned and walked to the cabin door. He opened it and poked his head out.

"Yes, Sir?" Lieutenant Rahzmahn said, looking up and then rising from his seat behind Manthyr's desk, where he'd been working on the squadron's accounts.

"I'll want to meet with Pawal, Aiwain, Stywyrt, and Captain Mahgail after supper tonight, Dahnyld," Manthyr told him. "See to it that they're informed, please. And I suppose you'd better warn Naiklos, too."

.VI.
### HMS *Ahrmahk*, 58,
### The Charis Sea,
### and
### HMS *Dawn Wind*, 54,
### Carter's Ocean

W hat do you think about Gwylym's new plans, Merlin?" Bryahn Lock Island asked quietly.

At the moment, the high admiral was stretched out in his cot aboard HMS *Ahrmahk*, his fifty-eight-gun flagship. Given the normal sounds of a ship underway through six-foot seas, no one was likely to overhear him even if he spoke in a normal conversational tone. He had no intention of risking being wrong about that, however.

Merlin Athrawes, sitting on the stern galley of HMS *Dawn Wind* while he gazed out at the early dawn several thousand miles to the east, had no problem with that. He was just grateful Cayleb had made it a priority on his return to Tellesberg to bring Lock Island fully into the inner circle before the high admiral returned to his fleet at sea. For the moment, Lock Island—like everyone else immediately after being told the truth—was being compulsively cautious, which was a trait of which Merlin approved.

"I think they make a lot of sense under the circumstances," he said now, in reply to the earl's question.

"I have to admit I was a bit taken aback myself by how effective Raisahndo's squadron was," he continued. "I don't suppose I should've been—we've all been reminding ourselves for months that Thirsk is probably the most dangerous commander on the other side—but I was." His lips quirked. "Maybe

I've been a Charisian long enough to start suffering from that . . . exuberant self-confidence that makes you so universally beloved by every other navy."

" 'Exuberant self-confidence,' is it?" Lock Island snorted.

"I think it's a fair term," Merlin responded, smiling at the rising sun. "Mind you, I never said it wasn't justified. Normally, at least."

"I only wish we could talk to Gwylym this way," Lock Island said in a rather more fretful tone. "I'm beginning to realize how maddening it must have been for Domynyk to be able to talk to you and to Cayleb—to see Owl's . . . 'imagery'—" (he pronounced the still-unfamiliar word carefully) "and not be able to tell *me* about it. But with Gwylym that far out on the end of a limb . . . ."

He shook his head, and Merlin's smile faded.

"I know," he sighed. "In fact, it was something we discussed—Domynyk and I—before Gwylym ever left. Unfortunately, we can only move so fast in bringing more people into the circle, and—"

He broke off with a shrug, and Lock Island nodded.

"I won't pretend I was happy to discover how long it took the Brethren to finally decide I was a sufficiently stalwart and trustworthy soul." The high admiral's lips twisted with wry humor. "At the same time, I can see why they might want to think about it for a bit before they start blabbing away about things like 'spaceships' and counterfeited religions. And, to be honest, I think it was probably a good idea to wait until Cayleb got home to tell me about it in person." He snorted again, a bit more loudly. "At least he had the authority to sit on me if I started running around in circles like a wyvern with its head cut off!"

"That thought did pass through our minds," Merlin acknowledged amiably.

"I'm sure," Lock Island said. Then he paused for a moment, frowning.

"In regards to that sort of decision," he said slowly, then, "I've been thinking about Ahlfryd."

"Don't worry." Merlin chuckled. "They're planning on telling him as soon as he pays one of his visits to Tellesberg. The healers aren't letting Sharleyan stir a step out of the palace until the baby's born, and she's determined *she's* going to be the one to tell him!"

"That wasn't my point," Lock Island said even more slowly. He hesitated, like a man steeling himself to say something he didn't want to, then continued anyway. "My point was that I don't know if it would really be a good idea to tell him at all."

Merlin blinked in astonishment. Despite the difference in their ranks, Baron Seamount was one of Lock Island's personal friends. The high admiral had an even better appreciation than most for the sharp agility of Sir Ahlfryd Hyndryk's mind. For that matter, if anyone in the entire Charisian Empire understood exactly how critical Seamount's innovations had been, it had to be Lock Island. So why—?

"Are you afraid he won't accept the truth about Langhorne and Bédard?" Merlin asked after a moment.

"You mean like Rayjhis and Green Mountain?" Lock Island shook his head. "Oh, no. That's the least of my worries where Ahlfryd's concerned!"

"Then may I ask why you have any reservations about telling him?"

"It's just . . . ."

Lock Island paused again, obviously marshaling his own thoughts.

"Look, Merlin," he said then, "I've known Ahlfryd for the better part of thirty years. There's not a man on the face of the world I'd trust more implicitly. And God knows I've never met anyone with a sharper brain! But there are actually three points I think need to be considered here.

"First, he's producing new ideas faster than we can put them into production already. Not only that, he's got his entire Experimental Board doing the same thing now, and all without knowing the truth or having access to all those . . . 'computer records' you've been talking about. I'll admit, I still don't really understand much about them, but my point is that Ahlfryd's been forging ahead on the basis of the handful of hints you've already given him. As I understand it, your whole idea in the long run is for people to start thinking of these sorts of things for *themselves*, and Ahlfryd's doing exactly that. Do we really need—or want—to divert him from stretching his own mind and the minds of people like Commander Mahndrayn into picking over someone else's records for ideas?

"Second, I *do* know Ahlfryd. The instant he finds out he can have access to such advanced knowledge, he's going to dive in headfirst, and we won't see him again for months. He won't be able to resist it any more than a drunkard could resist whiskey, Merlin, and you know it. We can probably come up with some sort of explanation for his sudden disappearance, but it's going to be awkward. And, in the same vein, once he knows what *can* be done, he'll move heaven and earth to *get* it done. I think there's a real chance he might end up pushing ahead too quickly. You've been very careful about not openly violating the Proscriptions, but I have to believe restraining Ahlfryd, keeping him from doing something that would clearly represent a violation, may turn out to be harder than you think. And, conversely, if we avoid that, he's going to be miserably unhappy knowing how much he *could* have done if only he'd been allowed to.

"But my third concern—and in many ways, it's the most serious one—is how he's going to react to the truth, to the discovery that he could have been running ahead—learning things, discovering things, *doing* things—for his entire life if not for the Proscriptions of Jwo-jeng . . . and that the Proscriptions themselves have been nothing more than a colossal lie. Cayleb told me the Brethren were concerned about his possible 'youthful impetuosity' if they told him the truth. Well, Ahlfryd's no impetuous teenager, but I literally don't know if he'll be able to go on pretending he doesn't know the truth once he does."

"Um."

Merlin frowned into the strengthening sunlight. He wasn't certain he shared Lock Island's concerns, but as the high admiral said, he'd known Seamount for a long time. In fact, he'd known him longer—and better—than anyone else in Cayleb's inner circle.

"I hadn't really thought about it from that perspective," he admitrted finally, slowly. "I'm not sure I agree—I'm not saying I don't; just that I'm going to have to think about it, first—but I think it's definitely something worth raising with Cayleb and Sharleyan before they tell him." He grimaced. "Sharleyan is *not* going to like it if we decide against telling him, you realize?"

"Oh, believe me, I do—I do!" It was Lock Island's turn to grimace. "And, to be honest, in a lot of ways I won't regret it if I get overruled on this one. I'll worry about it, but, damn it, Ahlfryd's my *friend*. I *want* to tell him the truth, Merlin. I just think this is something that needs to be considered very carefully."

"I agree with you about that much, at least," Merlin sighed.

"So you'll bring it up with Cayleb and Sharleyan?"

"Instead of *you* bringing it up, you mean?"

"Well, actually . . . yes," Lock Island admitted.

"Coward."

"Absolutely," the high admiral acknowledged rather more promptly, and Merlin chuckled.

"All right, I'll do it. Maikel and I need to talk to her and Cayleb about Rayjhis' correspondence with Gorjah, anyway. We think it may be time to, ah, push that process along a bit faster. I can probably work your little brainstorm into the conversation in my usual diplomatic fashion. On the other hand, she *is* pregnant, you know, and she's been more than a little irritable for the last month or so. I don't promise she won't hit the ceiling, however tactful I am. Still," he chuckled again, louder, "*I'm* still thousands of miles away. So if she *does* . . . take it poorly, guess which one of us she'll be able to get her hands on first?"

.VII.
Archbishop's Palace,
City of Tellesberg,
Kingdom of Old Charis

The Bishop is ready to see you now, Father."

Father Paityr Wylsynn looked up from the small volume of *The Testimonies* he'd been reading as he waited to find out why Bishop Hainryk had summoned him to the Archbishop's Palace. The fact that he'd been summoned *here*, rather than to the bishop's own residence, suggested that it was both official and that it dealt directly with either the Church of Charis as a whole, since the bishop was deputizing for Archbishop Maikel during his absence, or with the affairs of the Royal Council of Old Charis, upon which the bishop also sat at the moment as Staynair's deputy. Beyond that, however, he didn't have a clue, and so he'd striven to possess his soul in patience while he waited to find out.

Now he stood and followed the under-priest into the archbishop's office.

Bishop Hainryk stood, holding out his hand across the desk, as Wylsynn entered the office. The intendant bent over the hand, kissing Waignair's ring, then straightened. Wylsynn liked the bishop, and he respected him, yet it still seemed subtly *wrong* to see him sitting behind Staynair's desk, be it ever so temporarily.

*Just how Charisian have I become?* Wylsynn wondered wryly, then brushed the thought aside, folded his hands in the sleeves of his cassock, and regarded Waignair with polite attentiveness.

"You sent for me, My Lord?"

"Yes. Yes, as a matter of fact, I did, Father," Waignair replied, and pointed at the armchair beside Wylsynn. "Please, sit."

"Thank you, My Lord."

Wylsynn settled into the chair, but he never took his eyes from Waignair's face, and the bishop smiled slightly. Then he leaned back in his own chair, smile vanishing, while his right hand toyed with the scepter he wore around his neck.

"I'm sure you've been at least mildly curious about why I asked you to come visit me today, Father."

"I must admit the question did cross my mind," Wylsynn conceded when Waignair paused.

"There were two things I needed to speak to you about, actually, Father." Waignair's voice was suddenly much graver, and Wylsynn felt his own eyes narrow in reaction to the shift in tone.

"Before I deal with those, however, Father Paityr, I want to express, once again, my condolences for the execution—the murder—of your father and your uncle. I have no wish to reopen the wound I know their deaths inflicted upon you, but I bring it up once more at this point because there are two additional things I need to say to you, and both relate to your loss."

Wylsynn's face tightened. Not simply with the memory of past grief but with the tension of present worry. He hadn't heard a word from Lysbet Wylsynn since her single letter had arrived. At least he hadn't heard of her or the children's being taken, yet that was very little comfort for his ignorance about where they were, how they were faring, or if they were even still alive. By now, even someone with his deep personal faith was beginning to feel almost frantic with worry.

"The first thing I wanted to say to you," Waignair continued, "is that the manner in which you've dealt with this news has only deepened my already profound respect for you as a person, as a child of God, and as a priest." The bishop held Wylsynn's eyes steadily. "It would have been only too easy to fall into personal despair upon receiving such news, especially in the absence of any news about the rest of your family. And when the murders of so many of your father's friends—and their familes—were confirmed, it would have been equally easy to turn against God Himself for permitting such hideous crimes to be committed in the name of His Church. You did neither of those things. Nor, despite your own loss, your own lack of information about your brothers and sisters and stepmother, did you falter for a moment in your duties as one of God's priests. Archbishop Maikel has frequently mentioned to me the high regard in which he holds you. What I wish to say to you today, Father, is that over the last few months I've come to understand—fully understand—precisely why he feels that way about you."

Paityr wondered what in the world he was supposed to say in reply. Whatever Bishop Hainryk might say, Paityr Wylsynn knew himself too well to recognize the candidate for sainthood Waignair had just described. It was horribly embarrassing, and yet he couldn't deny it was also . . . comforting. Not because he believed he was superior to anyone else, more important in God's eyes, but because . . . because it demonstrated that the bishop and the archbishop he served recognized that he was at least trying. And, even more important, that someone whose judgment he deeply respected found his efforts satisfactory.

Waignair watched the young priest on the other side of his desk, and knew exactly what Wylsynn was thinking. He couldn't have thought anything else and been who he was. And the bishop never doubted that he'd just embarrassed the intendant. But there were times when any child of God needed to be commended. Needed to be given the positive reinforcement of knowing he or she was truly valued, truly important in his or her own right. And when someone had given—lost—as much as this young man had in the service of God, it was at least as important to Hainryk Waignair to tell him how much he was valued as it could ever be for Paityr Wylsynn to hear it.

"I—" Wylsynn began, then hesitated. He closed his mouth, then opened it again, but Waignair raised his right hand in a "stop" gesture and smiled gently.

"Father, you're young. And I just embarrassed you horribly, didn't I?"

His smile grew broader, his brown eyes twinkling, and Wylsynn, despite the cocoon of grief he could never quite break free of, felt himself smiling back.

"Well, actually . . . yes, My Lord."

"Of course I have. But the *Writ* tells us it's as much our responsibility to know and to acknowledge virtue as it is to recognize and condemn sin. Or, as the Archangel Bédard put it, simply learning what it's wrong for us to do isn't enough unless we're also given examples of what it's *right* for us to do. In that regard, you can think of this as an example of my discharging my pastoral responsibility to you in obedience to both those commands. And you might also think of it as a lesson by example for you to apply in your own ministry when it comes time for *you* to praise someone else."

"I'll . . . try to remember that, My Lord."

"I'm sure you will. However, that was only the first thing I wished to speak to you about."

"Yes, My Lord?" Wylsynn said when Waignair paused yet again.

"Actually," the bishop said in the tone of a man who'd suddenly been struck by a happy inspiration, "perhaps it would be simpler—or better, at least—for me to let someone else talk to you about this particular point, Father."

Wylsynn frowned, perplexed by the bishop's almost whimsical smile, but Waignair simply stood, walked to his office door, and opened it.

"Would you ask them to step in now, please, Father?" he said to the under-priest who had escorted Wylsynn into the office. Wylsynn couldn't hear the reply, but he twisted halfway around in his chair so he could watch as the bishop stood to one side of the door, waiting patiently.

Then someone stepped through it.

Paityr Wylsynn never remembered—then or later—getting out of that chair. Never remembered how he crossed between it and the door. Never remembered what—if anything—he said as he did it.

The only thing he *ever* remembered was the feel of his arms around Lysbet Wylsynn, the feel of her arms around him, the sight of his sisters, his brothers, his brother-in-law, his infant nephew—all of them—*all* of them—crowding into Maikel Staynair's office while tears poured down their cheeks . . . and his.

▾　　▾　　▾

Bishop Hainryk Waignair watched for a moment, smiling, seeing the tears, the joy, the grief . . . the love. Listening to the babble of voices, the exclamations of wonder. Then, very gently, he stepped out into the anteroom and closed the door behind him.

He turned to find his secretary looking at him, beaming hugely, and he smiled back.

"Some days, Father," he said quietly, "it's easier than others to remember how good God truly is."

# JULY, YEAR OF GOD 894

## King Gorjah's Bedchamber,
## Royal Palace,
## City of Tranjyr,
## Kingdom of Tarot

K ing Gorjah woke up rather abruptly.
        A hand suddenly clamped over one's mouth in the middle of the
night tended to have that effect. Especially upon a king whose bedchamber was
at the top of the central keep of an old-fashioned castle well provided with
guardsmen.

His eyes flew open, and he started to struggle, only to stop almost instantly.
There were two reasons for that. One was that the hand over his mouth might
as well have been a gentle, hand-shaped steel clamp. The other was that he'd
just become aware of the tip of what seemed to be an exceedingly sharp dagger pressed against the base of his throat.

The night, he decided, was going rapidly from bad to worse.

"I'd appreciate it if you'd be calm, Your Majesty," a tenor voice he'd never
heard before in his life said. "If I'd only wanted to cut your throat, I wouldn't
have bothered to wake you up first."

The calm voice sounded almost insanely reasonable, like that of a man
simply pointing out that thunderclouds often meant rain.

Gorjah could just make out the silhouette of a man's head against the dim
glow of the bedchamber's gauzy, moonstruck drapes, and he felt a stab of gratitude that Rholynd was having a fretful night and Maiyl had insisted on having
her own bed made up in the nursery tonight. At the time, he'd thought it was
charmingly sweet of her to want to personally oversee the nurses; at the moment, he was deeply grateful that at least his wife and son were somewhere else.

"On the other hand," the voice went on pleasantly, "I'm quite sure that if,
for some reason, I decided I *did* want to cut your throat, I could do it long before any of your guardsmen could respond to any shout on your part. If I decided to take my hand off of your mouth, so the two of us could speak as one
civilized man to another, do you think you could bear that in mind? The bit
about my being able to kill you before anyone else gets here, I mean?"

Gorjah decided the owner of the voice must be mad. Still, he was very
much in favor of anything which left him with his throat uncut, and so he nodded firmly.

"Excellent!"

The hand left his mouth, and the man to whom it belonged bowed slightly. Gorjah's eyes were able to pick out a little more detail now, and he realized the intruder in his bedchamber was considerably taller and broader in the shoulders than he himself. He also appeared to be clean-shaven, and he spoke with what Gorjah now recognized as a Silkiahan accent.

"I apologize for my . . . unconventional methods, Your Majesty. I really do need to speak to you, though, and I'm of the opinion that neither of us would like your guardsmen, your courtiers, or—especially—Vicar Zhaspahr to become aware of the fact that we have."

Gorjah's stomach seemed to congeal. He couldn't be certain in the dimness, but it looked to him as if his visitor had smiled.

"The thing is, Your Majesty," the Silkiahan continued chattily, "I thought it might be a good idea for me to give a little nudge to your correspondence with Earl Gray Harbor. You may not be aware that by this time Their Majesties will have arrived back in Tellesberg, but I imagine that probably means the somewhat desultory pace of that correspondence will be picking up in the next few five-days."

Gorjah felt as if someone had just punched him. No one in Tranjyr—*no one*, with the exception of Sir Ryk Fharmyn—knew about the cautious notes which had passed back and forth between him and the Empire of Charis' first councilor. He hadn't mentioned them even to Baron Stonekeep! So how did whoever this was—?

"I . . . don't know what you're talking about," he managed to get out. Even to his own ears, though, it sounded like an automatic, instinctive denial with very little relationship to the truth.

"Your Majesty!" the Silkiahan chided, and actually clicked his tongue at the king. "You know perfectly well what I'm referring to," he continued scoldingly. "I'm afraid we don't have time to stand around all night while you deny it, though. And, no, Sir Ryk isn't how I found out about it."

The casual reference to Fharmyn was the final blow. Obviously whoever this lunatic was, he knew everything.

"All right," Gorjah sighed. "Of course I know what you're talking about. But who the Shan-wei are *you*, and what are you doing in my bedchamber?!"

"Much better, Your Majesty," the other man said in an approving tone. "As for introductions, my name is Ahbraim Zhevons. I know that doesn't mean anything to you, but you can think of me as a close friend of Merlin Athrawes'. I'm sure you're familiar with that name."

"Of course I am," Gorjah said slowly, and his eyes narrowed. Everyone in the world knew Merlin Athrawes was a *seijin*. If this fellow—this . . . Zhevons—was "a close friend" of his, that might explain how he came to be in Gorjah's bedroom in the middle of the night. Even as he considered that, the king was aware of a vast sense of ill usage. After so many centuries without a single confirmed, genuine sighting of a *seijin*, it seemed particularly unfair that

Cayleb of Charis should have an apparently unlimited number of them when Gorjah didn't have even one.

"Should I take it, then," he asked his visitor, "that you're also a *seijin*?"

"Let's just say that, like Merlin, I possess a few of the talents and abilities *ascribed* to *seijins*," Zhevons replied. "And since he's unfortunately still some five-days out of Tellesberg on his way home from Corisande at the moment, you might say I'm . . . deputizing for him."

"I see."

Gorjah gazed at the dimly seen profile for a few moments, then shrugged.

"Since you appear to be here as a messenger, may I at least sit up in bed without your dagger doing anything . . . hasty?"

"By all means, Your Majesty," Zhevons agreed courteously.

"Thank you."

Gorjah would really have liked to stand, if only to assert a modicum of control over the situation. On the other hand, he doubted he'd be all that imposing in his nightshirt. So he settled for arranging his pillows behind his shoulders, then cocked his head.

"Very well, *Seijin* Ahbraim. What exactly did you want to discuss?"

"Basically, I just thought it might be a good idea to drop by and introduce myself." Teeth gleamed in a fleeting smile. "I feel reasonably confident that, in the fullness of time, your correspondence with Earl Gray Harbor is going to lead to a satisfactory outcome for all concerned. In the meantime, though, it seemed likely to me that while I was here—just introducing myself, you understand— you'd also like to know Admiral Rock Point's about to be reinforced. I believe it's what's known as bringing an additional argument to bear."

"I beg your pardon?" Gorjah said a bit more sharply.

He knew exactly what Rock Point's current strength was, given the fact that the cheeky Charisian had set up permanent housekeeping in Holme Reach. Of course, most of his galleons were usually out cruising around, enforcing the blockade around the rest of the Tarotisian coast and carrying out the occasional raid on some minor Desnairian port on the other side of the Tarot Channel. By now, however, all of them had cycled through the anchorage off Hourglass Island at least once. There'd been plenty of time for his observers to identify each of them by name.

Which was about *all* he'd been able to do about the Charisian infestation of his territorial waters.

"I said Admiral Rock Point is about to be reinforced," Zhevons repeated obligingly. "At the moment, I believe, he's scheduled to be brought up to forty galleons." Gorjah resisted a sudden urge to swallow. "And, by a peculiar coincidence, there happen to be about twenty thousand Imperial Marines available to go aboard transports in Old Charis if they should find it necessary to make a cruise."

This time, Gorjah went ahead and swallowed. Twenty thousand Charisian Marines? With the new rifled muskets and artillery? And siege guns to deal with any fortifications that happened to get in their way? They'd go through his own small army like shit through a wyvern!

"Are you saying Cayleb is going to invade my kingdom?" he asked very carefully.

"I'm saying Cayleb—and Sharleyan—would very much prefer *not* to invade your kingdom," Zhevons said pleasantly. "Which brings me back to the little matter of your correspondence with Earl Gray Harbor. I think everyone would be happier if this could be settled without any . . . unnecessary unpleasantness."

Gorjah stared at his mostly invisible visitor for a moment. Then he surprised himself with a harsh crack of laughter.

"I must say, *Seijin* Ahbraim, that you have a peculiar negotiating style!"

"Oh, I'm not *negotiating*, Your Majesty! I'm simply pointing out that you might consider whether or not it behooves *you* to negotiate a bit more briskly with the Earl."

"I see." Gorjah contemplated the other man for several more seconds. "May I ask whether or not Cayleb—and Sharleyan—are as prepared to be . . . as reasonable as the Earl has suggested?"

"I think you might look at Nahrmahn in that regard," Zhevons said in a rather more serious tone. "I'm not in a position to make any promises on Their Majesties' behalf, but it does seem to me that leaving aside that little matter of a violated treaty, Tarot's actually done less damage to Old Charis than Emerald had before they reached their understanding with him. And, frankly, considering Tarot's geographic position, you'd have quite a bit to offer the Empire. So . . . ."

He let his voice trail off and shrugged, and Gorjah felt his lips quivering on the edge of an involuntary smile.

"You *do* have a peculiar negotiating style," he said, "but I take your point. May I assume that if I were to give you a message for the Earl—or, for that matter, for 'Their Majesties'—you could see to it that it was delivered?"

"Not immediately," Zhevons said, and Gorjah's eyebrows rose in surprise. "I have a couple of other small missions I have to take care of before I head back to Old Charis, Your Majesty," the *seijin* explained. "My transportation arrangements—and schedule—are based on my dealing with them. I think you'd probably be able to get a message back to Tellesberg through Sir Ryk's established channels rather more quickly than I could, actually."

"I see."

Gorjah's brain whirred as he tried to imagine what other "small missions" Zhevons might have on his calendar. Not that he had any intention of asking.

"If I might make one teeny-tiny suggestion," Zhevons continued, holding up an index finger and thumb about a half-inch apart, "I'd go ahead and address your next note directly to Cayleb and Sharleyan. If they're not already in Tellesberg, I'm sure they will be by the time it arrives."

"I see," Gorjah repeated. He shook his head. "I believe I'll probably take your advice, *Seijin*."

"Good! And in that case, Your Majesty, I suppose it's time I was going." The *seijin* moved across the room to an open fifth-floor window. "It's been an enjoyable chat," he continued, pushing the drapes to either side, sitting on the window sill, and then swinging his legs out the opening, "but I do have those other little responsibilities. Goodnight, Your Majesty."

He turned lithely, dropped off the window ledge, caught it briefly with his hands for a moment, then released it with one hand to wave cheerfully before he let go entirely and disappeared.

For an instant, Gorjah stared disbelievingly at the suddenly empty window. Then he flung himself out of bed, dashed over, and looked down.

Despite his disbelief, he wasn't really surprised when he didn't see a smashed *seijin* lying on the pavement of the courtyard below. Not that not seeing it told him a single damned thing about how his visitor had managed to get in and out of his bedchamber.

*Well,* he thought, one thing's certain—*at least now I* know *all of the "tall tales" about* seijins *are true!*

.II.
### Merlin Athrawes' Recon Skimmer,
### Above Howell Bay,
### Kingdom of Old Charis

You enjoyed that entirely too much, Merlin Athrawes!" Sharleyan Ahrmahk scolded.

"Nonsense," Merlin replied airily. He leaned back comfortably in the recon skimmer's flight couch, gazing down on the dark mass of the island continent of Charis. From his present location, he could actually see the lights of Tellesberg, one of which undoubtedly represented Sharleyan's bedroom window. "I was simply attempting to establish the proper . . . collegial atmosphere."

" 'Collegial atmosphere,' is it?" Cayleb snorted over his own com. " 'Do you think you could bear that in mind? The bit about my being able to kill you before anyone else gets here, I mean?' I believe you said?"

"Yes, that was a witty line, wasn't it?" Merlin observed in a pleased tone. "I thought it got his attention quite nicely."

"Merlin, diplomacy isn't supposed to be *fun*," Nahrmahn chimed in.

"Of course not, Your Highness. Now tell me with a straight face that you wouldn't have enjoyed doing exactly the same thing."

"Of course I would have. In fact, that's why it was particularly rude of you to do it, when you know perfectly well none of the rest of us *could* do it!"

"I'm sure you're all enjoying yourselves enormously," Maikel Staynair said. "If I might point out, however, it's going to be dawn in about another two hours here aboard ship, Merlin. Are you going to be back, and aboard, with all of your . . . foliage back in place before someone notices your absence?"

"Back and aboard, yes, Your Eminence," Merlin said, checking the steady regrowth of his mustachios and beard with the fingers of one hand. "I'm not entirely certain about the 'foliage,' though. You may have to cover for me for an hour or so."

"You know," Staynair said meditatively, "before I met you, I was very seldom forced to prevaricate, much less lie outright."

"Only because no one was asking you the right questions," Merlin pointed out. "Besides, this time you won't have to lie at all. I will be there, and I will be meditating. Or, at least, reviewing Owl's latest take, and that's basically the same thing. Besides, you're an archbishop! If you'd prefer, all you have to tell anyone who wants to visit me is 'Because I *said* not, and I'm the Archbishop, that's why.' "

"You really *are* in a cheerful mood, aren't you?" Cayleb observed.

"As a matter of fact, yes." Merlin lowered his hand and gazed up and out of his bubble canopy at the pinprick diamonds of Safehold's heavens. "All joking aside, I think my little meeting went quite well. I'm certain Gorjah is going to be writing to you soon, Cayleb, and it won't hurt a bit for him to remember a *seijin* can creep in and out of his bedroom window anytime he feels like it. I don't think he's one of those naturally traitorous souls like Zebediah, but giving him a little added incentive to keep any promises he makes—this time around, at least—is probably a good thing, don't you think?"

"I don't see how it could hurt," Cayleb agreed.

"Besides, I'm beginning to like '*Seijin* Ahbraim.' And he's turning out to be quite a useful fellow."

"That's true," Sharleyan said. "Being able to stay in touch with one another wherever you happen to be lets us do things like send you to Corisande with Maikel, but '*Seijin* Merlin' still can't be in more than one place at a time. I'd just as soon not have Clyntahn—or, especially, Trynair—starting to ask himself where all these *seijins* came from all of a sudden, but establishing that there's more than one of you—and that all of you are just as 'mysterious' as the original Merlin—gives us a lot more flexibility."

"Exactly." Merlin nodded. Then he sighed suddenly.

"What?" Cayleb asked.

"I just wish there were a way for us to drop another *seijin* in on Gwylym," Merlin said, his expression far more pensive.

"I agree, but he's doing well enough so far on his own," Cayleb replied, and Sharleyan nodded vigorously.

"I have to admit, I was a little nervous when you told me he was planning on sailing straight into Shwei Bay," she said. "I was afraid he was displaying a bit too much of that thing you told us about the other day. *Chutzpah.*"

"You weren't the only one," Merlin said feelingly.

Gwylym Manthyr was showing a pronounced gift for taking what the military liked to call "calculated risks" . . . at least when they succeeded. They tended to call them something else when they *didn't* succeed. Of course, Manthyr *had* been Cayleb's flag captain, Merlin reflected. Having watched his then-crown prince sail an entire squadron through a channel he couldn't even see in the middle of the night and in a howling gale, it was probably inevitable that his definition of "acceptable risk" should have acquired a certain elasticity.

*On the other hand, sailing his entire squadron through Shweimouth and then clear up the Yu-Shai Inlet was just a bit more "elastic" than would have been good for my circulatory system, assuming I still had one.*

Yet he had to admit it had worked out. Manthyr had made his final approach to the city under cover of darkness, using local fishermen as pilots. Yu-Shai's garrison hadn't expected him until early afternoon, at the earliest; when he'd actually launched his attack on the harbor at dawn, he'd caught them napping.

The local batteries had been more dangerous than they would have been as little as a year before, since the Harchongese had given a high priority to producing fortress artillery to protect their building capacity, but Manthyr had gone in close, anyway, anchored by the stern, and laid down rolling broadside fire from ten of his galleons. In the event, he'd been lucky in several ways, including the fact that the wind had been setting from the east-northeast when he actually attacked. It hadn't been a particularly strong wind, which had made things interesting for the nine galleons (including *Prince of Dohlar*) told off to attack the Harchongese's newly built warships when the harbor defense galleys sortied. On the other hand, it had also meant the blinding banks of smoke had built up in layered walls between his ships and the defensive batteries and then stayed there. The smoke screen of his own broadsides had done far more than the storm of grapeshot and round shot with which he'd swept the batteries to protect his galleons and schooners from the defenders.

HMS *North Bay* had lost her mainmast, anyway, and her sister ship, *Rock Point*, had suffered over sixty casualties when two of the new, big Harchongese galleys managed to claw through her broadsides and run alongside. Fortunately, that was about the best the galleys had managed. Not for want of trying or lack of courage, but in the face of such complete surprise, they'd never managed to get organized. They'd sortied from the inner harbor in whatever order they could, coming in piecemeal, and Manthyr's galleons, despite their own anemic wind-limited mobility, had cut them up badly as they attacked in dribs and drabs. In fact, his squadron had sunk two and captured seventeen of them, and the handful of shaken survivors had beaten a sullen retreat.

All the captured ships had been burned, once their crews had been taken off, which would have been eminently worthwhile in its own right. But Manthyr had also converted half a dozen captured coasters into fire ships, stuffed to the deckheads with turpentine, old sails, barrels of pitch, and every other flammable substance. One had drifted off course when the tiller ropes burned through too quickly. A second had been grappled by a particularly courageous galley skipper and towed clear. But the other four had made no mistake. Their volunteer crews had fired them at almost exactly the right moment and taken to their own boats just before their flaming vessels sailed directly into the closely moored hulls of fifteen Imperial Harchong Navy galleons still in the process of fitting out.

Twelve of those galleons had become total losses, and one of the survivors had been badly damaged. Two more had survived only because they'd been upwind from the initial fire and their fast-thinking crews had been given just enough time to scuttle them before the holocaust sweeping through their consorts reached them. They'd settled to the shallow bottom, with only their upper decks above water, and the Harchongese seamen had managed to keep the still exposed portions of their ships from catching fire. Even so, they were going to be out of service for months while they were pumped out, raised, and then repaired.

It would have been even better if Manthyr had been able to administer the same treatment to Gorath Bay, but, fortunately, he showed no signs of lapsing into outright insanity.

"I agree he's doing well—extremely well, especially considering that he doesn't have any access to the SNARCs," Merlin said. "In fact, the damage he's already done completely justifies sending him out in the first place. And if the Dohlarans are feeling more confident, after Yu-Shai, the *Harchongese* aren't. I just wish there were some way we could get him that access." The *seijin* shook his head. "I'm afraid he's underestimating how quickly Thirsk's strength is building up."

"He may be," Cayleb conceded. "Unfortunately, as you pointed out to me before Haryl's Crossing, there are still going to be times when we have information we just can't figure out how to share with the people who need it. And even though he probably doesn't realize how *badly* he's about to be outnumbered, he's taking it for granted he *will* be outnumbered when the moment comes. When you come down to it, aside from telling him exactly where

Thirsk is at any given moment, that's really all we could tell him from the SNARCs, anyway."

"I know. I know," Merlin sighed. "It's just—"

"Just that you worry about friends, Merlin," Cayleb said with a soft, sad little chuckle. "We know. Believe us, we know."

.III.
## Imperial Palace,
## City of Tellesberg,
## Kingdom of Old Charis

I'm sure Father Ohmahr is on his way, Your Majesty!"

It was a sign of just how flustered Sairaih Hahlmyn was that she'd slipped and forgotten the proper protocol here in the Kingdom of Old Charis, reverting to the older, more familiar form of address and forgetting that in Tellesberg Sharleyan was officially "Your Grace," and not "Your Majesty."

Not that Sharleyan was in any mood to correct such minor lapses. She was too busy pursing her lips and breathing out—hard—while she squeezed Cayleb's hand fiercely. The spasm eased, and she dropped her head back on the pillow, panting.

"He'd better get here soon," she said then, between pants. "Someone *else* is going to be here, whether he is or not!"

"This is ridiculous," Cayleb muttered, taking a fresh cloth from Sairaih and blotting sweat from Sharleyan's forehead. "You're the *Empress,* damn it! He's supposed to be here—*waiting*—when you go into labor!"

At the moment, he could cheerfully have strangled Father Ohmahr Arthmyn, despite the fact that he was normally very fond of Tellesberg's leading obstetrician.

*Starting tomorrow,* he told himself firmly, *Father Ohmahr has a nice suite right here in the Palace, damn it! I'll keep the thing handy for the next kid, by God! I am not supposed to have to send someone six blocks to a frigging hospital monastary when my wife goes into labor!*

"Don't panic." Sharleyan reached across to pat the hand she held with her other hand. "They're not all that close together yet, and my water hasn't even broken. There's time." Cayleb would have been happier if her tone had sounded a bit more positive and a bit less . . . hopeful. "Besides, he probably expected Sister Frahncys to give him more warning than this. And it's not his fault I decided to start doing this in the middle of the night, either!"

"No, but—"

"Oh, hush!" she commanded, and began breathing deeply once again.

The contractions were coming closer together, and she wasn't enjoying it one bit. On the other hand, it wasn't as bad as she'd been half-afraid it would be. Not yet, at least. And her mother had assured her that women in her family always had *easy* deliveries. Of course, there was a first time for everything . . . including *hard* deliveries. And there had been all that morning sickness. . . .

"And now that I think about it, where the hell *is* Sister Frahncys?" the emperor demanded.

"Little Tirian," his wife panted as the fresh contraction eased.

*"What?!"* Cayleb stared at her.

Sister Frahncys Sawyair, the Pasqualate nun who'd accompanied them back from Cherayth aboard *Empress of Charis,* was a sister of the Convent of the Blessed Hand, which specialized in pregnancies. Which meant (despite the rote nature of *The Book of Pasquale*'s teachings) that she was a skilled obstetrician.

"What in hell's name is she doing *there?*" he more than half snarled.

"My fault!" Sharleyan smiled apologetically while he blotted more sweat. "She wanted to go visit the convent there. With Father Ohmahr right here, I told her it would be all right. In fact, I insisted she go."

"You ins—?" Cayleb began incredulously, then made himself stop and draw a deep breath of his own. "I take it when you say 'insisted' you mean *insisted*," he said instead.

"Of course she did!" Sairaih's tone was the exasperated one of someone who'd served Sharleyan since she'd been a little girl. The maid shook her head, taking the cloth Cayleb passed to her and handing him a fresh one. "You *know* what she's like, Your Majesty! Stubborn, always knows best, never listens to anyone, always worrying about someone else, always has her own way, never—"

"I'm sure he's got the entire catalog, Sairaih," Sharleyan said dryly. "Not but what you're right. She did argue, and I did insist." She smiled crookedly at her husband. "And now that I think about it, I told her *I'd* tell Father Ohmahr she was going. And I sort of forgot to."

"Of course you did." Cayleb rolled his eyes and snorted. Then he smiled back at her and shook his head. "You do realize you're probably the only empress in the entire world who could arrange things so there was *no one* on call when she went into labor? I thought it was the husband who was supposed to be running around like a lunatic!"

"I am *not* running around like a lunatic," Sharleyan told him firmly. "I've just been a little . . . absentminded for the last few days."

"That's *one* way to put it," he said feelingly.

"Oh, hush," she said again. "Besides, I was really hoping this wouldn't happen until Maikel and—"

She broke off with another quick smile, and he patted the back of the hand he held and nodded. HMS *Dawn Wind* was becalmed, still three days out from Dolphin Reach. He and Sharleyan had both hoped the galleon would reach Tellesberg with Maikel Staynair and Merlin Athrawes before their child was born. They'd known the odds were against it when *Dawn Wind* made an unusually slow passage from Corisande, but they'd still hoped. And now—

"Um, Cayleb?" Sharleyan said.

"Yes?"

"You remember what I said about my water not having broken?"

"Yes?" he repeated rather more slowly.

"Well, I'm afraid that's no longer accurate."

"Wonderful." Cayleb looked across at Sairaih. "You go out that door," he said, pointing at the royal bedchamber's ornately carved panels, "and you find Ehdwyrd, and you tell him I said for *one* of you to find Father Ohmahr *now*."

His voice was completely calm, but Sairaih Hahlmyn's eyes widened.

"Yes, Your Majesty!" she squeaked and disappeared like a puff of smoke.

▼    ▼    ▼

Cayleb Ahrmahk looked at the lying clock. Sairaih Hahlmyn had been gone for at least two hours, so why did the deceitful device insist less than twenty minutes had passed? He made a mental note to have the royal clockmaker examine its clearly defective gizzards at the earliest possible moment.

He knew from Sergeant Seahamper's earlier reports that a sizable clutch of palace servants had gathered outside the royal suite. There were probably at least a couple of fairly experienced midwives out there somewhere, he thought. On the other hand, he didn't want just anyone—

The door opened again, abruptly, and he looked up.

"Well, it's about time!" He knew he sounded less than gracious, but at the moment, he didn't really care.

"I apologize, Your Majesty," Father Ohmahr Arthmyn said, stepping through the door. "I'm afraid I expected Sister Frahncys to alert me a bit sooner than this."

"Not her fault!" Sharleyan's voice got progressively higher and more breathless, then broke off in another bout of quick, hard breathing.

"I'm just glad Sairaih found you," Cayleb said in a less harassed, more moderate tone, looking down at his wife as her hand tightened on his once again.

"Sairaih?" Arthmyn sounded puzzled, and Cayleb looked back up, eyebrows rising.

It was a sign of just how focused on Sharleyan he'd been that he hadn't realized the person following Arthmyn through the door was another priest, not Sairaih. Like Arthmyn, he wore the green-on-green cassock and golden caduceus of an upper-priest of the Order of Pasquale, but Cayleb had never seen him before. He was a tall man, with dark brown hair and brown eyes.

"And this is?" Cayleb asked a bit brusquely.

"Forgive me, Your Majesty," the stranger said in a tenor voice, bowing deeply, "I'm Father Ahbraim."

Cayleb's eyes widened abruptly as "Father Ahbraim" straightened.

"Father Ahbraim has been visiting Bishop Hainryk, Your Majesty," Arthmyn said. "I hadn't realized he was in Tellesberg until the *Bishop* sent him to inform me Her Grace had gone into labor. I . . . haven't seen Sairaih this evening. Perhaps she passed me on the way here?"

"Ah!" Cayleb nodded. "She must have. Good evening . . . Father Ahbraim. Should I assume you have some small expertise in these matters?"

"I'm here primarily as support for Father Ohmahr, if he should feel he needs it," Father Ahbraim said, reaching up and casually brushing his right ear. "I assure you, however, Your Majesty, that if he should decide to call upon my services you'll find that I am, indeed, well instructed in this area."

"I'm delighted to hear that, Father," Sharleyan said. Her breathing had eased once again, and she smiled at the newcomer. "I trust Father Ohmahr completely, but I'm glad Bishop Hainryk sent you along, as well."

"Thank you, Your Grace," Father Ahbraim said simply. "It's an honor—and a privilege—to be here."

▼    ▼    ▼

"You could have told us you were coming, Merlin," Cayleb said very quietly, some hours later, sitting beside Sharleyan's bed while he stared down at the incredibly beautiful, red, wizened, fretful, eyes-screwed-shut face of Alahnah Zhanayt Naimu Ahrmahk. His wife was sound asleep, and his dark-haired daughter was snugly wrapped in a tight little cocoon of blankets. There were still traces of her mother's milk on her tiny, perfect rosebud lips, and he already felt the bone-deep programming of fatherhood sweeping over him.

"I wasn't certain I'd be able to," Merlin replied, equally quietly, through the plug in Cayleb's right ear as he gazed down through a remote at his sleeping goddaughter. "Finding a way to get me on or off the ship in daylight isn't something we can do at the drop of a hat, you know. I *wanted* to be there, and not just because I wanted to see the baby born, either. I trust Sister Frahncys—when Sharley doesn't absentmindedly send her off on a visit, anyway!—and Father Ohmahr completely, but I'd be lying if I said I wasn't relieved I could be there. They've both delivered a lot more babies than I have, but neither of them has a direct link to the med computer in my cave. Fortunately, Sharley was clever enough to go into labor in the middle of the night. And Safehold nights are long."

"You got back in time?"

"Like I said, Safehold nights are long. I'm afraid *Seijin* Merlin's going to be meditating until sometime around midday, though." Cayleb could almost feel the wry twitch of Merlin's lips. "I still don't *have* to eat, but at the rate I'm growing and losing hair lately, I need enough replacement organics that I'm actually beginning to develop an appetite."

Cayleb snorted, then reached down to trace his daughter's delicate lips with a wondering fingertip.

"She's so *small*," he murmured. "She fits in the palm of one hand, Merlin!"

"I know. But she'll grow. And with you for a father and Sharley for a mother, I'm sure she'll be a handful—in quite another sense of the word—when she does, too!" Merlin chuckled. Then his voice gentled once more. "But I know you, Cayleb. However big she gets, she'll always be small enough to fit into your heart."

"Oh, yes," Emperor Cayleb Zhan Haarahld Bryahn Ahrmahk whispered. "Oh, yes."

# AUGUST, YEAR OF GOD 894

I don't like the looks of *that*, Sir," Captain Raif Mahgail said quietly. Or, at least, as quietly as he could through the calliope-voiced wind shrilling through HMS *Dancer*'s rigging and the surge and crash of water as she labored hard to hold her course for Claw Island, close-hauled under courses and reefed topsails.

"Why on earth not?" Sir Gwylym Manthyr replied ironically.

The two of them stood on *Dancer*'s quarterdeck gazing at the western sky. The ship had been beating to windward against a steadily strengthening wind all day. That wind had backed constantly until, by late afternoon, it had been slicing almost straight into the Gulf of Dohlar across the Sea of Harchong. Now, with evening coming on, it was blowing a near gale, and *Dancer* pitched hard as twelve-foot seas came rolling up under her starboard bow.

It was evident that they weren't going to reach the island anytime soon.

The sun was setting, although neither of them could see it. The solid wrack of clouds boiling up against the western horizon was like an indigo landmass, its mountain peaks edged in fire as they reared up against the copper-streaked heavens beyond. Manthyr was no stranger to foul weather, and every instinct in his body had its hands cupped around its mouth while it shouted warnings at him.

*This,* he thought, *is a truly, outstandingly* bad *situation.*

He and the eleven galleons with him were supposed to be rendezvousing in Hardship Bay with the rest of the squadron to reprovision and regroup. The redoubtable Earl of Thirsk had made dismayingly steady progress preparing his fleet, despite Manthyr's depredations, and the admiral knew it was time to consider heading back to Old Charis. He'd have to decide one way or the other once he was able to gather all his ships in one place again, and he wasn't looking forward to it. At the moment, however, it didn't look like he was going to have to make it quite as soon as he'd thought he would. His eleven ships were six hundred miles from Claw Island, almost equidistant between the Harchong Empire's provinces of Tiegelkamp and Queiroz in the mouth of the Gulf of Dohlar, and with the wind where it was, and the way the weather was making up, they were probably about as far west as they were going to get.

Until the weather cleared, at least.

The good news, such as it was, was that they could afford to be blown a good seventeen hundred miles east before they'd run into the western coast of Shwei Province. The bad news was that if the wind continued backing, they were going to find themselves being driven towards the *Tiegelkamp* coast, and that would give them far less sea room before they found themselves off a lee shore. And the even worse news was that even if the wind *didn't* back, every mile eastward that it forced them would be directly away from Claw Island . . . and toward the Earl of Thirsk. Manthyr didn't know exactly what Thirsk was up to at the moment, but he suspected he wouldn't have liked it. According to the Harchongese fishermen whose catch *Flash* had purchased for the squadron last five-day, Thirsk had upward of thirty-five galleons in full commission now, and he was beginning to extend his "training cruises" well beyond Hankey Sound.

*You have to take that kind of "intelligence" with a grain of salt, Gwylym,* he reminded himself. *People who sell information about their own side aren't always the most reliable sources around.*

Which was true. And *Flash*'s "purchase" hadn't really been paying for fish. It did offer at least a threadbare excuse if anyone from Dohlar or Harchong should ask questions, since the fishing boat's skipper could always explain he'd had no choice but to hand over his catch when a ten-gun Charisian schooner sailed up alongside and "suggested" he do so. In fact, he'd been looking for *Flash*—or one of Manthyr's other ships—expressly to sell them his information. Which, under most circumstances, would have made Manthyr extremely suspicious.

But this particular fishing boat was one of the regulars on the Dohlar Bank, and during the squadron's tenure on Trove Island, its skipper really had sold them a lot of fish. Like most common-born Harchongese, he prayed daily that God and the Archangels would keep the officials of the Harchong bureaucracy safe, well, happy . . . and far, *far* away from him, and that had made the Trove Island base one of his favored ports. He got a far better price for his catch from the Charisian squadron than he was ever likely to get elsewhere, and he wasn't compelled to pay the customary rake off to the harbormaster and half a dozen other minor officials.

In the course of their discreet transactions, he and Manthyr had met several times. In fact, the admiral had made a point of sharing an occasional glass of whiskey with the man, and something a bit closer than a purely professional relationship, yet too distant to dignify with the description of "friendship," had sprung up between them during those meetings. Manthyr never doubted that the fisherman was as canny as they came. He had to know that the real reason for a foreign admiral to hobnob with the skipper of a lowly fishing boat was because the admiral in question was deliberately cultivating information sources. The interesting thing had been his clear willingness to be cultivated. Given how many reasons lowborn Harchongese had to dislike their own aristocracy and the corrupt bureaucrats which served it, a certain willingness to do those aristocrats and bureaucrats a disservice was understandable enough. Doing the same thing to the *Church,* however, was quite another thing, yet Manthyr had come to the conclusion that the skipper had reasons of his own for doing exactly that.

So, no, he wasn't prepared to disregard the man's information and implicit warning. That didn't mean he was prepared to accept it uncritically, either, but it did fit rather well with the other bits of information he'd been able to assemble. And it would be an eminently reasonable way for Thirsk to proceed.

*You've singed their beards pretty well at Yu-Shai,* he told himself, still watching the ominous wall of purple-black cloud marching towards him. *And Langhorne only knows how many thousands of marks worth of naval stores and artillery you've sent to the bottom. But if Thirsk really has that many ships at sea, it probably is time you headed for home. And it's for damned sure you don't want to get blown any deeper into the Gulf than you can help!*

The problem was that he might not have much control over where he got blown to.

"All right, Raif," he said. "I don't think this is going to get any better, and I'd just as soon none of us got dismasted in the middle of the night by something we couldn't see coming."

"Oh, I think I could live with that, Sir."

"Good." Manthyr bared his teeth, then grimaced. "I smell a lot worse than this. Pass the signal while we've still got light enough. Send down the upper yards. Then I want the royals and the topgallants housed and storm canvas ready."

Mahgail raised one eyebrow. Manthyr obviously did expect the weather to get a lot worse. Either that, or he was suddenly becoming far more timorous than Mahgail had ever seen him before.

He glanced back at the ominous western horizon and decided the admiral had a point.

"Yes, Sir. I'll see to it at once," he said.

.II.
### HMS *Rakurai*, 46,
### Gulf of Dohlar

Eighteen hundred miles east of Claw Island, HMS *Rakurai* sailed slowly but steadily west. Night had already fallen, and the Earl of Thirsk stood on *Rakurai*'s quarterdeck, pipe clenched between his teeth, gazing up at a clear, star-strewn sky.

He lowered his gaze from the heavens to another starscape—this one the running lights of a fleet.

*His* fleet.

There were forty-two galleons in that fleet, over half the Kingdom of Dohlar's entire share of Mother Church's enormous new navy. Twenty-eight were converted merchant galleons, like *Rakurai* herself; the other fourteen, though, were purpose-built *war* galleons, sisters of Sir Dahrand Rohsail's *Grand Vicar Mahrys*. In fact, as Thirsk had promised, *Grand Vicar Mahrys* was present herself, and flying the streamer of a division commander, at that. Thirsk still thought Rohsail was an arrogant, opinionated, aristocratic pain in the arse, yet there was no denying that the man was a fighter. Thirsk was prepared to overlook quite a lot when a man displayed the sheer guts Rohsail obviously had.

As nearly as he'd been able to estimate the strength of the Charisian squadron, it couldn't have more than twenty-five galleons. Nor did it have as many schooners as *he* would have sent along on an expedition like this. Since there was no evidence of any sudden shortage of light cruisers on the Charisians' part, he could only put their absence down as a serious oversight on someone's part. Which was rather reassuring. It was nice to realize even Charisians could screw up.

*The object, Lywys,* he reminded himself, *is to let* them *do the screwing up.*

His lips twitched at the thought, but it was one he made a point of contemplating at least once a day.

The action off Dragon Island had given Bishop Staiphan the ammunition he'd needed to stave off the demands for precipitous action from Thirsk's political enemies. The Dohlaran Navy might have lost *Prince of Dohlar,* the bishop had pointed out acidly, but its ships had done immeasurably better than anyone else who'd crossed swords with the Imperial Charisian Navy. Under the circumstances, it behooved the authorities ashore to bestir themselves meeting Admiral Thirsk's requirements so that he could prepare a decisive blow instead of complaining that he wasn't "trying hard enough." Thirsk wasn't certain exactly how Bishop Staiphan had reported the action in his semaphore dispatches to the Temple, but however he'd described it, Allayn Maigwair had come down firmly on the bishop's side.

And that, as they said, had been that. At least for now.

*All well and good,* he thought now. *In fact, better than you ever really expected you were going to get away with before Thorast got you beached . . . assuming you were lucky enough for it to stop there. But now it's up to you to prove Bishop Staiphan was right to support you. And that means finding yourself some Charisians and pounding the ever living shit out of them . . . which is what brings you three thousand miles from home this beautiful evening. So why aren't you happier about being here?*

There were times, however little he was prepared to whisper that fact to a living soul, when Lywys Gardynir, the Earl of Thirsk, found himself wondering if the Church of Charis didn't have a far better understanding of what God truly wanted than Mother Church. Or, at least, than the Group of Four. It was a thought which had gained a greater, more poisonous strength following Zhaspahr Clyntahn's purge of the vicarate and the formal declaration of Holy War. The stakes were starker than ever, and he didn't want to think he might be on the wrong side. Didn't want to contemplate the possibility that his sword might be serving the Dark rather than the Light. But he was who he was—a son of Mother Church, a Dohlaran aristocrat, a vassal of King Rahnyld, and an admiral in the Royal Dohlaran Navy—and all of those people were at war with the Charisian Empire.

He couldn't change that even if he'd wanted to, and to be totally honest, whenever he remembered Rock Point and Crag Reach . . . and the ultimatum Prince Cayleb had given him the morning *after* Crag Reach, he *didn't* want to.

*No,* he thought, taking the pipe out of his mouth and tamping the tobacco with his thumb. *Happy or not, pounding the shit out of a few Charisian galleons for a change does have a certain appeal, doesn't it?*

He put the pipe back into his mouth, then stuck a sliver of resinous wood into the flame of the binnacle lantern illuminating the helmsmen's compass card, and used it to relight the tobacco. He puffed until it was drawing properly, then tossed the sliver over the taffrail. It arced from the quarterdeck into the sea like a tiny shooting star, and he looked back over the lights of his fleet once more, nodded in satisfaction, and headed below.

.III.

### HMS *Dancer,* 54,
### Gulf of Dohlar

There were times, Gwylym Manthyr thought, when it would have been far more satisfying to have been wrong. No doubt his reputation as a weather prophet would have suffered, yet he would infinitely have preferred that to facing what was probably the worst storm he'd ever encountered at sea.

Sunset's purple-black clouds had continued their remorseless advance, and the wind had risen from shrill-voiced wailing, to howling, to a frenzied scream. As he'd feared, the storm's swelling strength had made it impossible for his galleons to maintain their course towards Claw Island. They'd been forced to lie-to under fore and main storm staysails and goose-winged main topsails. He'd ordered the royal masts and topgallant masts sent down more on a hunch—a feeling—than anything else, but he was glad he had.

He clung to the quarterdeck rail, lifeline snug around his chest, staring up at the heavens, awed despite a lifetime at sea, by the boiling indigo fury. Lightning stuttered and flashed, exploding like Langhorne's own *rakurai* in long, jagged streaks like cracks between Creation and Hell. The cannonade of

Heaven's own thunder could be heard even through the hell-born wind-howl and the sea's stupendous, crashing fury. Waves reared thirty feet high and more, with long overhanging crests. The surface of the sea was completely covered with long white patches of foam, lying along the direction of the wind, and wave crests were white explosions of wind-shredded froth. The impact of those mighty waves was shock-like, slamming at the bones and sinews of his ships, and ice-cold rain, beating down so heavily that it actually washed the salt taste of flying spray off his lips, pounded on his streaming oilskins like needle-tipped fists. He could see only three other ships, despite the fiery illumination of the blue-white lightning—the others were obscured by rain, spray, and the mountainous waves themselves.

It was perhaps the single most terrifying, exhilarating moment of his life, and he felt his lips drawing back from his teeth in challenge as he clung to his flagship's rail and felt her limber, vibrant strength fighting back against the fury of the sea.

He had no business on this deck, and he knew it. He was a flag officer, not a captain, and he held no direct responsibility for *Dancer*'s handling . . . or survival. He'd never been as fully aware of his passenger's status as he was at this moment, and he wondered if Captain Mahgail resented his presence on deck. Thought it was a case of a nervous admiral looking over his flag captain's shoulder?

He hoped not, for the truth was that he had total faith in Raif Mahgail. It was just that on this night, in the teeth of a storm like this, he simply couldn't stay in his cabin while his wildly swaying cot swung from its deckhead gimbals.

Yet there was another reason he was here, for unless his instincts played him false, this magnificent, malignant monster of a storm had yet to reach its full fury. He'd always heard that storms born in the Great Western Ocean were like no others, and he'd always regarded those claims with a hefty dose of skepticism. This night was turning him into a believer. He'd lived through two hurricanes, neither of them actually at sea, and as he peered into the luridly illuminated heart of this storm's living fury, he knew it was rapidly approaching that level of violence. And this time he *wasn't* safe ashore.

*Just what I don't need,* he thought grimly.

He knew the storm drove his galleons deeper into the Gulf of Dohlar with every passing hour. What he didn't know was whether they'd be able to keep any sail set at all or whether Captain Mahgail would have no choice but to put *Dancer* before the wind under bare poles. A landsman might not believe a ship could actually make headway without a single scrap of canvas set, but the wind resistance of her standing rigging and furled sails would be more than enough to drive her in conditions like these, while any sail she might have set—even the triple thickness of a storm staysail—could carry away like so much tissue at any moment, potentially inflicting serious damage aloft.

At the moment, despite the storm's roaring violence, it was clear to his experienced eye that *Dancer* was in no immediate danger. She might stagger, shaking her head like a belligerent drunk, as another huge sea hurled itself upon her, sweeping in green and cream fury across her decks. She might lurch drunkenly, might groan and creak in every plank and timber while wind shrieked through her shrouds. And he knew the pumps were working, dealing with the water which managed to spurt around the edges of even the most tightly sealed gunport, find its way through the most closely covered hatch gratings. No doubt more water was finding its way through her seams as she worked in the violent seaway, as well, but that didn't concern him. It was only another indication of her true strength, the limber toughness that let her flex and bend, yielding *just* enough to the forces pounding at her hull.

But however well she might endure the sea's fury, she couldn't stand motionless in its face. He couldn't see the land spreading away, hundreds of miles to the north and south, as the continents of West Haven and Howard reached out to envelop his ships, yet he knew it was there.

*One thing at a time, Gwylym,* he told himself. *One thing at a time. First we survive . . .* then *we worry about Thirsk. Besides*—he felt himself baring his teeth once more—*if he's at sea on a night like this with that bunch of pressed landsmen of his, he's got enough things of his own to worry about to be leaving us the hell alone!*

.IV.
Tellesberg Cathedral,
City of Tellesberg,
Kingdom of Old Charis

Merlin Athrawes suspected Empress Sharleyan was going to have a few pungent things to say to him once she figured out what was going on. For that matter, he was fairly confident he'd deserve the empress' pointed observations about his character, if not the ones she might tack on about his intellect. He was prepared to take that as it came, however.

*Besides, Cayleb was right,* Merlin thought grimly, glancing up at the multichromatic brilliance of the cathedral's stained glass, lit by Tellesberg's morning sun. *The* last *thing she needs today, of* all *days, is that sort of distraction!*

At the moment, Archbishop Maikel Staynair, in the full glory of his episcopal regalia, his crown glittering with rubies, stood before the altar, his face creasing with a huge smile, as Her Imperial Majesty Sharleyan Alahnah Zhenyfyr Ahlyssa Tayt Ahrmahk advanced towards him along the runner of rich crimson carpet through the raised voices of the cathedral choir. She was escorted by His Imperial Majesty Cayleb Zhan Haarahld Bryahn Ahrmahk, and in her arms she carried the lustily protesting Crown Princess Alahnah Zhanayt Naimu Ahrmahk.

The empress' long black hair spilled over her shoulders, confined only by the light golden circlet of a simple presence crown. Her gown was equally simple, devoid of elaborate embroidery, without a single gem to sparkle and dance in the cathedral's multi-hued sunlight, and Cayleb was just as plainly dressed as he walked beside her. He wore the emerald necklace that proclaimed an Old Charisian king, instead of a crown, but he was unadorned by any other jewelry except for the wedding bands they both wore. They could have been any Charisian couple come to have their newborn daughter blessed and baptized by their village priest, but no village church was ever as packed and vibrantly attentive as Tellesberg Cathedral was this day.

*No,* Merlin thought. *She's got enough on her mind already, and it's too important that neither of them be distracted until we get through this.*

Today was more than a simple Naming Day, of course. Everyone in Tellesberg already knew exactly who Crown Princess Alahnah was, but this morning was the formal expression of her identity—the legal testament of her parents and of the lords temporal and secular of the Charisian Empire that she was not simply the most recent of its subjects but in her tiny person the heir to its throne—to the combined crowns of Old Charis, Chisholm, Emerald, Zebediah, Corisande, and (though no one else knew it yet) Tarot. It was a formality, true, but an *essential* formality, and one which admitted of no competing distractions.

*She's still going to be pissed off, though,* he admitted to himself. *She's already mad enough over the fact that Seamount hasn't been brought fully inside. When she finds out I told Owl to close her out of any take from the SNARCs about Gwylym and his squadron, she's going to be ready to chew horseshoes and spit nails.*

The only good news was that, at Cayleb's own suggestion, he'd done the same thing where the emperor was concerned. Unlike Sharleyan, Cayleb knew about the howling storm which had enveloped Gwylym Manthyr's galleons, but his own access to the orbiting SNARCs had been temporarily shut down. He knew there *was* a storm, which was more than Sharleyan did, yet that was all he knew, and Merlin was freshly impressed by his acting ability.

*No, not "acting ability,"* Merlin corrected himself. *That's not the right term. It implies some sort of . . . falsity, and that's not what's happening here. He's simply focused, concentrating on this event, and there's nothing at all false or assumed about that focus. I guess what I'm really impressed by is the fact that he can focus on this ceremony while in the back of his brain he has to be worried sick over what could happen to Gwylym.*

Midmorning in Tellesberg was the middle of the night in the approaches to the Gulf of Dohlar, and in the back of his own brain, Merlin watched tiny beads of light creeping across a chart as Manthyr's squadron was driven deeper and deeper into the Gulf.

*I wish to* hell *he had a com,* Merlin thought bitterly behind his own composed expression. Yet even as he thought it, he knew it wouldn't have made one bit of difference. Knowing a storm was coming was all very well, but that foreknowledge became academic for a fleet of wooden sailing galleons too slow to get out of its path. Even Owl had been taken by surprise by the speed with which the massive storm system had burst into existence, and Manthyr had already been headed for Claw Island by the time the AI became aware of the threat. In the absence of any closer friendly port, he'd really had no option but to continue doing what he'd already begun.

All of that was true enough, but what had already happened wasn't what had Merlin concerned. Owl's models all concurred; when the center of the storm hit the Tiegelkamp coast, it was going to lose a lot of its force—which, in many ways, wasn't a bad thing. But those models also all insisted that Gwylym Manthyr's galleons were going to take the brunt—were already *taking* the brunt—of its full strength first . . . and the Earl of Thirsk's squadron, well to the northeast, wasn't. The Dohlarans were going to experience some heavy weather of their own, but nothing to compare with what Manthyr's ships were enduring, because Tiegelkamp was going to break the worst of its power before it reached them. Worse, if Thirsk reacted as quickly and intelligently as Merlin feared he would, his galleons would be able to beat their way into the protection of Saram Bay, on the coast of Stene Province, before the full fury of wind and wave reached them.

And while they were doing that, Gwylym Manthyr was being blown steadily, and helplessly, closer and closer to their waiting arms.

Merlin Athrawes could no more do anything to change that than Empress Sharleyan might have, and he knew it. But at least if Manthyr had had a com, he could have been warned about Thirsk's presence. He could have been alerted to the potential threat, and—

*And* what, *Merlin?* he asked himself harshly. *He's already fully aware that Thirsk is almost certainly at sea somewhere, looking for him. That's why he was headed for Claw Island in the first place! And if there was one damned thing he could do to avoid being driven east, do you think for one minute he wouldn't already be* doing *it?*

It was true, and he knew it, and he wished he could bring himself to cut his *own* access to the SNARC—long enough, at least, to complete this ceremony. But he couldn't. He simply *couldn't,* and so he took refuge behind the stern "on-duty" façade of *Seijin* Merlin while the back of his mind continued to watch those tiny beads of light creeping steadily, steadily east.

Gwylym Manthyr wasn't surprised by his fatigue. After the last three days, he would have been astounded if his knees *hadn't* felt just a bit too limber and his eyes hadn't ached.

He stretched and yawned as he looked around *Dancer*'s quarterdeck in the morning light. His flagship had come through the tempest more or less intact, but she hadn't gotten off unscathed. Despite his having sent down the royals and topgallants, she'd lost her main and mizzen topmasts when a rogue wave rolled her almost onto her beam ends. She'd recovered—something he wouldn't have been prepared to bet on at the moment—and the violent roll as she came back the other direction had whipped the topmasts out of her.

The good news was that the wind had continued backing. By now, it was out of the south-southeast, far enough abaft the bow for *Dancer* to hold a westerly heading once again, close-hauled on the port tack under her main and mizzen courses and her fore topsail. It was an awkward, ill-balanced spread of canvas, but it was the best Captain Mahgail could manage until he could sway up replacement masts and spars. Unfortunately, the main and mizzen topgallant and royal masts had been lashed to the since-vanished topmasts when they were brought down and housed. They'd gone over the side with the lower masts, which meant they had to be replaced, as well. Not only would that require extra time, but *Dancer* didn't have *that* many replacement spars onboard. Whatever they could cobble up was going to be jury-rigged, at best, at least until Captain Mahgail could get her back to Claw Island and do a proper job.

*Looks like some of those coasters full of naval stores you sent back to Claw Island will come in handy after all,* he thought with a certain relish. The notion of using the Royal Dohlaran Navy's own spars to repair his damages appealed to him strongly.

And it was as well he had them, he reflected, his smile fading, because *Dancer* wasn't the only galleon who'd suffered damage aloft. Not surprisingly, the storm had scattered his ships. Only six of them were in sight at the moment, including *Dancer,* and four had lost spars, sails, or masts of their own. In fact, HMS *Rock Point* had lost her entire foremast, and her decks were a swarm of activity as her captain prepared to step a replacement. From *Dancer*'s quarterdeck, it looked as if he was using a spare main yard, which would probably serve well enough until they could get a proper mast set up back at Hardship Bay.

The true miracle, as far as Manthyr was concerned, was that HMS *Messenger*, the smallest of the schooners attached to the squadron, had not only survived the storm intact, but had actually located the flagship afterward. Just how Lieutenant Commander Grahzaial had managed both those feats was more than the admiral was prepared to guess at this point, but it certainly confirmed his already high opinion of Grahzaial's seamanship.

*That young man's in line for bigger and better things,* Manthyr thought. Then his lips twitched. *Of course, giving up something as lively as* Messenger *in return for a great, lumbering galleon may not strike him as a "better thing," at least at first. I'm sure he'll get over it, though.*

At the moment, *Messenger* was well to the east, keeping a wary eye on the horizon. Manthyr still wasn't certain exactly how deep into the Gulf of Dohlar they'd been driven, but his best guess put him just east of the Harchong Narrows, the roughly four-hundred-and-fifty-mile stretch between Stene's Cape Samuel to the north and the northern coast of Kyznetsov to the south. That would put him the better part of twelve hundred miles from Claw Island, which, combined with his ships' damaged rigging, was going to make getting back to the island a slow, dragging, unmitigated pain in the arse. At the same time, he didn't really expect the entire Dohlaran Navy to come sailing right at him. As severely as the storm had handled his own experienced, well-trained, well-found ships, he hated to think what it would have done to a less experienced fleet. If the Earl of Thirsk and his galleons had gotten in the way of *that* storm, they'd be lucky if they hadn't lost entire ships, far less the occasional mast or spar.

He stepped back out of the way as Lieutenant Yairman Seasmoke, *Dancer's* first lieutenant, and her boatswain prepared to send the replacement mizzen topmast aloft. Mahgail was actually using a replacement *fore* topmast, which was a bit longer than the mizzen topmast it was replacing, but approximately the same diameter, which would allow it to fit through the hole in the lower mast cap once it was set up. The broken stub of the original topmast had been lowered to the deck, and the jeers, the top rope, and the top block attached to the underside of the cap were already in place. Now the men on the hauling end of the top rope took the strain and the replacement spar began inching upward, supported by the rope rove through the sheave in its heel. It was longer than the lower mast's height above deck, so it had been necessary to take the heel of the new topmast forward, lowering it through the removed spar deck gratings to get sufficient clearance for it to be started up, but Seasmoke and the boatswain had things well in hand, and Manthyr watched the evolution with satisfaction.

"Excuse me, Sir."

Manthyr turned toward the politely raised voice and smiled at Lieutenant Rahzmahn. The auburn-haired young Chisholmian looked as tired as Manthyr felt.

"Naiklos, ah . . . *requested* that I inform you your breakfast is ready. I believe he's a bit provoked at not being able to offer you fresh eggs this morning."

Rahzmahn's expression was admirably grave, but the corners of his lips twitched, and Manthyr snorted. Both the chicken coop and the wyvern coop (wyverns and chickens couldn't be confined together, because the former had a tendency to eat the latter) had been washed overboard during the storm. Manthyr was grateful it hadn't been far worse, but Naiklos Vahlain clearly took it as a personal affront that the first hot meal he'd been able to offer his admiral in four days was going to be less than perfect.

"I'm sure he is—a bit provoked, I mean," the admiral said. "Which probably means I shouldn't keep him waiting. I assume you'll join me, Dahnyld?"

"Thank you, Sir. I will."

"Then let's you and I go beard the dragon in his lair."

▼   ▼   ▼

Manthyr was just finishing his third cup of tea, feeling pleasantly fed (fresh eggs or no), when someone knocked on the cabin door.

Vahlain scurried over to open it, and the admiral looked up, then raised his eyebrows and lowered his cup as Captain Mahgail stepped into the cabin.

"I apologize for interrupting your breakfast, Sir Gwylym." The flag captain could not have spoken more courteously, but something about his manner jangled an alarm bell in the back of Manthyr's brain.

"That's quite all right, Raif," he replied, setting the cup on its saucer. "Dahnyld and I had just finished. What can I do for you?"

"Sir, we've just received a signal from *Messenger*. She reports five sail, all galleons, bearing almost due east. According to Commander Grahzaial, it's a chase and four pursuers. And"—he met Manthyr's eyes levelly across the breakfast table—"the lead ship is flying Charisian colors."

▼   ▼   ▼

Captain Caitahno Raisahndo stood on HMS *Rakurai*'s quarterdeck, hands clasped behind him, and watched with fierce anticipation as his ship slowly, slowly overtook the fleeing Charisian galleon while three of her consorts—including Captain Saigahn's *Guardsman*—drove hard in her wake under all the canvas they could carry. Under normal circumstances, the Charisian would have been faster than they were, but she'd obviously been handled hard by the storm which had charged up the Gulf of Dohlar. It looked as if her mainmast might have been sprung during the storm. There had to be *some* reason she wasn't carrying more sail when she was being pursued at four-to-one odds, at any rate.

At the moment, Raisahndo didn't really care what her problem was. What he cared about was that the Royal Dohlaran Navy was about to exact its

vengeance for the action off Dragon Island. And just as Earl Thirsk had promised, Raisahndo and his ship would be in the lead.

He turned and looked astern. Beyond HMS *Scimitar*, the rearmost ship of
his own little force, he saw the mastheads and topgallants of at least two dozen
other ships. Some were very nearly hull-up from *Rakurai*'s quarterdeck; the
others were more strung out, scattered as each of them made the best speed
she could in obedience to Earl Thirsk's signal for "General Chase." Some of the
larger, purpose-built galleons, like Sir Dahrand Rohsail's *Grand Vicar Mahrys*,
which had been at the rear of the fleet's formation when the chase began, were
forging steadily ahead of their slower merchant-conversion consorts thanks to
their bigger, more powerful sail plans. But none of them were going to overtake
*Rakurai* before she overtook the Charisian she'd been pursuing since just before
dawn.

"Excuse me, Captain."

Raisahndo turned back forward and found himself facing Lieutenant
Mahntee, *Rakurai*'s first lieutenant.

"Yes, Charlz?"

"Sir, the forward masthead reports the chase is signaling."

"Signaling?" Raisahndo frowned. "I don't suppose the lookout can see
who she might be signaling *to*?"

"No, Sir. Not yet," Mahntee replied . . . which came as no particular surprise. Whoever the Charisian was signaling to must be well ahead, still over the
horizon from Raisahndo's own more distant lookouts. Although, he reflected,
whoever it was couldn't be *too* far ahead if he was close enough to read the
chase's signals.

He felt his hands folding more tightly together behind his back. Signal
flags implied someone to signal to, and Admiral Thirsk's most recent intelligence reports indicated the Charisian admiral had decided to retire on Claw Island, at least temporarily, which probably meant they'd met the storm head-on.
If they'd been scattered in the heavy weather, that might explain what the soli-
tary Charisian fleeing from Raisahndo was doing this far east all by herself.

But it also meant he and the three ships in company with *Rakurai* might be
rapidly closing with up to another twenty or so Charisian galleons.

*That would be like the old story about the hunting hounds that caught the slash
lizard,* he thought with grim humor. *On the other hand, I've got the Earl and all
the rest of the fleet handy for support. For that matter, it's always possible this fellow in
front of me's signaling to an empty ocean, hoping he can bluff me into thinking he's got
support handy.*

"Very well, Charlz. I don't know if the rest of the fleet's close enough to
read our signals, but signal *Scimitar*. Have her repeat to the Flag. 'Estimate unknown number enemy sail ahead. Chase signaling.' She's to keep that hoist flying until it's acknowledged by someone astern of her."

"At once, Sir."

Mahntee saluted, then beckoned for a midshipman while Captain Raisahn-do gazed ahead once more at the weather-stained canvas of the ship he was slowly overhauling.

▼　　▼　　▼

"Another signal from *Messenger,* Sir Gwylym."

Captain Mahgail's voice was harsher, and Manthyr warned his face to remain calm as he turned from the stern windows to face the flag captain. Lieutenant Commander Grahzaial had taken his small schooner farther to the east, trying to get into signal range of the Dohlaran galleon. That had taken her beyond any distance at which *Dancer's* signalmen could read her own signals. Now, the better part of two hours later, she was clearly close enough for that once more.

"Yes, Raif?" he inquired levelly, and Mahgail glanced at the sheet of paper in his hand.

"*Messenger* signals, 'Chase bears east-by-north, distance from Flag thirty miles. Chase identified HMS *Talisman*. *Talisman* reports damaged mainmast and four Dohlaran galleons in pursuit, range twelve miles, own speed six knots. Also reports many additional sail in sight to eastward.'"

"I see."

Manthyr turned back to the windows, listening to the sounds transmitted through the deck overhead as *Dancer's* crew attacked her repairs with redoubled energy. Not that it was going to make a great deal of difference.

Thirty miles to Captain Tymahn Klahrksain's *Talisman*. Twelve more to her pursuers, and, say, twenty to those "many additional sail" Klahrksain had reported. Fifty miles, then. The wind had freshened and backed still farther to the east. It was blowing a stiff topgallant breeze by now—not enough to significantly hamper *Dancer's* repairs, but it wasn't going to make them go any quicker, either. *Rock Point* was going to be rather more bothered by it, trying to replace her entire foremast, of course.

But what mattered was that *Talisman* was making at least six knots, even with damage—*And how much damage?* he wondered—aloft. If she could do that much but was still being overtaken, then her pursuers had to be capable of at least, say, seven. At the moment, *Dancer* could make possibly three, and *Rock Point* was even slower than that. Which meant the Dohlarans were overhauling him, whether they realized it or not, at somewhere around five knots.

*Ten hours,* he thought. *No more than five before their lookouts are able to see us, and it's not even lunchtime yet.*

The long summer Safeholdian day stretched out before him. There were at least another fourteen hours of daylight, and as if that weren't bad enough, the moon was just past full and he didn't see a cloud in the sky.

*They're going to overhaul you, Gwylym,* he told himself coldly. *It's going to happen. Now, what do you* do *about it?*

▼     ▼     ▼

Lywys Gardynyr, the Earl of Thirsk, looked down at the chart spread on his cabin table while he considered *Rakurai*'s signal.

By Thirsk's best estimate, anyone the fleeing Charisian galleon might be signaling to had to be at least fifty or sixty miles ahead. Normally, the chance of overtaking Charisians in this sort of weather wouldn't be very good—on average, Charisian galleons were bigger, able to carry more sail for a given wind condition, and despite any improvements to the Dohlaran Navy's sail plans, Charisian sails were still individually larger and more efficient.

*But that assumes they're undamaged, Lywys, and it's pretty obvious the fellow in front of Raisahndo isn't undamaged. Which means. . . .*

He suppressed the surge of anticipation, but it was hard. And what made it even harder was that the scenario unfolding in his mind's eye seemed so plausible.

He and his own galleons had been fortunate to make it into the shelter of Saram Bay when he realized the weather was making up. There, sheltered by the sharp fishhook shape of Cape Samuel, they'd ridden out the howling storm safe and snug. Even in their sheltered anchorage, two of his ships had dragged their anchors, but they'd managed to lay out additional anchors in plenty of time, and no one had ever been in any danger.

He'd been relieved by his ability to find shelter, because he'd been confident that, despite the vast improvement in his crews' sail drill, they would have lost ships if they'd been caught at sea. It wouldn't have been anyone's fault, either—just the consequences of inexperience, one of those little things landsmen didn't consider when they started blithely talking about throwing fleets around. He'd wondered at the time if any of his opponent's ships had been caught on the open sea, and he'd gotten his answer shortly before dawn.

Captain Raisahndo wasn't the only person pursuing a Charisian galleon this morning. Three more of Thirsk's galleons were the better part of forty miles to the *south,* pursuing a second Charisian at that very moment. Whether or not they were going to overtake her was another matter, but they were to windward of her, forcing her to flee farther *east*—deeper into the Gulf—to elude them. Unlike Raisahndo's quarry, the second Charisian's rigging appeared undamaged, and she was managing to open the range between her and her pursuers, albeit slowly. But even if she managed to shake them off completely, she'd still have to get back past the rest of Thirsk's fleet eventually if she wanted to escape the Gulf.

More to the point, the Charisians had no more than twenty galleons, all told, and if he already knew where *two* of them were, there couldn't be more than another eighteen—maximum—over *Rakurai*'s western horizon.

And even allowing for the ships off chasing the second Charisian, he had *thirty-nine*.

"Ahlvyn," he said, never looking away from the chart.

"Yes, My Lord?" Commander Khapahr replied.

"Have Captain Baiket signal all ships in company. 'Suspect maximum eighteen enemy sail bearing approximately due west, distance fifty miles. Make all possible sail. Prepare for battle.' "

▼    ▼    ▼

It was just after midday when the first Dohlaran galleon came into sight from *Dancer's* quarterdeck. There were four of them, actually, and the two leading ships had been exchanging long-range fire with *Talisman* for over an hour before Manthyr found them with his own spyglass. It was unlikely *Talisman's* long fourteens were going to inflict serious damage at such extended range, and even less likely the Dohlarans' lighter twelve-pounders were going to accomplish a great deal. Especially when none of the pursuers could bring more than two guns each to bear, compared to *Talisman's* four stern chasers. The possibility always existed, of course, and as *Dancer's* own lamed condition demonstrated only too clearly, damage aloft could impose severe constraints on a ship's ability to maneuver. More than that, the breeze was stiff enough, and everyone was carrying such a heavy press of canvas, that even damage which would normally have been minor could quickly become serious.

But *Talisman* hadn't been lucky enough to inflict that sort of damage on any of her pursuers, and as the range had dropped, Captain Klahrksain's reports had become ever more detailed . . . and hopeless.

There were at least thirty Dohlaran ships back there. For that matter, Manthyr could see the topgallants of at least twenty of them from his own quarterdeck now. And, unlike his own ship, *they* were obviously undamaged.

*How the hell did Thirsk pull that off?* a corner of Manthyr's brain wondered almost conversationally. *He sure as hell can't have been through what we went through! So how . . . ?*

Saram Bay, he decided. That was the only answer, given the relative positions of the two forces and the Dohlarans' present heading. They'd managed to get into the bay's shelter, ridden out the storm, and then come hunting again.

And this time, they'd gotten lucky.

There wasn't a defeatist bone in Sir Gwylym Manthyr's body, but he was a realist, and even adding *Talisman* to the ships already in company with *Dancer*, he'd have only eight. Eight . . . and only four of them were truly anything he'd call maneuverable. *Rock Point* and *Dancer* certainly weren't. *Damsel,* one of his converted merchantmen, had lost her fore and main topmasts. She was in little better shape than *Dancer,* and her repairs had been going more slowly. *Avalanche,* yet another converted merchantman, had lost her jibboom and bowsprit when she buried her head in a massive wave. The total sail area she'd lost wasn't all that vast, but headsails were particularly important when it came to maneuvering. Almost worse, she'd lost all four of the essential stays which set up from the complex structure of the foremast to the bowsprit, providing every bit of its forward support, which seriously weakened the entire structure of her rigging. Her crew had steeved a spare main topgallant yard as a stubby substitute, lashing it to the remnants of the shattered bowsprit, but it projected forward for barely twenty feet. That was a poor substitute for the bowsprit and jibboom's original *ninety* feet of length. They were rigging the new stays now—or working on it, at any rate—but even once they'd done that, her foremast would be far more fragile than before the storm.

*Dasher* and *Destruction*, his remaining two galleons, were undamaged aloft. In this sort of weather, with any sort of head start, they should be able to show a clear pair of heels to any Dohlaran galleon ever launched. Except that none of their consorts could do the same thing.

Gwylym Manthyr had considered his limited options and alternatives carefully. And then, unflinchingly, he'd made his decision.

"Hoist the signal to *Dasher* and *Destruction,* if you please," he said quietly.

"Yes, Sir," Lieutenant Rahzmahn replied, equally quietly.

Within minutes, the gaily colored bunting was streaming to the wind, stiff and starched as so much hammered metal. Manthyr didn't look up at the signal himself, although he saw some members of *Dancer*'s company craning their necks as the flags broke. Every man aboard knew what the signal said; Manthyr had agreed with Raif Mahgail that they had a right to know—know both what their admiral had decided, and why he had decided it.

The answer was simple enough. *Dancer, Rock Point, Damsel,* and *Avalanche* couldn't run. *Dasher, Destruction,* and—possibly—*Talisman* could. So those who couldn't were going to cover the escape of those who could.

A battle at eight-to-one odds could have only one outcome. On the other hand, the short end of ten-to-three odds was no better, when all was said. For that matter, it wasn't at all certain *Talisman* would be able to disengage from her pursuers, after all. But this way, those who *could* get free would have the best chance to do that, and at least Thirsk was said to be an honorable man. When the time came for Manthyr's ships to strike, he hoped they'd find that was true.

He watched *Dasher* and *Destruction* setting more sail, beginning to lean more heavily to the press of their canvas while *Rock Point, Damsel,* and *Avalanche* turned towards the invisible coast of Tiegelkamp, far to the north, taking the wind almost dead aft as they formed line of battle ahead and astern of *Dancer* . . . directly across the Dohlarans' course.

"Hoist Number One, Captain Mahgail," Manthyr said, watching *Talisman* surge closer and closer to his truncated line. All four of Klahrksain's pursuers were firing their bow chasers now, and he even saw a wind-shredded puff of gunsmoke from the forecastle of yet another of the Dohlaran galleons, much farther astern.

He heard cheers as the signal—"Engage the enemy"—broke from *Dancer's* yardarm, but they were more subdued than usual, those cheers. No less determined, but without the high, confident dragon's snarl of sublime Charisian confidence, the knowledge that Charis reigned supreme wherever there was saltwater. He didn't blame the men for that. Indeed, his heart swelled with pride as they produced a cheer at all, even as he wept inside for what he was about to demand of them.

He stood as the endless minutes ticked past, listening to the approaching gunfire, watching *Talisman* foam ahead, watching the white water burst around her cutwater, the clouds of spray fly like sun-struck diamonds. She was close enough now for him to see splinters fly when a Dohlaran round shot slammed into her quarter galley. He could see holes in her spanker, her mizzen topsail, her main topgallant. Severed shrouds trailed over the side, hanging from her mizzen chains as evidence yet another Dohlaran shot had found its target. And he could see the damaged mainmast leaning dangerously, even under its reduced canvas, despite the spare mainyard her crew had fished to it in an effort to strengthen it.

She came closer, charging towards the line of her consorts, and Manthyr heard her crew cheering as her crippled sisters prepared to cover her escape. He saw Captain Klahrksain standing on his quarterdeck, raising his hat in silent salute to the ships standing to die so his own ship might live.

Her pursuers slowed abruptly, unwilling to sail directly into the prepared broadsides of four waiting Charisian galleons, and the distance between them and *Talisman* grew suddenly wider as the Charisian ship drove straight through the gap Manthyr had deliberately left between *Dancer* and *Damsel*.

He wasn't surprised to see the quartet of Dohlarans split, two trying to work around ahead of his short line while the other two tried to pass astern of it. He didn't doubt that if they could get close enough, find the position they wanted, they'd rake his leading and trailing ships heavily as they passed. He didn't intend to give them that opening, and he doubted they expected him to. They were simply continuing their pursuit of their original quarry—slowed, forced to drop astern, by the roadblock of Manthyr's battleline, but not stopped. He could only hope the delay he'd imposed would be sufficient for *Talisman* to regain enough ground to stay away from them at least until dark.

*Or, for that matter, for* Dasher *and* Destruction *to fall back enough to cover her,* he thought grimly.

He hoped it would work out that way, but it was out of his hands, now. His duty and his task, like his options, had become brutally simple, and he remembered the Battle of Darcos Sound. Remembered the decision a monarch had made that day. The example and the challenge a dead king had presented to his navy and his kingdom.

"We'll have that final signal now, Dahnyld," he said, almost softly, and another hoist of flags replaced Number One. It was a longer hoist, using more flags, because one of the words wasn't in the numerical vocabulary and had to be spelled out in its entirety, yet it was only three words.

For a moment, there was no sound except wind and wave. Even the gunfire of *Talisman*'s pursuers had died away as their new headings took her out of the play of their chasers. But then, as men aboard the other ships of Gwylym Manthyr's short, doomed line read those flags, or had them read to them, the cheering began. The hard, harsh, defiant, *savage* cheering—the wolf howl's cheering—he'd known those three words would awaken. He felt himself taking off his own hat, waving it over his head, waving it at those signal flags, and the flagship's cheering redoubled.

Such a simple message, yet one whose meaning, whose significance, no Charisian could ever mistake, just as Manthyr knew the men of his ships had not mistaken it.

"Remember King Haarahld," it said. And as he listened to those cheers, he knew that was all it had to say.

.VI.
Imperial Palace,
City of Tellesberg,
Kingdom of Old Charis

It was very quiet in the Tellesberg Palace library. The sun had set, darkness was settling over the landscaped grounds, and the tall grandfather's clock in one corner ticked loudly, steadily, in the stillness. Crown Princess Alahnah slept in her bassinet at her mother's side, although it wasn't going to be long before she roused again, demanding her next meal.

Merlin Athrawes was glad she would. All of them needed that reaffirmation of life and hope and growth. Needed it badly, at this particular moment.

"I should have insisted on sending more ships," High Admiral Lock Island said quietly over his com from his distant flagship.

"We didn't have them to send, Bryahn," Domynyk Staynair replied, equally quietly. "Not then."

"Besides, it's not as if it would've made a lot of difference," Cayleb said. "Not in this situation. And it's not as if Gwylym made any mistakes, for that matter. The problem is that *Thirsk* didn't make any, either."

"That and the storm," Merlin agreed, subvocalizing over his own built-in com from his post just outside the library door. "I think that at the very worst he could have fought a running engagement clear back to Claw Island if he'd had all eleven ships concentrated when Thirsk happened across him. Assuming he couldn't simply have outrun the Dohlarans."

"Of course it was the storm." Cayleb nodded. "But it wouldn't have mattered against someone like the Harchongese—or even against the Desnairians, at this point—because *they* wouldn't have been at sea when it hit." His nod turned into a headshake. "We all knew Thirsk was their most dangerous admiral. The relationship he's managed to forge with Maik makes him even more dangerous, since it covers his back against his political enemies, but we always knew he wasn't going to make the mistakes the rest of their so-called naval commanders are going to make."

"At the moment, it's rather cold comfort to have the accuracy of our predictions confirmed," Lock Island said bitterly, and once again, Merlin found himself in complete agreement.

Gwylym Manthyr's stand had successfully covered *Dasher* and *Destruction*'s escape, even though the two of them had dropped back to protect *Talisman*. Caitahno Raisahndo had realized none of his consorts were going to be able to join him . . . and that his quartet of galleons were no match for three purpose-built Charisian war galleons. Once he'd accepted that, he'd turned back to join the general assault on Manthyr's crippled line of battle.

In fact, the only real flaws in Thirsk's handling of the engagement, if they could be called "flaws," were the way his captains had permitted themselves to all be drawn in against Manthyr's line and the lack of order as his ships crowded in to engage the Charisians. In their eagerness to get to grips, his captains flung themselves on the formation right in front of them and allowed the ships which had kept running to escape. And as they swarmed around Manthyr's short line, they'd gotten in one another's way, turning what should have been the methodical demolition of a vastly outnumbered force into a wild melee.

It wasn't really anyone's fault. Thirsk's order for a "general chase" had undoubtedly been the correct one. Rather than limit his entire fleet to the speed of its slowest unit, it had freed his faster units by ordering every ship to pursue independently. But it also meant his own flagship had been too far astern of those faster consorts for him to exercise tactical control once action was actually joined. His division commanders had made efforts in that direction, but most of them were still too new to their own command responsibilities—and to the potential control their new signal systems permitted—to impose true discipline.

The good news from the Dohlaran perspective was that discipline had broken down in a surfeit of *aggressiveness,* not hesitation. But the bad news was that Gwylym Manthyr had given them an extraordinarily costly lesson about the difference between an ordered formation and a mob.

The Charisian line had maintained iron discipline, pounding its opponents with deadly accurate broadsides. The smashing power of those heavy Charisian guns had savaged the Dohlaran galleons as they attempted to close, and more than one Dohlaran warship—hammered by the Charisian artillery—had staggered aside, at least briefly. Half the time, it seemed, that had brought them into collision with one of their consorts, and several of them had drifted completely out of the action, locked together by fouled rigging until their chastened crews could get them untangled.

Yet, in the end, not even Charisian discipline could overmatch such superior numbers. Not when their foes were just as willing to fight as they were. Eventually, a degree of order had been sorted out of the chaos, with Sir Dahrand Rohsail taking a leading role in the sorting, and a Dohlaran line of battle had coalesced. *Two* Dohlaran lines of battle, in fact, and the Charisian galleons had found themselves engaged from both sides simultaneously and pounded slowly into ruin.

That had been the end. Not immediately, of course. Charisian seamen were too stubborn to yield easily, and Gwylym Manthyr had been determined to attract as many of Thirsk's ships onto his own as he could. To inflict as much damage, lame as many of them, as possible.

The brutal engagement had lasted almost four hours—lasted until all four Charisian galleons had been completely dismasted. Until their sides had been beaten in by point-blank cannon fire. Until blood ran from their scuppers, and the remaining gunners could scarcely serve their pieces because of the bodies in their way. They'd inflicted as many casualties as they'd taken—Merlin was certain of that—but their own losses were heartbreaking. It was impossible to be positive yet, even with the SNARCs, but he would be surprised if Gwylym Manthyr's crews hadn't taken at least sixty percent casualties before it was all over. He hoped he was overestimating, that the sheer fury of the engagement had caused him to be too pessimistic. Unfortunately, he couldn't convince himself he had been.

Nor had *Dancer* and her three consorts been Manthyr's only losses. HMS *Silverlode* had been driven ashore and wrecked at the height of the storm. Half her crew had been lost when she drove onto the rocks amid thirty-five-foot waves; the other half had been rounded up by the Harchong Army . . . who'd killed over half of the survivors in the process. HMS *Defense* had simply foundered, driven over on her beam ends by a huge sea no one could have seen or avoided in the darkness. She'd filled almost instantly and gone down with her entire company. And *Dagger* had ultimately been cornered against a lee shore by a trio of Thirsk's galleons. Forced to fight against such heavy odds, she'd given a good account of herself before she was forced to surrender, but it was obvious the Dohlaran Navy's days of letting itself be bullied into allowing Charis to dictate the terms of battle were over. And, finally, HMS *Howell Bay* and HMS *North Bay* were still deep inside the Gulf of Dohlar, trying to work their separate ways back out again without being intercepted.

Of Gwylym Manthyr's nineteen galleons, including the captured *Prince of Dohlar,* eight had been captured or destroyed by the storm, and two might yet be intercepted before they could break free of the Gulf. The others had reached Claw Island by now, or would reach it shortly, and Captain Pawal, the senior officer left, had received Gwylym Manthyr's final orders. Given the losses he'd already anticipated, and the obvious Dohlaran strength in the western portion of the Gulf of Dohlar, those instructions had been clear, concise, and unwavering.

It was only a matter of time—and not much of that—before Thirsk moved to attack Claw Island. So it was time to go, and Pawal was ordered to evacuate the Marines and all of the transports, covered by the remaining galleons.

Instead of heading east to return to Old Charis, however, he was to sail *west,* to Chisholm. It would actually be a shorter journey, and given the Dohlaran performance, reinforcing Chisholm had just become a significantly higher priority.

Yet the truth remained that the Charisian expedition wasn't simply withdrawing, its mission accomplished. Oh, it would have been withdrawing even without the storm. And if it had—if Manthyr had evacuated Claw Island as planned and sailed home again—it would have been a very different matter. But that wasn't what had happened. For the first time, one of the Church's subject navies had scored an unambiguous victory over the Imperial Charisian Navy. What had happened off Dragon Island could be argued either way, claimed as a tactical victory by either side. What had happened in the Harchong Narrows could not.

*And the truth is,* Merlin told himself unflinchingly, *that Thirsk damned well earned that victory. The weather might have let him collect it, but it's entirely possible we would have gotten hurt even worse if not for the storm. He was closer behind Gwylym than Gwylym realized, and even if his crews were less disciplined than he might have wished, they were full of fight. If he'd managed to get all forty-two of his ships into the approaches to Claw Island the way he'd planned, especially with him right there to impose tactical discipline, while Gwylym had to claw his way out with only nineteen warships and all those transports to protect . . .*

Manthyr's decision to fight had prevented that much, at least. In what Merlin privately considered to be Thirsk's only real mistake of the entire campaign, the Dohlaran earl had decided to take his own damaged ships and their prizes to Yu-Shai in Shwei Bay for repairs before resuming his offensive. In some ways, given the fact that he didn't know where Manthyr's other galleons were, it had made sense to avoid the risk that his cripples and captures might be pounced upon by undamaged Charisian warships. In fact, though, Merlin was certain Thirsk's decision had been shaped more by a desire to show Yu-Shai what the Dohlaran Navy had done to the squadron which had attacked the city. And to ensure that his prizes did get home to Gorath Bay in the end. Not just because they were his trophies, either, although Merlin never doubted Thirsk had at least enough of common human vanity to want to display his prizes as exactly that. No. Those captured Charisian ships were going to be the proof his methods, his strategy, and his tactics actually *worked*. That Charisian squadrons could be defeated . . . and that he was the admiral who could do the defeating.

*Maybe I should reconsider that decision not to simply assassinate him,* he thought. He didn't want to get into the habit of doing things like that but still . . .

"At least Sir Gwylym's still alive," Sharleyan said into the stillness. She was the only member of the conversation who'd never gotten to know Manthyr personally, but what she had known about him she'd liked. Now she looked across the bassinet at her husband and reached out to lay a comforting hand on his knee. "We have that much," she reminded him.

"Yes." He covered her hand with his own, then inhaled deeply and smiled at her. "Yes, we do. And it looks as if Thirsk has forgiven me for marooning him and his men on Armageddon Reef after Crag Reach."

He actually managed a chuckle, and Merlin snorted mentally. He'd been there when Cayleb delivered his ultimatum to Thirsk, and he knew the emperor had been at least a little anxious about how Thirsk might react the first time Charisians had to surrender to him.

In the event, he'd treated Manthyr and his officers and men with rigorous propriety under the Safeholdian customs of war. His healers had tended Manthyr's wounded as conscientiously as they had looked after their own, and the surviving officers had been shown every courtesy by their captors. To be honest, that was exactly what Merlin had expected out of Thirsk, although it was a vast relief to have his expectations confirmed.

*And it would be an even vaster relief if I could be certain Thirsk was going to be allowed to hang on to them,* he thought grimly. *Which is* another *reason not to assassinate him, damn it.*

He snorted to himself, wondering why it was that he found the thought of assassinating someone he respected, even admired, so repugnant when he would have killed the same man in open battle with barely a qualm.

*I guess everyone has to have a sticking point somewhere. And it's not as if there weren't logical reasons* not *to kill him off. If we did, and if it was an obvious assassination—or even something Clyntahn could simply claim* might *have been an assassination—it would only reinforce the suspicions of everyone who thinks Cayleb had Hektor murdered. But even that's not the worst of it. Killing him off would only make room for someone else, probably one of his "disciples," someone who's already imbibed his own theories and plans, like Hahlynd. They might not be quite as good as he is, but they'd probably be good enough. And for another, he* has *treated his prisoners decently, at least so far. Can we afford to kill off someone on the other side who seems determined to do that? Especially in the wake of what Clyntahn did to the Wylsynns and their friends?*

That was what worried him most, at the moment, he admitted to himself. Would Thirsk be allowed to retain possession of "his" prisoners? Or would someone else be given charge of them?

*For the first time, the Church has the opportunity to get its hands on an entire clutch of Charisian "heretics," and I hope to God they don't do what I'm afraid they might. Clyntahn's purge of the vicarate was bad enough. If he decides to turn this into the kind of religious war Old Earth saw entirely too many of, with atrocities provoking counteratrocities, even from* Charisians . . .

"How do you think Clyntahn's going to respond to this, Merlin?" Lock Island asked, almost as if he'd been reading Merlin's mind, and Merlin shrugged.

"I don't know," he said honestly. "On *so* many levels, I don't know. But I do know one thing."

"What?" Cayleb asked when he paused.

"I know we'd damned well better get Seamount and Howsmyn started cranking out those new shells of theirs," Merlin told him.

# SEPTEMBER,
# YEAR OF GOD 894

.I.
Sir Koryn Gahrvai's Townhouse
and
Royal Palace,
City of Manchyr,
Princedom of Corisande

Sir Koryn Gahrvai walked into his study carrying a glass of Chisholmian whiskey and crossed to his desk. He used his free hand to turn up the wick on the oil lamp one of the servants had lit earlier in the evening and started to set down the whiskey, then stopped abruptly.

There was an envelope on his desk. *He* hadn't left it there; in fact, he'd never seen it before. On the other hand, he did recognize the handwriting. *That* he'd seen before.

*Well,* he thought after a moment, *at least this time there's no broken glass.*

He finished setting down the whiskey and seated himself. He gazed at the envelope for a few more seconds, then shrugged and picked it up.

As the last time, there were several sheets of paper, but instead of the pair of hand-drawn maps which had accompanied the first letter, there were three. Not of secret rooms in monasteries this time, but of the city of Telitha in the Earldom of Storm Keep. One was a precisely annotated street map, indicating names and addresses. He recognized some of the names already; others, he'd never heard of, but he suspected that when he got around to the rest of the letter, he'd find out who they were. The second map was a diagram of Storm House, the Earl of Storm Keep's residence, this one marked with neat arrows indicating concealed caches of correspondence and other documentary evidence, and one small suite simply marked "the Bishop Executor's rooms." And the third . . .

His eyes lit as he saw the warehouses and followed more neat arrows to the areas in which camouflaged crates which had arrived in Corisande by way of Zebediah had been stored.

*You know, I didn't really believe you when you told me about all this,* Seijin Merlin, he thought, sipping whiskey before he started reading the letter itself. *Oh, I guess I did intellectually. But deep inside, I never really believed there truly was this vast network of seijins scattered around the world. But*—he looked around the study, looked at the closed and locked glass doors leading to the central garden, thought about the sentries around the townhouse—*I don't see who else could've gotten in here and left this for me!*

He snorted a laugh, took another sip, then stood and crossed back to the study door. He opened it and looked out at the sentry outside it.

"I need some messengers, Corporal."

"Of course, Sir! How many?"

"Well, let me see. I need one to Sir Charlz Doyal, one to my father, one to Earl Tartarian, and one to Viceroy General Chermyn." The corporal's eyes had widened a bit farther with each name, but he only nodded, and Gahrvai smiled at him. "Tell Major Naiklos I said to pick good, reliable men he knows will keep their mouths shut. I'll have notes for them to deliver by the time they can assemble here. Oh, and find Yairman Uhlstyn. I'll want him . . . and he'll want to be here."

"Yes, Sir!" the sentry said, and dashed off down the hallway. Gahrvai watched him go, then went and sat behind his desk, pulled several sheets of stationery out of a drawer, dipped a pen, and began writing.

▼　　▼　　▼

"What's this all about, Koryn?" Sir Rysel Gahrvai grumbled as he marched into the meeting chamber. "I'd just settled in for the evening when your man came thundering on the front door!"

"I apologize for disturbing you, Father, but something's come up."

"Damn it, you *know* how I hate those words!" the Earl of Anvil Rock groused, crossing to his chair at the council table. " '*Something*' has been '*coming up*' at the most inconvenient possible moment for the last two damned *years*!"

He plunked himself down, leaned back, and regarded his eldest son and the apple of his eye with remarkably scant favor. His august and trusted fellow councilor, Earl Tartarian, chuckled, and Anvil Rock turned his glower upon him.

"I suppose you think this is humorous?" he demanded, his tone irate, although there might have been just a spark of amusement in his eyes. "I happen to know that you usually stay up until all hours, anyway, instead of going to bed at a *sane* hour. You probably hadn't even had supper yet when this young jackanapes' note reached you!"

"Of course I hadn't," Tartarian soothed. "Whatever you like, Rysel. And now, if you've got that out of your system, perhaps we could get down to business?"

"Spoilsport," Anvil Rock muttered, but he also turned his attention back to his son. "All right, Koryn," he said in quite a different tone. "What is it?"

"I just received a note of my own, Father," Gahrvai replied. "The one *Seijin* Merlin warned me I might be receiving."

"Ah?" Anvil Rock sat up straighter, his eyes narrowing.

"You're certain this is really from one of Merlin's mysterious . . . assistants, Koryn?" Tartarian sounded a bit cautious, and Gahrvai didn't blame him.

"I don't see how anyone but another *seijin* could have delivered it the way it was delivered." Gahrvai shrugged. "It was on my desk in my locked study when I walked in after dinner, My Lord. And there's enough sensitive material in that study that it's under guard day and night. But *someone* got in, anyway. I'm not going to say it would have been *impossible* for someone other than a *seijin* to pull that off, but it would certainly have been difficult. And Charlz"—he twitched his head towards the foot of the table, where Charlz Doyal was poring over the letter even as he spoke—"is confident what he's seen so far is genuine. You know we've been doing a little checking of our own ever since *Seijin* Merlin warned us about this 'Northern Conspiracy' of his. We haven't wanted to overset any potato carts or step on any of the *seijin's* . . . associates' toes, so we haven't pushed too hard. Everything we've turned up, though, is consistent with this letter."

"I see." Tartarian looked at Anvil Rock. "Rysel?"

"If Koryn and Charlz are satisfied it's genuine, so am I." Anvil Rock's expression was as grim as Tartarian remembered ever having seen it. "And, to be honest, I'm just as glad to hear it. I *want* these bastards, Taryl. I want them badly."

Gahrvai watched his father's expression, as well, marveling at how Anvil Rock's attitudes had altered since he'd unwillingly assumed the role of the absent Prince Daivyn's regent. The earl was no happier than he had been at the notion that his princedom had been conquered by a foreign power, and as the man who'd commanded Prince Hektor's army, he continued to take that conquest as a personal failure. At the same time, however, it was obvious he'd come to genuinely accept that the Charisian occupiers were doing their best to be no more repressive than they had to. And, Gahrvai knew, little though his father cared to admit it, Anvil Rock had grudgingly, against his will, fighting every inch of the way, come to accept that Cayleb of Charis and Sharleyan of Chisholm were better rulers than Hektor had been, as well.

*Oh, how he fought that one!* Gahrvai thought ruefully. *It really stuck in his craw. And I suppose I understand that, too. They were cousins, and here at home, at least, Hektor always tried to ride with a light rein. But you were too close to him, Father, weren't you? You knew what he was like when it came to the "great game." Just like you knew—as well as I did—who really started the conflict between Corisande and Charis. And it wasn't Haarahld, was it?*

Even now Sir Koryn Gahrvai wasn't even tempted to think of his father as a Charisian partisan. In fact, the mind boggled at the concept. But, especially since Archbishop Maikel's visit, Anvil Rock had at least accepted that Charis was trying to make a bad situation better. And, Gahrvai suspected, while the earl might not yet have worked his way around to considering himself a Charisian subject, he *had* found himself much more firmly in agreement with the *Church* of Charis' doctrine—and the growing support that doctrine was finding among Corisande's own Reformists—than he'd ever anticipated.

*Which is the real reason you want "those bastards," Father,* Gahrvai thought affectionately. *Because you don't trust them as far as you could spit upwind. Because you know damned well people like Craggy Hill and Barcor and Zebediah aren't trying to make a bad situation better . . . unless they can do better for themselves in the process.*

"Your note said you were informing the Viceroy General?" his father said, and he nodded.

"Yes, Father." He shrugged slightly. "First, because it was my responsibility to inform him, and, second, because I figured it was entirely possible he was going to get a note of his own." Gahrvai smiled crookedly. "Under the circumstances, it seemed the most prudent thing to do. Although I did tell him I'd be meeting with you and Earl Tartarian and that you two would advise him of the Regency Council's decision in this matter."

"Tactful sort, aren't you?" his father observed, then looked at Tartarian. "Well, Taryl, I don't see that we have a lot of 'deciding' to do here, despite Koryn's efforts to spare our feelings. And I'm not sure I see any reason to go convening the entire Council, either. This clearly comes under the executive authority of the Crown, which is presently vested in me as Regent. Besides, we have—as Koryn just pointed out—an obligation to inform Chermyn and cooperate with him fully in this matter." He grimaced. "Comes with all those oaths the bunch of us and Parliament swore to Cayleb and Sharleyan. Would you agree?"

"With the observation that nobody in Zion or the Temple is ever going to accept those oaths as binding, yes," Tartarian said mildly.

"Huh!" Anvil Rock snorted contemptuously and shook his head. "Of course they aren't! But the truth is, Taryl, I've discovered I really don't give a fart for the damned Group of Four anymore. This whole mess is that lizard-loving bastard Clyntahn's fault in the first damned place. And 'Grand Inquisitor' or no, if *he* really gives a damn what God wants, I'm a frigging Harchong grand duke!"

Gahrvai's eyes widened. Despite his own earlier thoughts about Anvil Rock's attitude towards the Church of Charis, that was, by any measure, the strongest statement his father had ever made about the Temple's current leadership. Yet even though he'd never expected to hear it, what surprised him the most was that he felt so *little* surprise when the words were actually said.

He looked at Tartarian and felt another little spasm of surprise, because Tartarian was actually *smiling* at Anvil Rock.

"Took you a little while to figure that out, did it, Rysel?"

"His mother"—Anvil Rock twitched a thumb in his son's direction—"always did say I could be a little slow. But I'll tell you this, Taryl, it'll be a cold day in hell when you see someone like Grand Vicar Erek or that murderous asshole Clyntahn trekking all the way out to someplace like Corisande. You think they give a spider-rat's arse what happens to us out here?"

"Of course not," Tartarian said quietly. "I never did. On the other hand, I never thought there was any way to change that, either."

"Well, neither did I, really," Anvil Rock admitted. "And I didn't think there was when Cayleb sailed over here from Old Charis and kicked our arses up between our ears, either. Religious reform? Dragon shit! Old-fashioned imperial politics with a new justification, that's what it was, and I knew it. I'm still not entirely ready to give up on that interpretation, either, but . . ."

"But then there's Archbishop Maikel, isn't there?" Tartarian finished for him in a soft voice, and Anvil Rock nodded.

"There's Archbishop Maikel, and there's priests like Father Tymahn, and there's the cold-blooded bastards who *murder* priests like Father Tymahn. Bastards like Zhaspahr Clyntahn, who murder *children* and call it 'God's will.' "

Muscles bunched in Anvil Rock's jaw for a moment, and then he closed his eyes, inhaled deeply, and gave himself a shake. When he opened his eyes again, the jaw muscles had relaxed once more, and he smiled crookedly.

"I don't think Cayleb Ahrmahk is the Archangel Langhorne come back in glory, but I *do* think he's a basically good young man doing the best he can in one hell of a messy situation. A young man who refused to just roll over and die when the Group of Four decided to destroy his kingdom. I also think Clyntahn and the Inquisition have shown their true colors now. And I'll tell you this right now, Taryl—I'll side with anyone this side of Shan-wei herself who's willing to stand up to someone like that."

.II.
City of Telitha,
Telith Bay,
Earldom of Storm Keep,
Princedom of Corisande

There was nothing remarkable about the two merchant galleons lying to anchor well out from the harborside quays of the city of Telitha. They'd arrived separately, hours apart, one flying the house flag of a rather disreputable Manchyr trading house, and the other of Chisholmian registry. They'd anchored within a few hundred yards of one another, then proceeded to ignore each other as they awaited their own turns to go along quayside or lighter their cargo ashore.

Neither seemed in any particular hurry, since their skippers hadn't made any special push to arrange to land their cargoes, but no one in Telitha cared particularly about that. In fact, no one in Telitha paid them the slightest mind as they lay there, a handful of men moving about their decks, watching darkness settle slowly over the bay. Lights began to glow here and there ashore—nothing like the illumination one might have seen out of Tellesberg or Cherayth, or even Manchyr, but glittering like beached stars nonetheless. They seemed even brighter tonight than they might have been otherwise, since there happened to be no moon.

Complete darkness closed in, turning the galleons into all but invisible black blots against the only slightly brighter water. Stars came out overhead, briefly mirrored in the oily-smooth swell, but even as they appeared, cloud began sweeping in from the east.

▼    ▼    ▼

*This,* Sir Koryn Gahrvai thought, standing on the quarterdeck of one of those galleons and watching the incoming clouds steadily erase the stars, *is ridiculous. I'm willing to believe in* seijins, *I guess, and I suppose—especially after listening to Father; talk about conversions!—I can accept that God is on Archbishop Maikel's side. That's not the same thing as being on* Cayleb's *side, though! And even if it were, how did even a* seijin *arrange a night like this? It's like the Archangels delivered the damned weather to order!*

Under the circumstances, it was a reasonable enough question. Then again, Gahrvai didn't know about SNARCs, or an AI named Owl, or the meteorological projections he could make. Nor did he have any idea that Merlin Athrawes, thousands of miles away in Tellesberg, could arrange to have one of Owl's remotes quietly deliver his message on a timetable designed to get Gahrvai and his raiders here at precisely this time.

Actually, Merlin had aimed for any spot in a four-day window. In fact, he'd been prepared to settle for missing the window completely, given the vagaries of wind, weather, and the unpredictable interference of Murphy. It had seemed worth shooting for, though, and Gahrvai—and Hauwyl Chermyn—had surprised him with how quickly they'd moved. They'd been fortunate with the wind on their passage from Manchyr, as well.

Which was how Sir Koryn Gahrvai found himself watching the galleons sway their boats—rather larger and more numerous than most merchant galleons might have carried, if anyone had noticed—over the side on a calm, windless night blacker than the inside of an old boot. He was confident they would have managed under other weather conditions, but he wasn't about to look a gift dragon in the mouth when God decided to give him *perfect* weather conditions.

Even if he didn't know how the *seijins* had arranged it.

Now he waited as the first wave of Imperial Charisian Marines and Corisandian guardsmen who'd hidden below decks all day swarmed quietly up out of the galleons' hatches and then down into the waiting boats. In all, there were almost a thousand men spread between the two merchantmen. Even with a larger than usual complement of boats, they couldn't land that many troops at once. On the other hand, after carefully studying charts of the harbor (and the maps which had accompanied the mysterious letter), Gahrvai and Major Danyel Portyr, commanding the Imperial Charisian Marine's First Battalion, Third Regiment, had picked likely spots to land the first wave.

Gahrvai waited until the last man—but one—of the first wave had climbed down, then dropped lightly over the galleon's side, himself. He slid down the rope until Yairman Uhlstyn, waiting below, reached up and grabbed the heel of one boot. Uhlstyn guided his foot down to one of the boat's thwarts, and Gahrvai released the rope and dropped the last inch or so.

"All right," he said quietly. "Let's go."

▼　▼　▼

Four boats rowed silently, oarlocks muffled, across Telith Bay.

The city's lights offered a sufficient navigation beacon for experienced Imperial Navy coxswains. In fact, the hard part was less finding their way to their destination than making certain they gave other anchored vessels a sufficiently wide berth. It was no part of Gahrvai and Portyr's plans for some civilian anchor watch to hail them and raise any sort of alarm ashore.

Nothing of the sort happened, and Gahrvai's boat slid quietly under one of the city's older, more rickety piers. It was almost low water, and he was pleased to see his mysterious correspondent's notes were, indeed, accurate. The receding tide had exposed a wide expanse of rocky shingle, roomy enough for half again as many men as he'd brought with him, nestled in the ink-black shadow of the abandoned pier. The first two boats were already disembarking their passengers—a full company of guardsmen equipped with their personal weapons and a dozen bull's-eye lanterns with firmly closed slides—when Gahrvai stepped ashore. He looked around just long enough to reassure himself of the spot's suitability for landing, then nodded to the senior of the quartet of coxswains.

"This'll do," he said quietly. "Head back for the next lot."

"Aye, Sir."

The petty officer had a Chisholmian accent, Gahrvai noticed. Now the coxswain looked thoughtfully at the gentle waves rolling up onto the shingle.

"Tide's going to start making in another half hour or so, Gen'ral," he said. "Be at least twice that long till I can get the next load ashore. Might be you and your lads're going to find yourselves wading afore that happens."

"If we do, we do." Gahrvai shrugged. "The good news"—he twitched his head at one of the pier's pilings and the necklace of high-water shellfish and weeds which encircled it—"is that it's not going to get a lot more than knee-deep, even when the tide's all the way back in. Not that we won't appreciate your moving things right along."

"Oh, o' course, Sir!" the coxswain chuckled. "We'll do that little thing."

"Good." Gahrvai's teeth flashed in a smile so white it was dimly visible even in the pier's shadow, then he smacked the coxswain on the shoulder. "In that case, though," he said a bit pointedly, "I suppose you'd best get started."

▼    ▼    ▼

The coxswain's estimate turned out to have been almost uncannily accurate, the sort of offhand precision twenty or thirty years' experience at sea could provide.

The water was little more than ankle-deep by the time all four boats came sliding silently out of the night once more, although the guardsmen had been standing there long enough to demonstrate that none of their boots were truly watertight. Gahrvai could feel the cold water squishing around his own toes, seeming to swirl a bit, even inside his boots, as small wavelets slopped across the shingle. It wasn't the most pleasant sensation he'd ever experienced. On the other hand, he could think of quite a few which had been worse, and few of them had come his way in such a good cause.

"Captain says Major Portyr's first lot made it ashore all right and tight, too, Gen'ral," the Chisholmian coxswain said softly as the second load of guardsmen climbed out of the boats. "Reckon his second lot'll be going ashore in 'bout another fifteen, twenty minutes."

"Good," Gahrvai said again. He looked around as Major Naiklos (who'd been promoted to command his own battalion since the Manchyr raid) and Uhlstyn got things organized. He considered what the coxswain had said and the street map which had come with the letter. He compared overland distances from his current position to his objective, then considered how long it would take Portyr to reach *his* primary objective. Allow another fifteen minutes or so for slippage, and . . .

"All right, Frahnk," he said quietly, his mouth a foot from Naiklos' ear, "it's time we got them started moving. Your scouts have their bearings?"

"Yes, Sir," Naiklos replied equally quietly, and grinned tightly. "And they're good men, too. As a matter of fact, Yairman picked them."

"I figured he would." Gahrvai snorted, giving his armsman a look of affectionate exasperation. "Give him an inch, and he'll take a mile, Major. Never has known his place."

"Now, you know that's not true, Sir," Uhlstyn said. "Know my place perfectly, I do. Right here." He pointed at the water slopping over the shingle approximately two feet behind Sir Koryn Gahrvai. "As for the rest, well—"

The armsman shrugged with the confidence of a trusted family henchman, and Gahrvai shook his head.

"All right, Major," he said resignedly. "If Yairman's deigned to sign off on the suitability of your scouts, let's move out."

▼    ▼    ▼

In point of fact, Major Naiklos' scouts did their job perfectly. They'd had ample opportunity to study a copy of the map which had come with Gahrvai's letter. Their copy omitted all of the detailed information whose origin would have been difficult to explain, but it was more than sufficient for them to pick up their landmarks as they circled around the harbor district. Gahrvai's men moved through the shadows of warehouses, avoiding the glow of lanterns where still-open taverns served their customers. The lead scouts were far enough ahead to spot even the occasional prostitutes before they could notice that the better part of three hundred guardsmen were slipping through the darkened streets of Telitha.

Most of those prostitutes, and the handful of other pedestrians who fell into the scouts' clutches, were more than a little uneasy to find themselves "requested" to accompany Gahrvai's troopers. None were foolish enough to mistake the politeness of the invitation as an indication that they had any choice, however, and one look at the grim-faced guardsmen was enough to convince any of them to keep his—or her—mouth shut rather than risk raising the alarm. They might not know exactly what Gahrvai and his men were up to, but they knew enough to be certain it was none of *their* business . . . whatever it was.

Despite his own careful planning, and despite the experience of the scouts Naiklos and Uhlstyn had chosen, Gahrvai was actually surprised when they managed to get all the way to their initial objective without raising a single alarm. Aside from a handful of dogs who'd taken exception to their presence—and the handful of involuntary fellow travelers they'd swept up along the way—no one in the entire city seemed to have taken the least note of their presence.

*Doesn't say much for the local guard's alertness,* Gahrvai mused. *Not that I'm going to complain about it . . . tonight, at least. But, Langhorne—! I know we were taking precautions, but I have to wonder if these clowns would've noticed us if I'd come in with a brass band and a torchlight parade!*

On the other hand, he supposed Earl Storm Keep and his fellow conspirators might have been discouraging the city guard from noticing anything they weren't supposed to notice.

*In fact,* he thought slowly, *maybe we aren't the first bunch of armed men to be creeping around in the middle of the night. If they've been working on this as long as our letter-writing friend says they have, they may have marched quite a few men through Telitha to collect arms from the warehouses here. That could explain why all the locals are being so careful to avoid noticing us.*

That thought made him even more grateful for the ten additional transports—and the six escorting war galleons—which ought to be about five miles out at the moment. Of course, they'd hoped for a bit more wind when they were laying their plans, and it was entirely possible their reinforcements— an entire regiment each of Imperial Marines and Corisandian Guardsmen— were going to be delayed.

*Well, if everything goes the way it's supposed to, we won't* need *reinforcements,* he encouraged himself, resolutely not thinking about how seldom "everything" actually did go the way it was supposed to.

He wished he had a better notion of exactly how Portyr was doing, but timing was actually less critical than it might have been. Portyr's objective was, ultimately, as important as Gahrvai's. But unlike Gahrvai, Portyr was supposed to be pouncing on a mostly empty—or at least currently unoccupied— building. Gahrvai's objective, on the other hand, was most definitely occupied. Which, considering who the occupants were, was the real reason it had been assigned to a completely Corisandian force.

He peered down the boulevard at the luxurious, walled mansion. Like the city itself, Storm House was of fairly recent construction—no more than fifty years old—and it had little in common with old-fashioned, fortified seats like Baron Larchros' manor in Serabor. Or, for that matter, even Earl Craggy Hill's residence in Vahlainah. It had lots of doors and windows, and very little in the way of built-in defensive features. The wall around Storm House, no more than seven or eight feet tall, was more for privacy than protection, although it was probably enough to at least delay any intruders. Especially if anyone be- hind it knew the intruders were coming.

According to the letter which had been delivered to his study, Storm Keep had no more than a couple of dozen armed retainers here in his townhouse. Telitha might be his city, but there was a limit to just how openly he dared to operate, even here. On the other hand, Gahrvai had to assume any retainers he did keep here knew all about his plans and were fully committed to them. Which suggested they might well offer resistance . . . especially if they didn't immediately realize just how outnumbered they actually were. And it wouldn't take a great deal of delay for the really important fish to slither out of the net before he could scoop them up.

"Get your second company in position, Major," he whispered to Naiklos, and heard the major's own murmured order being relayed from man to man.

A few moments later, the designated company moved off, gratifyingly qui- etly, and he settled back down in the shadows, waiting. He gave the moving company long enough to get into its pre-chosen position, covering the back side of the townhouse from the spacious park attached to it, then waited that long again, as a cushion. Only then did he turn back to Naiklos and nod.

"Go," he said simply.

▼　　▼　　▼

The first inkling any occupant of Storm House had that something untoward was happening was the sudden, voiceless rush of booted feet on cobblestones. It was understandable that it should take at least a few seconds for anyone to recognize that sound, especially when it came out of absolutely nowhere in the middle of the darkest night of the month. The pair of armsmen assigned to the gate were reasonably alert, but they'd never actually expected to be assailed here in the middle of the earl's own city. The idea was preposterous! And so, even after their instincts had begun to recognize what they were hearing, their brains insisted they had to be wrong. There must be some other explanation!

Unfortunately, there wasn't. And, perhaps even more unfortunately, Sir Koryn Gahrvai's instructions to his guardsmen had been very clear. No one was to be allowed to raise the alarm. As a consequence, the earl's armsmen were . . . neutralized with a maximum of efficiency and a minimum of gentleness while they were still trying to figure out what that "other explanation" was. Still, the guardsmen weren't actually trying to kill them, and both of them recovered consciousness within two days.

As the gate guards went down under vigorously applied Guard musket butts, Gahrvai and the bulk of his men went flooding into Storm House's courtyard. There was some jostling as they funneled through the constricting gate, but this was the same company Gahrvai had selected for the raid which had netted Aidryn Waimyn. By now, they'd become experts at raiding monasteries or townhouses in the middle of the night, and they'd been even more carefully briefed tonight than they'd been *that* night. As soon as they were clear of the gate, they spread out once more, individual squads heading for individual objectives under their sergeants.

▼   ▼   ▼

Bishop Executor Thomys Shylair had been delighted to accept Earl Storm Keep's invitation to visit Telitha. While he was confident of Earl Craggy Hill's security in Vahlainah, Shylair was of the opinion that it was better to stay on the move. Allowing himself to loiter too long in any one location was too likely to give some potential informant the chance to recognize him, however secure his hiding place might appear, or even actually be.

Craggy Hill had disagreed, arguing that it was wiser for him to find a single, really safe hiding place—obviously, in Craggy Hill's opinion, in Vahlainah—and then simply stay there. If he never went out, Craggy Hill had reasoned, the chance of someone recognizing him would be nonexistent.

Shylair could appreciate the logic, but there were four telling points against it, in his opinion. First, wherever he set up his headquarters, there was going to be a steady flow of messengers and visitors in and out. It had to be that way, if he was going to stay in contact with the princedom's Temple Loyalist clergy. All that traffic was likely to draw attention sooner or later, if he stayed in one place, whether or not anyone realized he himself was present. Second, he simply wasn't prepared to stay cooped up in a single suite of rooms, no matter how luxurious, for literally months on end. He *had* to get out, breathe at least a little fresh air, and moving about—cautiously—between the residences of the senior members of the resistance was the best way to stay on top of the situation. Third, he was uneasy about trusting men with whom he had no personal contact. He wanted to see them, look them in the eye, listen to the firmness of their voices, and, in his opinion, it was safer for one man and his personal aide—him—to move around discreetly than it would have been for all of the others to come to *him*.

And fourth—though he was unprepared to discuss this one with *any* of his secular allies—he had less than absolute faith in the selflessness of Craggy Hill's motives. For that matter, he nursed at least some suspicion about the altruism of all of those allies. Which meant he had no desire to find himself as the permanent guest of, and (just coincidentally) under the physical control of, any of them.

His own logic was not universally accepted, yet there wasn't a great deal anyone could do about it. Shylair suspected his fellow conspirators had recognized that and organized their own schedule of "invitations" as the best compromise available to them, but that was fine with him. He didn't mind being "managed" a bit, as long as he did have the opportunity to avoid permanent incarceration.

Of all of the townhouses and manors in which he'd been a guest since fleeing Manchyr, Storm House was his favorite. It was the newest and most modern, the rooms assigned to him had a magnificent beachside view, and he loved the climate here. The soothing sound of surf helped him to sleep, as well, and that was what he was doing, deeply and peacefully, at the moment Sir Koryn Gahrvai's guardsmen put the Storm House gate guards into an even deeper slumber than his own.

Less than three minutes later, however, the bishop executor's repose found itself rudely interrupted.

▼　▼　▼

Sahlahmn Traigair, the Earl of Storm Keep, was sound asleep, snoring peacefully beside his wife, when something penetrated his slumber.

Unfortunately for the earl, while Storm House might not have been designed as a fortress, it was solidly built. In fact, it had intentionally been constructed with an eye towards holding down noise from the nearby city streets, especially in the earl's personal apartments and bedchamber, and that same noise-baffling design meant the muffled sound wasn't loud enough to actually wake him. His sleeping brain roused a bit, trying to identify it, but before the fish of consciousness reached the surface of his sleeping mind's pool, the door to his bedchamber burst violently open.

Storm Keep bolted up into a sitting position even as his wife screamed and clutched at the blankets.

"*What the h——?!*" he began thunderously.

"Earl Storm Keep," a flat, cold voice interrupted him, "I arrest you on the charge of treason and conspiracy against the Crown."

Storm Keep froze, mouth still open, as he recognized that icy voice. A flood of adrenaline brought him fully awake, but his brain was still slithering across a surface of shock, like a man trying to find his feet on the surface of a frozen lake. He blinked against the light streaming from the opened slides of three bull's-eye lanterns, and as he looked past Sir Koryn Gahrvai he saw half a dozen of Gahrvai's guardsmen . . . and the lantern light glinting on the razor edges of their bayonets.

▼    ▼    ▼

Bishop Executor Thomys was in the midst of a dream—inspired by the surf sound coming to him even in his sleep, no doubt—of a sunny day on one of the beaches outside Manchyr when the door to *his* bedchamber flew open. He was also a sounder sleeper than Earl Storm Keep. He sat up, blinking in the sudden light, startled, yet too sleep-sodden and groggy to feel truly alarmed.

"Wh—?" he started.

"Thomys Shylair," a voice said, and even in his confused sleepiness, a corner of Shylair's rousing brain noticed the absence of any ecclesiastic title, "I arrest you on a charge of treason and conspiracy."

.III.
### Imperial Palace,
### City of Tellesberg,
### Kingdom of Old Charis

S o it went well, did it?" Sir Rayjhis Yowance asked.

"Yes, My Lord. Very well," Merlin Athrawes replied with a smile.

He and Earl Gray Harbor were alone in the earl's office in Tellesberg Palace, and despite his smile, Merlin found himself once again regretting the fact that they dared not tell Gray Harbor the entire truth. He knew it bothered Cayleb and Sharleyan, as well, just as it bothered them in Baron Green Mountain's case. It wasn't simply that not telling their two most senior councilors prevented them from getting the best out of two very able men's advice and counsel, either. What really bothered them—and Merlin—was that they felt as if they were sneaking around behind the backs of men who were also friends. Confidants. In Green Mountain's case, a second father, even, at least in Sharleyan's case.

Because of that, Merlin was particularly happy Gray Harbor, at least, knew about *Seijin* Merlin's "visions." The earl had also adjusted quite well to the notion that there might be additional *seijins* scattered around Safehold. He even accepted Merlin's explanation—truthful, as far as it went—that all those other *seijins,* and Merlin, himself, were part of an organization which had been carefully concealed for many years (Merlin figured nine hundred years qualified as "many," and given how many personalities he seemed to be developing calling himself and Owl an "organization" didn't seem *too* outrageous) until its members finally believed there was an opportunity to do something about the Church's corruption. Of course, there weren't a huge number of those *seijins,* but his acceptance of their existence had let him take things like the suddenly increased reasonableness of King Gorjah's clandestine correspondence in stride.

It had also prepared him to accept that Merlin's . . . associates in Corisande were in a position to tell Anvil Rock and Viceroy General Chermyn when the proper time to move against the Northern Conspiracy arrived. And he didn't have any problem accepting Merlin's "vision" of how well the raid had gone.

*I'm glad,* Merlin thought affectionately as he smiled at the first councilor. *And not just because it means we can call on his insight where both Corisande and Tarot are concerned, either. I* like *Rayjhis, and this feels good.*

"So they got Storm Keep and Shylair," Gray Harbor said now, leaning back in his chair with a smile of his own. In fact, he actually allowed himself to rub his hands together in satisfaction, and Merlin chuckled.

"Gahrvai and his men took both of them into custody," he confirmed. "I think he and Hauwyl were wise to decide he'd do most of the arresting, at least of our more . . . prominent suspects, too. It gave the rest of Storm Keep's supporters a lot less chance to whip up some kind of resistance to the 'Charisian oppressors' before their reinforcements could land. Of course, it helped that they had a list of all of the more important supporters actually in Telitha." His smile turned into a rather nasty grin. "They grabbed almost all of them in the first pounce, as well."

"And the weapons?"

"Major Portyr secured the warehouses without firing a shot, and the rifles were still in the Zebediahan shipping crates . . . even if the crates were labeled as 'general hardware.' Funny how the cargo and custom manifests in both Telitha and Zebediah didn't catch that little error."

"A most unfortunate oversight, I'm sure," Gray Harbor agreed with a grin which was just as nasty as Merlin's.

*And it's going to be "most unfortunate" for Zebediah in* oh *so many ways,* Merlin thought cheerfully. *The customs manifests, his correspondence with Craggy Hill and Earl Swayle, and that unfortunate business with the serial numbers.*

The one real problem with going after Storm Keep first had been that while the weapons had been landed in Telitha, Zebediah's incriminating correspondence was still in Craggy Hill's safe in Vahlainah. On the other hand, Vahlainah was far enough inland that any operation against Craggy Hill would have to be mounted overland, with—unfortunately—ample time for him to realize it was coming. Since it would be virtually impossible to achieve surprise in his case, Cayleb and Sharleyan had decided it was more important to scoop up the weapons before they could be dispersed, especially if they could grab Shylair at the same time. They'd recognized that Craggy Hill would almost certainly learn what had happened in Telitha in time to dispose of any incriminating documents before he himself could be arrested, but they'd been willing to accept that for several reasons.

One was the importance of getting their hands on Shylair and seizing the weapons, but another was that they didn't really *need* the correspondence between Craggy Hill and Zebediah to prove the grand duke's complicity.

Ehdwyrd Howsmyn had adopted a novel practice which had since spread to the majority of Old Charisian manufactories: assigning serial numbers to items he produced. It had been customary for centuries to use maker's marks, and arbalests, matchlocks, and artillery pieces had carried proof marks, as well. But Howsmyn (at the suggestion of a certain *Seijin* Merlin) had begun stamping actual serial numbers into things like musket barrels, sword blades, breastplates, and cannon. In fact, he'd extended the practice to *everything* he manufactured.

That had never been very practical before Merlin introduced Arabic numerals, which helped explain why no one had ever done it before . . . and why no one had ever considered tracking inventory by *recording* serial numbers. That practice had now been generally introduced throughout the Charisian military, and it was beginning to spread to civilian goods, but some people—like Earl Swayle and Grand Duke Zebediah—were a little slow to realize the implications. Like the minor fact that it would be possible for prosecutors to demonstrate in any court of law that the weapons seized in Telitha had passed directly through Swayle's and Zebediah's hands before reaching their destination.

*We don't need any correspondence promising to provide them when we already have proof he* did *provide them sitting in front of the judge,* Merlin thought with profound satisfaction. *For that matter, it doesn't really matter if Craggy Hill destroys the originals of all his documents. I've already got perfect duplicates, right down to the odd inkblot, tucked away, and somehow I don't think Cayleb or Sharleyan—or even Maikel!—would have any great qualms about introducing them into evidence as the originals. And if we do, what good is it going to do Craggy Hill to protest that they can't possibly be the originals because he personally* burned *the originals before they could have been seized?*

"I think we can safely assume Cayleb's deviousness has paid off in Zebediah's case," he said out loud, and Gray Harbor chuckled.

"He always was such a *clever* boy," the first councilor agreed, remembering Merlin's report of a conversation between him and the emperor aboard HMS *Empress of Charis,* anchored in the waters of Hannah Bay.

"He was, was he? I wonder who taught him to be that devious?" Merlin mused.

"I'm sure I wouldn't know," Gray Harbor replied in his most innocent tone.

"Of course you wouldn't." Merlin shook his head, then his expression grew more serious. "The question in my mind, now that Zebediah's fulfilled Cayleb's prediction and given him an unambiguous justification for removing him, is who he and Sharleyan will *replace* Zebediah with."

"I can think of several possible replacements," Gray Harbor said. "At the moment, though, I think the leading contender is Hauwyl Chermyn."

Merlin blinked in surprise, then castigated himself for feeling it. Chermyn was about the least politically ambitious person he could think of, and he certainly didn't have much experience with court politics. Or, at least, he *hadn't* had much. Given his responsibilities in Corisande that wasn't really the case any longer. And given how well he'd discharged those responsibilities, he was a logical choice for Zebediah, as well. Not only had he amply earned consideration for the position of the island's senior noble, but his performance in Corisande would give him plenty of experience when it came to establishing his own authority in Zebediah.

*And the fact that he did his job so well in Corisande is going to make any Zebediahan who might think about resisting the "outsider" think twice. Or even three or four times, for that matter!*

"Actually, I think that's an excellent idea, My Lord," Merlin said out loud. Then he laughed again. "Of course, Hauwyl will probably consider cutting his own throat if Cayleb and Sharleyan do nominate him as the new grand duke!"

"He may think about it, but he won't do it," Gray Harbor replied. "In fact, once he gets over the initial shock, I think he'll probably adjust quite nicely to the notion of becoming a great—and very wealthy—noble."

"And having Zebediah in the hands of someone absolutely trustworthy would take a huge load off Cayleb's and Sharleyan's minds."

"Not exactly a minor factor in my own thinking," Gray Harbor agreed.

The earl drummed the fingers of his right hand lightly on his desktop, looking off into space and obviously considering the situation in Corisande and Zebediah. Then he gave himself a shake.

"I have to say, at the risk of tempting fate, that things are looking up," he said. "I hate what happened to Admiral Manthyr, but on the *political* front, this has been a very good month. Anvil Rock and Hauwyl are in the process of ripping the guts out of the only serious, organized conspiracy in Corisande; Zebediah's for the long drop in Carmyn, whether he knows it or not; Swayle and his little clutch of friends in Corisande are about to go the same way; and our friend Gorjah has effectively accepted Their Majesties' terms for inclusion in the Empire."

He nodded slowly, and his eyes refocused on Merlin.

"With Tarot in hand, we've secured the Empire's 'natural frontiers,'" he said, and there was no hiding the satisfaction—or the relief—in his voice. "I don't think Clyntahn and Trynair are going to be *at all* pleased to hear about that!"

"No," Merlin agreed. "No, I don't imagine they will."

.IV.
The Temple,
City of Zion,
The Temple Lands

A ll right, Zhaspahr. We're all here now, so suppose you tell us what this is all about?"

Zahmsyn Trynair put what he hoped was a precisely metered bite into his tone. Over the last few months, he'd come to feel more and more like an animal trainer who specialized in man-eating beasts. And, like the animal trainer, he found it necessary to never show fear. To occasionally remind Clyntahn that the Grand Inquisitor wasn't the only one with a Temple power base, and that Trynair remained confident of his control of the Temple hierarchy.

Whether or not he was succeeding in *convincing* Clyntahn of that was a bit more problematical.

"Actually, Zahmsyn, I was rather hoping you might be able to shed a little illumination on a disturbing rumor which has reached my attention," Clyntahn said now, and *his* tone was dangerously affable.

"What sort of rumor?" Trynair asked just a bit guardedly.

"Well, I realize that, as Chancellor, you're in charge of Mother Church's diplomacy, but according to Father Frahnklyn, Gorjah of Tarot seems to be . . . losing some of his zeal for Mother Church's struggle."

"What?" Trynair straightened in his chair, eyebrows lowering. "I just had a report from Narth last five-day. He didn't report anything untoward!"

Rhobair Duchairn watched impassively as Clyntahn smiled at Trynair. It was unpleasant, that smile, but Duchairn had grown accustomed to that. Just as he'd grown accustomed to Clyntahn's smirking satisfaction at the way the rest of the vicarate had come obediently to heel. So far, he seemed to have restricted his most unseemly displays to the circle of his immediate subordinates and his "colleagues" in the Group of Four. Some days, Duchairn hoped he would continue to be at least that discreet . . . other days, he longed for Clyntahn's mask to slip where every other surviving vicar could see it.

*The problem is that even if it does slip, it won't tell anyone anything they don't already know. Zhaspahr may not gloat openly—yet—but that doesn't mean there's anyone left who isn't perfectly well aware of how he truly feels.*

For his own part, Duchairn had completely stopped deferring to Clyntahn. He didn't go out of his way to provoke the Grand Inquisitor, but he'd made his indifference to Clyntahn clear. Not surprisingly, the Inquisitor had responded with profound disdain and contempt, yet he seemed curiously loath to actually attack Duchairn. He wasn't even needling the Treasurer the way he once had. It was clear to Duchairn that Clyntahn had accepted the bargain he'd proposed by way of Trynair. It was even remotely possible the Grand Inquisitor actually understood the necessity for Mother Church to show a kinder, more caring face rather than relying solely upon the mailed fist, the whip, and terror.

*More likely he's simply satisfied I'm either too terrified of him to challenge him, or else that I've become such a "bleeding heart" I no longer really care about worldly power. It may even be a combination of the two. At any rate, he seems to've taken my declaration of neutrality at face value, so far at least. Which probably means I'm beneath contempt now, as far as he's concerned.*

If that *was* Clyntahn's attitude, it suited Duchairn just fine. Not that he intended to take any stupid, overly optimistic chances.

Behind his impassive façade, however, the Treasurer found himself wondering what Clyntahn was up to this time. Father Frahnklyn Sumyr, the Church's intendant in Tarot, was a Schuelerite, like almost all intendants. As such, he reported directly to the Inquisition, although any report touching on political affairs was supposed to be copied to Trynair's office in the Chancellery, as well. Bishop Executor Tyrnyr Narth, on the other hand, was supposed to report to Archbishop Failyx Gahrbor, the Archbishop of Tarot, whose deputy he officially was. Of course, he was also supposed to be copying *his* reports to the Chancellery, as well. Theoretically, then, Trynair should have been informed about anything which had reached Clyntahn's ears.

Which, obviously, was not the case.

"I'm not really surprised Narth didn't mention anything about it," Clyntahn said now, almost carelessly. "Probably not his fault, really. I mean, I know he's our official representative in Tarot, and that he's been conferring regularly with Gorjah, so I'm sure he's confident he's on top of the situation."

"But you're suggesting he *isn't* on top of it, correct?" Trynair asked sharply.

"Oh, I'm sure he's fully conversant with all the diplomatic correspondence and negotiations—all that sort of thing. But according to Father Frahnklyn, there's been a mysterious drop in Charisian naval activity in Thol Bay. As a matter of fact, the entire Charisian blockade seems to have suddenly become about as watertight as a fishnet."

"Excuse me?" Trynair's puzzlement was obvious, and Clyntahn snorted.

"We already know Gorjah changed sides once," he said in the tone of a man explaining something to a very young child in very simple words. "We also know, despite any investigations which might have cleared him, that only someone in Tarot could've warned Haarahld of what was about to happen. I've always wondered just who could have had the authority and reach to both pass that information along and make certain no one was ever able to identify him as the source. Of course, as the rest of you have pointed out, we can't just go around deposing kings and princes on suspicion, can we?"

"Zhaspahr, if you were really convinced Gorjah was the leak, you should have said so at the time." There was a pronounced edge of asperity in Trynair's voice. "Your own Inquisitors conducted the investigation—at *his* request, I remind you! If they turned up any evidence that you failed to share with us, I suggest you tell us about it now."

"If I'd had any such evidence, I would've shared it with you *then*," Clyntahn said coolly. "Obviously, I didn't. But riddle me this, Zahmsyn. Why should the Charisians suddenly begin going easy on Tarot? After locking that damned island up tight—sticking it in a cask and then driving in the bung for the better part of two years—why is their blockade suddenly so porous? You know as well as I do that that bastard Rock Point's been basing himself *inside* Thol Bay. Frankly, I've always found it just a bit suspicious that Gorjah and his precious White Ford weren't even able to keep him from doing that! But now, all of a sudden, 'blockade runners' are managing to slip past the eagle-eyed Charisians in droves."

"You're suggesting Gorjah's negotiated some sort of secret arrangement with Cayleb and Sharleyan?"

Trynair and Clyntahn both looked at Duchairn as he asked the question. His own expression was one of indifference, almost boredom, and there might actually have been a hint of amusement in his tone.

"That's exactly what I'm suggesting, Rhobair," Clyntahn said after a moment. "You find the idea humorous?"

"Oh, by no means," Duchairn said calmly. "What I *do* find a bit amusing, though, is that you—well, you and Zahmsyn, I suppose—should be more concerned with scoring points off of one another here in the council chamber than in keeping all of us fully informed on whatever information comes into our hands."

Trynair's eyebrows rose. Clyntahn's didn't, and an ugly light flickered in his eyes. He started to open his mouth, but then he stopped. He glowered at Duchairn for a moment, and then, to Trynair's surprise, he actually chuckled.

"Point taken," the Grand Inquisitor said, and turned his gaze to Trynair.

"Rhobair's right. And I'll admit there's a part of me that wants to rub everyone else's nose in it, if it turns out Gorjah really is turning his coat . . . again. Because the truth is I never did trust the slimy little bastard, and I did let myself be overruled by the rest of you. So, yes, I guess I would take a certain satisfaction if it turns out I was right about him. Which, as Rhobair has just pointed out, isn't really all that smart of me."

Trynair managed not to blink, although the sight of Zhaspahr Clyntahn in reasonable mode wasn't one that had come along all that often of late.

"I don't imagine any of us are really at our best these days," the Chancellor said after a moment. "I know I'm not, at any rate. And you're right, Narth didn't mention anything about blockade runners. To be fair, though, matters of trade and shipping have always been rather outside his area of expertise."

"I know." Clyntahn waved one hand. "In fact, I knew it when I was twisting your tail. But my point stands. I think we have to take this sudden shipping upsurge in and around Tarot seriously. I think it's possible—even probable—that Gorjah *has* worked out some sort of under-the-table deal with Cayleb."

"What sort of a deal?" Duchairn asked.

"I don't know," Clyntahn said thoughtfully, pursing his lips. "It could be something as simple as an unofficial, effective neutrality. Or it could indicate he *was* the one who passed our original plans along and that he's reopened that channel of communications. In either of those cases, the Charisians might let enough shipping through to ease his own shortages without either side making any official admission about what they were up to."

"But what you're really afraid of is that he's becoming a second Nahrmahn," Trynair said.

"Yes." Clyntahn shrugged his beefy shoulders. "That would be the most damaging thing he could do to us, at any rate, so on the theory that it's best to assume the worst, that's exactly what I'm afraid he's doing."

"In that case, why don't we arrest him?" Allayn Maigwair asked. All three of the others turned to look at the Temple's Captain General, and Maigwair raised his hands a bit defensively. "I mean, if we're afraid he's going to betray us, why not have the Inquisition take him into custody while we investigate?"

"Under other circumstances, that might not be such a terrible idea, Allayn," Trynair said almost gently. "If Gorjah's really planning on emulating Nahrmahn, though, and if his plans are so far along Cayleb and Sharleyan have already eased their blockade, we have to assume Gorjah's also following Nahrmahn's example in terms of covering his back. Let's face it, that far from Zion, the Inquisition relies more on its moral authority and its power to require the secular authorities to support Mother Church rather than on the Temple Guard. You know—better than anyone else, probably—that we've never had anything remotely like enough guardsmen to cover everything that needs to be covered all over the world! I doubt there are more than a couple hundred guardsmen in all of Tarot. So if Gorjah has a few thousand men who are prepared to follow his orders and defy Mother Church, actually arresting him would be almost impossible."

"And trying to arrest him and *failing* would be even worse," Duchairn pointed out. His colleagues swiveled their gazes to him, and he shrugged. "Think about it. If we order him arrested when we don't have any evidence he's done anything wrong, we hand him a ready-made pretext to turn against Mother Church. Faced with such serious 'false accusations,' he'd simply be reacting in self-defense . . . and claiming our decision to arrest him as yet one more example of the corruption and capriciousness of Mother Church."

"I really hate to say it, but I think Rhobair has a point," Clyntahn said heavily. "As a matter of fact, it occurred to me to wonder if that wasn't exactly what Gorjah was trying to provoke me—us—into doing. If he really is ready and waiting, I mean. And let's face it, as Rhobair says, Tarot *is* a long way from Zion. Father Frahnklyn's a good man, but we can't possibly read the situation in Tranjyr from here without better information than he's been able to give us . . . so far, at least. If I were Cayleb, and if I could manipulate things to create a situation in which Mother Church 'drives' Gorjah into his arms—for general consumption, at least—I'd damned well do it. It would be one more way to make everybody who's still loyal to Mother Church nervous . . . not to mention the way it would play into that son-of-a-bitch Stohnar's hands."

Duchairn squelched his smile before it ever got anywhere near his lips. He'd wondered how long it would take for Clyntahn's compulsive suspicion of Greyghor Stohnar to surface.

"But if we don't arrest him, what *do* we do?" Maigwair asked.

"I don't think we *can* do a great deal inside Tarot," Trynair said thoughtfully. "About all that's really available to us, I think, is to encourage Father Frahnklyn to pursue this matter—discreetly, of course. I'll send a message to Bishop Executor Tyrnyr instructing him to assist Father Frahnklyn, as well. And I think it might be a good idea to transfer a few more agents of inquisition into Tarot from Desnair and Siddarmark, Zhaspahr. Let's get some more eyes and ears into Tranjyr. If we can find evidence Gorjah's already in contact with the Charisians, I'd be a lot more inclined to try to arrest him, even if the attempt is likely to fail."

"You know," Duchairn said pensively, "I have to wonder—aside from the example of yet another secular ruler deserting Mother Church, how much would losing Tarot really hurt us? You haven't actually been counting on the galleons they're building being available in our order of battle, have you, Allayn?"

"Not really," Maigwair admitted unhappily. "We went ahead and ordered them, but the chances of Tarot's actually getting them completed, manned—and armed—and then getting them to sea past the Charisians are pretty damned slim."

"That's what I was thinking," Duchairn said, and looked at Trynair and Clyntahn. "As Mother Church's Treasurer, I may be more aware than the rest of you of how much money we're putting into Tarot . . . and for how little return. That blockade's been damnably effective, and Tarot's paid less than a third of its usual tithe ever since the war began. For that matter, this year the Exchequer doesn't expect Gorjah to be able to pay at all! To be brutally frank, losing the Kingdom completely would be barely a bump as far as our finances are concerned. So I think what we really need to think about are the political and military consequences. And as Allayn's just said, losing Tarot from our side would have very little impact on our capabilities. So how much would *gaining* Tarot *help* the other side?"

"An interesting point," Clyntahn said thoughtfully. "The political damage would be worse, I think, if only as an example of ongoing erosion. Militarily, I doubt Tarot would add much to Cayleb's capabilities. In fact, it would give the Charisians still more territory to protect, which would spread their forces even thinner."

"By the same token, though," Maigwair pointed out, "it would give them a naval base right off the Siddarmark coast. It would dominate the Gulf of Tarot and close off the Tarot Channel, which would pretty much isolate the Gulf of Mathyas."

"Drive a wedge between our northern squadrons and Desnair, you mean?" Trynair asked.

"Exactly."

"But how realistic a concern is that?" Duchairn asked. "I mean, if Rock Point's already basing his squadron in Thol Bay, then they've already got a 'naval base' right there on the Tarot Channel, don't they?"

"Well . . . yes," Maigwair admitted slowly.

"Then the only real difference is that it would become an *official* naval base," Duchairn pointed out.

"So what you're suggesting, Rhobair, is that we not act precipitously and give Gorjah a pretext for deserting us, but continue to investigate cautiously," Trynair said. "If we find proof—real proof, or at least strongly suggestive evidence—we can go ahead and try to arrest him. And if it should happen he either surprises us by actually changing sides, or goes over to Cayleb after we give him that 'pretext,' it's not really going to hurt us that much militarily or economically?"

"More or less." Duchairn shrugged. "This is your area of expertise—yours and Zhaspahr's, where the politics are concerned, and Allayn's, where the military's concerned. I'm simply trying to examine this question from all perspectives. It's not," he finished dryly, "as if we haven't gotten ourselves into trouble upon occasion by acting too precipitously."

Clyntahn flushed at the none-too-oblique reference to his own "final solution to the Charisian problem." He chose to let it pass, however. At the same time, his eyes took on a thoughtful look. He sat silently pondering for several seconds, then nodded to himself and refocused his eyes on the other three.

"I'm not sure keeping our hands off Tarot is the right way to proceed. On the other hand, I'm not sure it *isn't* the right way, either." He shrugged. "Under the circumstances, I think a wait-and-see attitude's less likely to go *catastrophically* wrong, though. At the same time, I think we ought to think about ways to . . . disaster proof our position, as it were, if Tarot does switch sides."

"What do you have in mind?" Trynair sounded a bit cautious, and Clyntahn smiled.

"I'm not planning on running off in a bout of excessive enthusiasm, Zahmsyn! I was just thinking about what Allayn said about Tarot's strategic position. About its offering the Charisians a naval base between our northern squadrons and Desnair."

"And?"

"And it occurred to me that one way to prevent that from becoming a problem would be to concentrate our forces in the Gulf of Mathyas right now. Before Tarot does whatever it is Gorjah's planning to do."

"What?" Trynair blinked.

"Look, it's already September," Clyntahn said, and twitched his head in the direction of the council chamber's window. Icy rain pounded down outside, and nearly leafless branches swayed in the wind. "It won't be long before Hsing-wu's Passage starts to freeze over again. When that happens, our northern squadrons—the ones we've built here in the Temple Lands and all the ships Harchong's built in her northern ports—are going to be stuck. If we get them out now, before the ice closes in, and send *all* of them to Desnair, we'll have all seventy-four Desnairian galleons and at least fifty or sixty each from Harchong and the Temple Lands—that's between a hundred and seventy and *two hundred* galleons—in one concentrated force, less than two thousand miles from Tarot and barely three thousand from Charis. If we get them there before Gorjah changes sides, it might suggest to him that treason would be a bad idea. And even if they don't get there until after he changes sides, or if he goes ahead and betrays us despite their presence, we'd have a serious force in place both to threaten Tarot and Charis and to force them to redeploy against it. After what Thirsk did in the Gulf of Dohlar, they'd have to take that threat seriously, don't you think?"

Trynair and Duchairn were both looking at him in surprise now. As a general rule, Clyntahn didn't much concern himself with military movements. Partly, Duchairn thought cynically, because it had been his breezy confidence where military affairs he'd known nothing about were concerned which had launched this entire disaster in the first place.

"I don't know, Zhaspahr," Maigwair said slowly. "The new construction's scattered up and down the length of the Passage. We'd have to get it all into one place, first. And a good quarter of the ships we've managed to launch and rig still don't have their artillery." He grimaced. "I'm afraid our foundries have been slower to really hit their stride than we'd anticipated, and, frankly, *Harchong's* foundries are nowhere near as efficient as they could be, either. They've got a lot of them, but their output's lower even than ours. For that matter, their best ones are in South Harchong—in Shwei and Kyznetsov. And before Thirsk ran the Charisians out of Claw Island, they put a major hole in the delivery of the guns South Harchong had managed to produce."

"Well, Desnair's foundries are doing pretty well, aren't they?" Clyntahn riposted, and cocked an eyebrow at Duchairn.

"Production numbers are rising," Duchairn acknowledged. "It's not that their individual foundries are particularly big or especially efficient, but they do have a higher output per furnace than Harchong, and they've been establishing a lot of little cannon foundries. They're still having problems with *iron* guns, though. Everybody is"—*except for Charis*, he carefully did not say out loud—"but even more of Desnair's iron pieces seem to be failing when they're proofed."

"That's just a matter of experience," Clyntahn said dismissively. "Of course they're not going to get it right the first few times they try! But if they've got the foundries, sooner or later they'll be able to produce the guns we need."

"Why not send them to Dohlar, instead?" Duchairn suggested. Maigwair and Trynair looked thoughtful, but Clyntahn's face turned expressionless as the shutters went up behind his eyes. "Thirsk seems to've straightened out the Dohlaran foundries—at least, he's been able to compensate for the Harchong guns the Charisians took. By now, according to the invoices I'm getting, he's actually far enough ahead of his own demand that he's in a position to export guns to *Harchong,* instead of the other way around."

"Dohlar's too far from Tarot and Charis," Clyntahn said flatly, and Duchairn felt one eyebrow arch.

He glanced at Trynair and saw the same speculation on the Chancellor's face.

Just as Clyntahn had never truly been prepared to give Gorjah of Tarot a clean bill of health over the betrayal of the Group of Four's original plan of attack, he'd never forgiven Thirsk for first losing the battle of Crag Reach and then surrendering his surviving ships to Cayleb Ahrmahk. The Dohlaran ought to have fought until every one of his galleys went to the bottom, in Clyntahn's opinion. The fact that he hadn't—that he'd put the lives of his men above his service to Mother Church—made him automatically and permanently suspect to the Grand Inquisitor. Clyntahn had acquiesced only grudgingly in Thirsk's appointment to his present post, and only when all three other members of the Group of Four had voted against him. And he'd bitterly resented Thirsk's "demands" that Mother Church pay the wages of his sailors. As far as Clyntahn was concerned, those sailors should be eager to volunteer in God's Own cause! Besides, the Church had dozens of other things it could have used that money for. And that didn't even consider Thirsk's ridiculous insistence that the Church ought to pay *pensions* to the survivors of men who were killed in her service.

The Grand Inquisitor hadn't been happy when Duchairn supported Thirsk's policies. Having the Church's Treasurer agree that the outrageous demands were "reasonable" and "manageable" had cut the ground out from under his own arguments. Maigwair's unusually stubborn insistence that Thirsk had the best grasp of the new naval tactics hadn't made him any more cheerful. And rather than agreeing with Duchairn and Maigwair that Thirsk's performance in the Harchong Narrows demonstrated that the earl had been right all along, Clyntahn sided with the opinion (coming, Duchairn suspected, from Duke Thorast) that Thirsk had simply been lucky. Lucky in the weather, lucky in outnumbering the Charisians by such a huge margin, and—probably—lucky the Charisians had withdrawn from Claw Island before he was *finally* ready to attack it, since they would undoubtedly have defeated him—*again*—if he'd actually had to fight to evict them.

Only the fact that the Duke of Fern and Bishop Staiphan Maik, Clyntahn's own intendant for the fleet, strongly supported Thirsk had held the Grand Inquisitor's ire in check. Well, that and the fact that Thirsk's victory was the *only* victory any of the Church's squadrons had so far achieved.

*And as far as I can tell, the fact that Thirsk allowed the Charisians to surrender has only pissed him off even more.* Duchairn very carefully did not grimace. *As far as Zhaspahr's concerned, the only good Charisian is a dead one. He sees absolutely no reason Thirsk should have let them surrender. Even Allayn understands that if our admirals don't allow* them *to surrender, then* their *admirals won't allow* our *crews to surrender. I don't think Zhaspahr really cares about that, though. In fact, I wonder if he wouldn't actually prefer a situation in which the other side flatly refused to give quarter. He probably sees it as the best way to motivate our people to fight to the bitter end . . . exactly the way Thirsk didn't do at Crag Reach.*

"I admit Dohlar's a long way from Charis and Tarot," the Treasurer said out loud. "On the other hand, as Allayn says, our ships are scattered all over the Passage . . . and nothing the Charisians have is close enough to *threaten* the Passage. We could send them all the way to Gorath Bay without having to worry about their being intercepted. And Dohlar's much closer to Chisholm—and Corisande, for that matter—going west."

"Of course it is." Clyntahn waved an impatient hand dismissively. "And the Charisians who evacuated Claw Island went straight to Chisholm to reinforce the ships they already had there. In fact, that's another reason to send *our* ships to Desnair."

Duchairn looked at him quizzically, and he snorted.

"They've had to disperse strength to cover Chisholm and Corisande, Rhobair." Clyntahn was back to that adult-lecturing-a-particularly-slow-child tone of his, but Duchairn was too accustomed to it to rise to the baiting. For that matter, he wasn't even certain Clyntahn was still doing it on purpose. "Our best estimate is that Rock Point has about twenty or twenty-five galleons based on Thol Bay, and Lock Island has another thirty-five or forty operating out of Rock Shoal Bay. That's sixty-five total. The rest of their galleons are dispersed protecting Chisholm and Corisande. What I'm proposing is that we take advantage of that dispersal to punch our ships through to Desnair. By the time they can redeploy the ships they have on distant stations, we'll be concentrated in the Gulf of Mathyas and there won't be anything they can do about it."

Trynair was looking thoughtful, and even Duchairn had to admit there was a certain logic to Clyntahn's argument. Still, the thing which had most impressed Duchairn about the failure of their initial attack on Charis was that sending fleets on lengthy voyages with coordinated timetables which didn't consider little things like, oh, weather, seemed to be significantly more problematical than sending armies on lengthy *marches*.

"You're talking about sending a hundred to two hundred and twenty of our galleons past Tarot to Desnair," he said now. "According to Allayn, a quarter of them would be completely unarmed. So, say we have your higher number available for the trip—a hundred and twenty. That means only *ninety* of them would actually be armed, and none of our ships are as well trained as Earl Thirsk's were. If the sixty or seventy Charisians manage to intercept them, I don't know how well our ninety would make out, Zhaspahr. I don't like saying that any more than you like hearing it," he added as Clyntahn's face tightened, "but we have to be realistic. And it's not their fault, either. They simply haven't had the time to train."

"Rhobair has a point," Trynair said in a reasonable tone.

"Yesssss," Maigwair said slowly. The others all looked at him, and he held up his right hand, index finger extended. "Yes," he repeated, "but we've got the semaphore."

"And?" Duchairn prompted when the Captain General paused again.

"First," Maigwair said, "we ought to have the advantage of surprise when we actually start moving the ships. Distance alone ought to see to that, but let's assume the Charisians' spies here in the Temple Lands have access to the commercial messages we allow the semaphore to pass. Or, for that matter, just that they have a network of homing wyverns to carry messages. Whatever. It's obvious they do have spies somewhere in the system, right?"

Duchairn nodded, impressed despite himself. Thinking things through wasn't something he normally associated with Allayn Maigwair.

"All right. In that case, we openly send orders to our squadrons all along Hsing-wu's Passage. For that matter, let's send them in one of the ciphers we're pretty sure the Charisians may have compromised in Delferahk or Corisande. We order them to rendezvous at Angelberg, but we tell them that's a ruse. They're concentrating there to help any Charisian spies assume we're going to send them to Desnair, but they're to prepare to sail to *Dohlar*. Even if the message isn't compromised along the semaphore chain, you *know* at least some of their crew will talk about their upcoming trip to Dohlar whenever they get a chance to go ashore in Angelberg. So any Charisian spies are going to hear about that destination, and as far as *preparing* for the voyage is concerned, it doesn't matter whether they're going to Dohlar or Desnair, really."

His eyes were beginning to sparkle now as his enthusiasm mounted.

"So, our cover story is that their preparations are to take them west. Any spies who spot them in Chantry Bay will almost certainly find out about their orders to Dohlar, and we don't tell even our *admirals* differently until they're all ready to sail. At that point, we use the semaphore to send them their actual sailing orders. Surely that ought to insure that we have strategic surprise. In fact, if the Charisians do get wind of their original orders, they may shift their own deployments to protect Chisholm and Corisande!

"Then, once we have our ships in motion to the east, instead of the west, we use the semaphore to order the Desnairians to sortie to meet them. We'll be able to tell Desnair to sail more quickly than the Charisians will be able to tell their squadrons to concentrate. So, ideally, Lock Island will still be lying to anchor in Rock Shoal Bay when Rock Point and his twenty-five ships find themselves caught between seventy-odd Desnairian galleons coming up from the south and a hundred to a hundred and twenty Harchongese and Temple Lands galleons coming down from the north."

"That's a very good thought, Allayn," Clyntahn congratulated. "And there's another aspect to it, as well. We can keep track of both forces as long as they stay in coastal waters, so if one of them hits a snag, or if it turns out the Charisians have somehow managed to concentrate against one of them, we can order the other one to turn around and avoid action."

Maigwair beamed, clearly basking in the unaccustomed light of the Grand Inquisitor's approval. Even Trynair was nodding, slowly at first, but then more firmly.

Duchairn, on the other hand, still had profound reservations. Maigwair's and Clyntahn's ideas about coordinating two separate fleets sounded good in theory, but he couldn't quite convince himself it would work out that smoothly in practice. On the other hand, Maigwair did have a point about achieving surprise. If no one outside the Group of Four itself knew where the northern ships were really going to go, no one could possibly betray that information to Charis. And it really didn't matter how quickly the information got to Charis once the ships actually began moving, because Charisian warships as far away as Chisholm or Corisande would be so badly out of position that they might as well have been on the bottom of the sea. They couldn't possibly reach the Gulf of Tarot or the Sea of Justice before the Church's fleets had either united with one another or turned around and returned separately to their original ports.

He watched the other three and realized that whatever qualms he might feel, all of them were in favor. That being the case, he wasn't going to prevent it, whatever he did. So he wouldn't try. He would content himself with voicing his own reservations—reservations mild enough he could brush them away later with a smile for his own timidity if they proved unfounded, but sufficiently pointed to position him, if things turned out badly after all, to remind them all that he'd warned them against overconfidence.

He sat back in his chair, waiting while Maigwair and Clyntahn worked out the details to their own satisfaction. There'd been a time when Rhobair Duchairn hadn't worried all that much about political calculations. He'd risen to his post as Treasurer mostly because he'd been the consummate bureaucrat, content to leave politics—Mother Church's and secular politics, alike—to Trynair and Clyntahn.

*And the fact that we're having this discussion is proof of how well* that *worked out, isn't it, Rhobair?* he asked himself acidly. *On the other hand, even* you *can learn if God hits you with a heavy enough club. The real trick's going to be convincing them— and especially Zhaspahr—that you still don't have a clue.*

He smiled inwardly behind an expression that mingled patience with just a touch of boredom. It was ironic, he thought, that his "bargain" with Clyntahn should do so much to convince the Grand Inquisitor to completely disregard any threat he might represent. That the man who was supposed to be the keeper of Mother Church's conscience regarded Duchairn's insistence on actually discharging his responsibilities as one of God's vicars as proof of maudlin foggy-mindedness.

*You just go right on seeing things that way, Zhaspahr,* Rhobair Duchairn thought coldly. *Because one of these days, you're going to find out just how wrong you truly are.*

I was wondering when they'd get around to this," Cayleb Ahrmahk said sourly.

He, Sharleyan, their daughter, and one Captain Merlin Athrawes were afloat once more. *Empress of Charis* was still in yard hands, so he and Sharleyan flew their standard aboard HMS *Royal Charis*, one of the new fifty-eight-gun galleons designed to avoid *Empress of Charis'* problems. They wouldn't actually be leaving Tellesberg for their return to Chisholm until the morning tide, but they'd decided to get Princess Alahnah aboard ship and settled that afternoon.

Of course, that also meant they had to be a bit more careful about keeping their voices down, given the thinness of cabin bulkheads.

"Well," Bryahn Lock Island said rather more philosophically from his own flagship, "we figured they'd have to decide what to do with all those ships before Hsing-wu's Passage froze. Now we know. I have to admit, though—I didn't expect them to be quite this subtle. Gather their fleet in an *eastern* port, then send them all *west*?" He shook his head. "That's a lot sneakier than I anticipated, frankly."

Lock Island had a point, Merlin conceded. The port of Angelberg, on Chantry Bay, lay on the southern shore of Hsing-wu's Passage, almost three thousand miles *east* of Temple Bay. It was nearly halfway to the eastern mouth of the Passage, where it debouched into the Icewind Sea . . . and well over seven thousand miles from the Passage's *western* mouth. Had it not been for the orders to the various squadron commanders, he would have assumed they were planning on coming east, instead of west. Fortunately, they *had* been able to read those orders, which confirmed that what they were really planning was what Merlin and Lock Island had both considered to be their smartest move all along.

"They *are* being clever, aren't they," Prince Nahrmahn remarked from Eraystor, where his own galleon was waiting to join *Royal Charis* for the voyage to Chisholm.

"Maybe so, but now that we've caught them at it, the problem's deciding what we do about it," Domynyk Staynair put in from Thol Bay over his own com.

"No," Cayleb said, his tone ever more sour than it had been. "It isn't deciding *what* we do about it; it's deciding how we go about *doing* it. We're all agreed that this is the most logical thing for them to be doing, after what happened to Gwylym. And I think we have to honor the threat. Which means reinforcing both Corisande and Chisholm."

"I'm afraid you're right," Merlin sighed.

"So am I," Lock Island conceded. "But while we're worrying about what Thirsk might do, let's not forget about Kholman and Jahras."

Merlin grimaced.

The fact that he dared not insert remotes into the Temple itself always left a blank area at the very apex of their intelligence analyses. There was simply no way to get eyes and ears inside the innermost councils of the Group of Four, and their ignorance of what went on there was all the more frustrating because of their ability to penetrate every other council of war on the planet.

He kept reminding himself that he and his allies had better intelligence on their enemies' plans and capabilities than anyone else in the history of mankind. The problem was that they *needed* that kind of advantage if they were ever going to prevail against someone so numerically superior to themselves. And they'd been waiting for five-days to find out which way the Church's new navy was going to jump as autumn came on.

As Lock Island had pointed out, they'd known Allayn Maigwair and his colleagues would have to choose a course of action before the northern ports started to freeze. Of course, they *could* have decided to just sit there, but no one had really expected that. After the declaration of Holy War and the bloody fashion in which Clyntahn had secured the Group of Four's rear in the Temple and Zion, it had seemed a foregone conclusion that they weren't going to simply leave a hundred or so brand-new galleons frozen into the ice for several months.

As Merlin, Cayleb, Lock Island, and Rock Point had considered the Church's options, they'd concluded that there were three possible ice-free destinations: Shwei Bay, Gorath Bay, and the Gulf of Mathyas. There were arguments in favor of all three. For that matter, there'd been a fourth possibility—Bédard Bay, in the Republic of Siddarmark. North Bédard Bay would actually have been the most defensible of all the ice-free ports available, and given Clyntahn's near-psychotic suspicion of all things Siddarmarkian, basing a sizable contingent of the Church's new fleet right off the capital city's waterfront as a suggestion that the Lord Protector should behave himself could have been tempting.

There was also the question of just how the Church might choose to split up the ships it was moving south. In fact, Merlin had rather hoped they'd parcel the northern units out between several possible destinations, instead of keeping them concentrated. Having the opposing navy scattered around in as many separate sub fleets as possible struck him as a very good idea from Charis' viewpoint.

But whatever he might have hoped, Merlin had always expected the Church to end up choosing the strategy it had now selected. Given the Earl of Thirsk's accomplishments, combining as much as possible of the Church's total naval strength under his command made a lot of sense. Not only that, but under Thirsk's energetic management, Dohlaran foundries were now churning out more—and better—guns than anyone else outside of Charis. They were mostly still casting in bronze while they tried to get a handle on the greater difficulties involved in producing reliable iron guns, but their output had risen steadily. And if they were much less innovative than Charisian foundry operators, they were enormously *more* innovative than the Harchongese.

The Harchong economy still ran on what was essentially slave labor. The Empire had long-established, labor-intensive ways of doing things, and its innately reactionary conservatism—and ultra-orthodox adherence to the Proscriptions of Jwo-jeng—left it strongly disinclined to make changes. Its sheer size and population had allowed its economy to dominate western Howard and Haven for the last century and a half, despite its inherent inefficiency, however, and when the Church began its massive armament programs, the number of Harchongese foundries had suggested the Empire would provide at least a third, and more probably half, of all the required artillery. In fact, however, those plans had capsized when all those small foundries turned out to be so much less productive than expected. Against that sort of backdrop, the way in which Thirsk and Duke Fern had managed to improve the output of *Dohlaran* guns was one of the genuine bright spots for the Church. And given how badly cannon production continued to lag in both Harchong and the Temple Lands, it made a lot of sense to sail as many as possible of the Church's still unarmed galleons to Gorath Bay. With Claw Island now firmly in Thirsk's hands, the voyage would be both shorter and far more secure than trying to send them to any other destination.

It would also just happen to put the better part of two hundred galleons, under the Church's best admiral, in an ideal position to strike at Chisholm or Corisande from the east. And since the Imperial Charisian Navy had only about ninety-seven galleons of its own after Sir Gwylym Manthyr's losses in the Harchong Narrows, redeploying to meet that threat was going to be . . . difficult.

*Especially since, as Bryahn's just been kind enough to point out, we still have to worry about the frigging Desnairians, too,* Merlin thought disgustedly.

Duke Kholman and Admiral Jahras reminded Merlin rather forcibly of an Old Terran general named McClellan. They were pretty fair managers, all things considered. Despite ongoing problems with their own artillery production, they'd managed to get around seventy galleons launched, armed, and (more or less) manned. It was a significant accomplishment, particularly given the fact that there'd been no real Desnairian shipbuilding industry before the Church's massive program. Of course, there'd been an enormous amount of graft, some of the ships weren't all that well built, and Desnairian guns had a tendency to blow up more often than most, but seventy-plus galleons were still seventy-plus galleons.

The good news (and the main reason Kholman and Jahras made Merlin think about McClellan) was that, having built their navy, they were disinclined to have anything unfortunate happen to it. What Dunkyn Yairley and HMS *Destiny* had done to Commodore Wailahr clearly loomed large in their thinking, and especially in Baron Jahras'. In fact, he'd refused to venture outside of the Gulf of Jahras' sheltered waters to train his crews, which suited Charis just fine.

But if they redeployed enough strength to protect Chisholm and Corisande against an admiral as capable as Thirsk, even Jahras might find it within himself to operate with a modicum of aggressiveness. And if that happened . . .

"We're going to have to make some deep cuts in home waters, Bryahn, no matter what the Desnairians may be thinking about doing," Cayleb said finally. "Thirsk is just too damned good. If he comes at Chisholm with two hundred galleons, we need a lot more than Sharpfield has in the area now to stop him."

Lock Island nodded heavily. Sir Lewk Cohlmyn, the Earl of Sharpfield, had been the commanding officer of the Royal Chisholmian Navy. As such, he was now the second-ranking officer, after Lock Island himself, in the Imperial Charisian Navy. That rank, plus his intimate familiarity with Chisholmian waters, made him the logical—indeed, the only—choice to command the squadrons protecting Sharleyan's kingdom. As a peacetime officer, he'd been outstanding, especially with his determination to root out corruption at all levels, and no one doubted his personal courage. Yet all his combat experience was with *galleys*. He'd never commanded even a single galleon in action. Now he was in command of an entire *fleet* of them, and the thought of giving him his first experience with it outnumbered six- or seven-to-one wasn't particularly appealing.

"It would help if we had someone in Chisholm or Corisande with a com," Sharleyan pointed out. "If Sir Lewk and Admiral Mahndyr had access to the SNARCs, they could combine their strength into a single force that would have a far better chance of matching Thirsk."

It was Merlin's turn to nod. Gharth Rahlstahn, the Earl of Mahndyr, had been Sharpfield's Emeraldian equivalent. He was younger than Sharpfield, without as many years of experience at sea, but he'd proven he was a fighter at Darcos Sound, and years of service under Prince Nahrmahn had given him a degree of political acumen which the bluff, apolitical Sharpfield completely lacked. That was why he'd been chosen to command the squadron covering Corisande.

"Unfortunately, the only flag officer we could send would be you, Domynyk," Lock Island said. "Which—"

"Which," Cayleb interrupted in a slightly odd, almost amused tone, "would be . . . politically awkward at this particular moment."

"Awkward, but survivable, Your Majesty," Rock Point said respectfully. "I know Gorjah wants me right where I am when we finally have him announce he's coming over, but I can think of a half-dozen other officers who could hold down this command as well as I can. Kohdy Nylz comes to mind, among others."

"I'm sure Admiral Nylz could handle your naval duties perfectly adequately, My Lord," Nahrmahn put in. "The problem is that all Gorjah's calculations are built around having *you* covering Thol Bay to make sure no nasty Desnairians come sailing in to attack him when the Church finds out he's changing sides. He's nervous enough already, and I don't think he shares our navy's contempt for Jahras. Which, given how much closer he is to Desnair than we are, probably isn't all that unreasonable, when you come down to it. It's obvious he's developed enough faith in *you* to feel confident, but if we reorganize everything on the fly, I think there's at least a fair chance he'll back off at the last moment."

"Especially if he should happen to become aware of the fact that the Inquisition's sending more investigators into Tarot," Merlin agreed.

"I think Merlin and Nahrmahn have a point, Cayleb," Sharleyan said unhappily.

"So do I," Cayleb agreed, but the amusement in his tone was even more pronounced, and then he shook his head mock regretfully at his wife and surprised all of them with a laugh.

"Did I miss something humorous?" Sharleyan asked a bit tartly, and he nodded, still chuckling.

"As a matter of fact, you did," he said. "Came as a bit of a shock to me, too, since you're not usually so slow."

"Slow?" she repeated even more tartly. Indeed, one might have described her tone as ominous.

"Well, you *do* seem to have overlooked the minor fact that *we're* both going to be in Chisholm. And so is a fellow named Merlin, unless I'm mistaken."

Sharleyan's eyes widened. For a moment, she sat staring at him with the expression of a very smart woman who very seldom made foolish mistakes. Then it was her turn to laugh.

"Of course we are! And if memory serves, you've had a modicum of naval combat experience yourself, haven't you?"

"A modicum," her husband agreed, holding up his thumb and index finger about an inch apart.

"With all due respect, Your Majesty, I'm not in favor of risking you at sea,"

Lock Island said. Cayleb arched an eyebrow, and the high admiral shrugged. "At Armageddon Reef and Darcos Sound, your father was right about how important it was for the fleet to know you were there. I don't think this situation's exactly comparable, though, and there are all sorts of reasons why having you killed would be politically disastrous."

It was obvious from Lock Island's voice that he had some highly personal reasons for not wanting to see his cousin killed, as well, and Cayleb's eyes softened. But then he shook his head.

"First, we have a firmly secured succession now," he said, reaching out and taking Sharleyan's hand in his own. "There's not a single soul in Old Charis who wouldn't accept Sharley as Empress in her sole right if something happened to me. And there's also Alahnah, now. So the arguments about how 'utterly indispensable' I am seem just a bit less compelling than they used to be.

"Second, with all due modesty, the Navy has a certain degree of confidence in me. I think they'll probably find it reassuring to have me with them if they've got to go into battle at such unfavorable odds."

Saying the Imperial Charisian Navy had "a certain degree of confidence" in Cayleb Ahrmahk was rather like saying there was "a certain amount of water" in the Great Western Ocean, Merlin reflected.

"But third, and most important of all, I'm the only person we've got—aside from you, Bryahn—we could possibly send to Chisholm who has both access to Owl's SNARCs and enough seniority to give Sharpfield orders. There's no way in the world we could justify leaving me ashore for this one, and you know it."

"He's right, Bryahn," Sharleyan said quietly, and grimaced. "I'm pretty sure I'm even unhappier than you are at the notion of letting him go and get shot at again," her hand tightened on Cayleb's, "but he's still right."

There was silence for a moment while the emperor sat, fingers of his free hand drumming lightly on a side table while he thought. Then he inhaled deeply.

"All right," he said. "That's what we're going to do. And I'm going to have to take more of your fleet strength than I'd like to, Bryahn. We can't *not* reinforce Chisholm and Corisande strongly when we know what's coming at them, and we can't wait. This time of year, it's going to take longer for us to get reinforcements to Chisholm than it'll take Maigwair's new construction to get to Gorath Bay. I know we'll have a little bit of time in hand, at least, after they get there, but I don't want to give Thirsk a gift of any *more* time than we have to. On the other hand, we can't organize all of this in a flash. It's going to take at least a few days, and I don't want to delay our own departure for Chisholm.

"I think I agree with Merlin and Nahrmahn that we need to leave Domynyk where he is, and with me there, we'll have SNARC access without him. So, we'll send the reinforcements out after *Royal Charis* under Admiral Nylz. He's a good man, and I can use him."

"Yes, Your Majesty," Lock Island said formally, half bowing to his distant emperor. "How much strength do you want me to send with him?"

"That's what really scares me," Cayleb said frankly. "I don't see how we could possibly cover both Chisholm and Corisande with less than sixty sail."

The silence which greeted that number was profound, and Cayleb's lips twitched.

"I can eke that out with the best of the old carronade-armed galleys," he continued, "but even with the SNARCs, I can't magically reproduce galleons like rabbits. I'll be able to see what Thirsk is up to, but if he fights as smart as we all expect him to, he's not going to split up into smaller forces I can pick off one at a time. He's going to come at me with everything he's got in one concentrated fleet, and I'm going to need enough firepower to stop him when he does. Which, even with sixty galleons, is going to be a tall order, now that he knows exactly what broadside fire can do. That's where, hopefully, the SNARCs will come in by letting me choose the tactical situation when we finally engage."

"Your Majesty," Rock Point said after a moment, "I can't dispute anything you've just said. But if we deploy sixty sail to Chisholm and Corisande, that's only going to leave about *thirty* to keep an eye on waters closer to Old Charis."

"I know," Cayleb said. "But even with sixty, we'll still be outnumbered in Chisholmian waters by better than three-to-one. And, frankly, if I'm going to be outnumbered *three*-to-one up against someone as good as Thirsk, then I think we have to be willing to take a chance on people as good as you and Bryahn being outnumbered *two*-to-one against a second-rater like Jahras."

Rock Point said nothing for a moment, then nodded.

"At the same time, though, I'm not repeating the mistake we made with Gwylym," Cayleb said, his brown eyes hardening. "We've got a lot more schooners than we need for blockade duty, especially now that Tarot's joining the Empire, so I want at least fifteen or twenty of them sent out with Nylz. That ought to give me plenty of fast cruisers to picket Claw Island and the Harchong Narrows closely—which, hopefully, will explain how I'm managing to keep an eye on Thirsk—with enough more left over for effective hit-and-run raids in the Gulf to generally make his life as miserable as possible. I don't think we're likely to panic him into a misstep just by throwing commerce raiders at him, but I'm certainly willing to try.

"And it's not as if Thirsk is operating in a political vacuum," he continued. "Even with Maik in his corner, Thorast's still doing his best to stab him in the back. If I can raise enough havoc in the Gulf of Dohlar and the same waters where Gwylym was operating, I may be able to give Thorast a hand." Cayleb grimaced. "Part of me hates doing that to an honorable man, but he's just too damned capable. I'll settle for getting him out of the way any way I can, I'm afraid."

"Actually, I think that's a very good idea," Lock Island said. "If we hit them with an offensive of our own, we may preempt their plans. And I'll probably be able to send you even more schooners over the next couple of months."

That, Merlin reflected, was true enough. Not only was the Navy's requirement for blockade vessels going to decline, as Cayleb had just pointed out, but privateering was nowhere near as profitable as it once had been. By now, most of the Church's merchant shipping was traveling in convoys which were increasingly protected by ships with enough artillery to make any attack upon them a chancy proposition. More to the point, though, there simply wasn't very much enemy merchant shipping left. Which meant dozens of fast, agile, heavily armed schooners were being disposed of by privateering consortiums who no longer needed them. In fact, they were glutting the market so badly they could be picked up for the proverbial song.

"Good thinking," Cayleb agreed. "And as for the situation in Charisian and Tarotisian waters, Domynyk, don't forget Ehdwyrd's making progress with Ahlfryd's shells now. He ought to be starting production in another month or so."

"*Starting* production," Rock Point repeated dryly.

Ehdwyrd Howsmyn was as frustrated as anyone had ever seen him over the delays in putting Seamount's shells into production. Not that it was his fault. Not even his access to Owl could magically produce the equipment, the techniques, and—above all—the trained workforce he needed overnight, especially since he was rather in the position Merlin had always been in. He could make suggestions, even have an occasional flash of brilliance, but to avoid charges of violating the Proscriptions, he had to be able to demonstrate a development *process* . . . and, given the declaration of Holy War, that was more important than ever. By now, he'd managed that, but he'd been deeply frustrated by how long it had taken. And once he'd managed *that* part, it had been only to run into almost intolerable weather delays in getting his new shell-producing manufactory up and running. Torrential rains which went on seemingly forever, weather-spawned avalanches which imposed blockages on the canal system serving his ironworks, and then no less than three tropical storms blowing in off the Sea of Justice in a single two-month period . . . If he hadn't known the truth about the "Archangels," the industrialist would have been inclined to think God really *was* on the other side.

But at least he finally had the foundations in, a roof on, and the furnaces under construction. Even so, it was going to be at least another two or three months, possibly even into March, before he was able to provide the new projectiles to the Navy in anything like adequate numbers.

"I know we're not going to be able to start issuing them until spring," Lock Island said now. "On the other hand, they're sending the vast bulk of their naval strength to Thirsk. Even if he decides to try a galleon-equipped version of the original Armageddon Reef plan, we'll have something like six or seven months before he could possibly get to Old Charis. Frankly, I don't think there's a chance in hell they'll try that again, though—not after what happened last time, and not when Chisholm and Corisande are so much closer to Gorath Bay. So the important thing is to get His Majesty reinforced heavily enough to deter Thirsk until Ehdwyrd does have enough shells for us. Once *that* happens"—the high admiral smiled nastily—"*we'll* be the ones going looking for *them,* and they won't like it a bit when a shell-armed battleline catches up with them, either."

# OCTOBER,
# YEAR OF GOD 894

.I.

HMS *Royal Charis*, 58,
Zebediah Sea,
HMS *Ahrmahk*, 58,
Charis Sea,
and
HMS *Destroyer*, 54,
Thol Bay

S hit."
Merlin Athrawes pronounced the single word with a quiet, terrible emphasis as he gazed at the latest download from Owl. *Royal Charis* was crossing the Zebediah Sea, six five-days out of Tellesberg and almost exactly halfway to Cherayth. It was just after Langhorne's Watch, the Safeholdian midnight, and Cayleb and Sharleyan were sound asleep.

*Waking them up won't help a damned thing,* Merlin thought grimly. *On the other hand, if I don't wake them up and tell them about this, they're both going to be pissed as hell.*

He considered the time, then grimaced as he decided on a compromise. Crown Princess Alahnah would be waking up to demand her early feeding in no more than another hour. He could let the emperor and empress have at least that much more sleep.

On the other hand, it was four hours earlier in Tellesberg, so. . . .

▼　　▼　　▼

Bryahn Lock Island's eyes narrowed as the invisible plug in his right ear chirped at him, then began a soft rendition of a peculiar piece of music. The sound—the opening bars of something which had once been called "Anchors Aweigh"—sounded very . . . strange to any Safeholdian. It also identified the caller as Merlin Athrawes, however, and Lock Island hadn't expected to hear from him for at least another couple of hours. For that matter, Merlin always tried to avoid calling when anyone who wasn't already part of the inner circle was present.

Which suggested the high admiral had better take this particular call.

"All right, Henrai," he said to the lieutenant commander sitting across the table from him. "I think that covers just about everything. There are a couple of other points I'd like to discuss before the meeting tomorrow, but let me mull them over tonight."

"Of course, Sir."

Henrai Tillyer had been Lock Island's flag lieutenant for over three years. Since his promotion to lieutenant commander, Lock Island had decided to emulate Earl Thirsk and turned Tillyer into his chief of staff. Unlike Thirsk, however, who was inventing the concept on his own, Lock Island had benefited from researching the historical development and organization of staff officers in Owl's data banks. As a result, he was well along the way to creating a genuine staff, with specific, designated areas of responsibility, and he was already making mental selections for the flag officers—Navy, Army, and Marine—he intended to nominate to Cayleb when the emperor inaugurated the concept of a *general* staff for the entire empire in another few months.

At the moment, it was obvious Tillyer, who knew him far better than most, was more than a little perplexed by the high admiral's abrupt termination of their meeting. But whatever questions might be running through his brain, he wasn't about to ask them. Instead, he gathered up the notes he'd been taking, jogged them together, and slid them into a folder. Then he smiled at Lock Island, finished the last swallow in his whiskey glass, and cuffed Lock Island's rottweiler Keelhaul gently and affectionately on his massive head.

Keelhaul chuffed in acknowledgment of the goodbye without ever opening his eyes, and Tillyer chuckled.

"I'll see you in the morning, Sir."

"By all means. In fact, join me for breakfast, if you would."

"Of course, Sir."

Tillyer nodded respectfully and withdrew, shutting the door behind him. Lock Island looked at the closed door for a moment, then stood and opened the many-paned glass door to HMS *Ahrmahk*'s sternwalk. He leaned on the rail, gazing up at a sky that was fading from blue into indigo. A few of the brightest stars were visible, but it would be a while before darkness actually fell.

"Yes, Merlin?" he said then, quietly, his voice inaudible through the sound of wind and water to anyone more than two or three feet away from him.

"I'm sorry to disturb you," Merlin's voice said in his earplug, and Lock Island felt his eyebrows knitting in quick alarm as the *seijin*'s grim tone registered. "Unfortunately," Merlin continued, "we've got a problem. A *big* one."

"What do you mean?" Lock Island asked quickly, and heard a distant sigh.

"We've been had," Merlin said flatly. "They aren't sending the fleet to Thirsk, after all. They're sending it to Desnair."

▼    ▼    ▼

Two hours later, Merlin, Cayleb, and Sharleyan sat on *Royal Charis'* sternwalk.

"It's my fault," Merlin said.

"Oh, kraken shit!" Cayleb snapped. "Just how the hell is this supposed to be *your* fault? Or at least *all* your fault—which seems to be where you're headed!"

"They're my SNARCs, and I was the one who was so sure they'd be sending everything to Thirsk," Merlin replied. "If I hadn't predisposed everyone to think—"

"Cayleb's right, Merlin—that *is* kraken shit." Lock Island sounded even more impatient than the emperor had. "You weren't the only one who thought Gorath Bay was the logical destination! And whatever you may've *thought,* we had confirmation—*written* confirmation, official orders, mind you—that all of us had examined through Owl's SNARCs. At which point *all* of us concluded the ships were going where they'd been *ordered* to go by none other than Allayn Maigwair. So just how were you supposed to realize they'd decide to go somewhere *else* at the last minute?"

"I don't think they did decide at the last minute," Nahrmahn Baytz said. Like Cayleb and Sharleyan, he was returning to Chisholm, but he and his wife were aboard HMS *Eraystor,* one of the two galleons escorting *Royal Charis.* "I think this is what they intended to do all along."

"Then why tell their own captains they were going *west*?" Domynyk Staynair asked from his own flagship in Thol Bay.

"Disinformation," Nahrmahn said simply. "Whatever we think of the Group of Four, they really aren't drooling idiots. Fools, perhaps. And arrogant and corrupt and any other pejorative anyone would care to add, certainly. But I think sometimes we forget that a lot of their 'mistakes' are the result of the fact that they don't have a clue what they're really up against. They still think the old rules apply to things like spying, communication times, and everything else. That's the reason they've persistently assumed their semaphore means their communications—what people used to call the 'communications loop'—must be faster than anyone else's, when they're actually *slower* . . . for some of us, at least.

"My point is that we've been guilty of underestimating them. We know they turned Tarot upside down trying to figure out how their plans leaked before Armageddon Reef. We also know they never found an answer, since Tarot didn't actually have anything to do with it. But what should have occurred to us when we were analyzing their 'cover plan' is that eventually they were going to have to assume we have some fiendishly effective spy network in place. Obviously, that's exactly what they did . . . as the fact that they were bothering with a cover plan at all should *damned* well have told someone as clever as *I'm* supposed to be!"

The portly little prince sounded about as bitter as Merlin had ever heard him, and his self-anger was painfully apparent when he paused for a deep breath.

"As I say, we should have realized they were going to think of something like this," he went on in a more controlled tone. "And, given all the coded messages all of them have passed through the semaphore at one time or another, they have to be aware someone else could be sending coded messages under the guise of simple commercial transactions or personal letters. The only way they could stop that would be to shut down all secular use of the semaphore, and that would cause all sorts of dislocations, not to mention costing them a hefty chunk of their revenue. Not only that, but once they start thinking in that direction, it's going to occur to them that there could be other ways to cobble up an alternative communications system even if they *did* shut down the semaphore stations. Like carrier wyverns."

He paused again, and Cayleb snorted. Back when Prince Nahrmahn of Emerald had been conspiring to assassinate King Haarahld and Crown Prince Cayleb of Charis, his chief agent in Tellesberg had been one of the kingdom's most prestigious providers of hunting and homing wyverns. Which had just happened to provide Nahrmahn with a swift, clandestine means of communication between Charis and Emerald.

"If they've decided we do have spies in the Temple Lands, and if they've accepted that those spies can get information to us as quickly—or even just almost as quickly—as they can send messages using the semaphore, then it was only a matter of time before they started taking precautions. That's what happened here. They told their captains to prepare to sail west *expecting* any of our spies who intercepted those orders to send them along to us, while all the time they were planning on changing their captains' orders at the last minute."

"I think Prince Nahrmahn's right, Your Majesties," Rahzhyr Mahklyn offered from his apartment in Tellesberg Palace. "It makes sense, anyway."

"Maybe it does," Merlin acknowledged. "And maybe that will make me feel better about the way they snookered us someday. It doesn't help much when it comes to deciding what to do about it, though."

"No, you've got a point there," Cayleb agreed in a much grimmer tone.

"Frankly, there's not much we *can* do," Lock Island said bleakly. "Kohdy Nylz and your reinforcements are barely a five-day behind you and Sharleyan, and the prevailing winds are out of the west. Even if we could communicate with him instantly—and explain how the hell we'd done it—he'd still need at least a month, more probably seven or eight five-days, to get back here."

"Thanks to my eagerness to get him started early, you mean," Cayleb said.

"If you don't want Merlin kicking himself over things that aren't his fault, don't kick *yourself* over things that aren't *your* fault," his cousin told him tartly. "Given what all of us 'knew,' you made the right decision. They just—as Merlin said—'snookered us.'" The high admiral chuckled harshly. "Assuming 'snookered' means what I think it means!"

"Well, assuming the orders they've sent to Kholman and Jahras aren't more of Nahrmahn's 'disinformation,' they're obviously planning on catching you and Domynyk between two forces," Sharleyan said. "So I'd say the first priority is to make sure they don't do that."

"I could agree with that," Lock Island said feelingly.

"Of course, there *is* the little problem of how twenty-seven of our galleons fight a hundred and thirty of theirs, even assuming we can engage them without Jahras hitting us from behind," Rock Point pointed out.

"Only ninety of them are armed," Lock Island replied, and Rock Point snorted.

"All right, how do twenty-seven of our galleons fight *ninety* of theirs? I'm willing to count one of ours as worth two of theirs, maybe even two and a half. Hell, let's make it three! But even assuming we turn the northern force back, we're going to get hurt, Bryahn, and you know it. So what happens if we get whittled down against one force, then get jumped by the other one?"

"We get hurt *badly*," Lock Island said grimly. "And we see to it that they get hurt a hell of a lot worse."

"They don't have a few hundred transports loaded with troops sailing along with them," Sharleyan pointed out. "Even if they manage to get through to Desnair, they don't have an army ready to land anywhere."

"You're thinking we could avoid action? Play for time?" Cayleb said.

"More or less," she agreed. "All they can really do is sail around. They certainly can't invade Old Charis or Emerald—not against the garrisons we've got in place with rifles and the new artillery!"

"The problem is that we can't afford to let these two forces unite," Cayleb replied. "They'd have over two hundred galleons in the Gulf of Mathyas. And if they could bring Thirsk and his Dohlarans down around Howard, they'd have three hundred." He shook his head. "We have to keep them from concentrating."

"And let's not forget Tarot." Rock Point's tone was bleak. "You're probably right that they don't have the troop strength for a serious landing in Old Charis or Emerald, Your Majesty. Unfortunately, I'm sure they *do* have enough strength to carry out raids at least as destructive as the ones *we* carried out in Corisande. And whether they can do that or not, between the seamen and the soldiers they've got aboard all those ships, they've got more than enough strength to invade Tarot. Gorjah doesn't have any of the new weapons, and while I don't think there are as many Tarotisian Temple Loyalists as the Group of Four thinks there are, there are enough to create a genuine civil war if they think the Church is invading. If Clyntahn and Trynair get a couple of hundred galleons into Thol Bay, Tarot's gone."

"Wonderful," Cayleb sighed.

"What are your latest numbers on shell production, Ehdwyrd?" Lock Island asked.

"About what they were when you asked me yesterday," Ehdwyrd Howsmyn replied from his bedroom. His normally affable voice was considerably more tart than usual. "Effectively zero, in other words. We're still setting up the production line, Bryahn. You know that, and—"

"I'm not criticizing," Lock Island said quickly. "But with only twenty galleons, we're going to need an edge if we're going to stop these bastards."

"Well, I'm not going to have the new line up for at least another two five-days." It was obvious from Howsmyn's tone that he was kicking himself for not having gotten it up sooner, although given the weather problems he'd faced . . .

"Well, you've got at least eight five-days before they can reach the Gulf of Tarot," Rock Point replied. "That's almost a month and a half, Ehdwyrd!"

"Yes, it is." Howsmyn's tone was suddenly far more thoughtful.

There was silence for several seconds, then he shrugged.

"I can go ahead and start making fuses now," he said. "Once I have the furnaces in and the molds ready to go, I can probably produce about a hundred or a hundred and fifty thirty-pounder shells a day. I might be able to edge that up a little higher if I forget finishing the insides of the shell chambers. In *another* couple of five-days, I can probably get two more furnaces online, and that will get me up to somewhere around three hundred shells a day. So, figure everything works *perfectly* from this point—which it damned well hasn't so far!—and I can produce, say, a hundred and twenty-five shells a day for two five-days, and then three hundred a day for another six five-days. Call it a total of ten thousand."

That sounded like an awful lot, Merlin reflected, but it wasn't really, given the normal ammunition allotments of ICN galleons. The "establishment" was forty rounds of round shot, ten rounds of grapeshot, and five rounds of chain shot per gun. That was almost *three* thousand rounds for a single fifty-four-gun galleon. Replacing just the round shot in her shot lockers on a one-for-one basis would require the next best thing to twenty-two hundred shells.

On the other hand, if the other side didn't anticipate yet another new Charisian weapon, they might well break and run the moment they encountered it.

*And they might* not, *too,* he reminded himself grimly. *This isn't going to be like Armageddon Reef or Darcos Sound. These ships are coming directly from Harchong and the Temple Lands themselves, and Mother Church has proclaimed Holy War. Then there's the little fact that we've already been denounced as Shan-wei-worshippers and demon-worshippers by Clyntahn's propaganda. If we start firing exploding shells at them, that's only going to confirm Clyntahn's lies, at least in the short term. And the fact that they're headed down this way on a* jihad *against the Powers of Darkness may actually help them take it in stride. . . .*

"Not good enough, I'm afraid," Cayleb said. Merlin and Sharleyan looked at him, and he shrugged.

"Ehdwyrd's estimate is the number of shells he can deliver eight five-days from now. But by that time, they'll be halfway across the Markovian Sea . . . and ships sailing from Old Charis at that point won't possibly be able to intercept them before they're into the Tarot Channel. We *might* be able to catch them at the southern end of the Channel, before they cross the Gulf of Mathyas, but we'll never stop them from getting into Thol Bay, if they decide to do that. And, to be honest, even the chance of intercepting them in the Gulf's probably no better than even."

"We could load them aboard transports and deliver them at sea," Lock Island said.

"We could try," Cayleb conceded, "but we'd run the risk of getting caught by the other side while we were doing it. For that matter, just to get transport galleons to the northern end of the Tarot Channel would take a good four five-days, Bryahn. Which means Ehdwyrd would lose four of the eight five-days he's planning on. And according to my numbers, that would cost six thousand or so of his total."

"Maybe we don't have any choice but for me to go call on Admiral Nylz the way I did on your father before Darcos Sound," Merlin said unhappily.

"Forget it." Cayleb shook his head. "Father was already at sea against an opponent he knew about. Not only that, but it was reasonable—if risky—for him to adopt the strategy he did, given that he knew I was going to be headed back from Armageddon Reef as quickly as I could. But Kohdy and his entire fleet are headed towards Chisholm to confront a threat *there*. There is absolutely no logical, reasonable argument he could use to turn the fleet around against his existing orders, even if we were lucky enough for him to take the truth in stride. I think it's probable he *would,* as a matter of fact, but that doesn't change the fact that if we turn him around *without* a good, solid reason everyone can grasp, no explanation short of demonic—or angelic—intervention could explain to anyone *else*—including his own officers and men!—why we did it."

He was right, Merlin realized.

"All right," Lock Island said. "You're right, Your Majesty. We can't turn Kohdy around, and we don't have eight five-days to produce shells and ship them to the fleet. So, the way I see it, we only have one real option."

"We have an option? Really?" The humor in Cayleb's voice was biting but genuine, and the high admiral chuckled harshly.

"I didn't say it was a *good* option," he pointed out.

"All right, in that case tell us about this *not*-so-good option."

"The way I see it, we're going to have to take the pressure off the Desnairians. I don't want to do that, and if anyone can think of *any* way we can encourage them to stay home despite Maigwair's direct orders to sortie, I'll be delighted to hear about it. In the meantime, though, it'll be up to me to sail north. I doubt they're going to just turn around and head home when they see my topsails, but knowing I'm in the area—and *not* knowing how much of our strength we've sent off to Chisholm in response to their 'disinformation'—they'll have to regard me as a potentially significant threat, at least initially. I'll take enough schooners with me to keep them under close observation, try to make them nervous. With a bit of luck, I should at least be able to instill enough caution to slow them down. On the other hand, if they're feeling frisky and adventurous, I may even be able to tempt them—or some of them, at any rate—into chasing me and draw them off."

"And this will achieve exactly what?" Cayleb asked, although his tone suggested he was already following his cousin's thinking.

"While I'm doing that, Domynyk will sail for home. We'll be in touch by com, and we'll both know where the Church fleet is. He'll load however many shells Ehdwyrd's able to manufacture before he has to pull out. Then, assuming the other side's stayed concentrated and I'm still shadowing them, he'll sail to rendezvous with me. If they've divided and sent some of them to pursue me, he'll ignore them and go for the main fleet. He'll be badly outnumbered—hell, for that matter we'll be badly outnumbered if both our forces manage to rendezvous before the battle!—but he should have at least a few thousand shells in his lockers. If he does, and if we can catch them at sea, and if the shells work out as well in practice as Ahlfryd's tests suggest, and *if* the other side panics when it realizes what we're doing to it, we *may* manage to turn them back."

"You do remember how often Father pointed out that a flag officer who builds his strategy based on the assumption that *all* of it will work the way he expects it to is an idiot, don't you, Bryahn?"

"Of course I do. And if I had a choice, I wouldn't be suggesting anything of the sort this time, either. Unfortunately, I don't think we do have a choice."

"Bryahn's right, Your Majesty," Rock Point said. "God only knows how we're going to convince the Desnairians to stay home, or at least make them hesitant enough to let us deal with the northern fleet first! But this is the only approach I see which *could* work, no matter how many things may go wrong with it. And there's this, too, I'm afraid. As long as we can avoid a close action that ends up doing to us what Thirsk did to Gwylym, we're no worse off if this doesn't work than we would be if we didn't try to do anything about it at all."

"And if you don't have enough shells, and if they don't work the way we expect them to, then just how the hell do you plan to avoid that?" Cayleb demanded. "Correct me if I'm wrong, but my powerful intellect suggests to me that to get into your range of them, you have to come into *their* range of *you*. Which means the only way you're going to find out you *don't* have enough shells, or that they *don't* work the way we expected them to, is going to put you into exactly that sort of an engagement!"

"That may be what happens," Lock Island said quietly. "If it does, though, then it does. And you'll still have two-thirds of the Navy to come back and do something about it."

.II.
HMS *Destiny*, 54,
Off Terrence Point,
Gulf of Mathyas,
and
The Duke of Kholman's Office,
City of Iythria,
Desnairian Empire

Sir Dunkyn Yairley had always hoped to someday fly his own admiral's streamer. He hadn't expected it to come quite this soon, however, or under precisely these circumstances. He stood on HMS *Destiny*'s quarterdeck, gazing up at that striped strip of steel thistle silk flying from his ship's foremast, and wondered exactly what the watchers ashore were making of his current antics.

He turned his gaze aft. Twenty-six galleons followed in *Destiny*'s wake, each in the severe livery of the Imperial Charisian Navy. Other fleets, other navies, painted their ships in gaudy colors, decorated them with gold leaf and ornate carvings. Charisian warships were painted in black, the only color they boasted the white stripes, marking the lines of their gunports, and the red-painted lids of the ports themselves. In its own way, it was the most arrogant decoration available, Yairley thought. First, because the Empire was the only navy which painted its ships in that fashion, which made them instantly recognizable at any range. And, secondly, because it was a statement that *Charisian* seamen needed no ornamentation to overawe any foe.

Despite the severity of their paint scheme, the ships forging along behind him made a brave show, although it was obvious to any observer that he had rather more of the Imperial Navy's refitted merchantmen than he might have chosen. On the other hand. . . .

He turned his head, gazing out at the second column of mastheads, paralleling his own. A trio of schooners lay between his own column and those distant masts to relay his signals, and he'd kept young Ensign Aplyn-Ahrmahk occupied for the past several hours reporting his observations to them.

More schooners slid smoothly through the water between him and Terrence Point, and others hovered farther to the northwest, covering the waters between Terrence Point and Howard Island. With the light breeze blowing almost directly into the Howard Passage from the Gulf, the schooners' speed and ability to work to windward made them ideal for keeping an eye peeled for the Imperial Desnairian Navy.

Assuming, of course, that the Imperial Desnairian Navy felt adventurous enough to poke its collective nose out of its snug little hidey-hole in the Gulf of Jahras when so much of the Imperial *Charisian* Navy was obviously waiting—longingly—for it to do precisely that.

▼    ▼    ▼

"Oh, *crap,*" the Desnairian Army lieutenant in charge of the observation post on the tip of Terrence Point muttered quietly, but with great feeling, as he bent to peer through the tripod-mounted telescope at the apparently endless column of Charisian ships.

"See what I mean, Sir?" his sergeant asked respectfully.

"I do, indeed, Sergeant," the lieutenant acknowledged, straightening his back and glaring out to sea. "What I *don't* see is what kind of bee got up their arses for them to suddenly be doing this kind of shit!"

He stood glowering at the Charisians, then sighed.

"Well, I suppose we'd better get the message off."

▼    ▼    ▼

"And so yet another brilliant strategy goes astray," the Duke of Kholman murmured, gazing at the transcript of the semaphore message from the Terrence Point observation post. He shook his head, then laid the transcript on his desk, very carefully and precisely, and looked at Baron Jahras.

"You know," he said almost whimsically, "I don't know how much Cayleb Ahrmahk pays his spies, but it obviously isn't enough. They must've known about our instructions almost as soon as we did!"

"Not necessarily," Jahras disagreed. The duke frowned, and Jahras chuckled sourly. "Oh, I agree they know what's going on, but they could have found out as much as a five-day or more after we did and still managed to arrange this."

He flicked an index finger at the sheet of paper on Kholman's desk.

"You're right about another 'brilliant' plan going straight into the crapper, though," he continued. "And it's obviously another case of Vicar Allayn getting too clever for his own good. I can understand why he didn't want us sailing prematurely. But the way it's worked out, we're screwed, at least until—and unless—Harpahr and Shaiow get close enough to threaten these people from the north."

"That's not precisely what we're supposed to be doing," the duke observed, and Jahras shrugged.

"Tell me something I *don't* know, Daivyn! I'm not too clear on exactly how we're supposed to 'follow the plan,' though. They haven't put anything heavier than schooners and three or four galleons into our coastal waters for months now. Oh, I don't doubt they've had more ships farther out to sea, ready to whistle up if we'd been foolish enough to come out, but they've obviously been relying on a distant blockade strategy. They didn't want to keep us sealed in *port*; they wanted to draw us out where they could pounce on us in deep water, which is precisely why I had no intention at all of going there!

"Now, suddenly, they've got the next best thing to *thirty* galleons trailing their coats less than fifteen miles offshore. And there are more of the bastards farther out to sea. I'd say it's pretty obvious they know we've been ordered to sortie . . . and they don't plan on us doing anything of the sort!"

"The Captain General's orders aren't exactly discretionary, Urwyn," Kholman pointed out.

"Oh, yes they are," Jahras demurred. Kholman arched an eyebrow, and the baron snorted. "They say we're supposed to make all preparations to insure that, when ordered to by semaphore, the fleet can sail—and I quote—'at the earliest practicable moment.'"

"Which obviously means as soon as we get the order to put to sea. I *am* assuming that's why they want us to *prepare* to go to sea, you know."

"But that isn't what they said." Jahras smiled thinly. "If that's what they meant, they should have said to sail 'immediately upon receipt of the order.' *That's* nondiscretionary. 'Practicable' means I'm supposed to sail as soon as I can *successfully* get to sea and carry out my assigned mission. Which is going to be just a bit difficult, given that it looks very much as if the Charisians have massed at least fifty or sixty of their own galleons—bigger, faster, more heavily *armed* galleons—specifically to intercept us as we try to clear the Howard Passage. And, just to make bad worse, the wind's in their favor and it'll probably *stay* in their favor, three days out of five, for the foreseeable future." He shook his head. "If I try to tack out of the Gulf of Jahras into the broadsides of that many galleons, they'll pound my ships into driftwood before I ever clear the Passage, much less make it to the Tarot Channel. Which isn't exactly the definition of 'practicable,' according to any dictionary with which I'm familiar."

Kholman tipped back in his chair, frowning. He rather doubted Allayn Maigwair and Zhaspahr Clyntahn were likely to share his cousin-in-law's interpretation of the order they'd meant to give him. Despite that, Jahras obviously had a point about what would happen if he took his own inexperienced ships into the teeth of that much highly experienced firepower. And even a confirmed landsman like Kholman could see the baron was also right about the added, deadly disadvantage of the wind. The Howard Passage was less than sixty miles across. After allowing for various banks and shoals, it was actually considerably narrower than that . . . and at the moment, the wind was blowing almost directly into it off the Gulf of Mathyas.

"They aren't going to like hearing that," he said mildly, and Jahras shrugged.

"They also haven't sent us the execute order yet," he pointed out. "In fact, our instructions are very clear on that point. We're supposed to *prepare* to sail but wait until they tell us Harpahr and Shaiow are far enough along, *then* sortie. It's always possible Harpahr will never get close enough for them to issue that order. And if they do and it's clearly not 'practicable' for us to obey it, we can tell them that then. If they want to amend our orders and tell me to sail *at any cost,* obviously I will. But not until they get a message back to us telling me they're prepared for us to sustain the sort of losses I'll take trying to obey. Which, even with the semaphore, will take a five-day or so."

Kholman considered that, as well. Then he shook his head.

"I don't disagree with you about how . . . unwise it would be to sortie into that kind of opposition. And this is clearly the sort of situation where the exercise of a certain discretion by the officers actually on the ground seems indicated. But the Temple's declared Holy War. That kind of letter-of-my-orders argument may not work for the Grand Inquisitor. Especially if it comes at him cold."

"I'm not a lunatic, Daivyn, and I don't want Vicar Zhaspahr pissed off at me any more than the next man." Jahras' voice and expression alike were grimmer than they had been. "At the same time, I'm not going to lead our Navy into a sausage grinder when I know damned well what's going to happen to it."

"I don't think you should. I just said this better not come at the Temple cold. I think we should send them a report on the current situation. We need to formally acknowledge our receipt of their instructions, anyway. So we tell them we're storing the ships, rounding up as many of the men we still need as we can lay hands on, and generally preparing to sortie—as soon as 'practicable'—when they order us to. But we also tell them we've got somewhere around two-thirds of the entire damned Imperial Charisian Navy offshore. Then, if they send us the execute order, and if the weather's still against us and the Charisians haven't reduced their strength, we send them another message that says that in light of the Charisian numbers *which we had previously reported,* coupled with unfavorable wind conditions, we believe the sortie isn't 'practicable' without our suffering losses severe enough to prevent us from carrying out our end of the mission."

It was Jahras' turn to frown thoughtfully. It was always possible—even probable—the message Kholman was proposing to send would pass the actual execution order in transit. It might not, too, given how long it would take the northern force of galleons to approach the Gulf of Mathyas. In either case, though, preparing the ground ahead of time offered obvious advantages.

*And the truth is,* he reflected, *with this damned many Charisians mucking around in the Gulf of Mathyas, we've already drawn off a huge chunk of their available strength. As Daivyn says, this has to be two-thirds of their total galleon strength. If Harpahr and Shaiow can't break through Cayleb's remaining thirty or so ships with over a hundred of their own, we're all totally and completely screwed already, anyway. Hmmmmm . . .*

"I'd say you're on the right track," he said out loud. "The one thing I think we should add, though, is to point out how large a percentage of the

Charisians' strength we've drawn into our own waters. It might not hurt to plant a seed or two of our own by suggesting that what we have here is the opportunity to trap the Charisians between the anvil of our coast and Harpahr and Shaiow's hammer."

"Now *that,* Urwyn, strikes me as a very good notion!" Kholman said approvingly. "In that case, it would make perfect sense for us to sit tight, continuing to keep them drawn into our waters, until Harpahr and Shaiow can hit them from the other side, wouldn't it? They may actually go ahead and change our orders to do exactly that, in light of the Charisians' change in deployment."

"I certainly won't object if they do," Jahras agreed. *And not just because it's a lot less likely to get my crews slaughtered,* he added silently. *Because the fact is, you're right—that would be the most effective blow we could strike out of this whole over-elaborate operation of Maigwair's.*

▼　　▼　　▼

"All right, Master Lathyk," Sir Dunkyn Yairley told *Destiny*'s first lieutenant as the sun settled into a glowing bed of red and purple embers on the western horizon. "I think it's time to stand a bit farther offshore before we snug everyone down for the night. We'll bring the column to a north-by-northwest heading, if you please."

"Aye, aye, Sir," Rhobair Lathyk replied, and gestured to the signals midshipman to pass the order to the other ships.

Yairley left him to it, walking aft to stand at the taffrail, watching the galleons astern of *Destiny* while Lathyk's orders sent the signal flags soaring up the halyards. He hoped the other ships were already prepared for the course change, which had been due about now under his standing orders. Sail drill was actually what most worried him about his entire mission, since it was what seemed most likely to alert the enemy to the truth. Those other galleons simply didn't have the sort of manpower *Destiny* did, which was going to make it more difficult for them to carry out sailing evolutions with the sort of snap, precision, and speed that were hallmarks of a Charisian man-of-war.

Not too surprisingly, Yairley supposed, since *Destiny* and her sister *Mountain Root* were the only two real men-of-war in that entire long column.

*We must've used up every can of black, white, and red paint in the entire city of Tellesberg,* he thought now, shaking his head as he watched evening settle in. *Who would've thought we could disguise an entire fleet of merchantmen just by slapping paint on their sides? Now all I have to do is make sure no one from Desnair gets close enough to smell the fresh turpentine.*

High Admiral Bryahn Lock Island stood pondering the chart on his table. Brilliant sunshine reflections danced across the cabin's beams and deckhead, bouncing in through HMS *Ahrmahk*'s stern windows. They glittered and flashed in the hearts of the crystal paperweights anchoring the chart's corners, and his brass dividers gleamed like tarnished gold where they lay across the heart of the Markovian Sea.

*Ahrmahk*'s estimated position was indicated on that chart, eight hundred miles northeast of Hammer Island and three hundred and sixty miles southwest of Selekar's Point. In actual fact, as Lock Island knew, that "estimated" position was almost exactly correct. And, as he also knew courtesy of Owl, the reports from his schooners thirty miles farther north were also accurate . . . if somewhat incomplete.

He leaned forward, bracing himself on the table, trapping his position and the enemy's between the index fingers and thumbs of his two hands.

*Right about where you expected them,* he thought. *Well, actually, be honest—you didn't really expect them to come this close to keeping their schedule, did you?*

He pursed his lips, considering what he knew of the opposing commanders.

He knew quite a lot, actually, given Owl's remotes. The commanding officer of the Temple Lands–built contingent—and the overall commander of the entire force—was Bishop Kornylys Harpahr, of the Order of Chihiro, who'd been named Admiral General of the Church's navy. Of course, the Church had never had a navy before, and Harpahr had no experience commanding warships. He did, however, have extensive peacetime experience in the Temple Guard, and despite his silver hair, he was also relatively young—little more than fifty—and vigorous. Smart, too, from everything Lock Island had been able to see. That was unfortunate. And so was the fact that he was obviously a Temple hardliner.

Fortunately, no one in the Temple had any idea of the sort of staff arrangements towards which Earl Thirsk was working, but the men responsible for planning the organization of the newly christened "Navy of God" clearly possessed working brains. They'd divided their galleon strength into six-ship squadrons, each under the command of a senior prelate with Guard experience, and then assigned each admiral-bishop a flag captain from the Church's coast guard, customs, and courier service. That experience wasn't remotely the same as commanding a warship in action, but it meant each of the bishops at least had an adviser with an understanding of the limitations on a ship's maneuverability.

Bishop Kornylys' flag captain was Father Ahrnahld Taibahld, the Schuelerite upper-priest who commanded NGS *Sword of God*, Harpahr's flagship. He was ten years younger than his admiral, and even more energetic. Dark-haired and dark-eyed, he was anything but a fool, and he'd spent close to twenty years in the Church's coast guard. The two of them got along well—another unfortunate thing, from Lock Island's perspective—and, even worse, Taibahld knew Harpahr was not only willing to listen to his advice but expected him to *volunteer* it.

*They're going to make mistakes,* Lock Island mused, *but they won't be* stupid *mistakes. Not like the ones Malikai made at Rock Point. No, they'll be inexperienced mistakes. The sort smart people make when they have to do something they're not really trained to do. I'm going to have to keep that in mind.*

The Harchong contingent, on the other hand, had a far more satisfactory command structure. Lock Island found the Imperial Harchongese Navy's rank titles a little ridiculous, but that was probably to be expected from a force that was technically the largest navy in the world, yet kept fewer ships in commission than Corisande, alone. Of course, they'd always maintained an officer corps big enough to command all of the ships they *didn't* have in commission, as well. Worse, once a man earned the equivalent of captain's rank, *all* promotion in the IHN was based solely on seniority.

As a consequence, the senior officer afloat was one Chyntai Shaiow, the Duke of Sun Rising, who rejoiced in the title of Admiral of the Broad Oceans. A cousin of Emperor Waisu, he'd served (officially) in the IHN since two years before his actual birth. That, coupled with the appropriate bribes and the inherent corruption of all things Harchongese, had gotten him commissioned a captain of winds the month he turned sixteen. Of course, he'd never actually set foot on a naval vessel until he was twenty-one, but that sort of subterfuge was standard in Harchong, probably because it was the only way for anyone to attain flag rank when he was still at least theoretically young and vigorous enough to do some good.

Admiral of the Broad Oceans Sun Rising flew his streamer in IHNS *Flower of Waters*. He was currently seventy-five years old, his health was poor, and he tended to go off on long rambling discourses at captains' conferences. No one would have dared say anything of the sort—not in Harchong!—yet Lock Island knew at least some of Sun Rising's subordinates realized he was the wrong man in the wrong place. Unfortunately for them, he probably came the closest to being the right man of anyone of the appropriate seniority. Besides, his towering birth made him the only possible candidate for such a prestigious and important command.

Captain of Winds Shoukhan Khowsan, who commanded Sun Rising's flagship, was rather a different sort. Obviously, he had to be oppressively well-born to hold his current command, and although his own title was simply that of the Count of Wind Mountain, he was also the second son of the Duke of Dancing Water. And the Duke of Dancing Water, like every other Harchongese duke, was one of the emperor's cousins.

That was about the sole point of similarity between Wind Mountain and Sun Rising, however. The captain of winds was twenty years younger than the admiral of the broad oceans, and there was nothing wrong with *his* brain. He had far less experience than a Charisian officer chosen for his position would have had, but he was more experienced than just about anyone else the IHN might have chosen. Fortunately, his father and Sun Rising detested one another, which meant his relations with *his* admiral weren't remotely like the mutual respect which flourished between Harpahr and Taibahld. "Icily correct" was probably the best way to describe them, which suited Bryahn Lock Island just fine.

*What was it that fellow Merlin was talking about the other day said?* Lock Island frowned, trying to remember the man's name. *Napoleon? Something like that, anyway.*

The high admiral's frown turned into a grimace at his inability to remember the name, yet as he pondered the other side's command arrangements, he understood exactly what whatever-his-name-was had meant when he called another general fortunate because he only had to fight coalitions.

*Any coalition's only as good as its coordination,* he thought. *And until the Group of Four have been smacked around enough, I don't think they're likely to do the kind of arse-kicking necessary to make something like the Harchongese Navy coordinate with anybody. For that matter, I don't know if anyone short of God or a genuine Archangel could kick that kind of aristocratic arse!*

The thought was comforting . . . but only until he remembered that only nineteen of the ninety-three armed galleons coming his way were Harchongese. The other seventy-four had all been built, armed, and manned by the Temple Lands. That was another kraken entirely, and not just because of the difference in the officers corps involved, either.

The Temple Lands had officially abolished serfdom decades ago. Despite that, there were still serfs on virtually every major Temple Lands estate; they just weren't *called* that. By the same token, there were still men in Emerald and even Chisholm who were *called* serfs, but who'd actually become small landowners in their own rights. In fact, the phased abolition of the legal status of serf (a firm requirement of the Charisian Empire) had raised scarcely a ripple in Emerald or Chisholm. Within another two years, the process would be completed.

The situation was a little more complicated in Corisande and—especially—

Zebediah, where the conditions of serfdom had varied widely between one feudal territory and another. There'd been no serfs at all in Manchyr, Tartarian, or Airyth, for example, and the institution had been very similar to the Chisholmian variety in Rochair, Coris, Barcair, and Anvil Rock, and on Wind Daughter Island. It probably wasn't a coincidence that almost all the lords who'd joined the Northern Conspiracy in Corisande practiced a rather more severe version of serfdom, on the other hand, and phasing it out in Corisande was going to take longer.

But they not only had serfs in Harchong, they had outright slaves. Lots of them. Whereas Charis—and Emerald, Chisholm, and Corisande, in varying degrees—had a bustling, vibrant free labor force, supporting a steadily growing middle class as well as wealthy entrepreneurs like Ehdwyrd Howsmyn, Harchong had vast slave-worked plantations, and the workforce in Harchongese manufactories was almost always composed of slave laborers, as well. There *was* no Harchongese middle class, no free labor force, and definitely no equivalent of the Charisian treasure chest of experienced seamen. Harchongese warships were crewed by men who'd literally been driven aboard with the lash in many cases, and who were controlled by a brutal, often capricious discipline which would have provoked an almost instant mutiny aboard any Charisian vessel.

And, not surprisingly, their crews gave them exactly the degree of loyalty and initiative they deserved. There might be a modicum of enthusiasm—or, at least, willingness—aboard the IHN's ships now that the Group of Four had declared Holy War. The deep reservoir of faith among the Harchongese peasantry and serfs was one of the things which held the Empire together, and the priests aboard those ships had appealed fervently to that faith. Yet dumb acceptance of brutal conditions, even born of religious fervor, was no substitute for the enthusiasm and high morale which routinely prevailed aboard Charisian warships.

The Navy of God had its own share of conscripted serfs, but unlike its Harchongese counterpart, they formed a definite minority within its crews. Not only that, but each had been promised relief from the legal obligation which bound him to the land, and they were actually being paid the same wage as their non-serf crewmates. They were even eligible for promotion to petty officer status!

That would have been a big enough difference all by itself, but the majority of the Navy of God's crews were composed of freemen. Many came from the same sort of class backgrounds as their Charisian counterparts, although only a handful of them had been seafarers before their enlistment. The Church's dominant position within the Temple Lands' economy also meant a great many of them—probably even the majority—had personal, direct connections to the Church or one of its myriad business enterprises, which gave them a direct, personal stake in the Church's secular future. The reservoirs of faith in the Temple Lands were probably just as deep as those in the Harchong Empire, as well, although it had less of the dumb, patient, almost bovine acceptance of the Harchongese serfs.

Which meant that although they were nowhere nearly so experienced or well trained as the ICN, and although it was obvious that most of them were more than a little anxious, even frightened, at the prospect of meeting Charisians in battle, they were highly motivated, well integrated, and tightly knit, and Harpahr and his subordinate admirals had them training hard. Their sail drill had improved markedly in the five-days since they'd departed Chantry Bay, and Harpahr had ordered every ship to spend a minimum of two hours a day at gun drill, as well.

The Harchongese ships were supposed to be doing the same thing, and some of them actually were, although their results were . . . problematical. The Navy of God, on the other hand, was improving steadily. There was no way of knowing how well their training would stand up once round shot started tearing their ships apart around them, yet even by Lock Island's most optimistic assessment, each Temple Lands–built ship had to be worth at least three—probably four—Harchongese galleons of the same armament.

And eighty percent of the armed vessels coming at him had Temple Lands crews and Navy of God officers.

*What a truly not-good situation,* he thought, reflecting on the grand and glorious total of his own thirteen galleons. *Outnumbered by close to six-to-one, and the rotten, cheating bastards have had the unmitigated gall to actually* train *their crews! What a revolting development!*

A faint smile twitched his lips, but it faded quickly, and he straightened. He walked to the stern windows and stood gazing out them, thinking.

The good news—such as it was—was that Harpahr and Taibahld had no counterweight for his own reconnaissance capabilities. Like Cayleb before Rock Point and Darcos Sound, he had plenty of scouting cruisers scattered out to keep an eye on his enemies, but (also like Cayleb before Rock Point and Darcos Sound) their true function was to explain how he could have the information Owl's SNARCs had already provided. As a consequence, he knew precisely where his enemies were and what they were doing . . . and they *didn't* know that about him.

*That ought to be enough to let me pick my own time to engage,* he thought, unseeing eyes staring out at the waves of the Markovian Sea. *Let me pick the time, the weather conditions, make sure I've got the weather gauge . . . All of that's going to be a huge advantage. But once we get in amongst them, once it's broadside-to-broadside and all any of my captains will know is what he can see through the gunsmoke with his own eyes, all those advantages disappear. Then it's experience, and numbers, and guts, and gun power, and right this minute the only one of those where I really have an edge over Harpahr is experience. Which is not going to be enough.*

His head turned, tracking around, almost as if he actually thought his own unaided eyes could see across the endless miles of saltwater to Old Charis, and his mouth tightened.

*Get your arse here in time, Domynyk,* he thought, almost prayerfully. *Get your arse up here while there's still time to do some good.*

He drew a deep breath and turned away from the windows. It was time he went on deck and saw what he could do to slow the enemy down long enough for Domynyk Staynair to answer his prayer.

.IV.
HMS *Destroyer,* 54,
Larek,
Howell Bay,
Kingdom of Old Charis

Sir Domynyk Staynair had no way of knowing what Bryahn Lock Island was thinking at that particular moment, but he knew what Lock Island *ought* to be thinking.

He paused in his peg-legged pacing, standing by the starboard quarterdeck hammock nettings, and gazed out across the port city of Larek.

It was an interesting city, Larek. Five years ago, it had been little more than a sleepy fishing village. The navigable Delthak River had linked it to Ithmyn's Lake in the Earldom of High Rock, but that had meant little until Ehdwyrd Howsmyn broke ground for his foundry complex at Delthak on the lake's northwestern shore. When Merlin Athrawes first arrived in Charis, there'd been nothing there but the tiny town—a hamlet, really, with no more than fifty or sixty inhabitants—which had taken its name from the river. Today, Delthak was the largest foundry operation in the history of Safehold. The output from Howsmyn's complex of manufactories alone was greater than that of the iron industry of the entire Harchong Empire.

The consequences for Larek had been . . . significant. The onetime fishing village might well have become the only port in the world which was actually busier than Tellesberg. It was smaller, with a smaller total number of ships coming and going, but it never slept, and there was never—ever—enough room dockside for all the ships trying to land or take on cargo.

It helped, some, that even seagoing ships could sail up the Delthak, if they were careful, although many captains considered it more prudent to let river barges handle that part of the transportation loop. Rock Point had been tempted to take *his* ships upriver, but not very strongly. Under other circumstances, he might have been willing to take the chance. Not this time, though. His galleons drew more water than the majority of ships that plied the river, and he couldn't afford—literally *could not* afford—to ground one of his twelve priceless warships. They were going to be far too desperately needed far too soon for him to risk stranding one of them on a sandbar or a rock.

Which was why he had to lie at anchor, pacing his quarterdeck, watching through the SNARCs, as Bryahn Lock Island began the delicate, dangerous task of buzzing about Kornylys Harpahr's ears. He knew what Lock Island was supposed to do—distract Harpahr, annoy him, make him anxious about protecting the unarmed galleons he was escorting to Desnair. It was Lock Island's job to slow Harpahr down, any way he could . . . and it was Rock Point's job to sit here, waiting, while Ehdwyrd Howsmyn worked frantically to produce the explosive shells which might—*might*—give the Imperial Charisian Navy a chance to actually stop the enemy.

Personally, Rock Point gave them a slightly better than even chance, assuming Howsmyn was able to produce enough shells . . . and that *he* was able to get them to Lock Island's assistance in time. There was, however, a significant difference between inflicting enough damage to cripple Harpahr's fleet and surviving the experience.

*Even with the shells, we're going to have to come in close,* he thought once more. *If we can reach them, then they can reach us, and they'll have one hell of a lot more guns than we will. If the shells surprise them badly enough, if they break, if they aren't willing to come to close action with us, then,* maybe . . .

He inhaled deeply.

*Either we do it, or we don't, but there are times I wish I had the same depth of faith Maikel does. It's not that I don't believe in You anymore, God. It's just that looking at what You've allowed to happen here on Safehold so far, I have to wonder what* else *You're ready to allow. Maikel's all right with that—with the acceptance of Your will, whatever it is. I try to be the same way, but I can't. Or, maybe I can, where I'm concerned, at least. It's just . . . just that Your will can be so hard, sometimes. Like what happened to Gwylym. What happened to Samyl Wylsynn and his circle. Father Tymahn in Corisande.*

He closed his eyes for a long moment, standing motionless. And then he gave himself a shake, opened his eyes once more, and actually smiled crookedly.

*All right,* he thought. *I know. Free will. Maikel's explained it to me often enough, and I guess it makes sense. I've done my damnedest to figure out what it is You want me to do, too, and I think I've got it. I hope I do, anyway, and I promise I'll give it my best shot. But, please, if You could, keep an eye on us. We need You more now than we've ever needed You before. I may be too busy to tell You that, or to think about You the way I ought to, when the balls begin to fly, but don't You forget about us. And especially not about my men. I may not be Maikel, but I'm ready to accept whatever it is You have in mind for me. Only look after my men. Please, God, Whoever You really are, whatever it is You really want of us—of me—look after my men.*

# NOVEMBER,
# YEAR OF GOD 894

I'm finding it difficult of late to remember that God and Langhorne send all good things in their own time," Kornylys Harpahr remarked as he reached for his hot chocolate. He looked across the table at his flag captain and smiled crookedly. "Or, perhaps, I should actually say I'm finding it difficult to possess my soul in patience until Langhorne tumbles the minions of Shan-wei into the pit prepared for them."

"The minions in question do seem to be . . . exceptionally pestiferous, don't they, My Lord?" Father Ahrnahld agreed. "I think that's what makes it so difficult to remember that to all things, there come a season."

"And I suppose this is the season for provoking my ulcers." Harpahr shook his head, then sipped chocolate.

Ahrnahld Taibahld snorted and began spreading butter on another biscuit. Stowed down in the coolness of the flagship's bilge, the butter had kept remarkably well so far. It was finally beginning to turn rancid—it always did—but it was still more palatable than dry biscuit, especially with a little jam, and at least the hens and wyverns were both still producing fresh eggs.

Harpahr had already finished his own eggs and bacon, and he pushed back his chair. Taibahld began to rise himself, but the admiral general waved him back.

"Finish breakfast, Ahrnahld!" he scolded. "Not even a batch of Shan-wei-damned heretics is going to come calling on us in the next fifteen minutes."

"Of course, My Lord. Thank you."

Taibahld would actually have preferred to go ahead and stand, if Harpahr was going to. It seemed disrespectful not to, but he knew it would irritate the admiral general. For that matter, Harpahr would scold him again if he seemed to be bolting his food to get finished quickly. So he made himself chew slowly and methodically while Harpahr stepped out onto *Sword of God*'s sternwalk.

The flagship sailed steadily on a roughly southwesterly heading with the wind on her larboard quarter under topsails and topgallants. She was doing well to make four knots under that little canvas, given the current wind conditions, and Harpahr would really have preferred to make more sail. Unfortunately, Duke Sun Rising's ships' seamanship didn't seem to be quite as good as his own.

*Not surprisingly,* the admiral general thought grumpily. *I'm glad the Duke is so eager to coordinate with us, and I'm awed by his—or his secretary's, at least—command of the language. Still, I probably could survive without those incredibly flowery letters if he'd just actually institute the sail drill I asked for.*

He carefully did not apply to the Harchongese fleet commander a term bishops weren't supposed to use to describe faithful sons of Mother Church. Under the circumstances, it required more self-discipline than usual.

*Maybe I should have let Ahrnahld deal with it—let him talk to Wind Mountain, one flag captain to another flag captain. Maybe we could have finessed it past Sun Rising that way. Of course, given the fact that Sun Rising hates Wind Mountain's father's guts, that might've worked out even worse. Or as badly, at least; I don't really think it could have worked out worse. Unless Sun Rising could've figured out how to actually* undo *the drill they* have *carried out!*

His lips twitched, although the thought really wasn't all that humorous. It was entirely possible Sun Rising *could* have figured out a way to do that. If anyone on Safehold was capable of such a feat, it would have to be the duke.

The admiral general wrapped both hands around the chocolate cup. The sun was bright, and he'd been delighted to leave the bitter cold behind. The Icewind Sea had been bad enough in October; the Passage of Storms and the Markovian Sea had been still worse, in their own ways, even if they had been (marginally) warmer. The Passage of Storms, especially, had done everything possible to live up to its name. In fact—his face tightened—he'd lost two ships to one of the furious gales which had swept over his fleet. That storm had scattered his formation badly, too. If the Charisians had happened upon him then, with his ships spread out all over the ocean, Langhorne only knew what they might have done to him!

But they were nearing the equator, now, and the Gulf of Tarot was a far more pleasant experience in November than the Markovian Sea in October. It was still cool, this early in the morning, but by late afternoon he'd be wishing he could have hung on to the morning chill. Especially if the wind didn't strengthen.

He gazed into the east wind, eyes slightly squinted against the still low-lying sun. There'd been a distinctly reddish cast to the dawn, and a smear of cloud seemed to be swelling up along the horizon.

"Red sun at morning, sailor take warning," he quoted to himself. *The* Writ *warns against self-prideful predictions. I wonder if I could have been a bit hasty congratulating myself on having left the heavy weather behind.*

He sipped chocolate, then looked up as the cries of gulls and shrill whistles of wyverns came down from above. The winged creatures swarmed out from the coast of the Republic of Siddarmark's Windmoor Province, and as he watched, one of the wyverns swooped down to snatch something from the sea. He couldn't tell whether it was a fish or a bit of garbage scooped out of *Sword of God*'s wake, but he found himself wishing the wyvern well, whatever it had found.

"I see the Admiral of the Broad Oceans is still with us, My Lord," a voice said, and Harpahr turned to find Taibahld had joined him on the sternwalk. Like the admiral general, the flag captain had brought along his chocolate cup. Now he leaned his hip against the sternwalk's rail and nodded in the direction of a particularly untidy gaggle of sails trailing along to the north-northwest.

"More or less," Harpahr agreed, yet he also gave Taibahld a moderately quelling look. The title the upper-priest had just bestowed upon Duke Sun Rising was absolutely correct, but the admiral general knew the flag captain had *not* used its grandiloquent entirety as a compliment. Harpahr couldn't fault Taibahld's opinion, but certain appearances had to be maintained, and the flag captain half dipped his head, acknowledging the unspoken rebuke.

"Actually," the admiral general went on, "they do seem to be keeping somewhat better station this morning, don't they?"

"It may have something to do with those schooners yesterday, My Lord," Taibahld said dryly, and Harpahr snorted.

The humor in that snort was minimal. He'd found himself wishing more than once—in fact, he doubted there'd been a single half hour during this entire miserable, interminable trek in which he *hadn't* wished—that Captain General Maigwair had decided against lumbering him with his Harchongese "allies." Their miserable seamanship, lack of discipline, and prickly self-importance would have made them a questionable asset at the best of times; the fact that the majority of their ships were completely or almost completely unarmed only made bad worse. Even one of the Charisian schooners could strike at an unarmed galleon with impunity, and the handful of armed, wretchedly handled Harchongese galleons were woefully inadequate to fend them off. Which was why Harpahr had been forced to detach an entire squadron of his own galleons to do the job for them.

*Maybe we can convince Sun Rising to sell his ships to Desnair after we reach Iythria?* he wondered wistfully. *Jahras isn't exactly a brilliant master of the seaways, but he's got to be better than the Harchongese! And the whole idea was to get Desnairian guns put aboard them because their own foundries weren't up to the task. . . . Surely I can convince Vicar Allayn we ought to put Desnairian crews aboard to make sure the guns actually get used eventually!*

"I wonder when the Charisians are going to stop dancing and actually attack, My Lord," Taibahld said in a considerably more somber tone. He waved his chocolate cup to windward, where a trio of those omnipresent, maddeningly maneuverable Charisian schooners paced Harpahr's formation. "I admit it's irritating when the schooners dart in, but Cayleb can't really think they're going to do any sort of significant damage."

"Not as long as our formation holds," Harpahr agreed. "But remember what it was like in the Passage of Storms. If those schooners had turned up *then . . .*"

He let his voice trail off, and shrugged, and Taibahld nodded.

"I understand what you're saying, My Lord. But unless another gale makes up—which it could, in these waters, at this time of year—it's unlikely we'll get scattered again. Cayleb's too smart to be *counting* on something like that, and he's running out of time. Once we get through the Tarot Channel and Jahras sorties to meet us, it'll be too late. Unless he wants to wade into *all* of us, at any rate!"

It was Harpahr's turn to nod. He and Taibahld had discussed this very point often enough, and he knew the flag captain was right. If Cayleb of Charis didn't strike soon, he'd lose the opportunity completely.

"Well, according to our latest dispatches, he's still blockading the Howard Passage," the admiral general pointed out now. "I know anything from Jahras is at least two or three five-days out-of-date by the time it gets to us, semaphore or no semaphore, but even allowing for that, the majority of Cayleb's strength still has to be south of us." Harpahr grimaced. "I suppose it's possible he really is going to let us catch him between us and the Desnairian coast."

"No, My Lord, he's not," Taibahld disagreed, respectfully but firmly. "I'm astonished he's spent so long off Desnair already, but he'll never let us pin him against the coast. You're probably right that he's still south of us, but in that case, my money's on his sailing to meet us somewhere inside the Tarot Channel itself. He's going to be badly outnumbered whatever happens, and if Vicar Allayn's little sleight-of-hand worked, he may have diverted a sizable portion of his total strength to Chisholm and Corisande. In that case, he's going to be outnumbered *very* badly, and he may figure engaging us in the Channel would constrict our movements enough to offset some of that. But, one way or the other, he'll hit us before we reach the Gulf of Mathyas. Either that, or else he's going to realize we're too strong for him to challenge at sea and concentrate on getting out of the way and then defending his own harbors, instead."

Harpahr raised one eyebrow, but he didn't dispute Taibahld's analysis. First, because it made sense. But secondly, because Taibahld had demonstrated to Harpahr's satisfaction that he had a superior grasp of both tactical and strategic implications. In many ways, the bishop felt Taibahld would have made a better admiral general than *he* did. Unfortunately, the upper-priest lacked the seniority for that assignment, and Harpahr considered himself extraordinarily lucky to have him for an adviser. And a teacher, really, the bishop admitted to himself.

"Well," it was Harpahr's turn to indicate the watching schooners with a flick of his head, "at least we can be pretty sure Cayleb's going to know where to find us when he wants us."

.II.
HMS *Ahrmahk*, 58,
Gulf of Tarot,
and
Imperial Palace,
Cherayth,
Kingdom of Chisholm

". . . where to find us when he wants us."

Bryahn Lock Island snorted as the parasite perched on Admiral General Harpahr's shoulder transmitted his conversation to him in real time.

"Knowing where to find you's never been the problem," he muttered in the general direction of Harpahr's fleet, and heard someone else's snort—even harsher than his own—in his earplug.

"True," Cayleb Ahrmahk said from Prince Tymahn's Suite in snowy Chisholm. At the moment, he was the next best thing to eight thousand miles away from, and ten hours behind, Lock Island's flagship. "I only wish it *was* me who knew where to find him. Or get *to* him, anyway," he added.

"What?" Lock Island smiled thinly out over another stretch of the blue water Harpahr was even then considering from his own flagship. "Should I take that to indicate a certain lack of confidence in the command team you do have on the spot, Your Majesty?"

"Of course not!" Cayleb chuckled at the humor in his cousin's voice, but his own tone turned considerably more serious. "If I can't be there myself, I can't think of any two people I'd rather have standing in for me. It's just that I hate asking it of you and the men when I *can't* be there with you."

"I understand," Lock Island said quietly, and he did. Just as he understood that being able to watch everything happen even as it did was going to make things infinitely worse for his emperor and empress.

"We'll be praying for you, Bryahn," Sharleyan said softly, as if she'd read his mind across all those weary miles of stormy saltwater.

"Thank you." Lock Island smiled again, whimsically. "It can't hurt, anyway!"

"Actually, I think it might help a great deal," Maikel Staynair said from his office in his Tellesberg Palace. "Of course, it's my job to think that way, I suppose."

Lock Island could almost see the twinkle in the archbishop's eye, and he shook his head.

There was a curious parallelism with his adversary, he reflected. Both of them were standing on the sternwalks of their flagships, looking east, thinking and planning. Unlike Harpahr, however, Lock Island knew there were barely fifty miles of water between those two flagships. He knew exactly what his enemy's formation was, and he'd sat in invisibly when Harpahr and Taibahld discussed the course they intended to steer. As the admiral general said, he knew *exactly* where to find him, and exactly what he'd face when he did.

*The one thing I don't know is what's going to happen when I do.*

"Show me the map, Owl," he requested.

"Yes, High Admiral," the AI said, and a chart of the Gulf of Tarot and surrounding landmasses projected itself across Lock Island's contact lenses.

It hadn't changed since the last time he'd checked, but he gazed thoughtfully at the icon representing Rock Point's ships. They were coming up fast from the southeast under every stitch of canvas, and his eyebrows rose as he glanced at the information sidebars Owl updated continuously. Those *had* changed, at least a little, and he frowned as he contemplated the new data.

The wind had strengthened more—or, at least, more rapidly—for Rock Point's ships than originally projected. Owl's present estimate was that the twelve galleons would arrive almost four hours earlier than projected. And that meant. . . .

"I wonder . . ." the high admiral murmured out loud.

"You wonder what?" There was something remarkably like suspicion in Cayleb's voice, and Lock Island smiled.

"Domynyk's going to get here sooner than I'd anticipated," he replied. "And that weather front's moving in from the east more quickly than anticipated, as well. If the current projections hold up, and if Domynyk and I were to shift our rendezvous point a few miles, I think we might be able to come in right on the front's heels."

"That," Cayleb said in the tone of a man whose suspicions have just been confirmed, "sounds like a really bad idea. Sailing into the middle of a fleet that outnumbers you four-to-one in the middle of the night—in the *rain*—strikes me as a wonderful recipe for disaster."

"Odd," Rock Point put in from his own flagship, still two hundred miles from HMS *Ahrmahk*. "If you and Gwylym had discussed your tactical notions with *me* before Crag Reach, that's exactly what I would've said then. Oh, except that I probably would've added that *you* were planning on sailing in through a narrow channel you couldn't even see in the middle of a full gale. Obviously a far better and more maturely considered battle plan all round, Your Majesty."

"The situation was entirely different, and you know it," Cayleb riposted. "Thirsk's fleet's morale was already broken, and I had a huge firepower advantage. Not only that, *he* was anchored! I had every maneuver advantage there was, and his people were more than half-defeated before we ever fired the first shot! You may have noticed there's just a bit of difference between the Dohlarans' condition then and what Harpahr and Taibahld have accomplished with *their* ships!"

"That's true," Lock Island acknowledged. "By the same token, though,

Thirsk wasn't handicapped by having fifty unarmed Harchongese galleons hanging on his coattails. Not only that, Harpahr's formation's spread out between six columns—seven, counting the squadron he's got covering that gaggle of Sun Rising's. And I don't care how well he's managed to drill his crews, none of them will expect a night action. You know how confusing and terrifying that can be, Cayleb—you *counted* on it at Crag Reach. And however much training they've done, our people are a lot more experienced, so any confusion's going to work a lot more in our favor than theirs."

"The only way you're going to stand a chance against that many enemy ships is to maintain tight tactical control," Cayleb argued, his voice flat, "and every one of your signal systems depend on people being able to *see* them. If you lose cohesion, if your formation comes apart in the middle of all those Church galleons, you lose, Bryahn. I don't care how good our people are. I'll even concede that you'll give better than you get, but in the end, you'll lose."

"If he manages to maintain *his* tactical control, we lose anyway, because we won't be able to get deep enough to break him up," Lock Island replied. "We can nibble around the edges, but we can't *stop* him without ripping the brain—and the heart—out of his fleet, and you know it. For that, we *have* to penetrate his formation."

"And there's another point, Cayleb," Rock Island said. "Ehdwyrd only had time to manufacture a couple thousand shells, and the gun crews haven't had the time—or the spare ammunition—to train with them." The baron shrugged where he sat in his day cabin's comfortable armchair. "We've dry fired and rehearsed, but they've never actually *used* them, and despite the Navy's confidence in Ahlfryd, they're going to be a little . . . tentative, at first. We're going to have to get in really close to make them count, and I've only got about a hundred and seventy in each ship. That's less than eight broadsides for each of them. So if we can't make each of those broadsides count, we lose. And if we have to spar around the fringes, fight our way through just to get to decisive range in the first place, we may lose one or more of the shell-armed ships on our way in. Worse, we may have to use shellfire to get inside in the first place, in which case the people we're really after may have time to figure out what's coming before we hit them with it."

"But—" Cayleb began.

"They're right, Cayleb," a deep voice said quietly. The emperor's head turned, eyes sweeping towards the door beyond which Merlin Athrawes stood guard over Prince Tymahn's Suite.

"They're right," the *seijin* repeated, subvocalizing over his own built-in com. "They can't win this one by just killing ships; they can't kill *enough* of them. They have to defeat the fleet's *cohesion,* and to do that, they have to get in close. Worse, Harpahr's signal system may not be as good or as flexible as ours, but it's good enough for him to mass his squadrons if he's able to see Bryahn and Domynyk coming. For that matter, there's going to be enough gunsmoke once close action is joined it would be almost impossible for Bryahn to pass signals reliably, anyway. The fact that he and Domynyk, at least, will be able to see exactly what's going on will offer a significant advantage over Harpahr, but they won't be able to give detailed orders to anyone else, whatever happens. Better for them to go in in the dark, when the other side can't exercise any sort of tight control and the confusion lets us maximize our ships' individual superiority."

Cayleb sat silent for several endless seconds, and his wife's hand reached out across the bassinet between them. She laid it on his knee, and he looked at her quickly.

"Let them do it their way," she said very softly. "They're the best you've got, they're the ones actually on the spot, and they deserve for you to have enough confidence in them to let them fight their battle the way they think best. I know it's not easy for you, and I know why, but let them do it their way."

Cayleb inhaled deeply, and then, slowly, he nodded.

"All right, Bryahn. Domynyk. We'll do it your way," the Emperor of Charis said quietly.

.III.

## Off the Windmoor Coast,
## Gulf of Tarot

Ahrnahld Taibahld grimaced as a fresh wall of tropical rain swept across NGS *Sword of God*'s poop deck.

Rain in the Gulf of Tarot wasn't like rain in more northern waters. It didn't start gradually, there was no gentle warning. A handful of enormous raindrops smacked into his already-streaming oilskins, like cavalry hooves clattering down a stone street. Then, almost before his mind had time to register their impact, a solid wave of water pounded down. Visibility dropped instantly to almost nothing. Of course, visibility had already been limited at the moment, given the overcast night's total lack of moon or stars, but he could barely see the glow of the binnacle through the deluge, and when he looked down, he saw what looked like ground mist where splintered raindrops bounced back up off the deck planking.

*Me and my wiseass comments about bad weather,* he reflected.

Still, compared to the Passage of Storms, this *wasn't* bad weather. Not really. The wind had risen—enough for the fleet to furl its topgallants—but it came steadily out of the east, without rage or violence. It had veered almost two full points, to broad on *Sword of God*'s beam on her present heading, but the sea's motion hadn't caught up with the wind shift. The waves continued to come in under her quarter, imparting an uncomfortable corkscrew motion. There was no indication of squalls, no thunder, no lightning flashing on the horizon, however.

*Not even Sun Rising's fumble-fists are going to have any trouble out of* this *kind of "storm,"* he thought, then reached out and rapped his knuckles on the wooden fife rail. *Let's not tempt fate, Ahrnahld,* he reminded himself sardonically.

▼    ▼    ▼

Bryahn Lock Island tucked both loaded, double-barreled pistols into their holster loops under his oilskins, then returned the pistol case to his desk drawer. Keelhaul sat beside him, and the big dog whined softly, as if he could read his master's mind.

*Which he probably* can, *after this long,* the high admiral reflected.

He went down on one knee, putting an arm around the rottweiler's massive neck. Then he straightened and slapped the enormous dog on the shoulder.

"Time to go below," he said out loud. Keelhaul cocked his head, ears lifted, and whined again, louder. "No arguments," Lock Island said more sternly. "There's not a damn thing you can do up here. Now go with Henrai!"

Keelhaul gave him one more piteous look. Then the big dog's ears drooped and he heaved unhappily to his feet and crossed slowly to Lieutenant Commander Tillyer, toenails clicking on the deck planks, audible even above the sound of rain drumming on the cabin skylights.

It wasn't really a lieutenant commander's job to take a pet below for safety, but Keelhaul and Tillyer were old friends. The dog was a lot more likely to actually go—and, even more importantly, to *stay*—if Tillyer saw to his incarceration in the bosun's storeroom well below *Ahrmahk*'s waterline. Given how hard it was to actually sink a wooden warship, that was one of the safest places in the entire ship, and Lock Island felt grateful it was so as Keelhaul gave him one more reproachful, over-the-shoulder glance, sighed heavily, and followed Tillyer out of the cabin.

"I trust the High Admiral won't take this wrongly, but it's always reassuring to see the way all about you leap instantly to obey your commands."

Lock Island turned, cocking his head at Sylmahn Baikyr, his flag captain. Baikyr was small, compact, dark-haired and dark-eyed, and an elegant dresser. It was said (probably accurately) that he'd spent more than a master's mate's yearly salary on his dress uniform.

He was also competent, smart, and as close to absolutely fearless as any man Lock Island had ever met. In fact, he reminded the high admiral a great deal of a younger version of Rayjhis Yowance.

*Well, I should sure as hell* hope *he's all those good things!* Lock Island thought with a mental snort. *The Navy's high admiral isn't supposed to choose flag captains by picking names out of a hat!*

"I'm glad you find it reassuring, Sylmahn," he said. "And considering how many years you've known Keelhaul, I'm sure you understand that getting him to do *anything* he doesn't want to do is akin to carrying a thirty-pounder from one end of the Tellesberg waterfront to the other on your back . . . only harder." He grimaced. "Trust me, winning that particular battle of wills is going to make kicking Harpahr's arse look like a walk in the park!"

"I'm glad to hear it, Sir," Baikyr said with a smile.

"Good. In that case, I'm sure you won't mind clearing the ship for action, Captain."

"At once, Sir!" Baikyr replied, and saluted sharply.

▼     ▼     ▼

Normally, the urgent tattoo of drums would have sent *Ahrmahk*'s crew scurrying to action stations. Not tonight, however.

Artificial sounds had an astonishing ability to carry preposterous distances across water. Wind and rain, the sound of waves, the hum of rigging, could be depended upon to deaden much of that sound, but no one was much inclined to take unnecessary chances this night. And so, aboard every one of the twenty-five Charisian galleons forging through the Stygian darkness, no drum sounded as men were sent to their stations by quiet orders.

Feet pattered across decks. Muffled thumps and bangs came from below as internal partitions were dismantled and sent down into the hold—along with furniture, paintings, officers' wine cabinets, flag officers' armchairs, cabin rugs. Gun trucks squeaked and rumbled as breech ropes were cast off and the massive carriages were trundled back from where they normally stood, nestled firmly against the side of the hull and lashed there. Lead aprons were removed from touchholes. Gun locks were fitted. Tompions were removed from muzzles. Rammers and worms came down from overhead racks, tubs of water were arranged between each pair of guns, buckets of sand were scattered over the decking to provide traction . . . and absorb blood.

Forward, the gunner issued cutlasses and boarding pikes. The newfangled pistols which had been invented for the Imperial Guard had become much more common, and now simpler, smoothbore versions were issued to senior petty officers and seamen. Wolves—the light, swivel-mounted anti-personnel weapons of choice—were issued and hauled up to the fighting tops. Carronade gunners swarmed along the upper deck, preparing their own weapons while rain bounced from the stubby barrels like freshwater spray. Until the upper-deck guns heated up, the flintlocks' reliability would be suspect, so lengths of old-fashioned slow-match were wrapped around linstocks and placed in canvas-screened tubs where the betraying glow would be sheltered from hostile eyes and extinguishing rain, alike.

Above the decks, more hands spread protective nets to catch falling blocks and severed cordage. Other seamen rigged chain slings to support the yards. Boats which were normally stowed amidships were hoisted out, put over the side to tow astern, where they could generate no lethal splinters if they were struck by enemy shot. Below decks, surgeons laid out knives and saws, healers laid out fleming moss and bandages, and sick-berth attendants scrubbed down the mess tables where wounded men would all too soon lie sobbing in agony.

The Charisian standard was to clear for action from a standing start, without warning, in no more than fifteen minutes. Tonight, it took twice that long, because there was time. Time to do it right. Time to make preparations without risking accident and injury. Time to double-check every single aspect of the process.

There was not a man aboard the flagship, or aboard any of the ships following in *Ahrmahk*'s wake, who didn't understand exactly what they faced. Who hadn't been told the odds, who couldn't compute the chances of their own survival . . . or grasp what would happen if the ships invisible to them through darkness and rain were allowed to unite with the Desnairian fleet in the Gulf of Jahras.

They were experienced, most of those men. They knew the Charisian tradition. They didn't think, didn't merely believe, that they were the finest sea fighters in the history of the world—they *knew* they were, just as they knew what the Church of God Awaiting and the Inquisition would do to their homes and their families if they lost this war.

Bryahn Lock Island stood on his quarterdeck, feeling rain beat on his own oilskins, watching the projected map only he could see, and felt that in his men. Felt their knowledge, their fear . . . their determination.

"Be sure your mind is fresh enough to make the decisions worthy of the men under your command," Domynyk Staynair had said to Cayleb Ahrmahk on another rainy night, before the Battle of Rock Point. Cayleb had told his cousin about it, and now Lock Island repeated that same sentence to himself.

"Sir, the ship is cleared for action," Sylmahn Baikyr told him, touching the chest of his streaming oilskins in salute.

"Very well, Captain," the high admiral said. "Be good enough to make the signal."

▼    ▼    ▼

"Sir! The Flag's hoisted the signal!"

Captain Zakrai Wayst turned from a quiet conversation with the ship's chaplain at the signal midshipman of the watch's excited announcement.

"Has it, indeed, Master Hahlmyn?" His tone was calculated to steady the lad, and the midshipman drew a deep breath.

"Yes, Sir," he said in a much calmer voice, and Wayst nodded.

The captain's eyes were no longer young, but he doubted that would have made a great deal of difference. The downpour was so heavy he could barely see as far forward as the mainmast. He *might* have been able to pick out a faint glow, diffused across the plunging raindrops, from *Ahrmahk*'s big stern lanterns, shaded to be invisible from anywhere but astern, yet he wouldn't have bet money on it. And he for damned sure couldn't see the three red lanterns hoisted to the flagship's mizzen yard.

But young Hahlmyn was a reliable lad, and Wayst was prepared to take his word for it.

"Have you acknowledged, Master Hahlmyn?"

"Aye, Sir! One red lantern at the fore topsail yard."

"Very well, then. Repeat the signal to our next astern, if you please."

"Aye, aye, Sir!"

▼　　▼　　▼

One by one, down the entire length of that rain-lashed line of galleons, the red lanterns rose. Their gleam was all but lost in the darkness and rain, but sharp-eyed lookouts had been awaiting them for hours. Ship by ship, they were sighted and acknowledged. It took time—a seeming eternity as Bryahn Lock Island waited on his quarterdeck at the head of that long column—but eventually Baikyr's signal lieutenant saluted.

"*Darcos Sound* has hauled down her lantern, High Admiral."

"Good," Lock Island said calmly.

Zakrai Wayst could be something of a fussbudget, and there was no denying he had a pompous streak at least two feet wide, but he was as steady and reliable as a rock, and the man who could frighten him had yet to be born. That was why he commanded *Darcos Sound,* the second ship in Lock Island's line. The lowering of the lantern from *Darcos Sound*'s fore topsail yardarm was the signal that Wayst's own next astern—HMS *Daffodil*—had just lowered *her* forward lantern. There'd been simpler and faster ways to pass that information—indeed, both *Ahrmahk* and Rock Point's flagship, *Destroyer,* were equipped to use those other ways, when the time came—but not yet. They were too . . . energetic. Too indiscreet. Still, *Darcos Sound*'s lowered lantern showed everyone astern of her had done the same thing, indicating receipt of *Ahrmahk*'s signal to prepare for battle.

As it happened, Lock Island knew that. He'd watched through the remotes Owl had deployed to smother the area.

*This must've been driving Merlin crazy ever since he got here,* the high admiral thought now. *He's been able to see so much—know so much—almost instantly, and he's still had to rely on signal flags and lanterns and the speed of mounted couriers because no one else could see it. And, of course, because he couldn't afford for his abilities to be labeled "demonic."*

"In that case, Captain Baikyr," he said out loud, turning once more to face his flag captain in the pounding rain, "I believe it's time we were about it."

▼          ▼          ▼

The red lanterns at *Ahrmahk*'s mizzen yard dipped, and Captain Baikyr put his helm up to windward.

Sodden canvas flapped as the ship fell off to leeward and the wind moved from broad on the the larboard beam to fine on the larboard quarter. Hissed commands trimmed sheets and braces, and Bryahn Lock Island stood gazing aft, where someone with unusually sharp eyes might have just made out the loom of *Darcos Sound*'s headsails. But he wasn't relying on anything as fallible as eyes, and he drew a deep, unobtrusive breath of relief as Zakrai Wayst's ship followed *Ahrmahk* around.

One by one, the ships of the Imperial Charisian Navy reached the point at which *Ahrmahk* had altered course, and one by one—each guided by the barely visible poop lanterns of her next ahead—they altered course, in turn.

Lock Island turned back forward. He stepped up close beside the helmsmen, looking down at the illuminated compass card, then raised his head once again and gazed forward while rainwater sluiced down his face.

There was nothing he could do now but project the posture and appearance of a man confident in his plan and its workings. He understood that, just as he understood that every sailor and Marine, every officer and petty officer, aboard *Ahrmahk* knew he couldn't actually see what was happening any better than they could. In point of fact, they were wrong about that, but there still wasn't anything else he could do. They *knew* he was playing a role, projecting the confidence they needed to see out of him, and it didn't matter. That, too, was part of the compact, part of the intricate, complicated network of responsibilities, commitments, duties, and trust between him and the men under his command.

*They can't see a damned thing,* he thought, almost wonderingly. *It's blacker than the inside of Clyntahn's heart, and they have no idea whether or not I'm really going to find Harpahr's fleet for them. Just as they have no idea what's going to happen when—if—we smash into one another in the dark, in the middle of a rainstorm. They're obeying my orders, following my plan, on the basis of nothing but duty . . . and faith. My God. What could anyone possibly do to* deserve *that kind of loyalty and obedience?*

He had no answer, but he knew he would do whatever it took, pay any price, to honor that trust. To be *worthy* of it, even if he couldn't deserve it.

He glanced at the nearer helmsman, a grizzled petty officer with a long pigtail, streaming with rain while his jaw worked on a chew of tobacco. The petty officer's attention was on the dimly visible sails, watching them, steering to keep them filled with the delicate touch of a man who'd spent twenty years at sea. He seemed to sense the high admiral's eyes, however, and turned his head to meet Lock Island's gaze.

"Just you be worryin' 'bout findin' the bastards, M'Lord," he said with a grin, raising his voice through the roar of rain on wet canvas, water sluicing across decks and runneling through the scuppers. "You find 'em, an' we'll kick their sorry arses proper fer 'em! You can lay to that, Sir."

He grinned again, then spat a stream of tobacco juice expertly into the spittoon lashed to the base of the binnacle housing.

▼   ▼   ▼

"Your move," Kornylys Harpahr observed, leaning back on his side of the chessboard. He knocked the ash out of his pipe and began methodically refilling it, never taking his eyes from the board while Taibahld considered it.

"That was nasty of you, My Lord," the flag captain said.

"Well, as the Archangel Chihiro said, we do our officers and men no favors by going easy on them," Harpahr replied comfortably. "The enemy isn't going to! Besides, you had it coming after what you did to *me* last night."

Taibahld chuckled. His thrice-a-five-day chess games with the admiral general had become a firm tradition, and he knew they both enjoyed them. They were well matched, and the companionable relaxation as they slaughtered one another's chessmen had helped build their close personal and professional relationship. They'd talked out more than one logistical problem, discussed more than one possible tactical scenario, across this chessboard, and Taibahld had been more than a little surprised by how fond he'd become of Harpahr in the process.

Now he rubbed his nose, considering the trap he'd been lured into. He could save his queen, but only by sacrificing his king's castle, which would open the right side of the board wide for Harpahr's attack. But if he let the admiral general *have* the queen, and used the move to slide his own queen's bishop between—

He was reaching for the bishop when he paused. His head came up, his eyes narrowing, just as Harpahr finished relighting his pipe. The admiral general looked at him curiously through a cloud of smoke.

"Ahrnahld?"

"I'm sorry, My Lord." The flag captain's tone was oddly taut. "I thought I heard someth—"

Then he heard it again.

▼   ▼   ▼

After an unconscionably shaky beginning, the Church of God Awaiting had actually gotten most of it right when it came to building its navy. Not *all* of it— that would have been expecting far too much out of a land animal. But once Allayn Maigwair had actually stopped to *think,* once Zhaspahr Clyntahn had pointed out that the galleys he was building were exactly the wrong ships, the

Church's Captain General had put a great deal of effort into recovering from his initial errors. He'd shown a surprising degree of insight in the process, and he'd found quite a few capable men—like Kornylys Harpahr—to help him do it.

There were still blind spots. His insistence on eschewing the shorter-ranged carronade, for example. He hadn't picked up on the huge advantage the Charisian ships' coppered bottoms gave them, either, and his galleons still boasted the fore-castles and aftercastles of pre-Merlin Safehold, although they *had* been reduced in height. Taken all together, though, he'd actually done almost as well as the Earl of Thirsk when it came to visualizing the threat and how to build a ship that could meet it.

And while the Temple Guard had no real naval tradition, it did understand discipline and the value of rigorous training. Unlike certain secular powers, the Guard had no institutional objection to finding experts who could teach it what it didn't know, either. Bad weather, ice, inefficient foundries, Charisian raids on essential shipping . . . all of them had helped to delay the Church's great project, but they hadn't been able to *stop* it, and men like Ahrnahld Taibahld and Kornylys Harpahr knew what to do with those ships once they were built.

Yet for all that, there were still weaknesses. For all their own courage, all the effort they'd spent on forethought and planning, it would never have oc-curred to Harpahr or Taibahld to attack a numerically superior enemy under the cover of a tropical front's waterfalls of rain. And for all the millions upon millions of marks the Church had invested in its fleet, it hadn't realized the im-portance of *light* units. It saw the fleet, graceful Charisian schooners as corsairs, as commerce raiders, without really appreciating their value as scouts. As swift bloodhounds to scent out an enemy fleet . . . or as the exquisitely sensitive whiskers of a cat-lizard to sense an approaching enemy before he could reach striking range.

And because of that, Admiral General Harpahr had snugged his columns of galleons down for the night without pickets to guard his flanks, reducing canvas to minimize the risk of collisions and avoid the possibility of damage if it turned out there were squalls hidden within the rain, after all. To keep his fleet from scattering and to be sure it would be the efficient, compact, concentrated force he and Taibahld had made of it when the sun rose and the rain ceased.

Which was why not a single lookout in a single ship of the Navy of God had seen a thing as twenty-five Charisian galleons came ghosting out of the dark.

▼　　▼　　▼

Bryahn Lock Island stood quietly, hands clasped behind him. The rain was eas-ing, although it still came down in sheets. That was fine with him, and so was the fact that there was actually going to be quite a lengthy break between this band of rain and the next one coming up from astern.

*Just last long enough for us to get in amongst them before you clear,* he thought at the weather. *Just last long enough.*

He'd made only a single minor course change since they'd turned in to attack. He could feel Captain Baikyr's tension, although the captain hid it well, but Lock Island himself was surprised to discover he was almost as calm as he looked. Unlike his flag captain, he knew they were on precisely the correct heading. On the other side of the rain lashing the surface of the sea to a white froth ahead of them, there was an enemy fleet, and HMS *Ahrmahk* and her sisters were stealing up upon the outermost column of that fleet like assassins.

He felt muscles and sinews tightening—not with fear, but with anticipation—and had to bite his tongue to keep from shouting for his gunners to stand to.

*Not yet. Not yet, Bryahn. Wouldn't do for the lookouts to be wondering how you saw the other side clear from the quarterdeck before they did. All sorts of unwelcome little questions could come out of that!*

And then—

"Sail two points abaft the larboard bow, Sir!"

The forward lookout had kept his wits about himself and passed the word aft, relayed from man to man, rather than raising a shout.

"Good," Lock Island said as an electric shock ran through the men on the quarterdeck about him. He sensed them stirring, backs straightening, eyes narrowing as they realized he had, indeed, found the enemy for them.

He felt himself leaning forward, squinting as if he could somehow physically see through the rain and the darkness, and then his eyes widened. The rain was beginning to taper off, and he discovered he *could* see. See a long, slowly moving column—fourteen high-sided galleons, poop lanterns gleaming, light showing through skylights or, here and there, through gunports opened for ventilation. Those lights picked them out of the night, illuminated his targets, while his own lean, black-painted ships came slinking out of the shadows.

"We'll cross their sterns, Captain Baikyr," High Admiral Lock Island said formally. "Then we'll come to larboard, take the wind on the beam, and pound them from leeward while we overhaul. Keep an eye out for their second column, though. We don't want some bright bastard over there to get any ideas about working up to windward."

"Yes, Sir!"

▼    ▼    ▼

The rearmost ship in Kornylys Harpahr's windward column was the fifty-gun galleon NGS *Saint Ithmyn.* Her ship's company had done well in the fleet's endless sail and gunnery drills. Over the thousands of miles they'd voyaged, hard work, training, and growing experience had transformed them from a crew only too conscious of its own *lack* of experience into one confident that it no longer had anything of which to be ashamed. And there was a great deal of truth to that.

But training or no training, growing experience or no experience, no one aboard *Saint Ithmyn* expected an attack any more than Harpahr or Taibahld had. Her lookouts had been more concerned with keeping track of consorts who represented potential collision hazards—and with finding ways to shelter from the downpour—than with the ridiculous possibility that the Imperial Charisian Navy might choose a night blacker than the pit of Shan-wei to assail them. And so no one was looking in the right direction when HMS *Ahrmahk* came sliding out of the dark like the Archangel of Death himself.

▼     ▼     ▼

*"What the h—?!"*

The crewman by *Saint Ithmyn*'s after rail wasn't a lookout. In fact, he wasn't supposed to be on deck—officially—at all. He was one of the servants assigned to the flagship's wardroom, and he'd nipped above decks when he heard the rain easing to empty one of the wardroom spittoons over the lee rail during the lull. He had no idea what had prompted him to look up at the moment he did. Perhaps it was the urging of some deeply buried instinct, or perhaps he'd already caught sight of something out of the corner of one eye without realizing that he had.

Whatever it was, he looked up just as *Ahrmahk*'s jibboom began crossing *Saint Ithmyn*'s wake barely fifty yards astern of her.

His inarticulate, half-strangled shout died in simple, paralyzing shock at the sight. Even then, it never occurred to him it might be a *Charisian* ship. If his brain had been working clearly, if it had been clear and daylight rather than a rainy, moonless night, he would have realized that low-slung, predatory shape couldn't possibly belong to one of *Saint Ithmyn*'s sisters. But the eye sees what the mind *expects* to see, and so he assumed it must be another of their own vessels, wandering out of formation and narrowly missing a collision with his own ship.

The lieutenant who had the watch looked up sharply at the chopped-off exclamation, then wheeled in the direction of the other man's stare. For a moment, his mind leapt down the same chain of assumptions, but unlike the servant, his had become a trained seaman's eye. His brain insisted that it was illogical, preposterous—*impossible*—yet he knew instantly that whatever and whoever that ship was, it didn't belong to *his* fleet.

"Strange ship, dead astern! Beat to quarters! Captain to the d—!"

The young lieutenant did everything right. More than that, he did it in the right *order*. Unfortunately, it was too late for the right thing to make any difference at all to NGS *Saint Ithmyn*.

▼     ▼     ▼

Bryahn Lock Island heard the shout even through the sound of wind and wave. The fact that HMS *Ahrmahk* was totally silent, no one speaking, the crew hardly even breathing, helped. He couldn't make out the words—partly because of the pronounced Temple Lands accent—but he recognized the tone of shock in the brief seconds before the shout was wiped away by another sound entirely.

"*Fire!*" Sylmahn Baikyr snapped, and the darkness came apart in fire and fury.

▼　　▼　　▼

The lieutenant was still shouting when *Ahrmahk*'s first broadside arrived. Twenty-seven thirty-pound round shot came howling out of a sudden, blinding flash of light. The lieutenant had never seen a heavy gun fired in total darkness—never imagined the incredible brilliance, the physical *pain* of abused optic nerves as that totally unexpected fist of light slammed into it. The Charisian artillery spewed flame and smoke, and the lieutenant never had the chance to fully appreciate the brutal beauty and savagery of that man-made lightning bolt.

One of the first round shot struck him just above the belt buckle and tore him in half. His severed torso flew over fifteen feet before it thudded to the deck, and no one heard the sodden impact through the shrieks and the screams and the sound of splintering wood.

*Ahrmahk*'s attack took her victim totally by surprise. Better than half the ship's company were in their hammocks, sound asleep or drowsing. Others were quietly playing cards, enjoying the companionship of their messmates on yet another rainy night. Some were darning holes in trousers, others were working on the scores of tiny repairs that were an incessant part of a wooden sailing ship.

And then, suddenly, without warning, Hell itself came for them. Six-inch round shots slammed into their ship, splintered her stern windows, ripped the full length of her crowded decks. Men in hammocks shrieked as those round shot plucked away arms and legs and victims woke from slumber and dreams of home to the agony of maimed and ruined bodies. The same round shot slammed into deck beams and framing members, spraying lethal clouds of splinters like wooden shrapnel to rip into still more sleeping or totally unprepared crewmen. *Saint Ithmyn*'s captain never had the opportunity to learn his ship was under attack—the third round shot of the first broadside killed him before he ever woke. A third of the galleon's officers were killed or wounded—the majority in their own cabins, or sitting around the wardroom table—as the Charisian fire ripped through them.

All the training, and all the motivation, and all the experience in the world were not—*could* not have been—enough to absorb that sudden, completely unexpected, unbelievably brutal onslaught. Officers and petty officers were dead or wounded. The ship was suddenly filled with screaming, broken men and the stink of blood and riven entrails. The Archangels themselves would have panicked in the face of that carnage, and *Saint Ithmyn's* discipline came apart.

Men bellowed in panic, fighting their way through strangling, clinging barriers of spread hammocks, sliding in blood, trampling on the broken, mewling bodies of what had once been messmates and friends. It wasn't cowardice; it was *shock,* the devastating impact of total surprise. And in the midst of that panic, in the depths of that carnage, someone dropped a lantern.

▼　　▼　　▼

HMS *Ahrmahk's* larboard guns recoiled in a squealing thunder of wooden gun trucks across thick planking. The upper-deck carronades had been fired with the slow-matches, at least for the first broadside, and their crews were delighted the rain had ceased, at least for the moment. They'd shrugged off their oilskins even before the rain stopped, freeing themselves of the encumbrance. Now they flung themselves on their weapons, swabbing the barrels, ramming home fresh cartridges, sliding in the fat round shot.

Below, on the main gundeck, men coughed and choked on the strangling brimstone of their own gunsmoke. They, too, embraced their multi-ton charges, swabbing bores to extinguish any lingering sparks, ramming home fresh charges. For the moment, at least, none of them had any attention to spare for their target—time enough for that when they'd reloaded.

But Bryahn Lock Island *did* have attention to spare for *Saint Ithmyn,* and his jaw tightened as he saw the first telltale flicker.

*Oh, those poor bastards,* he thought. *Those poor, damned bastards.*

▼　　▼　　▼

There is nothing more feared aboard a ship—especially aboard a *wooden* ship—than fire. And there is no emergency, no threat, which demands a quicker, more disciplined response. But there was no possibility of anything resembling a disciplined response aboard NGS *Saint Ithmyn* that night, at that moment. Too many men who would have responded instantly under other conditions were already dead, wounded, or maddened by panic, and the smell of wood smoke, the sudden crackle of flames, were the death knell of any hope of restoring order.

The fire spread with horrifying speed, overtaking men as they ran, crawling over the wounded who shrieked and tried to drag their broken bodies out of its embrace. Licking up heavily tarred rigging, despite the saturating rain which had come down for so many hours. Racing through shattered internal bulkheads, roaring jubilantly as it discovered the paint store and gorged itself on turpentine and gallons of cotton seed oil.

By the time *Ahrmahk* had reloaded, and *Darcos Sound* had crossed *Saint Ith-myn*'s stern and poured her own thundering avalanche of iron into the reeling ship, the savagely wounded galleon was clearly doomed. Men—some of them on fire—flung themselves over the side, seeking the temporary cooling salvation of the sea. Flames roared like one of Ehdwyrd Howsmyn's blast furnaces, and sparks were already cascading up out of the open hatchways.

And then *Ahrmahk*'s guns came to bear on their second target.

▼　　▼　　▼

The destruction of Kornylys Harpahr's windward column was total. Taken by surprise, unable to believe what was happening, rousing from the depths of sleep to face nightmare, and with the sudden, roaring inferno of *Saint Ithmyn* blazing against the night, the ships of that column never recovered.

It wasn't for want of trying.

The three rear ships never had a chance. Assailed out of the darkness, their crews were ripped to pieces before they could even begin to respond. The Charisian ships closed to as little as twenty yards, paralleling their targets, over-hauling them steadily and yet slowly enough to pound each of them mercilessly in turn. Masts went over the side. Guns were dismounted before their breeching ropes could even be cast off. It was a howling nightmare that shattered the fabric of the ships themselves almost as quickly and as brutally as it shattered the cohesiveness of the crews which manned them.

The eleven ships ahead of them had more time, at least some warning. Sailing ships, even *Charisian* sailing ships, are seldom as swift as slash lizards. It took time for *Ahrmahk* to overtake the ships ahead of *Saint Ithmyn,* and Lock Island's greatest fear had been that one of the Church column's leading units would turn out of line on her own initiative. Would steer to cut across the head of his own line in an effort to do to him what he'd done to *Saint Ithmyn*.

But surprise, confusion, and horror are poor soil for initiative. Especially for men who have never before experienced the violence of a point-blank broad-side. The officers and the crews of those ships did their best, and after the initial strobes of panic, they responded with courage and determination. But they *re-sponded*. They reacted. They made no effort to impose their own will. They defended themselves, getting their guns cleared away, bringing their batteries into action despite their surprise, despite the confusion. They fired back—raggedly, at first, then more steadily—even as an unending sequence of Charisian gunports sailed past them, every one of them belching flame and fury.

They had nothing to be ashamed of, those men, those officers. Most of them, when their time came, fell *facing* their enemies, shouting defiance, manning their weapons. But the only thing that could have saved them was swift, determined *offensive* action . . . and that was the one thing of which they were totally incapable.

▼    ▼    ▼

*Well, that was the easy part,* Lock Island thought as the shattered wrecks of the windward column fell astern.

Three more of them were on fire now, flames roaring up and painting the clouds in crimson and blood. It was obvious the other ten ships were out of action for hours, probably days. It was unlikely any of them would sink, and if they'd been going to catch fire, they would have already. But taken together, they represented almost twenty percent of Harpahr's total strength, and whatever else happened, they would play no part in any further combat this night.

*If we win, any one of them can be snapped up by a single schooner,* the high admiral thought. *If we lose, Harpahr will probably be able to recover and repair them all . . . eventually. But that's not going to happen.*

A part of Lock Island was tempted to break off, to vanish back into the darkness. What had already happened to the Church fleet was bound to have brutal repercussions for its morale. And if he could break off for now, do the same thing again once or twice, then—

*Forget it,* he told himself sternly. *Harpahr and Taibahld are too good for that kind of crap. Yes, you caught them with their trousers down and their bare arses hanging out tonight. What makes you think a pair as smart as they are is going to let you do that to them all over again? Besides, you only got away with it* tonight *because of the weather!*

No. He'd hurt them badly. Now it was time to hurt them even *more* badly, before they could recover.

"Captain Baikyr, we'll come about," he said, and waved at a distant red glimmer where firelight reflected on topsails to the northwest. "Those gentlemen are trying to get themselves into formation to greet us," he continued. "It would be rude to keep them waiting."

▼    ▼    ▼

Kornylys Harpahr stood on *Sword of God*'s poop deck and tried to look impassive.

It wasn't easy.

His flagship led what had been the centermost of five columns of warships. Now there were only four columns. *Saint Ithmyn* and her consorts had been too far away for him to make out any details, but the speed and savagery with which they'd been hammered into impotence had been only too easy to follow.

And there'd been nothing he could do about it. The Charisians had attacked from almost dead to windward, and the massacre of his column was over and done long before any of his other galleons could have beaten up to windward to assist it.

He'd almost tried, anyway—he'd almost hoisted the signal for a general chase in the hope at least some of his ships might see it and manage to scramble into action with the Charisians. But he hadn't. The one thing he absolutely could not do was to permit the Charisians to panic him into reacting without thinking, and so he'd locked himself in the icy armor of self-control. He'd forced himself to stand there, watching, feeling the destruction of each of those ships as if they were extensions of his own body, and refused to react blindly.

Instead, he'd started the process of forming his own line of battle. It wasn't going to be a *proper* line. That would have been impossible in these conditions. But it would be there, ready to his hand, and he bared his teeth at his foes.

By his estimate, there were between fifteen and thirty galleons in the attacking force, which suggested there were others somewhere about. If he'd been the Charisian commander, he'd have done his best to get at the Harchongese, so it was possible that was where at least some of the missing Charisians were.

At the same time, he reminded himself, it wouldn't do to start assigning superhuman powers to the enemy. He'd found during his own career in the Guard that competent officers had a tendency to make their own luck, but even allowing for that, the Charisians had been incredibly fortunate to come upon his outermost column on an almost perfect interception course. They'd exploited that good fortune for all it was worth, and the burning, crippled remnants falling astern were brutal evidence of just how effectively they'd done it.

But they weren't going to take the *rest* of his ships by surprise, and unless there were Shan-wei's own lot of them still wandering about out there in the darkness, he still had them outnumbered by better than two-to-one.

*Go ahead,* he thought at the Charisian commander. *Go ahead, come after us. We'll be here, waiting.*

▾   ▾   ▾

"All right, it's time," Lock Island said.

He was addressing Captain Baikyr, but it was Domynyk Staynair to whom he was actually speaking.

"We've whittled them down some," he continued, "but the rest are staying together. They're not going to let us pick them off in isolation, and I don't want to give them daylight to sort themselves out. Our own line's in pretty good shape, I think, and Admiral Rock Point's back there to take over if anything unfortunate happens to us. More to the point, the cloud cover's trying to break up and let some moonlight in here so we can actually see what we're doing. So it's time to get tucked in."

"Yes, Sir," Baikyr replied grimly.

He didn't seem to be looking forward to the experience, and Lock Island couldn't blame him. There were the next best thing to sixty galleons over there, and their very lack of formation was going to make things even uglier. He knew his captains, knew they would hold the line of battle together as long as humanly possible, supporting one another, massing their fire on single targets.

But he also knew that sooner or later—and probably sooner—that line was going to come apart, especially in the chaos and confusion of a night action. If Harpahr's crews proved as determined as he expected them to, this engagement was going to degenerate into a melee, with individual ships fighting desperately against individual enemies . . . and all too probably firing into friends in the madness.

Baikyr knew that as well as Lock Island did. Still, if there was any hesitation in the flag captain, the high admiral couldn't see it.

"Very well," he said. "Take us to them, Captain. Find us a way to their flagship."

▼    ▼    ▼

"Here they come, My Lord," Taibahld said flatly, and Harpahr nodded.

"Here they come, indeed," he murmured.

It had actually taken longer than he'd expected. Despite his experience on the long voyage, it was still vaguely surprising to an army officer, accustomed to how rapidly cavalry and even infantry could be moved about a field of battle, that it could take so long for ships to come to grips with one another.

There were no longer any flames on the horizon. One of his ships had erupted in spectacular, volcanic thunder when the flames finally reached her magazine. The other burning hulks had simply disappeared, burned to the waterline and gone. Over two and a half hours had passed since the rumble of guns had interrupted his chess game, and it was going to take at least another hour for the Charisians to reach him.

He had no doubt his captains had put the respite to good use, and he was grateful they'd had time to cope with the initial shock of the Charisians' sudden appearance. Despite that, he knew his crews' morale had to be badly shaken.

*And no doubt the* Charisians' *morale's been bolstered by their success,* he thought grimly. *Well, we'll just have to see what we can do about that.*

▼    ▼    ▼

Lock Island and Rock Point had given considerable thought to their formation.

Of their twenty-five galleons, only the twelve Rock Point had taken to Larek had shells in their magazines. For that matter, ten of Lock Island's thirteen galleons couldn't have fired the new ammunition if they'd had it. They mounted the "old-style" long krakens with which the Royal Charisian Navy's galleons had originally been armed, but the shells had been designed for the "new-model" krakens, which fired a thirty-pound shot instead of the older guns' thirty-*five*-pound shot.

The formation they'd adopted alternated Rock Point's shell-armed ships with Lock Island's own galleons. The only exception to that was the lead pair—*Ahrmahk* and *Darcos Sound,* both from Lock Island's original squadron. So far, there'd been no need for the shells, given the crushing surprise they'd achieved in the initial engagement, and Lock Island had no intention of allowing the other side to know the new weapon existed until he had an opportunity to use it *decisively.* So they were going to fight their way into Harpahr's sprawling formation with old-fashioned round shot, and only then would Rock Point's ships switch to shells.

*While they last, at any rate,* the high admiral thought grimly.

Now he watched as his flagship drew closer and closer to the Church squadrons and felt himself tightening internally once more.

*Whatever happens, these bastards are about to get hurt worse than they ever imagined,* he told himself.

▼　　▼　　▼

The leading Church galleons began to fire.

The range was still long, especially for inexperienced gun crews firing in such poor visibility. The thunder and lightning of their broadsides shredded the night, yet almost all of their twenty-five-pound and twelve-pound shot plunged harmlessly into the sea, and the Charisians held their fire. They sailed through the splashes, flinched at the thudding sledgehammer sounds as the occasional shot actually struck one of their ships. Most of the leading Charisians were purpose-built units, however, with the heavy framing and thick scantlings of true warships. The weak Church gunpowder and lighter shot were no match for their stoutness.

Here and there, round shot wailed through the air above a ship, or punched through a topsail like invisible fists. Shrouds were sliced away, and seamen swarmed up ratlines to splice severed lines. A few shots—a very few, luckier than their fellows—found targets of flesh and blood. A twenty-five-pound shot erupted through *Ahrmahk*'s quarterdeck hammock nettings. One of the carronade gunners dropped without a sound as his head vanished, and two more men on the same gun went down, writhing as their blood patterned the planking.

A casualty party hurried them below to the waiting surgeons and healers, and one or two of the flagship's men looked at one another uneasily. Most, however, simply stood there, watching the flashes of the enemy's guns, waiting. The high admiral could hear at least some of them commenting scornfully on the Church gunners' lack of accuracy, and he found himself grinning as one gray-haired gun captain turned his back on those gunners, pulled down his trousers, and waved his bare buttocks at the enemy.

A roar of laughter went up, mixed with catcalls and some incredibly obscene suggestions for how to improve the insult, and the gun captain redoubled his efforts. It was unacceptable, of course, and his division officer's snarled reprimand recalled him quickly to his own responsibilities, but Lock Island doubted the youthful lieutenant's heart had really been in it.

▼    ▼    ▼

"I think they're just wasting powder and shot, Ahrnahld," Harpahr said quietly, watching his lead ships fire, and his flag captain shrugged.

"I don't doubt it, My Lord. On the other hand, there's no way to stop them from here. It's possible they'll get lucky, for that matter—actually kill a Charisian or two, maybe even bring down a spar. And, frankly, I'd rather have them firing, even if they're not hitting anything, than eating themselves up with worry. Besides," his teeth gleamed faintly, reflecting the distant broadsides, "in another twenty minutes they'll be close enough they *will* be hitting something."

▼    ▼    ▼

The two fleets' slow, steady approach was totally different from the initial clash. There would be no ambush, this time. No sudden surprise of artillery thundering out of the night. *This* time both sides knew what was coming, and the Church gunners began to score more hits as the range was slowly but steadily pared away.

A crashing sound, and a chorus of screams from forward, told Lock Island that at least one Church round shot had finally gotten through. It might have found an open gunport, he thought, or it was possible the range had fallen enough for even Church gunpowder to start punching through his ships' sides.

He glanced at Sylmahn Baikyr. Moonlight poured through rents in the cloud cover now, turning sails to polished pewter, and *Ahrmahk*'s captain stood motionless, narrow eyes measuring ranges, evaluating firing arcs, looking for gaps between enemy ships. The fingers of his right hand drummed slowly, rhythmically, on the scabbard of his sheathed sword. Another round shot ripped through the midships hammock nettings. It killed a Marine, chewed a two-inch semicircle out of the back of the mainmast, then careened off into the darkness somewhere on the far side of the ship.

Baikyr didn't even flinch. He just stood waiting, and Lock Island felt a sudden surge of warmth—of affection—for his dapper little flag captain.

Still the range fell. *Ahrmahk*'s bowsprit thrust out ahead of her, aimed like some knight's lance, but at a solid mountain range of moon-washed canvas and waiting broadsides, not at another knight. Gunports began to flash ahead of her—scores of them, hundreds. Round shot howled through the air, punched into her bows, ripped through her sails. More of her crew went down, wounded or dead, and other men stepped into their places. Grips tightened on handspikes, on the staffs of rammers. Knuckles whitened, here and there lips moved in silent prayer, and *still* the range fell.

Even to Lock Island, it seemed incredible that so many guns could throw so many shot at a single target without ripping *Ahrmahk* to pieces. The thudding sounds grew more frequent, louder. Splinters flew. More men screamed. The fore topgallant mast pitched over the side. One of the foredeck carronades took a direct hit and its carriage disintegrated, throwing a deadly sheet of splinters across the deck.

And then, finally, his flagship—still without firing a single shot—began pushing her way physically through the gap between two of the Church galleons.

▼    ▼    ▼

Harpahr watched the leading Charisian come on like some moonlit, unstoppable juggernaut. His gunners were hitting her—he *knew* they were! Yet she seemed invulnerable, invincible. He saw holes appearing in her sails, and the sea around her was ripped and torn as tons of iron churned its surface. At least some of those shot *had* to be hitting her, had to be killing and maiming her men.

Then her fore topgallant toppled like a felled tree, and he held his breath, waiting to see her turn away at last, clear her own broadside so she could reply to her tormentors.

But she didn't. She just kept *coming,* and he felt a deep, formless emotion stirring within him. It wasn't *fear* he felt, yet it was something close. Dread, perhaps. He'd seen battle. He knew the sort of iron discipline it took to absorb that kind of pounding—to see that many cannon thundering away, hurling their hate at you—and still keep coming. He *knew* what he was seeing . . . and he could already sense the brutal price that courage and discipline were going to exact from his own men.

▼    ▼    ▼

An iron hurricane thundered into *Ahrmahk*'s bows just as she passed between NGS *Holy Warrior* and NGS *Crusade*. It came from yet a third galleon, lying almost directly across her own path, and her entire foremast swayed, then plunged downward, crashing into the water alongside. Her main topgallant mast went with it, and there were more screams and cries from forward. Two of her lieutenants went down, and Sylmahn Baikyr looked at his first lieutenant.

"You may fire, Master Vykain," he said.

▼    ▼    ▼

Harpahr winced as the lead Charisian fired at last.

For an instant, he thought the ship had exploded as both broadsides erupted simultaneously. Yet even as he thought that, he realized how wrong he was. Despite the pounding she'd taken during that long, slow, dreadful approach, there was a venomous precision to her fire. Her guns crashed out, two-by-two, spardeck carronades firing in unison with the heavier gundeck guns beneath them, and their accuracy was fearful to behold.

HMS *Ahrmahk* had paid a terrible price to break the Church line. A quarter of her crew were casualties. Her foremast was gone. She was slowed, lamed, with five guns out of action before she ever reached her enemies. But it was a price she had known she was going to pay, and she and her crew made no mistake.

Her guns had been double-shotted this time. They slammed their hate into *Holy Warrior* and *Crusade,* raking both ships simultaneously. Men shrieked and died aboard the Church galleons. *Holy Warrior* staggered, helm control obviously lost. She fouled one of her consorts in a crashing thunder of wooden hulls grinding together. Yardarms locked, masts snapped, and she and her sister wallowed aside.

HMS *Ahrmahk* was in little better state. *Crusade* swung round to larboard, turning to run before the wind, bringing her own larboard broadside to bear. A third of the Church ship's guns had been dismounted or disabled, but if her men were less experienced than *Ahrmahk*'s, they were no less determined. The remaining guns blasted at the Charisian flagship, and this time, most of them hit. The rest of *Ahrmahk*'s mainmast thundered down, and Bryahn Lock Island went to his knees as a heavy wooden block, swinging from the mizzentop like a lethal pendulum, literally picked a Marine up and hurled him into the high admiral.

"Larboard your helm!" Baikyr's clear voice cut through the bedlam, and *Ahrmahk* swerved to starboard even as her speed dropped. She slammed into *Crusade* bodily, the shock driving more men from their feet. *Crusade*'s mizzenmast went down with the impact, grappling irons flew, and Bryahn Lock Island drove himself to his feet, checked his sword, and drew his pistols.

"Away boarders, Master Vykain!" Baikyr shouted, and HMS *Ahrmahk*'s Marines and seamen howled the high, piercing Charisian war cry as they hurled themselves across onto the other ship's deck with their high admiral at their head.

▼    ▼    ▼

Behind *Ahrmahk*, *Darcos Sound* came driving through the gap the flagship had created. She bore down on *Holy Warrior* and her fouled consort, larboard broadside thundering, then drove past, deeper into the confusion and smoke and bedlam. Behind her, *Daffodil*, one of Rock Point's galleons, fought *her* way through, pounding with round shot, battering a road towards the heart of the Church formation. And behind her came *Crag Reach*, and *Margaret's Land*, and *Greentree*, and *Foam*.

The Charisians maintained their formation with iron discipline as they broke through the outermost Church line, but once they were past that ordered formation, the chaos Lock Island had envisioned enveloped them. There were simply too many Church galleons swarming towards them. There was no possible way to avoid all of them, and the indescribable confusion of a night action churned the chaos into a wild melee that no man could have hoped to sort out.

No one broke. No one ran. Perhaps one would have expected that of a navy with the ICN's traditions, yet its opponents were just as stubborn, just as determined. Say what one might about Zhaspahr Clyntahn, level whatever charge one wished at the corruption of the Group of Four, scorn the self-serving avarice of a corrupt and venal Church hierarchy if one would, there were no cowards aboard the Church's ships that night.

Lock Island and his officers and his men had known precisely what sort of action they intended to create. They'd embraced it with the cold, calculating courage of a navy with an all but unbroken record of victory, and they'd walked straight into it deliberately.

The crews of the Navy of God had *thought* they knew what was coming, but they'd been wrong. They'd trained, they'd practiced, they'd drilled, but they'd never *experienced* it, and nothing short of experience could truly have prepared them for it. Man-for-man and ship-for-ship, they were outclassed by their opponents in every category except one: courage. They were terrified, confused, with no clear idea of what was happening, and yet they stood to their guns. They were less accurate, they scored fewer hits, their round shot were lighter, but they poured fire back at the Charisians. And when Imperial Charisian Marines came storming aboard their ships after collision had locked them together, they met them at the bulwarks, on the gangways, with weapons in their hands and no give at all in their hearts.

The last, desperate defense of HMS *Royal Charis* at the Battle of Darcos Sound had been the closest, most brutal, most ferocious engagement in the history of the Royal Charisian Navy.

On this night, in this place, on these red-running decks, the *Imperial Charisian Navy* found its equal.

▼　▼　▼

"God wills it!"

Flame gushed up from the pistol's pan as Lock Island squeezed the trigger. The heavy, rifled bullet slammed into the Temple Guardsman's face in an explosion of blood, black in the moonlight. It was the pistol's second round, and there was no time to holster it as the dead guardsman's companion kept coming. Lock Island dropped the smoking weapon to the deck and his sword leapt into his hand.

"Langhorne and no quarter!" someone else was howling as the high admiral parried aside the guardsman's boarding pike. One of his own Marines lashed out with his musket, burying his bayonet in the guardsman's side, and the Temple Loyalist went down shrieking.

Lock Island staggered as another Church galleon came grinding in along *Crusade*'s other side. The newcomer had been badly battered—she'd lost her mizzenmast, and her larboard bulwarks looked as if they'd been pounded flat by some maniac with a sledgehammer—but her gangways were black with seamen and guardsmen, and steel gleamed dully in the smoke-choked moonlight.

"Charis! *Charis!*" he heard voices screaming.

"Death to the Inquisition!" someone else bellowed, and he felt the wild, half-maddened fury of his own Marines and seamen.

Then the new wave of boarders came streaming across onto *Crusade*'s deck in a torrent of hate and keen-edged steel.

"After me, lads!" Bryahn Lock Island screamed and charged to meet them.

▼    ▼    ▼

*Now*, Domynyk Staynair thought. *Now!*

*Destroyer* had finally broken through the fraying Church line. At least ten of his and Lock Island's galleons were yardarm-to-yardarm with Church galleons, cannon muzzles flaming at one another from as little as ten yards' range or even lashed together, with furious boarding actions raging back and forth.

Yet that island of madness had drawn in still more of Harpahr's ships. They were closing on the Charisian intruders, preparing to swarm them under before anyone could come to their aid. And in the process, they'd created a clear space, room into which *Destroyer* could lead the truncated line behind her.

"Now, Styvyn!" he barked.

"Aye, aye, My Lord!" Styvyn Erayksyn, his flag lieutenant, shouted through the chaos, and crossed to the larboard side of the quarterdeck.

Erayksyn had discarded his oilskins when the rain ceased. Now he reached into the pocket of his torn, smoke-grimed uniform tunic, extracted one of Commodore Seamount's "Shan-wei's candles," and struck it on the breech of a carronade. It flared and flashed and sputtered to life, and he touched it to the fuse of a curious-looking contraption lashed to *Destroyer*'s taffrail.

For a moment, nothing happened, and then something sputtered and glared even more ferociously. Erayksyn stepped back hastily . . . and the very first signal rocket ever used in combat on the surface of Safehold arced into the night sky. It soared upward, spewing a fiery trail that sent a stab of atavistic terror through men steeped in the restrictions of the Proscriptions of Jwojeng.

If it hadn't come at them cold, they would have recognized what it had to be. They'd worked and trained with gunpowder long enough to realize this was only one more application of a familiar material. But it *did* come at them cold, and when it exploded in a brilliant, thunderous flash high overhead, some of them—men who'd faced a maelstrom of howling round shot without flinching—panicked at last.

It didn't last, that panic. There were those who understood what they were seeing despite the surprise, and there were others who simply didn't care what Shan-wei-spawned deviltry the Charisian heretics might have brought with them. They rallied their more frightened companions, and the volume of fire which had faltered visibly when the rocket launched began to climb once more.

But the rocket was only a precursor. Only a sign of things yet to come. As it exploded overhead, ten Charisian galleons—every one of Rock Point's shell-armed ships which wasn't already mired in one of the furious boarding actions—stopped firing round shot.

▼   ▼   ▼

*"Langhorne!"* Kornylys Harpahr gasped.

*Sword of God* had so far avoided the melee, but his flagship was headed into the cauldron now, leading a dozen more galleons to seal off the Charisian penetration and crush the intruders. The admiral general had been as startled as anyone when the rocket hissed up from *Destroyer,* but he'd also been one of those who'd realized immediately that there was nothing demonic about it. In fact, he'd found himself wondering why the same idea had never occurred to him.

What he hadn't realized was what the rocket was *for.* For a few minutes, he actually hoped that it was a signal to break off, that the Charisians had realized they were too outnumbered to achieve victory. But then he discovered his mistake.

He was looking directly at HMS *King Sailys* when the fifty-eight-gun galleon fired a full broadside of thirty-pounder shells into NGS *Holy Writ* at a range of ninety yards. Only three of the twenty-seven shells missed. Two fuses malfunctioned—the gunners using them for the first time hadn't gotten them set properly. But that left twenty-two, and not even Commander Mahndrayn's tests had truly prepared Rock Point and his crews for what happened next.

*Holy Writ* blew up.

It was like some terrible avalanche of light. Baron Seamount's fuses were still in the developmental stage. Unlike the impact fuses he'd designed for the rifled shells he'd been forbidden to produce, the smoothbore shells used timed fuses ignited by the flash when the gun's propellant exploded, and he hadn't yet managed to come up with a fuse compound with a completely uniform combustion rate. As a result, the shells detonated in a staggered sequence. All of them exploded in the space of no more than three seconds, yet there were discernible intervals between them—gaps long enough for the Navy of God to realize that whatever ammunition *King Sailys* had just fired, it was the shells themselves exploding. It wasn't *Holy Writ*'s own ammunition; it was yet another new Charisian *weapon*.

And then, as the exploding shells reached a crescendo, *Holy Writ*'s ammunition *did* explode. Her main powder store went up like a disemboweling volcano, tearing her to pieces and scattering her fragments across the sea.

▼　▼　▼

A twelve-foot section of *Holy Writ*'s mainmast slammed into *Sword of God*'s hull like some demented giant's battering ram. It hit low enough, and the hull was stout enough, that it failed to penetrate, but Harpahr felt the impact run up through his legs as if the ship had just struck a reef.

Yet he hardly noticed. He was too busy trying to grasp the scale of the disaster which had just enveloped his fleet.

▼　▼　▼

*King Sailys* wasn't the only Charisian ship firing shells.

So were HMS *Green Hollow*, HMS *King Haarahld*, HMS *Port Royal*, HMS *Wave* . . . and the effect was terrible. The Imperial Charisian Navy had paid a dreadful price, but it had drawn virtually Harpahr's entire fleet into close-ranged, furious combat. Now shellfire ripped into a dozen of that fleet's galleons at once.

Not all those initial broadsides were as deadly as *King Sailys*' had been, and none of those other targets simply blew up in the very first exchange. But in some ways, the chains of exploding shells—the *repeated* chains of exploding shells—were even worse. They were proof that what had happened to *Holy Writ* hadn't truly been a fluke . . . and they showed how a ship could be demolished by explosion after explosion.

Hulls were ripped open, huge stretches of decking blew into the air, masts toppled, and flames began to dance and crackle in the wreckage.

▼　▼　▼

It was too much. Harpahr knew what was going to happen. He knew he couldn't stop it . . . and it never once occurred to him to blame his men for it. How could he? He knew what they'd given and endured. He knew they'd stood toe-to-toe with the vaunted Charisians, and if they hadn't been as good as the Charisians, they'd been good enough. They'd been *winning*, trumping Charisian experience and Charisian firepower with numbers and raw courage.

But there were limits in all things, and whatever this new and horrible weapon was, he couldn't ask them to face it. Not after all they'd already given him. And not when they had no counterweight for it, when the range was too short for the Charisians to miss . . . and when he had no sea room to run for it.

He never knew which ship's flag came down first. He supposed a careful enough investigation might have determined who it was, which galleon was the first to strike. But it was an investigation he never launched, a question he never sought to answer, because it didn't matter.

It was the right thing to do, and he knew it.

.IV.

Imperial Palace,
City of Cherayth,
Kingdom of Chisholm

It was cold on the battlements.

Cayleb Ahrmahk stood in the icy wind, staring sightlessly into the driving snow. He'd stood there for three hours, long enough for the front of his hooded parka to turn matted and white, and the tall, sapphire-eyed guardsman had stood at his back the entire time.

Merlin Athrawes, Edwyrd Seahamper, and Sharleyan Ahrmahk were the only people who knew where he was. Sharleyan had wanted to join him, but he'd only squeezed her hand gently, smiled sadly, and nodded at their sleeping daughter. Then he'd kissed her tear-streaked cheek, climbed into the parka, and headed out into the snowy evening.

It was possible the wetness on his own face was only the melting snow.

It was possible.

Finally, his shoulders moved as he drew a vast breath and turned to look at his guardsman, mentor, and friend.

"I didn't really think they could do it," he said quietly, the words barely audible, the voice that of the confessional. "I knew they had to try, that I had to *let* them try, but I didn't really think they could do it."

"I know," Merlin replied.

"It was worse than watching Gwylym," the emperor said, shaking his head. "All those men—on *both* sides. All that killing."

"And Bryahn," Merlin said softly, and Cayleb closed his eyes and nodded.

"And Bryahn," he whispered.

Merlin did something he'd never done before. He reached out, resting one hand on each of Cayleb's shoulders, and then he drew the Emperor of Charis into a tight embrace. He held him there, while Cayleb let his face rest—for a moment, at least—against his armsman's shoulder.

Merlin felt his own eyes burning as their composites faithfully mimicked the reaction of their flesh-and-blood originals.

The Battle of the Gulf of Tarot was going to go down beside Darcos Sound or Crag Reach. That much, he already knew. What neither he nor Cayleb yet knew, even with access to Owl's remotes, was how terrible the final cost was truly going to prove.

Lock Island's twenty-five galleons had been brutally hammered. Eleven of them had been reduced to shattered near wrecks. Three of the eleven had been completely dismasted, and a twelfth ship, HMS *Stonehill,* had burned to the waterline, then exploded. Merlin wasn't certain how it had happened, but he suspected the ship had been deliberately fired by one of the Church boarders. He hoped he was wrong, and not just because of the degree of fanaticism that act of self-immolation would represent.

Eight of Domynyk Staynair's galleons had gotten off with only negligible damage, or even completely untouched, but between them, the other seventeen Charisian ships engaged had suffered over three thousand casualties—four hundred of them aboard *Stonehill,* alone, when she blew up. That was nearly a third of their total complements, and of that total, half were dead, and many of the wounded were still going to die.

As High Admiral Bryahn Lock Island had died in the final, furious melee aboard NGS *Crusade.*

Yet terrible as Charis' losses had been, Kornylys Harpahr's had been worse. Of the Navy of God's seventy-four ships, only nine had escaped. Thirty-five of the Imperial Harchongese Navy's unarmed galleons had been taken, along with six of their armed galleons . . . five of which had surrendered to mere schooners, three without firing a single shot. The remainder of Harpahr's fleet had managed to escape mainly because there hadn't been enough Charisians with intact rigging to chase them, and only a handful of those escapees still had any interest in reaching Desnair. The rest were fleeing back the way they'd come.

The surrendered prizes were going to represent an enormous—and welcome—addition to the Charisian Navy's strength, and their loss represented a body blow to the Group of Four's plans. Merlin had no idea how the Group of Four was going to respond, but he didn't expect Zhaspahr Clyntahn to become any less fanatical in the face of this fresh defeat. And despite the Church's losses, the Temple still had the capacity to rebuild. The question was whether or not its leaders still had the will.

*Actually,* he thought, *I guess that's not the right question after all. The right question is probably whether or not they see any option* except *to rebuild and try again.*

"'The fortress of Charis is the wooden walls of her fleet,'" Cayleb quoted softly. He straightened, stepping back from Merlin's embrace, putting his own gloved hands on the *seijin*'s shoulders. "Old Zhan had that right, but he never mentioned the blood *inside* those walls."

"No, he didn't," Merlin agreed. "But it's not the walls themselves, Cayleb. And it's not the *blood* inside them; it's the *men* inside them. It's men like

Bryahn, and Domynyk. Like Captain Baikyr and Dunkyn Yairley. Like Hektor." He shook his head. "Cayleb, they knew exactly what they were doing . . . and they did it anyway. They walked straight into that holocaust because they thought it was their duty."

"*Duty!*" Cayleb repeated bitterly. "I am so sick—sick unto death—of seeing people die for 'duty,' Merlin!"

"Of course you are." Merlin smiled sadly, reaching out to cup Cayleb's head between his palms. "That's because you care. But riddle me this, Cayleb Ahrmahk. If you hadn't been here in Chisholm, instead, would you have been on the quarterdeck of one of those galleons?"

"Of course I would! It would've been—"

Cayleb broke off, and Merlin nodded.

"Your duty," he said softly. "And that's the true fortress of Charis, and of the Church of Charis, Cayleb. Duty. Responsibility. Love. Because that's the real basis of your sense of duty, and Bryahn's, and Maikel's, and Domynyk's, and Sharleyan's. You think *I* don't understand about 'duty,' Cayleb? That I don't know how much it hurts? The way it sticks in your throat sideways when you see everyone else you know and love laying down their *lives* out of 'duty'? But the reason they do it is the same reason you would—because they love something enough to die for it. They love their kingdom. They love their emperor and empress. They love their church and their God. They love freedom, and they love each other. And that, Cayleb—*that*—is the true fortress of Charis. I don't know where this war is going to go before it ends. I don't know how much more terrible the price is going to be. But I do know that as long as there are men like Bryahn and all the other men who followed him into that battle, the things you and Sharleyan and Maikel and Ahnzhelyk and Nahrmahn are fighting for will always have the champions they need."

"I know," Cayleb whispered, closing his eyes again. "And that's what terrifies me, Merlin. I'm going to need them, and I'm going to call on them, and I'm going to send them out, and they're going to *die.*"

"Everyone dies, Cayleb. Or at least, everyone but me." Cayleb couldn't see Merlin's smile through his closed eyes, but he felt the pain, the sorrow in it. "It's given to some of us, though, to die for the things we believe in. To know our lives—and our deaths—*mean* something. And it's your job, Your Grace— your *duty*—to see to it that those deaths *do* mean something."

"I know," Cayleb repeated very, very softly.

"I know you do." Merlin put his arm around the emperor's shoulders and gave him one last, quick hug.

"I know you do," he said again, more briskly. "But now, let's go inside and get you wrapped around a bowl of hot soup, Your Grace." He smiled again. "I think your wife and daughter are waiting for you."

# Characters

ABYLYN, CHARLZ—a senior leader of the Temple Loyalists in Charis.

AHBAHT, CAPTAIN RUHSAIL, IMPERIAL DESNAIRIAN NAVY—CO, HMS *Archangel Chihiro,* 40; Commodore Wailahr's flag captain.

AHBAHT, LYWYS—Edmynd Walkyr's brother-in-law; XO, merchant galleon *Wind.*

AHBAHT, ZHEFRY—Earl Gray Harbor's personal secretary. He fulfills many of the functions of an undersecretary of state for foreign affairs.

AHDYMSYN, BISHOP ZHERALD—previously Erayk Dynnys' bishop executor for Charis, now one of Archbishop Maikel's senior auxiliary bishops.

AHLBAIR, LIEUTENANT ZHEROHM, ROYAL CHARISIAN NAVY—first lieutenant, HMS *Typhoon.*

AHLDARM, MAHRYS OHLARN—Mahrys IV, Emperor of Desnair.

AHLVEREZ, ADMIRAL-GENERAL FAIDEL, DOHLARAN NAVY—Duke of Malikai; King Rahnyld IV of Dohlar's senior admiral.

AHRDYN—Archbishop Maikel's cat-lizard.

AHRMAHK, CAYLEB ZHAN HAARAHLD BRYAHN—Duke of Ahrmahk, Prince of Tellesberg, Prince Protector of the Realm, King Cayleb II of Charis, Emperor Cayleb I of Charis. Husband of Sharleyan Ahrmahk.

AHRMAHK, CROWN PRINCESS ALAHNAH ZHANAYT NAIMU—infant daughter of Cayleb and Sharleyan Ahrmahk; heir to the imperial Charisian crown.

AHRMAHK, KAHLVYN—Duke of Tirian (deceased), Constable of Hairatha, King Haarahld VII's first cousin.

AHRMAHK, KAHLVYN CAYLEB—Kahlvyn Ahrmahk's younger son.

AHRMAHK, KING HAARAHLD VII—King of Charis.

AHRMAHK, RAYJHIS—Duke of Tirian; Kahlvyn Ahrmahk's elder son and heir.

AHRMAHK, SHARLEYAN ALAHNAH ZHENYFYR AHLYSSA TAYT—Duchess of Cherayth, Lady Protector of Chisholm, Queen of Chisholm, Empress of Charis. Wife of Cayleb Ahrmahk. See also Sharleyan Tayt.

AHRMAHK, ZHAN—Crown Prince Zhan; King Cayleb's younger brother.

AHRMAHK, ZHANAYT—Queen Zhanayt; King Haarahld's deceased wife; mother of Cayleb, Zhanayt, and Zhan.

AHRMAHK, ZHANAYT—Princess Zhanayt; Cayleb Ahrmahk's younger sister, second eldest child of King Haarahld VII.

**AHRMAHK, ZHENYFYR**—Dowager Duchess of Tirian; mother of Kahlvyn Cayleb Ahrmahk; daughter of Rayjhis Yowance, Earl Gray Harbor.

**AHRTHYR, SIR ALYK, CORISANDIAN GUARD**—Earl of Windshare; Sir Koryn Gahrvai's cavalry commander.

**AHSTYN, LIEUTENANT FRANZ, CHARISIAN ROYAL GUARD**—the second-in-command of King Cayleb II's personal bodyguard.

**AHZGOOD, PHYLYP**—Earl of Coris; previously spymaster for Prince Hektor of Corisande; currently legal guardian for Princess Irys Daykyn and Prince Daivyn Daykyn.

**AIMAYL, RAHN**—a member of the anti-Charis resistance in Manchyr, Corisande. An ex-apprentice of Paitryk Hainree's.

**AIRYTH, EARL OF**—see Trumyn Sowthmyn.

**AIWAIN, CAPTAIN HARYS, IMPERIAL CHARISIAN NAVY**—CO, HMS *Shield,* 54.

**ALBAN, LIEUTENANT COMMANDER NIMUE, TFN**—Admiral Pei Kau-zhi's tactical officer.

**ANVIL ROCK, EARL OF**—See Sir Rysel Gahrvai.

**APLYN-AHRMAHK, ENSIGN HEKTOR, IMPERIAL CHARISIAN NAVY**—Duke of Darcos; acting lieutenant, HMS *Destiny,* 54. Cayleb Ahrmahk's adoptive son.

**ARCHBISHOP MAIKEL**—see Archbishop Maikel Staynair.

**ARCHBISHOP PAWAL**—see Archbishop Pawal Braynair.

**ARTHMYN, FATHER OHMAHR**—senior healer, Imperial Palace, Tellesberg.

**ATHRAWES, CAPTAIN MERLIN, CHARISIAN ROYAL GUARD**—King Cayleb II's personal armsman; the cybernetic avatar of Commander Nimue Alban.

**AYMEZ, MIDSHIPMAN BARDULF, ROYAL CHARISIAN NAVY**—a midshipman, HMS *Typhoon.*

**BAHLTYN, ZHEEVYS**—Baron White Ford's valet.

**BAHNYR, HEKTOR**—Earl of Mancora; one of Sir Koryn Gahrvai's senior officers; commander of the right wing at Haryl's Crossing.

**BAHR, DAHNNAH**—senior chef, Imperial Palace, Cherayth.

**BAHRDAILAHN, LIEUTENANT SIR AHBAIL, ROYAL DOHLARAN NAVY**—the Earl of Thirsk's flag lieutenant.

**BAHRMYN, ARCHBISHOP BORYS**—Archbishop of Corisande for the Church of God Awaiting.

**BAHRMYN, TOHMYS**—Baron White Castle; Prince Hektor's ambassador to Prince Nahrmahn.

**BAHRNS, KING RAHNYLD IV**—King of Dohlar.

**BAIKET, CAPTAIN STYWYRT, ROYAL DOHLARAN NAVY**—CO, HMS *Chihiro,* 50; the Earl of Thirsk's flag captain.

**BAIKYR, CAPTAIN SYLMAHN, IMPERIAL CHARISIAN NAVY**—CO, HMS *Ahrmahk,* 58. High Admiral Lock Island's flag captain.

**BAIRAHT, DAIVYN**—Duke of Kholman; effectively Emperor Mahrys IV's Navy Minister, Imperial Desnairian Navy.

**BANAHR, FATHER AHZWALD**—head of the priory of Saint Hamlyn, city of Sarayn, Kingdom of Charis.

**BARCOR, BARON OF**—see Sir Zher Sumyrs.

**BAYTZ, FELAYZ**—Prince Nahrmahn of Emerald's youngest child and second daughter.

**BAYTZ, HANBYL**—Duke of Solomon; Prince Nahrmahn of Emerald's uncle and the commander of the Emeraldian Army.

**BAYTZ, MAHRYA**—Prince Nahrmahn of Emerald's oldest child.

**BAYTZ, NAHRMAHN GAREYT**—second child and elder son of Prince Nahrmahn of Emerald.

**BAYTZ, NAHRMAHN HANBYL GRAIM**—See Prince Nahrmahn Baytz.

**BAYTZ, PRINCE NAHRMAHN II**—ruler of the Princedom of Emerald; Cayleb and Sharleyan Ahrmahk's Imperial Councilor for Intelligence.

**BAYTZ, PRINCESS OHLYVYA**—wife of Prince Nahrmahn of Emerald.

**BAYTZ, TRAHVYS**—Prince Nahrmahn of Emerald's third child and second son.

**BÉDARD, DR. ADORÉE, PH.D.**—Chief Psychiatrist, Operation Ark.

**BISHOP EXECUTOR WYLLYS**—see Bishop Executor Wyllys Graisyn.

**BISHOP ZHERALD**—see Bishop Zherald Ahdymsyn.

**BLACK WATER, DUKE OF**—see Ernyst Lynkyn.

**BLACK WATER, DUKE OF**—see Sir Adulfo Lynkyn.

**BLAHNDAI, CHANTAHAL**—an alias of Lysbet Wylsynn in Zion.

**BLAIDYN, LIEUTENANT ROZHYR, ROYAL DOHLARAN NAVY**—second lieutenant, galley *Royal Bédard*.

**BORYS, ARCHBISHOP**—see Archbishop Borys Bahrmyn.

**BOWAVE, DAIRAK**—Dr. Rahzhyr Mahklyn's senior assistant, Royal College, Tellesberg.

**BOWSHAM, CAPTAIN KHANAIR, ROYAL CHARISIAN MARINES**—CO, HMS *Gale*.

**BRADLAI, LIEUTENANT ROBYRT, CORISANDIAN NAVY**—true name of Captain Styvyn Whaite.

**BRAYNAIR, ARCHBISHOP PAWAL**—Archbishop of Chisholm for the Church of Charis.

**BREYGART, COLONEL SIR HAUWERD, ROYAL CHARISIAN MARINES**—the rightful heir to the Earldom of Hanth. Becomes earl 893.

**BREYGART, FRAIDARECK**—fourteenth Earl of Hanth; Hauwerd Breygart's great-grandfather.

**BROUN, FATHER MAHTAIO**—Archbishop Erayk Dynnys' senior secretary and aide; Archbishop Erayk's confidant and protégé.

**BROWNYNG, CAPTAIN ELLYS**—CO, Temple galleon *Blessed Langhorne*.

**BRYNDYN, MAJOR DAHRYN**—the senior artillery officer attached to Brigadier Clareyk's column at Haryl's Priory.

**BYRK, MAJOR BREKYN, ROYAL CHARISIAN MARINES**—CO, Marine detachment, HMS *Royal Charis.*

**BYRKYT, FATHER ZHON**—an over-priest of the Church of God Awaiting; abbot of the Monastery of Saint Zherneau.

**CAHKRAYN, SAMYL**—Duke of Fern, King Rahnyld IV of Dohlar's first councilor.

**CAHMMYNG, AHLBAIR**—a professional assassin working for Father Aidryn Waimyn.

**CAHNYR, ARCHBISHOP ZHASYN**—Archbishop of Glacierheart for the Church of God Awaiting; a Reformist member of Samyl Wylsynn's circle.

**CHAHLMAIR, SIR BAIRMON**—Duke of Margo; a member of Prince Daivyn's Regency Council.

**CHAIMBYRS, LIEUTENANT ZHUSTYN, IMPERIAL DESNAIRIAN NAVY**—second lieutenant, HMS *Archangel Chihiro,* 40.

**CHALMYR, LIEUTENANT MAILVYN, ROYAL CHARISIAN NAVY**—first lieutenant, HMS *Tellesberg.*

**CHALMYRZ, FATHER KARLOS**—Archbishop Borys Bahrmyn's aide and secretary.

**CHARLZ, CAPTAIN MARIK**—CO, Charisian merchant ship *Wave Daughter.*

**CHARLZ, MASTER YEREK, ROYAL CHARISIAN NAVY**—gunner, HMS *Wave,* 14.

**CHERMYN, VICEROY GENERAL HAUWYL, IMPERIAL CHARISIAN MARINES**—CO, Charisian occupation forces in Corisande. Cayleb and Sharleyan Ahrmahk's regent in Corisande.

**CHERYNG, LIEUTENANT TAIWYL**—a junior officer on Sir Vyk Lakyr's staff; he is in charge of Lakyr's clerks and message traffic.

**CLAREYK, GENERAL KYNT, IMPERIAL CHARISIAN ARMY**—Baron of Green Valley. Ex-brigadier, Imperial Charisian Marines.

**CLYNTAHN, VICAR ZHASPAHR**—Grand Inquisitor of the Church of God Awaiting; one of the so-called Group of Four.

**COHLMYN, ADMIRAL SIR LEWK, IMPERIAL CHARISIAN NAVY**—Earl of Sharpfield, second–ranking officer, Imperial Charisian Navy. Ex–Royal Chisholmian Navy.

**CORIS, EARL OF**—see Phylyp Ahzgood.

**CRAGGY HILL, EARL OF**—see Wahlys Hillkeeper.

**DAHNZAI, LYZBYT**—Father Zhaif Laityr's housekeeper at the Church of the Holy Archangels Triumphant.

**DAHRYUS, MASTER EDVARHD**—an alias of Bishop Mylz Halcom.

**DAIKHAR, LIEUTENANT MOHTOHKAI, IMPERIAL CHARISIAN NAVY**—XO, HMS *Dart,* 54.

**DAIKYN, GAHLVYN**—King Cayleb's valet.

**DAIVYS, MYTRAHN**—a Charisian Temple Loyalist.

**DARCOS, DUKE OF**—see Ensign Hektor Aplyn-Ahrmahk.

**DARYS, CAPTAIN TYMYTHY, IMPERIAL CHARISIAN NAVY**—CO, HMS *Destroyer*, 54. Sir Domynyk Staynair's flag captain.

**DAYKYN, DAIVYN**—Prince Hektor of Corisande's youngest child. Prince of Corisande in exile following his father's assassination.

**DAYKYN, HEKTOR**—Prince of Corisande, leader of the League of Corisande. Assassinated 893.

**DAYKYN, HEKTOR (THE YOUNGER)**—Prince Hektor of Corisande's second oldest child and heir apparent. Assassinated 893.

**DAYKYN, IRYS**—daughter of Prince Hektor of Corisande; older sister of Prince Daivyn.

**DAYKYN, RAICHYNDA**—Prince Hektor of Corisande's deceased wife; born in Earldom of Domair, Kingdom of Hoth.

**DEEP HOLLOW, EARL OF**—see Bryahn Selkyr.

**DEKYN, SERGEANT ALLAYN**—one of Kairmyn's noncoms, Delferahkan Army.

**DOBYNS, CHARLZ**—son of Ezmelda Dobyns; sometime supporter of the anti-Charis resistance in Manchyr, Corisande.

**DOBYNS, EZMELDA**—Father Tymahn Hahskans' housekeeper at Saint Kathryn's Church.

**DOYAL, SIR CHARLZ, CORISANDIAN GUARD**—former artillery commander in Prince Hektor's field army; now chief of staff and senior intelligence officer for Sir Koryn Gahrvai.

**DRAGONER, CORPORAL ZHAK, ROYAL CHARISIAN MARINES**—a member of Crown Prince Cayleb's bodyguard.

**DRAGONER, SIR RAYJHIS**—Charisian ambassador to the Siddarmark Republic.

**DRAGONMASTER, BRIGADE SERGEANT MAJOR MAHKYNTY ("MAHK"), RCMC**—Brigadier Clareyk's senior noncom during Corisande Campaign.

**DUCHAIRN, VICAR RHOBAIR**—Minister of Treasury, Council of Vicars; one of the so-called Group of Four.

**DYMYTREE, FRONZ, ROYAL CHARISIAN MARINES**—a member of Crown Prince Cayleb's bodyguard.

**DYNNYS, ADORAI**—Archbishop Erayk Dynnys' wife.

**DYNNYS, ARCHBISHOP ERAYK**—Archbishop of Charis. Executed for heresy 892.

**DYNNYS, STYVYN**—Archbishop Erayk Dynnys' younger son, age eleven in 892.

**DYNNYS, TYMYTHY ERAYK**—Archbishop Erayk Dynnys' older son, age fourteen in 892.

**EASTSHARE, DUKE OF**—see Ruhsyl Thairis.

**EDWYRDS, KEVYN**—XO, privateer galleon *Kraken*.

**EKYRD, CAPTAIN HAYRYS, DOHLARAN NAVY**—CO, galley *King Rahnyld*.

**EMPEROR CAYLEB**—see Cayleb Ahrmahk.

**EMPEROR MAHRYS IV**—see Mahrys Ohlarn Ahldarm.

**EMPEROR WAISU VI**—see Waisu Hantai.

**EMPRESS SHARLEYAN**—see Sharleyan Ahrmahk.

**ERAYK, ARCHBISHOP**—see Erayk Dynnys.

**ERAYKSYN, LIEUTENANT STYVYN, IMPERIAL CHARISIAN NAVY**—Sir Domynyk Staynair's flag lieutenant.

**ERAYKSYN, WYLLYM**—a Charisian textiles manufacturer.

**FAHRMAHN, PRIVATE LUHYS, ROYAL CHARISIAN MARINES**—a member of Crown Prince Cayleb's bodyguard.

**FAHRMYN, FATHER TAIRYN**—the priest assigned to Saint Chihiro's Church, a village church near the Convent of Saint Agtha.

**FAHRNO, MAHRLYS**—one of Madam Ahnzhelyk Phonda's courtesans.

**FAIRCASTER, SERGEANT PAYTER, CHARISIAN ROYAL GUARD**—one of Emperor Cayleb's personal guardsmen. A transferee from Crown Prince Cayleb's Marine detachment.

**FAIRYS, COLONEL AHLVYN, IMPERIAL CHARISIAN MARINES**—CO, First Regiment, Third Brigade, ICMC.

**FALKHAN, LIEUTENANT AHRNAHLD, ROYAL CHARISIAN MARINES**—CO, Crown Prince Cayleb's personal bodyguard. Later CO, Prince Zhan Ahrmahk's bodyguard.

**FATHER MICHAEL**—parish priest of Lakeview.

**FERN, DUKE OF**—see Samyl Cahkrayn.

**FHAIRLY, MAJOR AHDYM**—the senior battery commander on East Island, Ferayd Sound, Kingdom of Delferahk.

**FHARMYN, SIR RYK**—a foundry owner/ironmaster in the Kingdom of Tarot.

**FOFÃO, CAPTAIN MATEUS, TERRAN FEDERATION NAVY**—CO, TFNS *Swiftsure*.

**FORYST, VICAR ERAYK**—a member of the Reformists.

**FRAIDMYN, SERGEANT VYK, CHARISIAN ROYAL GUARD**—one of King Cayleb II's armsmen.

**FUHLLYR, FATHER RAIMAHND**—chaplain, HMS *Dreadnought*.

**FURKHAL, RAFAYL**—second baseman and leadoff hitter, Tellesberg Krakens.

**FYSHYR, HARYS**—CO, privateer galleon *Kraken*.

**GAHRBOR, ARCHBISHOP FAILYX**—Archbishop of Tarot for the Church of God Awaiting.

**GAHRDANER, SERGEANT CHARLZ, CHARISIAN ROYAL GUARD**—one of King Haarahld VII's bodyguards.

**GAHRMYN, LIEUTENANT RAHNYLD**—XO, galley *Arrowhead,* Delferahkan Navy.

**GAHRNAHT, BISHOP AMILAIN**—deposed Bishop of Larchros.

**GAHRVAI, GENERAL SIR KORYN, CORISANDIAN GUARD**—Prince Hektor's army field commander; now CO, Corisandian Guard, in the service of the Regency Council. Son of Earl Anvil Rock.

**GAHRVAI, SIR RYSEL**—Earl of Anvil Rock; Prince Daivyn Daykyn's official regent; head of Daivyn's Regency Council in Corisande.

**GAIRAHT, CAPTAIN WYLLYS, CHISHOLMIAN ROYAL GUARD**—CO of Queen Sharleyan's royal guard detachment in Charis.

**GAIRLYNG, ARCHBISHOP KLAIRMANT**—Archbishop of Corisande for the Church of Charis.

**GALVAHN, MAJOR SIR NAITHYN**—the Earl of Windshare's senior staff officer; Corisande Campaign.

**GARDYNYR, ADMIRAL LYWYS, ROYAL DOHLARAN NAVY**—Earl of Thirsk and King Rahnyld IV's best admiral.

**GARTHIN, EDWAIR**—Earl of North Coast; one of Prince Hektor's councilors; now serving on Prince Daivyn's Regency Council.

**GHATFRYD, SANDARIA**—Ahnzhelyk Phonda's/Nynian Rychtair's personal maid.

**GORJAH, FATHER GHARTH**—Archbishop Zhasyn Cahnyr's personal secretary.

**GORJAH, SAHMANTHA**—Father Gharth Gorjah's wife.

**GORJAH, ZHASYN**—firstborn child of Gharth and Sahmantha Gorjah.

**GRAHZAIAL, LIEUTENANT COMMANDER MAHSHAL, IMPERIAL CHARISIAN NAVY**—CO, schooner HMS *Messenger,* 6.

**GRAISYN, BISHOP EXECUTOR WYLLYS**—Archbishop Lyam Tyrn's chief administrator for the Archbishopric of Emerald.

**GRAIVYR, FATHER STYVYN**—Bishop Ernyst's intendant, Ferayd, Delferahk.

**GRAND VICAR EREK XVII**—secular and temporal head of the Church of God Awaiting.

**GRAY HARBOR, EARL OF**—see Rayjhis Yowance.

**GREEN MOUNTAIN, BARON OF**—see Mahrak Sahndyrs.

**GREEN VALLEY, BARON OF**—see General Kynt Clareyk.

**GREENHILL, TYMAHN**—King Haarahld VII's senior huntsman.

**GUYSHAIN, FATHER BAHRNAI**—Vicar Zahmsyn Trynair's senior aide.

**GYRARD, CAPTAIN ANDRAI, ROYAL CHARISIAN NAVY**—CO, HMS *Empress of Charis.*

**HAARPAR, SERGEANT GORJ, CHARISIAN ROYAL GUARD**—one of King Haarahld VII's bodyguards.

**HAHLEK, FATHER SYMYN**—Archbishop Klairmant Gairlyng's personal aide.

**HAHLMAHN, PAWAL**—King Haarahld VII's senior chamberlain.

**HAHLMYN, FATHER MAHRAK**—an upper-priest of the Church of God Awaiting; Bishop Executor Thomys Shylair's personal aide.

**HAHLMYN, MIDSHIPMAN ZHORJ, IMPERIAL CHARISIAN NAVY**—a signals midshipman aboard HMS *Darcos Sound,* 54.

**HAHLMYN, SAIRAIH**—Sharleyan Ahrmahk's personal maid.

**HAHLTAR, ADMIRAL GENERAL SIR URWYN, IMPERIAL DESNAIRIAN NAVY**—Baron Jahras; commanding officer, Imperial Desnairian Navy.

**HAHLYND, ADMIRAL PAWAL, ROYAL DOHLARAN NAVY**—the Earl of Thirsk's senior subordinate admiral.

**HAHLYND, FATHER MAHRAK**—Bishop Executor Thomys Shylair's personal aide.

**HAHSKANS, DAILOHRS**—Father Tymahn Hahskans' wife.

**HAHSKANS, FATHER TYMAHN**—a Reformist upper-priest of the Order of Bédard in Manchyr; senior priest, Saint Kathryn's Church.

**HAHSKYN, LIEUTENANT AHNDRAI, CHARISIAN IMPERIAL GUARD**—a Charisian officer assigned to Empress Sharleyan's guard detachment. Captain Gairaht's second-in-command.

**HAHVAIR, COMMANDER FRANZ, IMPERIAL CHARISIAN NAVY**—CO, schooner HMS *Mace,* 12.

**HAIMLTAHN, BISHOP EXECUTOR WYLLYS**—Archbishop Zhasyn Cahnyr's executive assistant in the Archbishopric of Glacierheart.

**HAIMYN, BRIGADIER MAHRYS, ROYAL CHARISIAN MARINES**—CO, Fifth Brigade, RCMC.

**HAINREE, PAITRYK**—a silversmith and Temple Loyalist agitator in Manchyr, Princedom of Corisande.

**HALCOM, BISHOP MYLZ**—Bishop of Margaret Bay.

**HALMYN, ARCHBISHOP ZAHMSYN**—Archbishop of Gorath; senior prelate of the Kingdom of Dohlar.

**HANTAI, WAISU**—Waisu VI, Emperor of Harchong.

**HANTH, EARL**—see Tahdayo Mahntayl. See also Sir Hauwerd Breygart.

**HARMYN, MAJOR BAHRKLY, EMERALD ARMY**—an Emeraldian army officer assigned to North Bay.

**HARPAHR, BISHOP KORNYLYS**—Bishop of the Order of Chihiro; Admiral General of the Navy of God.

**HARRISON, MATTHEW PAUL**—Timothy and Sarah Harrison's great-grandson.

**HARRISON, ROBERT**—Timothy and Sarah Harrison's grandson; Matthew Paul Harrison's father.

**HARRISON, SARAH**—wife of Timothy Harrison and an Eve.

**HARRISON, TIMOTHY**—Mayor of Lakeview and an Adam.

**HARYS, CAPTAIN ZHOEL, ROYAL CORISANDIAN NAVY**—CO, galley *Lance.* Later CO, galleon *Wing;* responsible for transporting Princess Irys and Prince Daivyn to safety.

**HARYS, FATHER AHLBYRT**—Vicar Zahmsyn Trynair's special representative to Dohlar.

**HASKYN, MIDSHIPMAN YAHNCEE, ROYAL DOHLARAN NAVY**—a midshipman aboard *Gorath Bay.*

**HAUWYRD, ZHORZH**—Earl Gray Harbor's personal guardsman.

**HENDERSON, LIEUTENANT GABRIELA ("GABBY"), TERRAN FEDERATION NAVY**—tactical officer, TFNS *Swiftsure.*

**HILLKEEPER, WAHLYS**—Earl of Craggy Hill; a member of Prince Daivyn's Regency Council; also a senior member of the Northern Conspiracy.

**HOLDYN, VICAR LYWYS**—a member of the Reformists.

**HOTCHKYS, CAPTAIN SIR OHWYN, ROYAL CHARISIAN NAVY**—CO, HMS *Tellesberg*.

**HOWSMYN, EHDWYRD**—a wealthy foundry owner and shipbuilder in Tellesberg.

**HOWSMYN, ZHAIN**—Ehdwyrd Howsmyn's wife.

**HUNTYR, LIEUTENANT KLEMYNT, CHARISIAN ROYAL GUARD**—an officer of the Charisian Royal Guard in Tellesberg.

**HWYSTYN, SIR VYRNYN**—a member of the Charisian Parliament elected from Tellesberg.

**HYLLAIR, SIR FARAHK**—Baron of Dairwyn.

**HYNDRYK, COMMODORE SIR AHLFRYD, IMPERIAL CHARISIAN NAVY**—Baron Seamount; Imperial Navy's senior gunnery expert. Effectively CO, Imperial Charisian Navy R&D.

**HYNDYRS, DUNKYN**—purser, privateer galleon *Raptor*.

**HYRST, ADMIRAL ZOHZEF, CHISHOLMIAN NAVY**—Earl Sharpfield's second-in-command.

**HYSIN, VICAR CHIYAN**—a member of the Reformists (from Harchong).

**HYWSTYN, LORD AVRAHM**—a cousin of Greyghor Stohnar, and a midranking official assigned to the Siddarmarkian foreign ministry.

**HYWYT, COMMANDER PAITRYK, ROYAL CHARISIAN NAVY**—CO, HMS *Wave*, 14 (schooner). Later promoted to captain as CO, HMS *Dancer*, 56.

**ILLIAN, CAPTAIN AHNTAHN**—one of Sir Phylyp Myllyr's company commanders.

**JAHRAS, BARON OF**—see Admiral General Sir Urwyn Hahltar.

**JYNKYN, COLONEL HAUWYRD, ROYAL CHARISIAN MARINES**—Admiral Staynair's senior Marine commander.

**JYNKYNS, BISHOP ERNYST**—Bishop of Ferayd.

**KAHNKLYN, AIDRYN**—Tairys Kahnklyn's older daughter.

**KAHNKLYN, AIZAK**—Rahzhyr Mahklyn's son-in-law.

**KAHNKLYN, ERAYK**—Tairys Kahnklyn's oldest son.

**KAHNKLYN, EYDYTH**—Tairys Kahnklyn's younger daughter.

**KAHNKLYN, HAARAHLD**—Tairys Kahnklyn's middle son.

**KAHNKLYN, TAIRYS**—Rahzhyr Mahklyn's married daughter.

**KAHNKLYN, ZHOEL**—Tairys Kahnklyn's youngest son.

**KAHRNAIKYS, MAJOR ZHAPHAR, TEMPLE GUARD**—an officer of the Temple Guard and a Schuelerite.

**KAILLEE, CAPTAIN ZHILBERT, TAROTISIAN NAVY**—CO, galley *King Gorjah II*.

**KAIREE, TRAIVYR**—a wealthy merchant and landowner in the Earldom of Styvyn.

**KAIRMYN, CAPTAIN TOMHYS**—one of Sir Vyk Lakyr's officers, Delferahkan Army.

**KAITS, CAPTAIN BAHRNABAI, IMPERIAL CHARISIAN MARINES**—CO, Marine detachment, HMS *Squall,* 36.

**KEELHAUL**—High Admiral Lock Island's rottweiler.

**KESTAIR, AHRDYN**—Archbishop Maikel's married daughter.

**KESTAIR, SIR LAIRYNC**—Archbishop Maikel's son-in-law.

**KHAILEE, MASTER ROLF**—a pseudonym used by Lord Avrahm Hywstyn.

**KHAPAHR, COMMANDER AHLVYN, ROYAL DOHLARAN NAVY**—effectively the Earl of Thirsk's chief of staff.

**KHATTYR, CAPTAIN PAYT, EMERALD NAVY**—CO, galley *Black Prince.*

**KHOLMAN, DUKE OF**—see Daivyn Bairaht.

**KHOWSAN, CAPTAIN OF WINDS SHOUKHAN, IMPERIAL HARCHONGESE NAVY**—Count of Wind Mountain; CO, IHNS *Flower of Waters;* 50. Flag captain to the Duke of Sun Rising.

**KING GORJAH III**—see Gorjah Nyou.

**KING HAARAHLD VII**—see Haarahld Ahrmahk.

**KING RAHNYLD IV**—see Rahnyld Bahrns.

**KING ZHAMES II**—see Zhames Rayno.

**KLAHRKSAIN, CAPTAIN TYMAHN, IMPERIAL CHARISIAN NAVY**—CO, HMS *Talisman,* 54.

**KNOWLES, EVELYN**—an Eve who escaped the destruction of the Alexandria Enclave and fled to Tellesberg.

**KNOWLES, JEREMIAH**—an Adam who escaped the destruction of the Alexandria Enclave and fled to Tellesberg, where he became the patron and founder of the Brethren of Saint Zherneau.

**KOHRBY, MIDSHIPMAN LYNAIL, ROYAL CHARISIAN NAVY**—senior midshipman, HMS *Dreadnought.*

**KRAHL, CAPTAIN AHNDAIR, ROYAL DOHLARAN NAVY**—CO, HMS *Bédard,* 42.

**KRUGHAIR, LIEUTENANT ZHASYN, IMPERIAL CHARISIAN NAVY**—second lieutenant, HMS *Dancer,* 56.

**LAHANG, BRAIDEE**—Prince Nahrmahn of Emerald's chief agent in Charis before Merlin Athrawes' arrival there.

**LAHFAT, CAPTAIN MYRGYN**—piratical ruler of Claw Keep on Claw Island.

**LAHFTYN, MAJOR BRYAHN**—Brigadier Clareyk's chief of staff.

**LAHRAK, NAILYS**—a senior leader of the Temple Loyalists in Charis.

**LAHSAHL, LIEUTENANT SHAIRMYN, IMPERIAL CHARISIAN NAVY**—XO, HMS *Destroyer,* 54.

**LAIMHYN, FATHER CLYFYRD**—Emperor Cayleb's personal secretary, assigned to him by Archbishop Maikel.

**LAIRAYS, FATHER AWBRAI**—under-priest of the Order of Schueler; HMS *Archangel Chihiro*'s ship's chaplain.

**LAITYR, FATHER ZHAIF**—a Reformist upper-priest of the Order of Pasquale; senior priest, Church of the Holy Archangels Triumphant; a close personal friend of Father Tymahn Hahskans'.

**LAKYR, SIR VYK**—SO, Ferayd garrison, Kingdom of Delferahk.

**LANGHORNE, ERIC**—Chief Administrator, Operation Ark.

**LARCHROS, BARON OF**—see Rahzhyr Mairwan.

**LARCHROS, BARONESS OF**—see Raichenda Mairwyn.

**LATHYK, LIEUTENANT RHOBAIR, IMPERIAL CHARISIAN NAVY**—XO, HMS *Destiny*, 54.

**LAYN, MAJOR ZHIM, ROYAL CHARISIAN MARINE CORPS**—Brigadier Kynt's subordinate for original syllabus development. Now the senior training officer, Helen Island Marine Base.

**LEKTOR, ADMIRAL SIR TARYL**—Earl of Tartarian; commanding officer, Royal Corisandian Navy under Prince Hektor during Corisande Campaign; Earl Anvil Rock's main ally since Hektor's death; another member of Prince Daivyn's Regency Council.

**LOCK ISLAND, HIGH ADMIRAL BRYAHN, IMPERIAL CHARISIAN NAVY**—Earl of Lock Island; commanding officer, Imperial Charisian Navy. Cayleb Ahrmahk's cousin.

**LORD PROTECTOR GREYGHOR**—see Greyghor Stohnar.

**LYAM, ARCHBISHOP**—see Archbishop Lyam Tyrn.

**LYNDAHR, SIR RAIMYND**—Prince Hektor's keeper of the purse; now serving on Prince Daivyn's Regency Council.

**LYNKYN, SIR ERNYST, CORISANDIAN NAVY**—Duke of Black Water (deceased), CO, Corisandian Navy; KIA, Battle of Darcos Sound.

**LYNKYN, SIR ADULFO**—Duke of Black Water; son of Sir Ernyst Lynkyn.

**LYWKYS, LADY MAIRAH**—Empress Sharleyan's chief lady-in-waiting. She is Baron Green Mountain's cousin.

**LYWYS, DR. SAHNDRAH**—faculty member, Royal College, Tellesberg, specializing in chemistry.

**MAHGAIL, CAPTAIN RAIF, IMPERIAL CHARISIAN NAVY**—CO, HMS *Dancer*, 56. Sir Gwylym Manthyr's flag captain.

**MAHGENTEE, MIDSHIPMAN MAHRAK, ROYAL CHARISIAN NAVY**—senior midshipman, HMS *Typhoon*.

**MAHKELYN, LIEUTENANT RHOBAIR, ROYAL CHARISIAN NAVY**—fourth lieutenant, HMS *Destiny*, 54.

**MAHKHYNROH, BISHOP KAISI**—Bishop of Manchyr for the Church of Charis.

**MAHKLYN, DR. RAHZHYR**—Chancellor, Royal College, Tellesberg. Chairman, Imperial Council of Inquiry.

**MAHKLYN, TOHMYS**—Rahzhyr Mahklyn's unmarried son.

**MAHKLYN, YSBET**—Rahzhyr Mahklyn's deceased wife.

**MAHKNEEL, CAPTAIN HAUWYRD**—CO, galley *Arrowhead*, Delferahkan Navy.

**MAHLDYN, LIEUTENANT ZHAMES, IMPERIAL CHARISIAN NAVY**—XO, HMS *Squall*, 36.

**MAHLRY, LIEUTENANT RHOLYND, EMERALD NAVY**—a lieutenant aboard galley *Black Prince*.

**MAHLYK, STYWYRT**—Captain Yairley's personal coxswain.

**MAHNDRAYN, COMMANDER URVYN, IMPERIAL CHARISIAN NAVY**—CO, Experimental Board. Commodore Seamount's senior assistant.

**MAHNDYR, EARL**—see Gharth Rahlstahn.

**MAHNTAIN, CAPTAIN TOHMYS, IMPERIAL DESNAIRIAN NAVY**—CO, HMS *Blessed Warrior*, 40.

**MAHNTAYL, TAHDAYO**—usurper Earl of Hanth.

**MAHNTEE, LIEUTENANT CHARLZ, ROYAL DOHLARAN NAVY**—XO, HMS *Rakurai*, 46.

**MAHNTYN, CORPORAL AILAS**—a scout-sniper assigned to Sergeant Edvarhd Wystahn's platoon.

**MAHRAK, LIEUTENANT RAHNALD, ROYAL CHARISIAN NAVY**—first lieutenant, HMS *Royal Charis*.

**MAHRLOW, BISHOP EXECUTOR AHRAIN**—Archbishop Zahmsyn Halmyn's executive assistant, Archbishopric of Gorath, Kingdom of Dohlar.

**MAHRTYN, ADMIRAL GAHVYN, ROYAL TAROTISIAN NAVY**—Baron of White Ford. Senior officer, Royal Tarotisian Navy.

**MAHRTYNSYN, LIEUTENANT LAIZAIR, IMPERIAL DESNAIRIAN NAVY**—XO, HMS *Archangel Chihiro*, 40.

**MAHRYS, ZHERYLD**—Sir Rayjhis Dragoner's secretary.

**MAIGEE, CAPTAIN GRAYGAIR, ROYAL DOHLARAN NAVY**—CO, galleon *Guardian*.

**MAIGEE, PLATOON SERGEANT ZHAK, IMPERIAL CHARISIAN MARINES**—senior noncom, Second Platoon, Alpha Company, ⅓rd Marines, ICMC.

**MAIGWAIR, VICAR ALLAYN**—Captain General of the Church of God Awaiting; one of the so-called Group of Four.

**MAIK, BISHOP STAIPHAN**—a Schuelerite auxiliary bishop of the Church of God Awaiting; effectively intendant for the Royal Dohlaran Navy in the Church's name.

**MAIKEL, CAPTAIN QWENTYN, ROYAL DOHLARAN NAVY**—CO, galley *Gorath Bay*.

**MAIKELSYN, LIEUTENANT LEEAHM, ROYAL TAROTISIAN NAVY**—first lieutenant, *King Gorjah II*.

**MAIRWYN, RAHZHYR**—Baron of Larchros; a member of the Northern Conspiracy in Corisande.

**MAIRWYN, RAICHENDA**—Baroness of Larchros; wife of Rahzhyr Mairwyn.

**MAIRYDYTH, LIEUTENANT NEVYL, ROYAL DOHLARAN NAVY**—first lieutenant, galley *Royal Bédard*.

**MAIYR, CAPTAIN ZHAKSYN**—one of Colonel Sir Wahlys Zhorj's troop commanders in Tahdayo Mahntayl's service.

**MAKAIVYR, BRIGADIER ZHOSH, ROYAL CHARISIAN MARINE CORPS**—CO, First Brigade, RCMC.

**MAKFERZAHN, ZHAMES**—one of Prince Hektor's agents in Charis.

**MAKGREGAIR, FATHER ZHOSHUA**—Vicar Zahmsyn Trynair's special representative to Tarot.

**MALIKAI, DUKE OF**—see Faidel Ahlverez.

**MANTHYR, ADMIRAL SIR GWYLYM, IMPERIAL CHARISIAN NAVY**—previously Cayleb Ahrmahk's flag captain for the Armageddon Reef and Darcos Sound campaigns. CO, Charisian expedition to Gulf of Dohlar.

**MARGO, DUKE OF**—see Sir Bairmon Chahlmair.

**MARSHYL, MIDSHIPMAN ADYM, ROYAL CHARISIAN NAVY**—senior midshipman, HMS *Royal Charis.*

**MATHYSYN, LIEUTENANT ZHAIKEB, ROYAL DOHLARAN NAVY**—first lieutenant, galley *Gorath Bay.*

**MAYLYR, CAPTAIN DUNKYN, ROYAL CHARISIAN NAVY**—CO, HMS *Halberd.*

**MAYSAHN, ZHASPAHR**—Prince Hektor's senior agent in Charis.

**MAYTHIS, LIEUTENANT FRAIZHER, ROYAL CORISANDIAN NAVY**—true name of Captain Wahltayr Seatown.

**MHULVAYN, OSKAHR**—one of Prince Hektor's agents in Charis.

**MYCHAIL, ALYX**—Rhaiyan Mychail's oldest grandson.

**MYCHAIL, MYLDRYD**—one of Rhaiyan Mychail's married granddaughters-in-law.

**MYCHAIL, RHAIYAN**—a business partner of Ehdwyrd Howsmyn and the Kingdom of Charis' primary textile producer.

**MYCHAIL, STYVYN**—Myldryd Mychail's youngest son.

**MYLLYR, ARCHBISHOP URVYN**—Archbishop of Sodar.

**MYLLYR, SIR PHYLYP**—one of Sir Koryn Gahrvai's regimental commanders, Corisande Campaign.

**MYLS, BRIGADIER GWYAHN, IMPERIAL CHARISIAN MARINES**—CO, Second Regiment, Third Brigade, ICMC.

**MYRGYN, SIR KEHVYN, ROYAL CORISANDIAN NAVY**—CO, galley *Corisande.* Duke Black Water's flag captain. KIA, Battle of Darcos Sound.

**NAIKLOS, CAPTAIN FRAHNKLYN, CORISANDIAN GUARD**—CO of Sir Koryn Gahrvai's headquarters company; later promoted to major.

**NARTH, BISHOP EXECUTOR TYRNYR**—Archbishop Failyx Gahrbor's executive assistant, Archbishopric of Tarot.

**NETHAUL, HAIRYM**—XO, privateer schooner *Blade.*

**NOHRCROSS, BISHOP MAILVYN**—Bishop of Barcor for the Church of Charis; a member of the Northern Conspiracy in Corisande.

**NORTH COAST, EARL OF**—see Edwair Garthin.

**NYLZ, ADMIRAL KOHDY, IMPERIAL CHARISIAN NAVY**—senior squadron commander, ICN; previously commodore, Royal Charisian Navy.

**NYOU, GORJAH**—King Gorjah III, King of Tarot.

**NYOU, MAIYL**—Queen Consort of Tarot; wife of Gorjah Nyou.

**NYOU, RHOLYND**—Crown Prince of Tarot; infant son of Gorjah and Maiyl Nyou; heir to the Tarotisian throne.

**OARMASTER, SYGMAHN, ROYAL CHARISIAN MARINES**—a member of Crown Prince Cayleb's bodyguard.

**OHLSYN, TRAHVYS**—Earl of Pine Hollow, Prince Nahrmahn of Emerald's first councilor and cousin.

**OLYVYR, AHNYET**—Sir Dustyn Olyvyr's wife.

**OLYVYR, SIR DUSTYN**—a leading Tellesberg ship designer; chief constructor, Royal Charisian Navy.

**OWL**—Nimue Alban's AI, based on the manufacturer's acronym: Ordoñes-Westinghouse-Lytton RAPIER Tactical Computer, Mark 17a.

**PAHLZAR, COLONEL AHKYLLYS**—Sir Charlz Doyal's replacement as Sir Koryn Gahrvai's senior artillery commander.

**PAHRAIHA, COLONEL VAHSAG, IMPERIAL CHARISIAN MARINES**—CO, Fourteenth Marine Regiment.

**PAWAL, CAPTAIN ZHON, IMPERIAL CHARISIAN NAVY**—CO, HMS *Dart,* 54.

**PAWALSYN, AHLVYNO**—Baron Ironhill, keeper of the purse (treasurer) of the Kingdom of Old Charis.

**PEI, KAU-YUNG, COMMODORE, TERRAN FEDERATION NAVY**—CO, Operation Ark final escort; husband of Dr. Pei Shan-wei.

**PEI, KAU-ZHI, ADMIRAL, TERRAN FEDERATION NAVY**—CO, Operation Breakaway; older brother of Commodore Pei Kau-yung.

**PEI, SHAN-WEI, PH.D.**—Commodore Pei Kau-yung's wife; senior terraforming expert for Operation Ark.

**PHALGRAIN, SIR HARVAI**—majordomo, Imperial Palace, Cherayth.

**PHANDYS, CAPTAIN KHANSTAHNZO**—an officer of the Temple Guard.

**PHONDA, AHNZHELYK**—an alias of Nynian Rychtair; one of the most successful courtesans in the city of Zion; an agent and ally of Samyl Wylsynn.

**PINE HOLLOW, EARL**—see Trahvys Ohlsyn.

**PORTYR, MAJOR DANYEL, IMPERIAL CHARISIAN MARINE CORPS**—CO, First Battalion, Third Regiment, Third Brigade.

**PRINCE CAYLEB**—see Cayleb Ahrmahk.

**PRINCE DAIVYN**—see Daivyn Daykyn.

**PRINCE HEKTOR**—see Hektor Daykyn.

**PRINCE NAHRMAHN**—see Nahrmahn Baytz.

**PRINCE RHOLYND**—see Rholynd Nyou.

**PRINCESS IRYS**—see Irys Daykyn.

**PROCTOR, DR. ELIAS, PH.D.**—a member of Pei Shan-wei's staff and a noted cyberneticist.

**QUEEN CONSORT HAILYN**—see Hailyn Rayno.

**QUEEN MAIYL**—see Maiyl Nyou.

**QUEEN SHARLEYAN**—see Sharleyan Tayt.

**QUEEN YSBELL**—an earlier reigning queen of Chisholm who was deposed (and murdered) in favor of a male ruler.

**QWENTYN, COMMODORE DONYRT, ROYAL CORISANDIAN NAVY**—Baron of Tanlyr Keep; one of Duke of Black Water's squadron commanders.

**QWENTYN, TYMAHN**—the current head of the House of Qwentyn banking and investment cartel.

**RAHLSTAHN, ADMIRAL GHARTH, IMPERIAL CHARISIAN NAVY**—Earl of Mahndyr; third-ranking officer, Imperial Charisian Navy. Ex–Royal Emeraldian Navy.

**RAHLSTYN, COMMODORE ERAYK, ROYAL DOHLARAN NAVY**—one of Duke Malikai's squadron commanders.

**RAHSKAIL, COLONEL BARKAH, IMPERIAL CHARISIAN ARMY**—Earl of Swayle; a senior supply officer, Imperial Charisian Army.

**RAHZMAHN, LIEUTENANT DAHNYLD, IMPERIAL CHARISIAN NAVY**—Sir Gwylym Manthyr's flag lieutenant.

**RAICE, BYNZHAMYN**—Baron Wave Thunder; royal councilor for intelligence, Kingdom of Old Charis.

**RAICE, LEAHYN**—Baroness Wave Thunder; wife of Bynzhamyn Raice.

**RAIMAIR, TOBYS**—head of Prince Daivyn Daykyn's unofficial guardsmen in Delferahk; ex-sergeant, Royal Corisandian Army.

**RAIMYND, SIR LYNDAHR**—Prince Hektor of Corisande's treasurer.

**RAISAHNDO, CAPTAIN CAITAHNO, ROYAL DOHLARAN NAVY**—CO, HMS *Rakurai*, 46.

**RAISLAIR, BISHOP EXECUTOR MHARTYN**—Archbishop Ahdym Taibyr's executive assistant, Archbishopric of Desnair.

**RAIYZ, FATHER CARLSYN**—Queen Sharleyan's confessor; killed in Sharleyan's attempted assassination.

**RAIZYNGYR, COLONEL ARTTU**—CO, ⅔rd Marines (Second Battalion, Third Brigade), Royal Charisian Marines.

**RAYNAIR, CAPTAIN EKOHLS**—CO, privateer schooner *Blade*.

**RAYNO, ARCHBISHOP WYLLYM**—Archbishop of Chiang-wu; adjutant of the Order of Schueler.

**RAYNO, HAILYN**—Queen Consort of the Kingdom of Delferahk; wife of King Zhames II; a cousin of Prince Hektor of Corisande.

**RAYNO, ZHAMES**—King Zhames II, Kingdom of Delferahk.

**RAZHAIL, FATHER DERAHK**—senior healer, Imperial Palace, Cherayth. Upper-priest of the Order of Pasquale.

**RHOBAIR, VICAR**—see also Rhobair Duchairn.

**ROCK POINT, BARON OF**—see Admiral Sir Domynyk Staynair.

**ROHSAIL, CAPTAIN SIR DAHRAND, ROYAL DOHLARAN NAVY**—CO, HMS *Grand Vicar Mahrys*, 50.

**ROHZHYR, COLONEL BAHRTOL, ROYAL CHARISIAN MARINE CORPS**—a senior commissary officer.

**ROPEWALK, COLONEL AHDAM, CHARISIAN ROYAL GUARD**—CO, Charisian Royal Guard.

**ROWYN, CAPTAIN HORAHS**—CO, Sir Dustyn Olyvyr's yacht *Ahnyet*.

**RUSTMAYN, EDMYND**—Baron Stonekeep; King Gorjah III of Tarot's first councillor and spymaster.

**RYCHTAIR, NYNIAN**—Ahnzhelyk Phonda's birth name; adopted sister of Adorai Dynnys.

**SAHBRAHAN, PAIAIR**—the Earl of Thirsk's personal valet.

**SAHDLYR, LIEUTENANT BYNZHAMYN, ROYAL CHARISIAN NAVY**—second lieutenant, HMS *Dreadnought*.

**SAHLMYN, SERGEANT MAJOR HAIN, ROYAL CHARISIAN MARINE CORPS**—Colonel Zhanstyn's battalion sergeant major.

**SAHNDYRS, MAHRAK**—Baron Green Mountain; Queen Sharleyan's first councilor.

**SAIGAHN, CAPTAIN MAHRDAI, ROYAL CHARISIAN NAVY**—CO, HMS *Guardsman*, 44.

**SAITHWYK, ARCHBISHOP FAIRMYN**—Archbishop of Emerald for the Church of Charis.

**SARMAC, JENNIFER**—an Eve who escaped the destruction of the Alexandria Enclave and fled to Tellesberg.

**SARMAC, KALEB**—an Adam who escaped the destruction of the Alexandria Enclave and fled to Tellesberg.

**SAWAL, FATHER RAHSS**—an under-priest of the Order of Chihiro; the skipper of one of the Temple's courier boats.

**SAWYAIR, SISTER FRAHNCYS**—senior nun of the Order of Pasquale, Convent of the Blessed Hand, Cherayth.

**SEABLANKET, RHOBAIR**—the Earl of Coris' valet.

**SEACATCHER, SIR RAHNLYD**—Baron Mandolin, a member of King Cayleb's council.

**SEAFARMER, SIR RHYZHARD**—Baron Wave Thunder's senior investigator.

**SEAHAMPER, SERGEANT EDWYRD**—Charisian Imperial Guardsman; Sharleyan Ahrmahk's personal armsman since age ten.

**SEAMOUNT, BARON**—see Sir Ahlfryd Hyndryk.

**SEASMOKE, LIEUTENANT YAIRMAN, IMPERIAL CHARISIAN NAVY**—XO, HMS *Dancer*, 56.

**SEATOWN, CAPTAIN WAHLTAYR**—CO of merchant ship *Fraynceen*, acting as a courier for Prince Hektor's spies in Charis. Alias for Lieutenant Fraizher Maythis.

**SELKYR, BRYAHN**—Earl of Deep Hollow; a member of the Northern Conspiracy in Corisande.

**SELLYRS, PAITYR**—Baron White Church; Keeper of the Seal of the Kingdom of Charis; a member of King Cayleb's council.

**SHAIKYR, LARYS**—CO, privateer galleon *Raptor.*

**SHAIN, CAPTAIN PAYTER, ROYAL CHARISIAN NAVY**—CO, HMS *Dreadful,* 48. Admiral Nylz's flag captain.

**SHAIOW, ADMIRAL OF THE BROAD OCEANS CHYNTAI, IMPERIAL HARCHONGESE NAVY**—Duke of Sun Rising, senior officer afloat, Imperial Harchongese Navy.

**SHANDYR, HAHL**—Baron of Shandyr; Prince Nahrmahn of Emerald's spymaster.

**SHARPFIELD, EARL OF**—see Sir Lewk Cohlmyn.

**SHOWAIL, LIEUTENANT COMMANDER STYV, IMPERIAL CHARISIAN NAVY**—CO, schooner HMS *Flash,* 10.

**SHYMAKYR, FATHER SYMYN**—Archbishop Erayk Dynnys' secretary for his 891 pastoral visit; an agent of the Grand Inquisitor.

**SHUMAY, FATHER AHLVYN**—Bishop Mylz Halcom's personal aide.

**SHYLAIR, BISHOP EXECUTOR THOMYS**—Archbishop Borys' executive assistant in the Archbishopric of Corisande.

**SMOLTH, ZHAN**—star pitcher for the Tellesberg Krakens.

**SOMERSET, CAPTAIN MARTIN LUTHER, TERRAN FEDERATION NAVY**—CO, TFNS *Excalibur.*

**SOWTHMYN, TRUMYN**—Earl of Airyth; one of Prince Hektor's councilors, now serving on Prince Daivyn's Regency Council.

**STANTYN, ARCHBISHOP NYKLAS**—Archbishop of Hankey in the Desnairian Empire.

**STAYNAIR, AHRDYN**—Archbishop Maikel Staynair's deceased wife.

**STAYNAIR, ADMIRAL SIR DOMYNYK, IMPERIAL CHARISIAN NAVY**—Baron of Rock Point, younger brother of Archbishop Maikel Staynair.

**STAYNAIR, ARCHBISHOP MAIKEL**—head of the Church of Charis; was senior Charisian-born prelate of the Church of God Awaiting in Charis; named prelate of all Charis by then-King Cayleb.

**STOHNAR, LORD PROTECTOR GREYGHOR**—elected ruler of the Siddarmark Republic.

**STONEKEEP, BARON OF**—see Edmynd Rustmyn.

**STORM KEEP, EARL OF**—see Sahlahmn Traigair.

**STYWYRT, CAPTAIN AHRNAHLD, IMPERIAL CHARISIAN NAVY**—CO, HMS *Squall,* 36.

**STYWYRT, CAPTAIN DAHRYL, ROYAL CHARISIAN NAVY**—CO, HMS *Typhoon.*

**STYWYRT, SERGEANT ZOHZEF**—another of Kairmyn's noncoms, Delferahkan Army.

**SUMYR, FATHER FRAHNKLYN**—Archbishop Failyx Gahrbor's intendant, Archbishopric of Tarot.

**SUMYRS, SIR ZHER**—Baron of Barcor; one of Sir Koryn Gahrvai's senior officers, Corisande Campaign; later member of Northern Conspiracy.

**SUN RISING, DUKE OF**—see Admiral of the Broad Oceans Chyntai Shaiow.

**SVAIRSMAHN, MIDSHIPMAN LAINSAIR, IMPERIAL CHARISIAN NAVY**—a midshipman, HMS *Dancer,* 56.

**SWAYLE, EARL OF**—see Colonel Barkah Rahskail.

**SYMKEE, LIEUTENANT GARAITH, IMPERIAL CHARISIAN NAVY**—second lieutenant, HMS *Destiny,* 54.

**SYMMYNS, TOHMAS**—Grand Duke of Zebediah; senior nobleman of Zebediah; a member of the Northern Conspiracy in Corisande.

**SYMYN, LIEUTENANT HAHL, ROYAL CHARISIAN NAVY**—XO, HMS *Torrent,* 42.

**SYMYN, SERGEANT ZHORJ, CHARISIAN IMPERIAL GUARD**—a Charisian noncom assigned to Empress Sharleyan's guard detachment.

**SYNKLYR, LIEUTENANT AIRAH, ROYAL DOHLARAN NAVY**—XO, galleon *Guardian.*

**TAHLAS, LIEUTENANT BRAHD, IMPERIAL CHARISIAN MARINES**—CO, Second Platoon, Alpha Company, ⅓rd Marines, ICMC.

**TAHLBAHT, FRAHNCYN**—a senior employee (and actual owner) of Bruhstair Freight Haulers; an alias of Nynian Rychtair.

**TAIBAHLD, FATHER AHRNAHLD**—upper-priest of the Order of Schueler; CO, NGS *Sword of God*; Bishop Kornylys Harpahr's flag captain.

**TAIBYR, ARCHBISHOP AHDYM**—Archbishop of Desnair for the Church of God Awaiting.

**TALLMYN, CAPTAIN GERVAYS, EMERALD NAVY**—second-in-command of the Royal Dockyard in Tranjyr.

**TANLYR KEEP, BARON OF**—see Donyrt Qwentyn.

**TANNYR, FATHER HAHLYS**—under-priest of the Order of Chihiro; CO, Temple iceboat *Hornet.*

**TANYR, VICAR GAIRYT**—a member of the Reformists.

**TARTARIAN, EARL OF**—see Sir Taryl Lektor.

**TAYSO, PRIVATE DAISHYN, CHARISIAN IMPERIAL GUARD**—a Charisian assigned to Empress Sharleyan's guard detachment.

**TAYT, ALAHNAH**—Dowager Queen of Chisholm; Queen Sharleyan of Chisholm's mother.

**TAYT, SAILYS**—King of Chisholm; deceased father of Queen Sharleyan.

**TAYT, SHARLEYAN**—Empress of Charis and Queen of Chisholm. See Sharleyan Ahrmahk.

**TEAGMAHN, FATHER BRYAHN**—upper-priest of the Order of Schueler, intendant for the Archbishopric of Glacierheart.

**THAIRIS, RUHSYL, DUKE OF EASTSHARE**—commanding officer, Imperial Charisian Army.

**THIESSEN, CAPTAIN JOSEPH, TERRAN FEDERATION NAVY**—Admiral Pei Kauzhi's chief of staff.

**THIRSK, EARL OF**—see Lywys Gardynyr.

**THOMPKYN, HAUWERSTAT**—Earl of White Crag; Chisholm's Lord Justice.

**THORAST, DUKE OF**—see Aibram Zaivyair.

**TIANG, BISHOP EXECUTOR WU-SHAI**—Archbishop Zherohm Vyncyt's bishop executor.

**TILLYER, LIEUTENANT COMMANDER HENRAI, IMPERIAL CHARISIAN NAVY**—High Admiral Lock Island's chief of staff; previously his flag lieutenant.

**TIRIAN, DUKE**—see Kahlvyn Ahrmahk.

**TOHMYS, FRAHNKLYN**—Crown Prince Cayleb's tutor.

**TOHMYS, FRAIDMYN**—Archbishop Zhasyn Cahnyr's valet of many years.

**TRAIGAIR, SAHLAHMN**—Earl of Storm Keep; a member of the Northern Conspiracy in Corisande.

**TRYNAIR, VICAR ZAHMSYN**—Chancellor of the Council of Vicars of the Church of God Awaiting; one of the so-called Group of Four.

**TRYNTYN, CAPTAIN ZHAIRYMIAH, ROYAL CHARISIAN NAVY**—CO, HMS *Torrent*, 42.

**TRYVYTHYN, CAPTAIN SIR DYNZYL, ROYAL CHARISIAN NAVY**—CO, HMS *Royal Charis*.

**TYOTAYN, BRIGADIER BAIRAHND, IMPERIAL CHARISIAN MARINES**—CO, Fifth Brigade, ICMC. Sir Gwylym Manthyr's senior Marine officer.

**TYRN, ARCHBISHOP LYAM**—Archbishop of Emerald.

**TYRNYR, SERGEANT BRYNDYN, CHISHOLMIAN ROYAL GUARD**—a member of Queen Sharleyan's normal guard detail.

**TYRNYR, SIR SAMYL**—Cayleb's special ambassador to Chisholm; were placed/supplanted/reinforced by Gray Harbor's arrival.

**UHLSTYN, YAIRMAN**—Sir Koryn Gahrvai's personal armsman.

**URBAHN, HAHL**—XO, privateer galleon *Raptor*.

**URVYN, ARCHBISHOP**—see Urvyn Myllyr.

**URVYN, LIEUTENANT ZHAK, ROYAL CHARISIAN NAVY**—XO, HMS *Wave*, 14.

**USHYR, FATHER BRYAHN**—an under-priest. Archbishop Maikel's personal secretary and most trusted aide.

**VAHLAIN, NAIKLOS**—Sir Gwylym Manthyr's valet.

**VAHNWYK, MAHRTYN**—the Earl of Thirsk's personal secretary and senior clerk.

**VYKAIN, LIEUTENANT MAHRYAHNO, IMPERIAL CHARISIAN NAVY**—XO, HMS *Ahrmahk*, 58.

**VYNAIR, SERGEANT AHDYM, CHARISIAN ROYAL GUARD**—one of King Cayleb II's armsmen.

**VYNCYT, ARCHBISHOP ZHEROHM**—primate of Chisholm for Church of God Awaiting.

**WAHLDAIR, LIEUTENANT LAHMBAIR, IMPERIAL CHARISIAN NAVY**—third lieutenant, HMS *Dancer,* 56.

**WAIGAN, FRAHNKLYN, IMPERIAL CHARISIAN NAVY**—chief petty officer and senior helmsman, HMS *Destiny,* 54.

**WAIGNAIR, BISHOP HAINRYK**—Bishop of Tellesberg; senior prelate (after Archbishop Maikel) of the Kingdom of Old Charis.

**WAILAHR, COMMODORE SIR HAIRAHM, IMPERIAL DESNAIRIAN NAVY**—a squadron commander of the Imperial Desnairian Navy.

**WAIMYN, FATHER AIDRYN**—intendant, Archbishopric of Corisande.

**WAISTYN, BYRTRYM**—Duke of Halbrook Hollow; Queen Sharleyan's deceased uncle and army commander.

**WALKYR, EDMYND**—CO, merchant galleon *Wave.*

**WALKYR, GREYGHOR**—Edmynd Walkyr's son.

**WALKYR, LYZBET**—Edmynd Walkyr's wife.

**WALKYR, MIDSHIPMAN FRAID, IMPERIAL CHARISIAN NAVY**—midshipman in HMS *Shield,* 54.

**WALKYR, MYCHAIL**—Edmynd Walkyr's youngest brother; CO, merchant galleon *Wind.*

**WALKYR, STYV**—Tahdayo Mahntayl's chief adviser.

**WALKYR, ZHORJ**—XO, galleon *Wave.* Edmynd Walkyr's younger brother.

**WALLYCE, LORD FRAHNKLYN**—Chancellor of the Siddarmark Republic.

**WAVE THUNDER, BARON OF**—see Bynzhamyn Raice.

**WAVE THUNDER, BARONESS OF**—see Leahyn Raice.

**WAYST, CAPTAIN ZAKRAI, IMPERIAL CHARISIAN NAVY**—CO, HMS *Darcos Sound,* 54.

**WHAITE, CAPTAIN STYVYN**—CO, merchant ship *Sea Cloud,* a courier for Prince Hektor's spies in Charis. Alias for Robyrt Bradlai.

**WHITE CASTLE, BARON**—see Tohmys Bahrmyn.

**WHITE CRAG, EARL OF**—see Hauwerstat Thompkyn.

**WHITE FORD, BARON OF**—see Gahvyn Mahrtyn.

**WIND MOUNTAIN, COUNT OF**—see Captain of Winds Shoukhan Khowsan.

**WINDSHARE, EARL OF**—see Sir Alyk Ahrthyr.

**WYLLYM, ARCHBISHOP**—see Wyllym Rayno.

**WYLLYMS, MARHYS**—the Duke of Tirian's majordomo.

**WYLSYNN, ARCHBAHLD**—younger son of Vicar Samyl and Lysbet Wylsynn; Father Paityr Wylsynn's half brother.

**WYLSYNN, HAUWERD**—Paityr Wylsynn's uncle; a Reformist member of the vicarate; ex Temple Guardsman; a priest of the Order of Langhorne.

**WYLSYNN, LYSBET**—Samyl Wylsynn's second wife; mother of Tohmys, Zhanayt, and Archbahld Wylsynn.

**WYLSYNN, PAITYR**—a priest of the Order of Schueler and the Intendant of Charis. He served Erayk Dynnys in that capacity and has continued to serve Archbishop Maikel.

**WYLSYNN, SAMYL**—Father Paityr Wylsynn's father; the leader of the Reformists within the Council of Vicars and a priest of the Order of Schueler.

**WYLSYNN, TANNIERE**—Samyl Wylsynn's deceased wife; mother of Erais and Paityr Wylsynn.

**WYLSYNN, TOHMYS**—older son of Vicar Samyl and Lysbet Wylsynn; Father Paityr Wylsynn's half brother.

**WYLSYNN, ZHANAYT**—daughter of Vicar Samyl and Lysbet Wylsynn; Father Paityr Wylsynn's half sister.

**WYNDAYL, MAJOR BRAINAHK, IMPERIAL CHARISIAN MARINES**—CO, First Battalion, Fourteenth Marine Regiment.

**WYNSTYN, LIEUTENANT KYNYTH, ROYAL CORISANDIAN NAVY**—first lieutenant, galley *Corisande.*

**WYSTAHN, AHNAINAH**—Edvarhd Wystahn's wife.

**WYSTAHN, SERGEANT EDVARHD, ROYAL CHARISIAN MARINES**—a scout-sniper assigned to ⅓rd Marines.

**YAIR, FATHER AIRWAIN**—chaplain and confessor to Rahzhyr Mairwyn, Baron Larchros.

**YAIRLEY, CAPTAIN ALLAYN, IMPERIAL CHARISIAN NAVY**—older brother of Captain Sir Dunkyn Yairley.

**YAIRLEY, CAPTAIN SIR DUNKYN, IMPERIAL CHARISIAN NAVY**—CO, HMS *Destiny*, 54.

**YOWANCE, EHRNAIST**—Rayjhis Yowance's deceased elder brother.

**YOWANCE, RAYJHIS**—Earl Gray Harbor, First Councilor of Charis.

**YUTHAIN, CAPTAIN GORJHA, IMPERIAL HARCHONG NAVY**—CO, galley IHNS *Ice Lizard.*

**ZAHCHO, FATHER DAISHAN**—an under-priest of the Order of Schueler; one of Father Aidryn Waimyn's Inquisitors in Corisande.

**ZAHMSYN, VICAR**—see Zahmsyn Trynair.

**ZAIVYAIR, AIBRAM, DUKE OF THORAST**—effective Navy Minister and senior officer, Royal Dohlaran Navy; brother-in-law of Admiral-General Duke Malikai (Faidel Ahlverez).

**ZEBEDIAH, GRAND DUKE OF**—see Tohmas Symmyns.

**ZHAKSYN, LIEUTENANT TOHMYS, ROYAL CHARISIAN MARINE CORPS**—General Chermyn's aide.

**ZHANSAN, FRAHNK**—the Duke of Tirian's senior guardsman.

**ZHANSTYN, BRIGADIER ZHOEL, IMPERIAL CHARISIAN MARINES**—CO, Third

Brigade, ICMC. Brigadier Clareyk's senior battalion CO during Corisande Campaign.

**ZHARDEAU, LADY ERAIS**—Samyl and Tanniere Wylsynn's daughter; Father Paityr Wylsynn's younger full sister; wife of Sir Fraihman Zhardeau.

**ZHARDEAU, SIR FRAIHMAN**—minor Tansharan aristocrat; husband of Lady Erais Zhardeau; son-in-law of Vicar Samyl Wylsynn.

**ZHARDEAU, SAMYL**—son of Sir Fraihman and Lady Erais Zhardeau; grandson of Vicar Samyl Wylsynn; nephew of Father Paityr Wylsynn.

**ZHASPAHR, VICAR**—see Zhaspahr Clyntahn.

**ZHASYN, ARCHBISHOP**—see Zhasyn Cahnyr.

**ZHAZTRO, COMMODORE HAINZ, EMERALD NAVY**—the senior Emeraldian naval officer afloat (technically) in Eraystor following the Battle of Darcos Sound.

**ZHEFFYRS, MAJOR WYLL, ROYAL CHARISIAN MARINES**—CO, Marine detachment, HMS *Destiny*, 54.

**ZHEPPSYN, CAPTAIN NYKLAS, EMERALD NAVY**—CO, galley *Triton*.

**ZHERMAIN, CAPTAIN MAHRTYN, ROYAL DOHLARAN NAVY**—CO, HMS *Prince of Dohlar*, 38.

**ZHESSYP, LACHLYN**—King Haarahld VII's valet.

**ZHEVONS, AHBRAIM**—alias and alternate persona of Merlin Athrawes.

**ZHOELSYN, LIEUTENANT PHYLYP, ROYAL TAROTISIAN NAVY**—second lieutenant, *King Gorjah II.*

**ZHONAIR, MAJOR GAHRMYN**—a battery commander in Ferayd Harbor, Ferayd Sound, Kingdom of Delferahk.

**ZHONES, MIDSHIPMAN AHRLEE, IMPERIAL CHARISIAN NAVY**—a junior midshipman in HMS *Destiny*, 54.

**ZHORJ, COLONEL SIR WAHLYS**—Tahdayo Mahntayl's senior mercenary commander.

**ZHUSTYN, SIR AHLBER**—senior minister for intelligence, Kingdom of Chisholm.

# Glossary

*Anshinritsumei*—literally "enlightenment," from the Japanese. Rendered in the Safehold Bible, however, as "the little fire," the lesser touch of God's spirit. The maximum enlightenment of which mortals are capable.

*Blink-lizard*—a small, bioluminescent winged lizard. Although it's about three times the size of a firefly, it fills much the same niche on Safehold.

*Borer*—a form of Safeholdian shellfish which attaches itself to the hulls of ships or the timbers of wharves by boring into them. There are several types of borer, the most destructive of which actually eat their way steadily deeper into a wooden structure. Borers and rot are the two most serious threats (aside, of course, from fire) to wooden hulls.

*Catamount*—a smaller version of the Safeholdian slash lizard. The catamount is very fast and smarter than its larger cousin, which means that it tends to avoid humans. It is, however, a lethal and dangerous hunter in its own right.

*Cat-lizard*—a furry lizard about the size of a terrestrial cat. They are kept as pets and are very affectionate.

*Chewleaf*—a mildly narcotic leaf from a native Safeholdian plant. It is used much as terrestrial chewing tobacco over most of the planet's surface.

*Choke tree*—a low-growing species of tree native to Safehold. It comes in many varieties and is found in most of the planet's climate zones. It is dense-growing, tough, and difficult to eradicate, but it requires quite a lot of sunlight to flourish, which means it is seldom found in mature old-growth forests.

*Commentaries, The*—the authorized interpretations and doctrinal expansions upon the *Holy Writ*. They represent the officially approved and sanctioned interpretation of the original scripture.

*Cotton silk*—a plant native to Safehold which shares many of the properties of silk and cotton. It is very lightweight and strong, but the raw fiber comes from a plant pod which is even more filled with seeds than Old Earth cotton. Because of the amount of hand labor required to harvest and process the pods and to remove the seeds from it, cotton silk is very expensive.

*Council of Vicars*—the Church of God Awaiting's equivalent of the College of Cardinals.

*Dagger thorn*—a native Charisian shrub, growing to a height of perhaps three feet at maturity, which possesses knife-edged thorns from three to seven inches long, depending upon the variety.

*Deep-mouth wyvern*—Safeholdian equivalent of a pelican.

*Doomwhale*—the most dangerous predator of Safehold, although, fortunately, it seldom bothers with anything as small as humans. Doomwhales have been known to run to as much as one hundred feet in length, and they are pure carnivores. Each doomwhale requires a huge range, and encounters with them are rare, for which human beings are just as glad, thank you. Doomwhales will eat *anything* . . . including the largest krakens. They have been known, on *extremely* rare occasions, to attack merchant ships and war galleys.

*Dragon*—the largest native Safeholdian land life-form. Dragons come in two varieties, the common dragon and the great dragon. The common dragon is about twice the size of a Terran elephant and is herbivorous. The great dragon is smaller, about half to two-thirds the size of the common dragon, but carnivorous, filling the highest feeding niche of Safehold's land-based ecology. They look very much alike, aside from their size and the fact that the common dragon has herbivore teeth and jaws, whereas the great dragon has elongated jaws with sharp, serrated teeth. They have six limbs and, unlike the slash lizard, are covered in thick, well-insulated hide rather than fur.

*Five-day*—a Safeholdian "week," consisting of only five days, Monday through Friday.

*Fleming moss*—an absorbent moss native to Safehold which was genetically engineered by Shan-wei's terraforming crews to possess natural antibiotic properties. It is a staple of Safeholdian medical practice.

*Grasshopper*—a Safeholdian insect analogue which grows to a length of as much as nine inches and is carnivorous. Fortunately, they do not occur in the same numbers as terrestrial grasshoppers.

*Gray-horned wyvern*—a nocturnal flying predator of Safehold. It is roughly analogous to a terrestrial owl.

*Great dragon*—the largest and most dangerous land carnivore of Safehold. The great dragon isn't actually related to hill dragons or jungle dragons at all, despite some superficial physical resemblances. In fact, it's more of a scaled-up slash lizard.

*Group of Four*—the four vicars who dominate and effectively control the Council of Vicars of the Church of God Awaiting.

*Hairatha Dragons*—the Hairatha professional baseball team. The traditional rivals of the Tellesberg Krakens for the Kingdom Championship.

*Hill dragon*—a roughly elephant-sized draft animal commonly used on Safehold. Despite their size, they are capable of rapid, sustained movement.

*Ice wyvern*—a flightless aquatic wyvern rather similar to a terrestrial penguin. Species of ice wyvern are native to both the northern and southern polar regions of Safehold.

*Insights, The*—the recorded pronouncements and observations of the Church of God Awaiting's Grand Vicars and canonized saints. They represent deeply significant spiritual and inspirational teachings, but as the work of fallible mortals do not have the same standing as the *Holy Writ* itself.

*Intendant*—the cleric assigned to a bishopric or archbishopric as the direct representative of the Office of Inquisition. The intendant is specifically charged with assuring that the Proscriptions of Jwo-jeng are not violated.

*Jungle dragon*—a somewhat generic term applied to lowland dragons larger than hill dragons. The gray jungle dragon is the largest herbivore on Safehold.

*Kercheef*—a traditional headdress worn in the Kingdom of Tarot which consists of a specially designed bandana tied across the hair.

*Knights of the Temple Lands*—the corporate title of the prelates who govern the Temple Lands. Technically, the Knights of the Temple Lands are *secular* rulers who simply happen to also hold high Church office. Under the letter of the Church's law, what they may do as the Knights of the Temple Lands is completely separate from any official action of the Church. This legal fiction has been of considerable value to the Church on more than one occasion.

*Kraken*—generic term for an entire family of maritime predators. Krakens are rather like sharks crossed with octupi. They have powerful, fish-like bodies, strong jaws with inward-inclined, fang-like teeth, and a cluster of tentacles just behind the head which can be used to hold prey while they devour it. The smallest, coastal krakens can be as short as three or four feet; deep-water krakens up to fifty feet in length have been reported, and there are legends of those still larger.

*Kyousei hi*—literally "great fire" or "magnificent fire." The term used to describe the brilliant nimbus of light the Operation Ark command crew generated around their air cars and skimmers to help "prove" their divinity to the original Safeholdians.

*Langhorne's Watch*—the thirty-one-minute period immediately before midnight in order to compensate for the extra length of Safehold's 26.5-hour day.

*Master Traynyr*—a character out of the Safeholdian entertainment tradition. Master Traynyr is a stock character in Safeholdian puppet theater, by turns a bumbling conspirator whose plans always miscarry and the puppeteer who controls all of the marionette "actors" in the play.

*Monastery of Saint Zherneau*—the mother monastery and headquarters of the Brethren of Saint Zherneau, a relatively small and poor order in the Archbishopric of Charis.

*Mountain spike-thorn*—a particular subspecies of spike-thorn, found primarily in tropical mountains. The most common blossom color is a deep, rich red, but the white mountain spike-thorn is especially prized for its trumpet-shaped blossom, which has a deep almost cobalt-blue throat, fading to pure white as it approaches the outer edge of the blossom, which is, in turn, fringed in a deep golden yellow.

*Narwhale*—a species of Safeholdian sea life named for the Old Earth species of the same name. Safeholdian narwhales are about forty feet in length and equipped with twin horn-like tusks up to eight-feet long.

*Nearoak*—a rough-barked Safeholdian tree similar to Old Earth oak trees, found in tropic and near-tropic zones. Although it does resemble an Old Earth oak, it is an evergreen and seeds using "pine cones."

*Nynian Rychtair*—the Safeholdian equivalent of Helen of Troy, a woman of legendary beauty, born in Siddarmark, who eventually married the Emperor of Harchong.

*Persimmon fig*—a native Safeholdian fruit which is extremely tart and relatively thick-skinned.

*Prong lizard*—a roughly elk-sized lizard with a single horn which branches into four sharp points in the last third or so of its length. They are herbivores and not particularly ferocious.

*Proscriptions of Jwo-jeng*—the definition of allowable technology under the doctrine of the Church of God Awaiting. Essentially, the Proscriptions limit allowable technology to that which is powered by wind, water, or muscle. The Proscriptions are subject to interpretation, generally by the Order of Schueler, which generally errs on the side of conservatism.

*Rakurai*—literally "lightning bolt." The *Holy Writ*'s term for the kinetic weapons used to destroy the Alexandria Enclave.

**Saint Zherneau**—the patron saint of the Monastery of Saint Zherneau in Tellesberg.

**Sand maggot**—a loathsome carnivore, looking much like a six-legged slug, which haunts beaches just above the surf line. Sand maggots do not normally take living prey, although they have no objection to devouring the occasional small creature which strays into their reach. Their natural coloration blends with their sandy habitat well, and they normally conceal themselves by digging their bodies into the sand until they are completely covered, or only a small portion of their backs show.

**Sea cow**—a walrus-like Safeholdian sea mammal which grows to a body length of approximately ten feet when fully mature.

**Seijin**—sage, holy man. Directly from the Japanese by way of Maruyama Chihiro, the Langhorne staffer who wrote the Church of God Awaiting's Bible.

**Slash lizard**—a six-limbed, saurian-looking, furry oviparous mammal. One of the three top predators of Safehold. Mouth contains twin rows of fangs capable of punching through chain mail; feet have four long toes each, tipped with claws up to five or six inches long.

**SNARC**—Self-Navigating Autonomous Reconnaissance and Communication platform.

**Spider-crab**—a native species of sea life, considerably larger than any terrestrial crab. The spider-crab is not a crustacean, but rather more of a segmented, tough-hided, many-legged seagoing slug. Despite that, its legs are considered a great delicacy and are actually very tasty.

**Spider-rat**—a native species of vermin which fills roughly the ecological niche of a terrestrial rat. Like all Safehold mammals, it is six-limbed, but it looks like a cross between a hairy gila monster and an insect, with long, multi-jointed legs which actually arch higher than its spine. It is nasty-tempered but basically cowardly, and fully adult male specimens of the larger varieties of spider rat run to about two feet in body length, with another two feet of tail. The more common varieties average between thirty-three percent and fifty percent of that body/tail length.

**Spike-thorn**—a flowering shrub, various subspecies of which are found in most Safeholdian climate zones. Its blossoms come in many colors and hues, and the tropical versions tend to be taller-growing and to bear more delicate blossoms.

**Steel thistle**—a native Safeholdian plant which looks very much like branching bamboo. The plant bears seed pods filled with small, spiny seeds embedded in fine, straight fibers. The seeds are extremely difficult to remove by hand, but the fiber can be woven into a fabric which is even stronger than cotton silk. It can also be twisted into extremely strong, stretch-resistant rope. Moreover, the plant grows almost as rapidly as actual bamboo, and the yield of raw fiber per acre is seventy percent higher than for terrestrial cotton.

*Surgoi kasai*—literally "dreadful (great) conflagration." The true spirit of God, the touch of His divine fire which only an angel or Archangel can endure.

*Tellesberg Krakens*—the Tellesberg professional baseball club.

*Testimonies, The*—by far the most numerous of the Church of God Awaiting's writings, these consist of the firsthand observations of the first few generations of humans on Safehold. They do not have the same status as the Christian gospels, because they do not reveal the central teachings and inspiration of God. Instead, collectively, they form an important substantiation of the *Writ*'s "historical accuracy" and conclusively attest to the fact that the events they collectively describe did, in fact, transpire.

*Wire vine*—a kudzu-like vine native to Safehold. Wire vine isn't as fast-growing as kudzu, but it's equally tenacious, and unlike kudzu, several of its varieties have long, sharp thorns. Unlike many native Safeholdians species of plants, it does quite well intermingled with terrestrial imports. It is often used as a sort of combination of hedgerow and barbed wire by Safehold farmers.

*Wyvern*—the Safeholdian ecological analogue of terrestrial birds. There are as many varieties of wyverns as there are of birds, including (but not limited to) the homing wyvern, hunting wyverns suitable for the equivalent of hawking for small prey, the crag wyvern (a small—wingspan ten feet—flying predator), various species of sea wyverns, and the king wyvern (a very large flying predator, with a wingspan of up to twenty-five feet). All wyverns have two pairs of wings, and one pair of powerful, clawed legs. The king wyvern has been known to take children as prey when desperate or when the opportunity presents, but they are quite intelligent. They know that man is a prey best left alone and generally avoid areas of human habitation.

*Wyvernry*—a nesting place and/or breeding hatchery for domesticated wyverns.

# A Note on Safeholdian Timekeeping

The Safeholdian day is 26 hours and 31 minutes long. Safehold's year is 301.32 local days in length, which works out to .91 Earth standard years. It has one major moon, named Langhorne, which orbits Safehold in 27.6 local days, so the lunar month is approximately 28 days long.

The Safeholdian day is divided into twenty-six 60-minute hours, and one 31-minute period, known as "Langhorne's Watch," which is used to adjust the local day into something which can be evenly divided into standard minutes and hours.

The Safeholdian calendar year is divided into ten months: February, April, March, May, June, July, August, September, October, and November. Each month is divided into six five-day weeks, each of which is referred to as a "five-day." The days of the week are: Monday, Tuesday, Wednesday, Thursday, and Friday. The extra day in each year is inserted into the middle of the month of July, but is not numbered. It is referred to as "God's Day" and is the high holy day of the Church of God Awaiting. What this means, among other things, is that the first day of every month will always be a Monday, and the last day of every month will always be a Friday. Every third year is a leap year, with the additional day—known as "Langhorne's Memorial"—being inserted, again, without numbering, into the middle of the month of February. It also means that each Safeholdian month is 795 standard hours long, as opposed to 720 hours for a 30-day Earth month.

The Safeholdian equinoxes occur on April 23 and September 22. The solstices fall on July 7 and February 8.